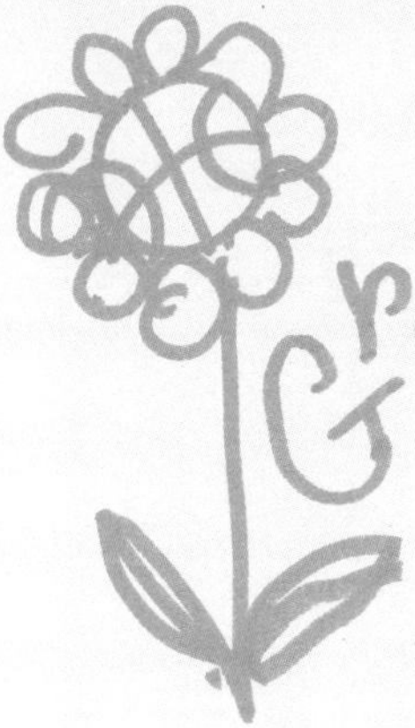

Grace!

p playing!! Gabi

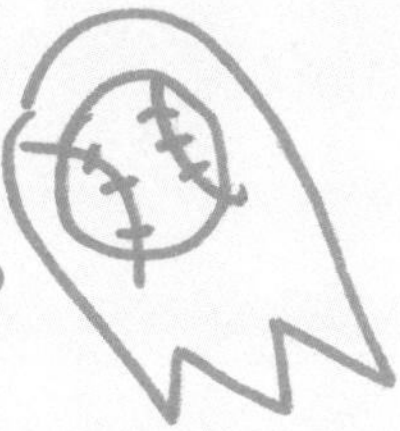

Mateo

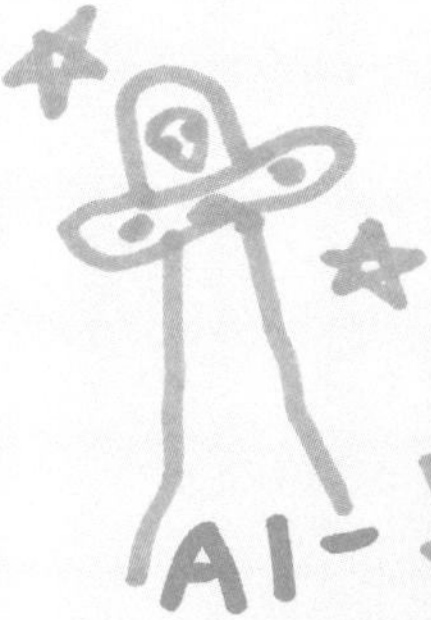

martians 4ever. -cal

Al- wrong.

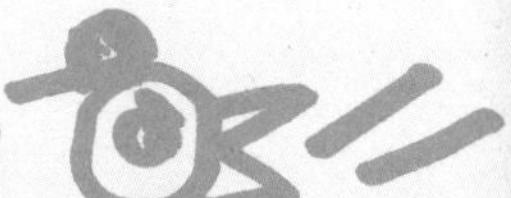

THE BEAK IS BACK

and is so PROUD OF YOU!

HONK!!! -Viv

(I will peck anyone who messes with you. I rly mean it.)

Tryouts

Sarah Sax

ALFRED A. KNOPF

NEW YORK

THIS IS A BORZOI BOOK PUBLISHED BY ALFRED A. KNOPF

Photographs on pages 282–283 courtesy of the author.

Visit us on the Web! rhcbooks.com

Educators and librarians, for a variety of teaching tools, visit us at RHTeachersLibrarians.com

Library of Congress Cataloging-in-Publication Data is available upon request.
ISBN 978-0-593-30691-8 (trade pbk.) — ISBN 978-0-593-30692-5 (trade) —
ISBN 978-0-593-30693-2 (lib. bdg.) — ISBN 978-0-593-30694-9 (ebook)

The text of this book is set in 12-point Brinkley Yearbook.
The illustrations were created digitally.

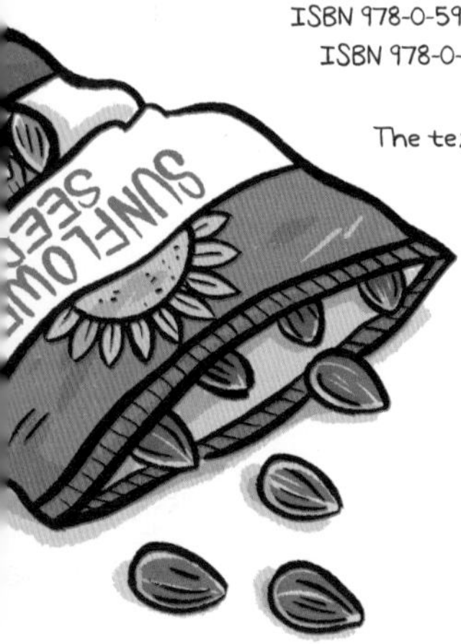

MANUFACTURED IN CHINA
May 2024
10 9 8 7 6 5 4 3 2 1
First Edition

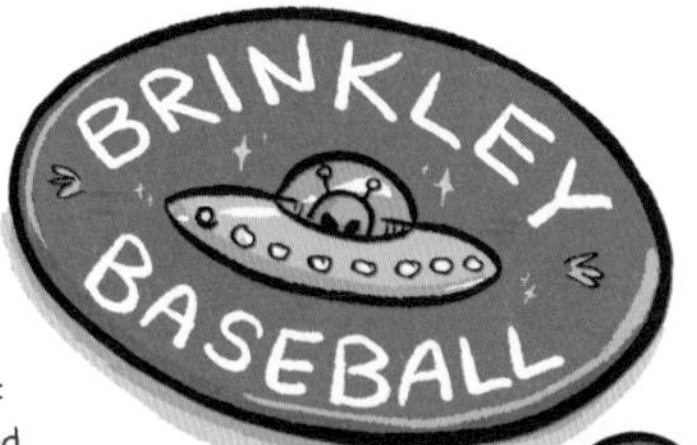
BRINKLEY
BASEBALL

Editor: Marisa DiNovis
Designer: Jade Rector
Copy Editor: Artie Bennett
Managing Editor: Jake Eldred
Production Manager: Claribel Vasquez

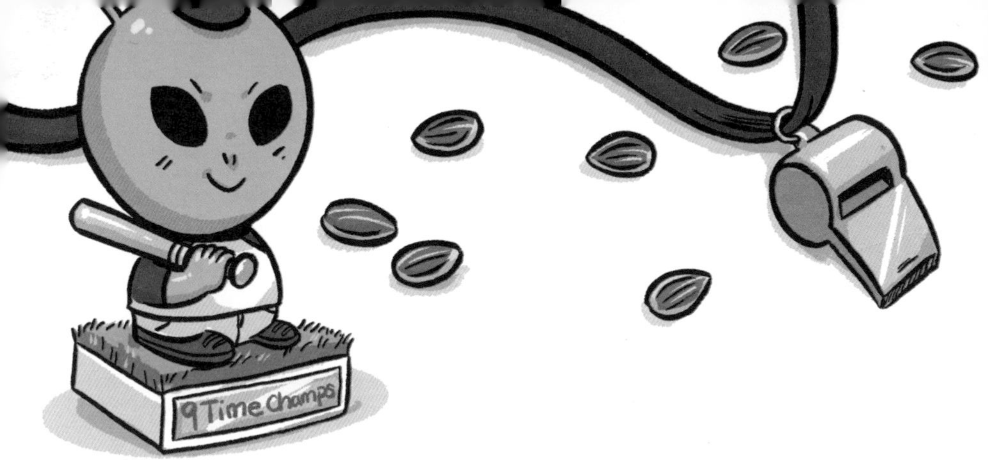
9 Time Champs

To all the kids looking
for their place on a team

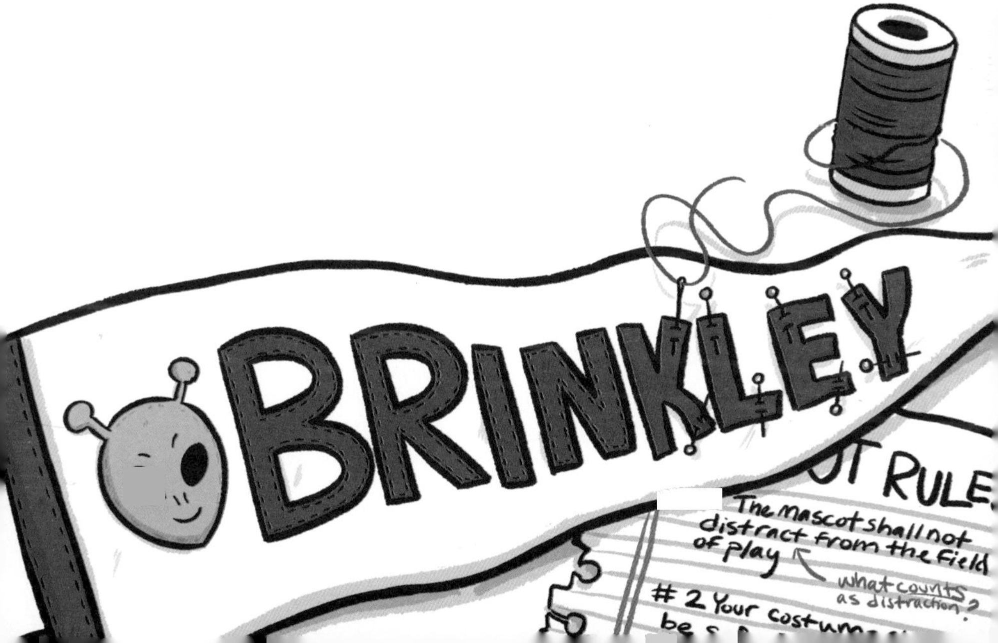
BRINKLEY
RULE
The mascot shall not distract from the field of play
what counts as distraction?
#2 Your

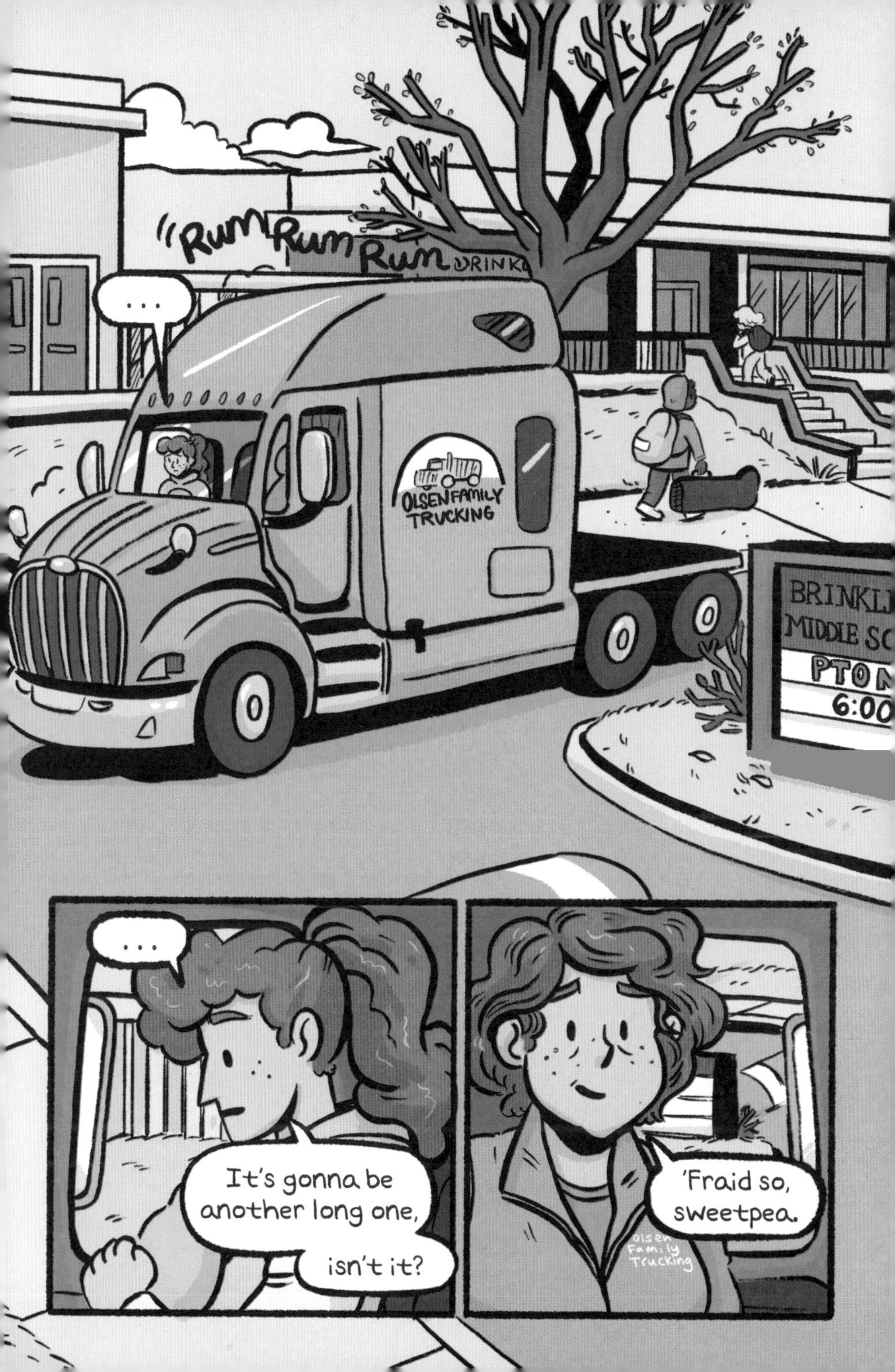
Rum Rum Run
BRINK
...
OLSEN FAMILY TRUCKING
BRINKL
MIDDLE SC
PTO N
6:00
...
It's gonna be another long one,
isn't it?
'Fraid so, sweetpea.
Olsen Family Trucking

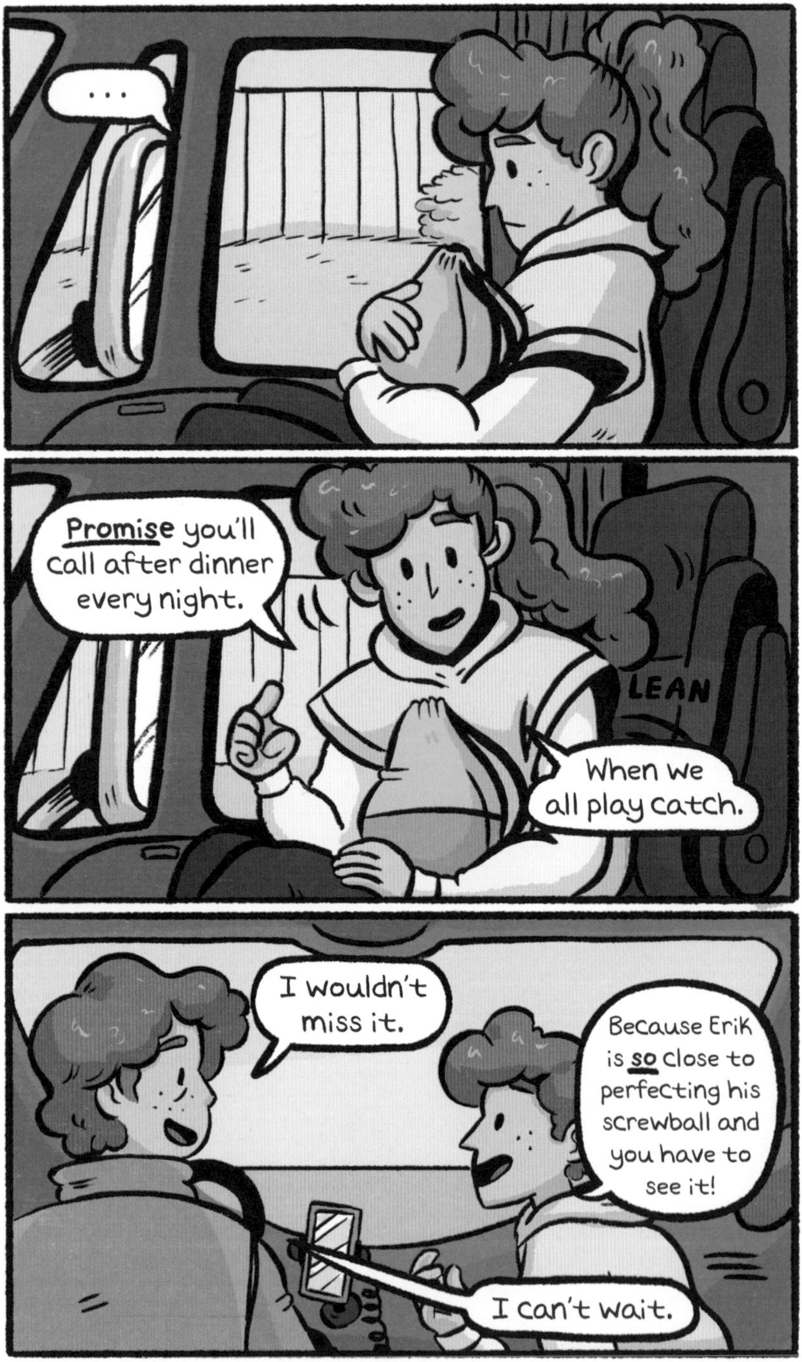
...
Promise you'll call after dinner every night.
LEAN
When we all play catch.
I wouldn't miss it.
Because Erik is so close to perfecting his screwball and you have to see it!
I can't wait.

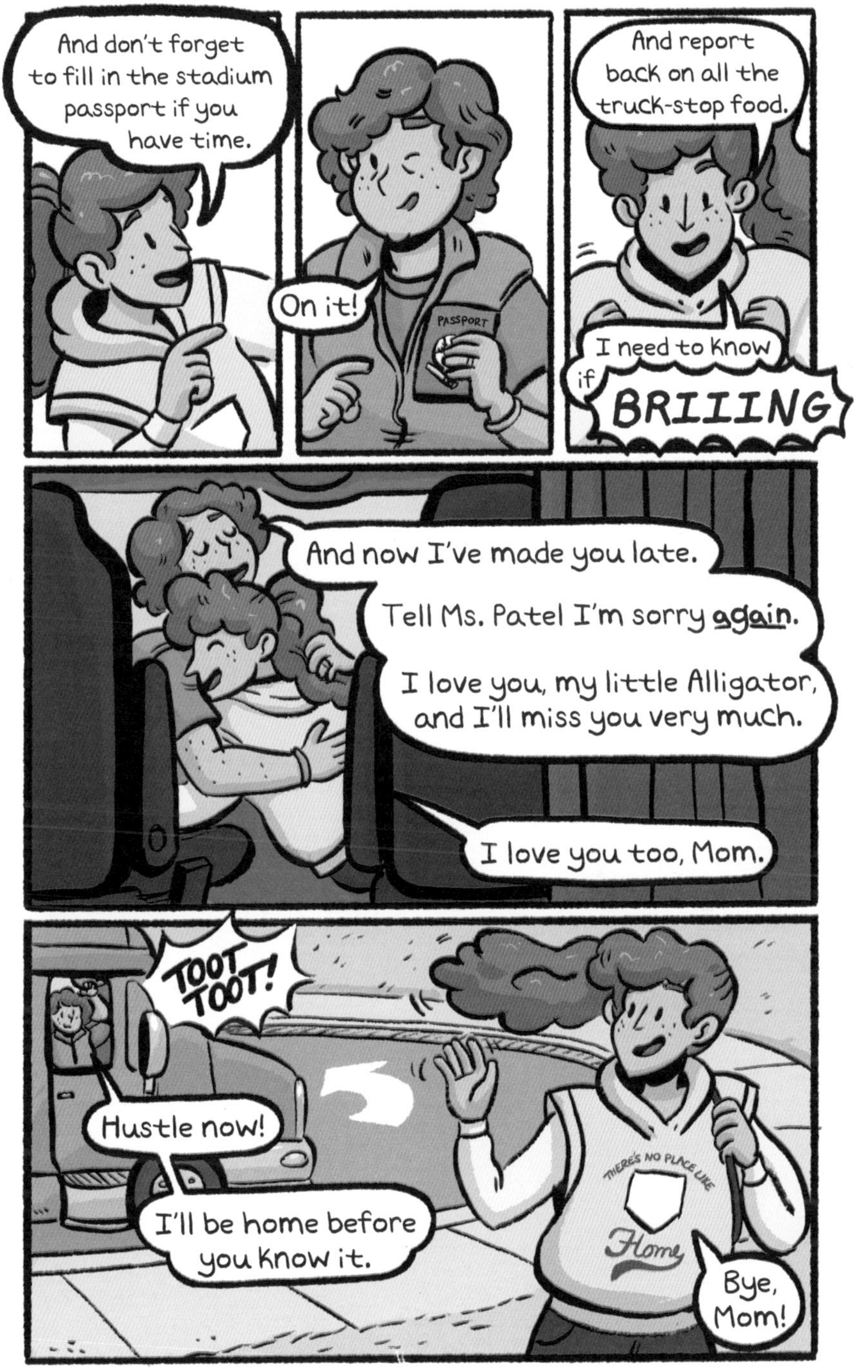
And don't forget to fill in the stadium passport if you have time.
On it!
PASSPORT
And report back on all the truck-stop food.
I need to know if
BRIIING
And now I've made you late.
Tell Ms. Patel I'm sorry again.
I love you, my little Alligator, and I'll miss you very much.
I love you too, Mom.
TOOT TOOT!
Hustle now!
I'll be home before you know it.
THERE'S NO PLACE LIKE Home
Bye, Mom!

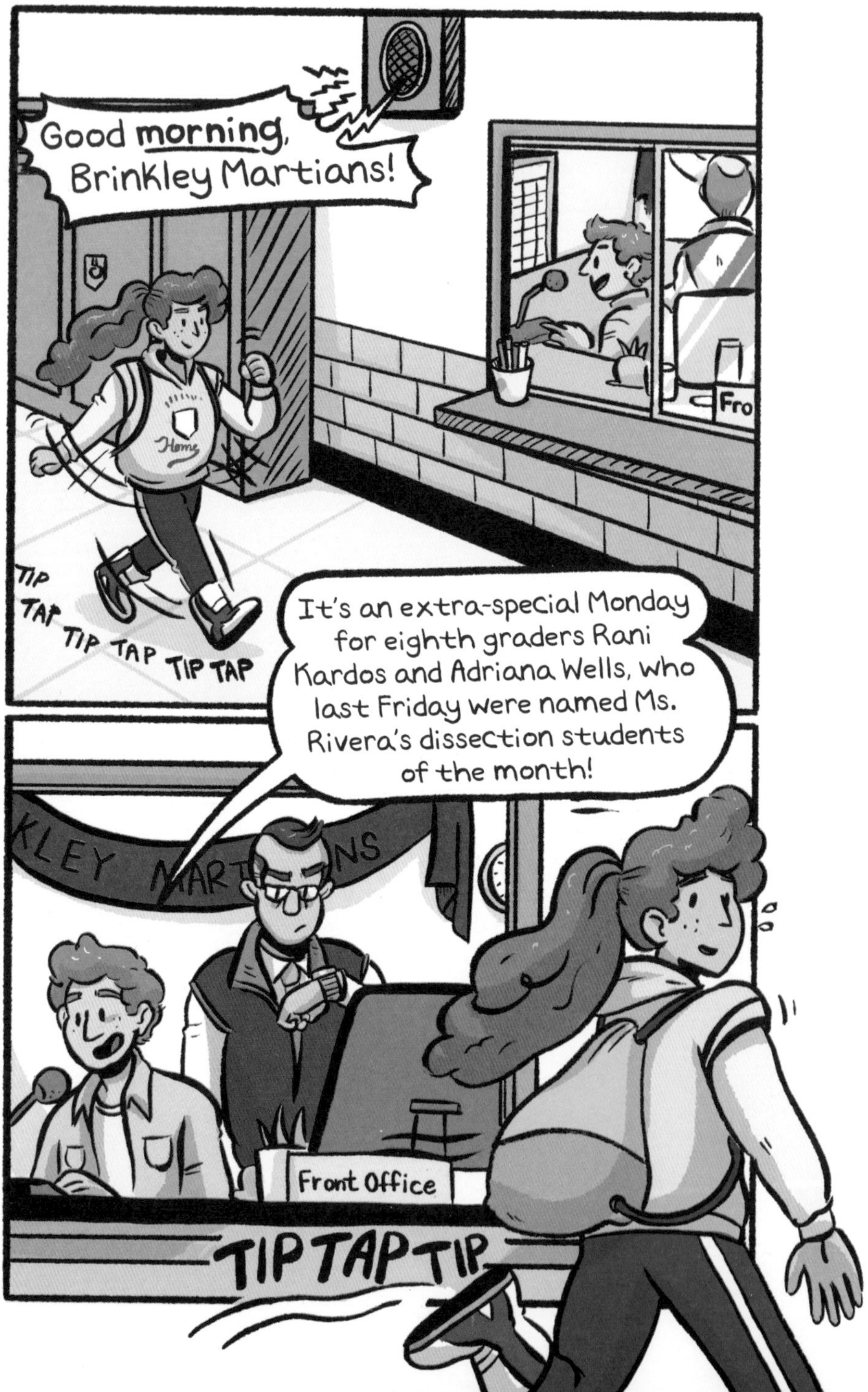
Good morning, Brinkley Martians!
TIP TAP TIP TAP TIP TAP
Fro
It's an extra-special Monday for eighth graders Rani Kardos and Adriana Wells, who last Friday were named Ms. Rivera's dissection students of the month!
KLEY MARTIANS
Front Office
TIP TAP TIP

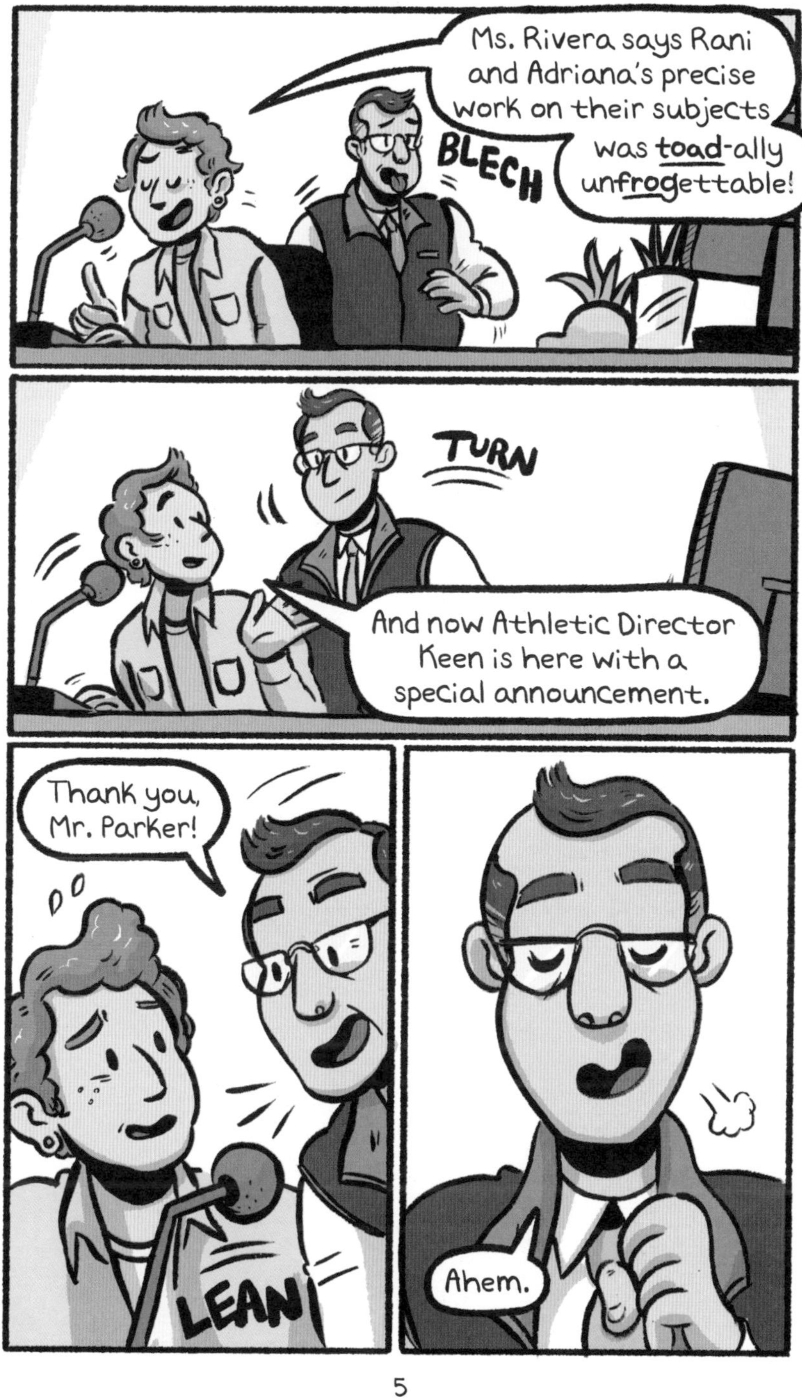
Ms. Rivera says Rani and Adriana's precise work on their subjects
was toad-ally unfrogettable!
BLECH
TURN
And now Athletic Director Keen is here with a special announcement.
Thank you, Mr. Parker!
LEAN
Ahem.

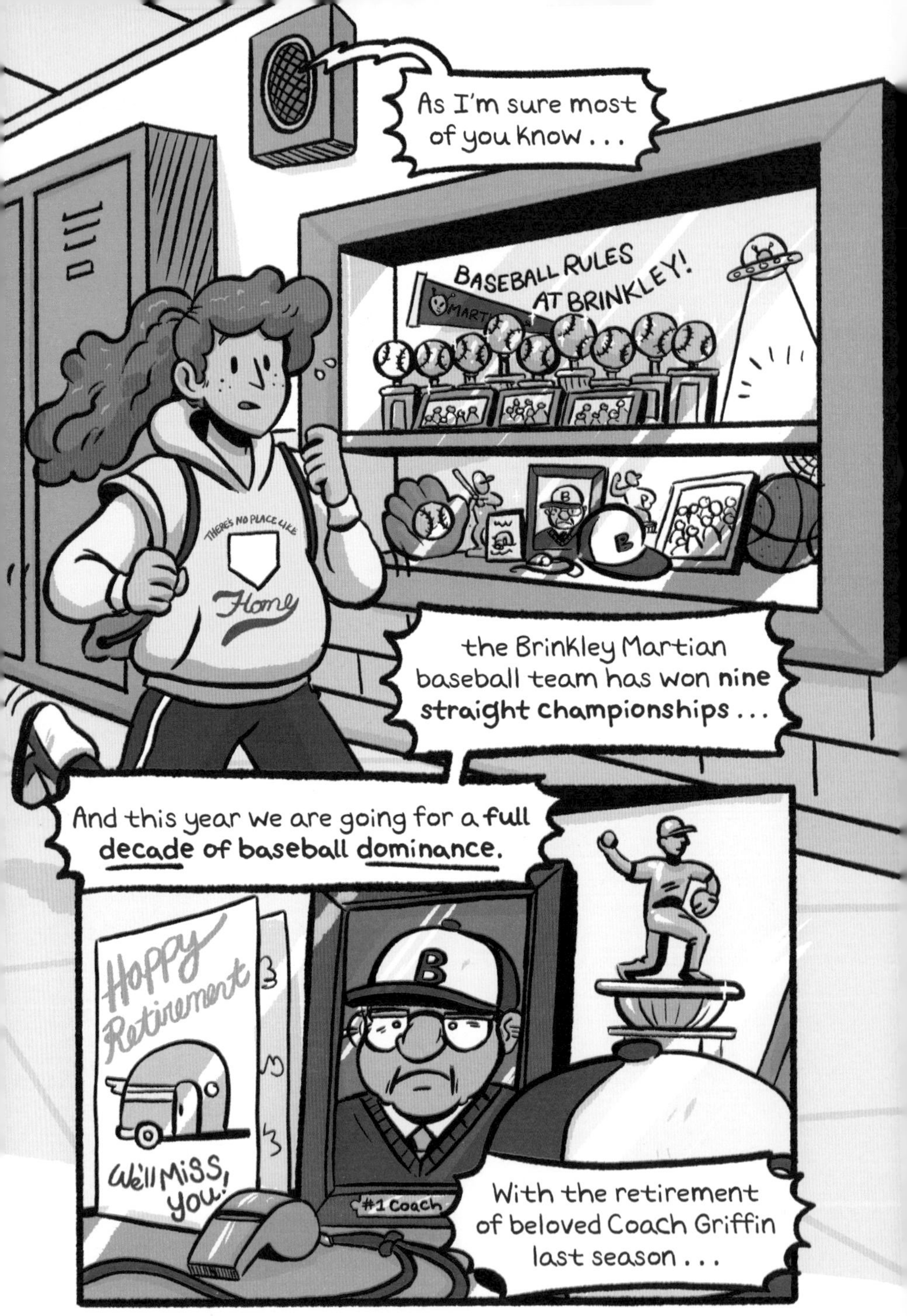
As I'm sure most of you know . . .
BASEBALL RULES AT BRINKLEY!
THERE'S NO PLACE LIKE Home
the Brinkley Martian baseball team has won nine straight championships . . .
And this year we are going for a full decade of baseball dominance.
Happy Retirement
We'll MISS you!
#1 Coach
With the retirement of beloved Coach Griffin last season . . .

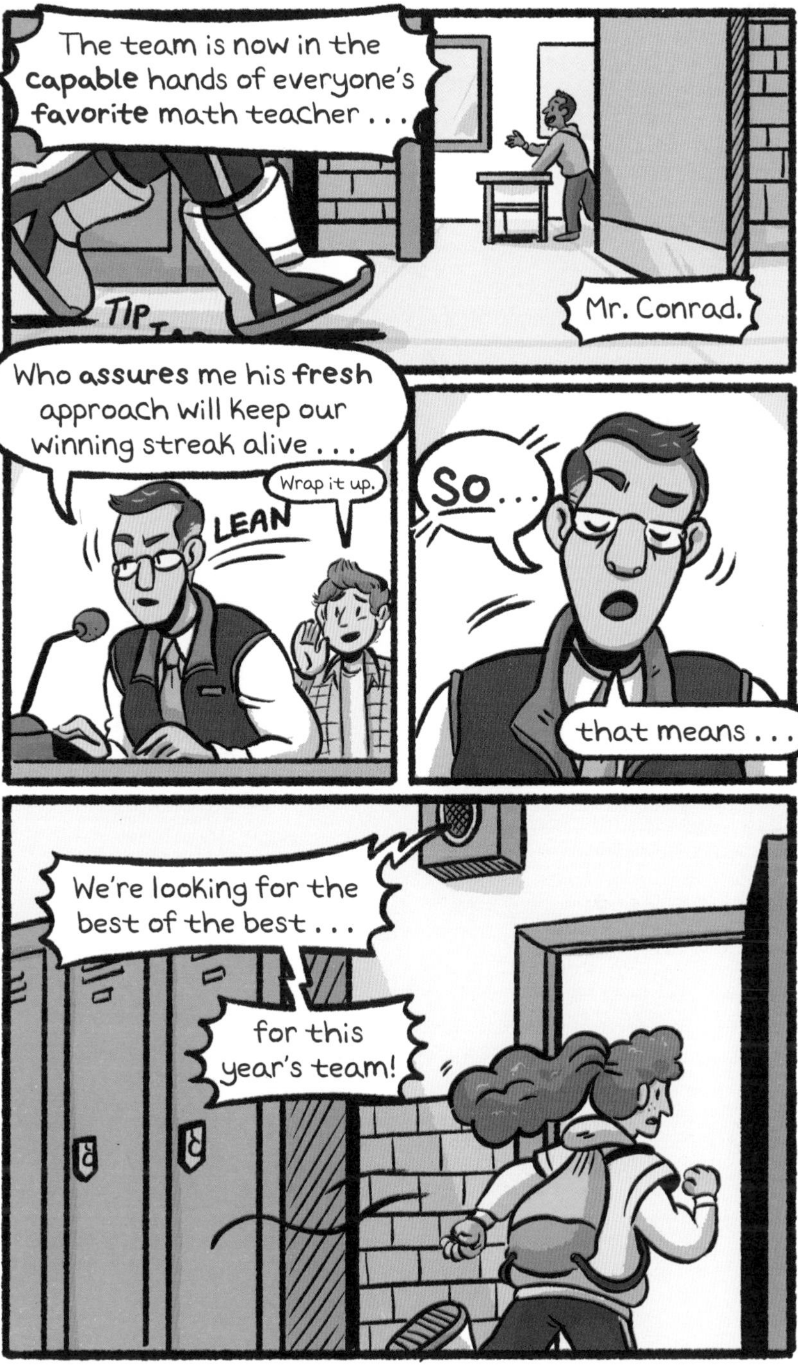
The team is now in the **capable** hands of everyone's **favorite** math teacher . . .
TIP
Mr. Conrad.
Who **assures** me his **fresh** approach will keep our winning streak alive . . .
LEAN
Wrap it up.
SO . . .
that means . . .
We're looking for the best of the best . . .
for this year's team!

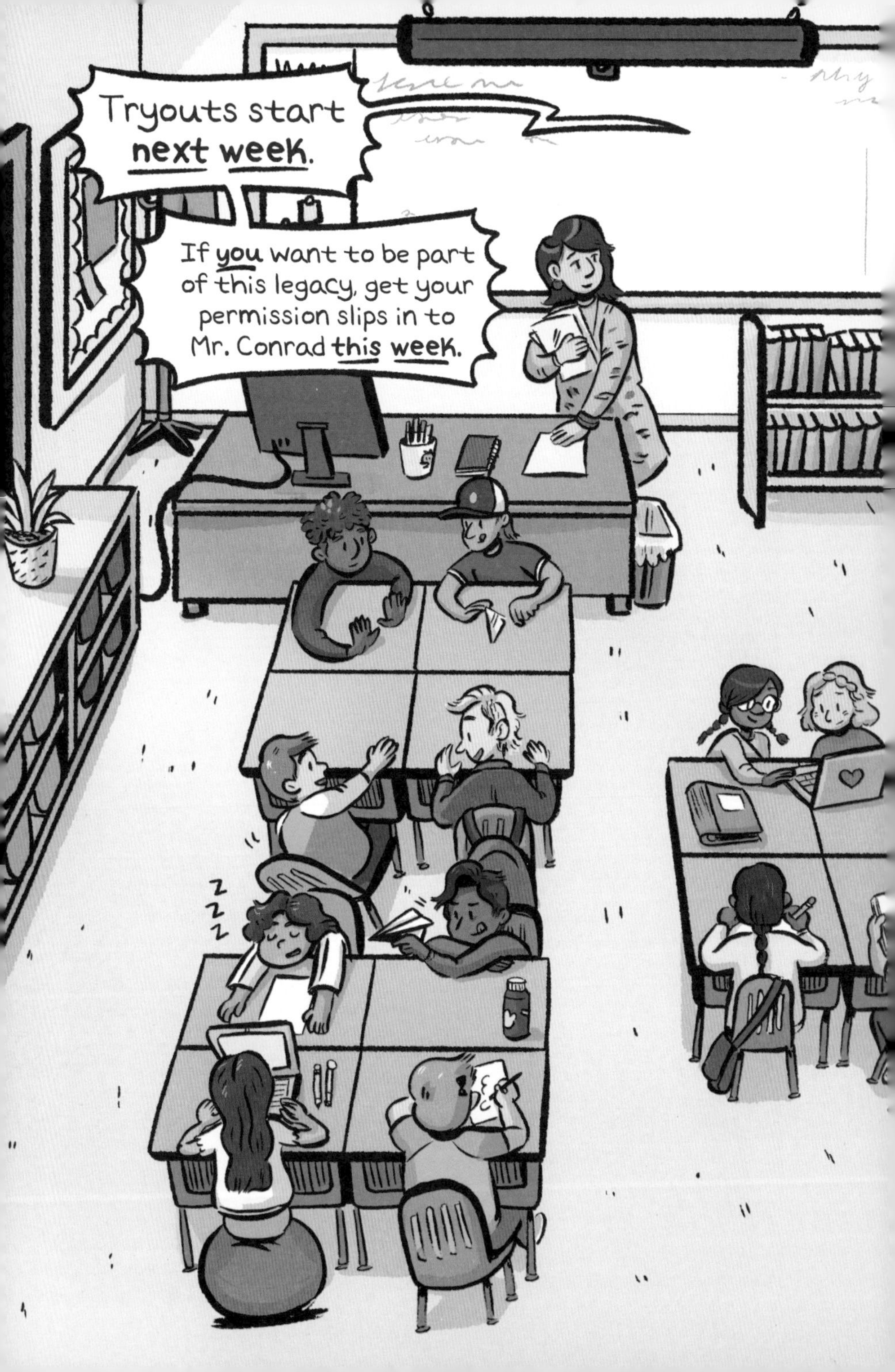
Tryouts start next week.
If you want to be part of this legacy, get your permission slips in to Mr. Conrad this week.

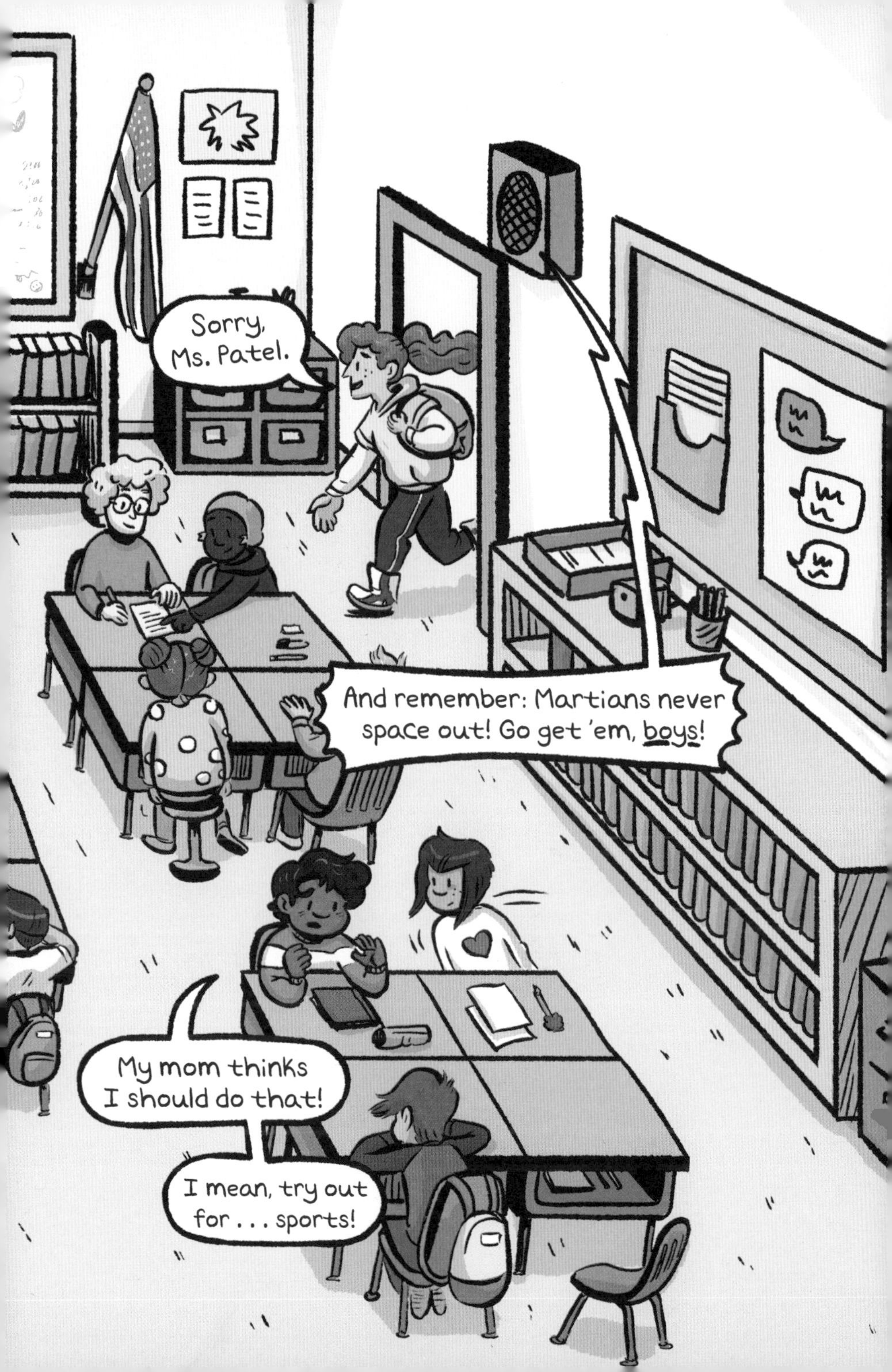
Sorry, Ms. Patel.
And remember: Martians never space out! Go get 'em, boys!
My mom thinks I should do that!
I mean, try out for . . . sports!

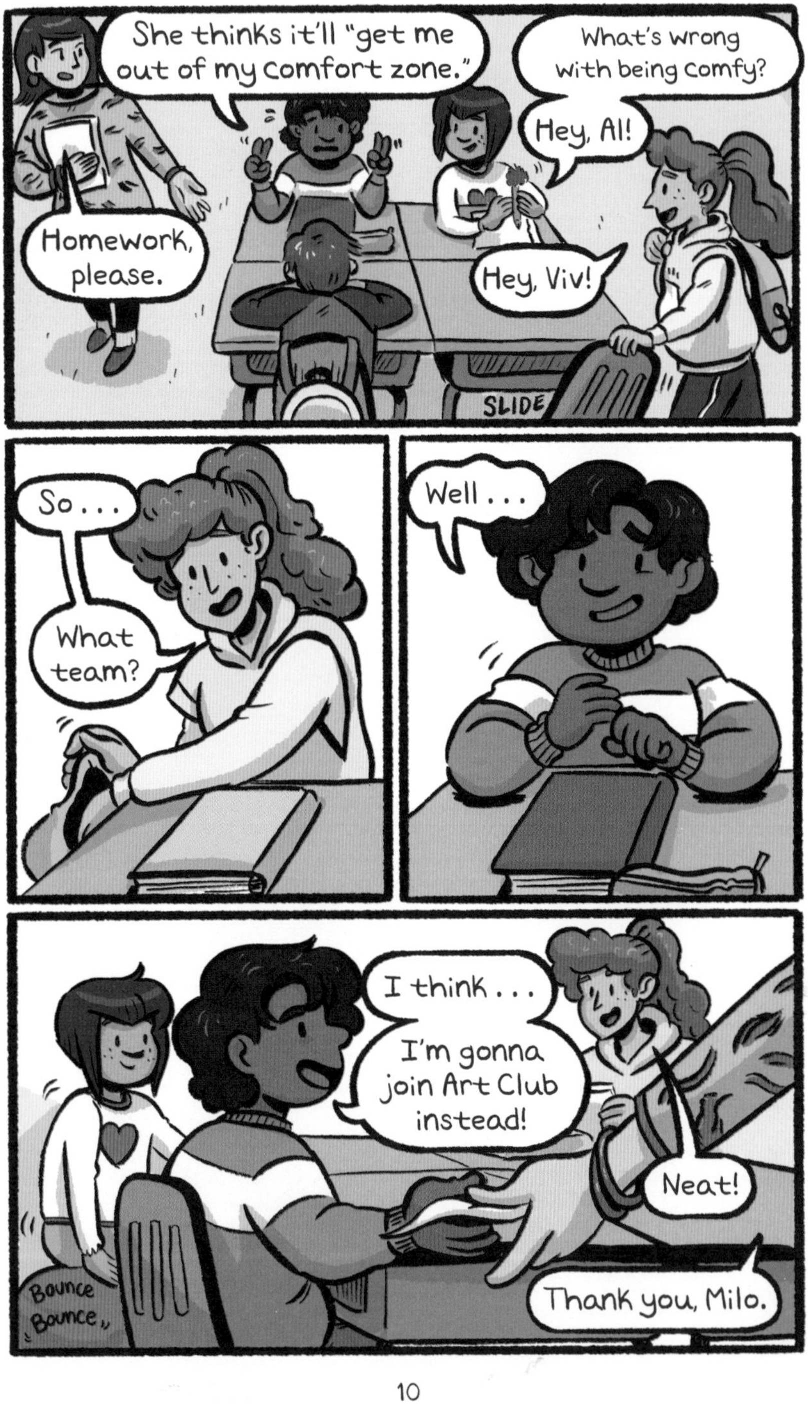
She thinks it'll "get me out of my comfort zone."
What's wrong with being comfy?
Hey, Al!
Homework, please.
Hey, Viv!
SLIDE
So . . .
What team?
Well . . .
I think . . .
I'm gonna join Art Club instead!
Neat!
Bounce Bounce
Thank you, Milo.

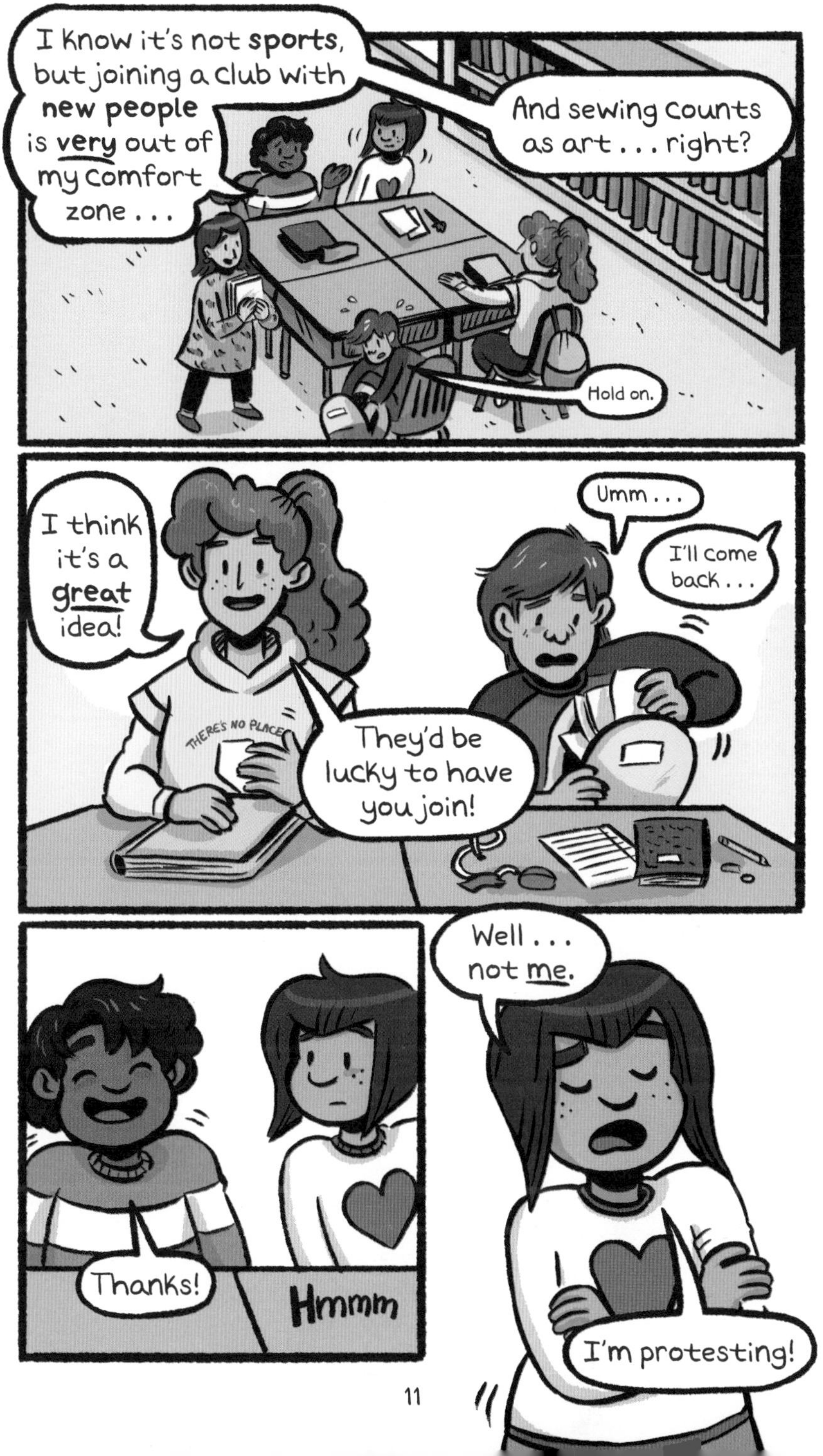
I know it's not sports, but joining a club with new people is very out of my comfort zone . . .
And sewing counts as art . . . right?
Hold on.
I think it's a great idea!
Umm . . .
I'll come back . . .
THERE'S NO PLACE
They'd be lucky to have you join!
Thanks!
Hmmm
Well . . . not me.
I'm protesting!

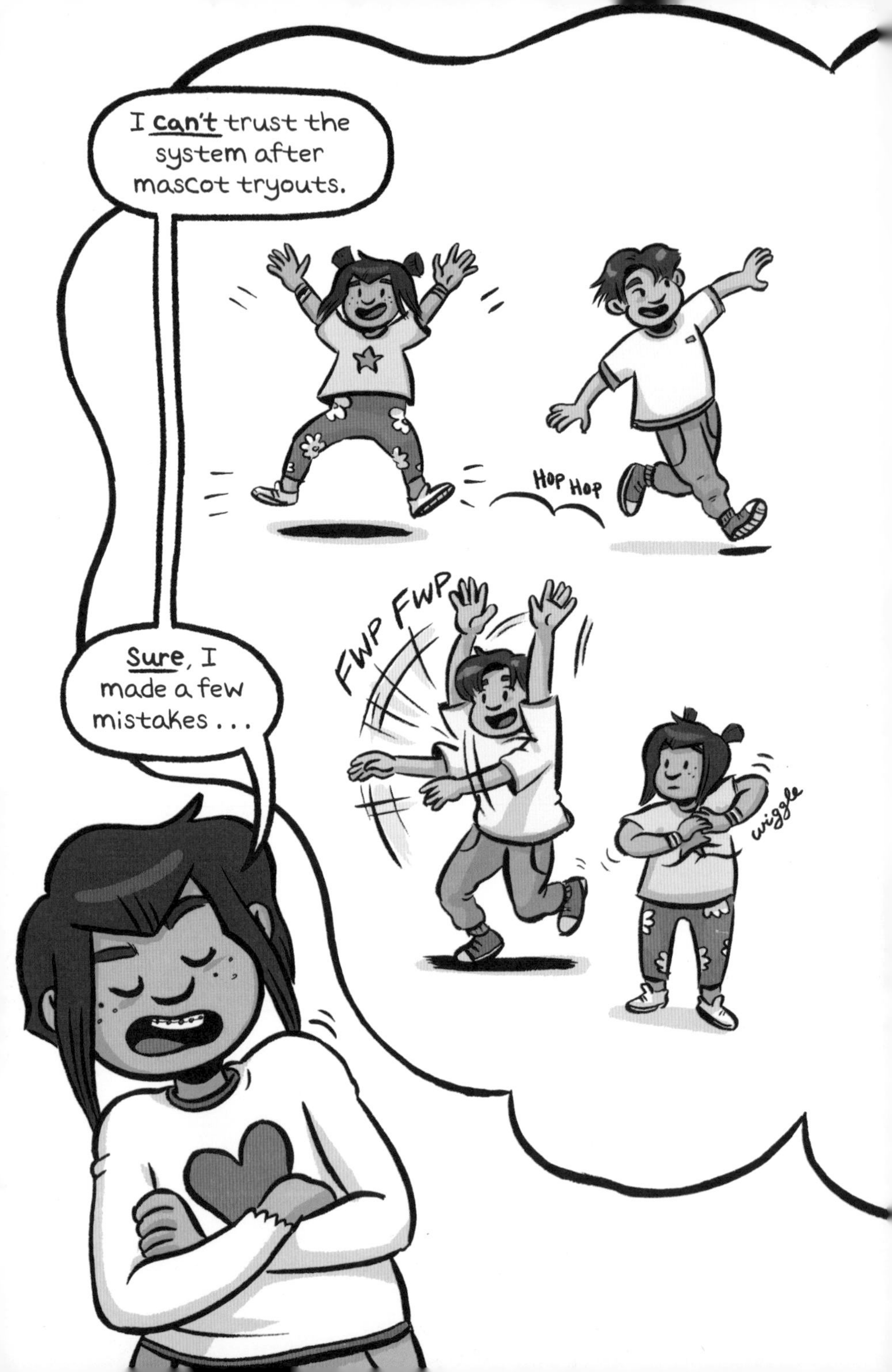

I can't trust the system after mascot tryouts.
HOP HOP
FWP FWP
Sure, I made a few mistakes . . .
wiggle

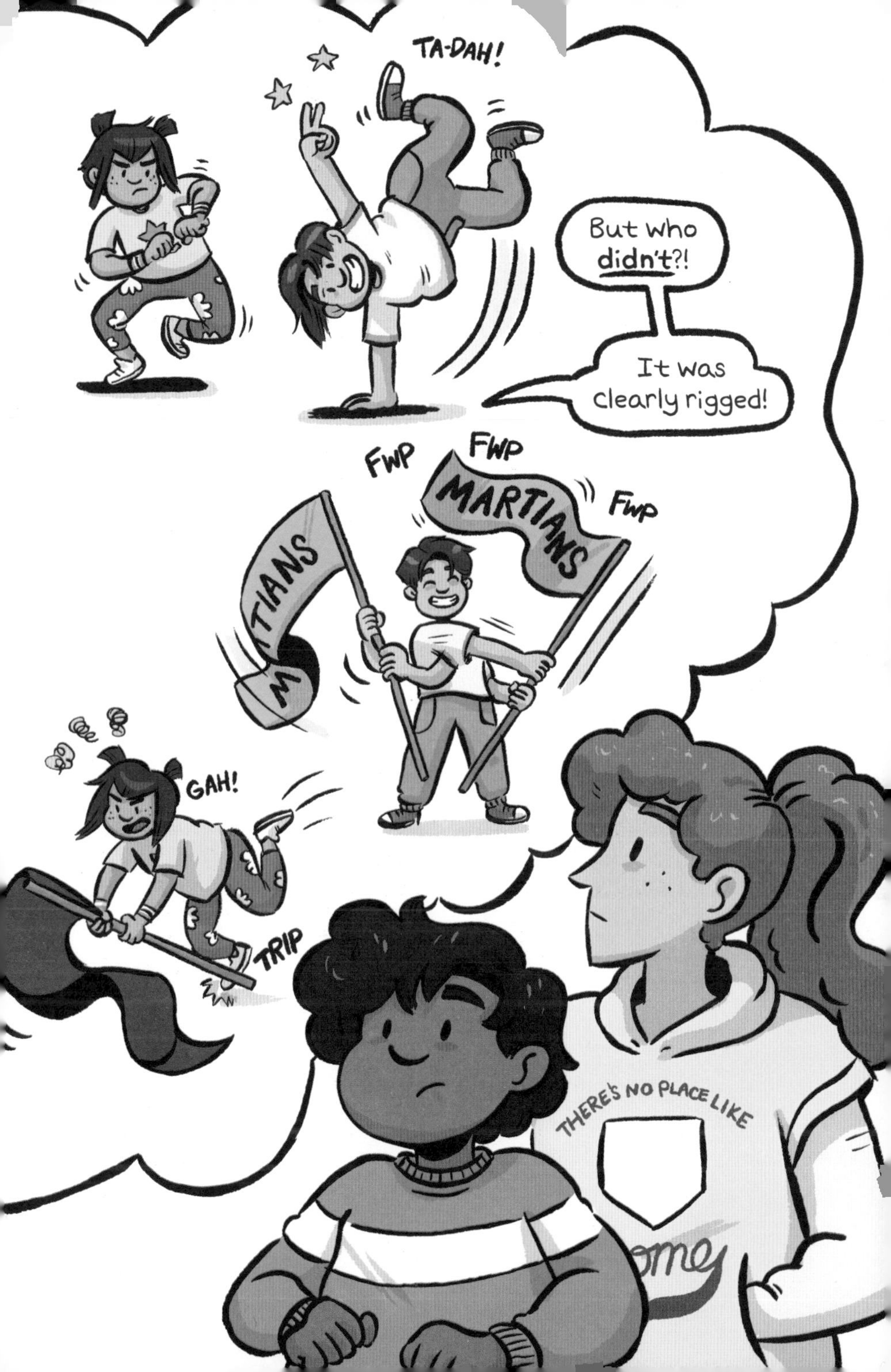
TA-DAH!
But who didn't?!
It was clearly rigged!
FWP
FWP
FWP
MARTIANS
MARTIANS
GAH!
TRIP
THERE'S NO PLACE LIKE
ome

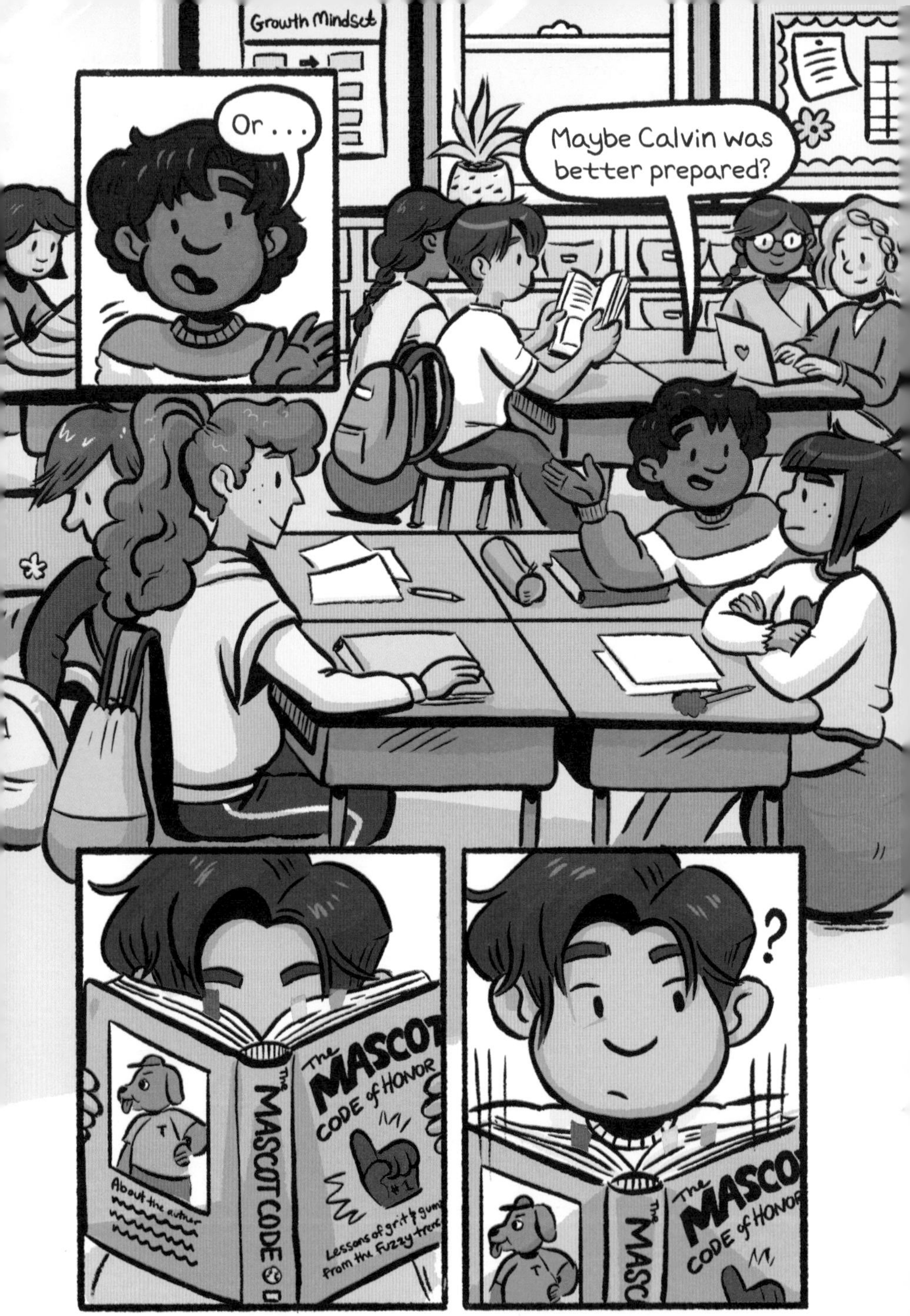
Growth Mindset
Or . . .
Maybe Calvin was better prepared?
The MASCOT CODE of HONOR
The MASCOT CODE
About the author
?

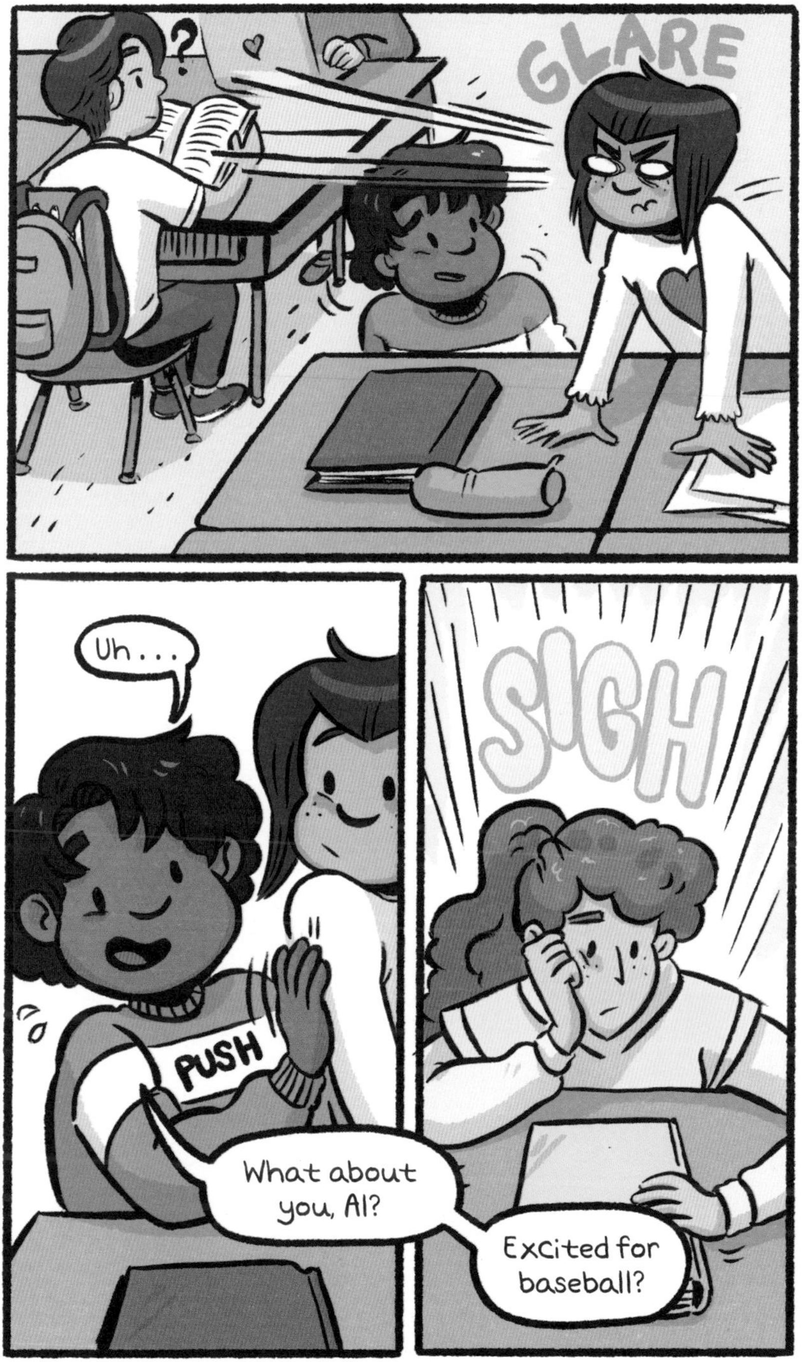
GLARE
?
Uh...
PUSH
SIGH
What about you, Al?
Excited for baseball?

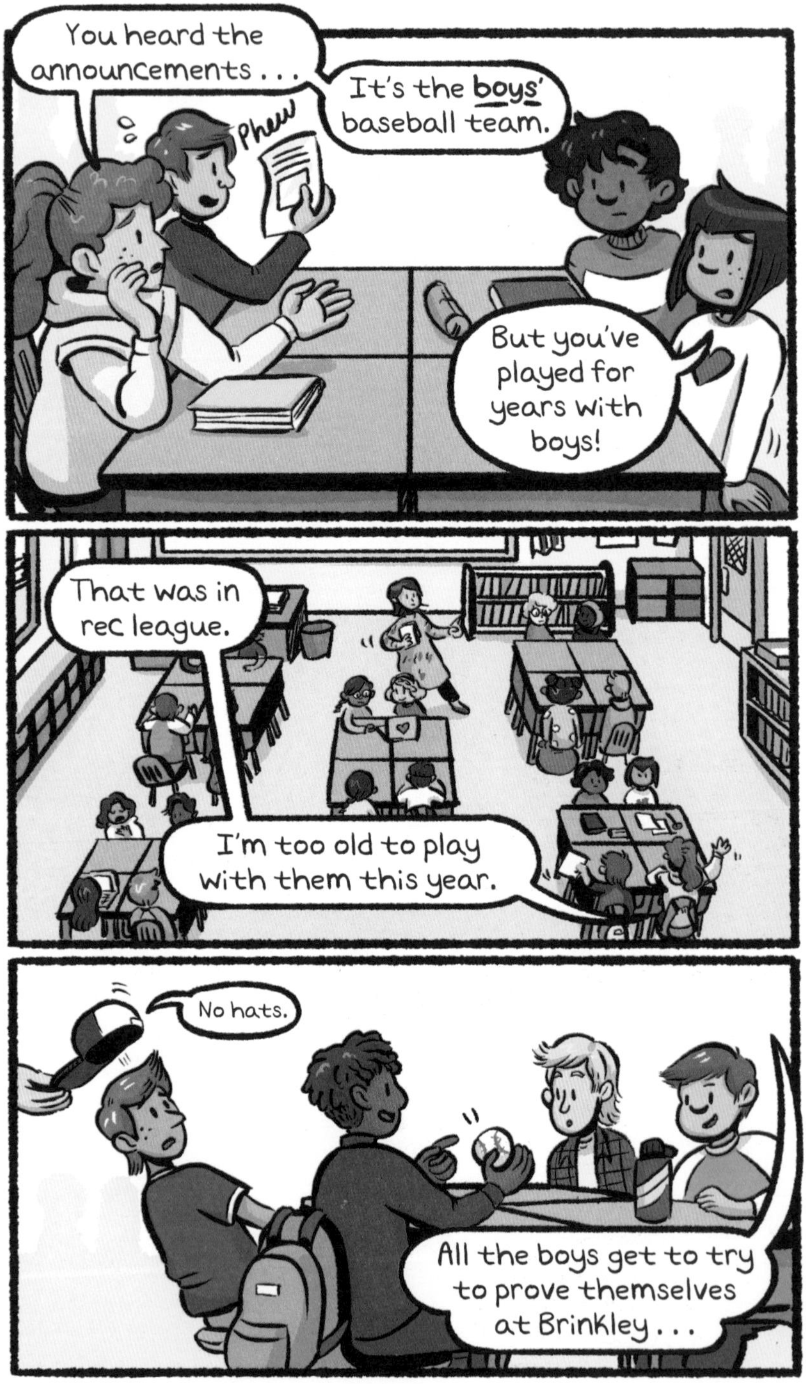
You heard the announcements . . .
Phew
It's the **boys'** baseball team.
But you've played for years with boys!
That was in rec league.
I'm too old to play with them this year.
No hats.
All the boys get to try to prove themselves at Brinkley . . .

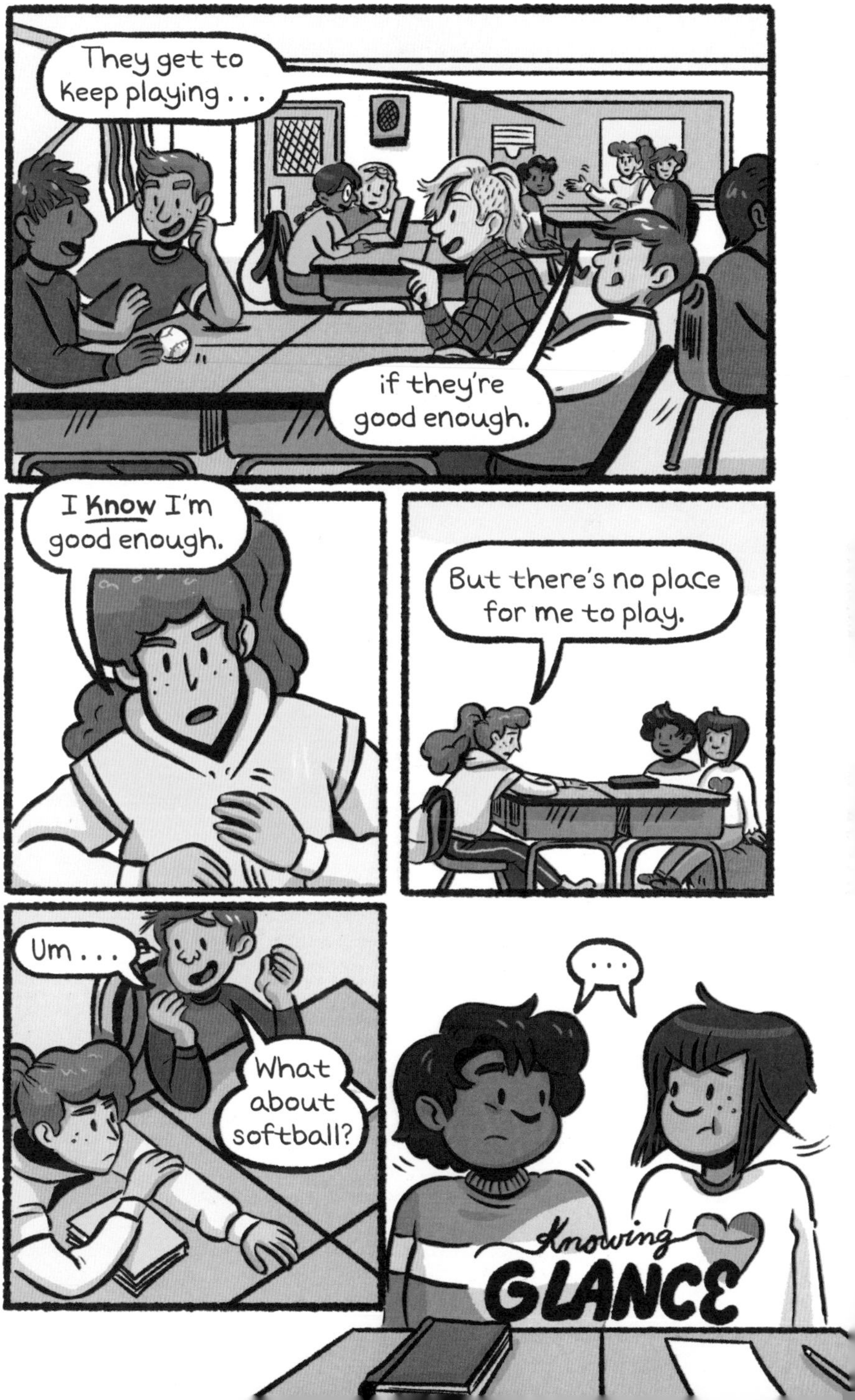
They get to keep playing . . .
if they're good enough.
I Know I'm good enough.
But there's no place for me to play.
Um . . .
What about softball?
. . .
Knowing GLANCE

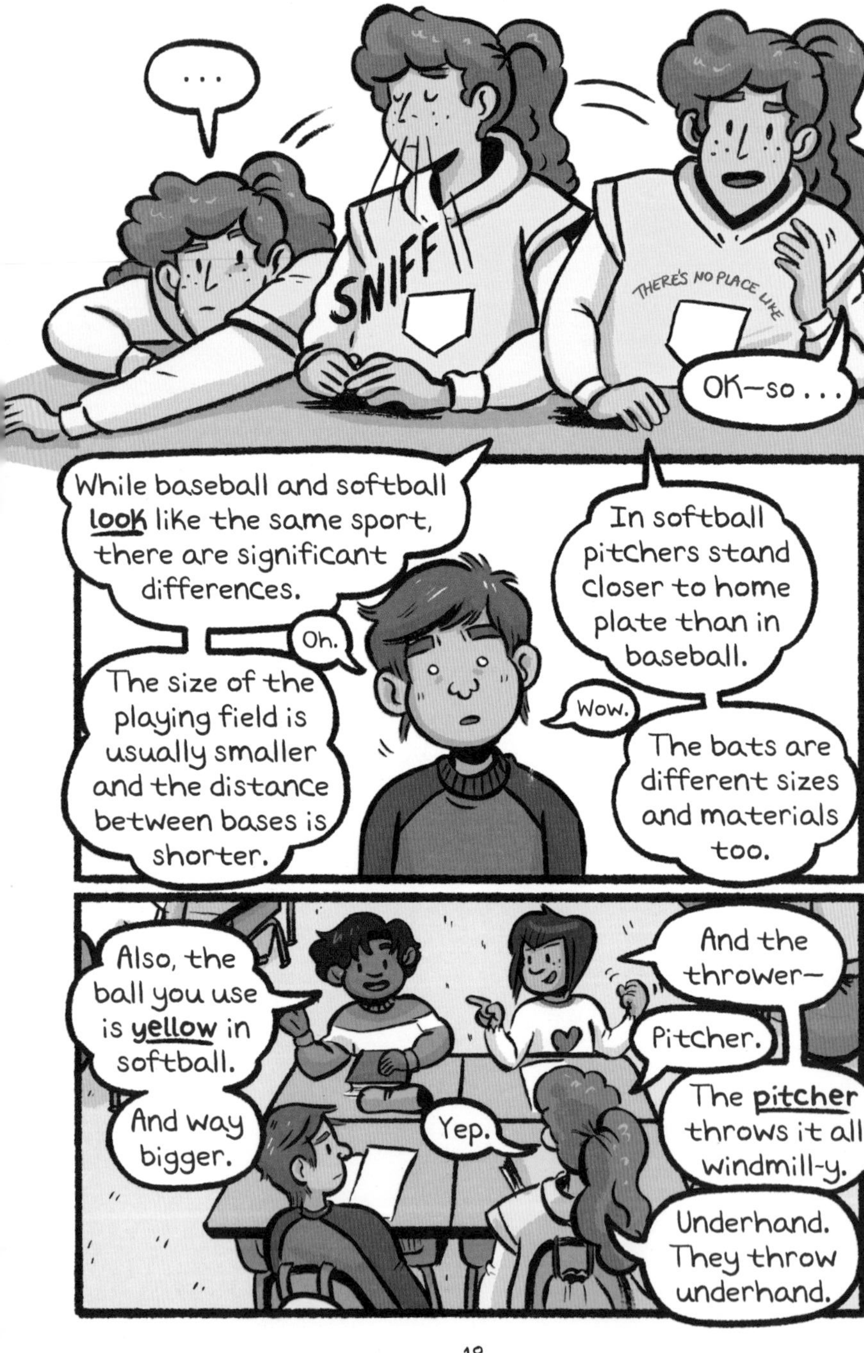
. . .
SNIFF
THERE'S NO PLACE LIKE
OK—so . . .
While baseball and softball look like the same sport, there are significant differences.
In softball pitchers stand closer to home plate than in baseball.
Oh.
The size of the playing field is usually smaller and the distance between bases is shorter.
Wow.
The bats are different sizes and materials too.
Also, the ball you use is yellow in softball.
And way bigger.
Yep.
And the thrower—
Pitcher.
The pitcher throws it all windmill-y.
Underhand. They throw underhand.

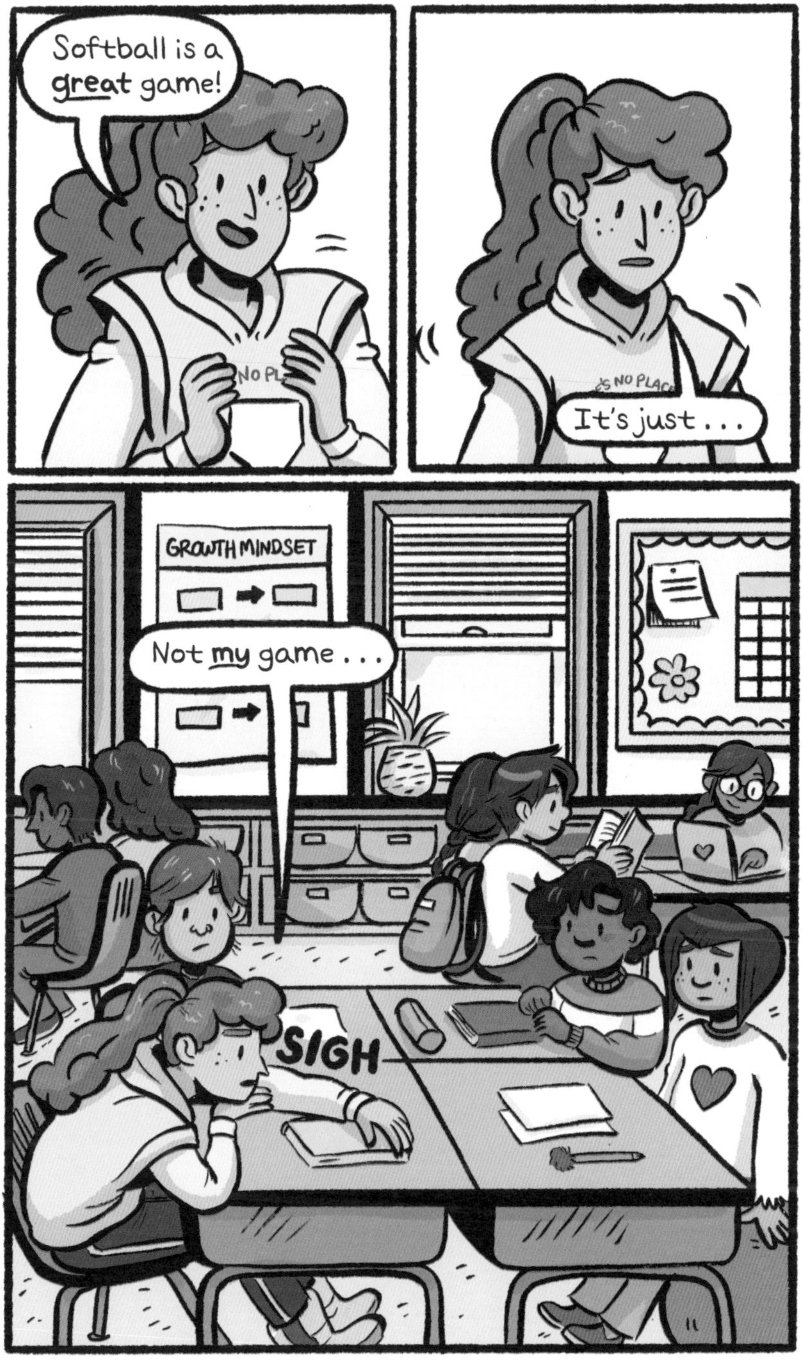
Softball is a great game!
It's just . . .
GROWTH MINDSET
Not my game . . .
SIGH

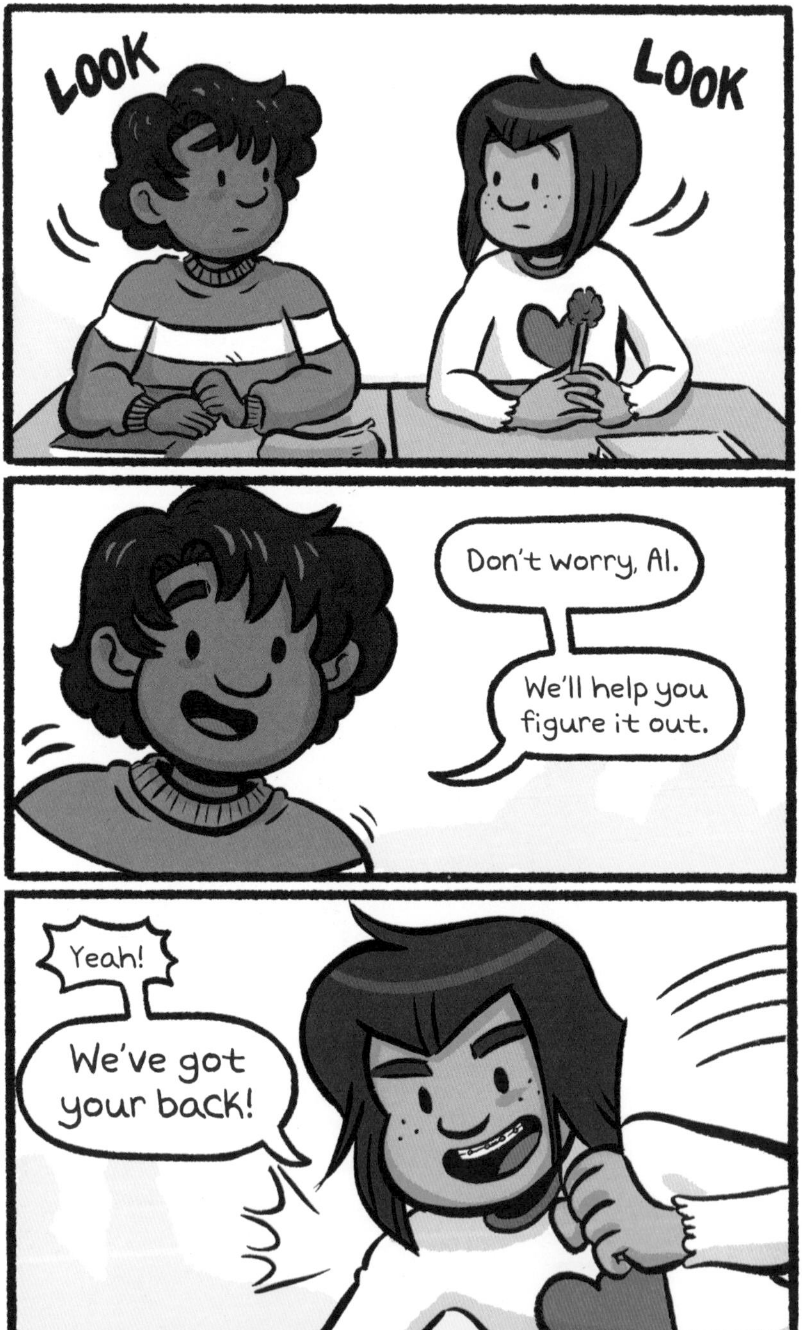
LOOK
LOOK
Don't worry, Al.
We'll help you figure it out.
Yeah!
We've got your back!

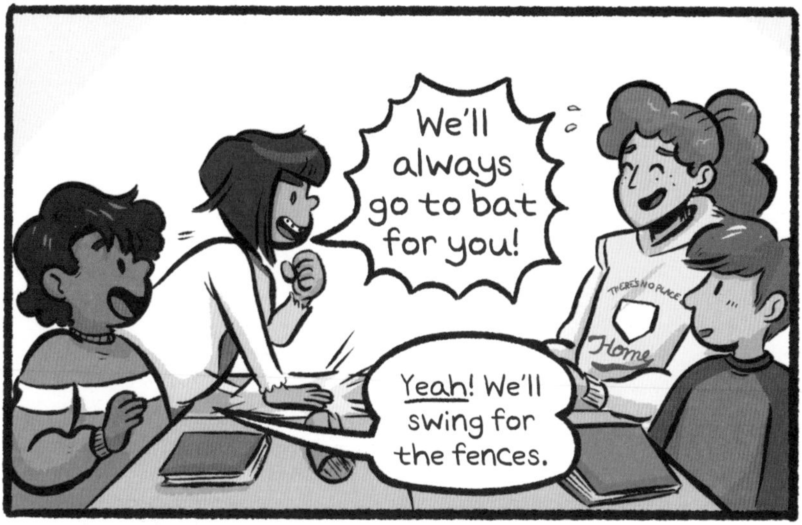
We'll always go to bat for you!
Yeah! We'll swing for the fences.
THERE'S NO PLACE
Home

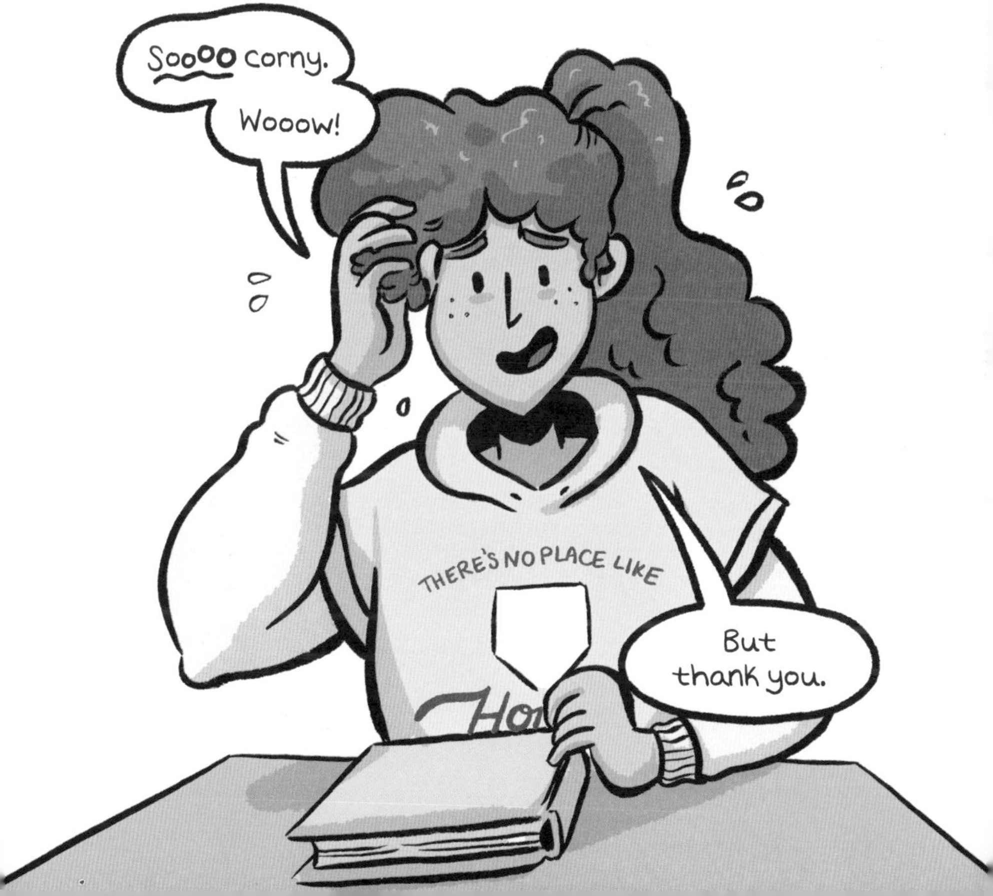
SooOO corny.
Wooow!
THERE'S NO PLACE LIKE
But thank you.

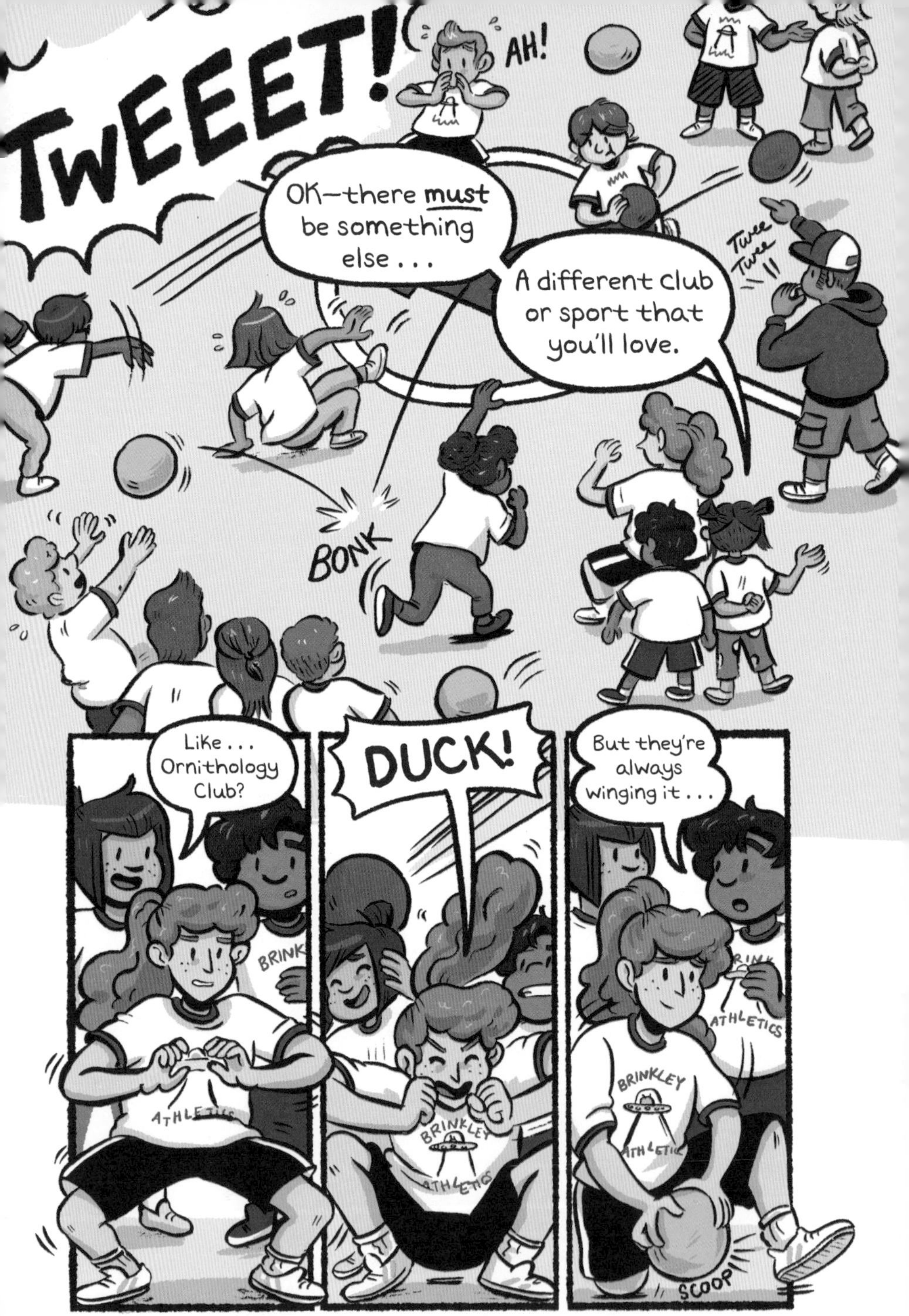
TWEEET!
AH!
OK—there **must** be something else . . .
A different club or sport that you'll love.
Twee Twee
BONK
Like . . . Ornithology Club?
DUCK!
But they're always winging it . . .
SCOOP
BRINKLEY
ATHLETICS

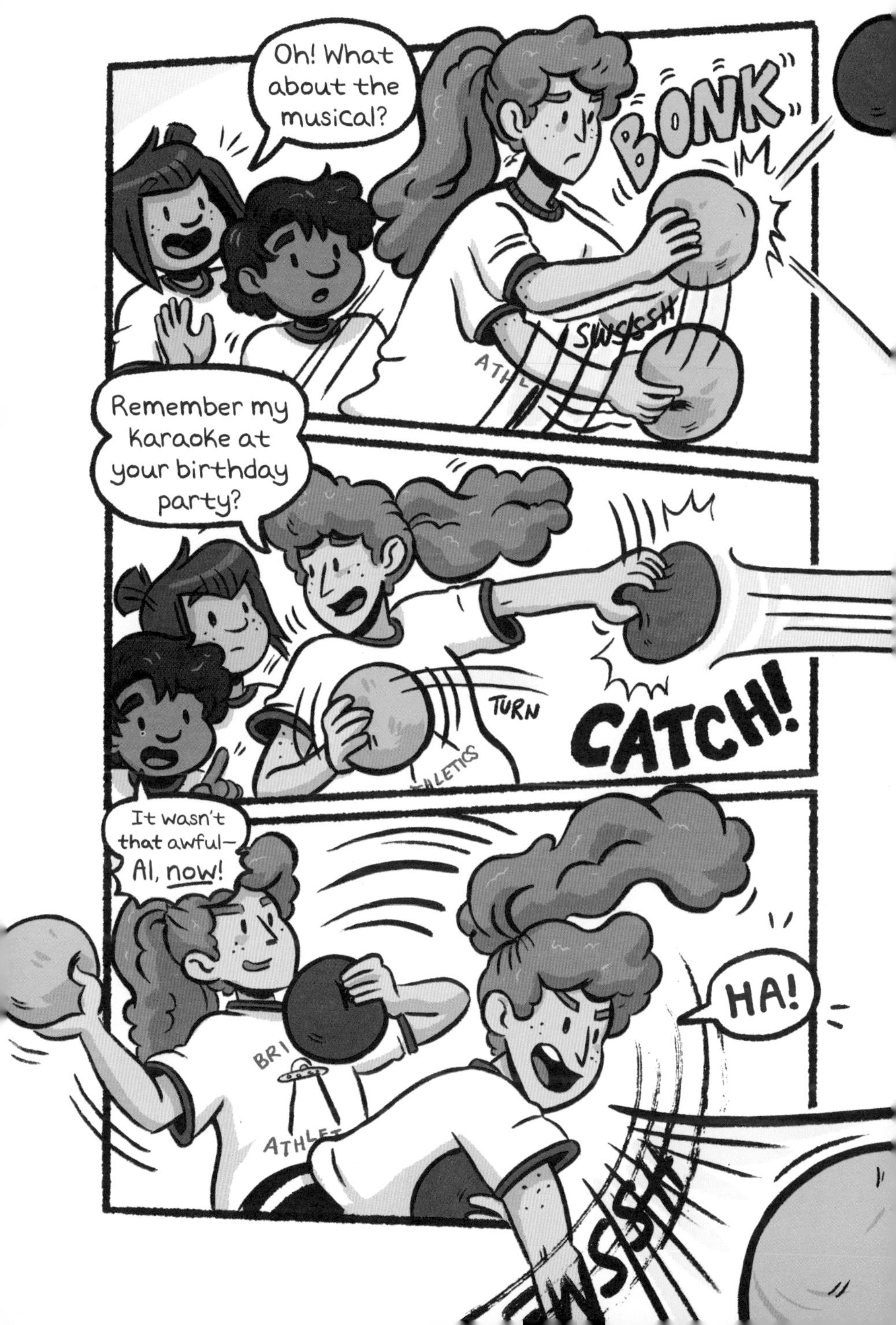

Oh! What about the musical?
BONK
SWSSSH
ATHL
Remember my karaoke at your birthday party?
TURN
LETICS
CATCH!
It wasn't that awful—
Al, now!
HA!
BRI
ATHLET
WSSSH

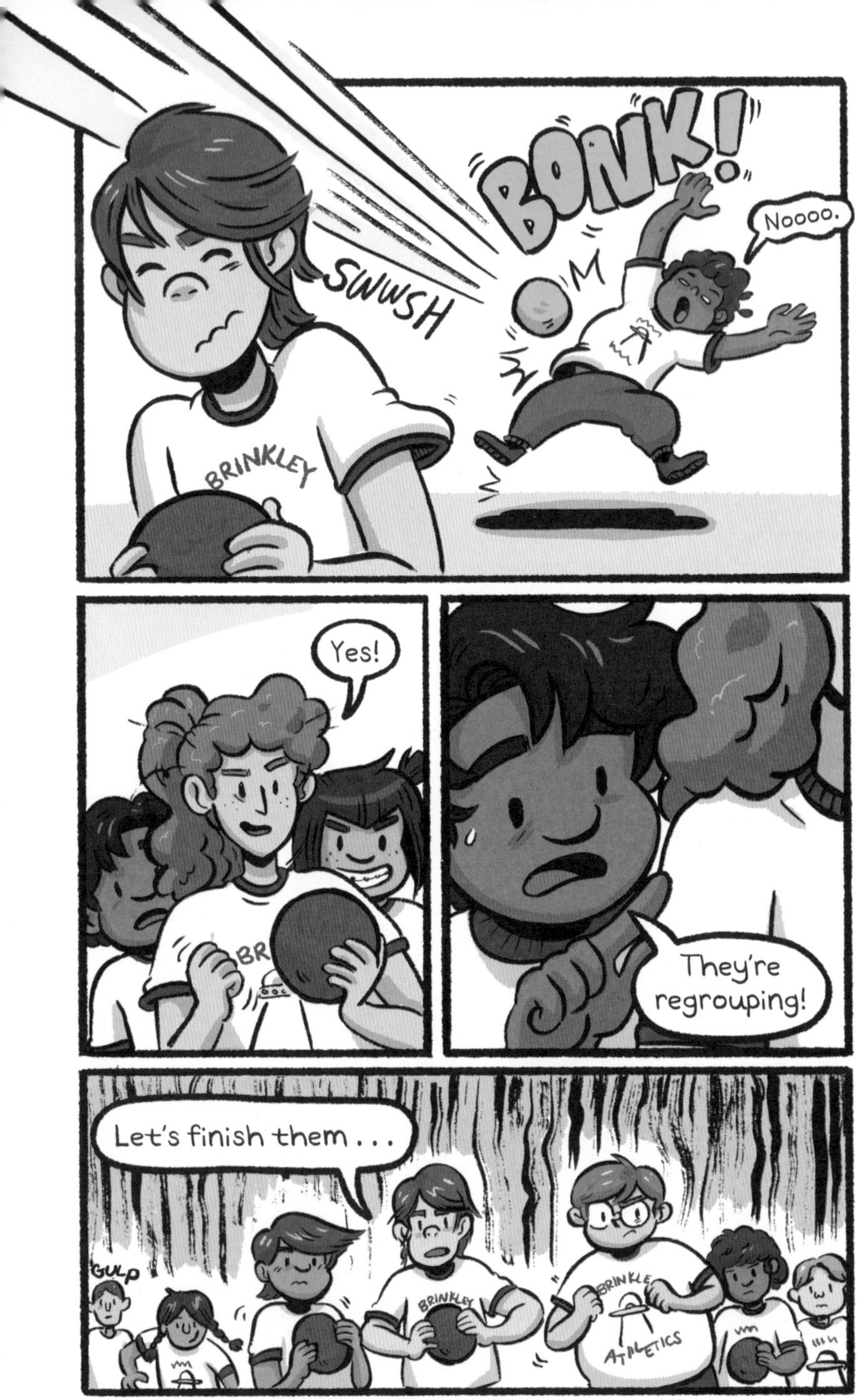
SWWSH
BONK!
WOMM
Noooo.
BRINKLEY
Yes!
They're regrouping!
Let's finish them . . .
GULP
BRINKLEY
BRINKLE
ATHLETICS

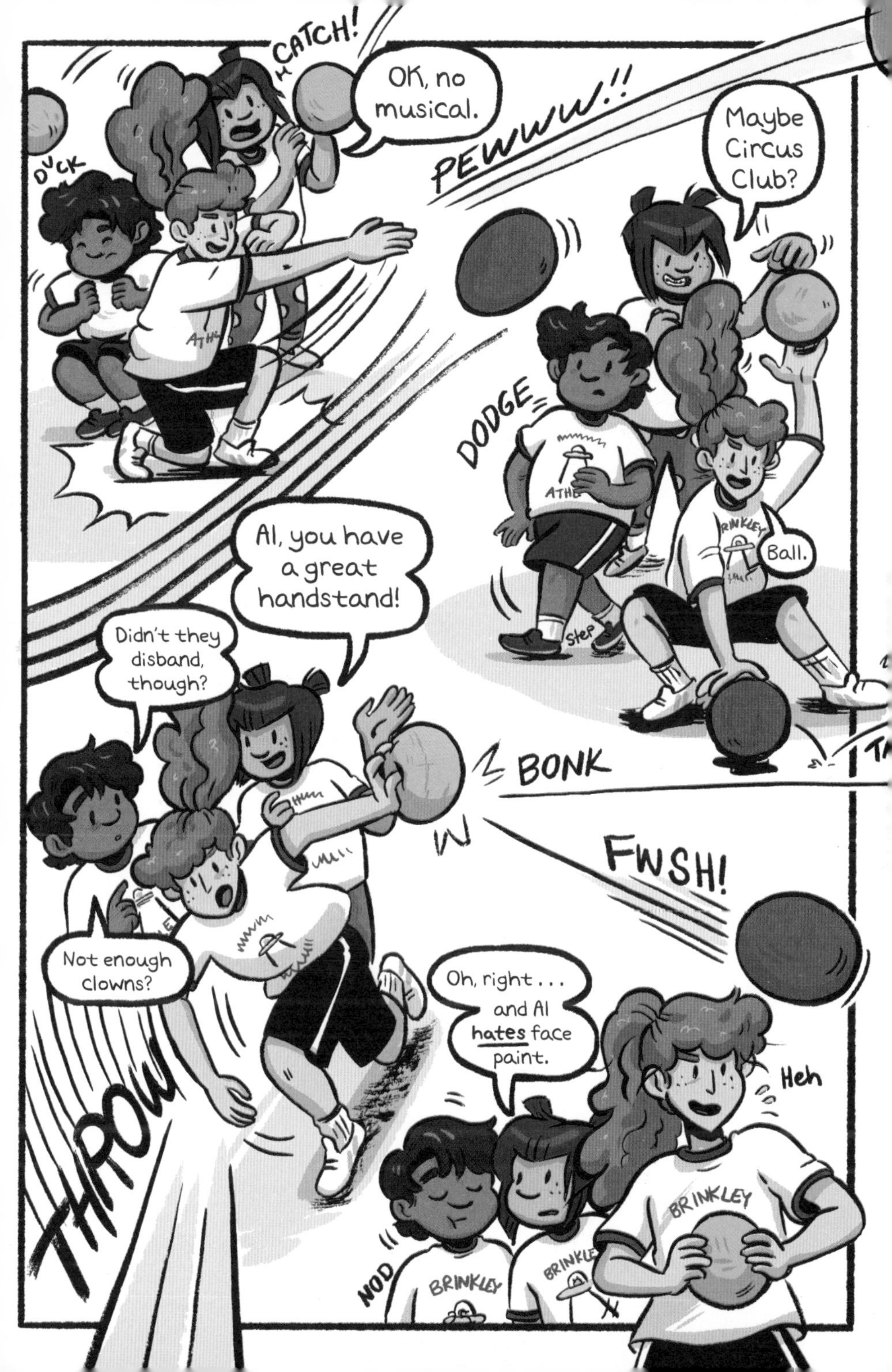
CATCH!
OK, no musical.
DUCK
PEWWW!!
Maybe Circus Club?
DODGE
ATHE
BRINKLEY
Ball.
STEP
BONK
Al, you have a great handstand!
Didn't they disband, though?
Not enough clowns?
FWSH!
THROW
Oh, right . . . and Al hates face paint.
Heh
NOD
BRINKLEY
BRINKLEY
BRINKLEY

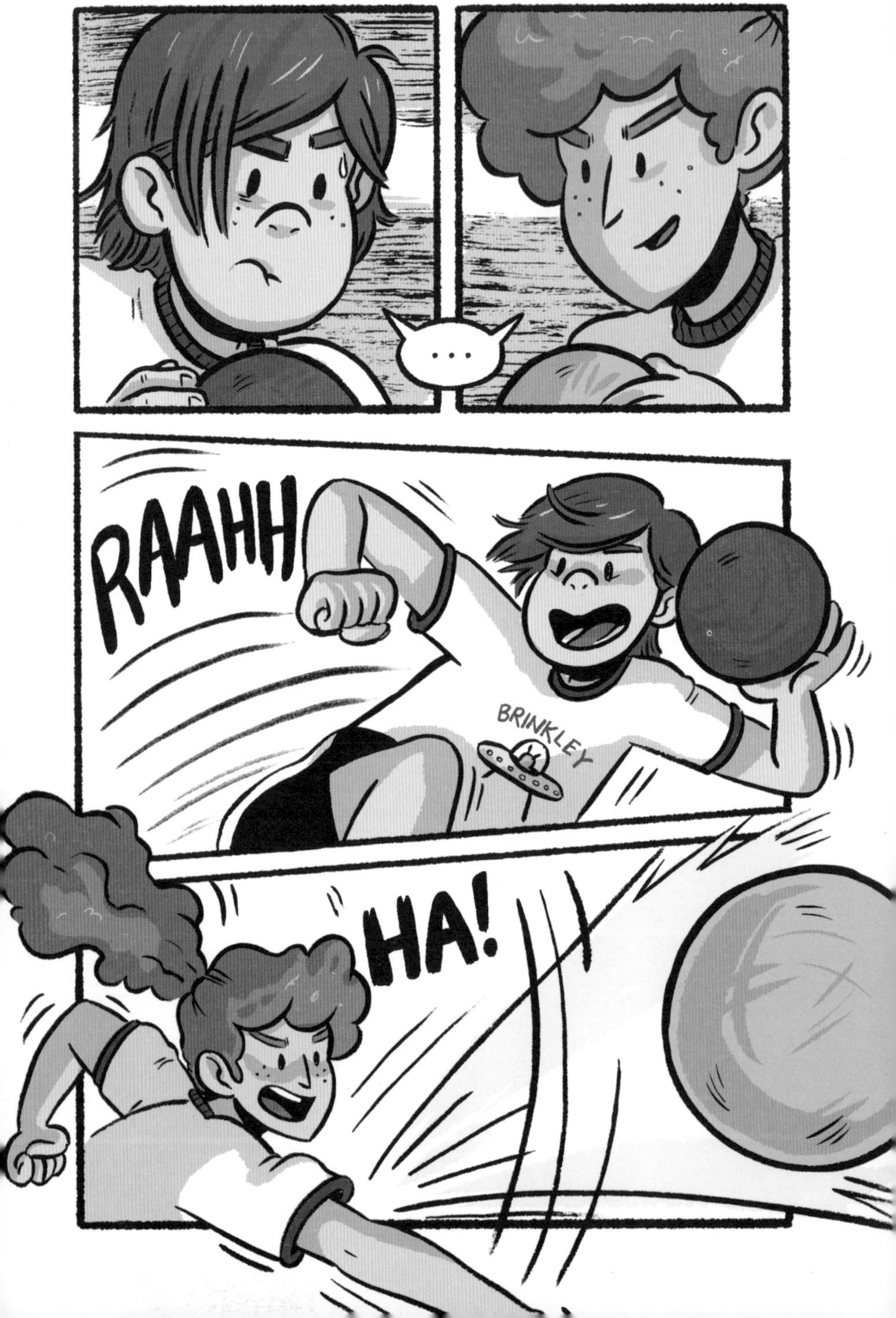
...
RAAHH
BRINKLEY
HA!

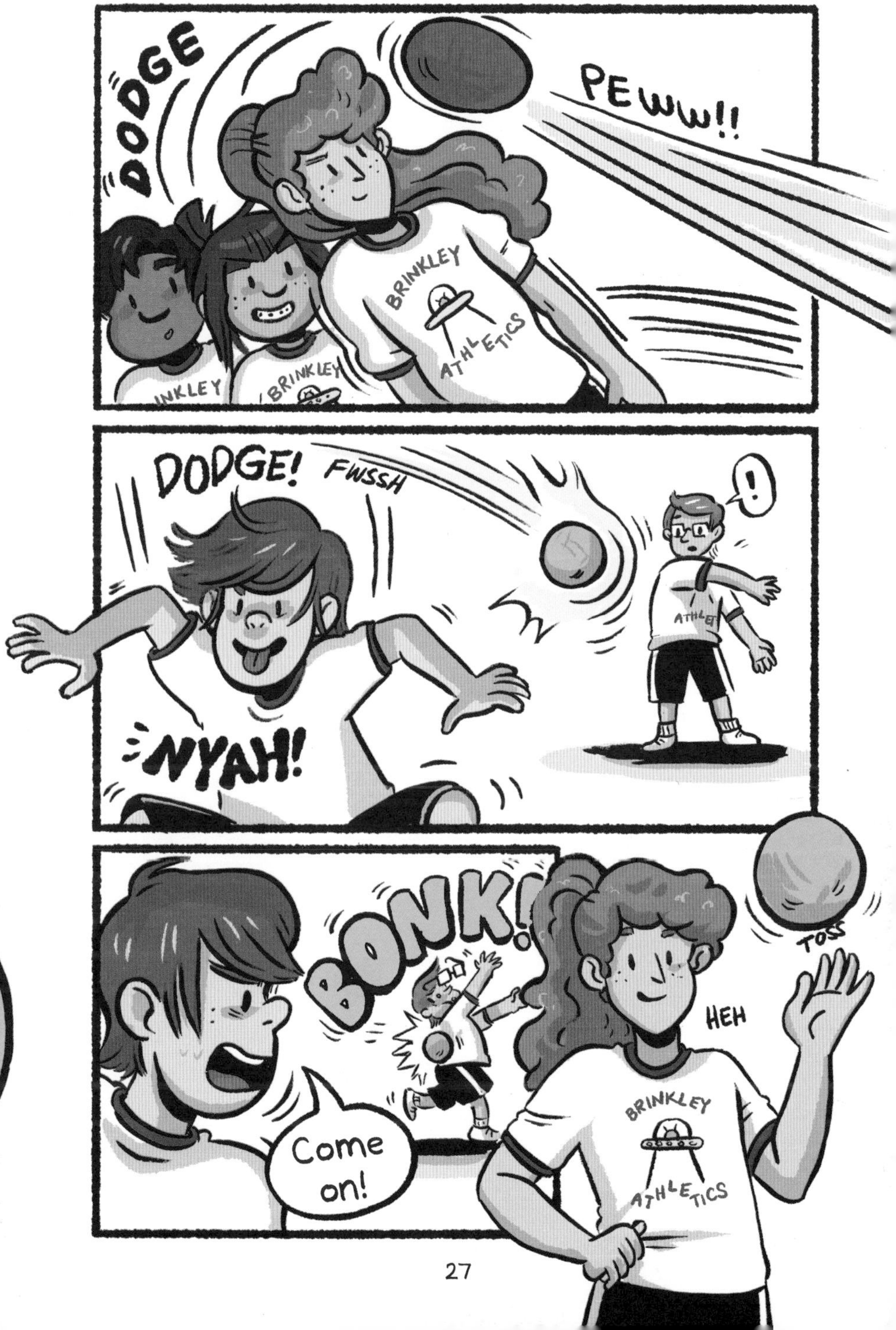
DODGE
PEWW!!
BRINKLEY ATHLETICS
DODGE! FWSSH
!
NYAH!
BONK!
Come on!
HEH
TOSS
BRINKLEY ATHLETICS

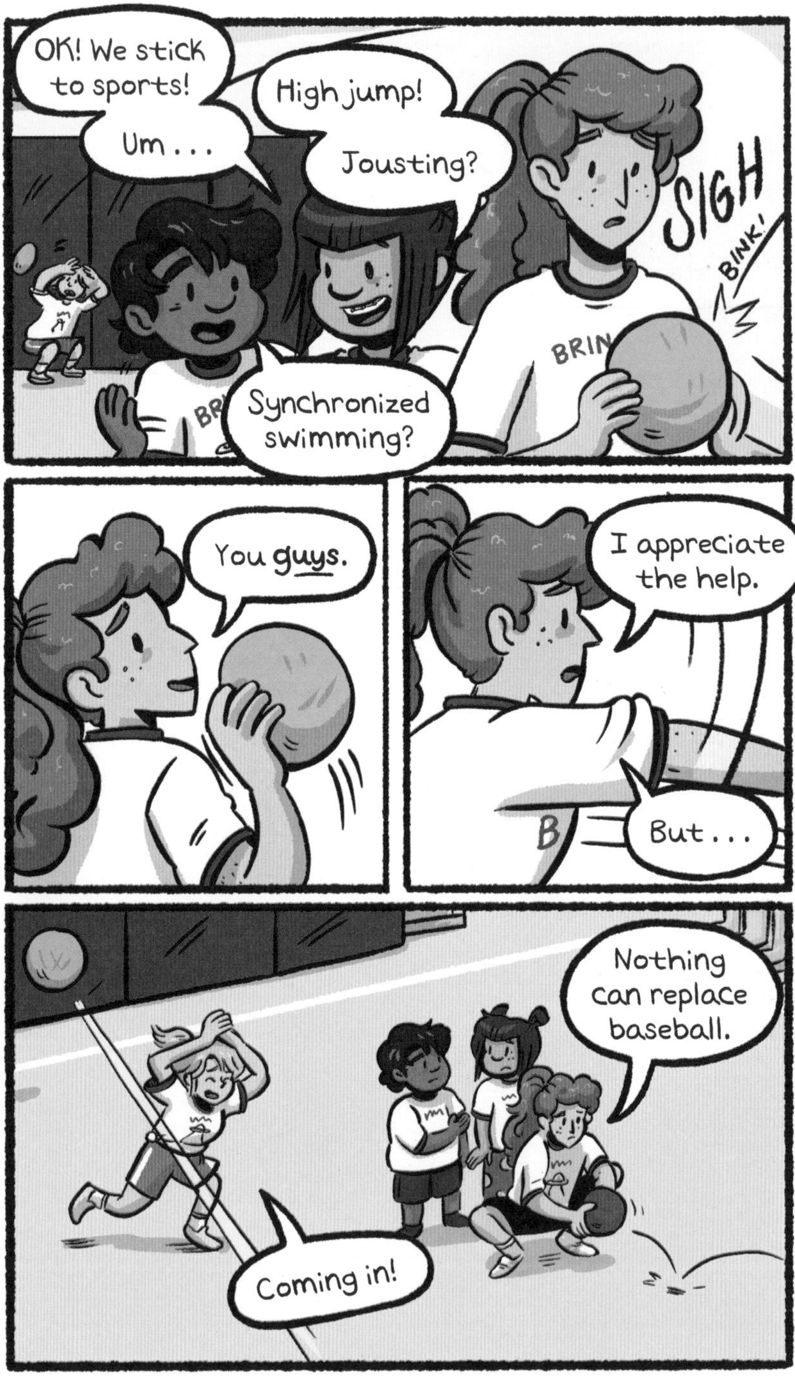
OK! We stick to sports!
Um . . .
High jump!
Jousting?
Synchronized swimming?
SIGH
BINK!
BRIN
You guys.
I appreciate the help.
But . . .
Nothing can replace baseball.
Coming in!

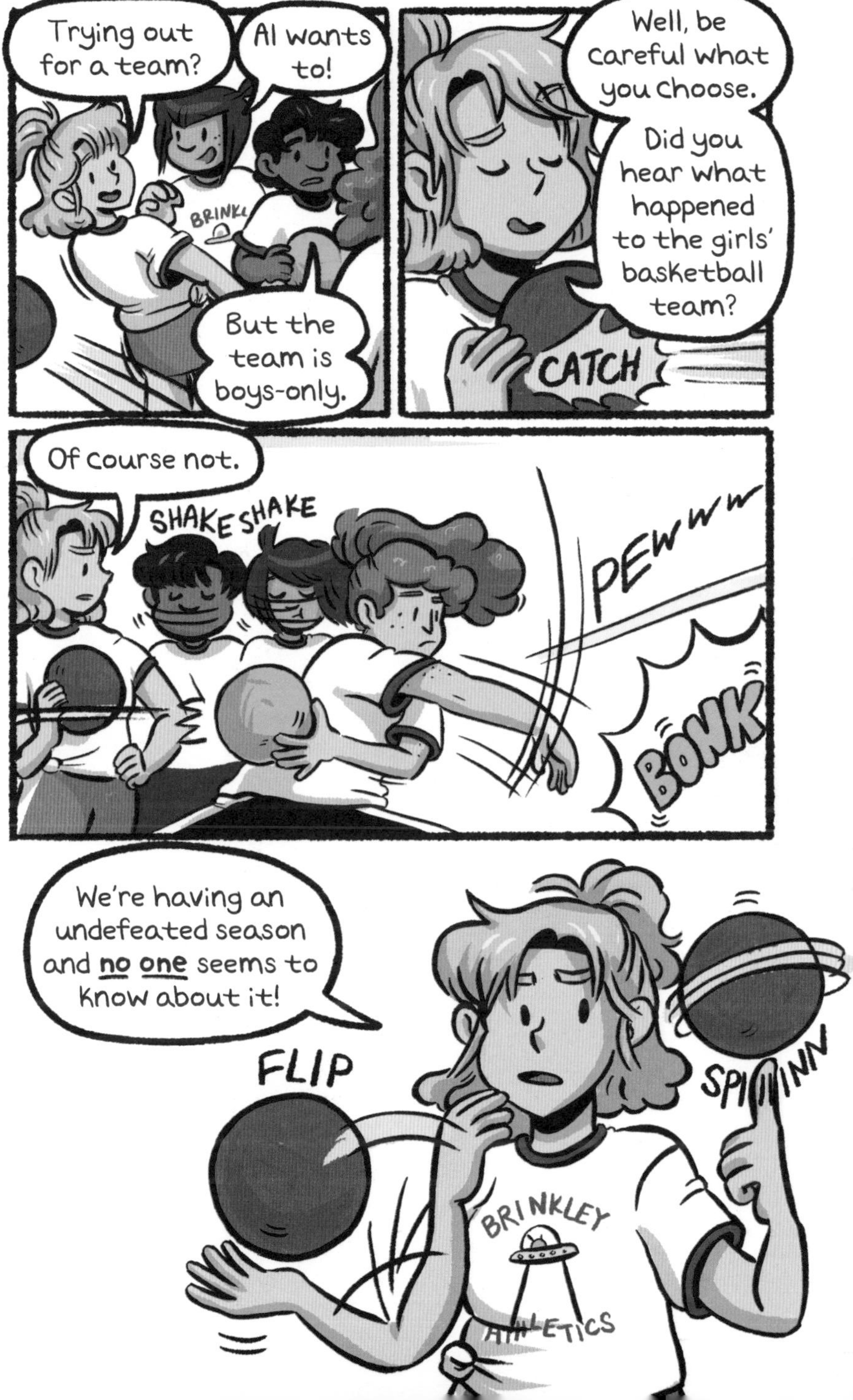
Trying out for a team?
Al wants to!
But the team is boys-only.
Well, be careful what you choose.
Did you hear what happened to the girls' basketball team?
CATCH
Of course not.
SHAKE SHAKE
PEWWW
BONK
We're having an undefeated season and **no one** seems to know about it!
FLIP
SPINNN
BRINKLEY
ATHLETICS

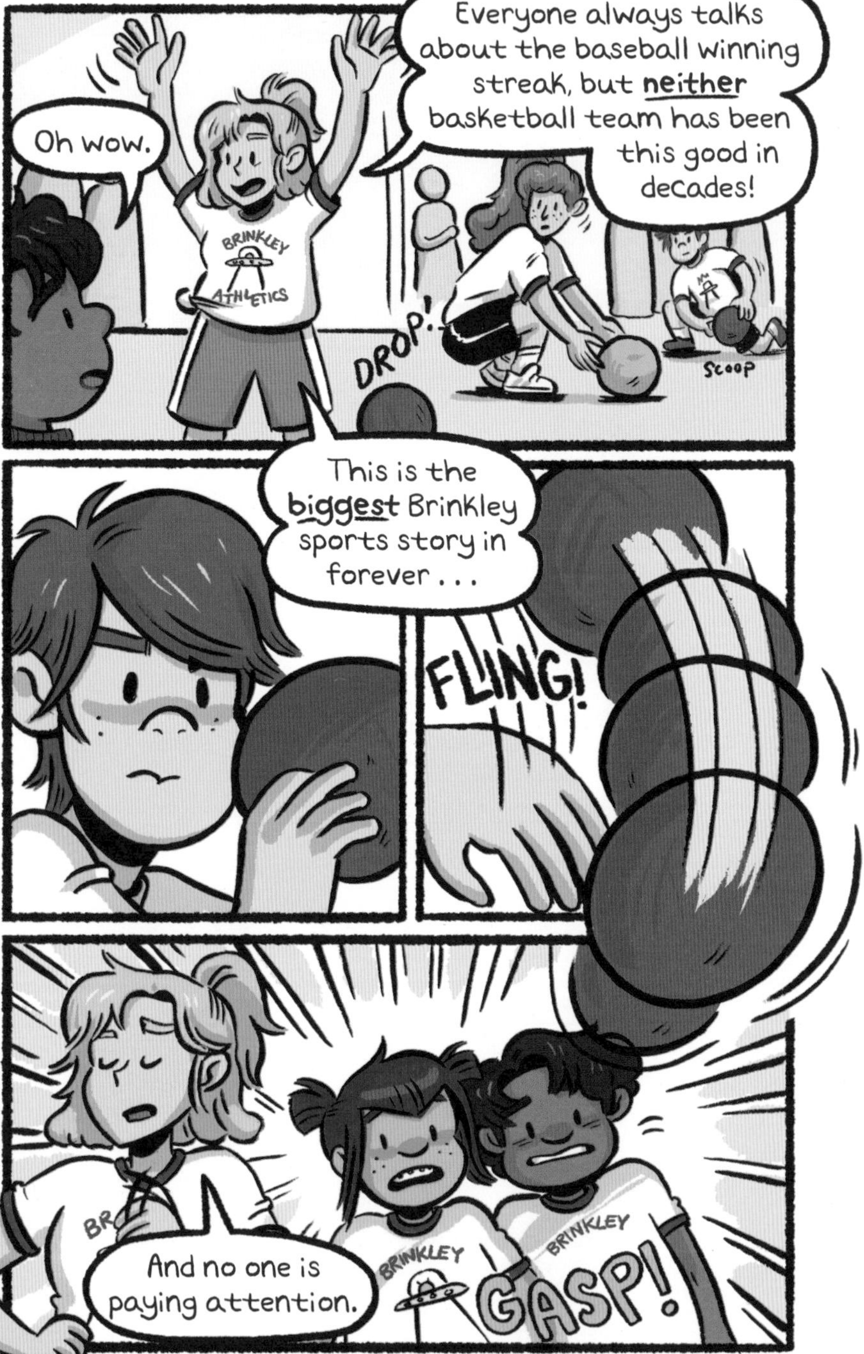
Oh wow.
Everyone always talks about the baseball winning streak, but neither basketball team has been this good in decades!
DROP!
SCOOP
BRINKLEY ATHLETICS
This is the biggest Brinkley sports story in forever . . .
FLING!
And no one is paying attention.
GASP!
BRINKLEY
BRINKLEY

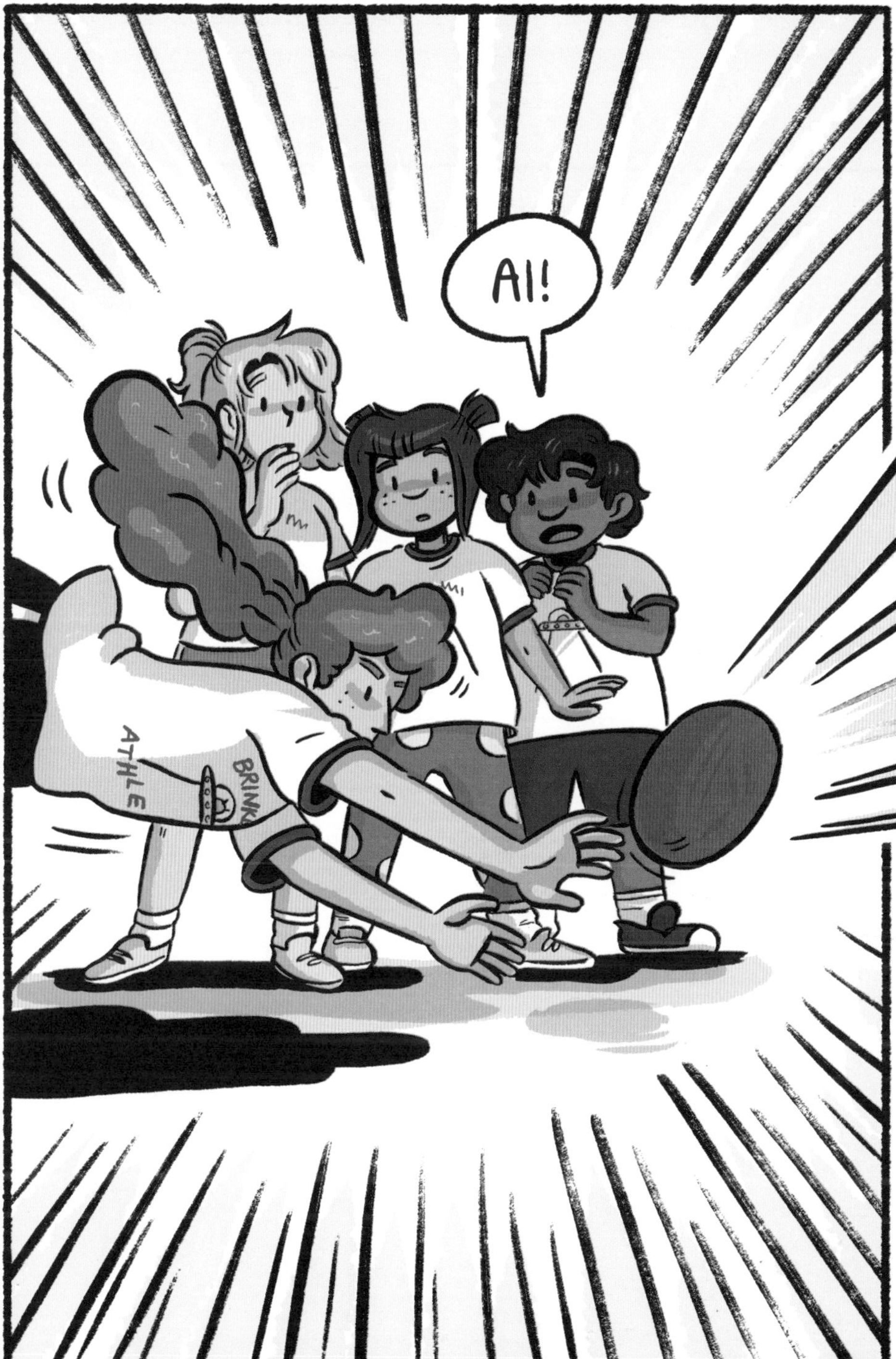
AI!

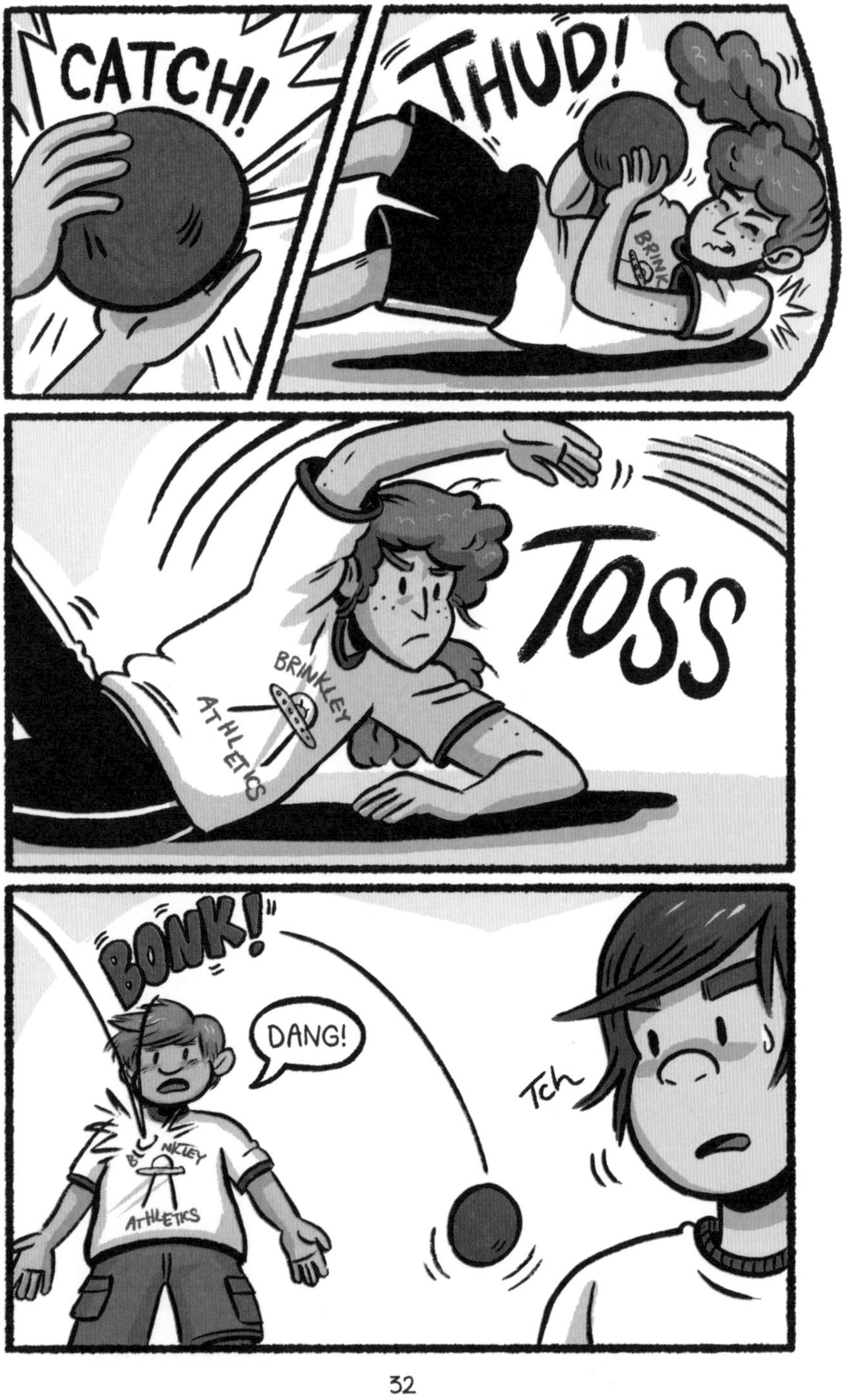
CATCH!
THUD!
BRINKLEY
ATHLETICS
TOSS
BONK!
DANG!
Tch
ATHLETICS

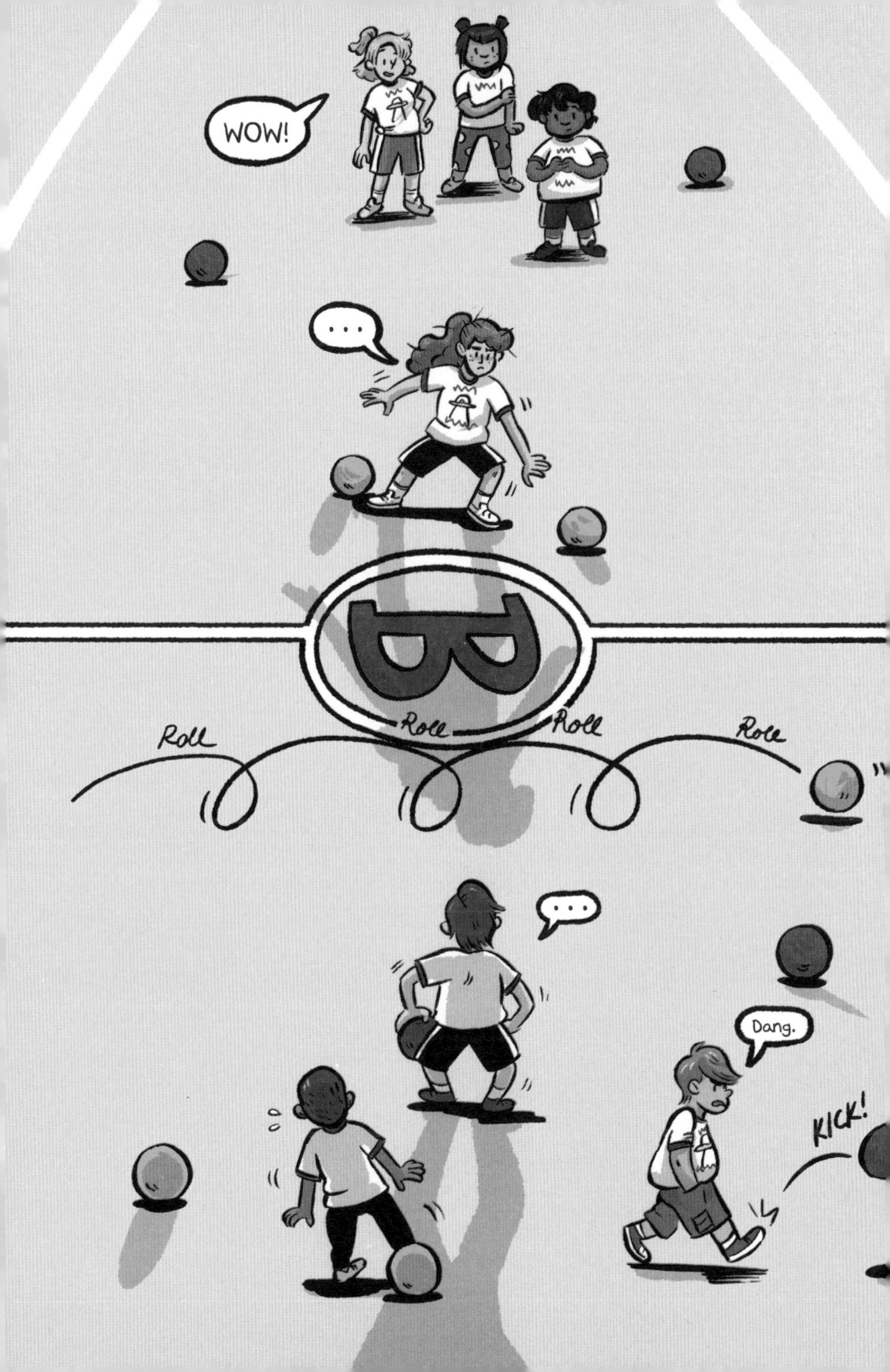
WOW!
...
Roll
Roll
Roll
Roll
...
Dang.
KICK!

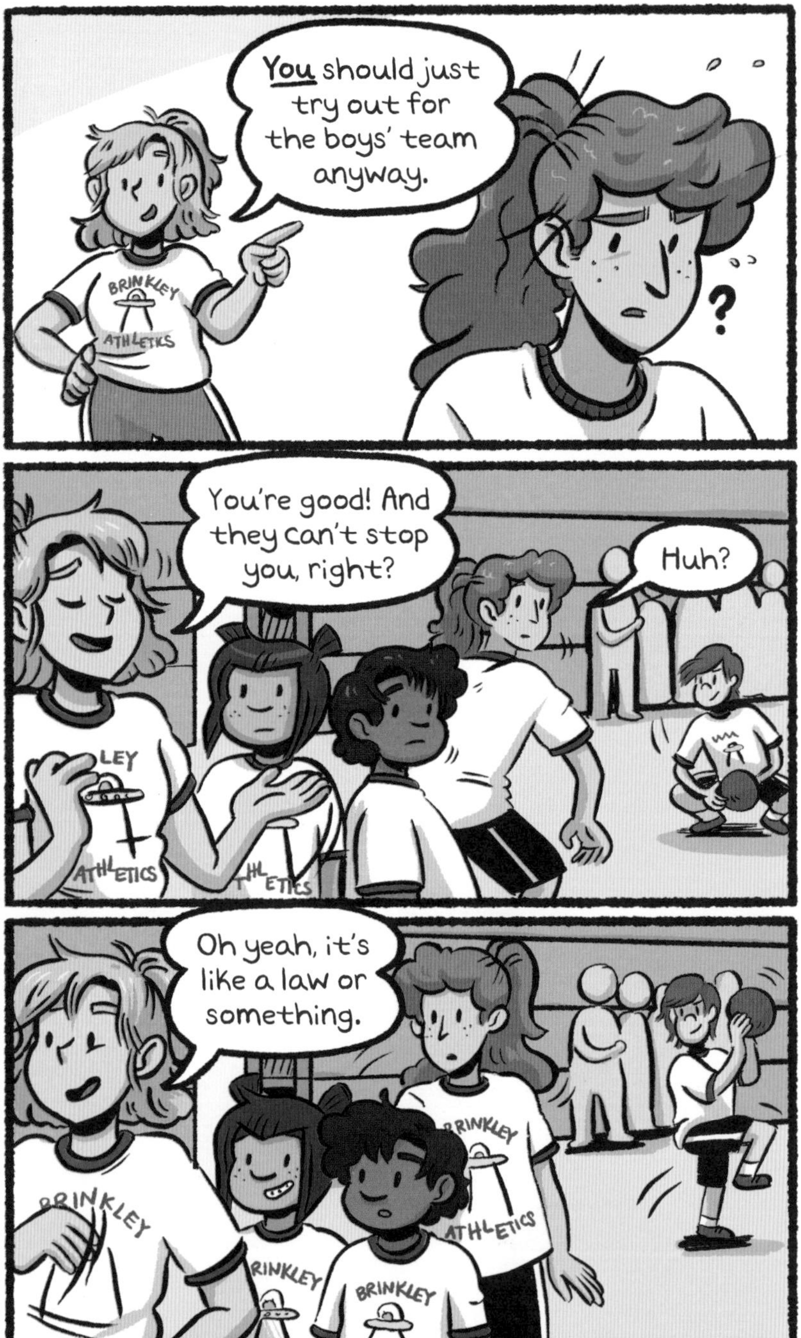
You should just try out for the boys' team anyway.
BRINKLEY ATHLETICS
?
You're good! And they can't stop you, right?
Huh?
Oh yeah, it's like a law or something.
BRINKLEY
ATHLETICS
BRINKLEY
BRINKLEY

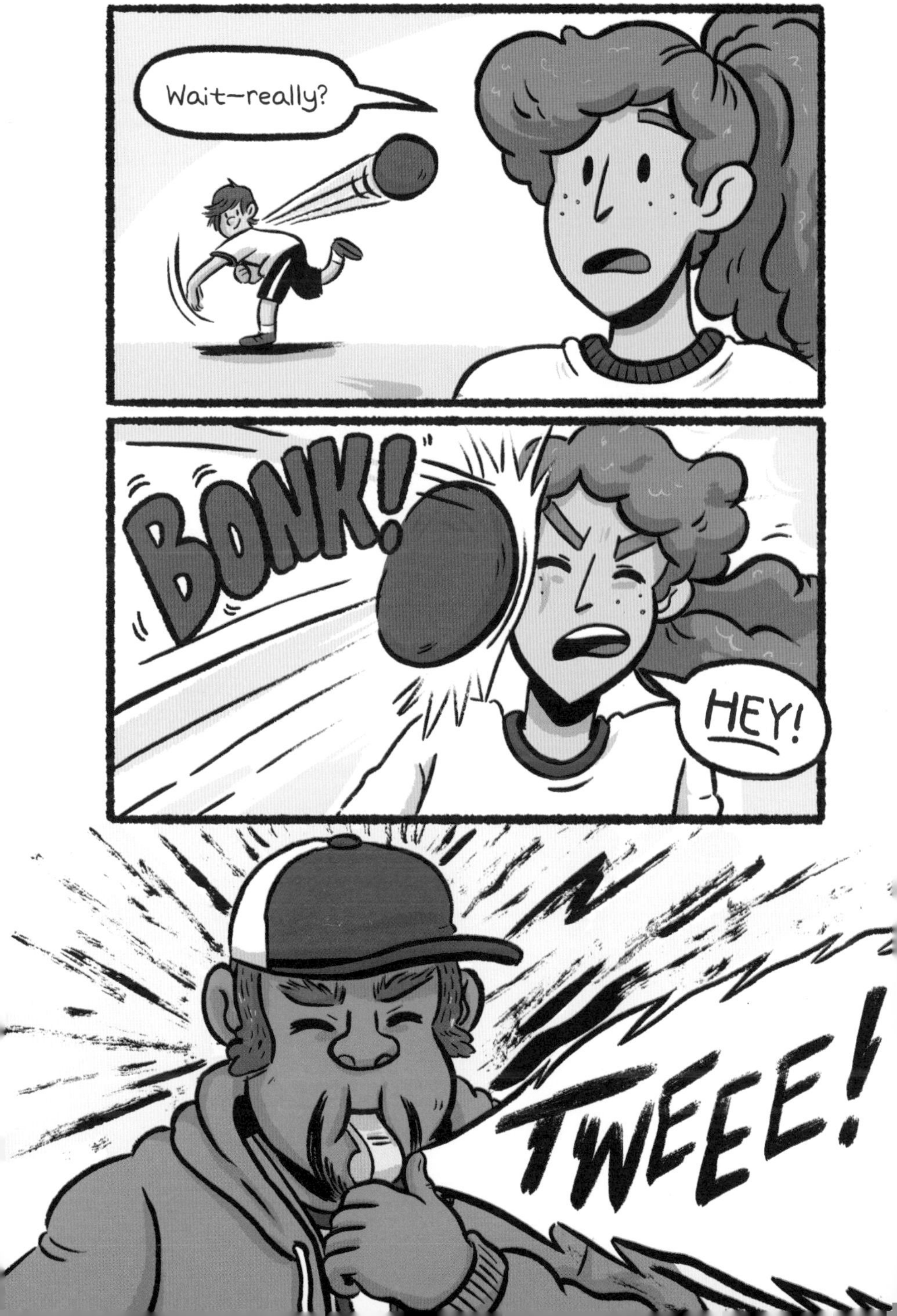

Wait–really?
BONK!
HEY!
TWEEE!

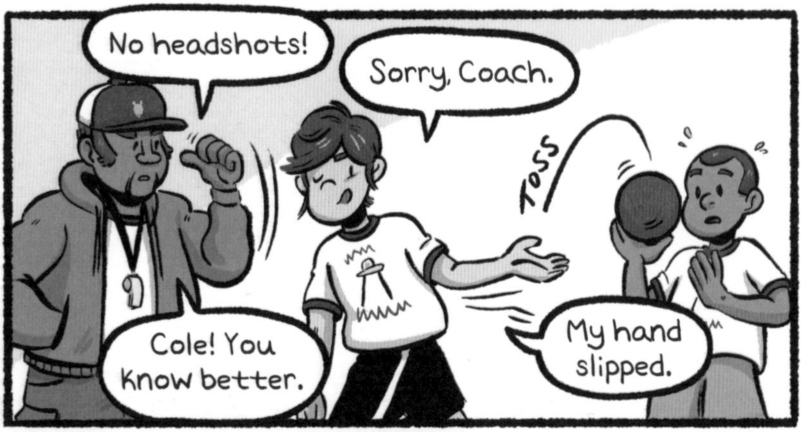
No headshots!
Sorry, Coach.
TOSS
Cole! You know better.
My hand slipped.

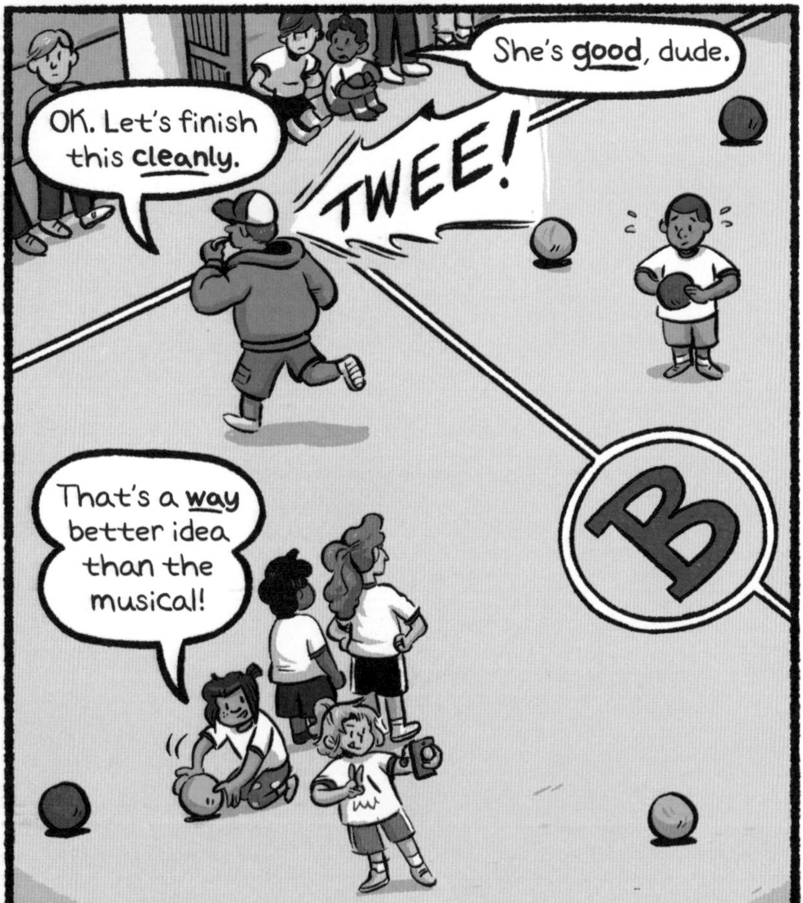
She's good, dude.
OK. Let's finish this cleanly.
TWEE!
B
That's a way better idea than the musical!

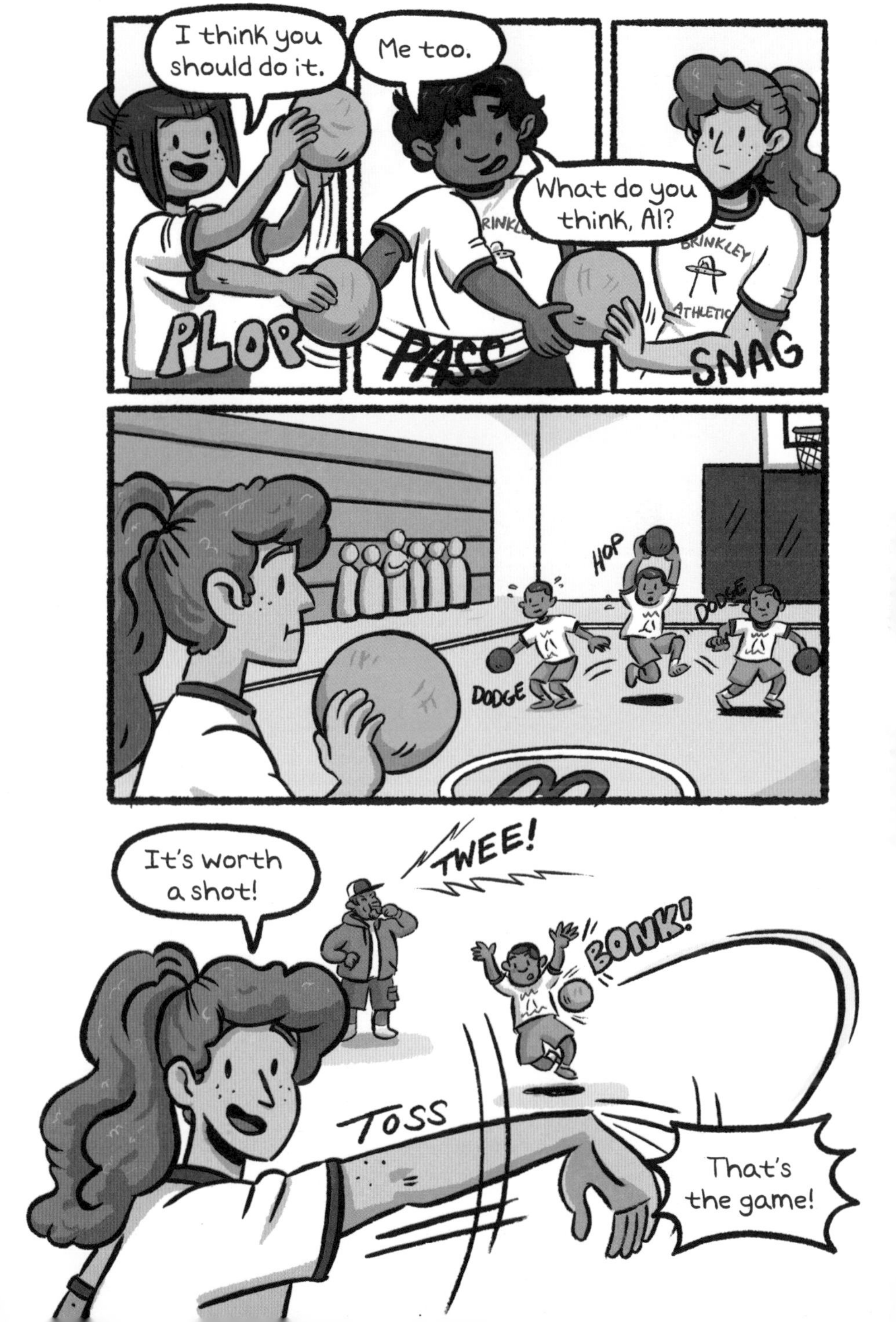
I think you should do it.
PLOP
Me too.
PASS
What do you think, Al?
BRINKLEY ATHLETIC
SNAG
HOP
DODGE
DODGE
It's worth a shot!
TWEE!
BONK!
TOSS
That's the game!

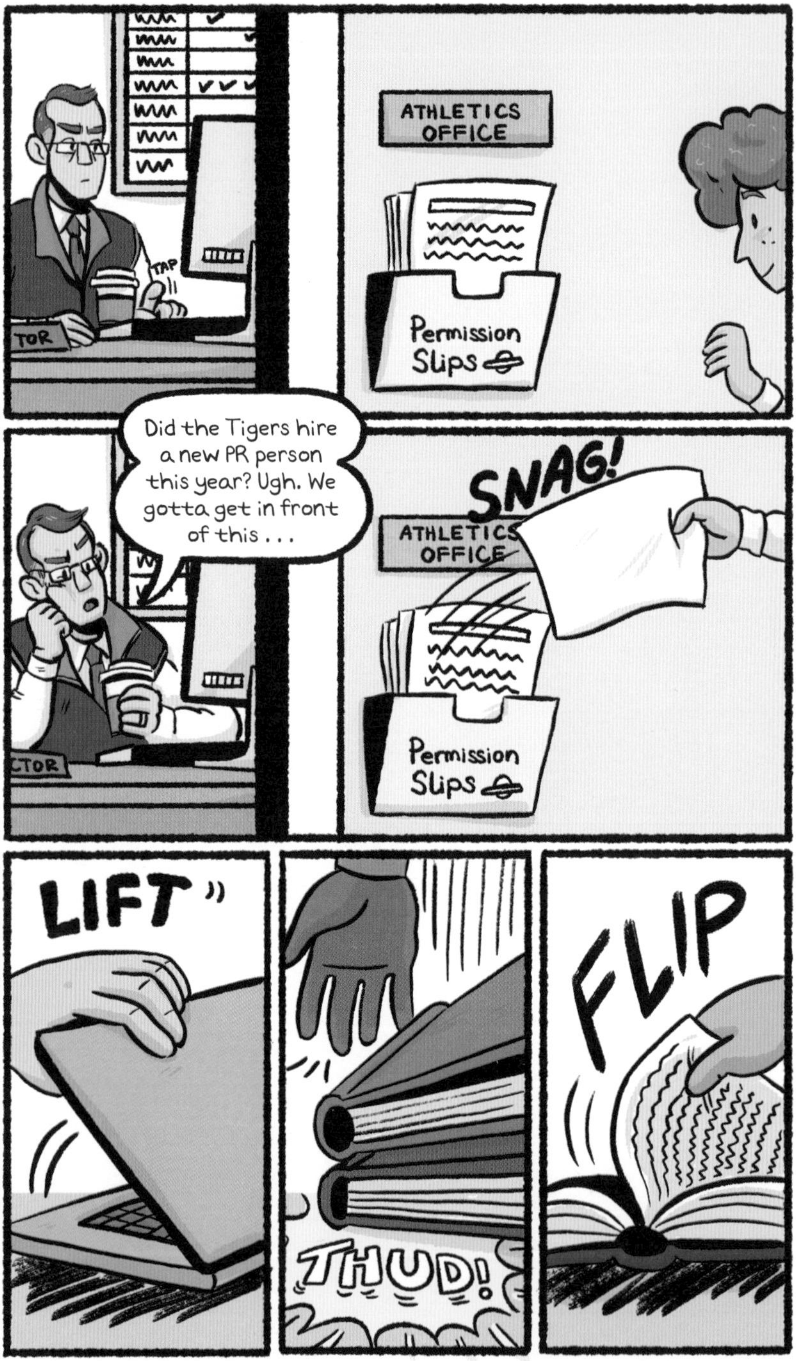
TAP
TOR
ATHLETICS OFFICE
Permission Slips
Did the Tigers hire a new PR person this year? Ugh. We gotta get in front of this . . .
SNAG!
ATHLETICS OFFICE
CTOR
Permission Slips
LIFT
THUD!
FLIP

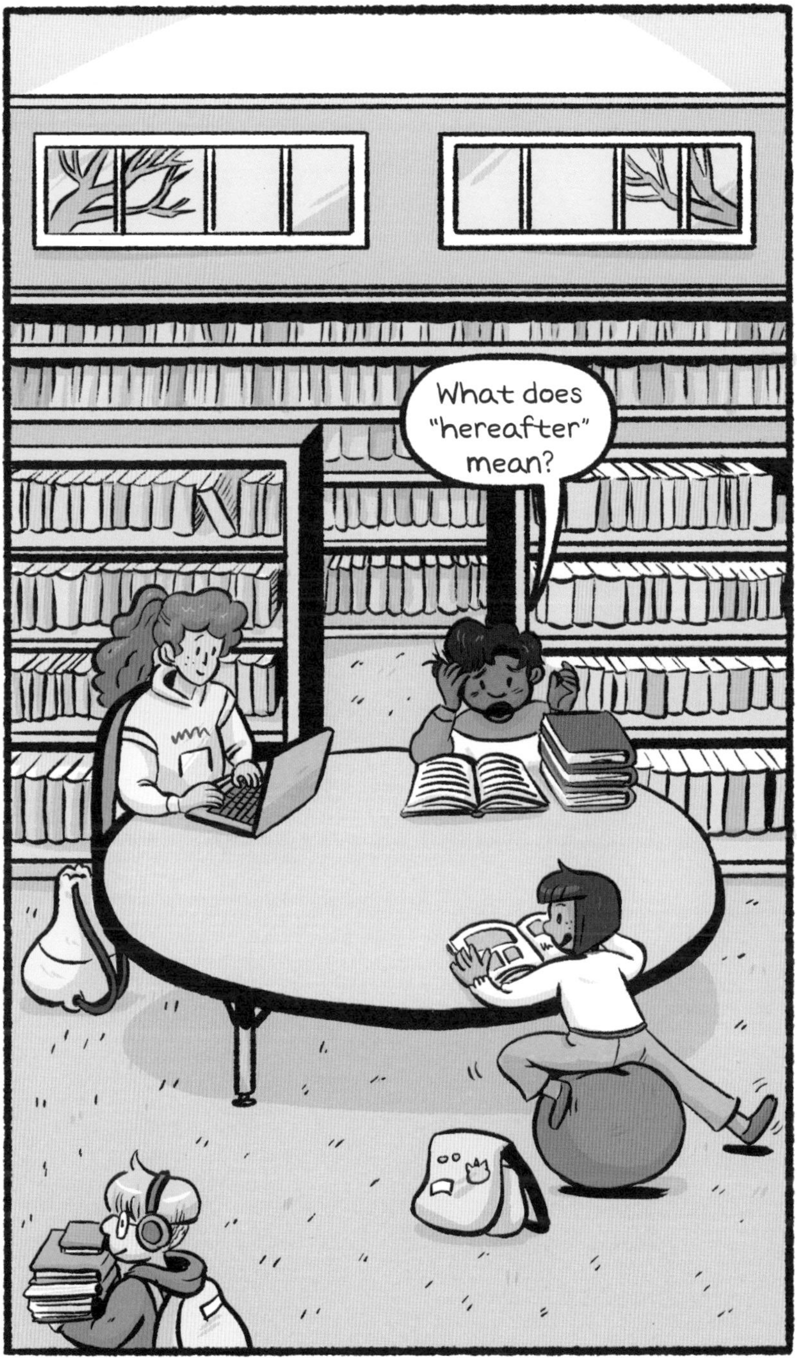
What does "hereafter" mean?

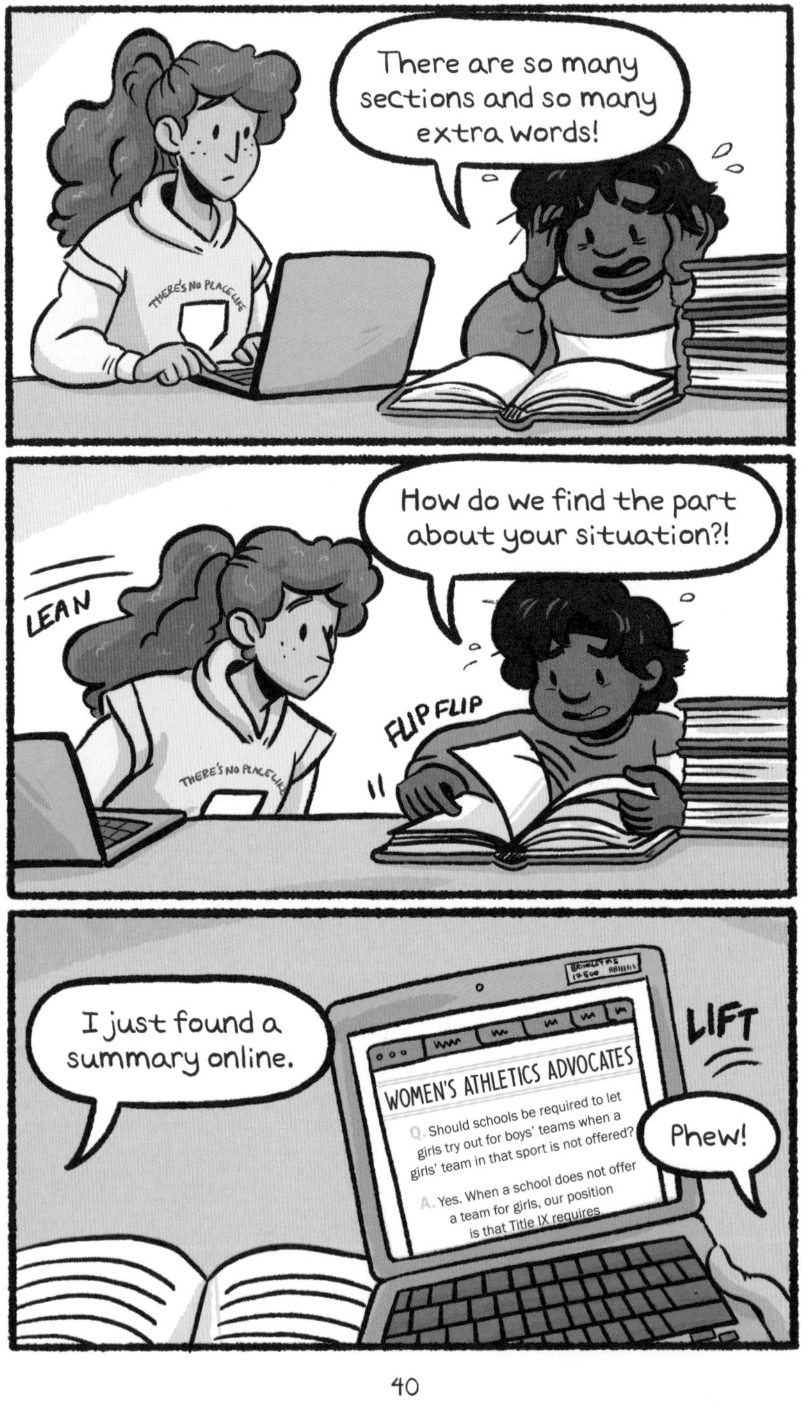
There are so many sections and so many extra words!
LEAN
How do we find the part about your situation?!
FLIP FLIP
I just found a summary online.
WOMEN'S ATHLETICS ADVOCATES
Q. Should schools be required to let girls try out for boys' teams when a girls' team in that sport is not offered?
A. Yes. When a school does not offer a team for girls, our position is that Title IX requires
LIFT
Phew!

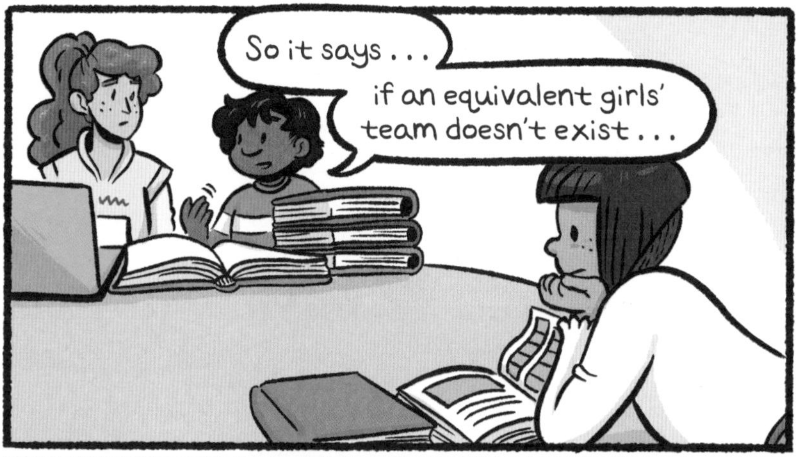
So it says . . .
if an equivalent girls' team doesn't exist . . .

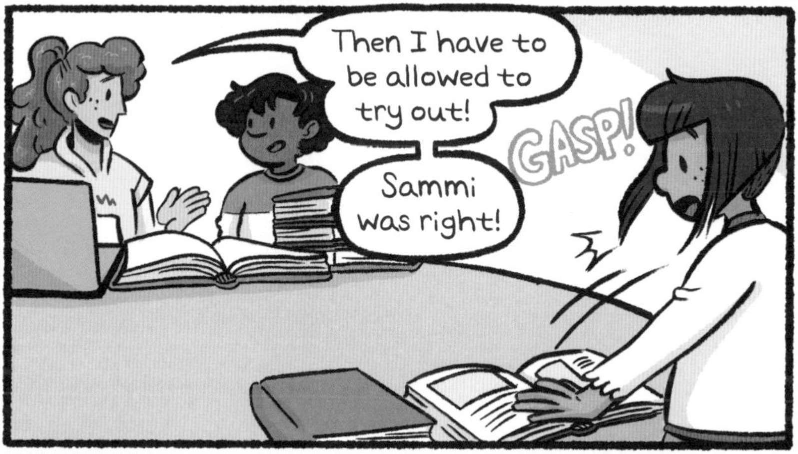
Then I have to be allowed to try out!
Sammi was right!
GASP!

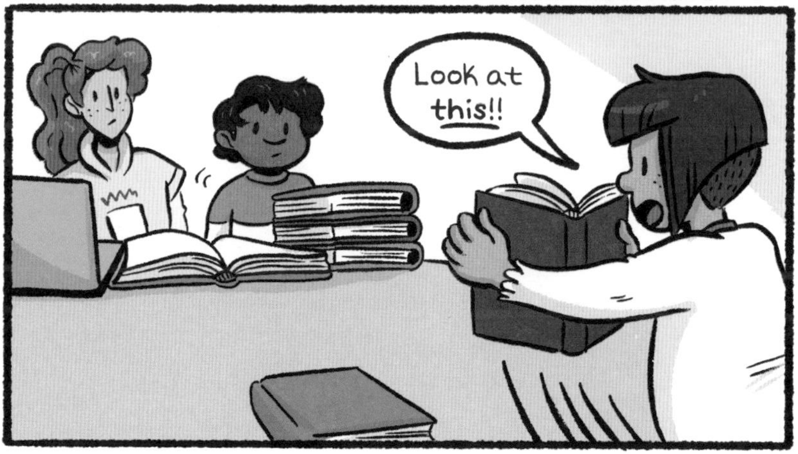
Look at this!!

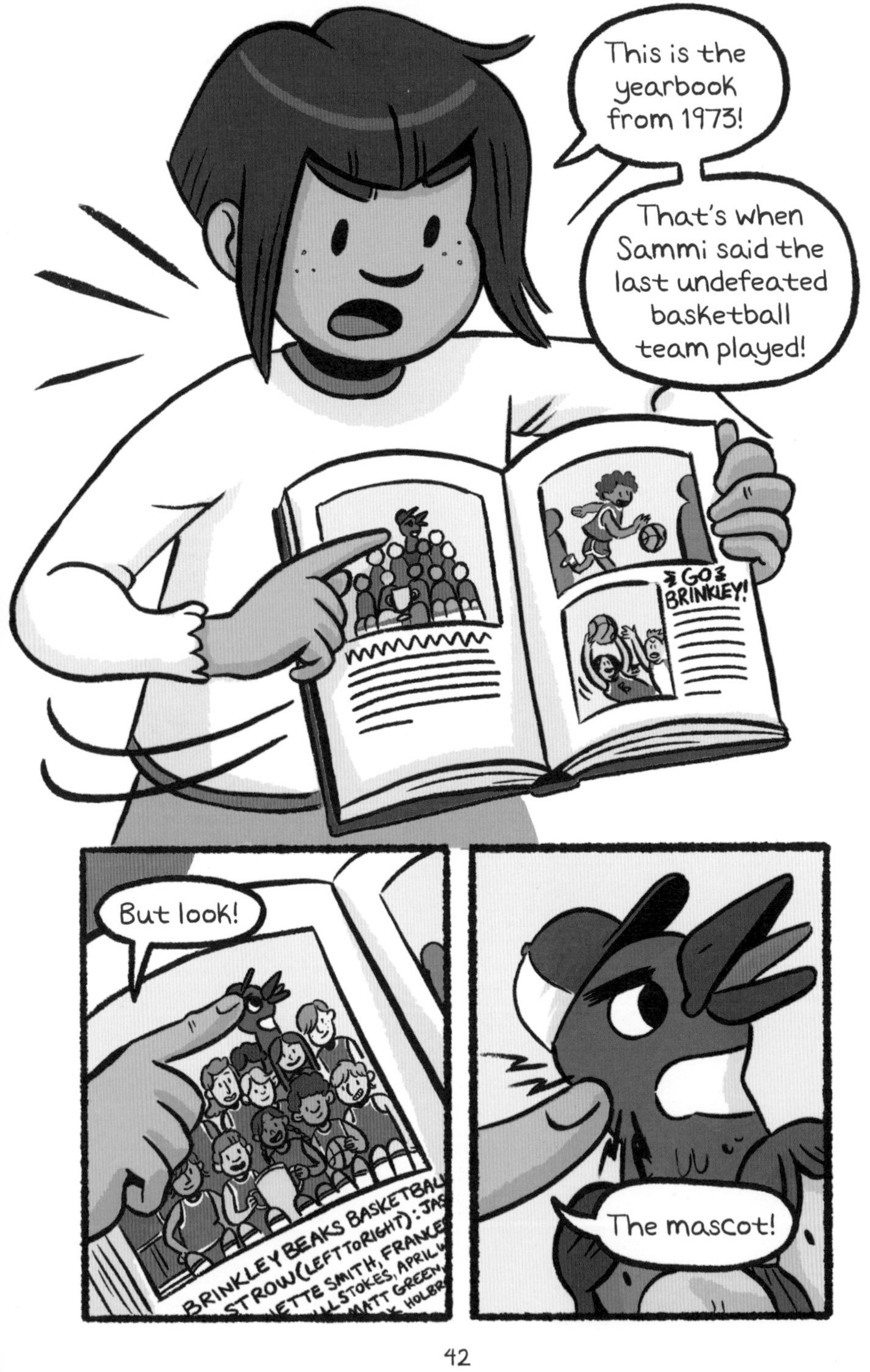
This is the yearbook from 1973!
That's when Sammi said the last undefeated basketball team played!
GO BRINKLEY!
But look!
The mascot!

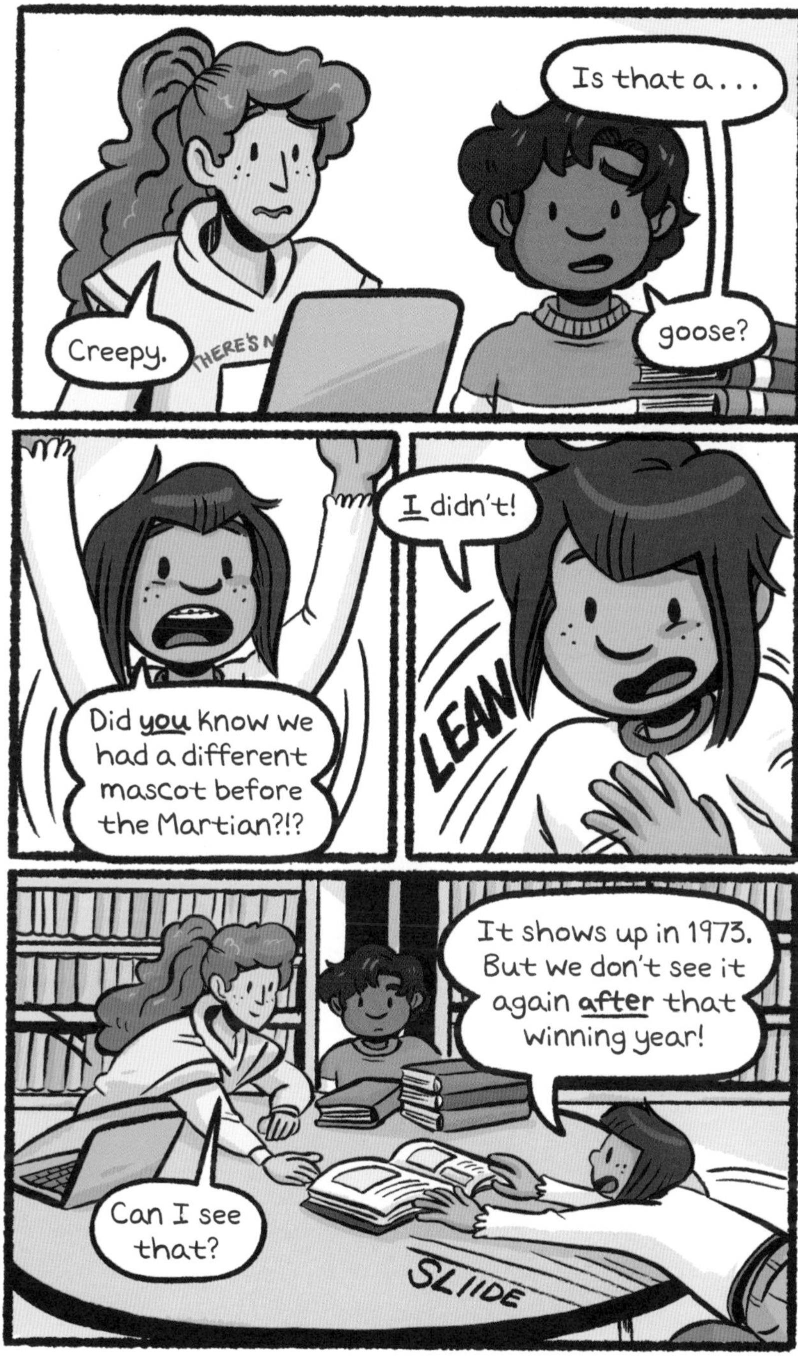
Is that a . . .
goose?
Creepy.
THERE'S N
Did you know we had a different mascot before the Martian?!?
I didn't!
LEAN
It shows up in 1973. But we don't see it again after that winning year!
Can I see that?
SLIIDE

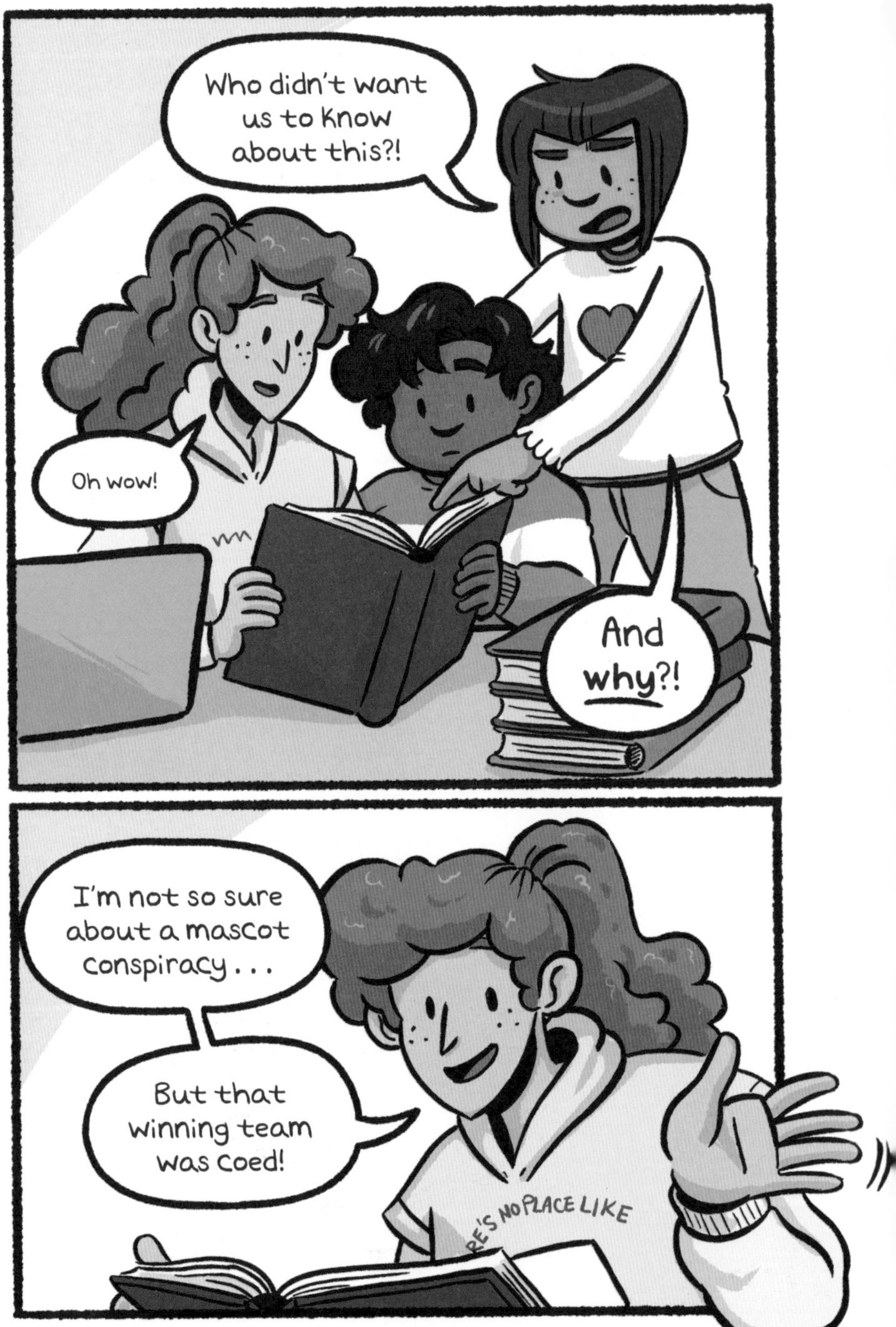
Who didn't want us to know about this?!
Oh wow!
And why?!
I'm not so sure about a mascot conspiracy . . .
But that winning team was coed!
RE'S NO PLACE LIKE

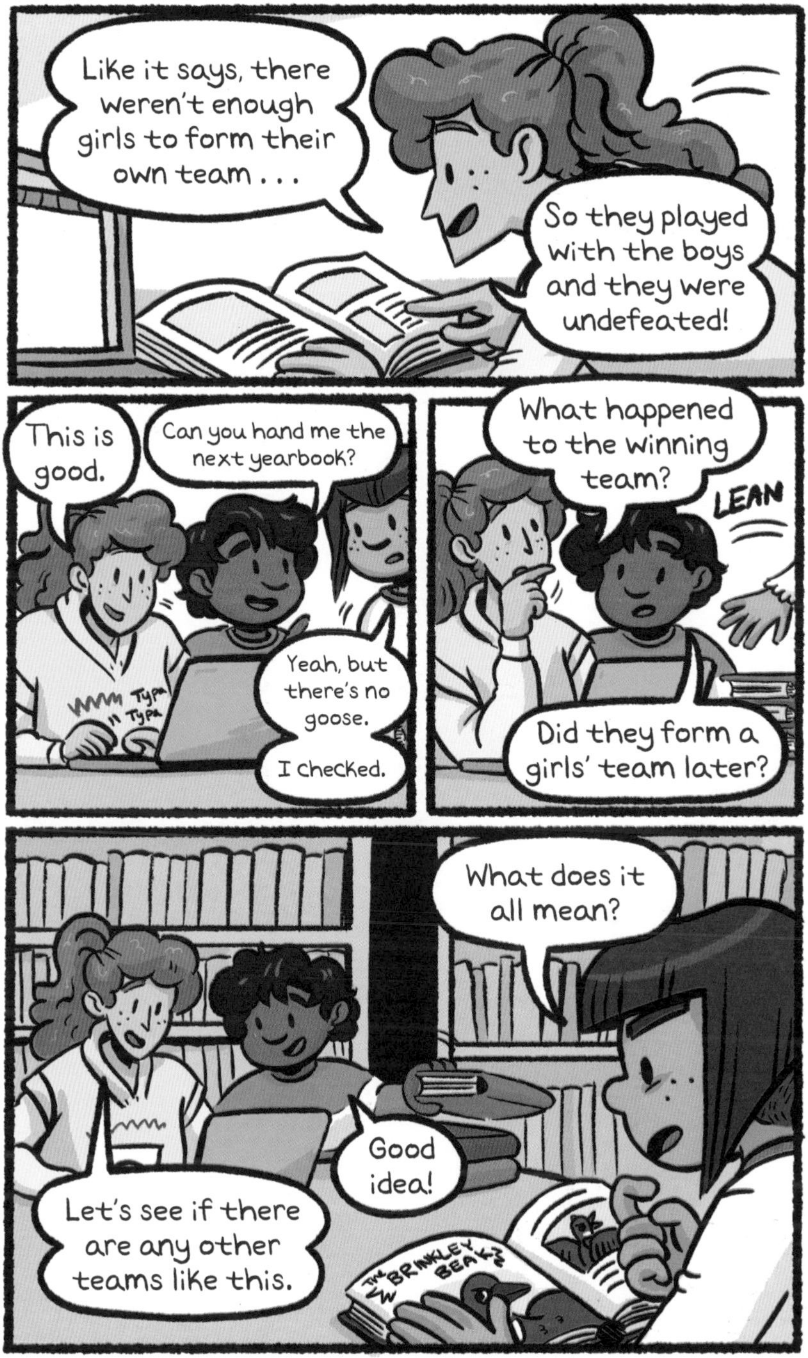
Like it says, there weren't enough girls to form their own team . . .
So they played with the boys and they were undefeated!
This is good.
Can you hand me the next yearbook?
Typa Typa
Yeah, but there's no goose.
I checked.
What happened to the winning team?
LEAN
Did they form a girls' team later?
What does it all mean?
Good idea!
Let's see if there are any other teams like this.
THE BRINKLEY BEAKS

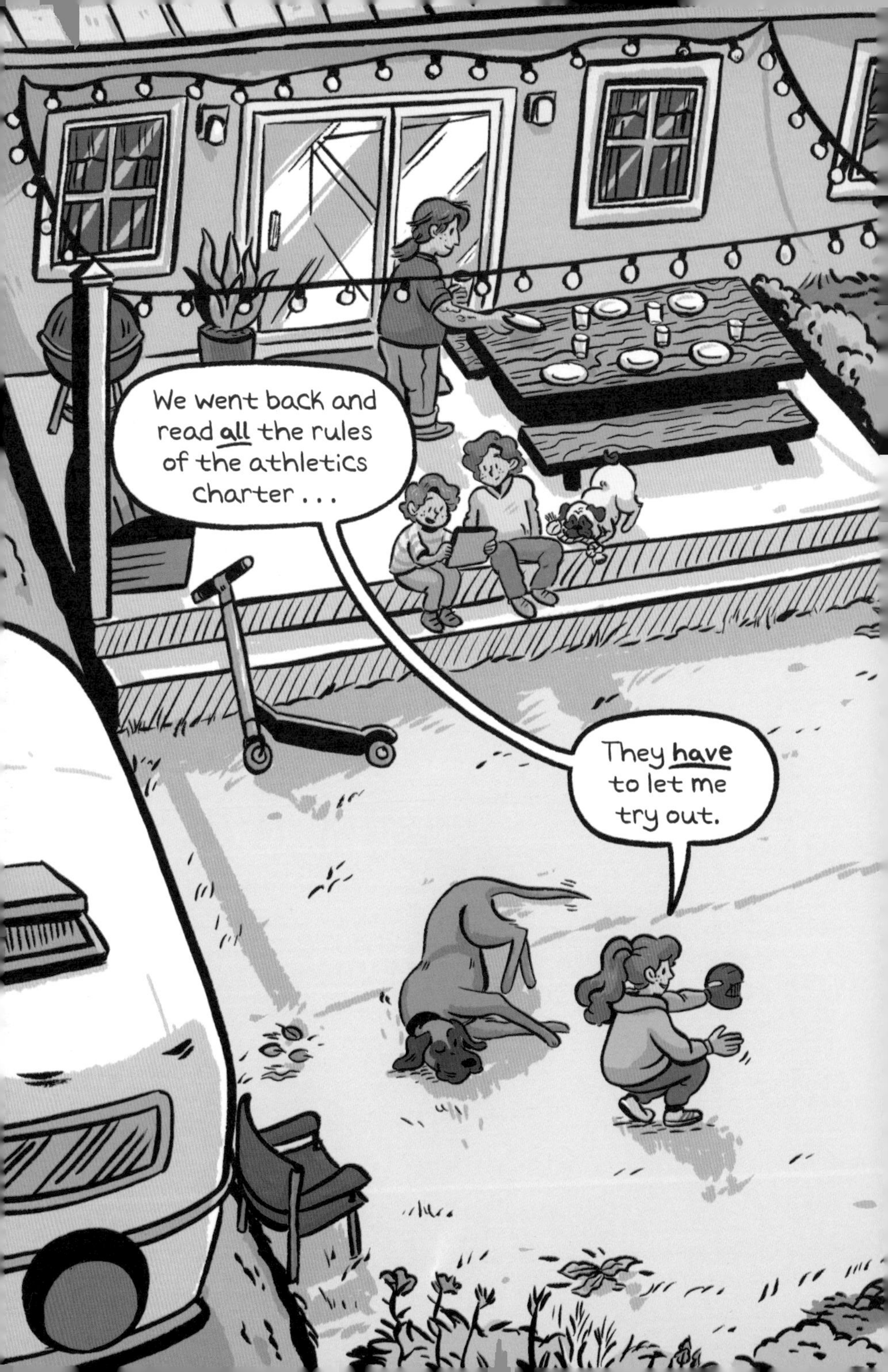
We went back and read all the rules of the athletics charter . . .
They have to let me try out.

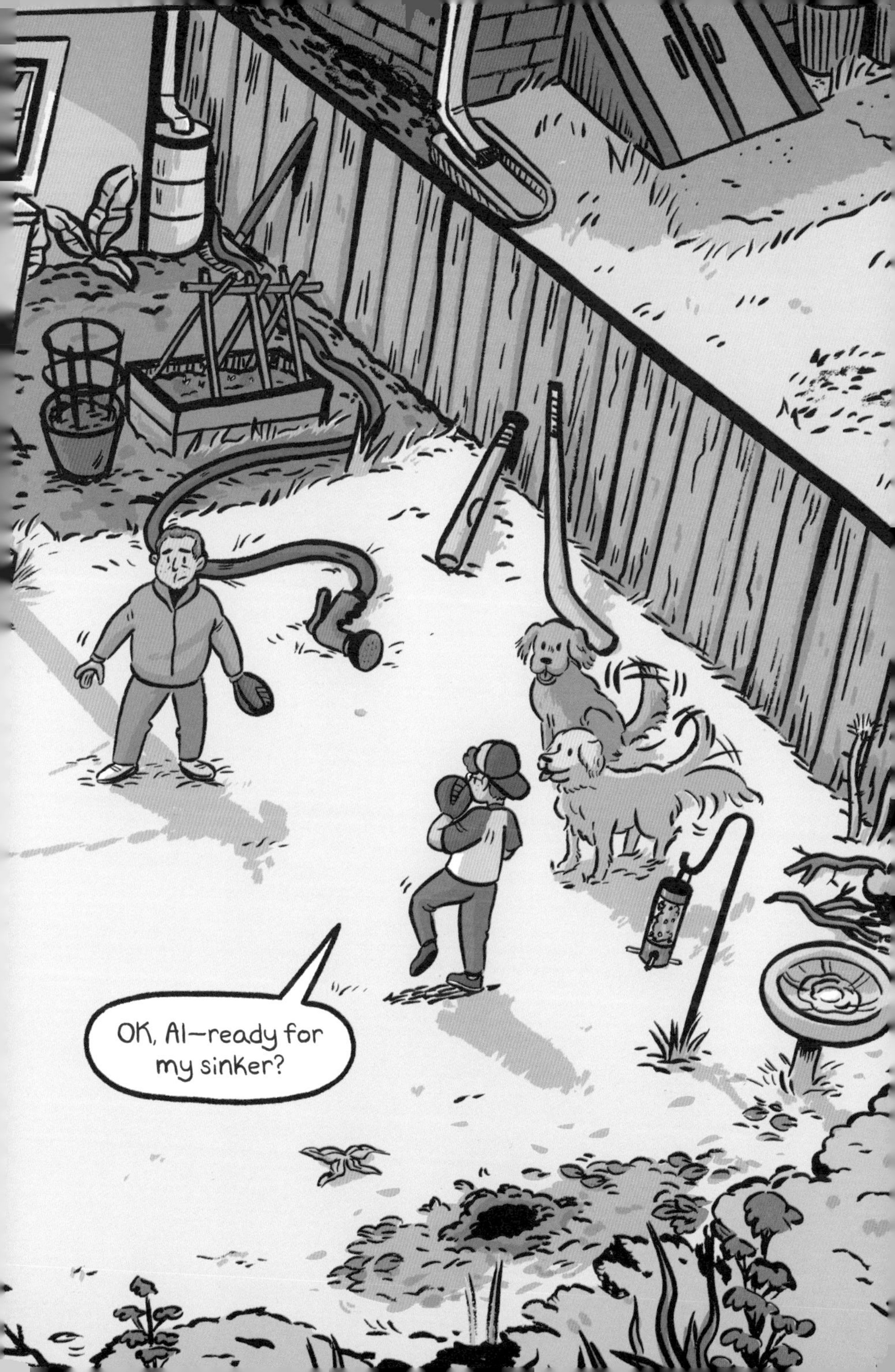
OK, Al—ready for my sinker?

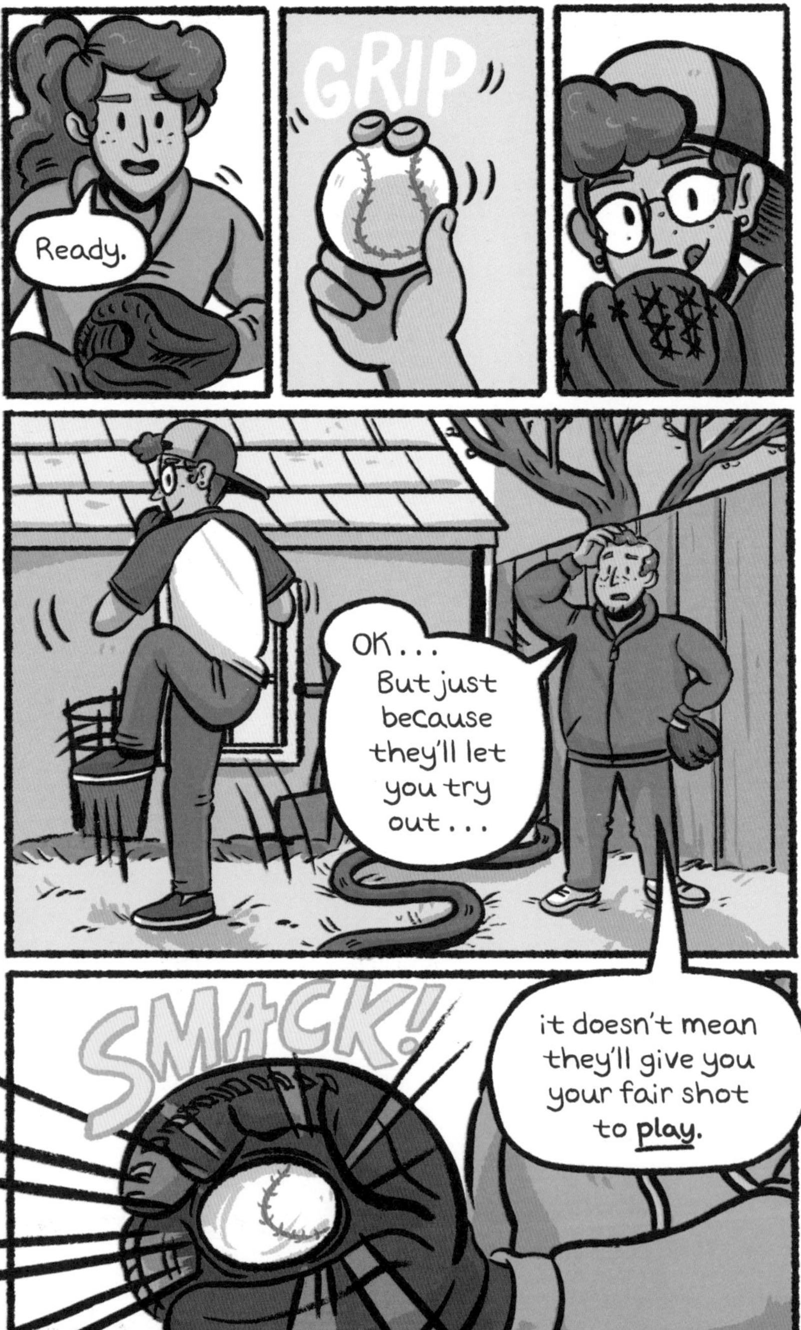
Ready.
GRIP
OK . . .
But just because they'll let you try out . . .
SMACK!
it doesn't mean they'll give you your fair shot to play.

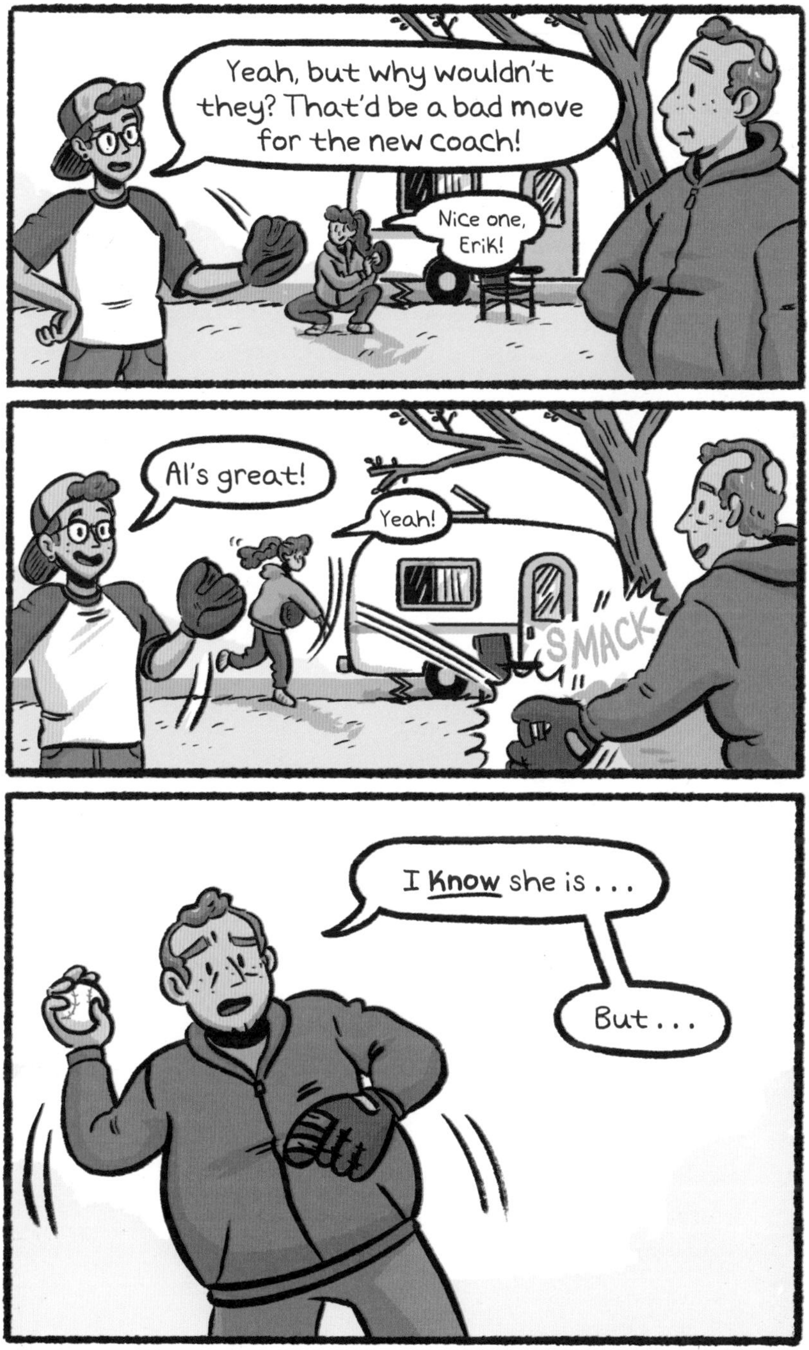
Yeah, but why wouldn't they? That'd be a bad move for the new coach!
Nice one, Erik!
Al's great!
Yeah!
SMACK
I Know she is . . .
But . . .

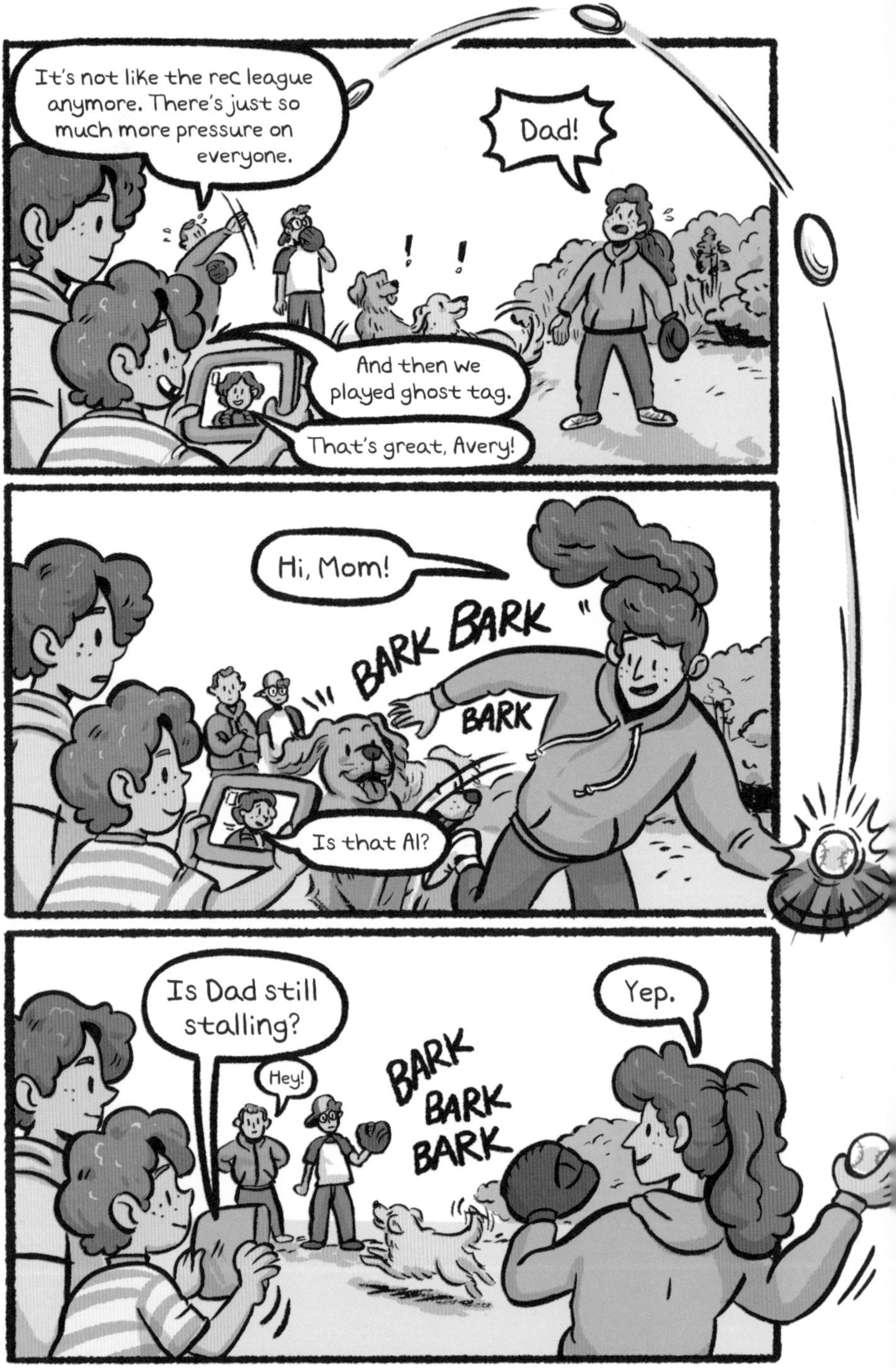
It's not like the rec league anymore. There's just so much more pressure on everyone.
Dad!
And then we played ghost tag.
That's great, Avery!
Hi, Mom!
BARK BARK
BARK
Is that Al?
Is Dad still stalling?
Yep.
Hey!
BARK
BARK
BARK

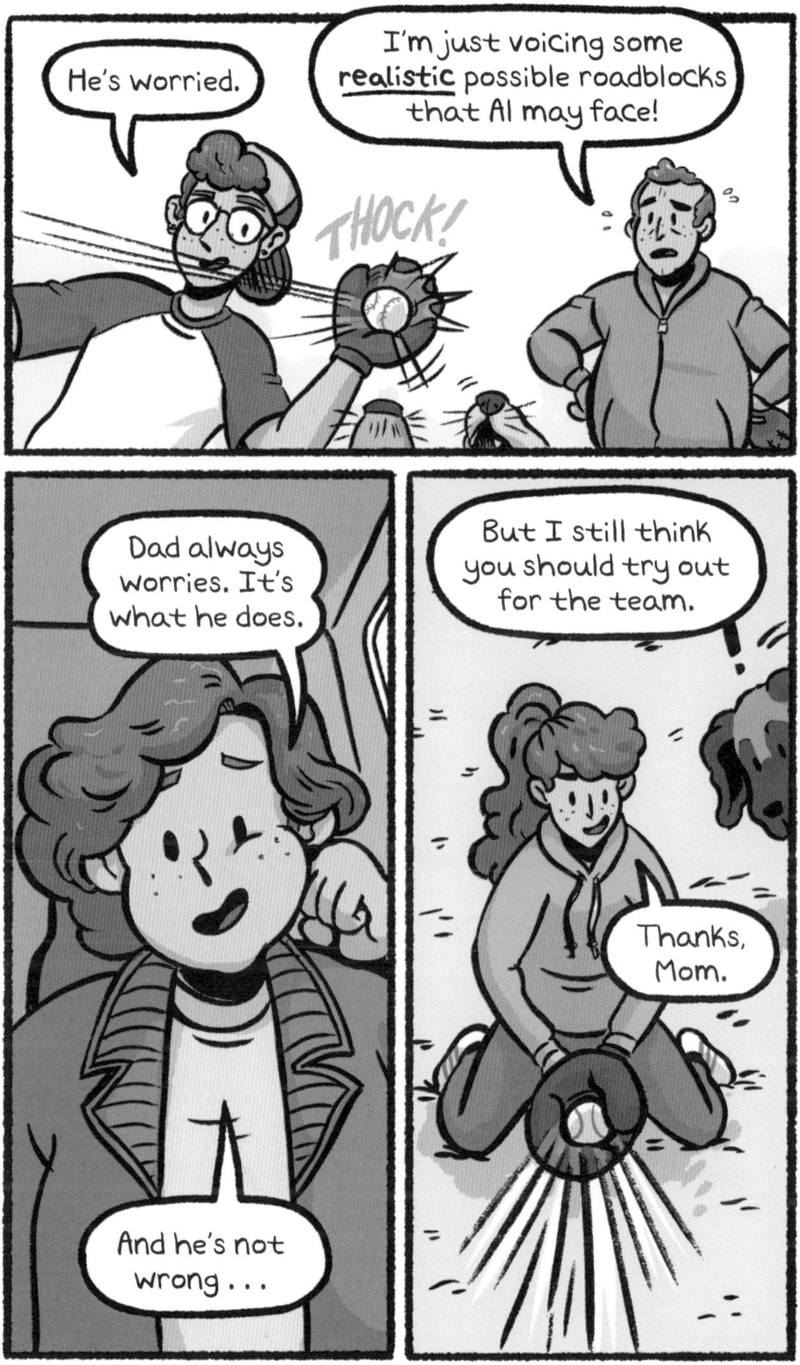

He's worried.
I'm just voicing some realistic possible roadblocks that Al may face!
THOCK!
Dad always worries. It's what he does.
And he's not wrong . . .
But I still think you should try out for the team.
Thanks, Mom.

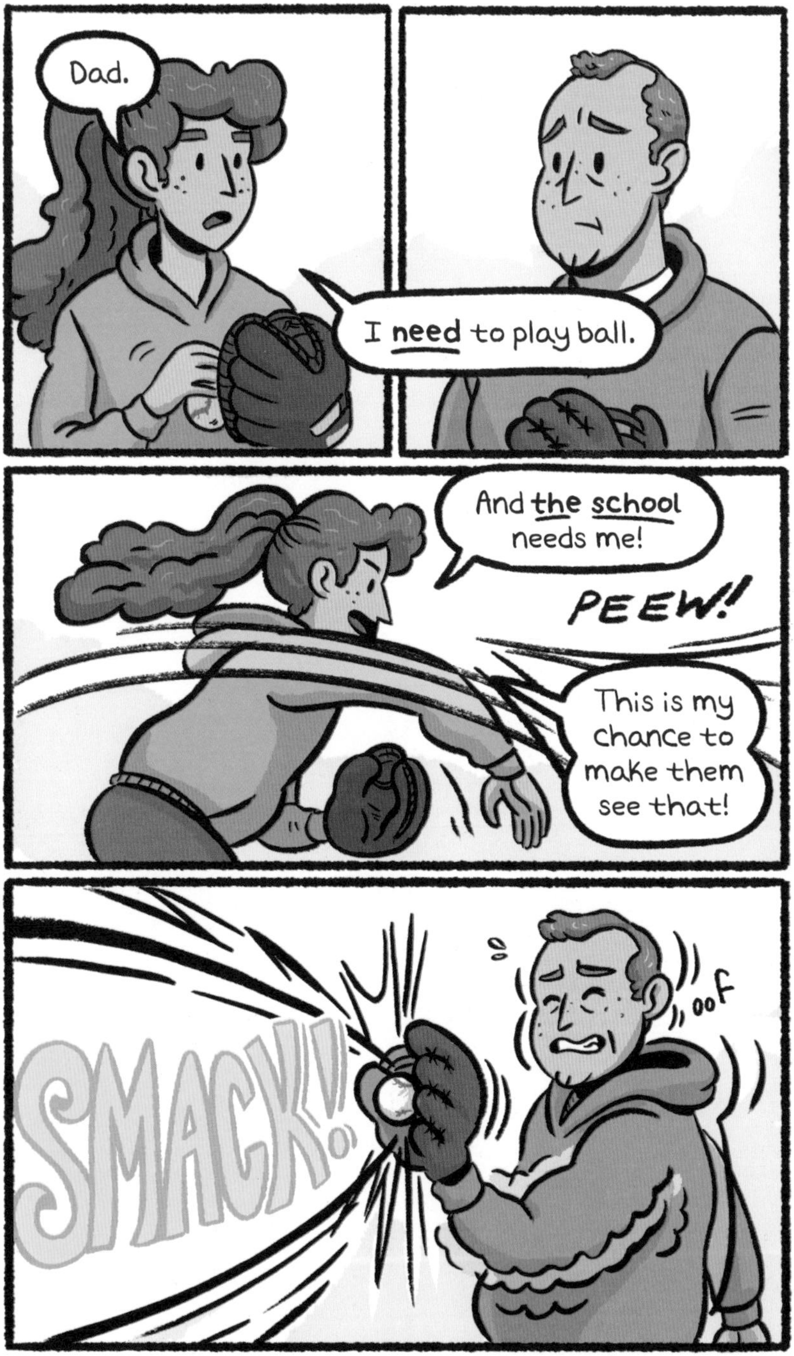
Dad.
I **need** to play ball.
And **the school** needs me!
PEEW!
This is my chance to make them see that!
SMACK!
oof

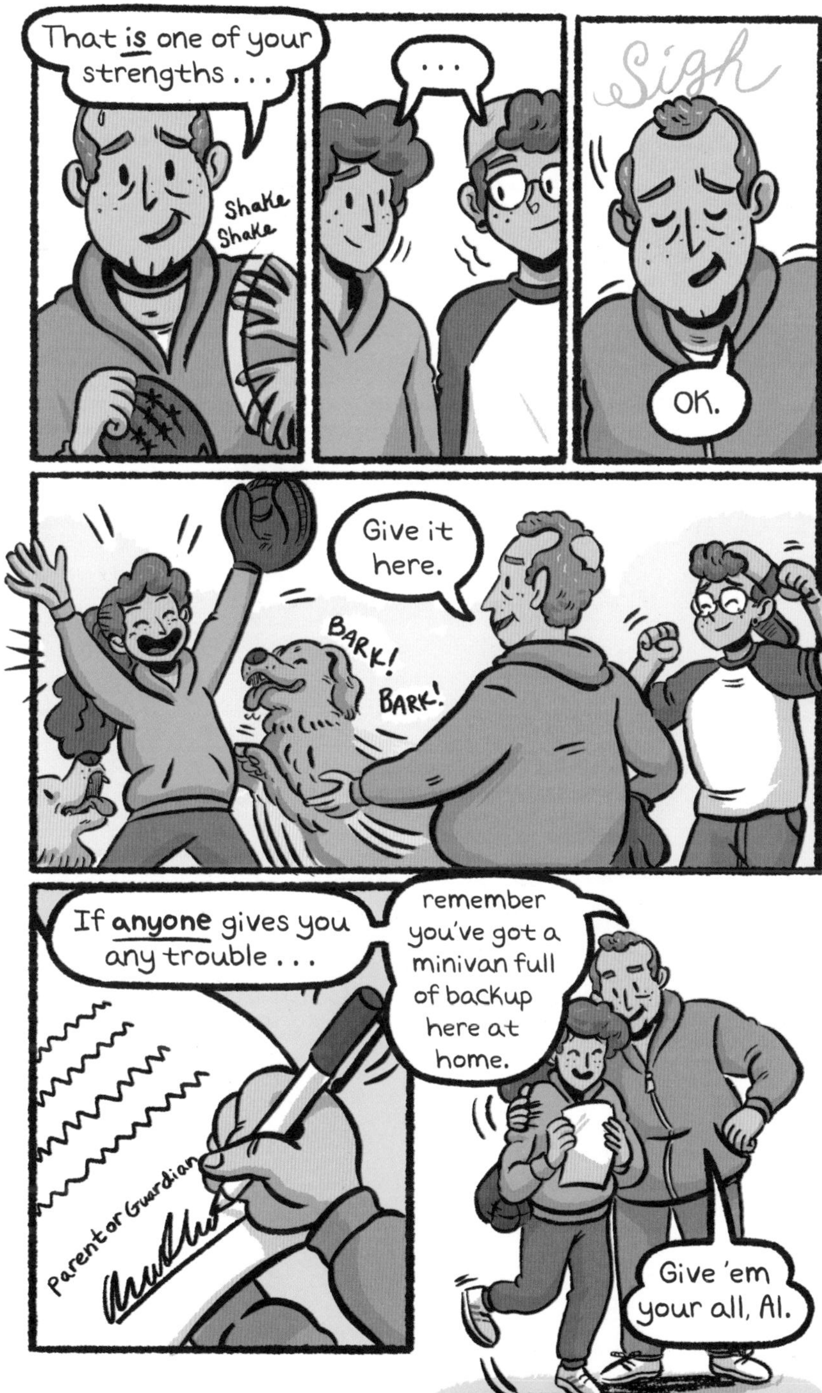
That is one of your strengths . . .
Shake
Shake
. . .
Sigh
OK.
Give it here.
BARK!
BARK!
If anyone gives you any trouble . . .
remember you've got a minivan full of backup here at home.
Parent or Guardian
Give 'em your all, Al.

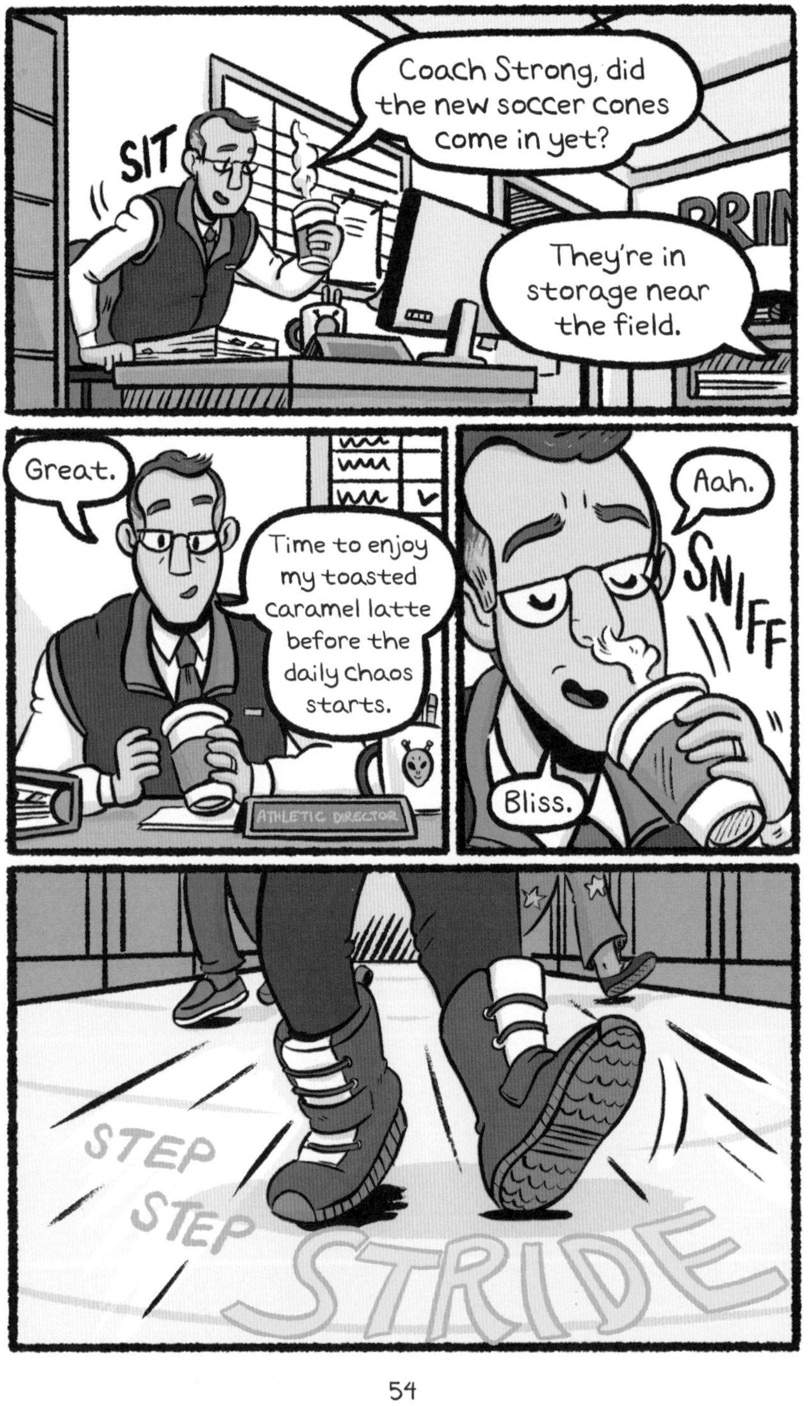
SIT
Coach Strong, did the new soccer cones come in yet?
They're in storage near the field.
Great.
Time to enjoy my toasted caramel latte before the daily chaos starts.
ATHLETIC DIRECTOR
Aah.
SNIFF
Bliss.
STEP
STEP
STRIDE

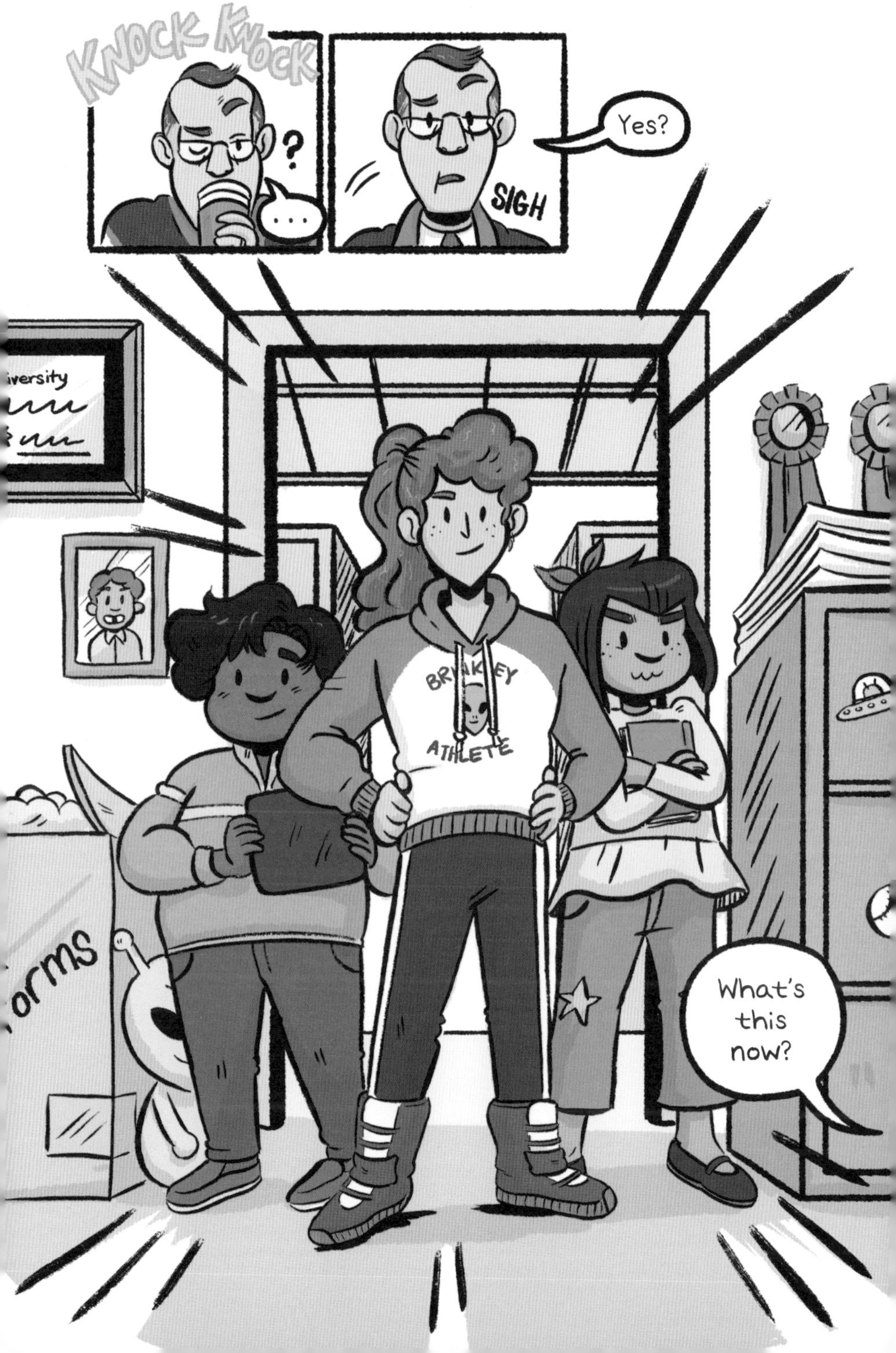

KNOCK KNOCK
?
...
Yes?
SIGH
What's this now?

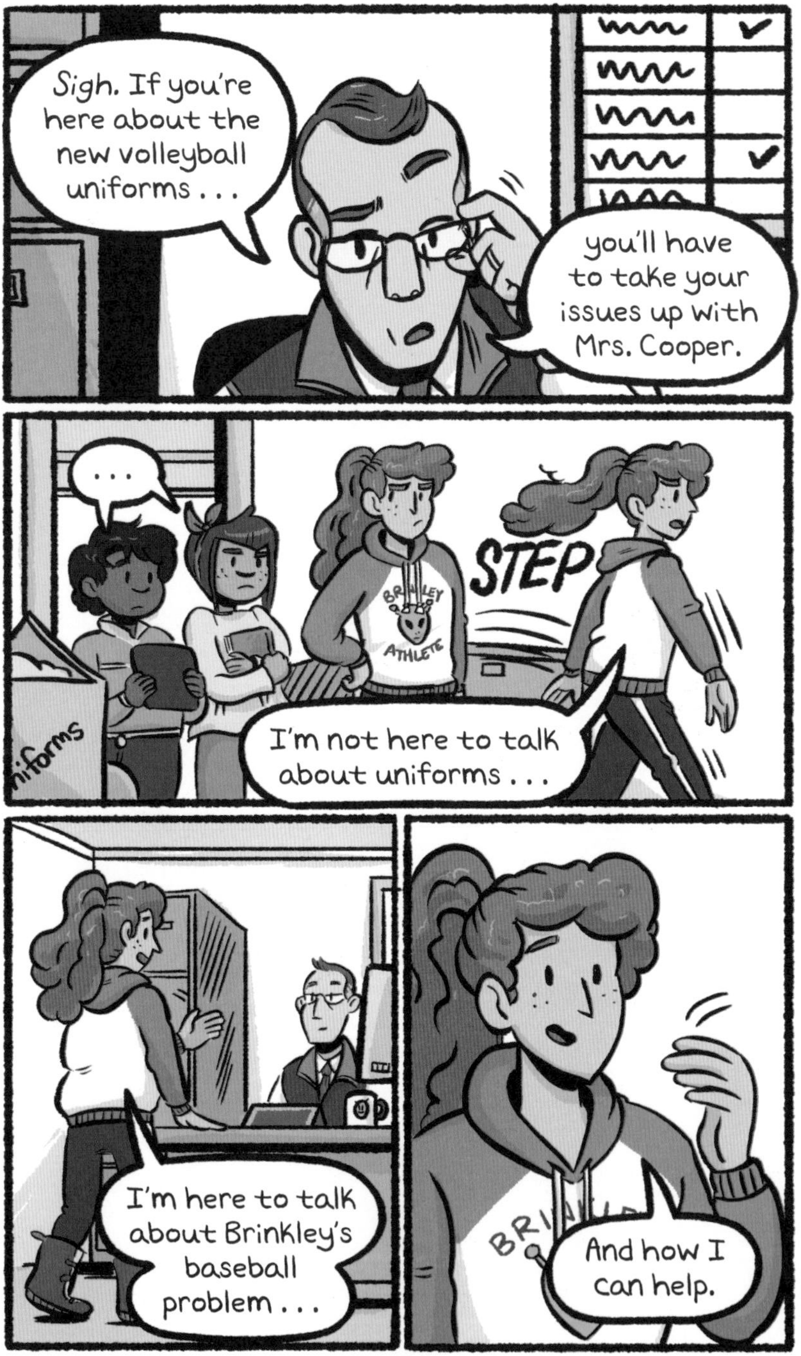
Sigh. If you're here about the new volleyball uniforms . . .
you'll have to take your issues up with Mrs. Cooper.
. . .
STEP
BRINKLEY ATHLETE
I'm not here to talk about uniforms . . .
uniforms
I'm here to talk about Brinkley's baseball problem . . .
And how I can help.

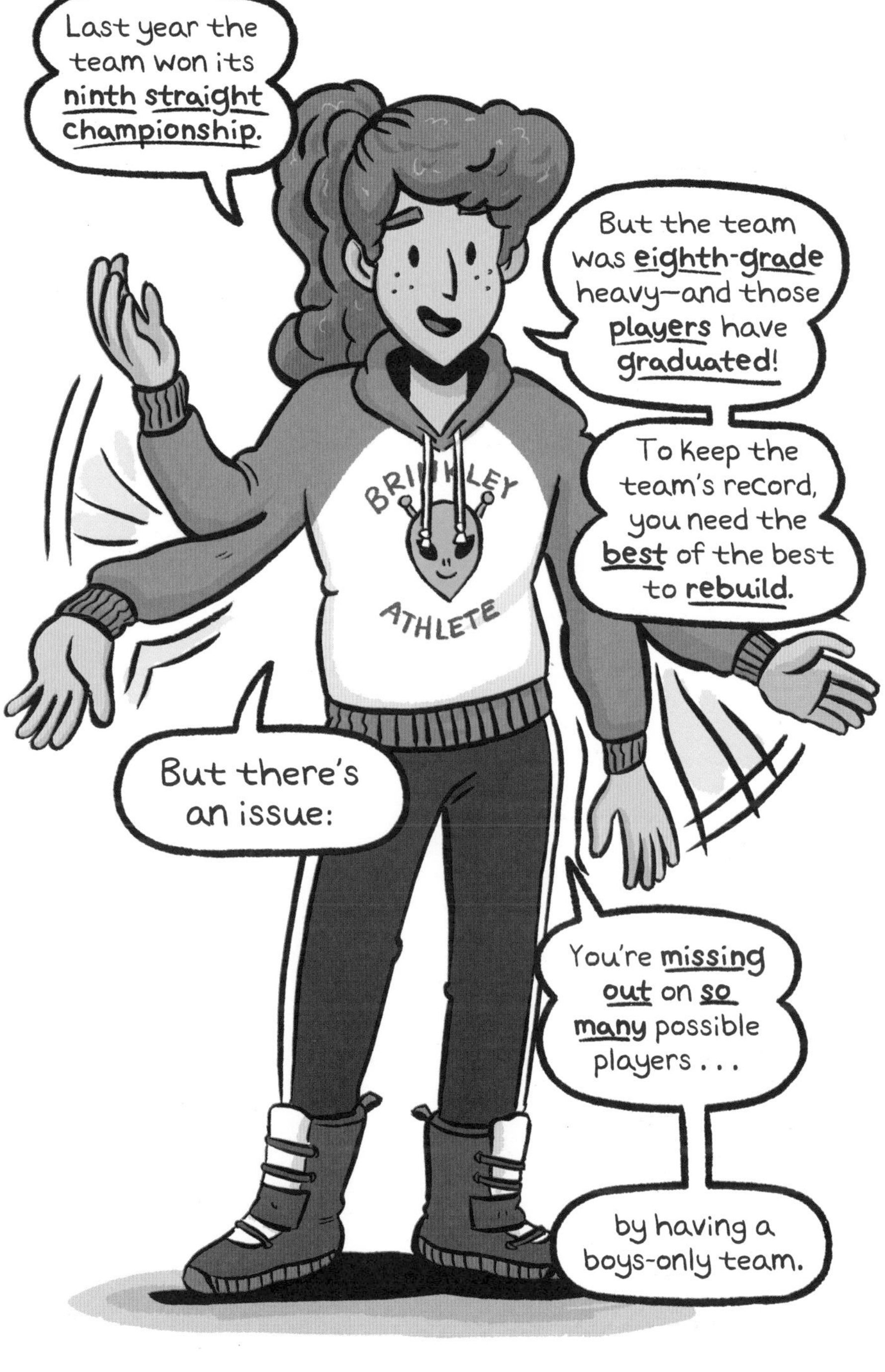

Last year the team won its ninth straight championship.
But the team was eighth-grade heavy—and those players have graduated!
To keep the team's record, you need the best of the best to rebuild.
BRINKLEY ATHLETE
But there's an issue:
You're missing out on so many possible players . . .
by having a boys-only team.

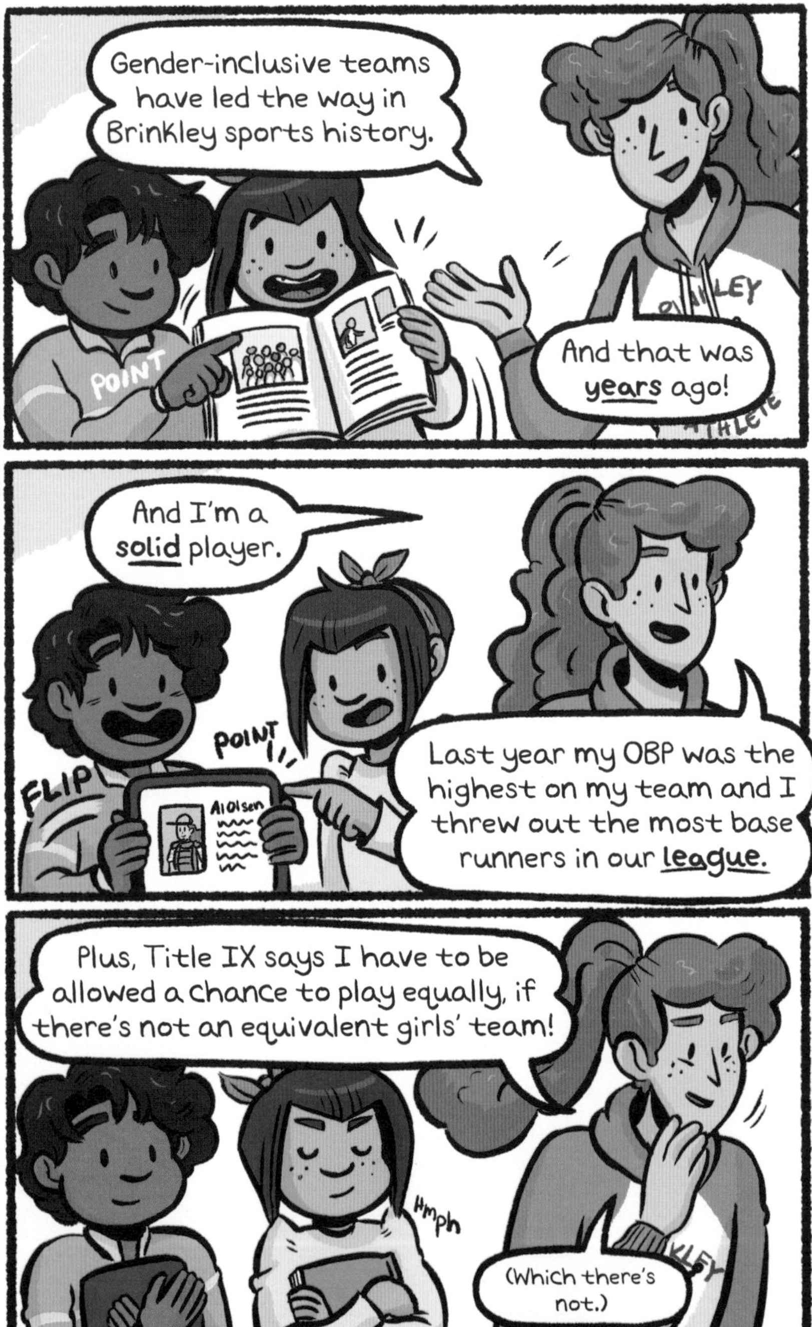
Gender-inclusive teams have led the way in Brinkley sports history.
POINT
And that was years ago!
And I'm a solid player.
FLIP
POINT
Al Olsen
Last year my OBP was the highest on my team and I threw out the most base runners in our league.
Plus, Title IX says I have to be allowed a chance to play equally, if there's not an equivalent girls' team!
Hmph
(Which there's not.)

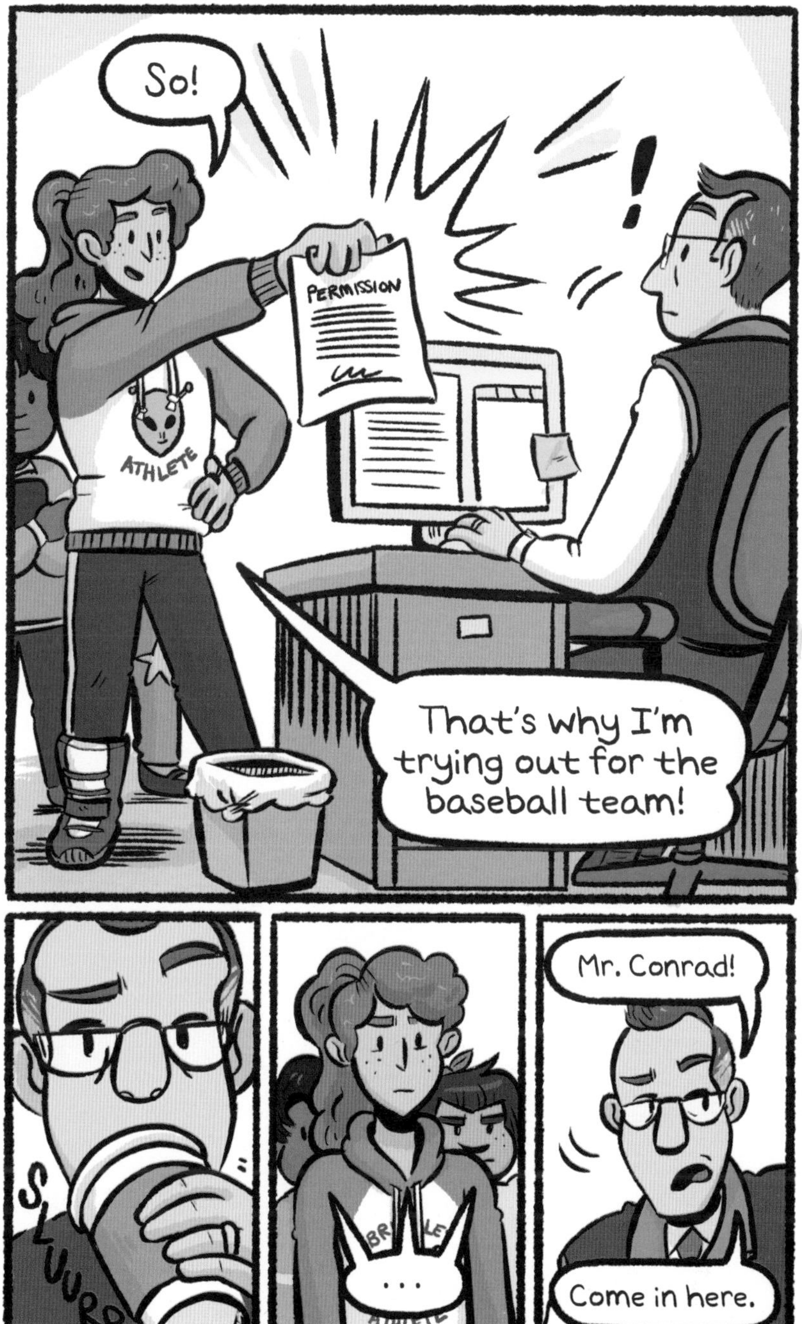
So!
!
PERMISSION
ATHLETE
That's why I'm trying out for the baseball team!
SLUURP
...
Mr. Conrad!
Come in here.

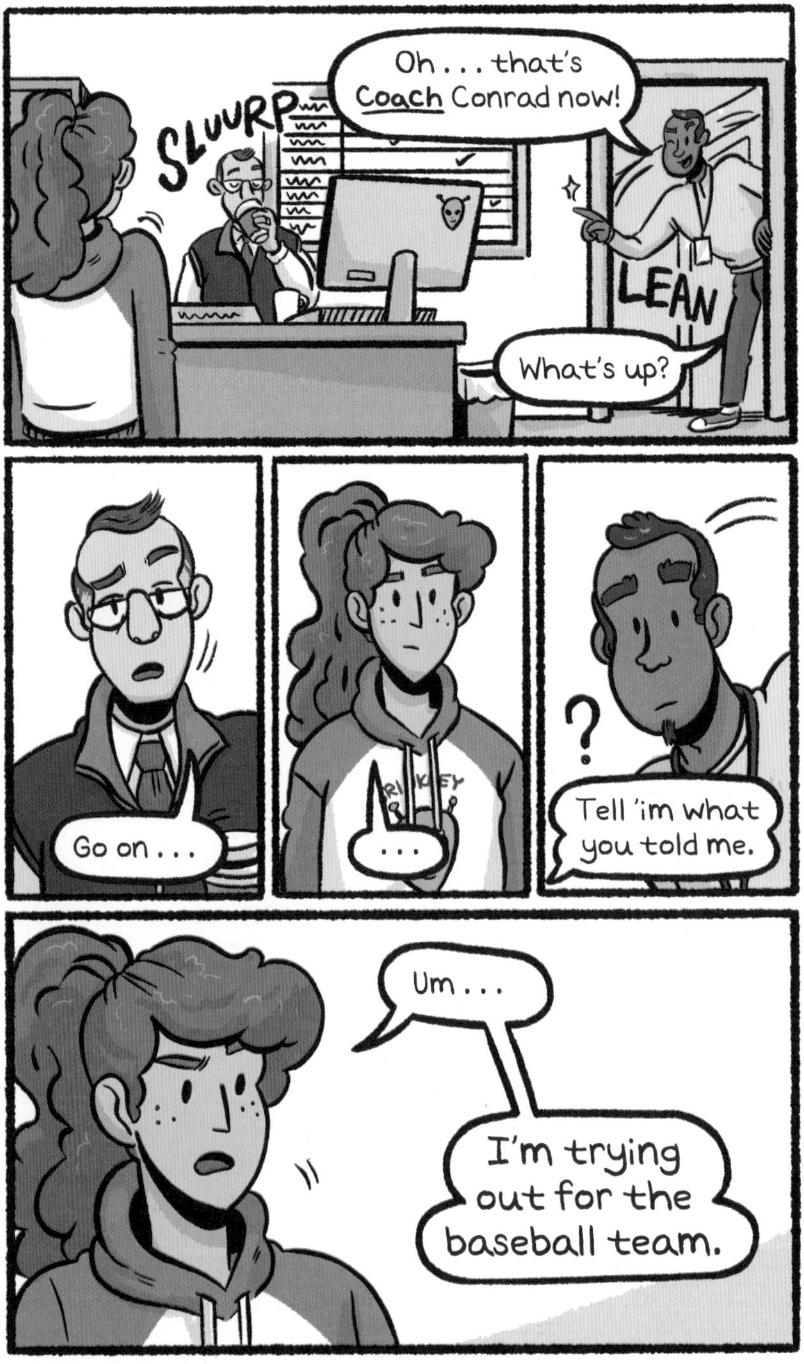
SLUURP
Oh . . . that's Coach Conrad now!
LEAN
What's up?
Go on . . .
. . .
?
Tell 'im what you told me.
Um . . .
I'm trying out for the baseball team.

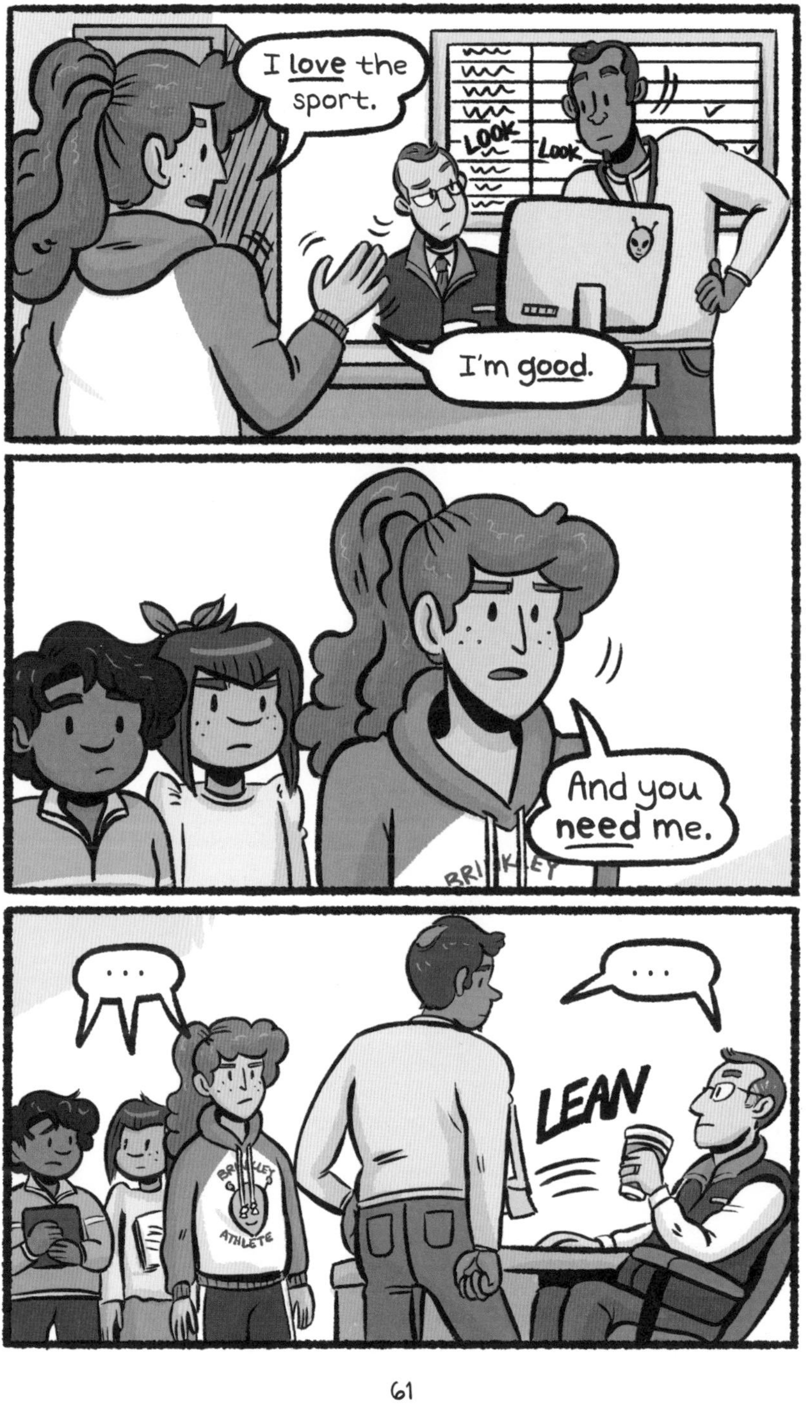
I love the sport.
I'm good.
LOOK
LOOK
And you need me.
BRINKLEY
. . .
. . .
LEAN
BRINKLEY
ATHLETE

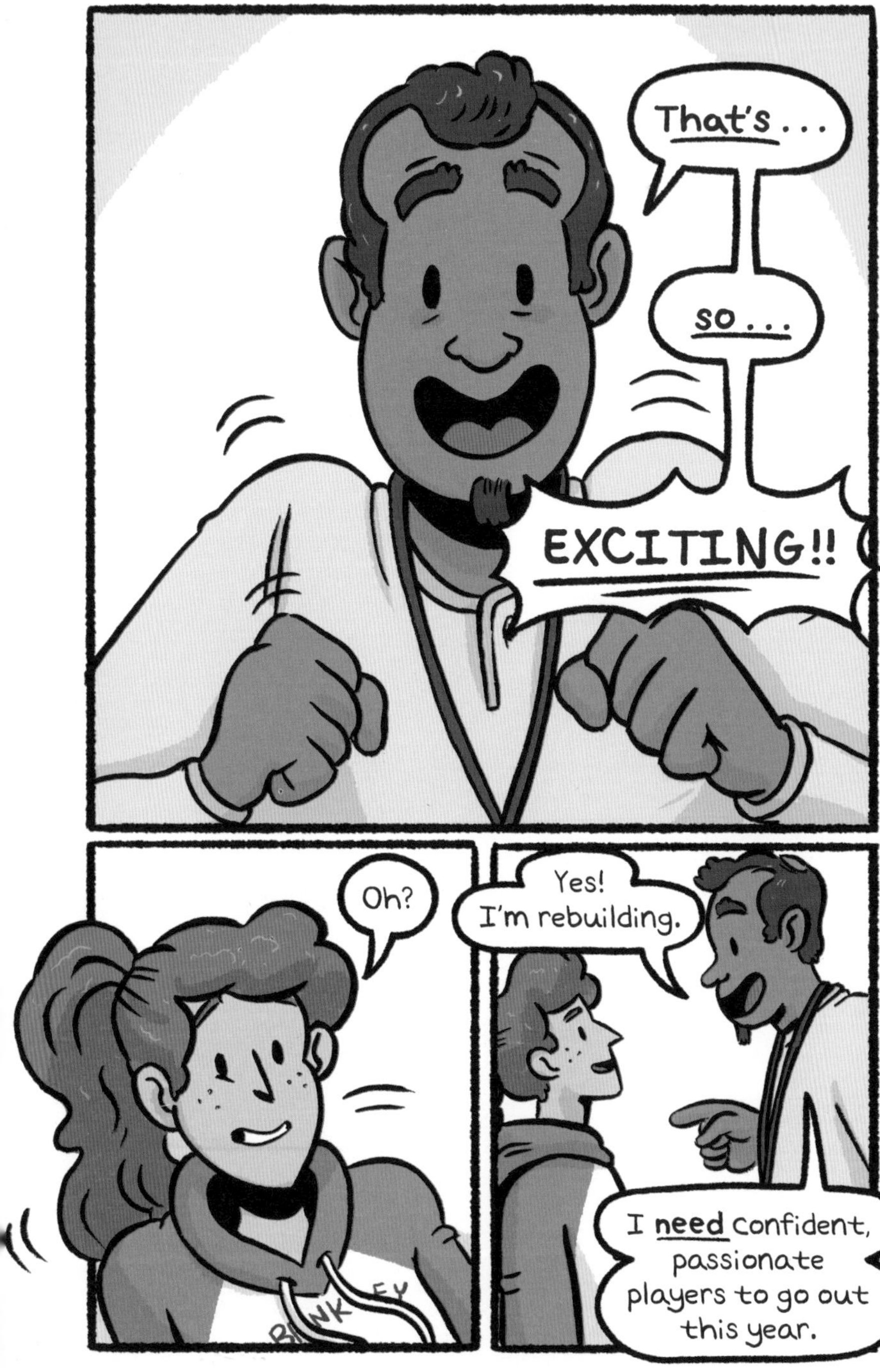
That's . . .
so . . .
EXCITING!!
Oh?
Yes! I'm rebuilding.
I need confident, passionate players to go out this year.

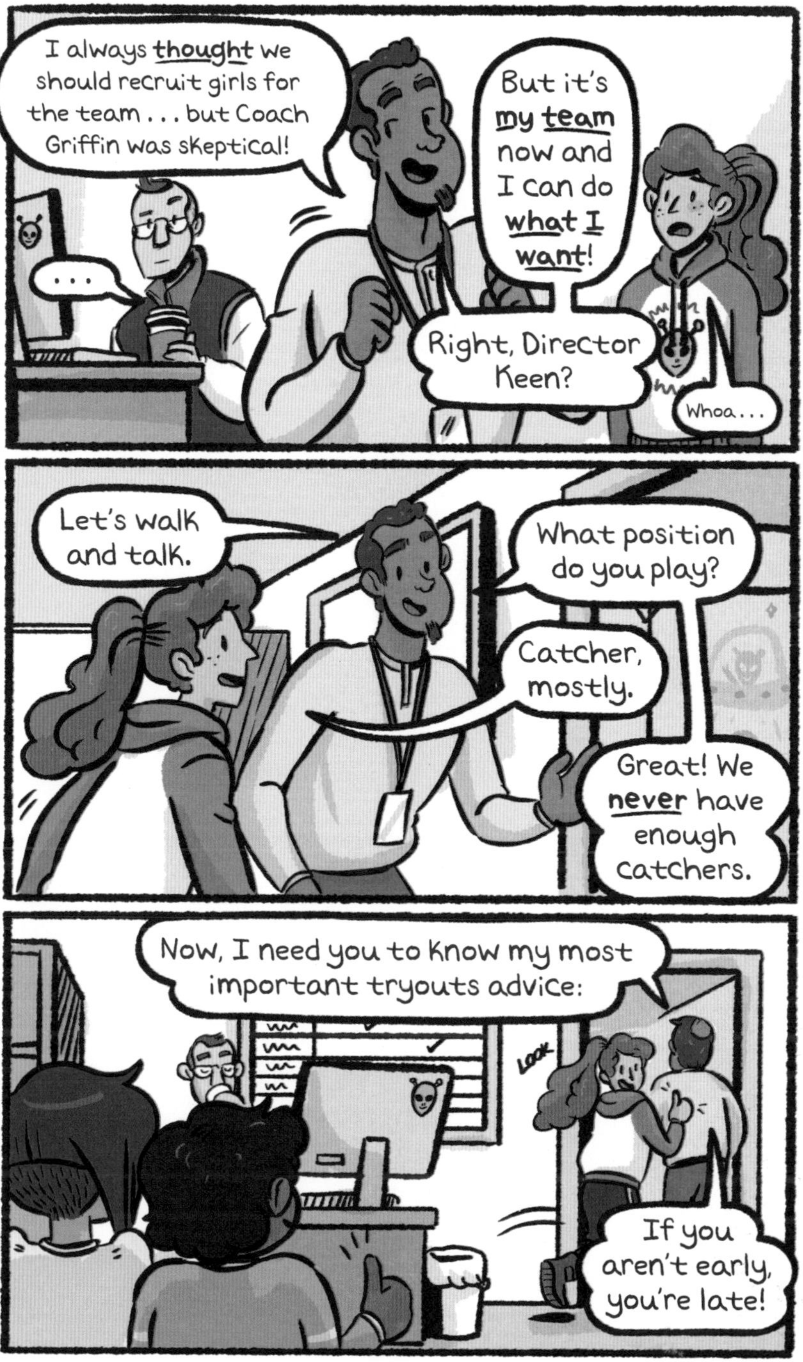
I always thought we should recruit girls for the team . . . but Coach Griffin was skeptical!
. . .
But it's my team now and I can do what I want!
Right, Director Keen?
Whoa . . .
Let's walk and talk.
What position do you play?
Catcher, mostly.
Great! We never have enough catchers.
Now, I need you to know my most important tryouts advice:
LOOK
If you aren't early, you're late!

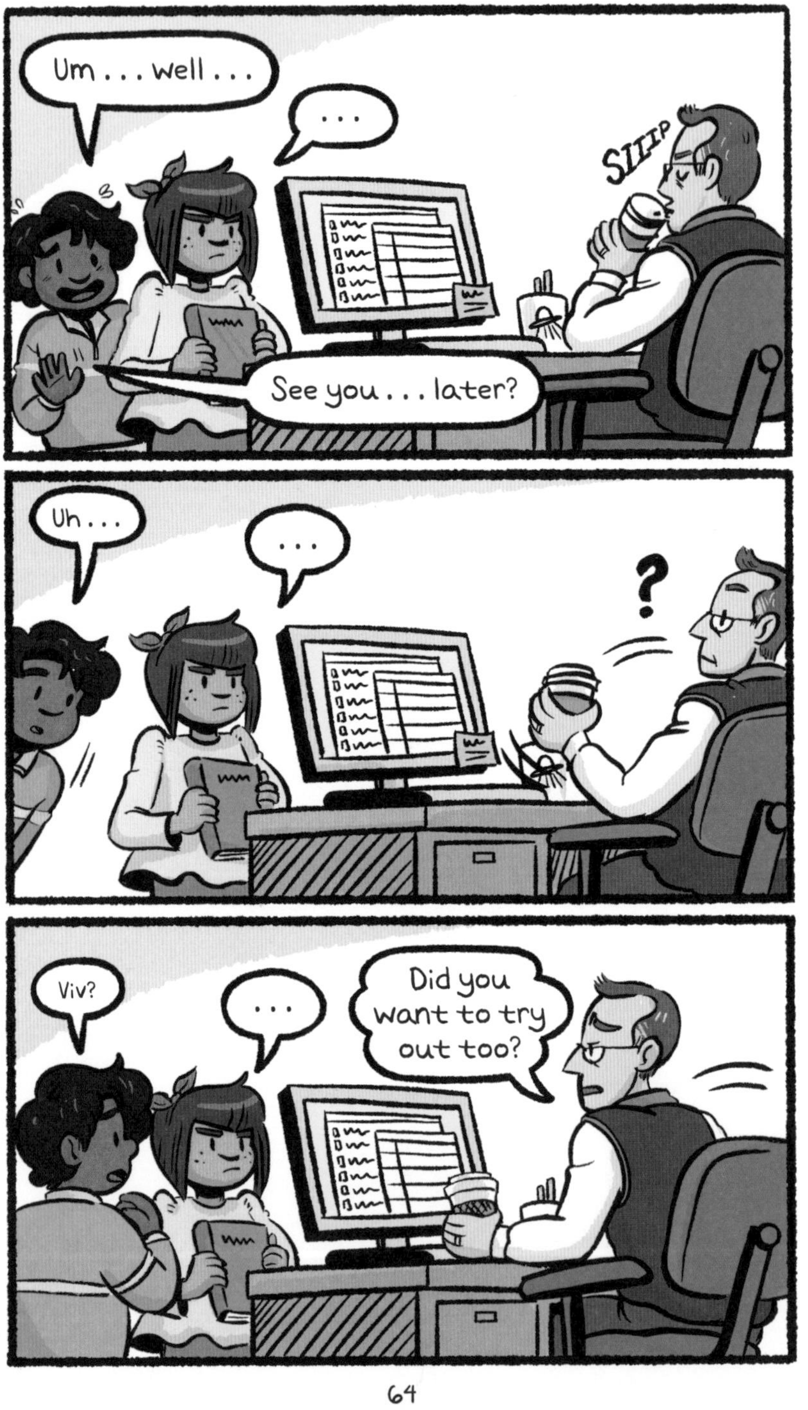

Um . . . well . . .
. . .
SIIIP
See you . . . later?
Uh . . .
. . .
?
Viv?
. . .
Did you want to try out too?

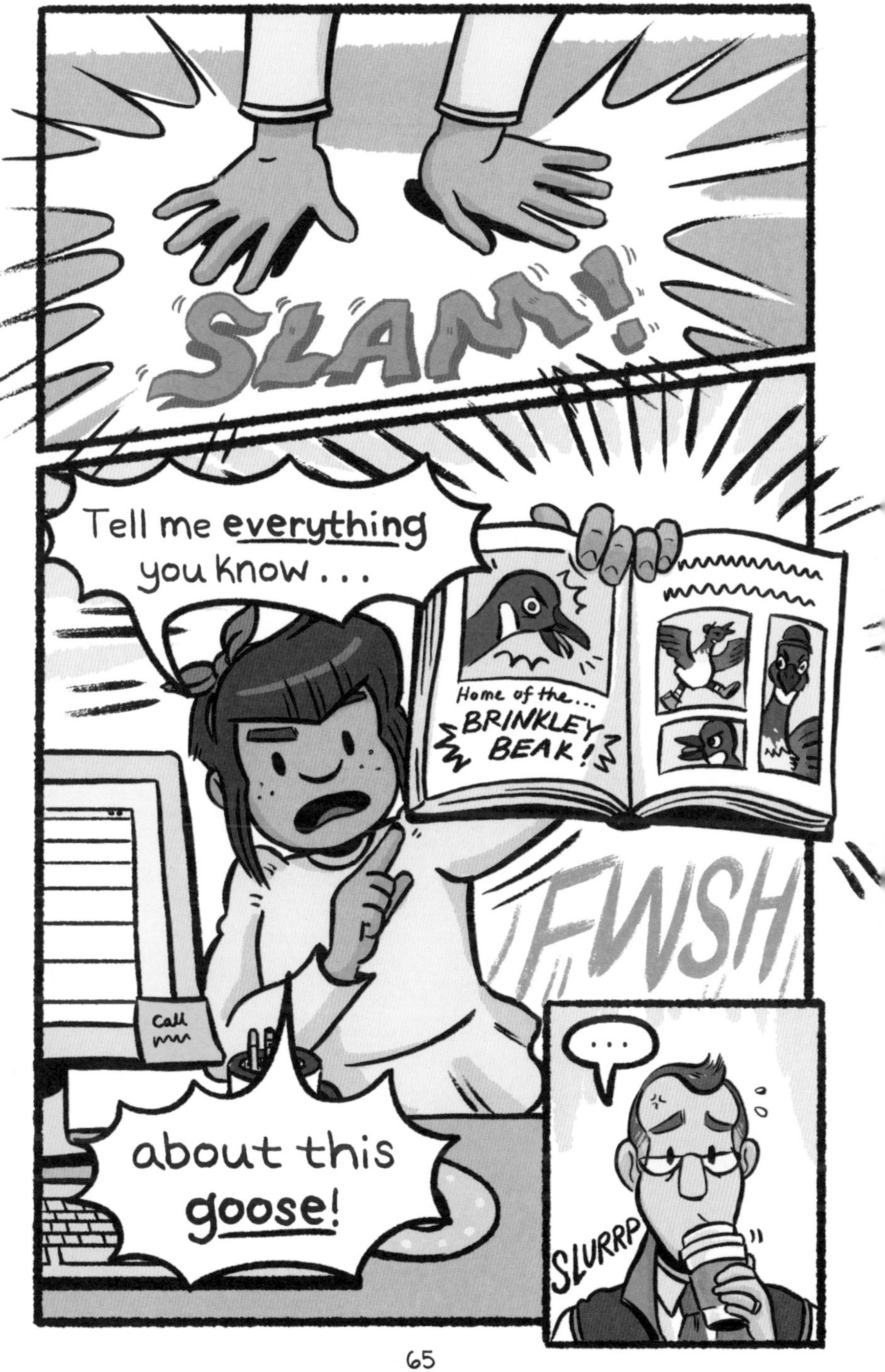
SLAM!
Tell me everything you know . . .
Home of the... BRINKLEY BEAK!
FWSH
Call
about this goose!
. . .
SLURRP

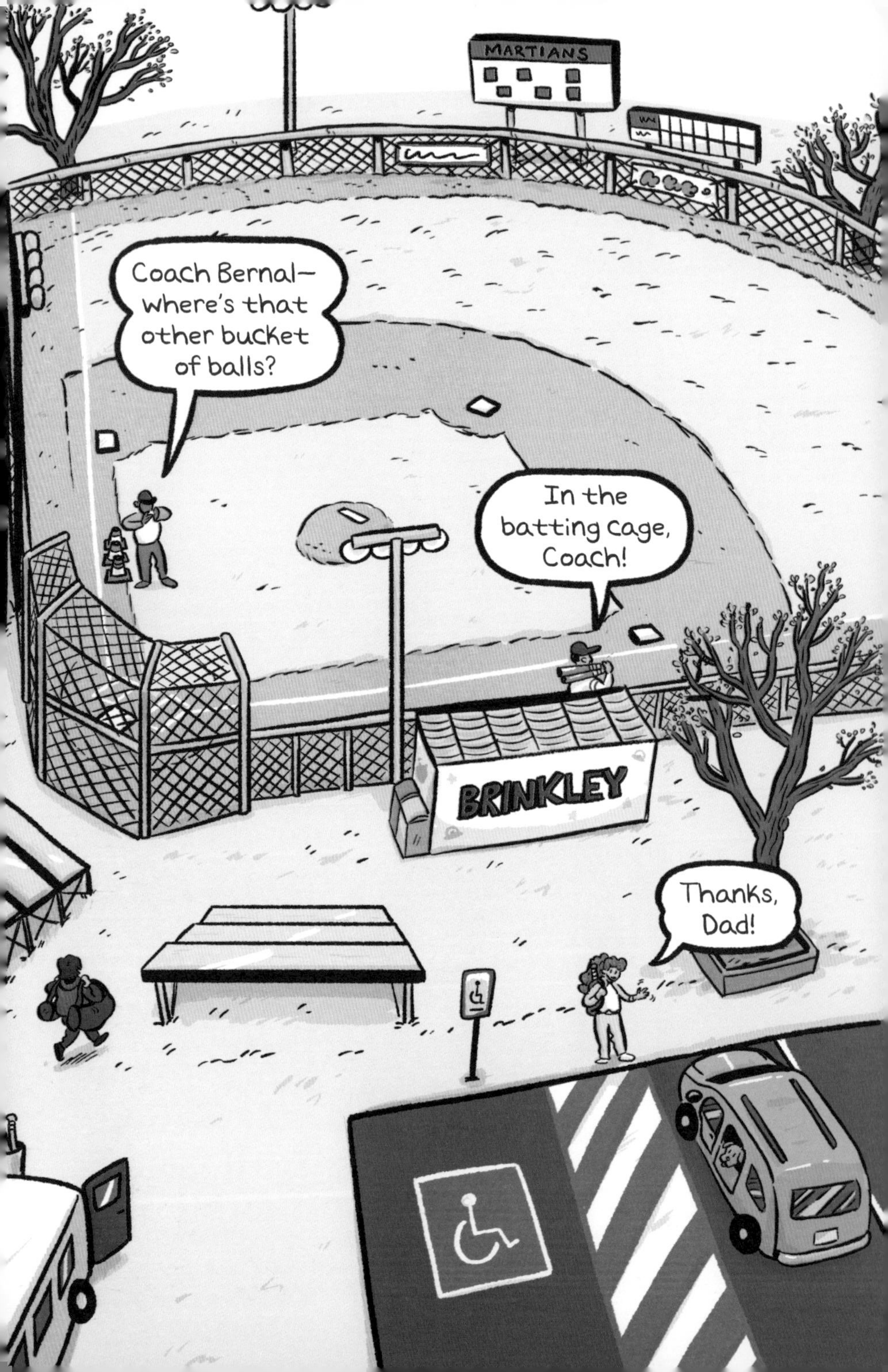
MARTIANS
Coach Bernal—where's that other bucket of balls?
In the batting cage, Coach!
BRINKLEY
Thanks, Dad!

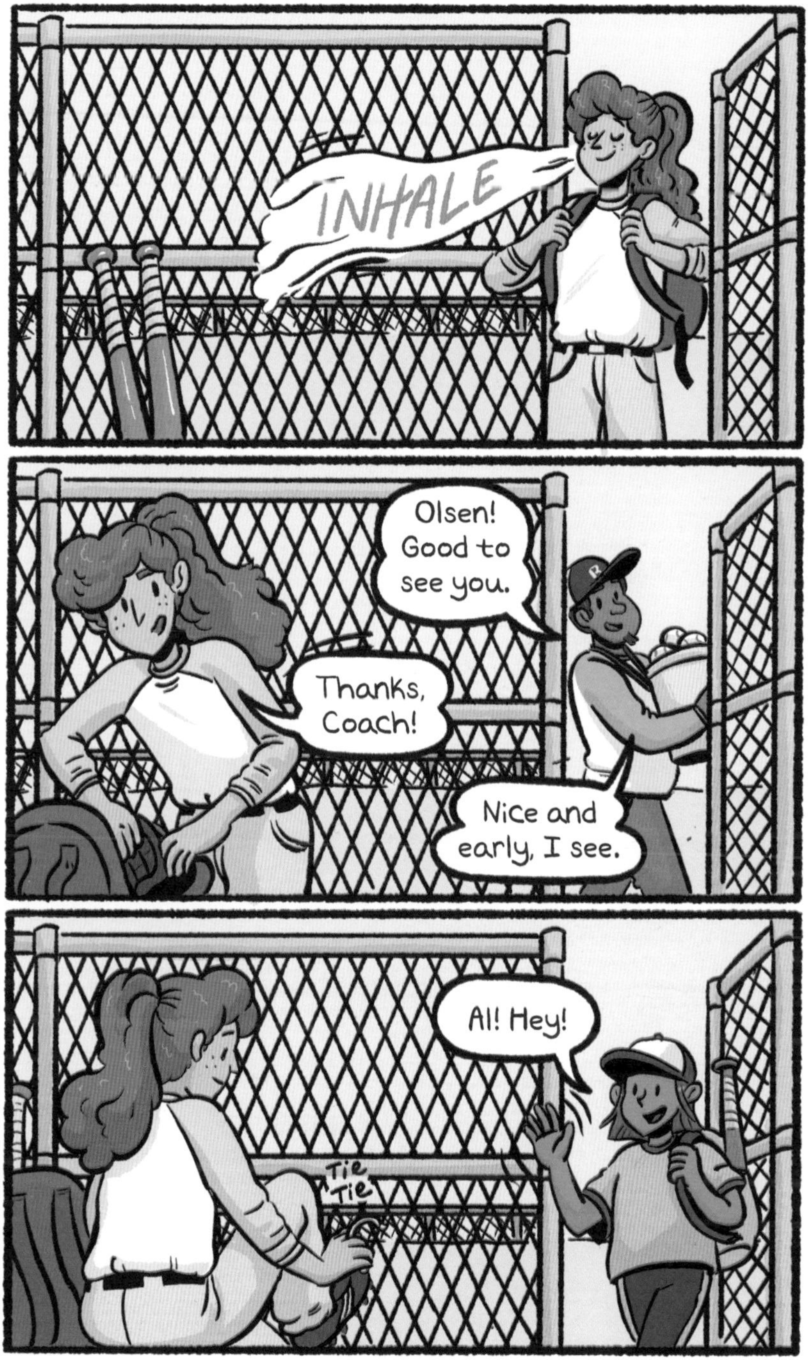
INHALE
Olsen! Good to see you.
Thanks, Coach!
Nice and early, I see.
Al! Hey!
TIE TIE

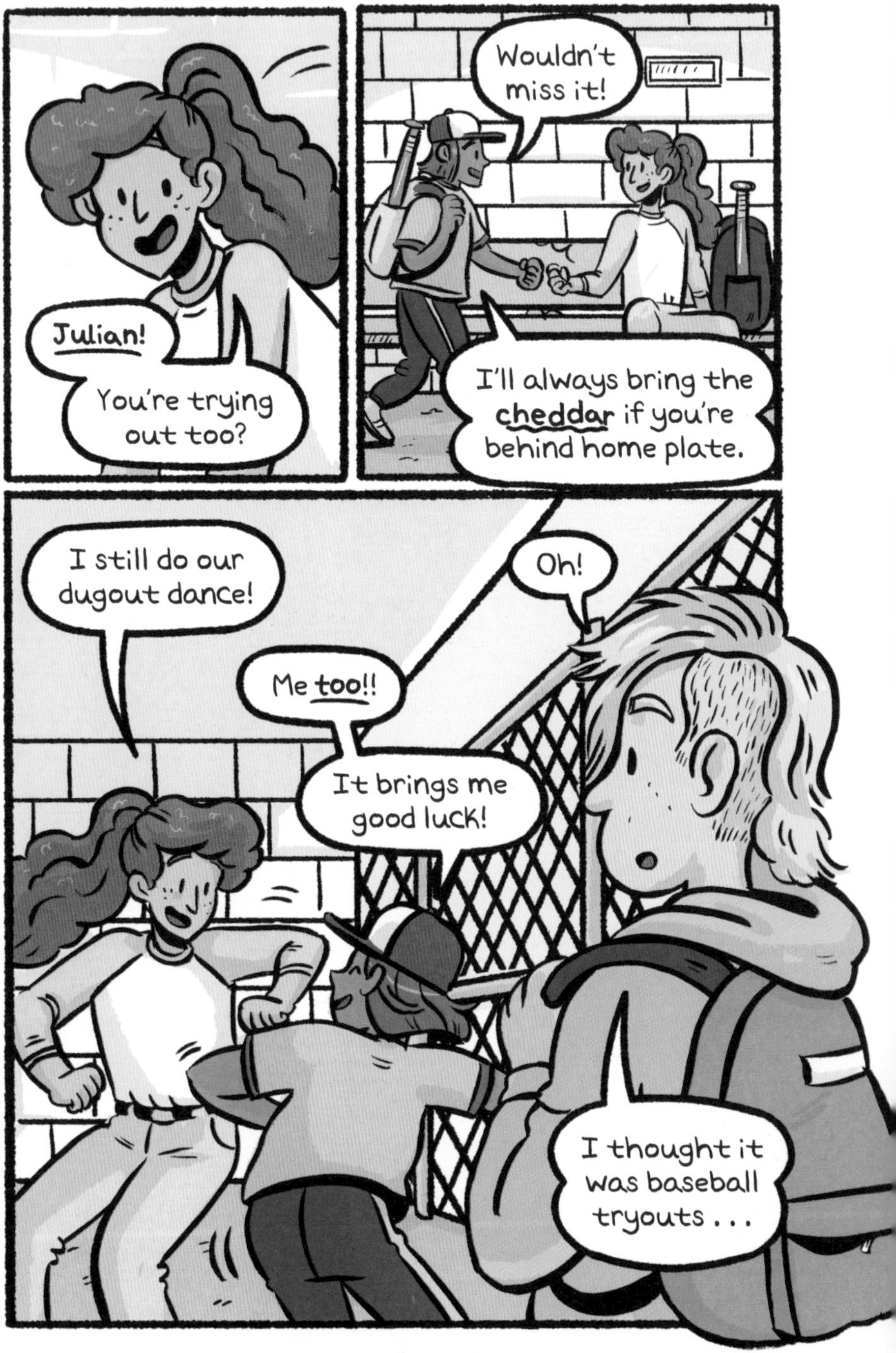
Julian!
You're trying out too?
Wouldn't miss it!
I'll always bring the cheddar if you're behind home plate.
I still do our dugout dance!
Me too!!
It brings me good luck!
Oh!
I thought it was baseball tryouts . . .

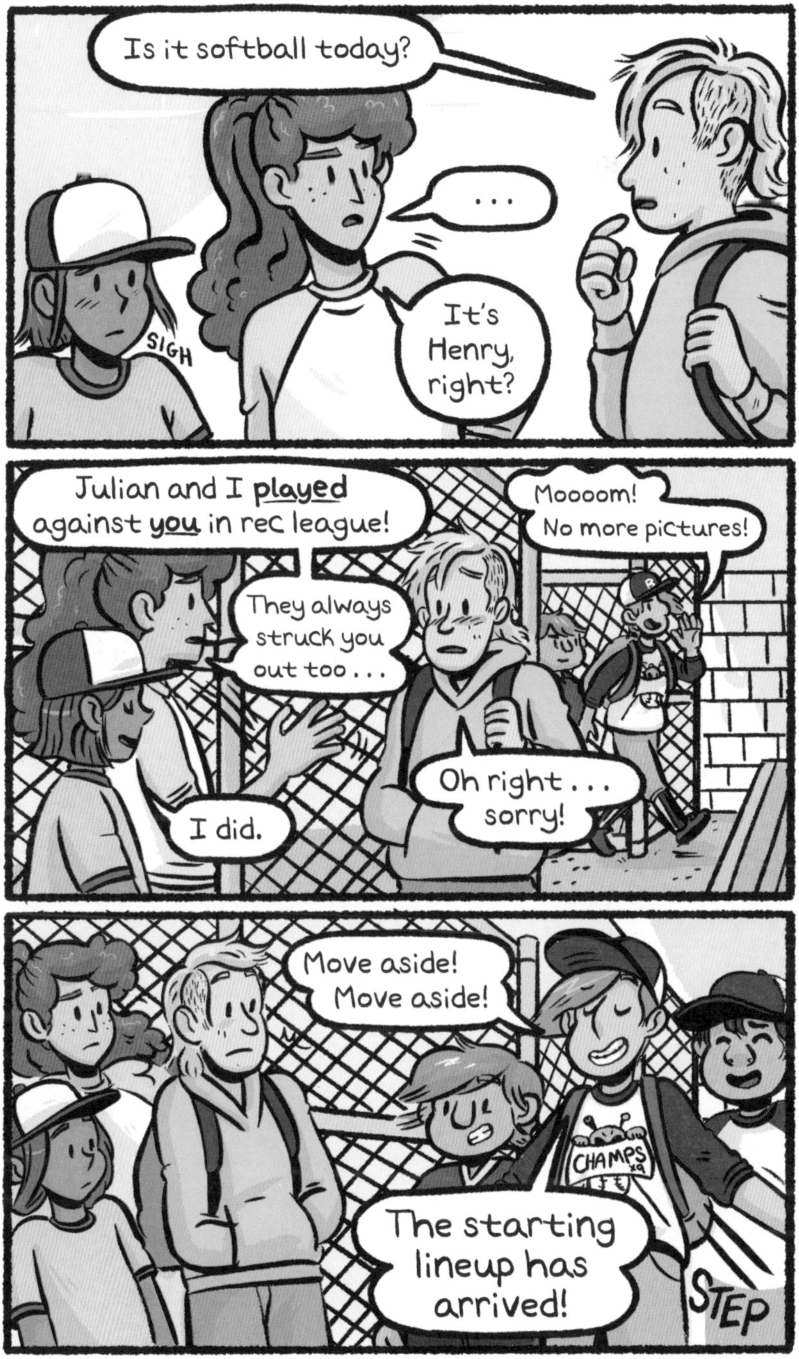
Is it softball today?
...
SIGH
It's Henry, right?
Julian and I played against you in rec league!
Moooom! No more pictures!
They always struck you out too...
Oh right... sorry!
I did.
Move aside! Move aside!
CHAMPS
The starting lineup has arrived!
STEP

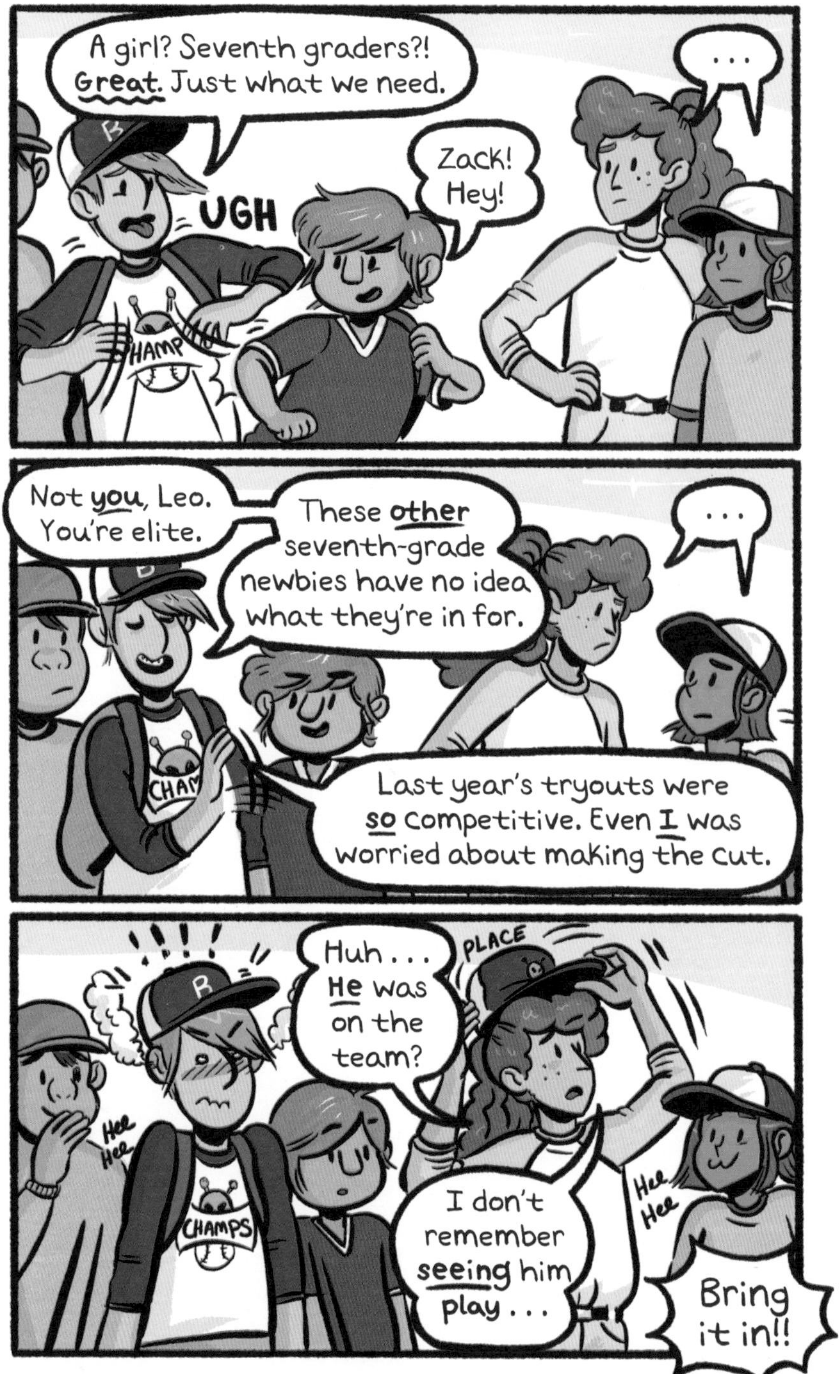
A girl? Seventh graders?! Great. Just what we need.
UGH
Zack! Hey!
...
Not you, Leo. You're elite.
These other seventh-grade newbies have no idea what they're in for.
...
CHAM
Last year's tryouts were so competitive. Even I was worried about making the cut.
Huh . . . He was on the team?
PLACE
Hee Hee
CHAMPS
I don't remember seeing him play . . .
Hee Hee
Bring it in!!

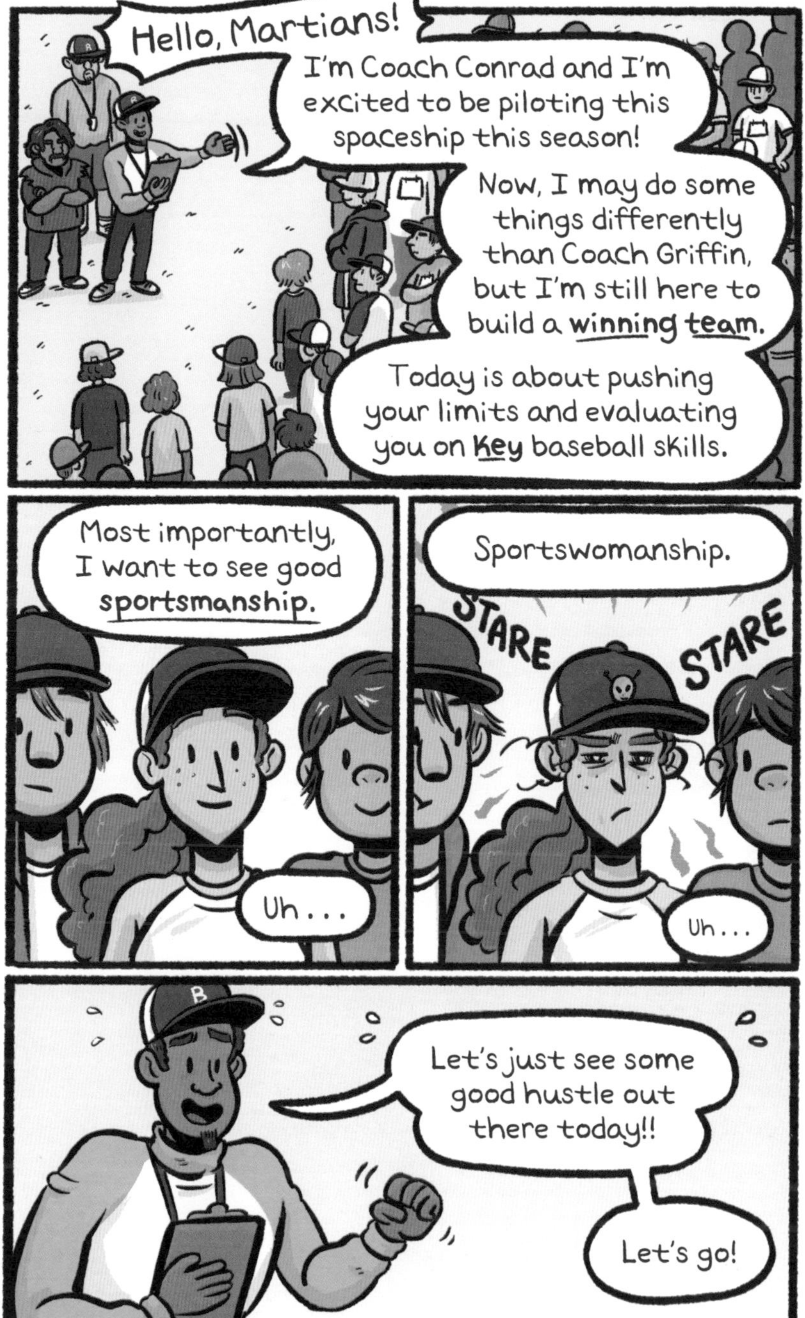
Hello, Martians!
I'm Coach Conrad and I'm excited to be piloting this spaceship this season!
Now, I may do some things differently than Coach Griffin, but I'm still here to build a winning team.
Today is about pushing your limits and evaluating you on key baseball skills.
Most importantly, I want to see good sportsmanship.
Uh . . .
Sportswomanship.
STARE
STARE
Uh . . .
Let's just see some good hustle out there today!!
Let's go!

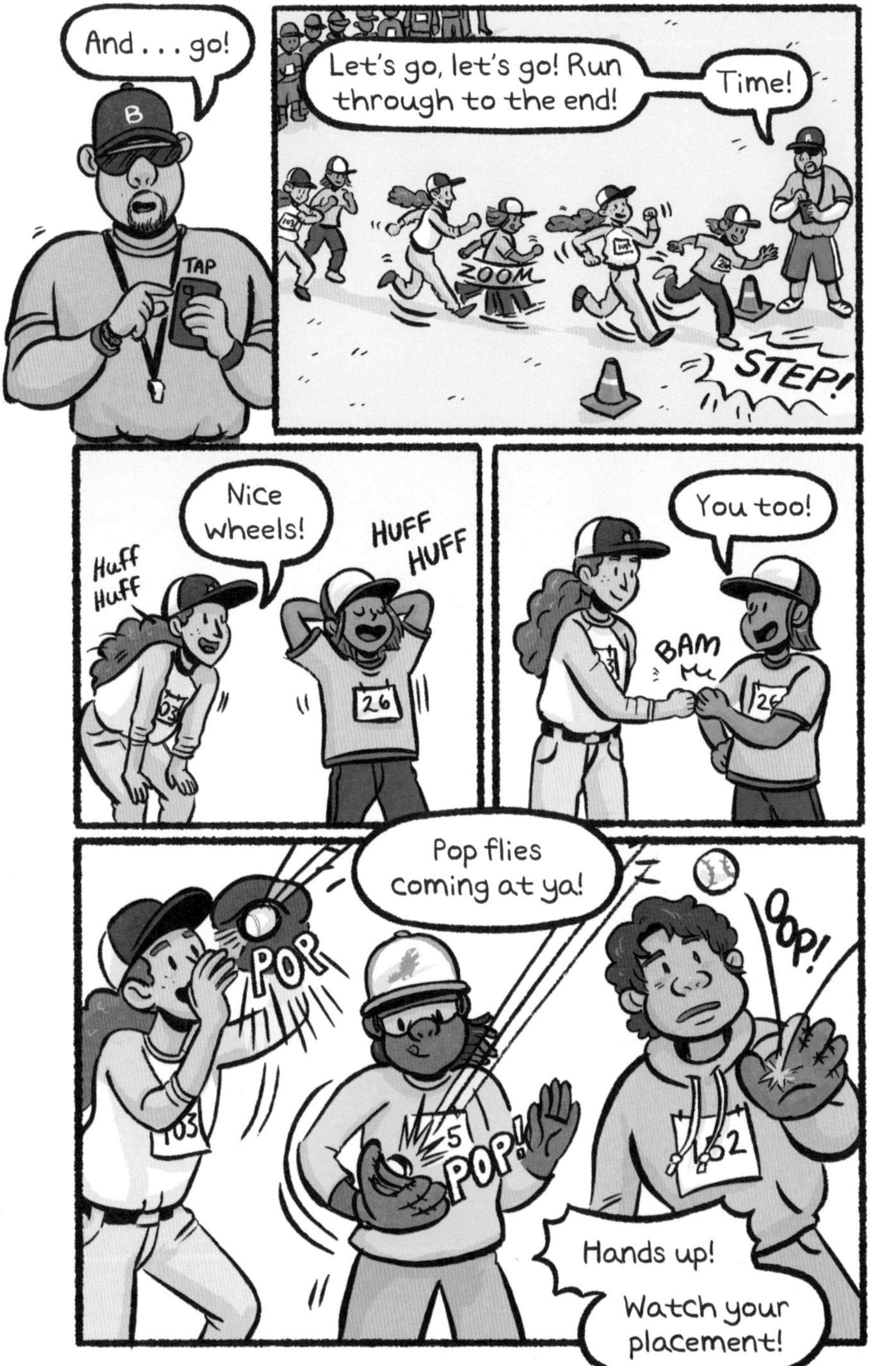
And . . . go!
TAP
Let's go, let's go! Run through to the end!
Time!
ZOOM
STEP!
Nice Wheels!
Huff Huff
HUFF HUFF
You too!
BAM
Pop flies coming at ya!
POP
POP!
OOP!
Hands up!
Watch your placement!

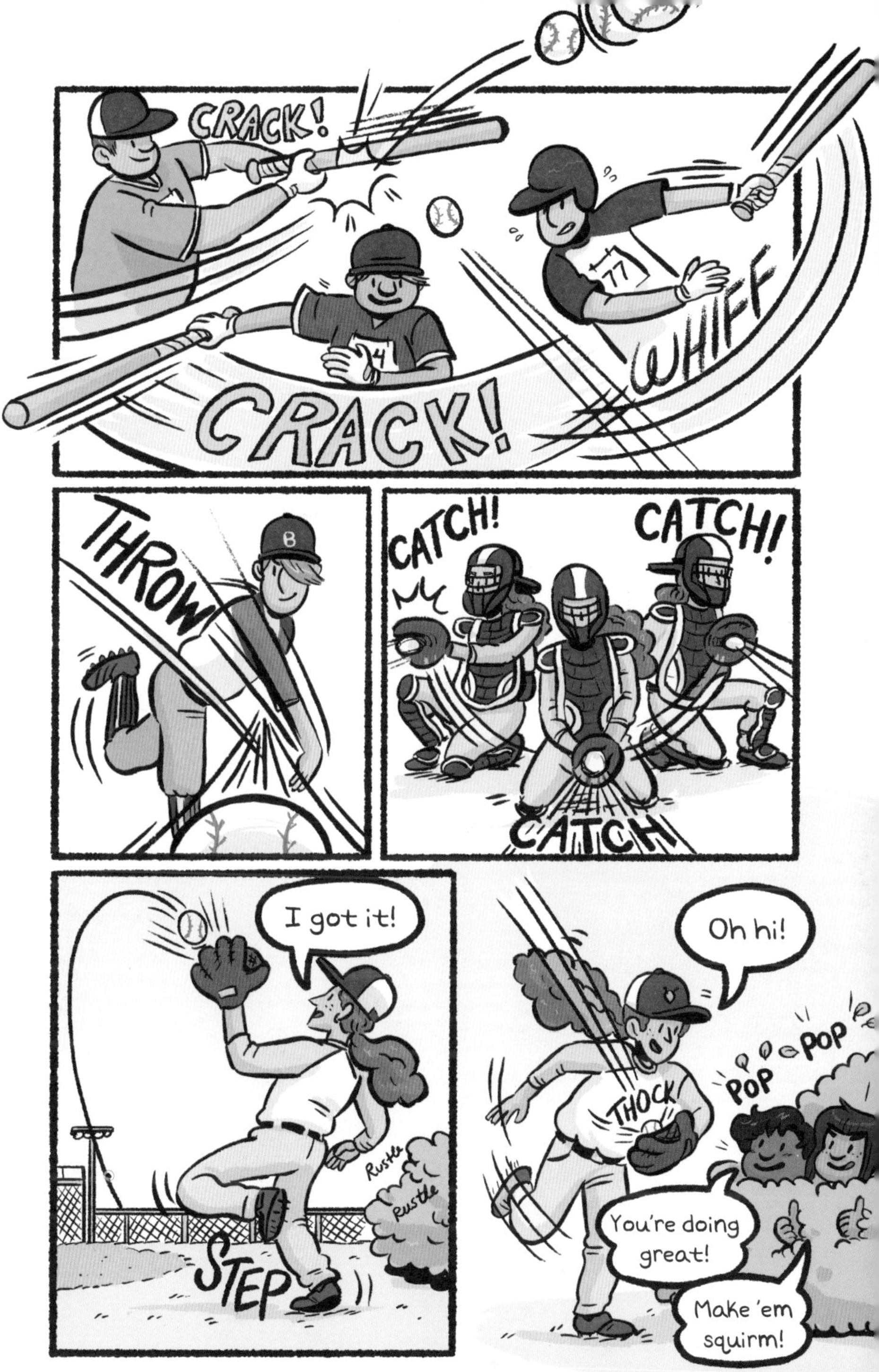
CRACK!
CRACK!
WHIFF
THROW
CATCH!
CATCH!
CATCH
I got it!
Rustle
Rustle
STEP
Oh hi!
POP
POP
THOCK
You're doing great!
Make 'em squirm!

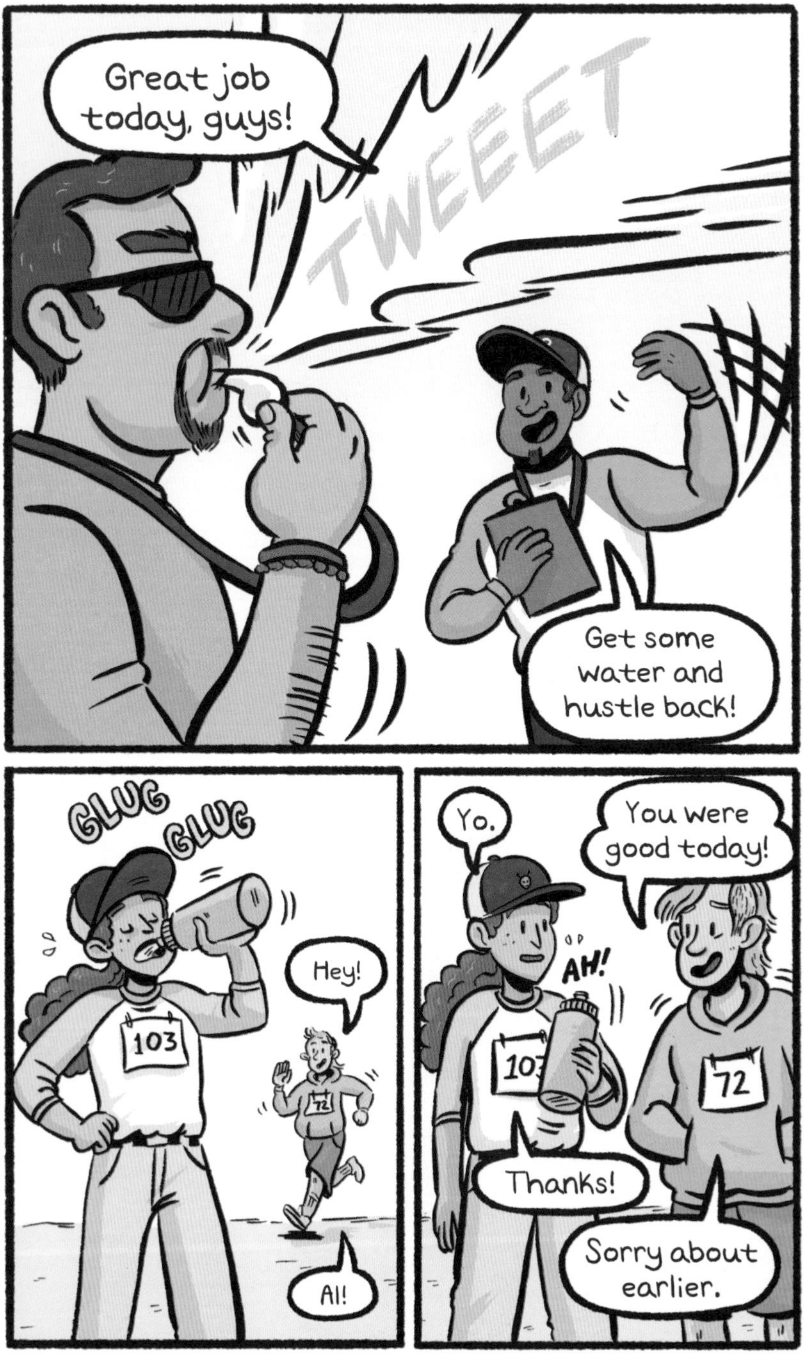
Great job today, guys!
TWEEET
Get some water and hustle back!
GLUG GLUG
Hey!
Al!
Yo.
You were good today!
AH!
Thanks!
Sorry about earlier.
103
72

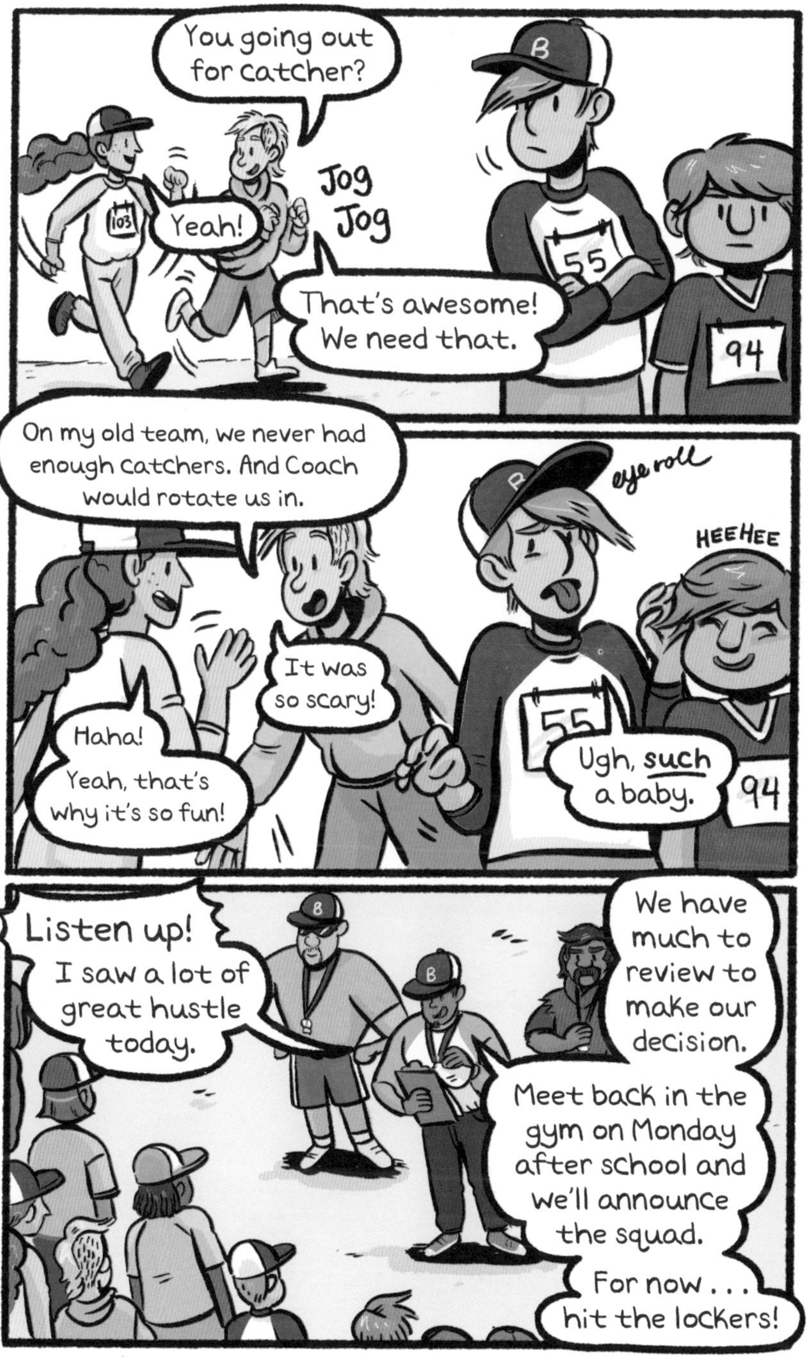

You going out for catcher?
Yeah!
Jog Jog
That's awesome! We need that.
On my old team, we never had enough catchers. And Coach would rotate us in.
eye roll
HEEHEE
It was so scary!
Haha!
Yeah, that's why it's so fun!
Ugh, **such** a baby.
Listen up!
I saw a lot of great hustle today.
We have much to review to make our decision.
Meet back in the gym on Monday after school and we'll announce the squad.
For now . . . hit the lockers!

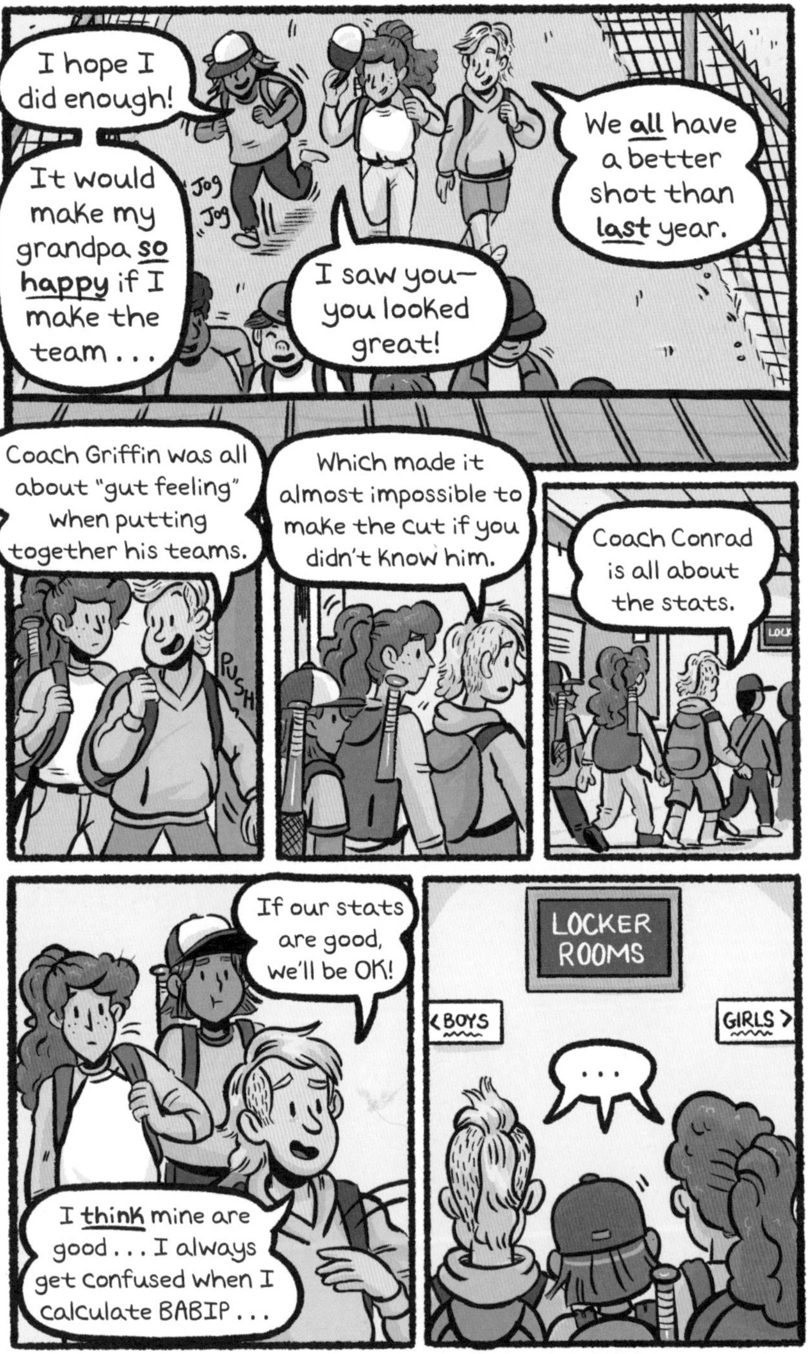
I hope I did enough!
It would make my grandpa so happy if I make the team . . .
Jog Jog
I saw you—you looked great!
We all have a better shot than last year.
Coach Griffin was all about "gut feeling" when putting together his teams.
PUSH
Which made it almost impossible to make the cut if you didn't know him.
Coach Conrad is all about the stats.
If our stats are good, we'll be OK!
I think mine are good . . . I always get confused when I calculate BABIP . . .
LOCKER ROOMS
< BOYS
GIRLS >
. . .

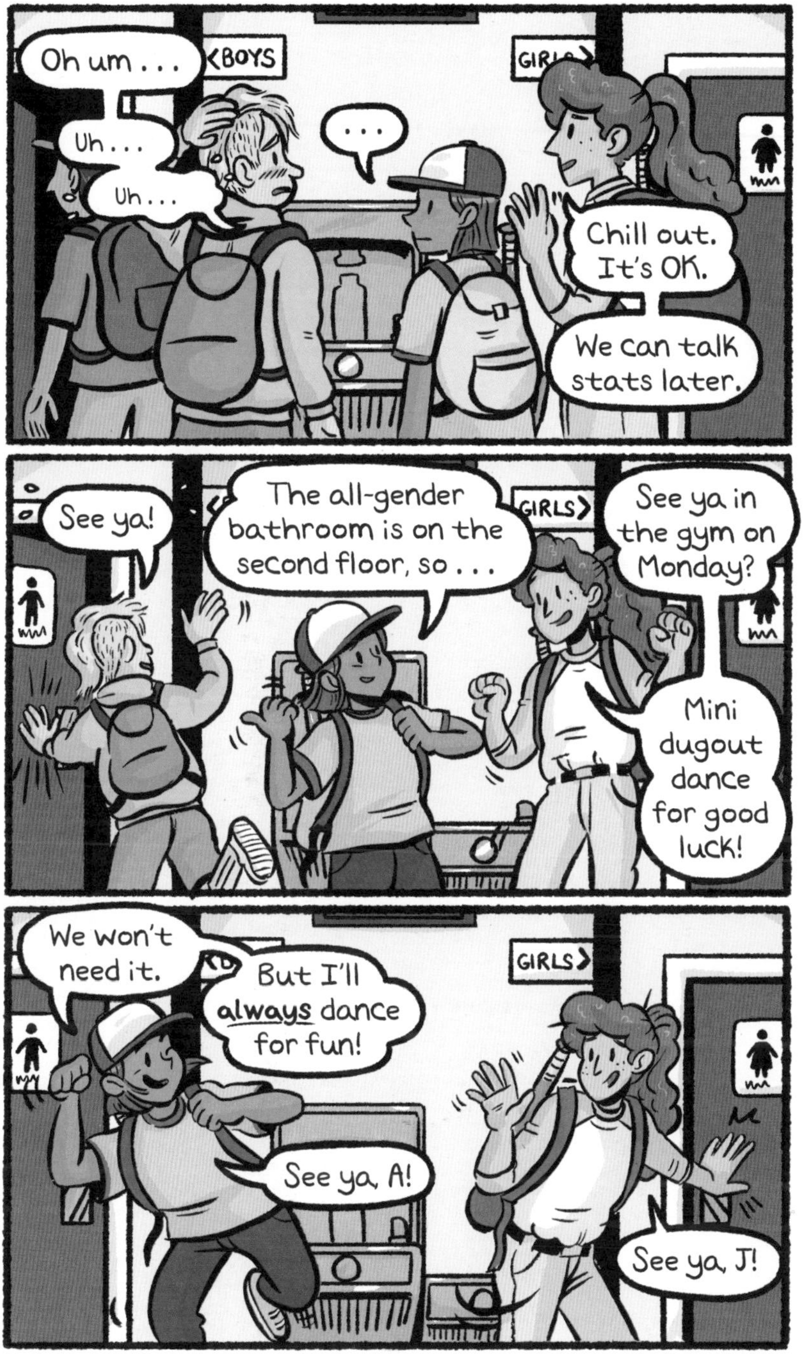
BOYS
GIRLS
Oh um . . .
Uh . . .
Uh . . .
. . .
Chill out. It's OK.
We can talk stats later.
GIRLS
See ya!
The all-gender bathroom is on the second floor, so . . .
See ya in the gym on Monday?
Mini dugout dance for good luck!
GIRLS
We won't need it.
But I'll always dance for fun!
See ya, A!
See ya, J!

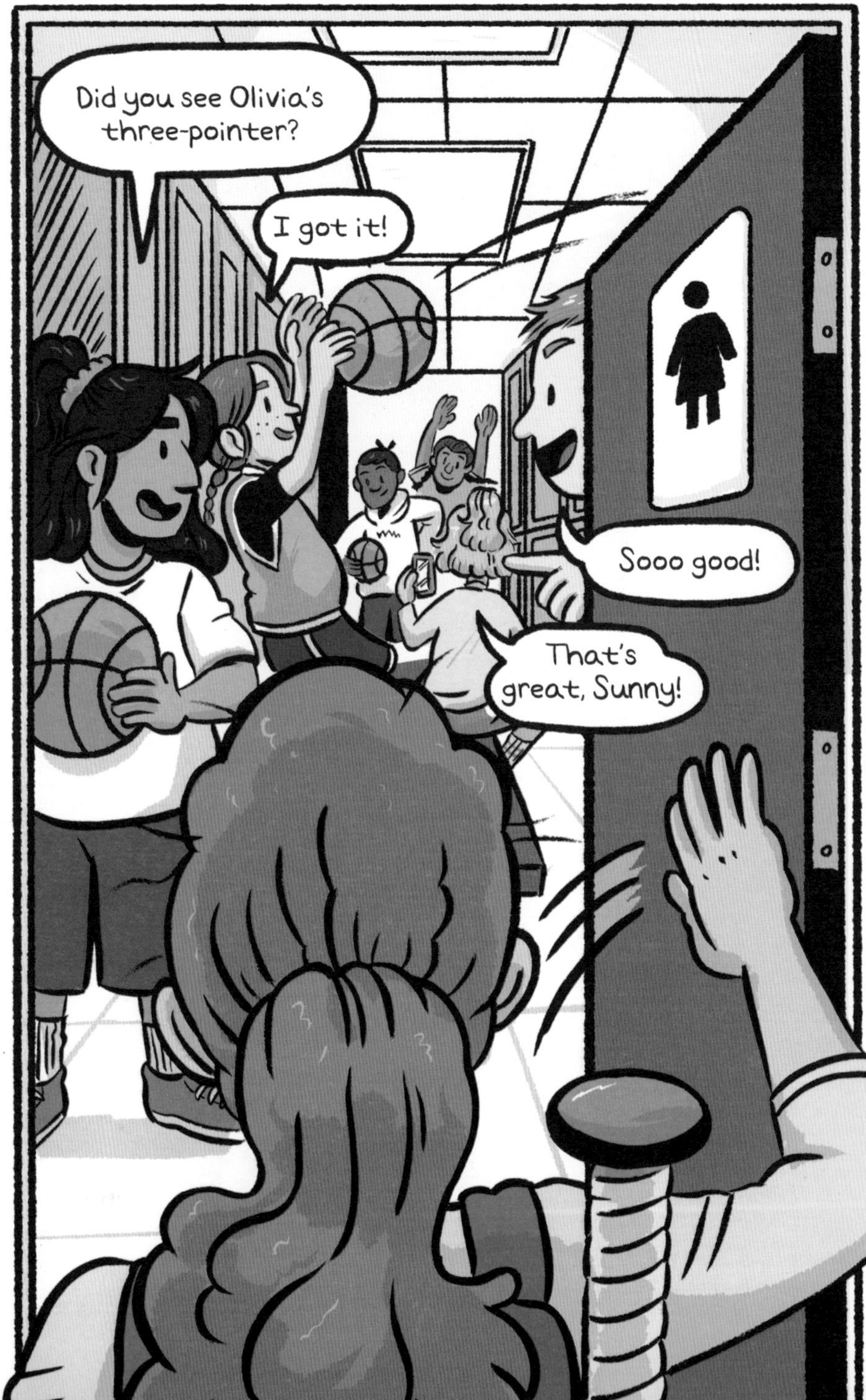
Did you see Olivia's three-pointer?
I got it!
Sooo good!
That's great, Sunny!

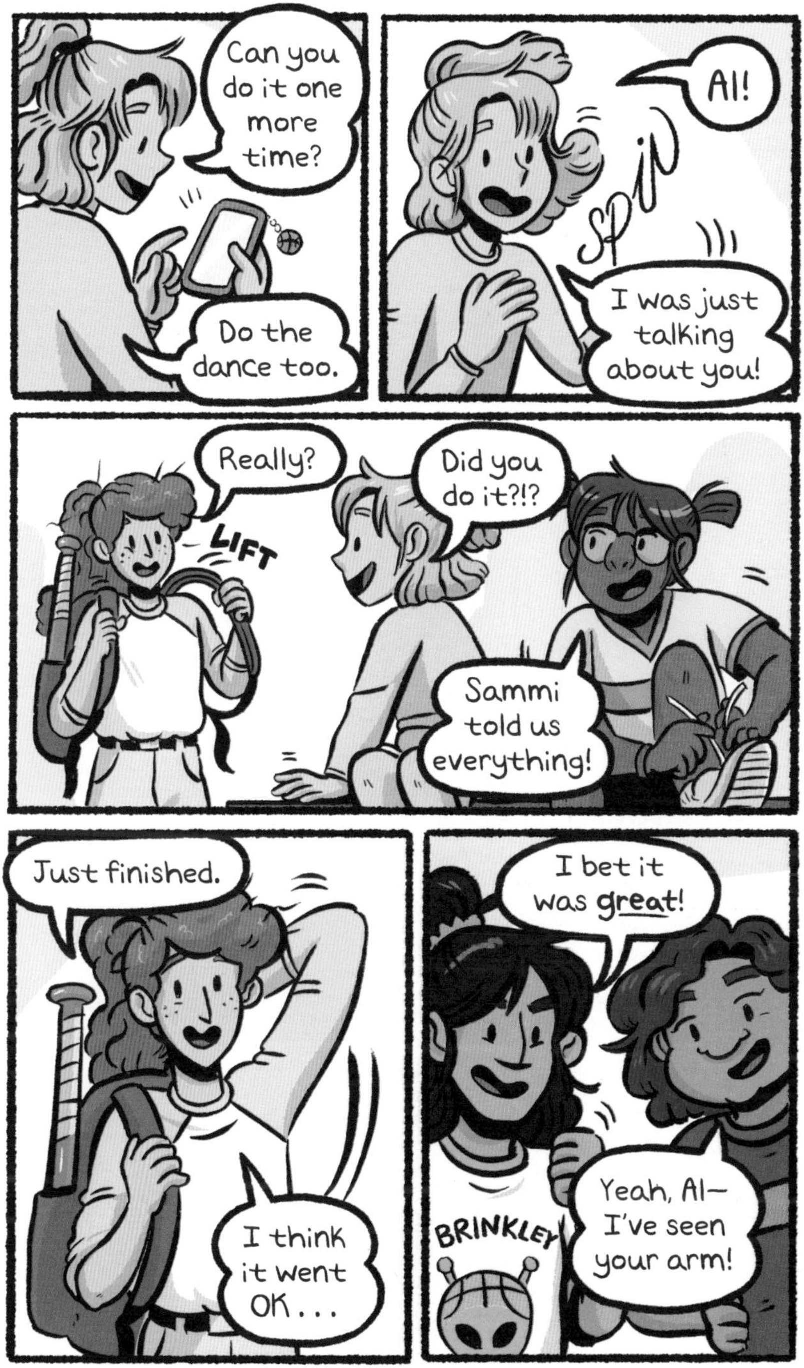
Can you do it one more time?
Do the dance too.
Al!
spin
I was just talking about you!
Really?
LIFT
Did you do it?!?
Sammi told us everything!
Just finished.
I think it went OK . . .
I bet it was great!
BRINKLEY
Yeah, Al— I've seen your arm!

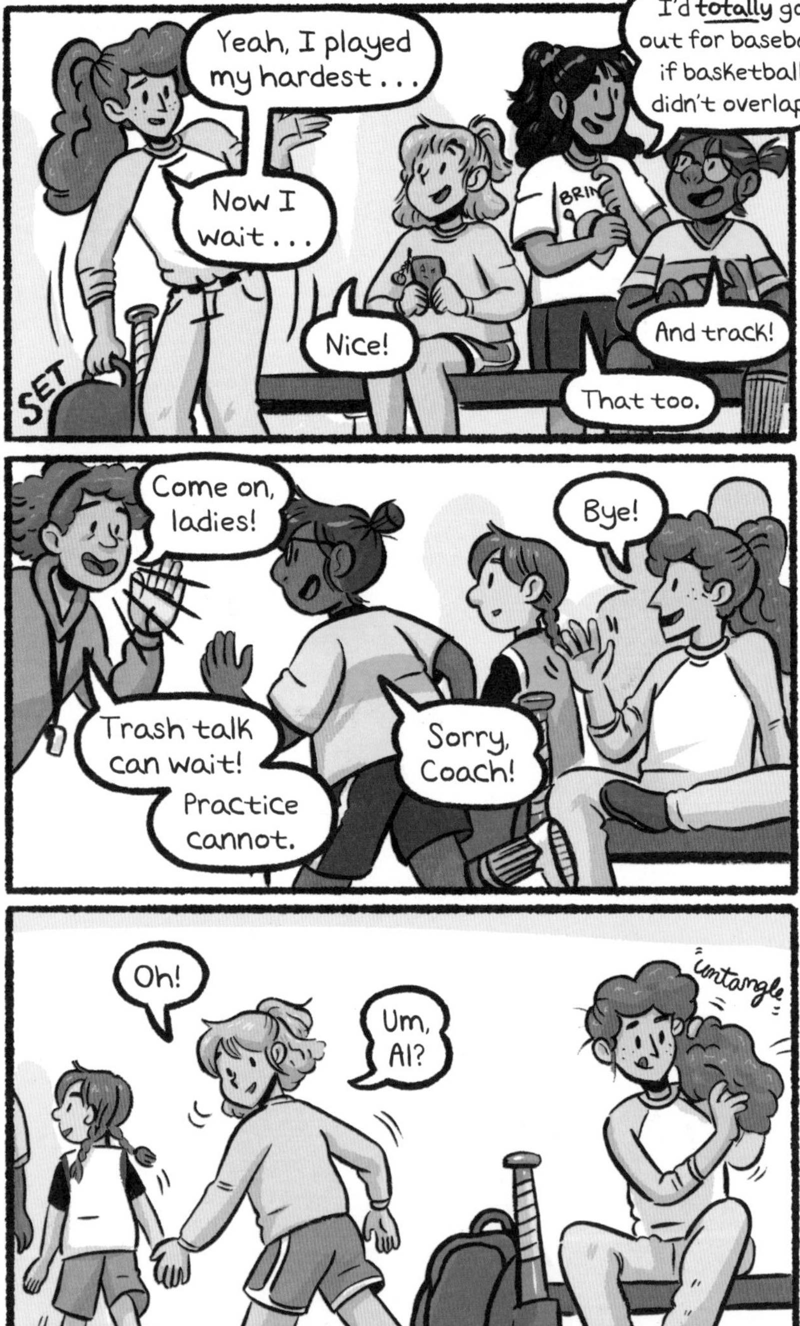
Yeah, I played my hardest . . .
Now I wait . . .
I'd **totally** go out for baseball if basketball didn't overlap.
Nice!
And track!
That too.
SET
Come on, ladies!
Bye!
Trash talk can wait!
Practice cannot.
Sorry, Coach!
Oh!
Um, Al?
untangle

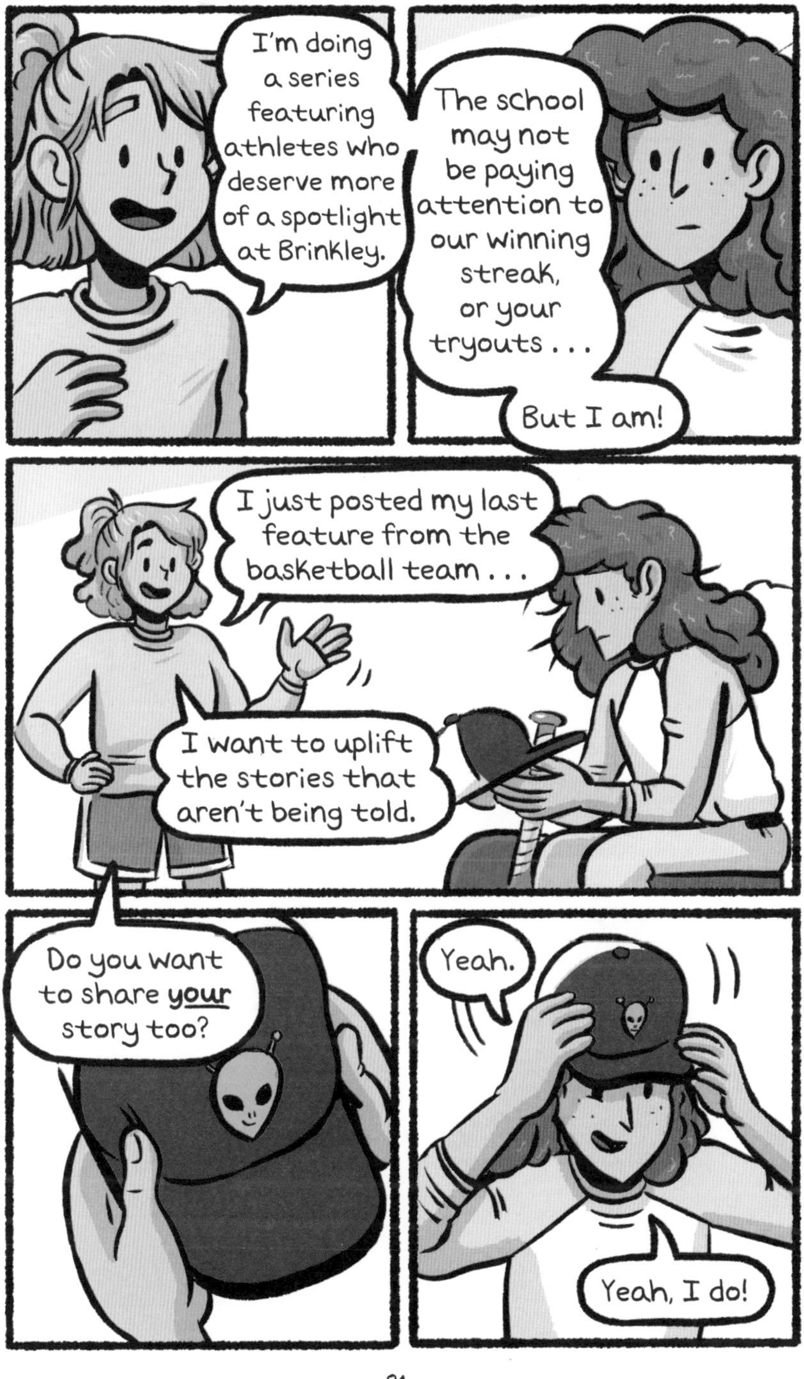
I'm doing a series featuring athletes who deserve more of a spotlight at Brinkley.
The school may not be paying attention to our winning streak, or your tryouts . . .
But I am!
I just posted my last feature from the basketball team . . .
I want to uplift the stories that aren't being told.
Do you want to share **your** story too?
Yeah.
Yeah, I do!

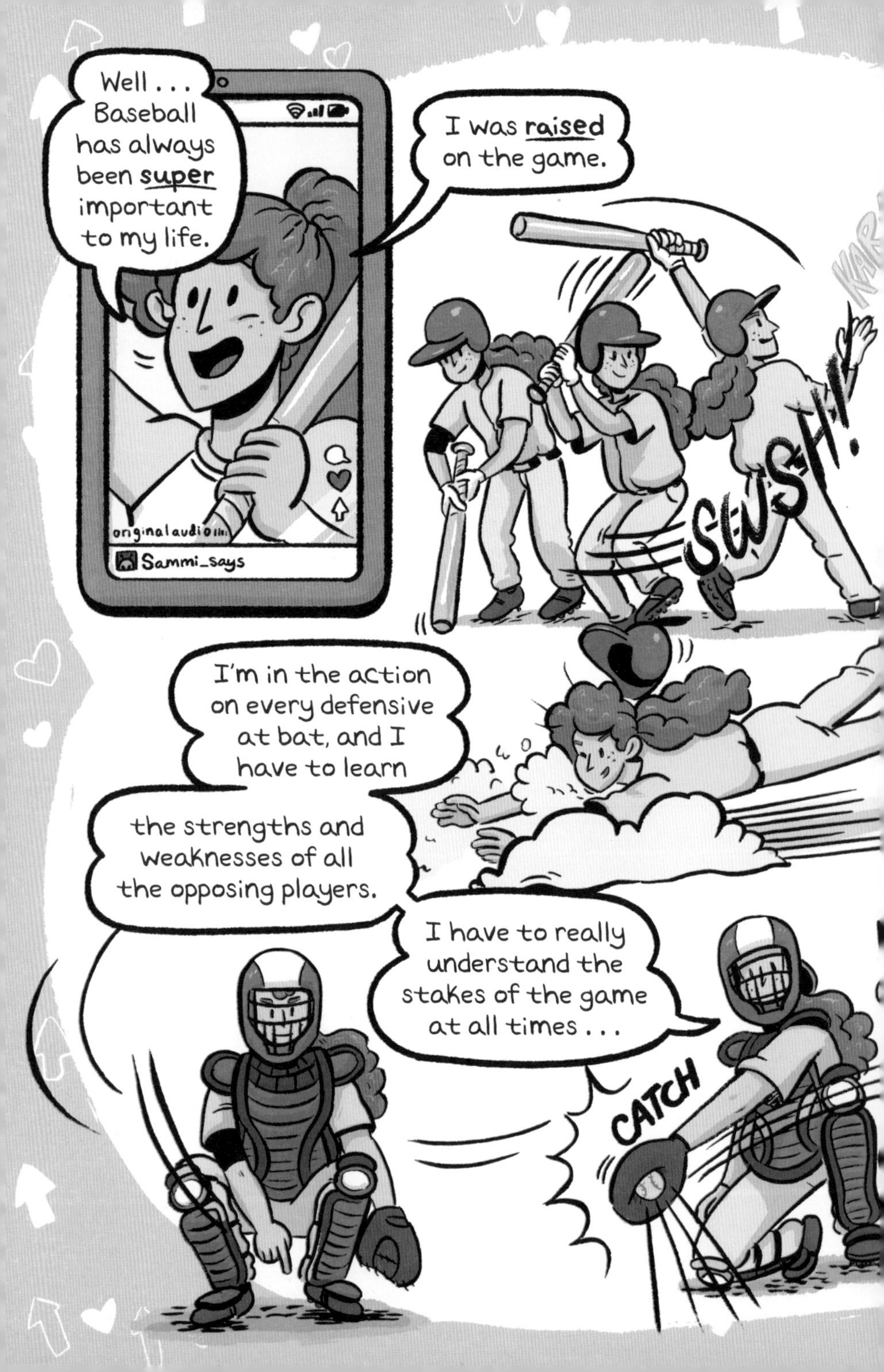
Well . . . Baseball has always been super important to my life.
original audio
Sammi_says
I was raised on the game.
SWSH!
I'm in the action on every defensive at bat, and I have to learn
the strengths and weaknesses of all the opposing players.
I have to really understand the stakes of the game at all times . . .
CATCH

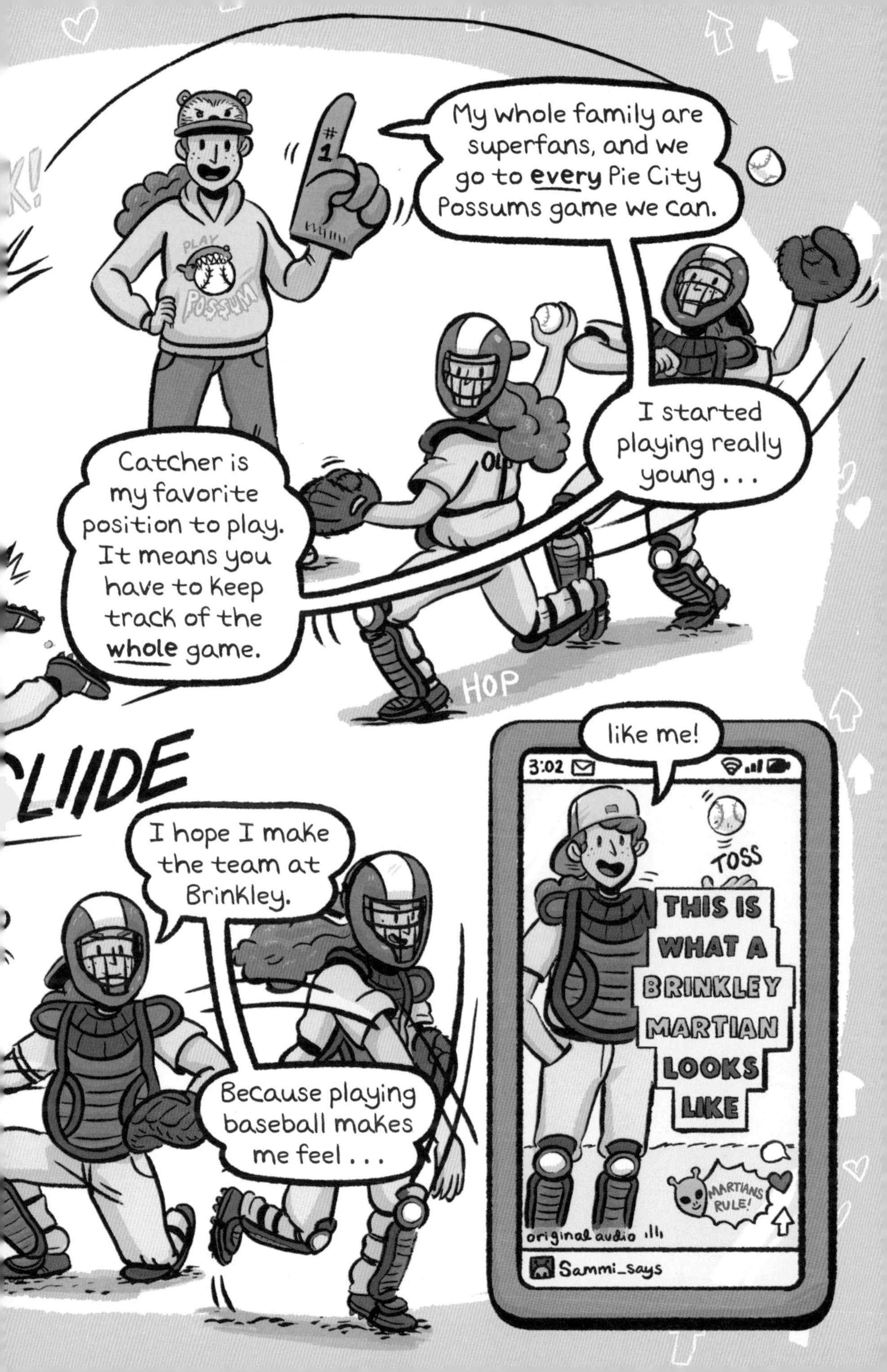
K!
My whole family are superfans, and we go to every Pie City Possums game we can.
PLAY POSSUM
I started playing really young . . .
Catcher is my favorite position to play. It means you have to keep track of the whole game.
HOP
SLIIDE
like me!
3:02
TOSS
THIS IS WHAT A BRINKLEY MARTIAN LOOKS LIKE
MARTIANS RULE!
original audio
Sammi_says
I hope I make the team at Brinkley.
Because playing baseball makes me feel . . .

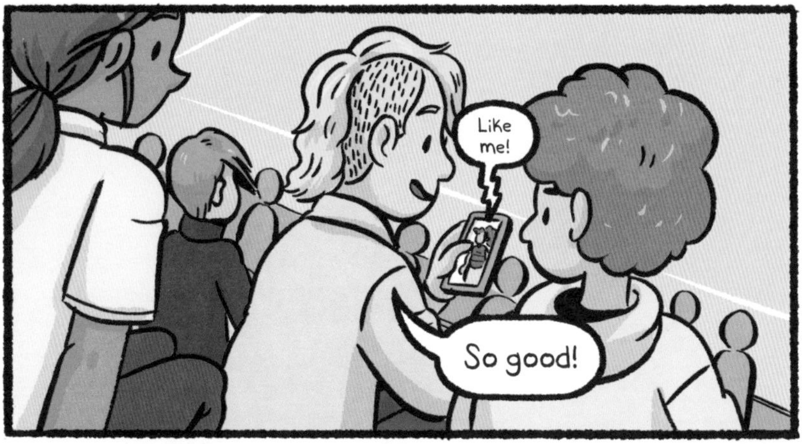
Like me!
So good!

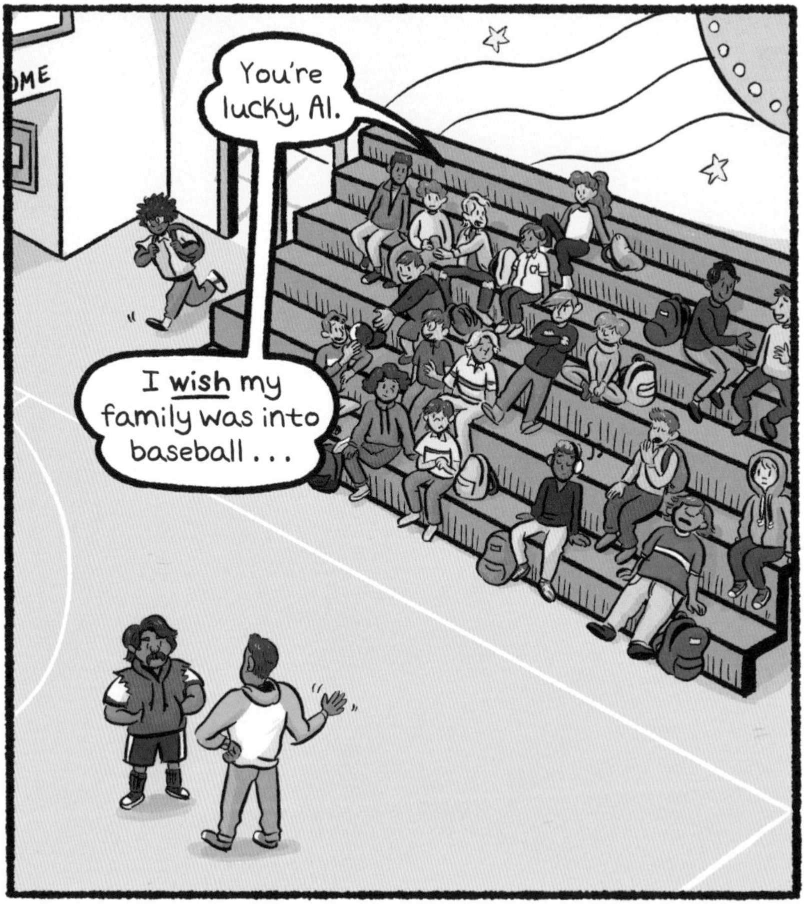
You're lucky, Al.
I wish my family was into baseball . . .

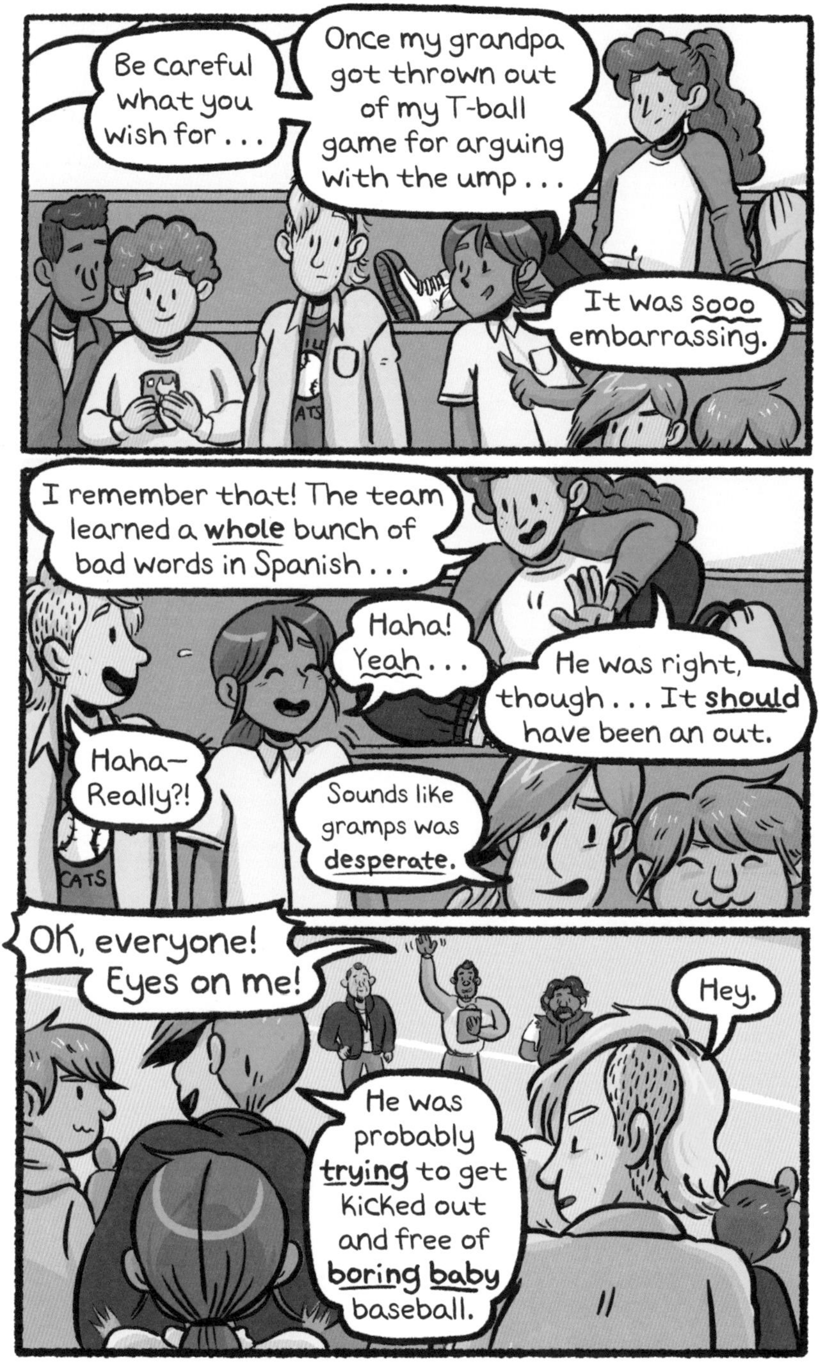
Be careful what you wish for . . .
Once my grandpa got thrown out of my T-ball game for arguing with the ump . . .
It was sooo embarrassing.
I remember that! The team learned a whole bunch of bad words in Spanish . . .
Haha! Yeah . . .
He was right, though . . . It should have been an out.
Haha— Really?!
Sounds like gramps was desperate.
OK, everyone! Eyes on me!
Hey.
He was probably trying to get kicked out and free of boring baby baseball.

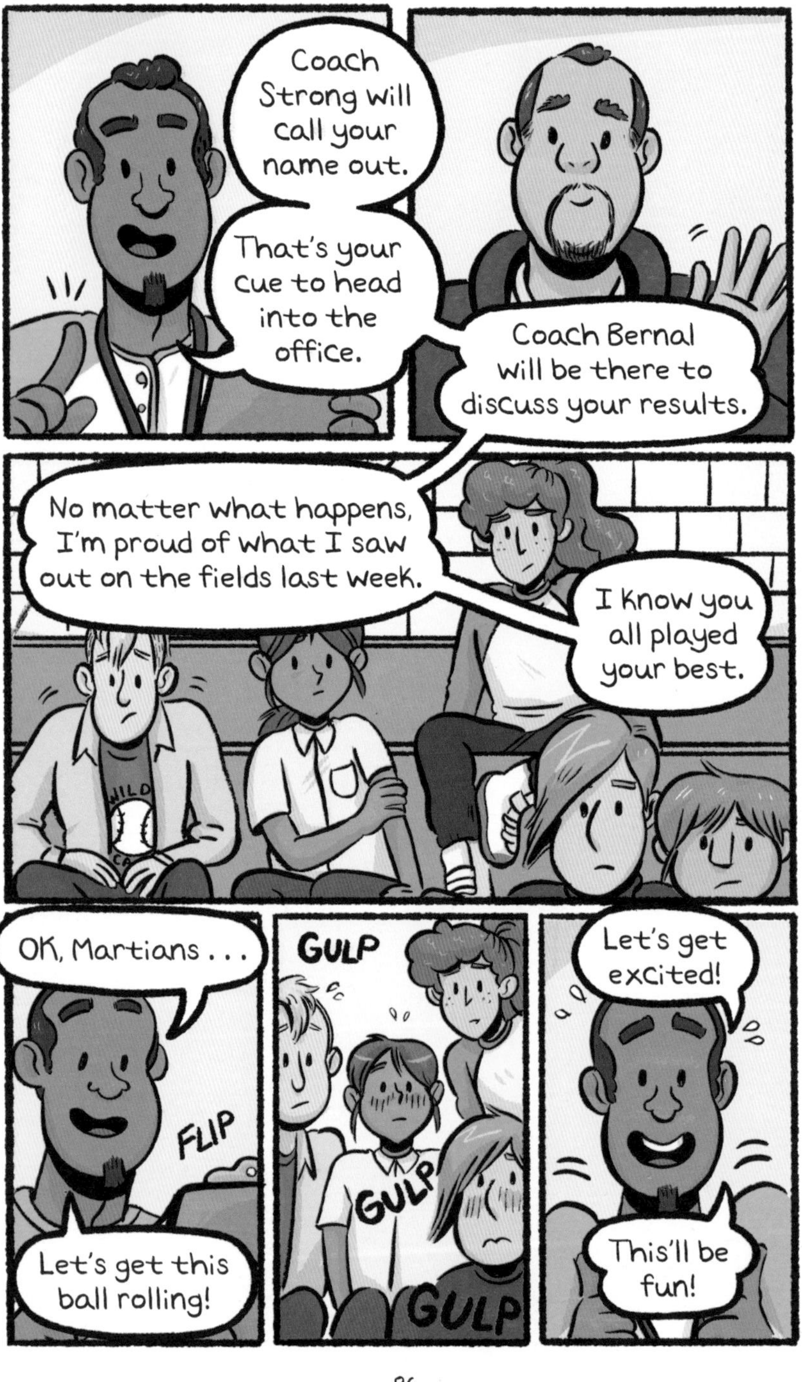
Coach Strong will call your name out.
That's your cue to head into the office.
Coach Bernal will be there to discuss your results.
No matter what happens, I'm proud of what I saw out on the fields last week.
I know you all played your best.
OK, Martians . . .
FLIP
Let's get this ball rolling!
GULP
GULP
GULP
Let's get excited!
This'll be fun!

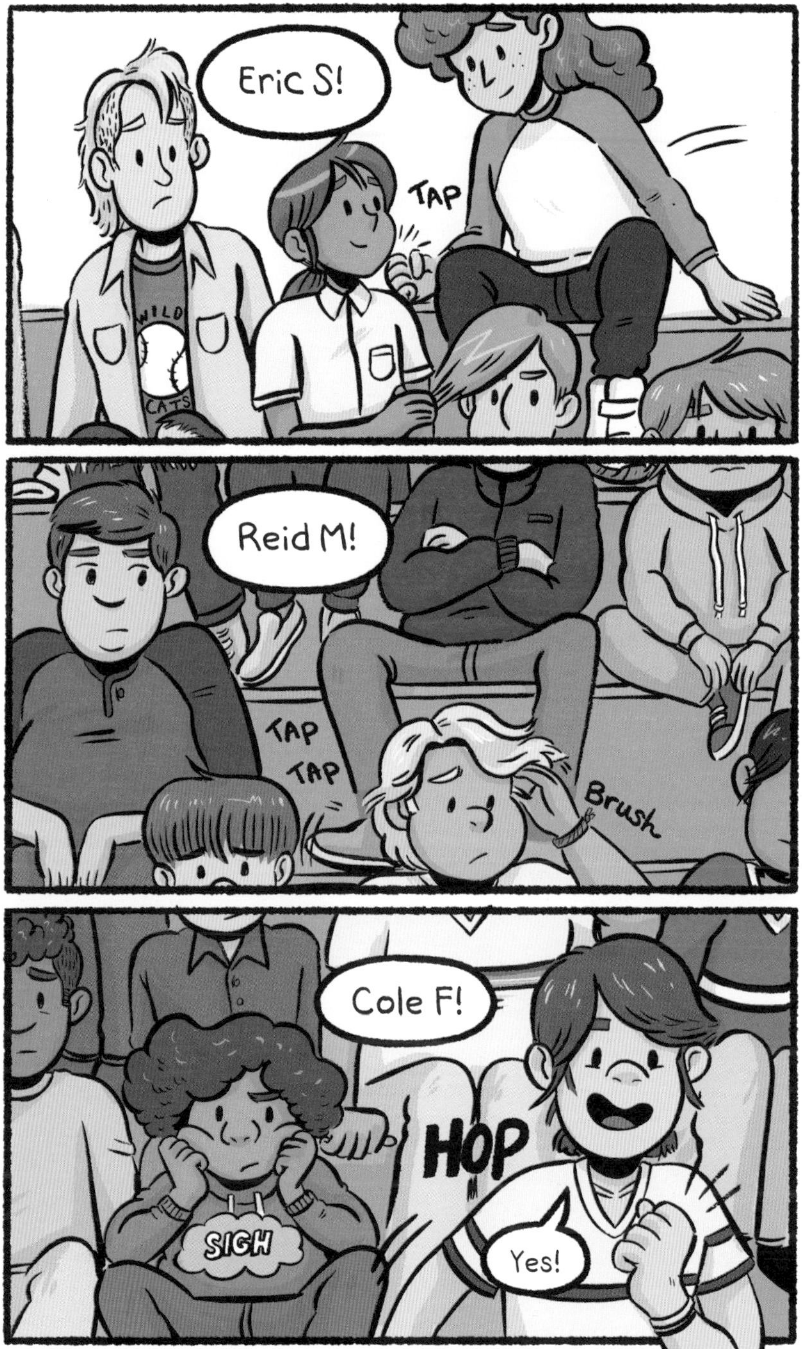
Eric S!
TAP
Reid M!
TAP
TAP
Brush
Cole F!
HOP
SIGH
Yes!

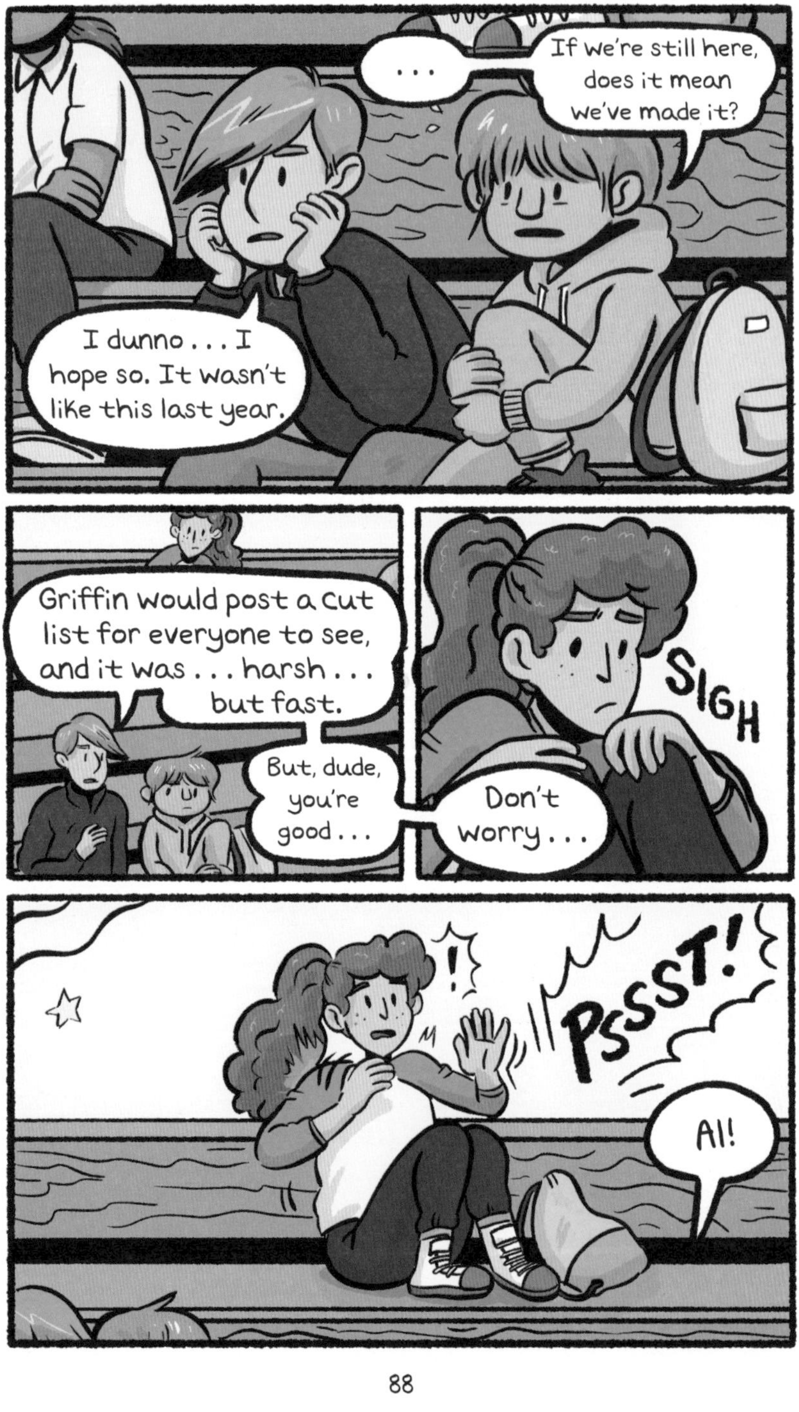
...
If we're still here, does it mean we've made it?
I dunno . . . I hope so. It wasn't like this last year.
Griffin would post a cut list for everyone to see, and it was . . . harsh . . . but fast.
But, dude, you're good . . .
Don't worry . . .
SIGH
!
PSSST!
Al!

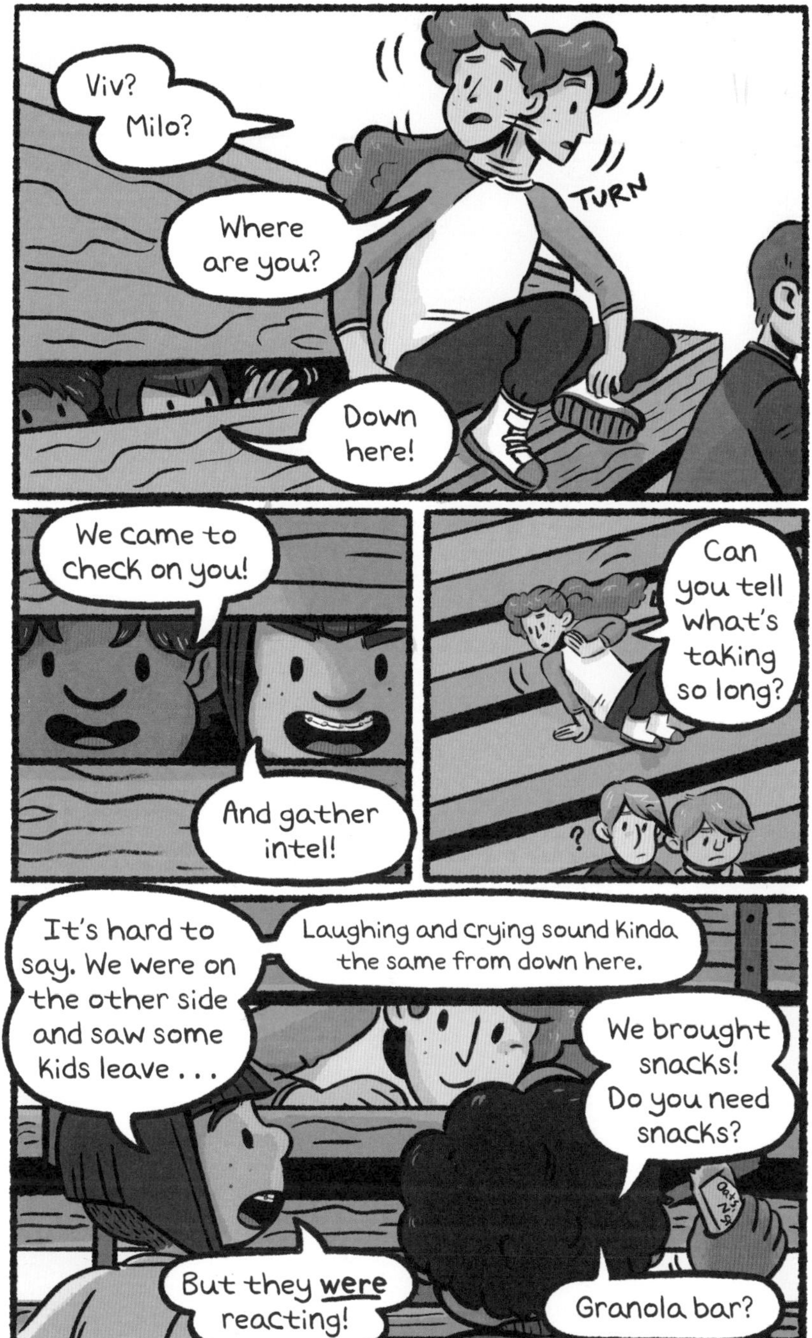
Viv?
Milo?
TURN
Where are you?
Down here!
We came to check on you!
And gather intel!
Can you tell what's taking so long?
?
It's hard to say. We were on the other side and saw some kids leave . . .
Laughing and crying sound kinda the same from down here.
We brought snacks! Do you need snacks?
But they were reacting!
Granola bar?

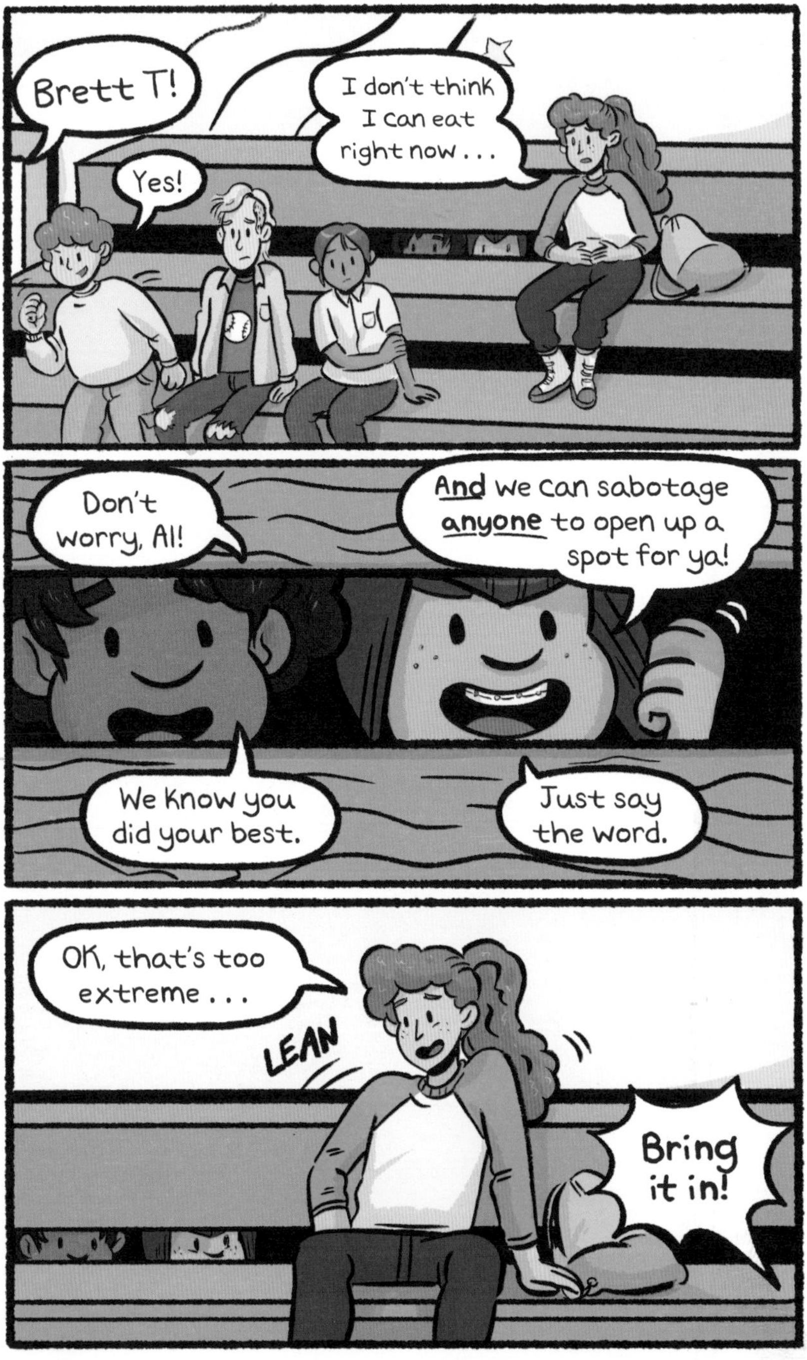
Brett T!
Yes!
I don't think I can eat right now . . .
Don't worry, Al!
And we can sabotage anyone to open up a spot for ya!
We know you did your best.
Just say the word.
OK, that's too extreme . . .
LEAN
Bring it in!

STAND
That's right. Come on down!
CLOMP
CLOMP
All in one row . . . good . . . good.
OK!
Thanks for your patience, everyone!
I know you all worked very hard . . .
So, if you are still here, I want to say emphatically . . .

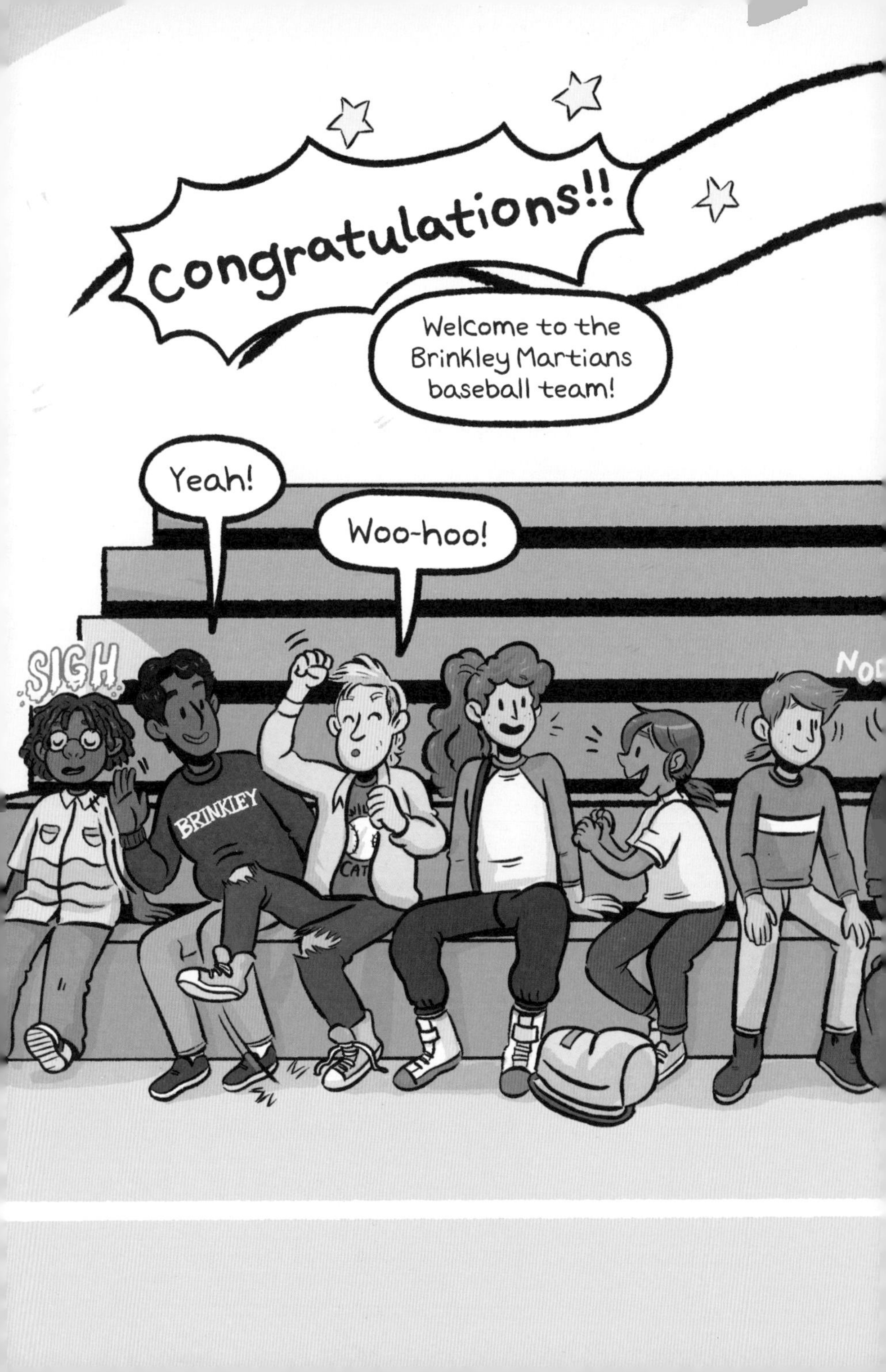
Congratulations!!
Welcome to the Brinkley Martians baseball team!
Yeah!
Woo-hoo!
SIGH
BRINKLEY

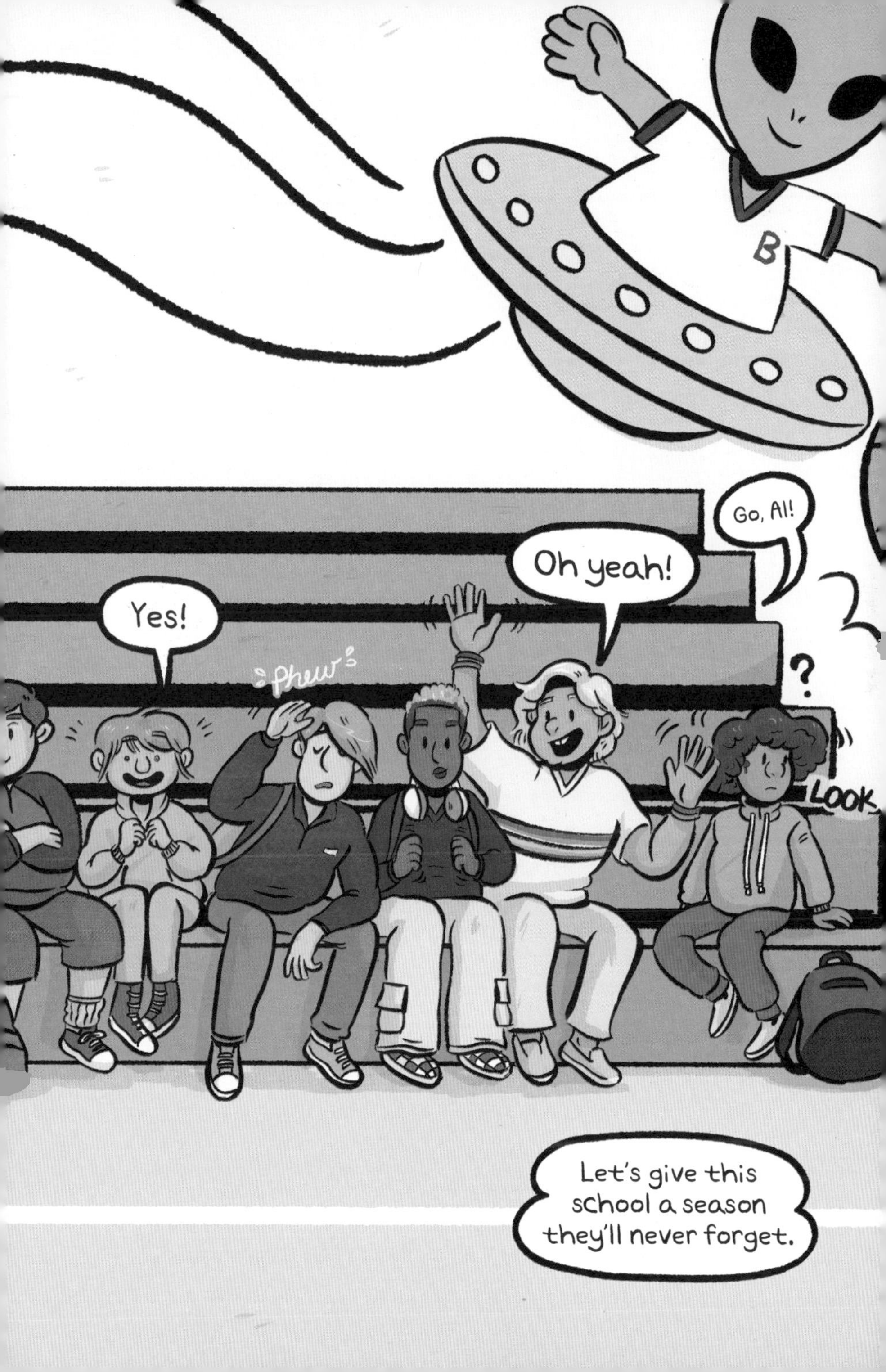
B
Yes!
Phew
Oh yeah!
Go, Al!
?
LOOK
Let's give this school a season they'll never forget.

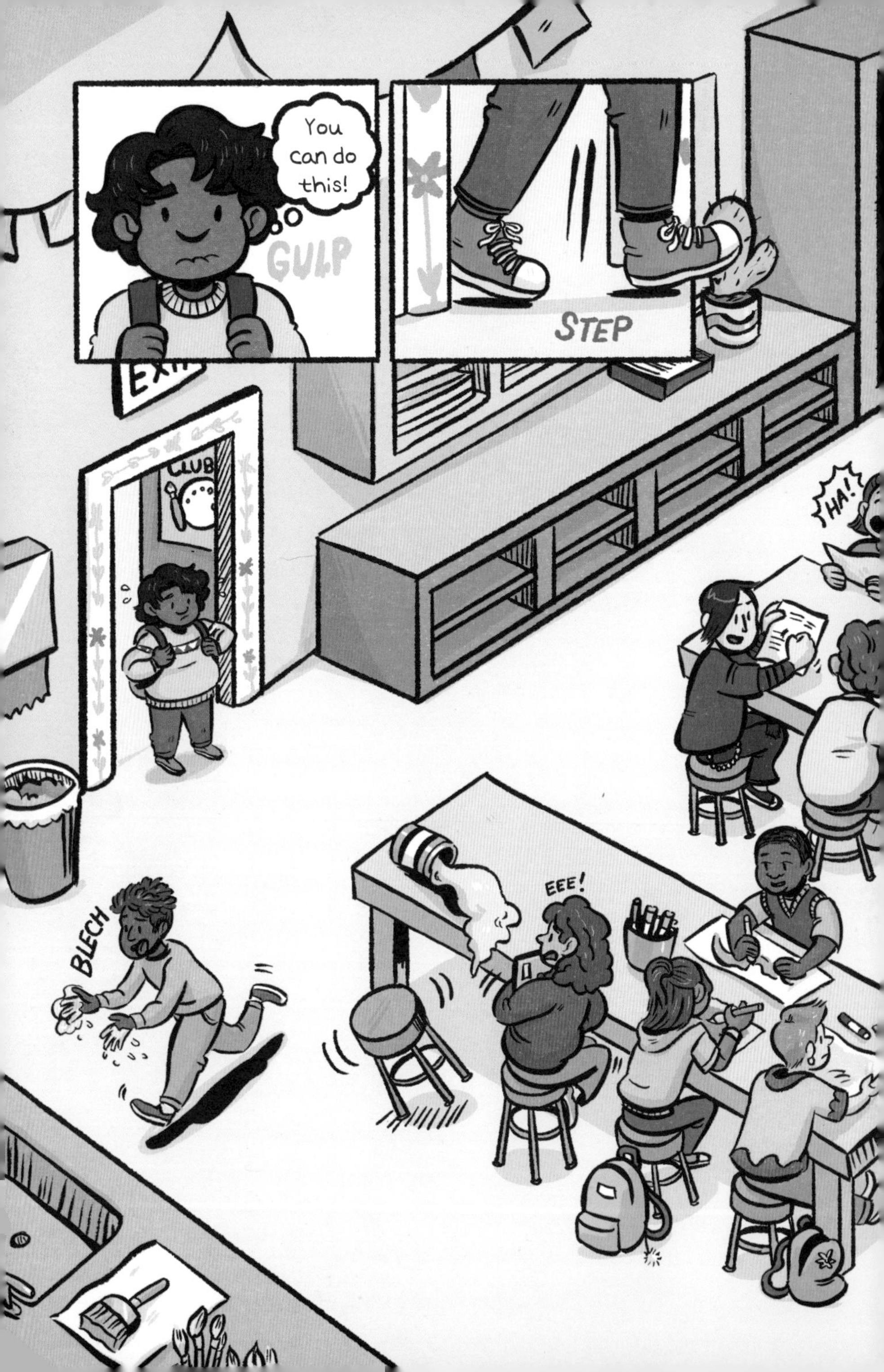
You can do this!
GULP
STEP
EXIT
CLUB
HA!
EEE!
BLECH

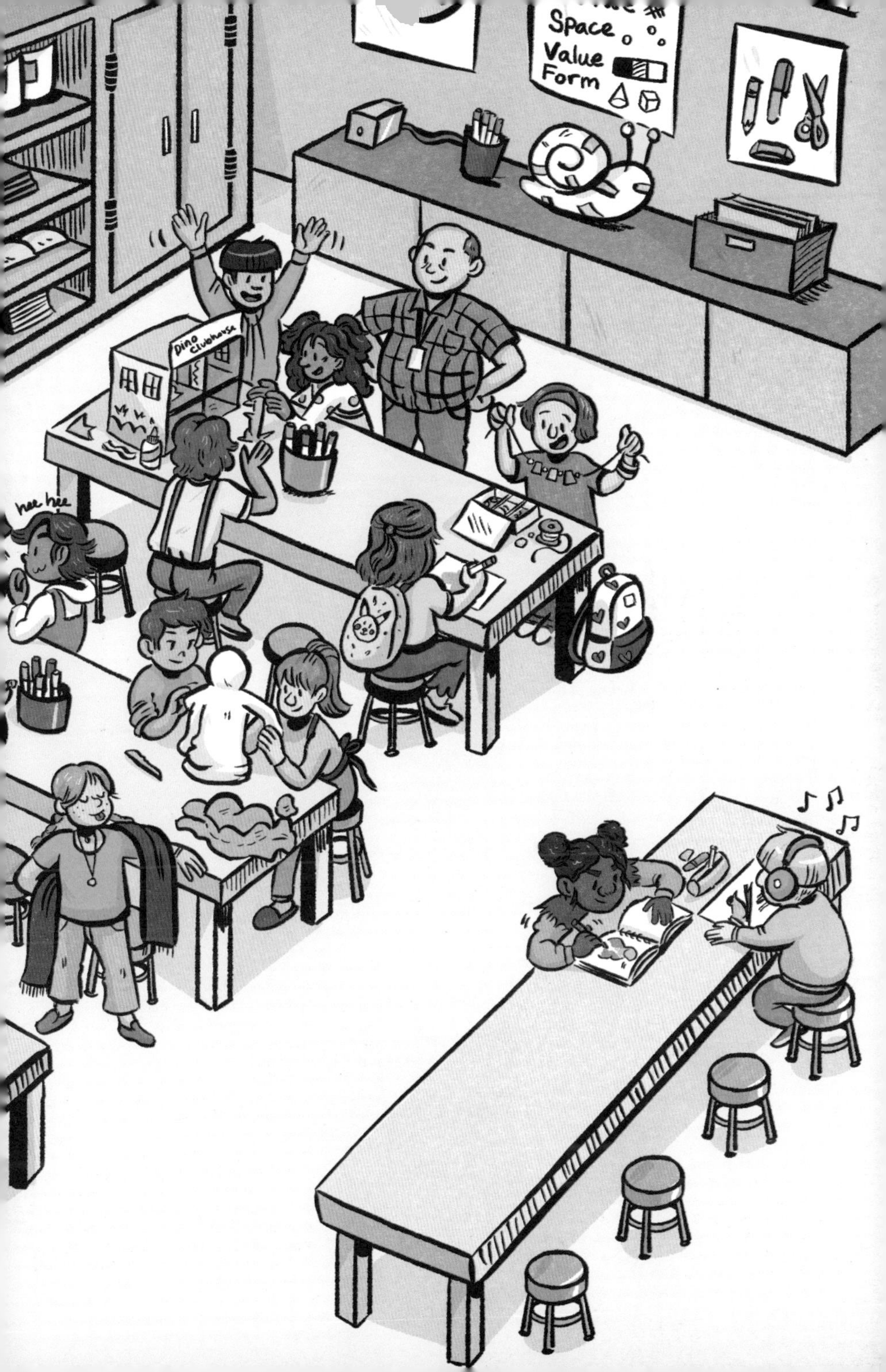

Space
Value
Form
Dino Clubhouse
hee hee

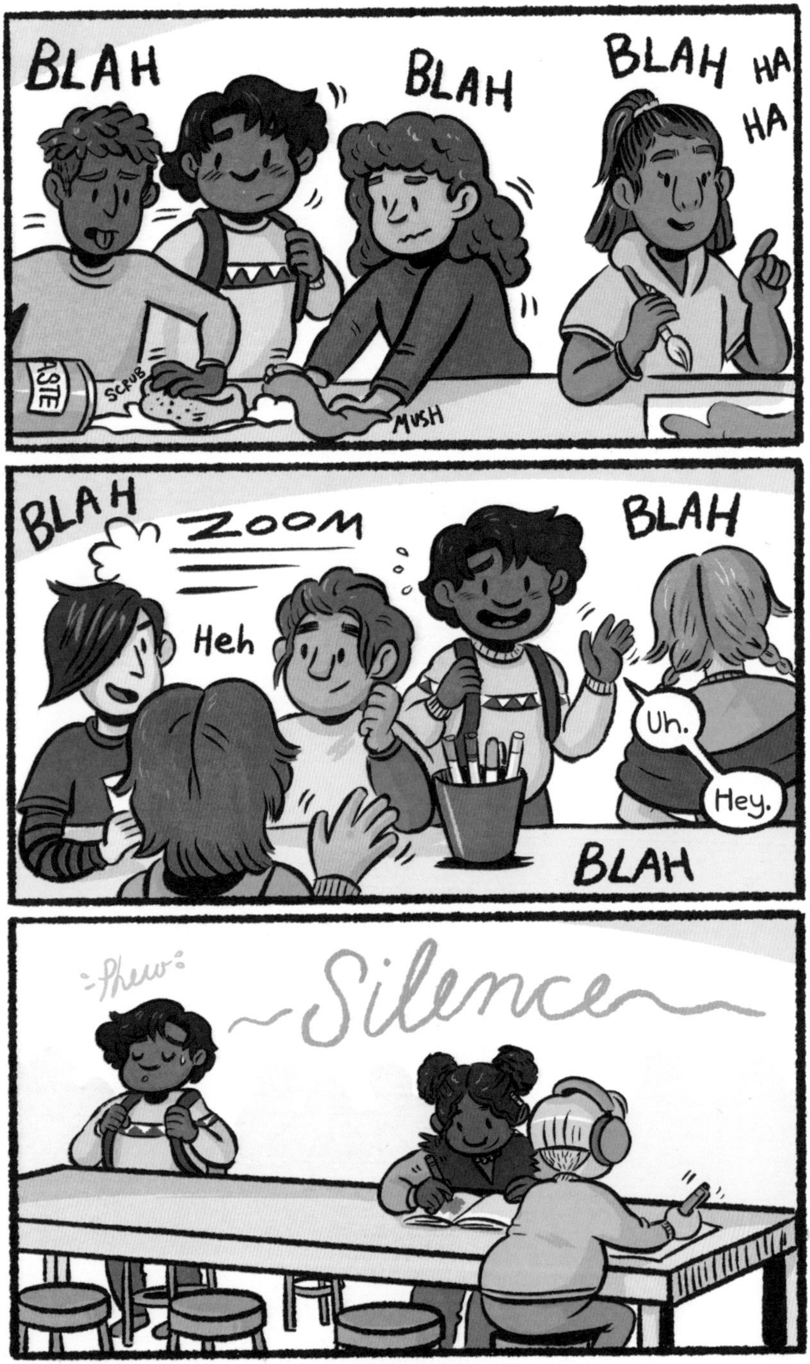
BLAH
BLAH
BLAH
HA
HA
PASTE
SCRUB
MUSH
BLAH
ZOOM
BLAH
Heh
Uh.
Hey.
BLAH
Phew
Silence

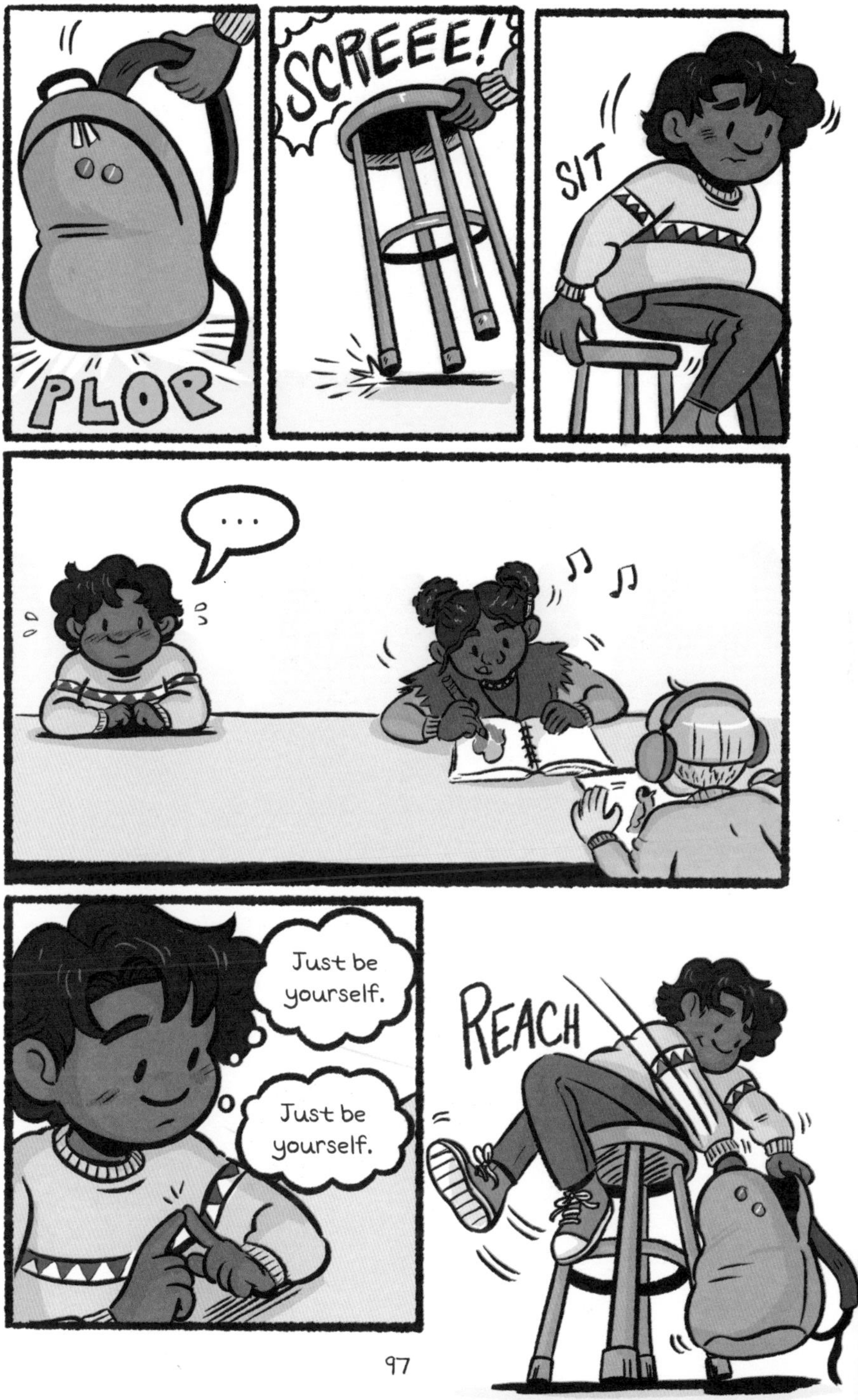
PLOP
SCREEEE!
SIT
...
Just be yourself.
Just be yourself.
REACH

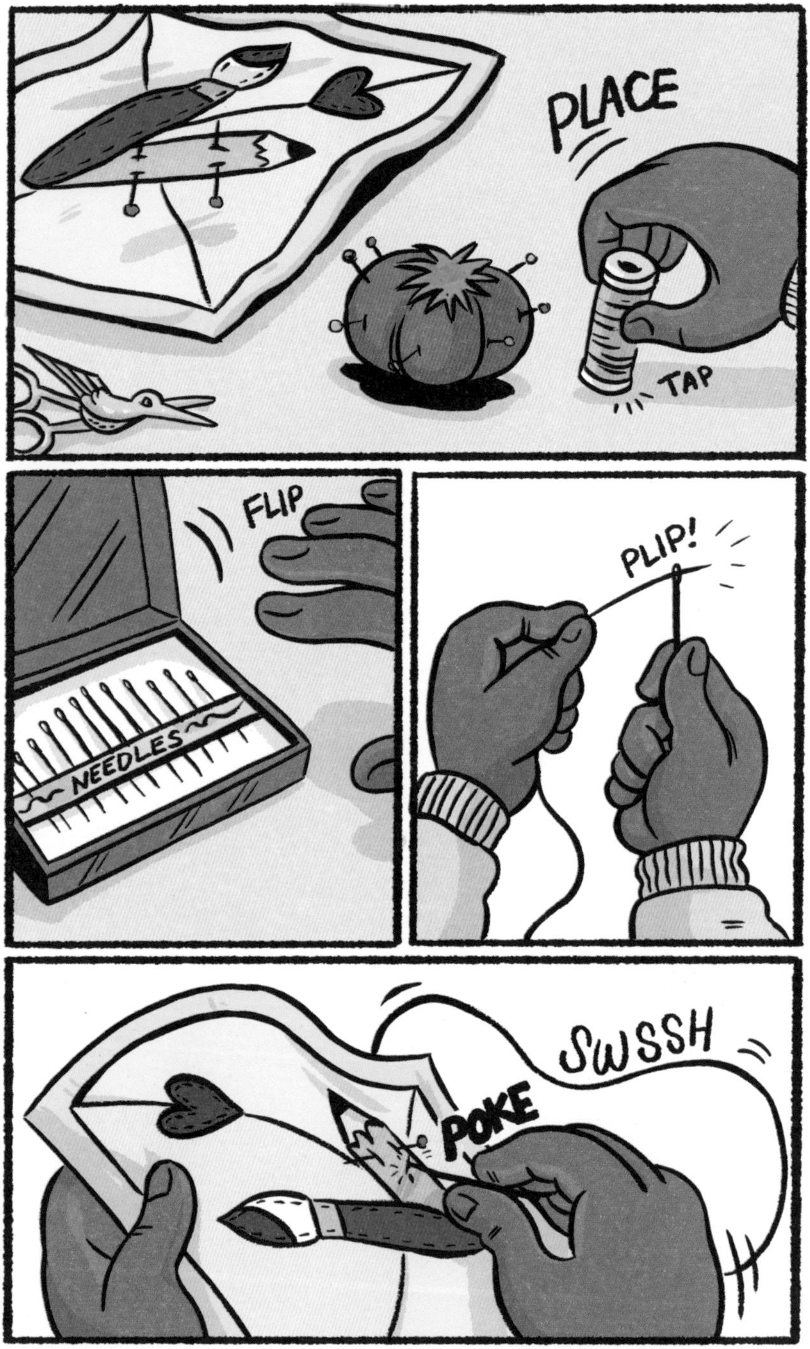
PLACE
TAP
FLIP
NEEDLES
PLIP!
SWSSH
POKE

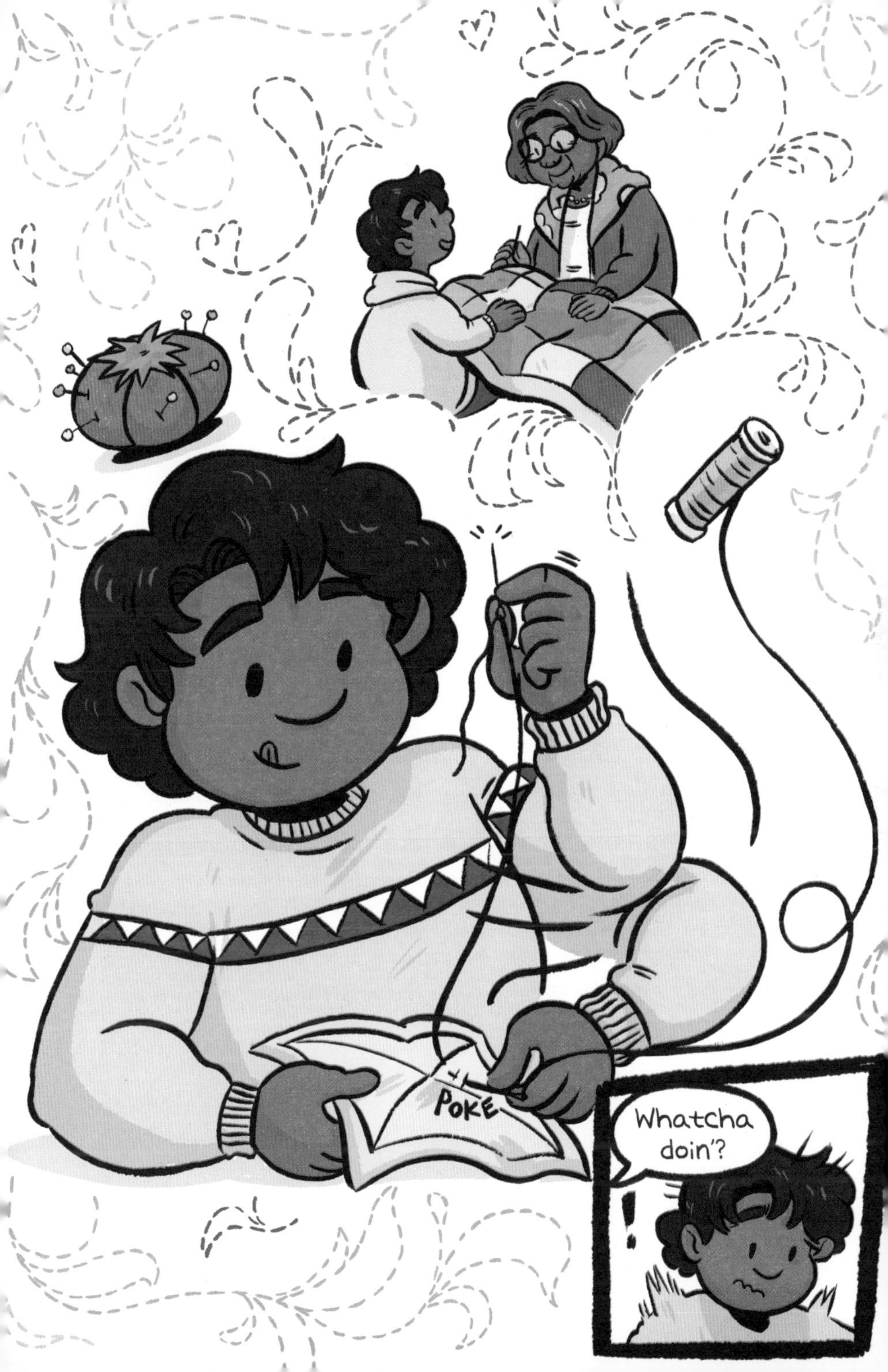
POKE
Whatcha doin'?
!

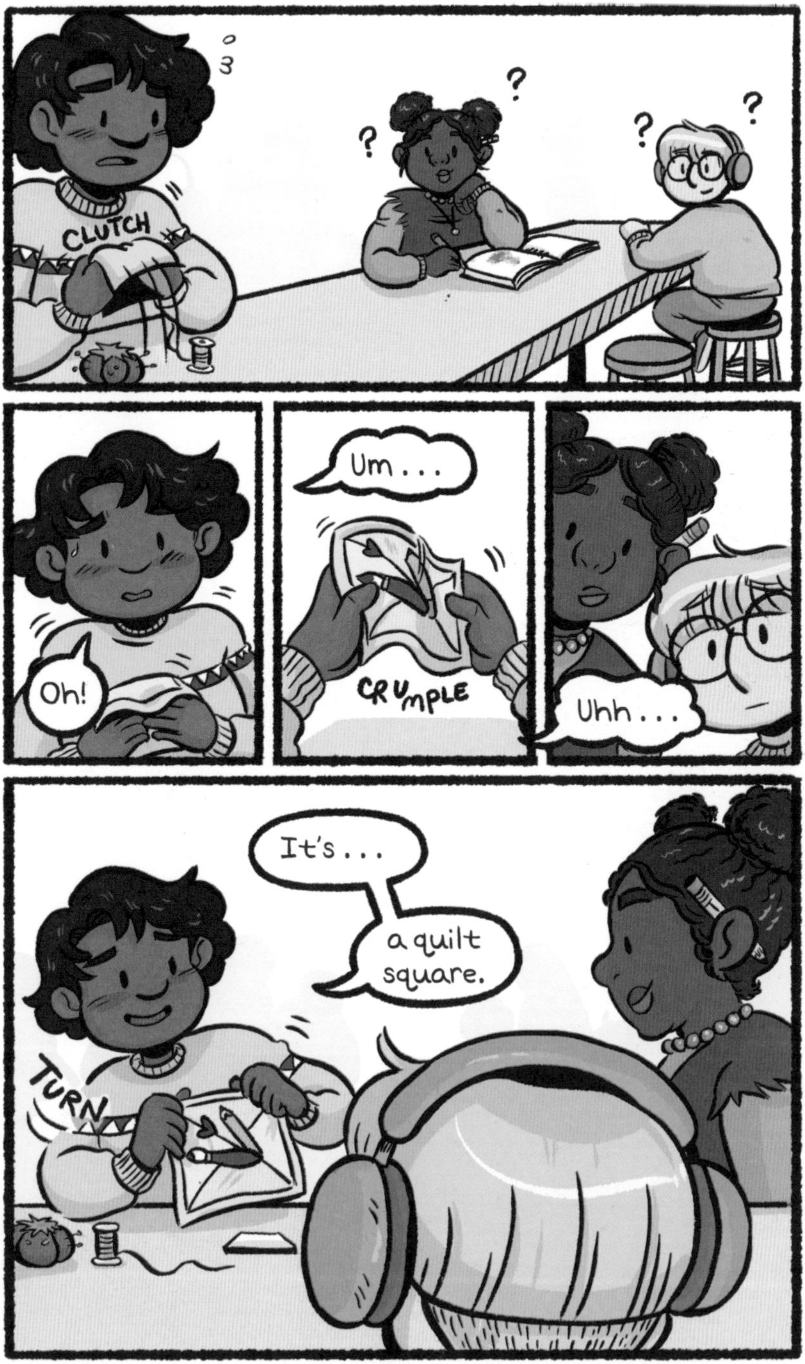
CLUTCH
?
?
?
?
Oh!
Um . . .
CRUMPLE
Uhh . . .
It's . . .
a quilt square.
TURN

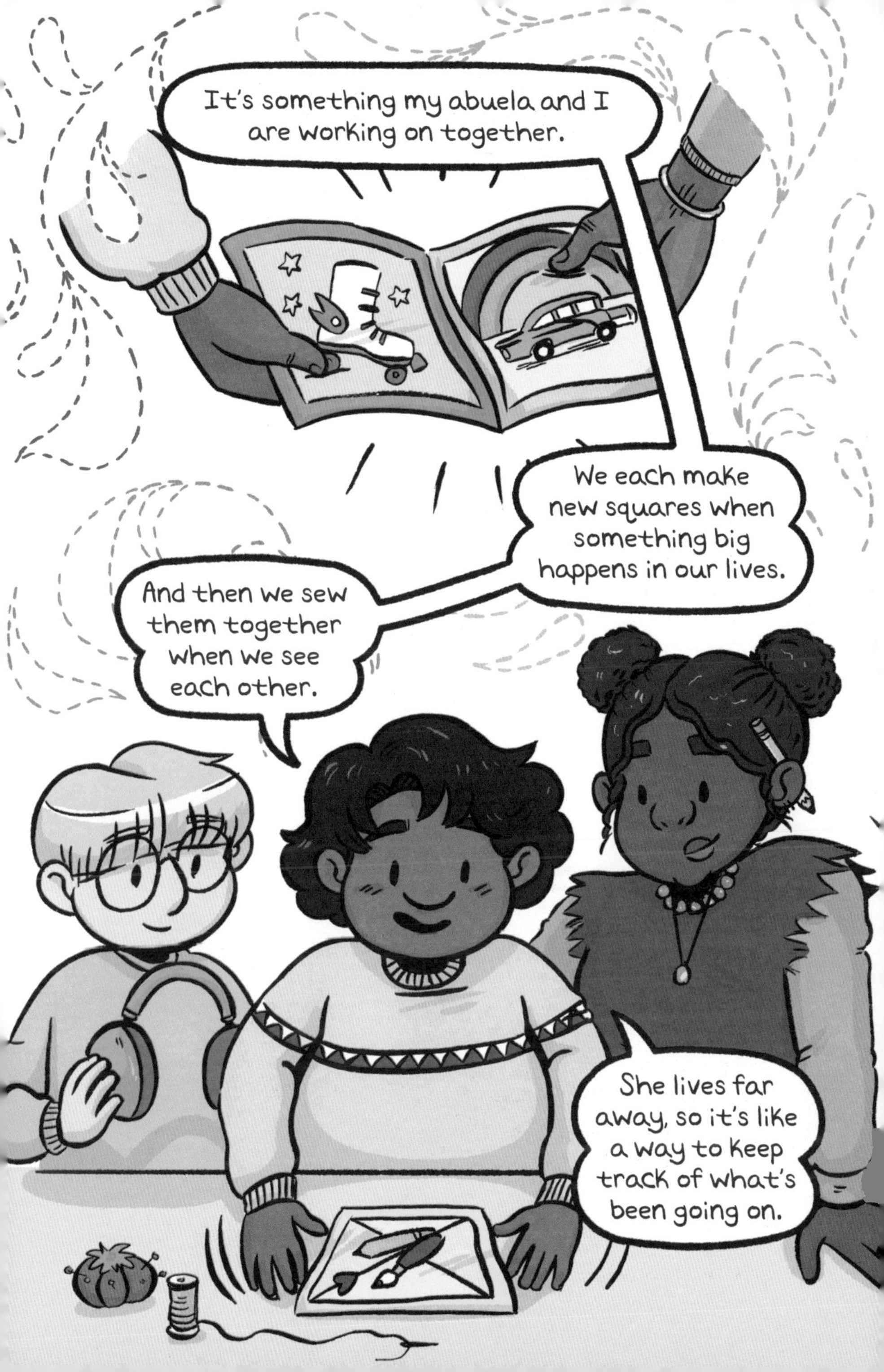
It's something my abuela and I are working on together.
We each make new squares when something big happens in our lives.
And then we sew them together when we see each other.
She lives far away, so it's like a way to keep track of what's been going on.

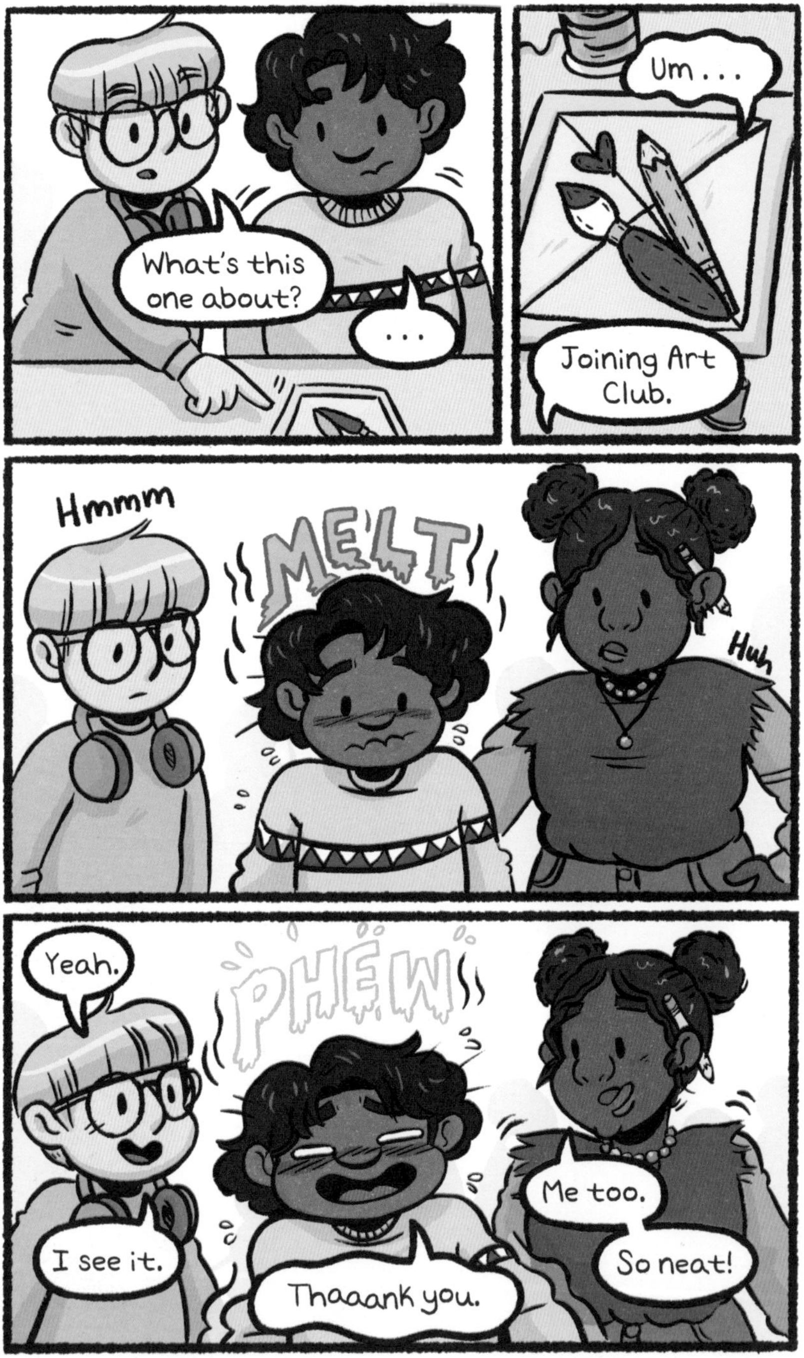
What's this one about?
. . .
Um . . .
Joining Art Club.
Hmmm
MELT
Huh
Yeah.
PHEW
I see it.
Thaaank you.
Me too.
So neat!

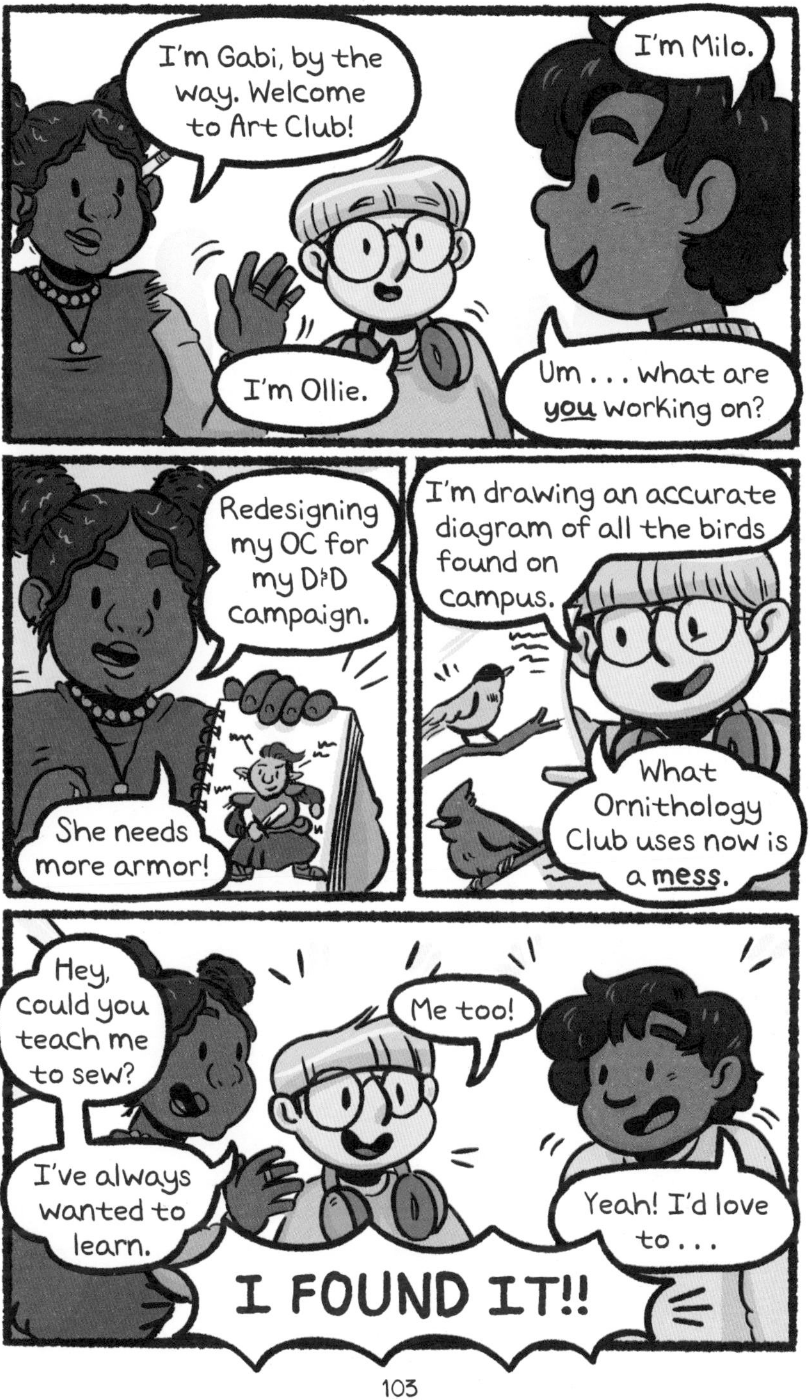
I'm Gabi, by the way. Welcome to Art Club!
I'm Milo.
I'm Ollie.
Um . . . what are you working on?
Redesigning my OC for my D&D campaign.
She needs more armor!
I'm drawing an accurate diagram of all the birds found on campus.
What Ornithology Club uses now is a mess.
Hey, could you teach me to sew?
I've always wanted to learn.
Me too!
Yeah! I'd love to . . .
I FOUND IT!!

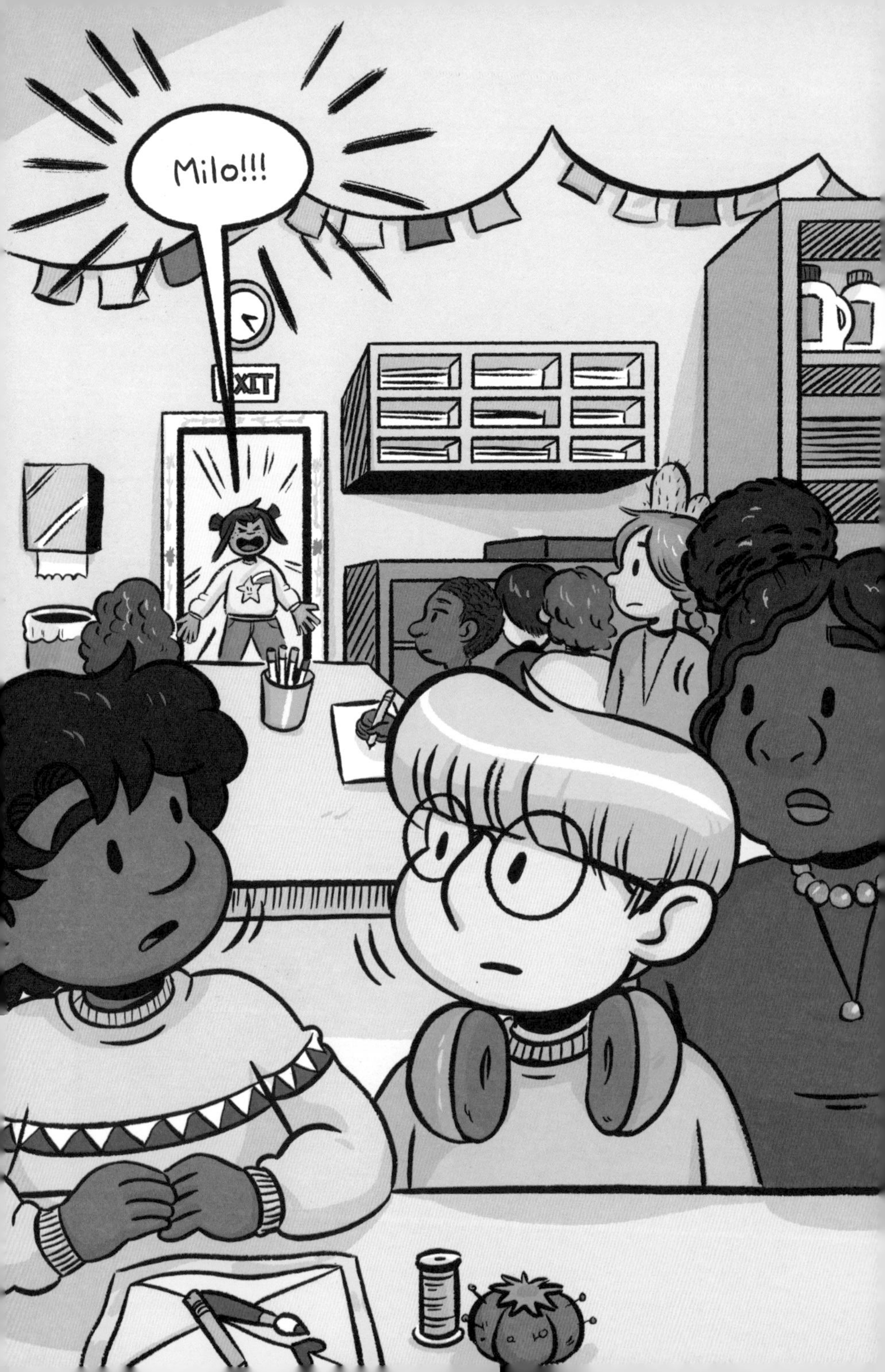
Milo!!!
EXIT

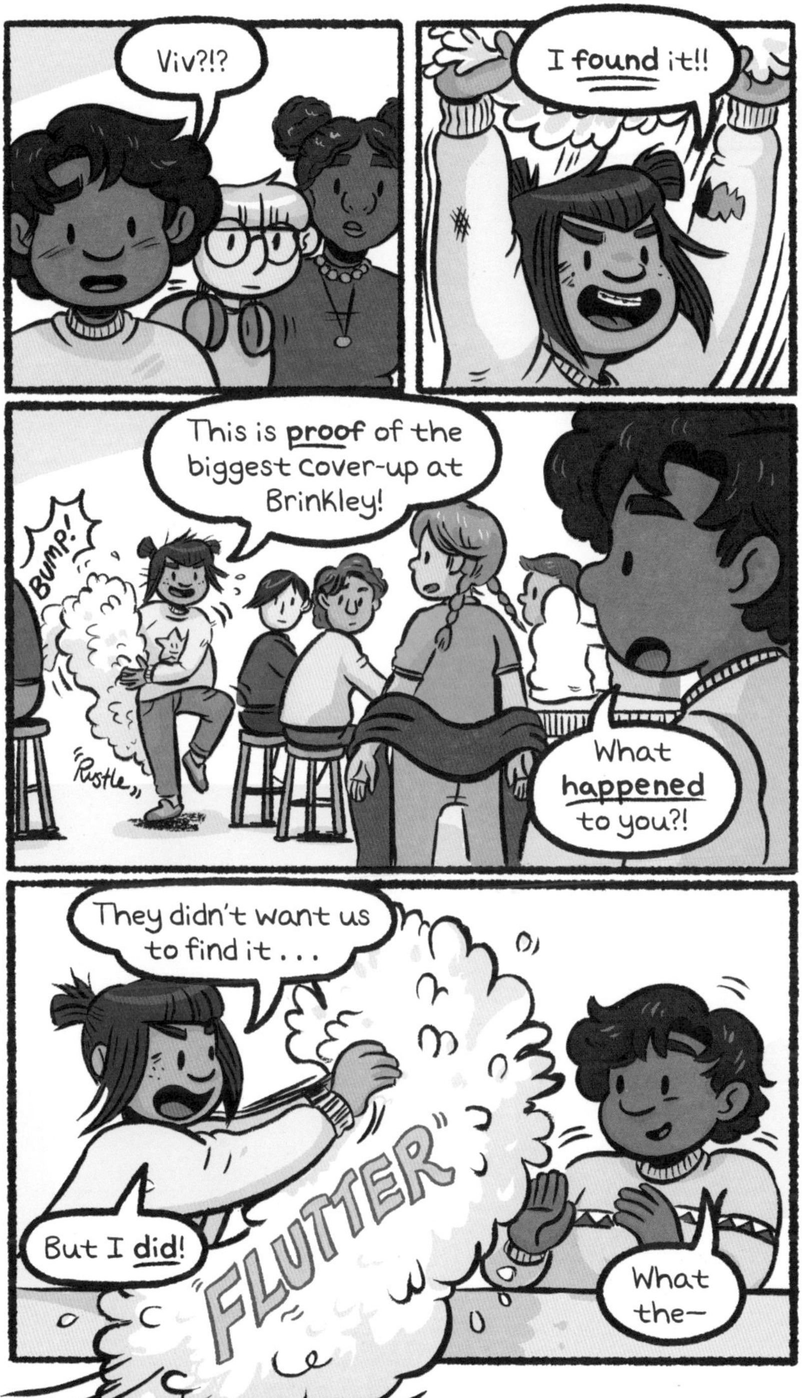
Viv?!?
I found it!!
This is proof of the biggest cover-up at Brinkley!
BUMP!
Rustle
What happened to you?!
They didn't want us to find it . . .
But I did!
FLUTTER
What the—

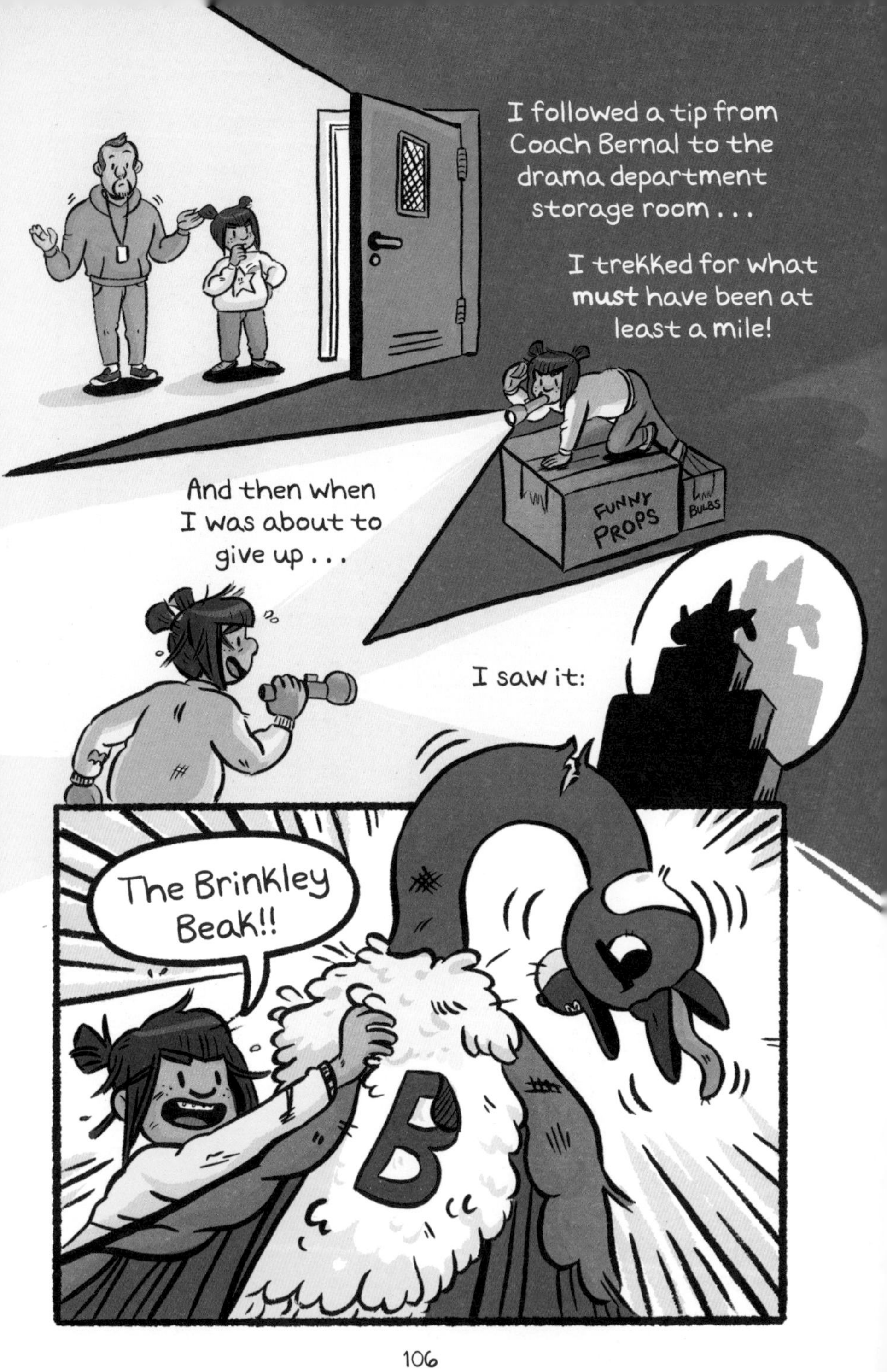
I followed a tip from Coach Bernal to the drama department storage room . . .
I trekked for what **must** have been at least a mile!
FUNNY PROPS
BULBS
And then when I was about to give up . . .
I saw it:
The Brinkley Beak!!

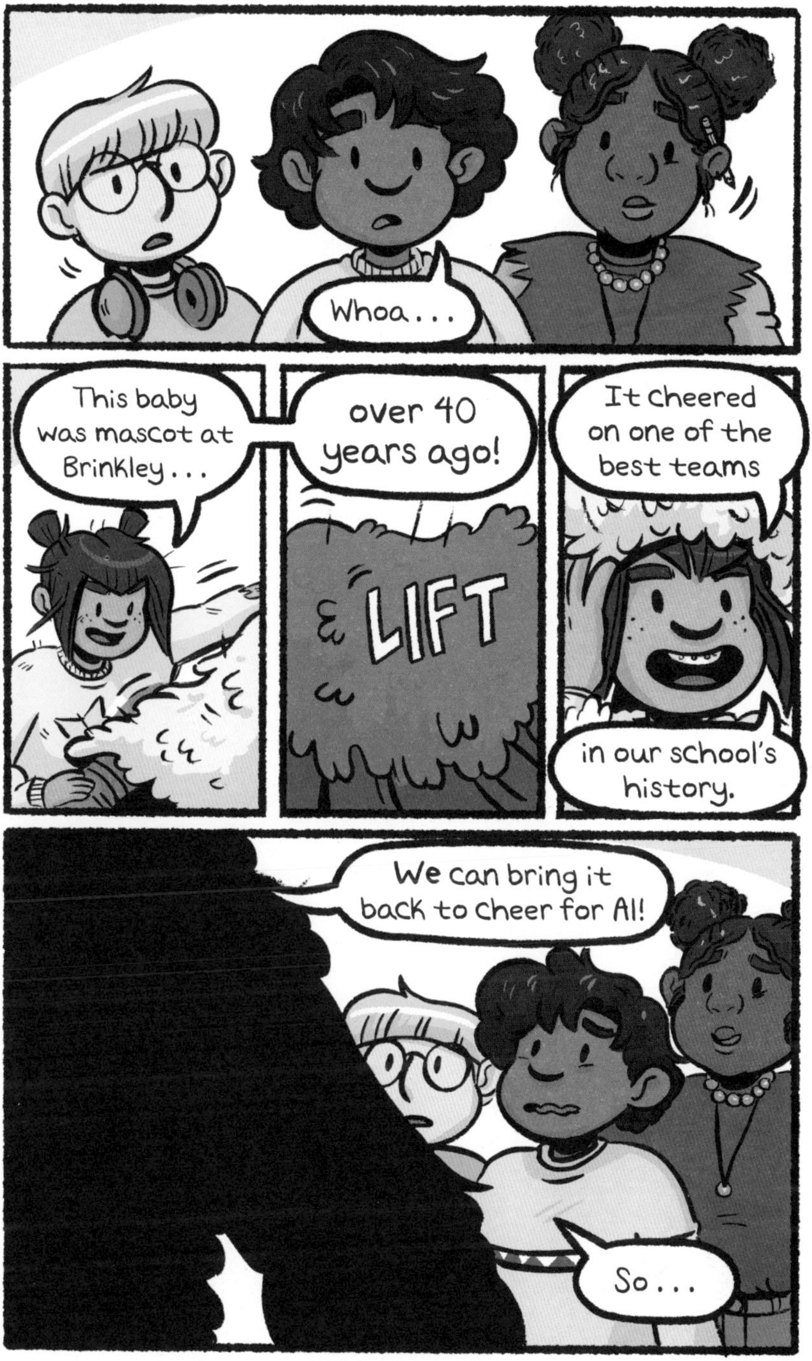
Whoa...
This baby was mascot at Brinkley...
over 40 years ago!
It cheered on one of the best teams
LIFT
in our school's history.
We can bring it back to cheer for Al!
So...

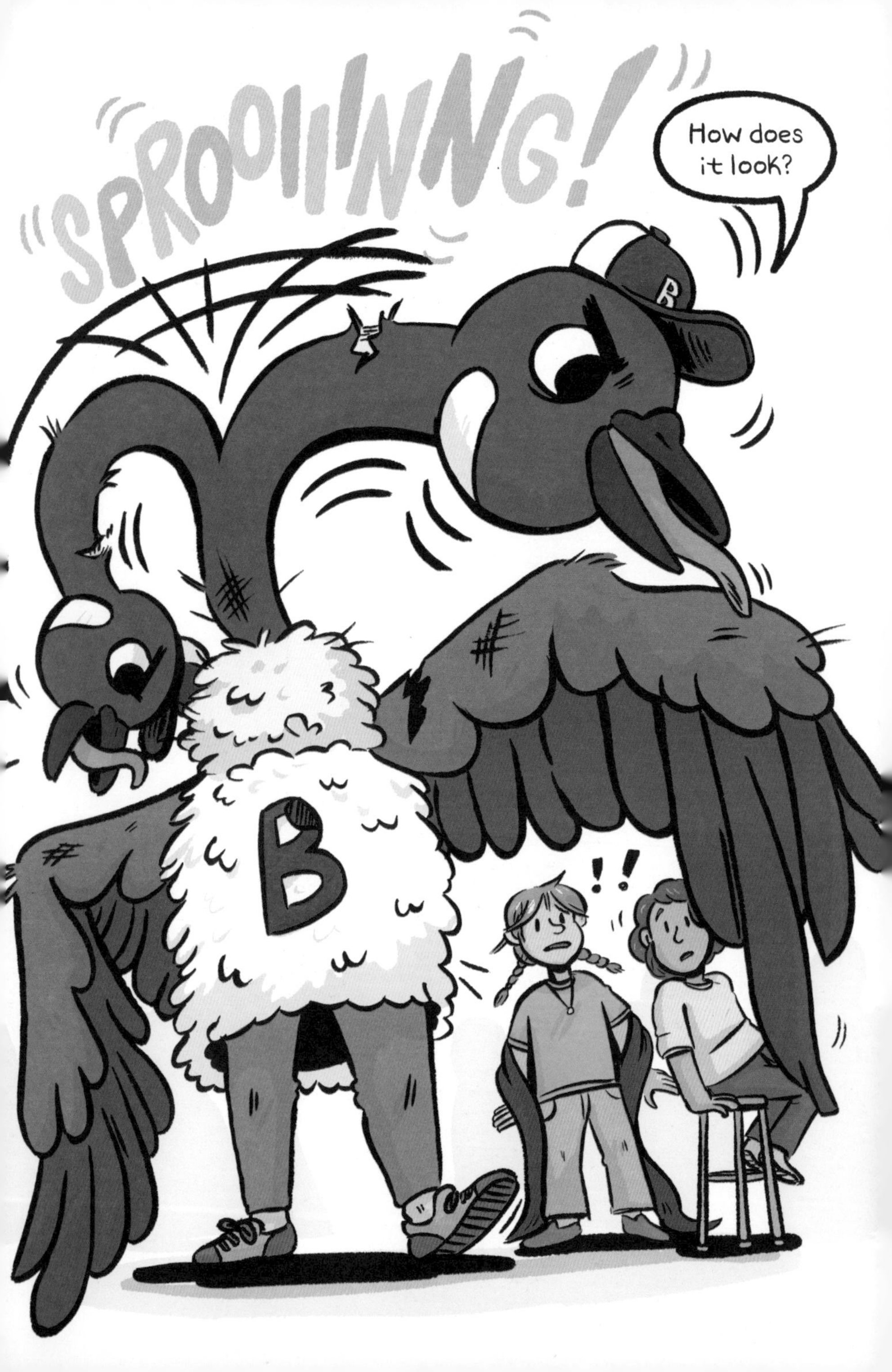
SPROOIIIINNG!
How does it look?
!!

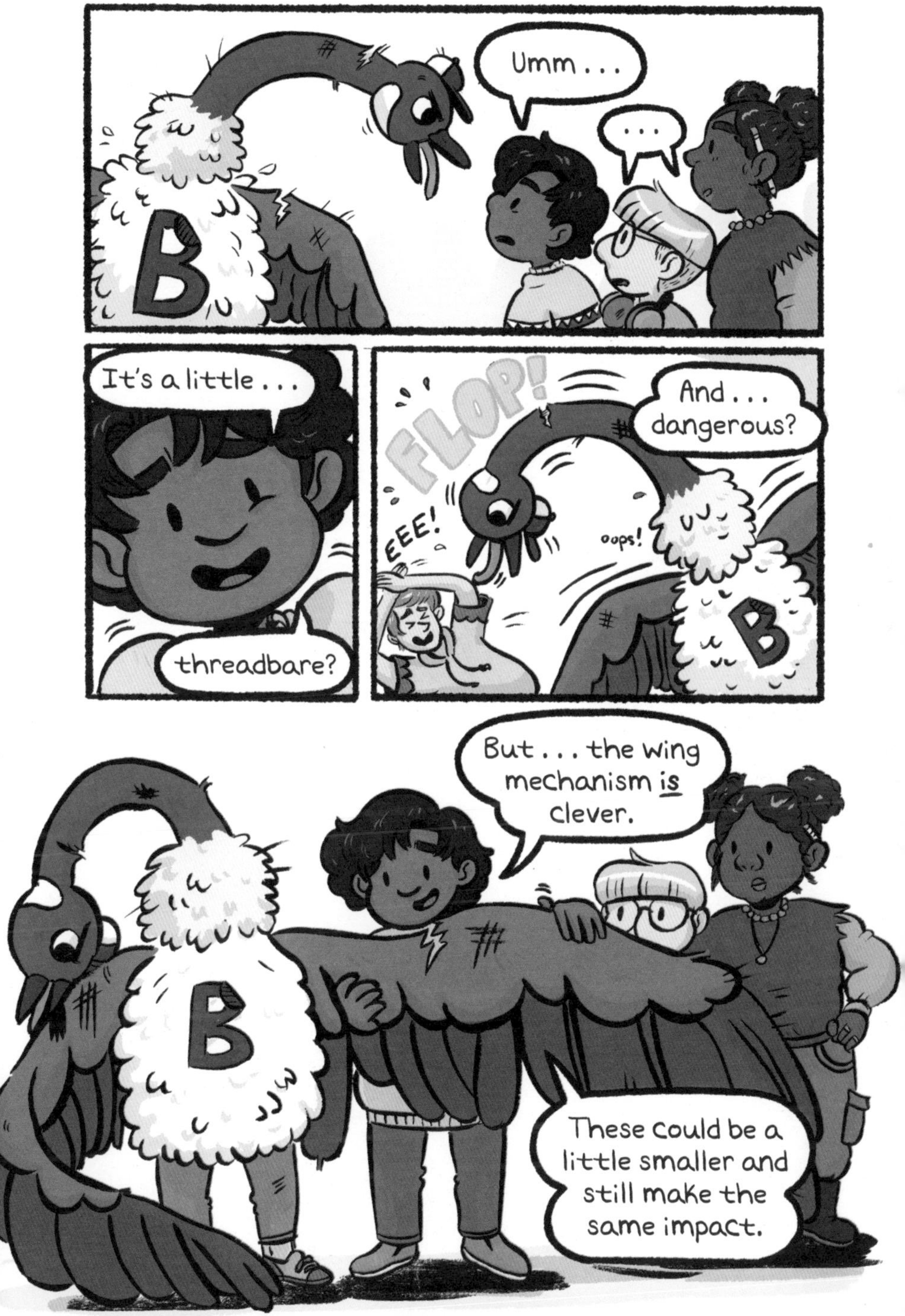
Umm . . .
. . .
It's a little . . .
threadbare?
FLOP!
And . . . dangerous?
EEE!
oops!
But . . . the wing mechanism is clever.
These could be a little smaller and still make the same impact.

It might be . . .

too lifelike.

Yeah, it needs a **major** character redesign.

What if the neck was retractable?

Yeah! And we could give it a new uniform.

ART CLUB

twee de do

I think we can fix it! Make it game-ready!

Hum Hmm Mmm

The Martian is cool and all . . .

Huh?

!

But this mascot has a **ton** of personality.

TURN

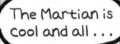

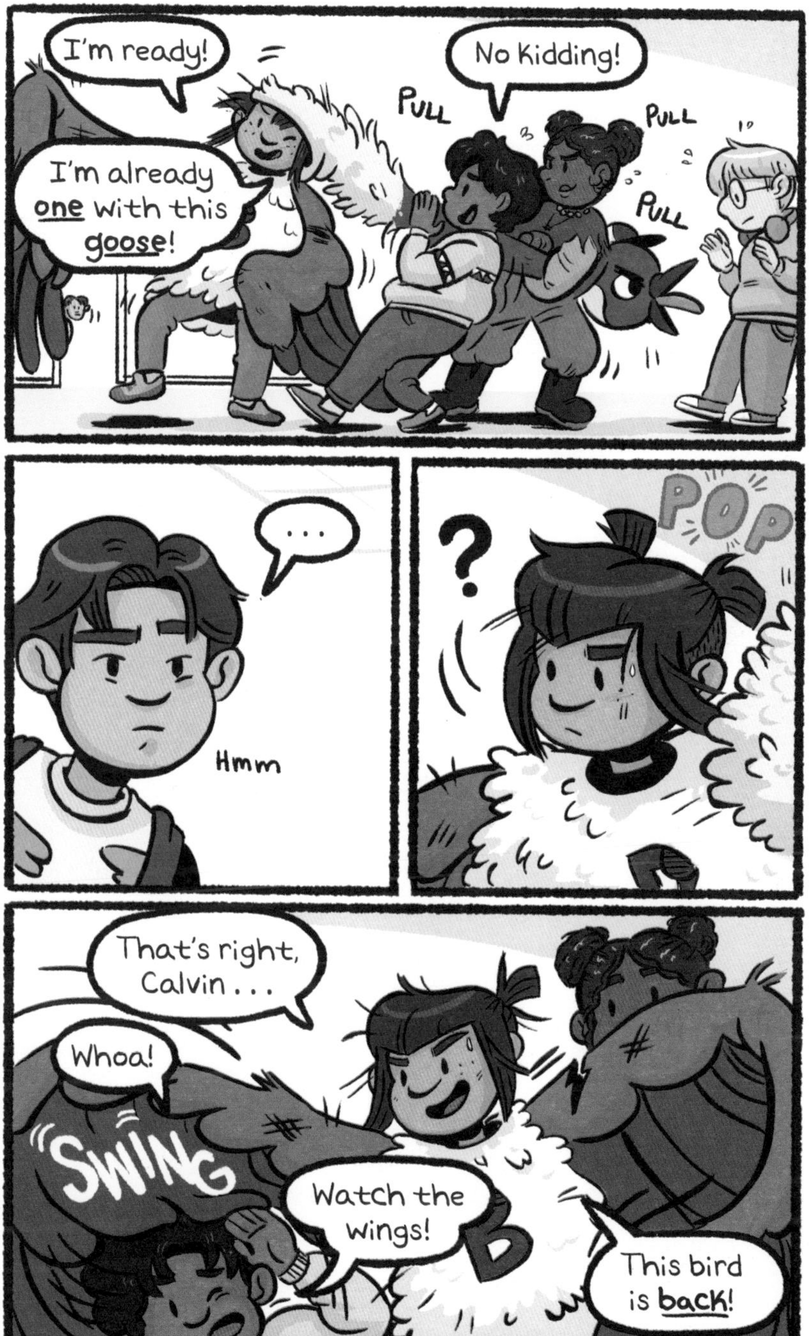
I'm ready!
I'm already one with this goose!
PULL
No Kidding!
PULL
PULL
...
Hmm
?
POP
That's right, Calvin . . .
Whoa!
SWING
Watch the wings!
This bird is back!

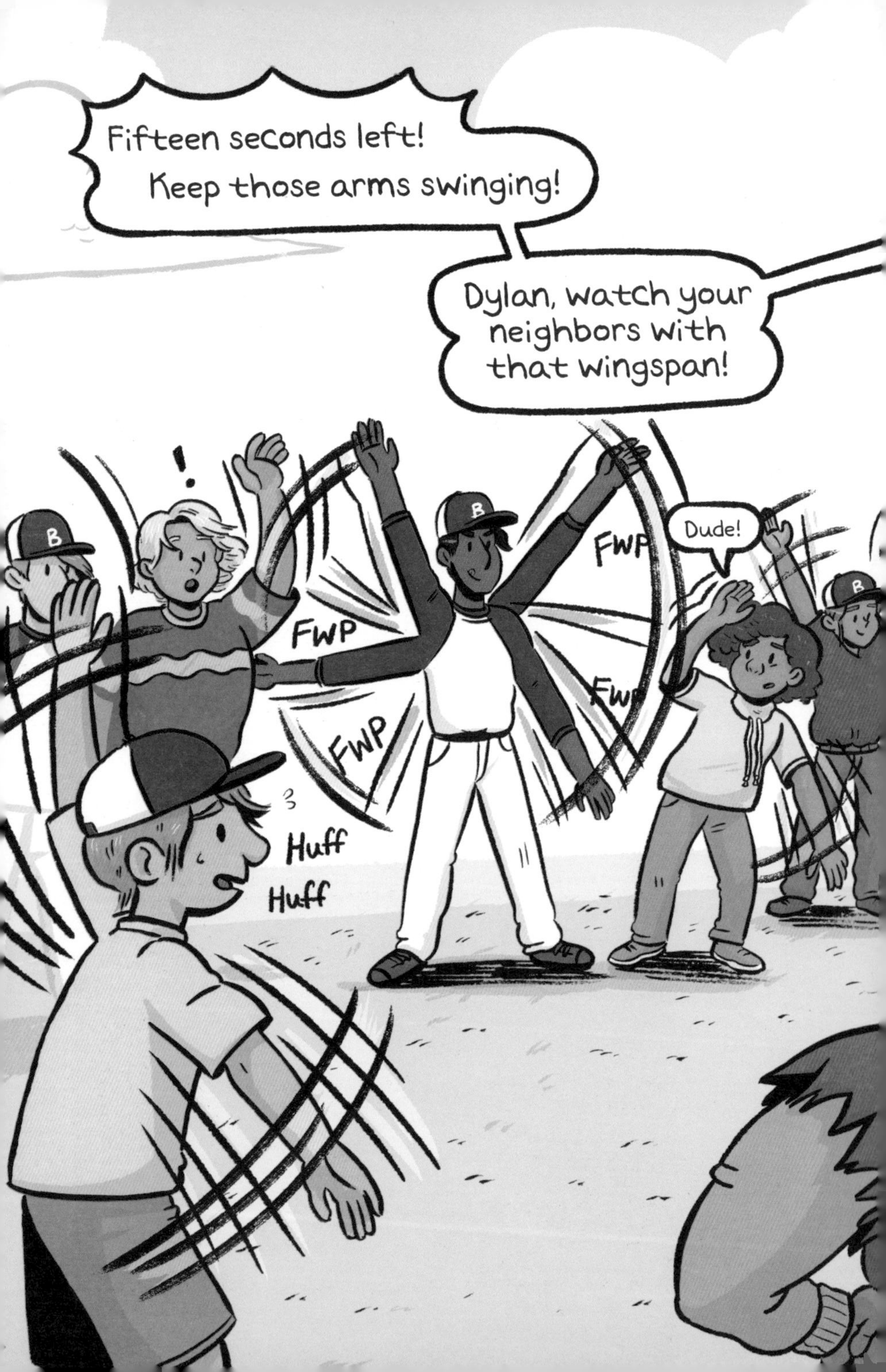
Fifteen seconds left!
Keep those arms swinging!
Dylan, watch your neighbors with that wingspan!
!
FWP
FWP
FWP
FWP
Dude!
Huff
Huff

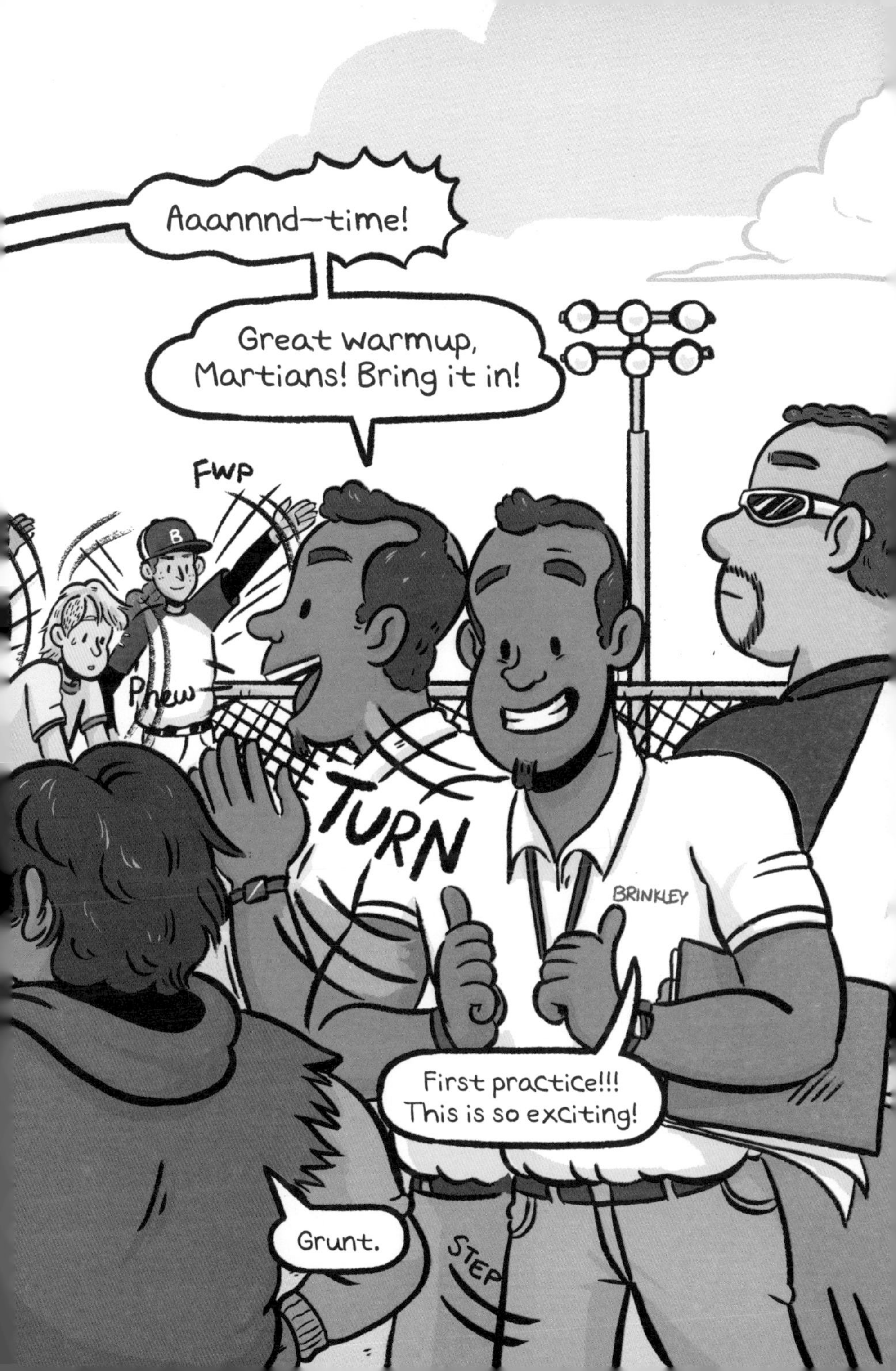
Aaannnd—time!
Great warmup, Martians! Bring it in!
FWP
B
Phew
TURN
BRINKLEY
First practice!!! This is so exciting!
Grunt.
STEP

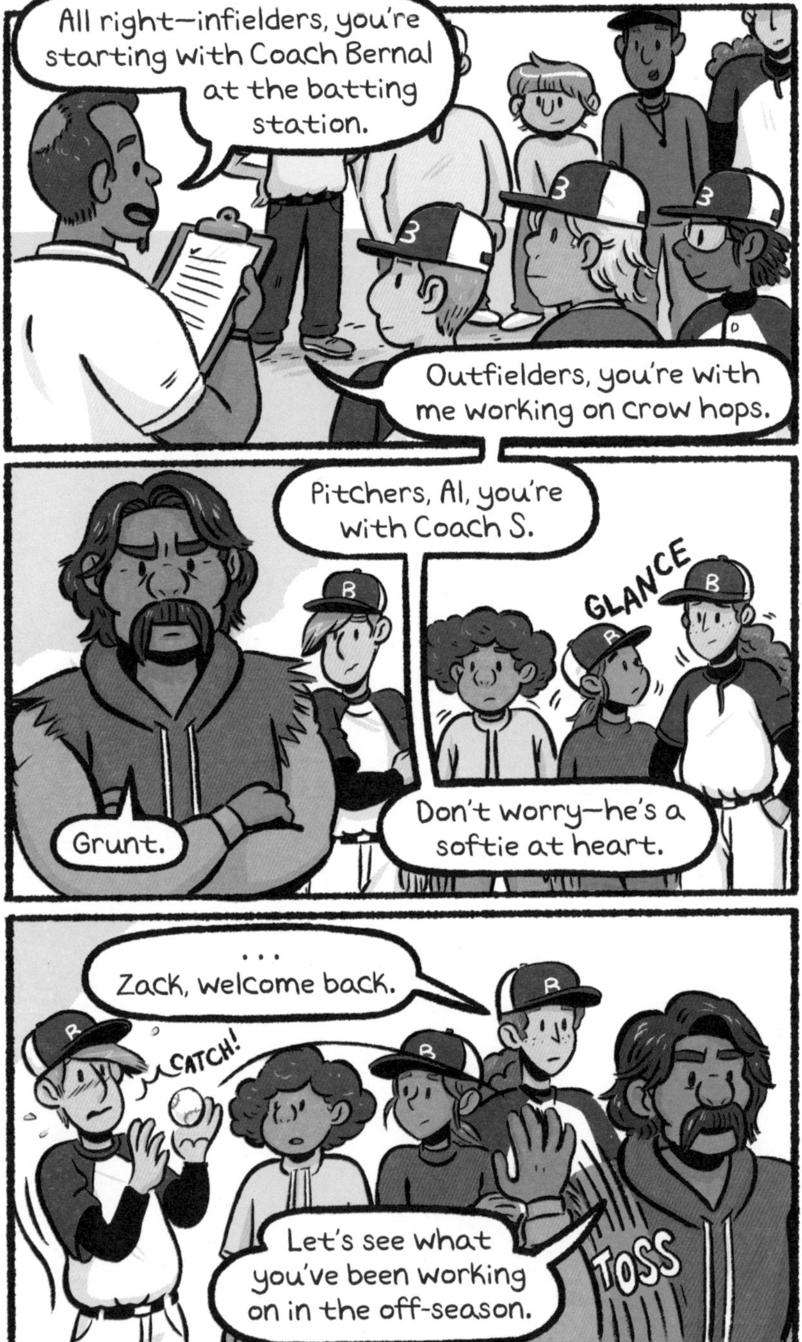
All right—infielders, you're starting with Coach Bernal at the batting station.
Outfielders, you're with me working on crow hops.
Pitchers, Al, you're with Coach S.
Grunt.
GLANCE
Don't worry—he's a softie at heart.
...
Zack, welcome back.
CATCH!
TOSS
Let's see what you've been working on in the off-season.

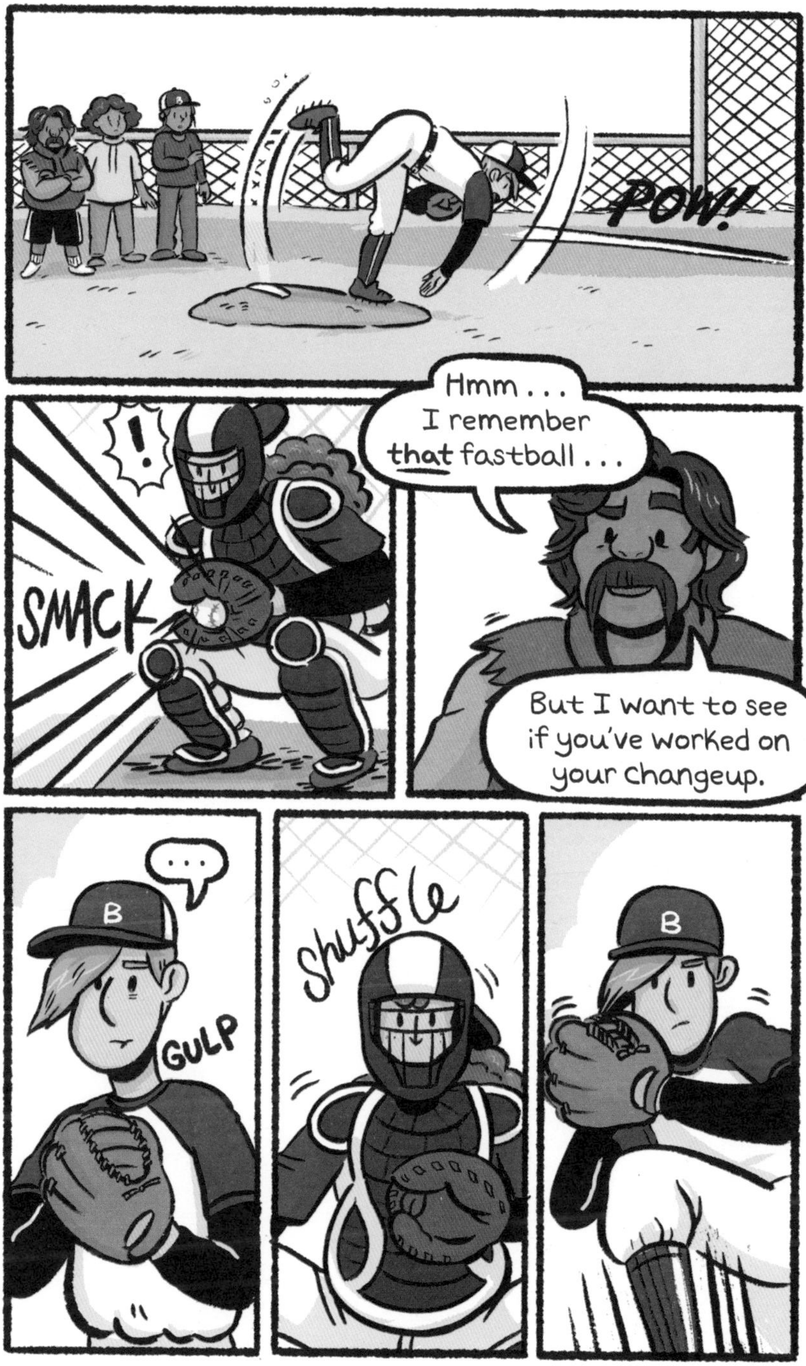
POW!
SMACK
!
Hmm . . . I remember that fastball . . .
But I want to see if you've worked on your changeup.
. . .
GULP
shuffle

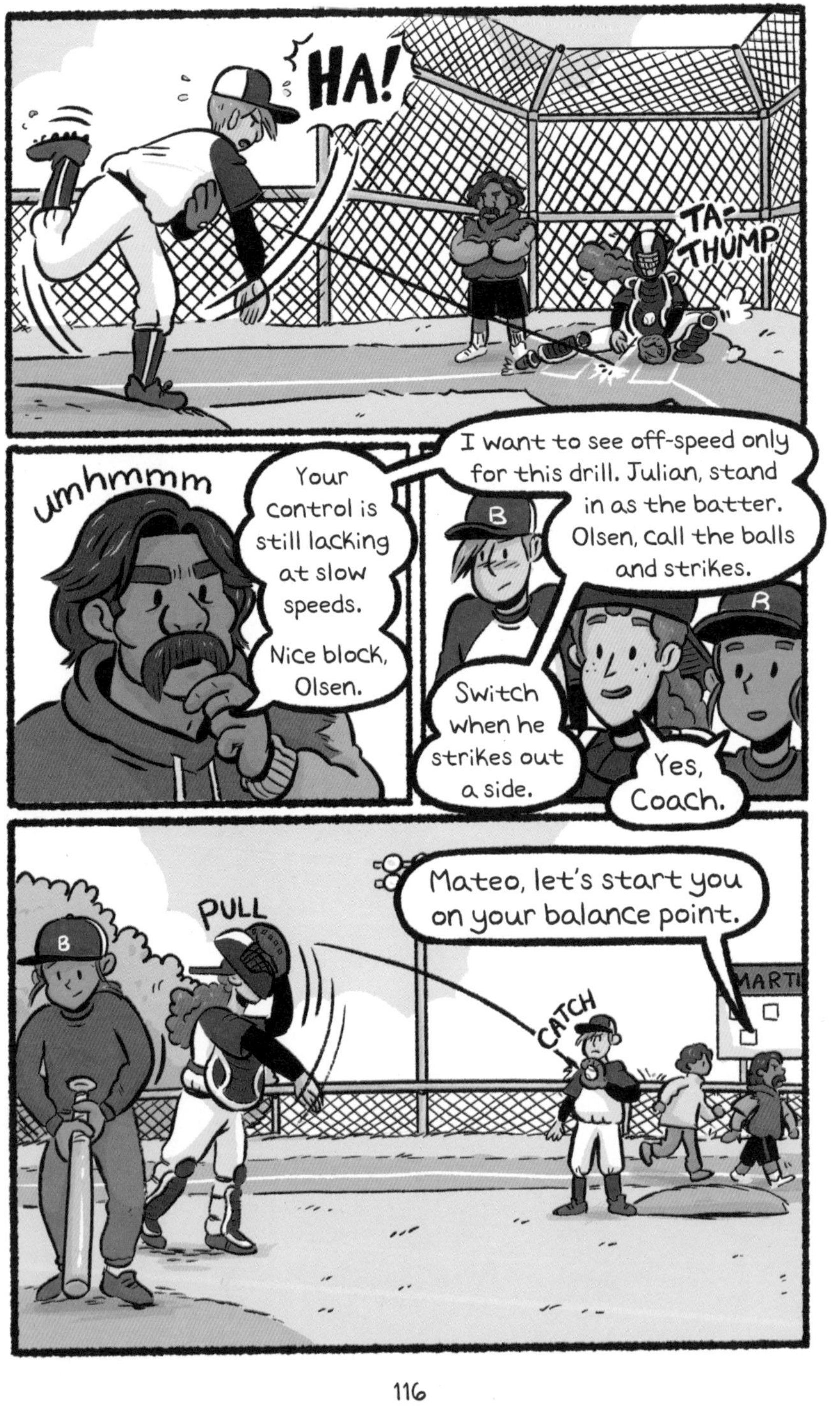
HA!
TA-THUMP
umhmmm
Your control is still lacking at slow speeds.
Nice block, Olsen.
I want to see off-speed only for this drill. Julian, stand in as the batter. Olsen, call the balls and strikes.
Switch when he strikes out a side.
Yes, Coach.
PULL
CATCH
Mateo, let's start you on your balance point.
MARTI

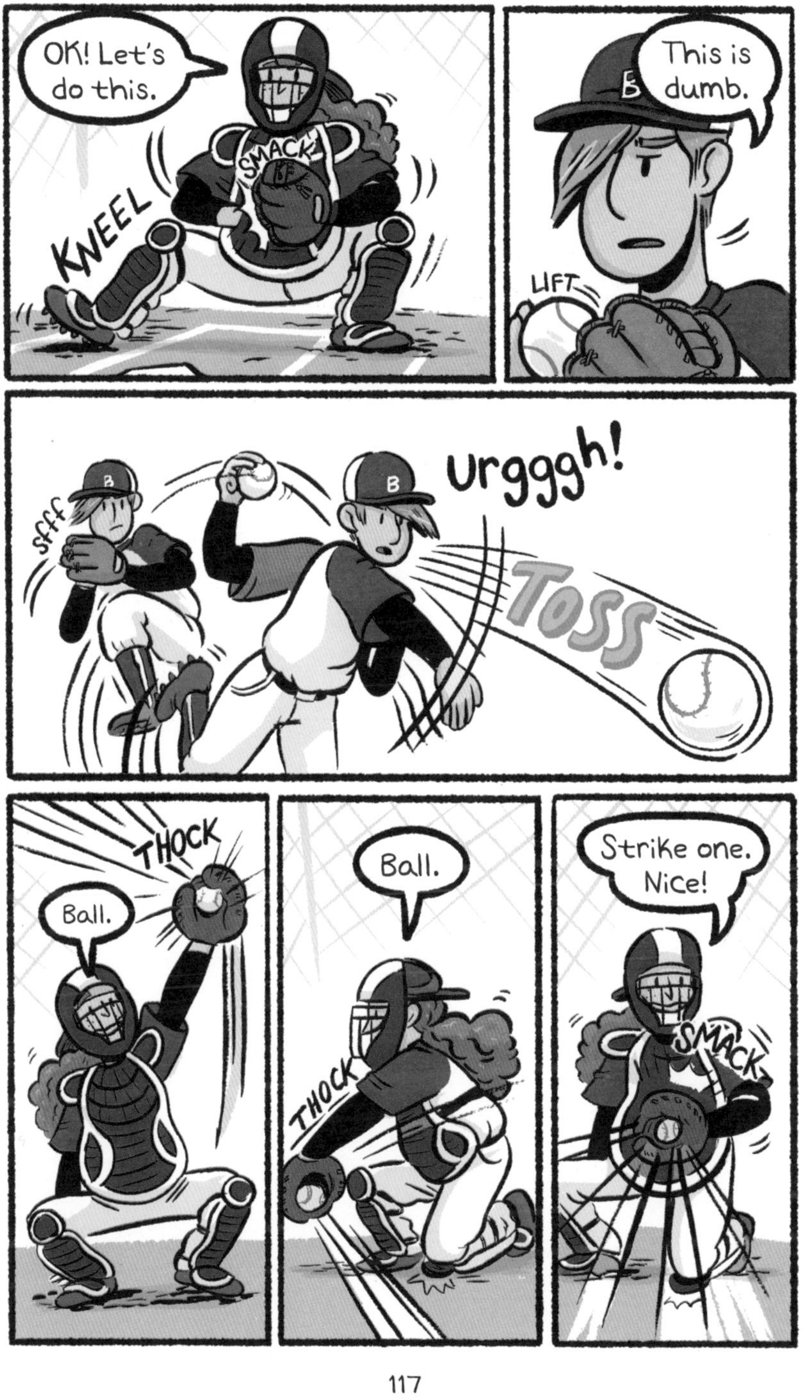
OK! Let's do this.
SMACK
KNEEL
This is dumb.
LIFT
sfff
Urgggh!
TOSS
THOCK
Ball.
Ball.
THOCK
Strike one. Nice!
SMACK

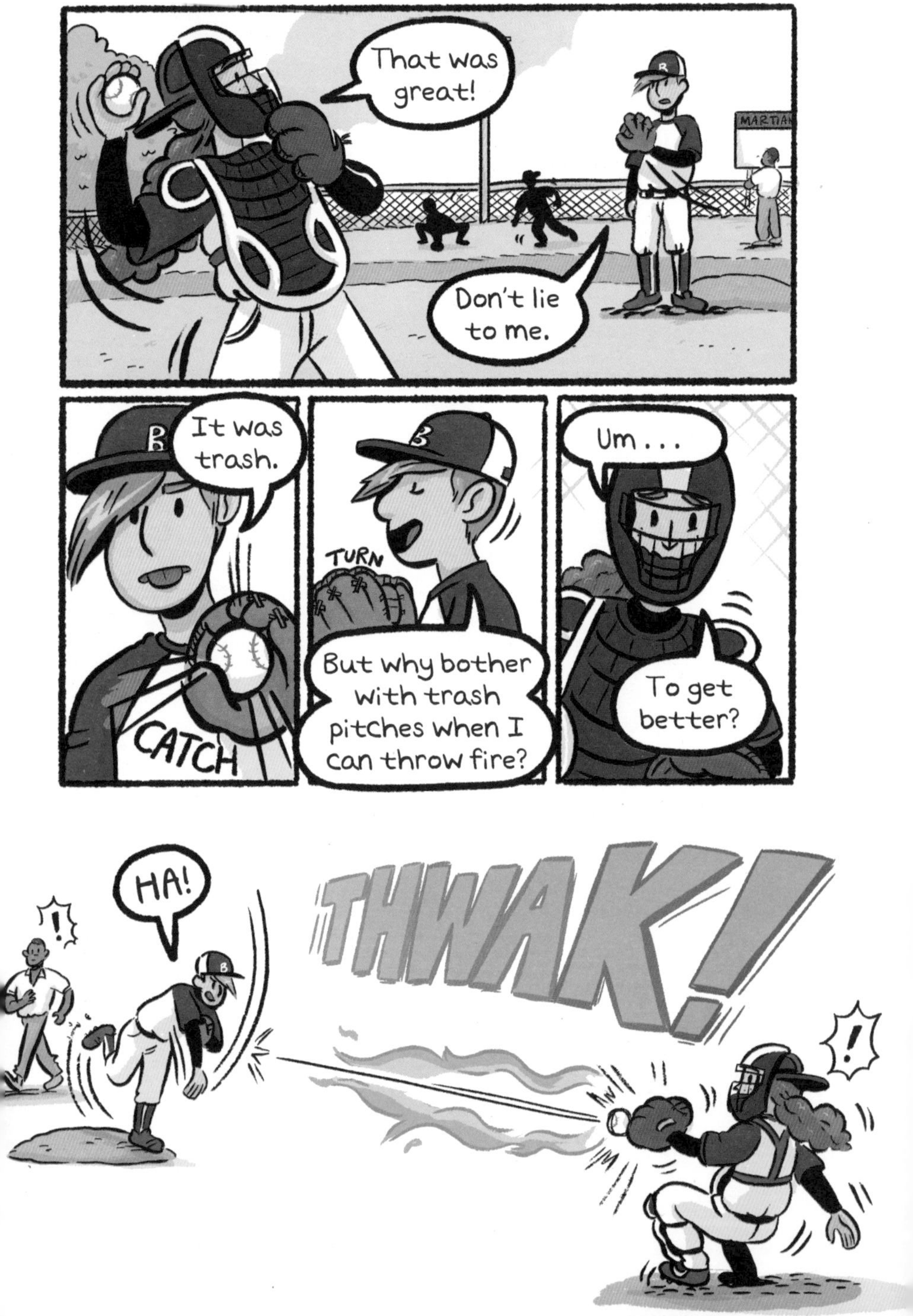
That was great!
Don't lie to me.
MARTIAN
It was trash.
CATCH
TURN
But why bother with trash pitches when I can throw fire?
Um . . .
To get better?
HA!
!
THWAK!
!

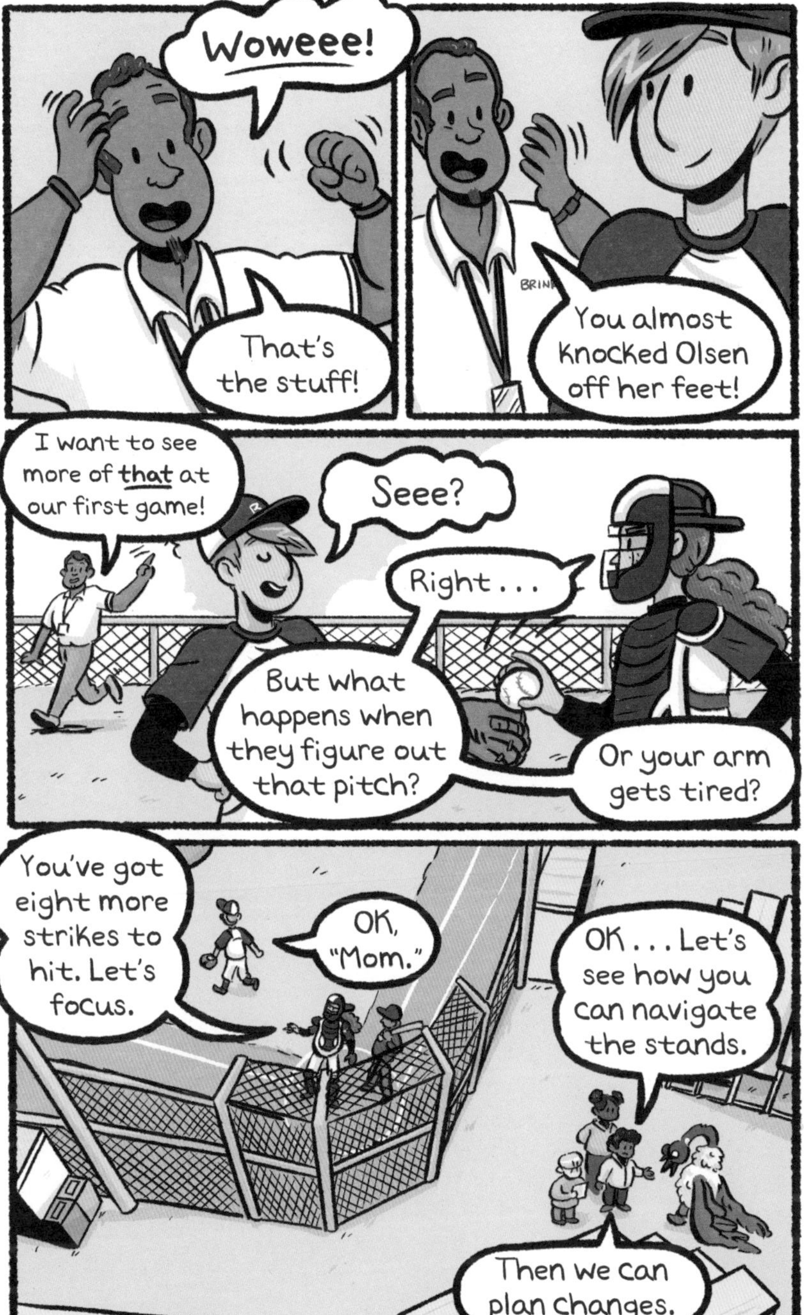
Woweee!
That's the stuff!
You almost Knocked Olsen off her feet!
I want to see more of **that** at our first game!
Seee?
Right . . .
But what happens when they figure out that pitch?
Or your arm gets tired?
You've got eight more strikes to hit. Let's focus.
OK, "Mom."
OK . . . Let's see how you can navigate the stands.
Then we can plan changes.

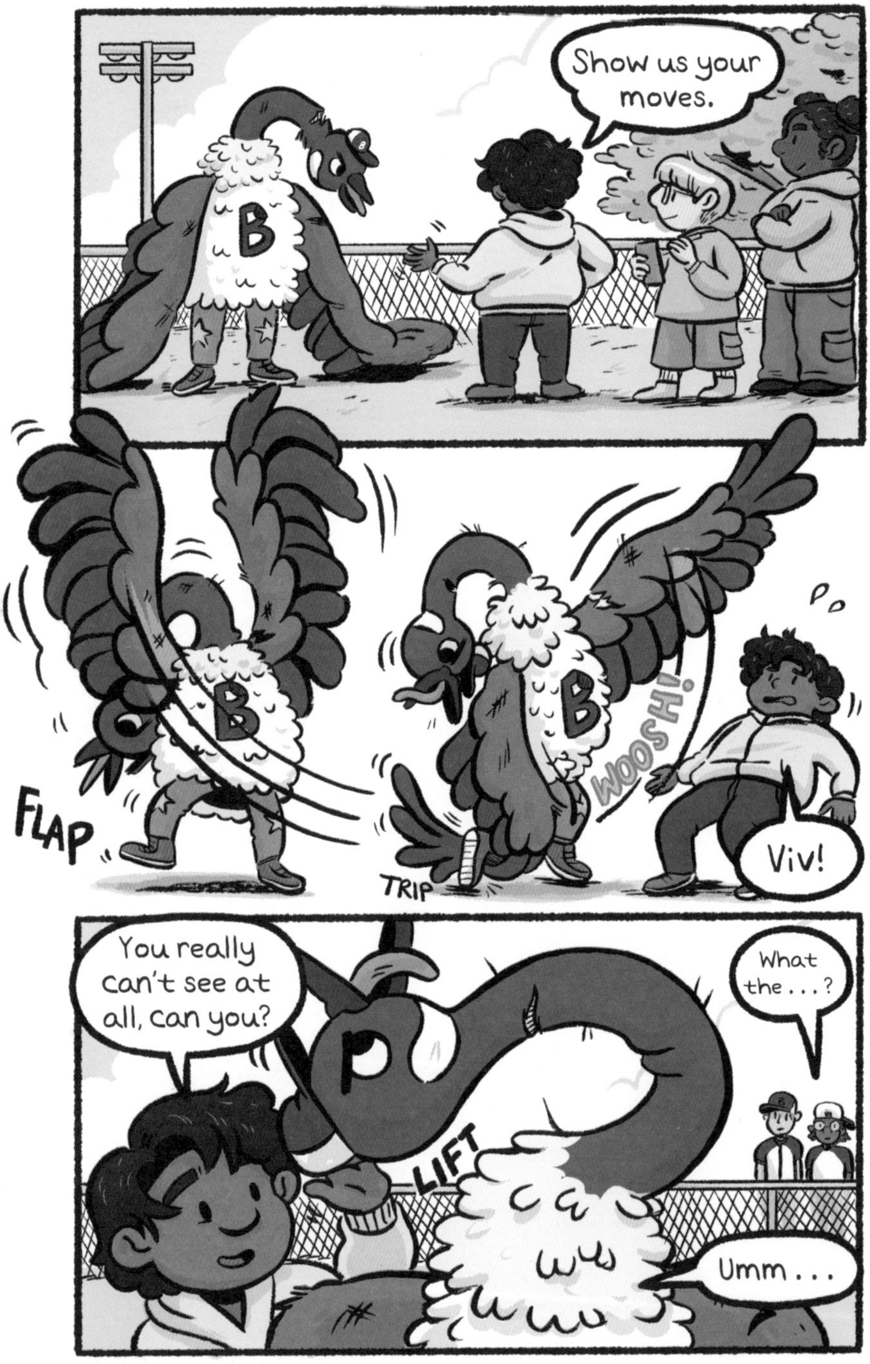
Show us your moves.
FLAP
TRIP
WOOSH!
Viv!
You really can't see at all, can you?
LIFT
What the . . . ?
Umm . . .

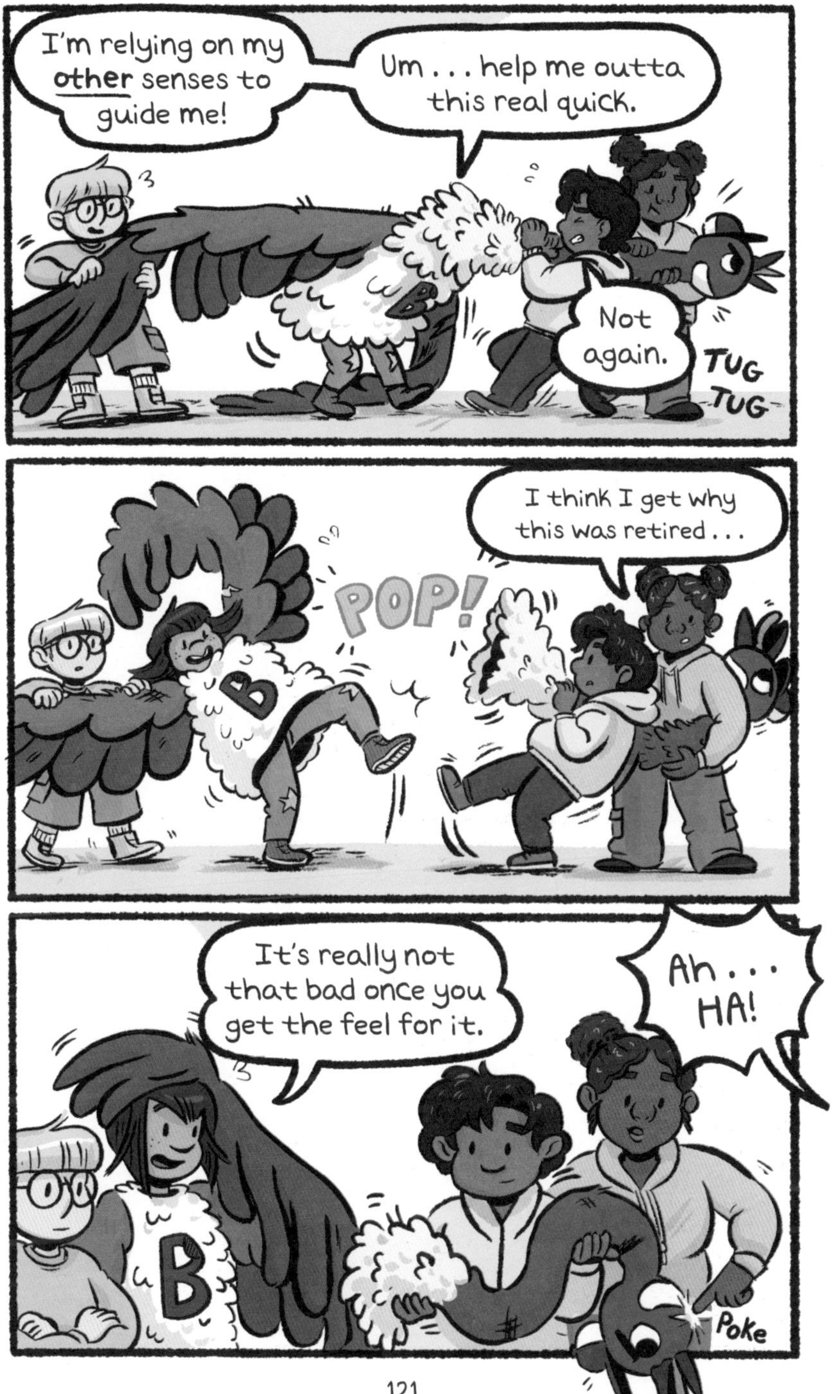

I'm relying on my other senses to guide me!
Um . . . help me outta this real quick.
Not again.
TUG TUG
I think I get why this was retired . . .
POP!
It's really not that bad once you get the feel for it.
Ah . . . HA!
Poke

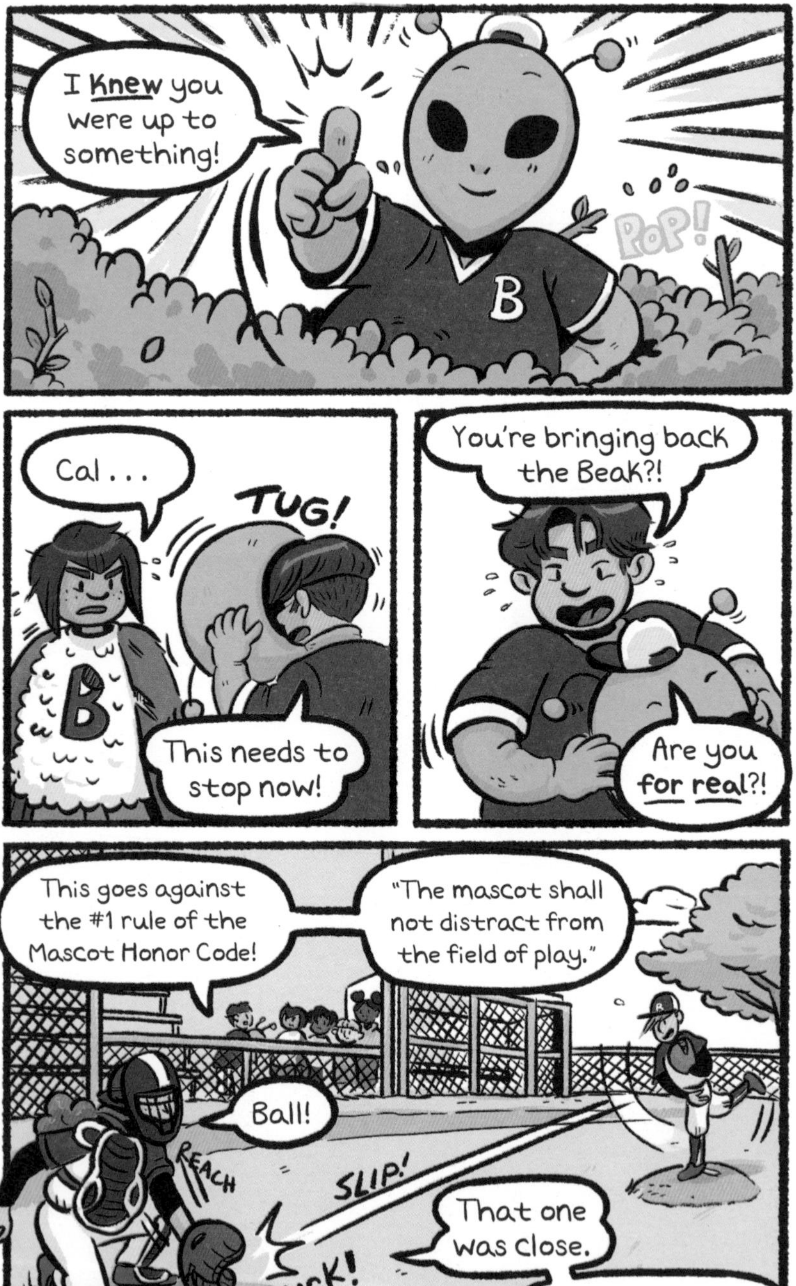
I **Knew** you were up to something!
POP!
Cal . . .
TUG!
This needs to stop now!
You're bringing back the Beak?!
Are you **for real**?!
This goes against the #1 rule of the Mascot Honor Code!
"The mascot shall not distract from the field of play."
Ball!
REACH
SLIP!
SMACK!
That one was close.
Try again! We're almost there.

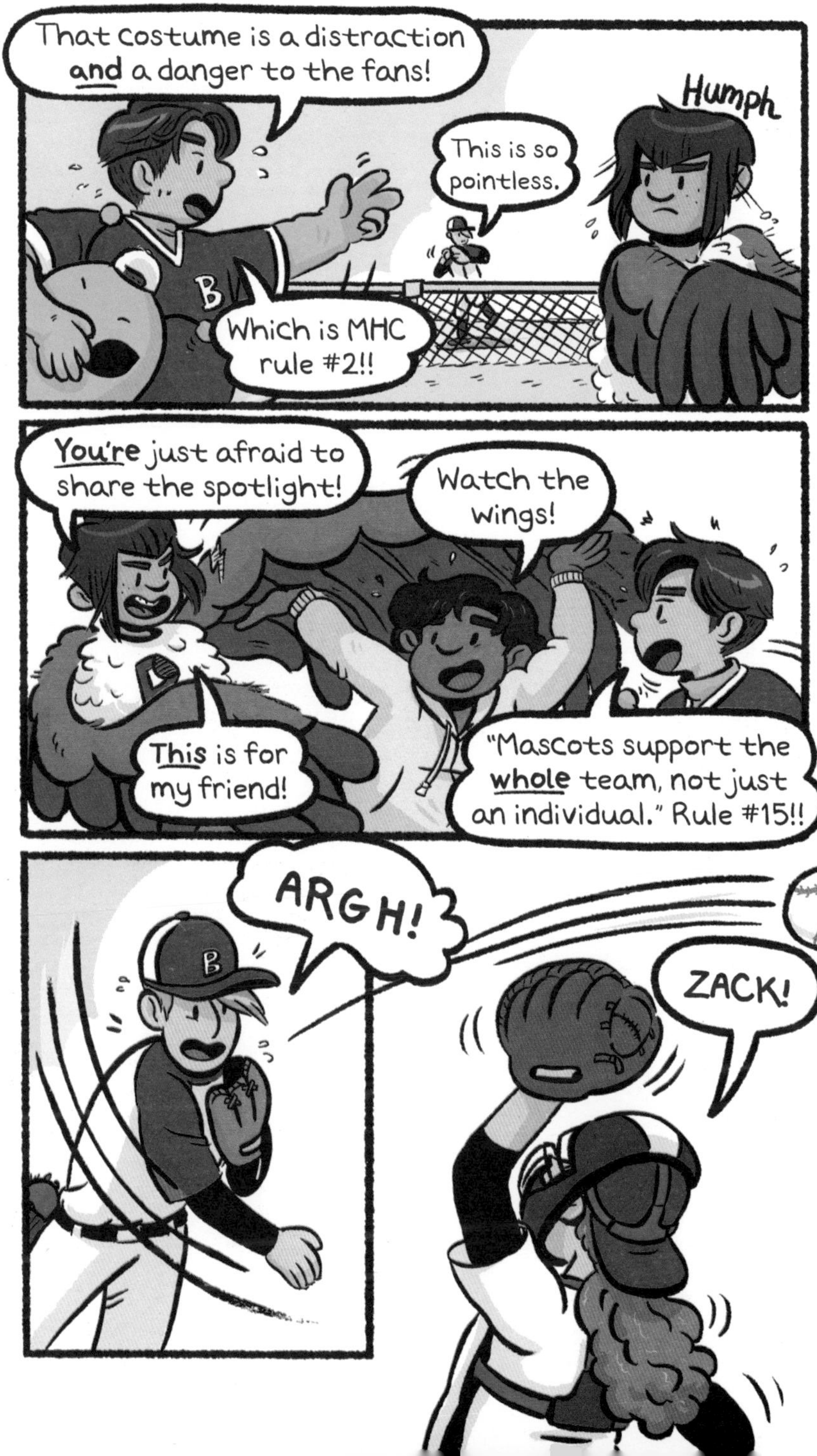
That costume is a distraction and a danger to the fans!
Humph
This is so pointless.
Which is MHC rule #2!!
You're just afraid to share the spotlight!
Watch the wings!
This is for my friend!
"Mascots support the whole team, not just an individual." Rule #15!!
ARGH!
ZACK!

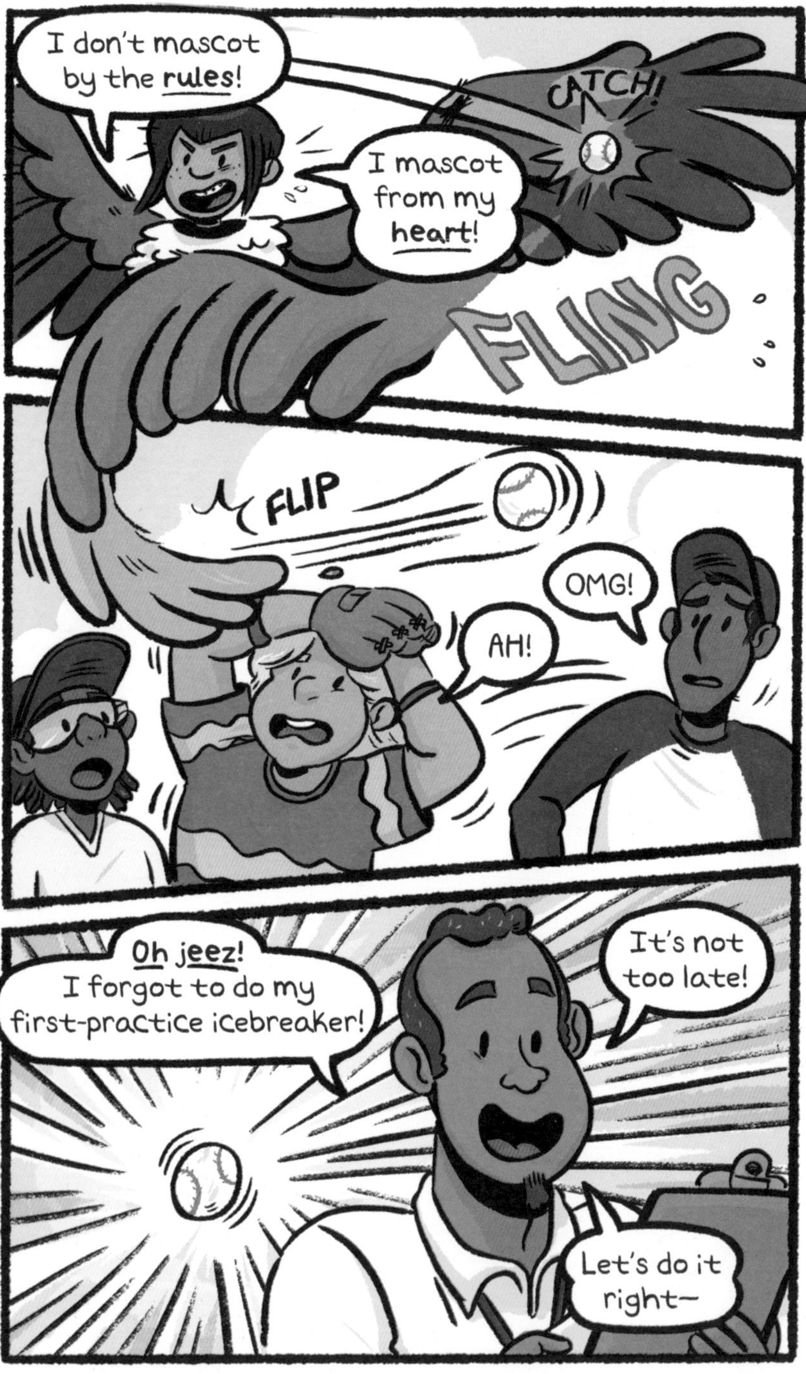
I don't mascot by the rules!
I mascot from my heart!
CATCH!
FLING
FLIP
OMG!
AH!
Oh jeez! I forgot to do my first-practice icebreaker!
It's not too late!
Let's do it right—

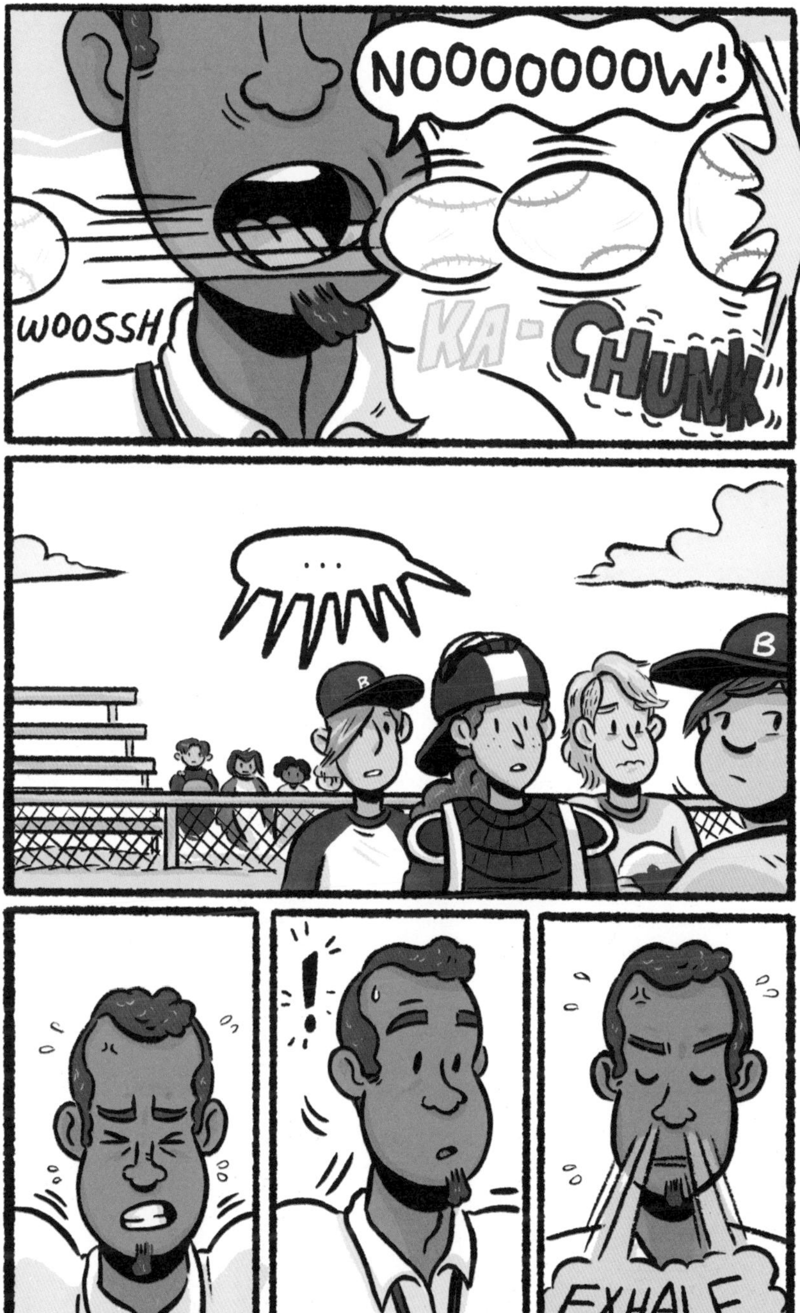
NOOOOOOOW!
WOOSSH
KA-CHUNK
...
!
EXHALE

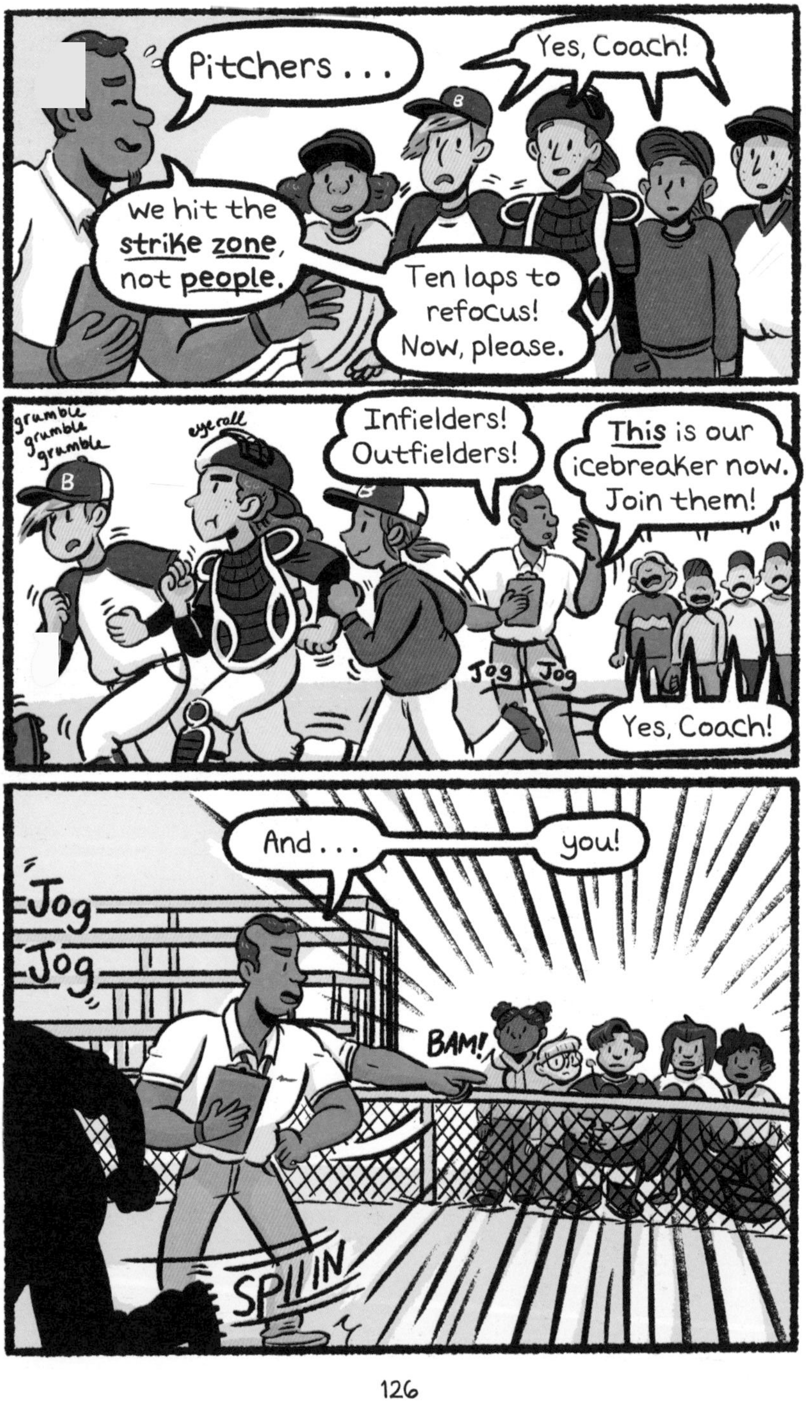
Pitchers . . .
Yes, Coach!
We hit the strike zone, not people.
Ten laps to refocus! Now, please.
grumble grumble grumble
eyeroll
Infielders! Outfielders!
This is our icebreaker now. Join them!
Jog Jog
Yes, Coach!
And . . .
you!
Jog
Jog
BAM!
SPIIIN

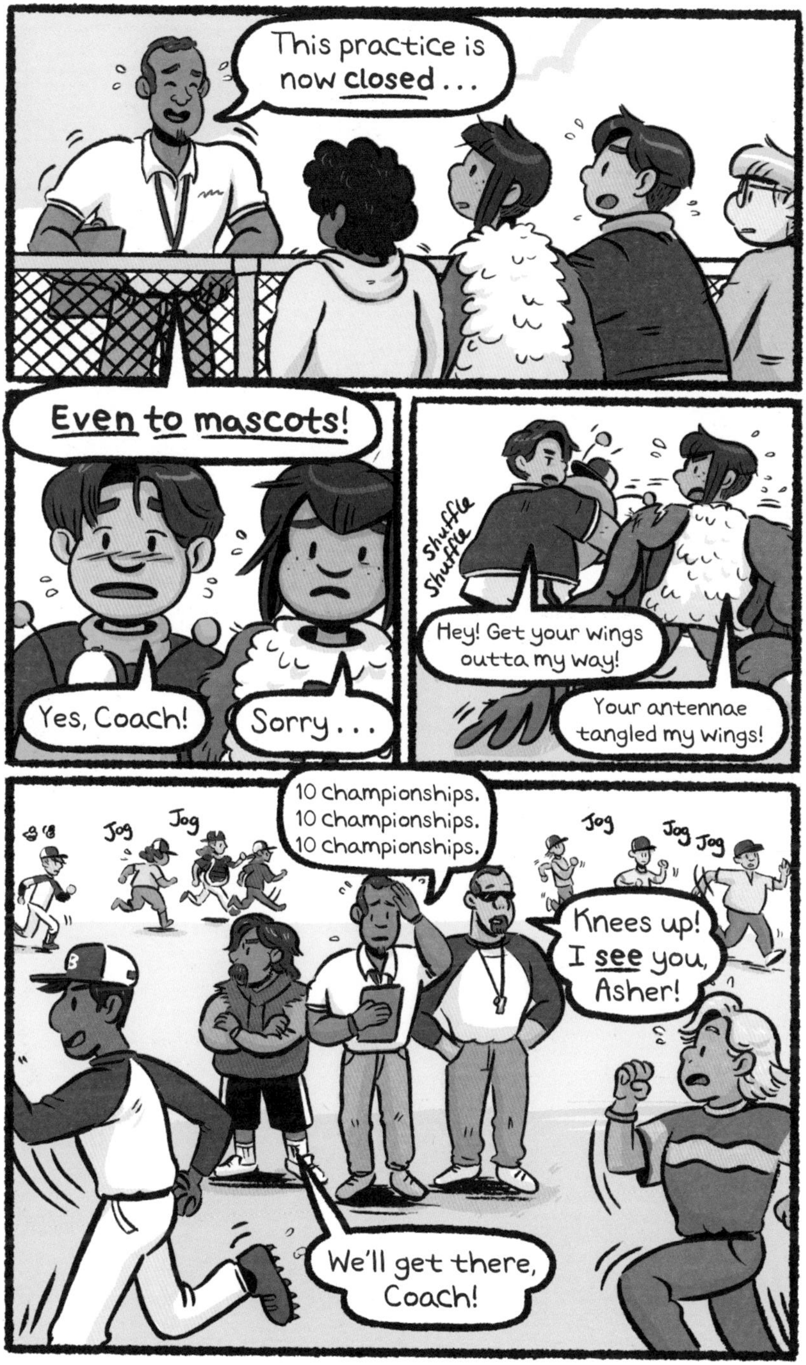
This practice is now closed . . .
Even to mascots!
Yes, Coach!
Sorry . . .
Shuffle Shuffle
Hey! Get your wings outta my way!
Your antennae tangled my wings!
10 championships. 10 championships. 10 championships.
Jog Jog
Jog Jog Jog
Knees up! I see you, Asher!
We'll get there, Coach!

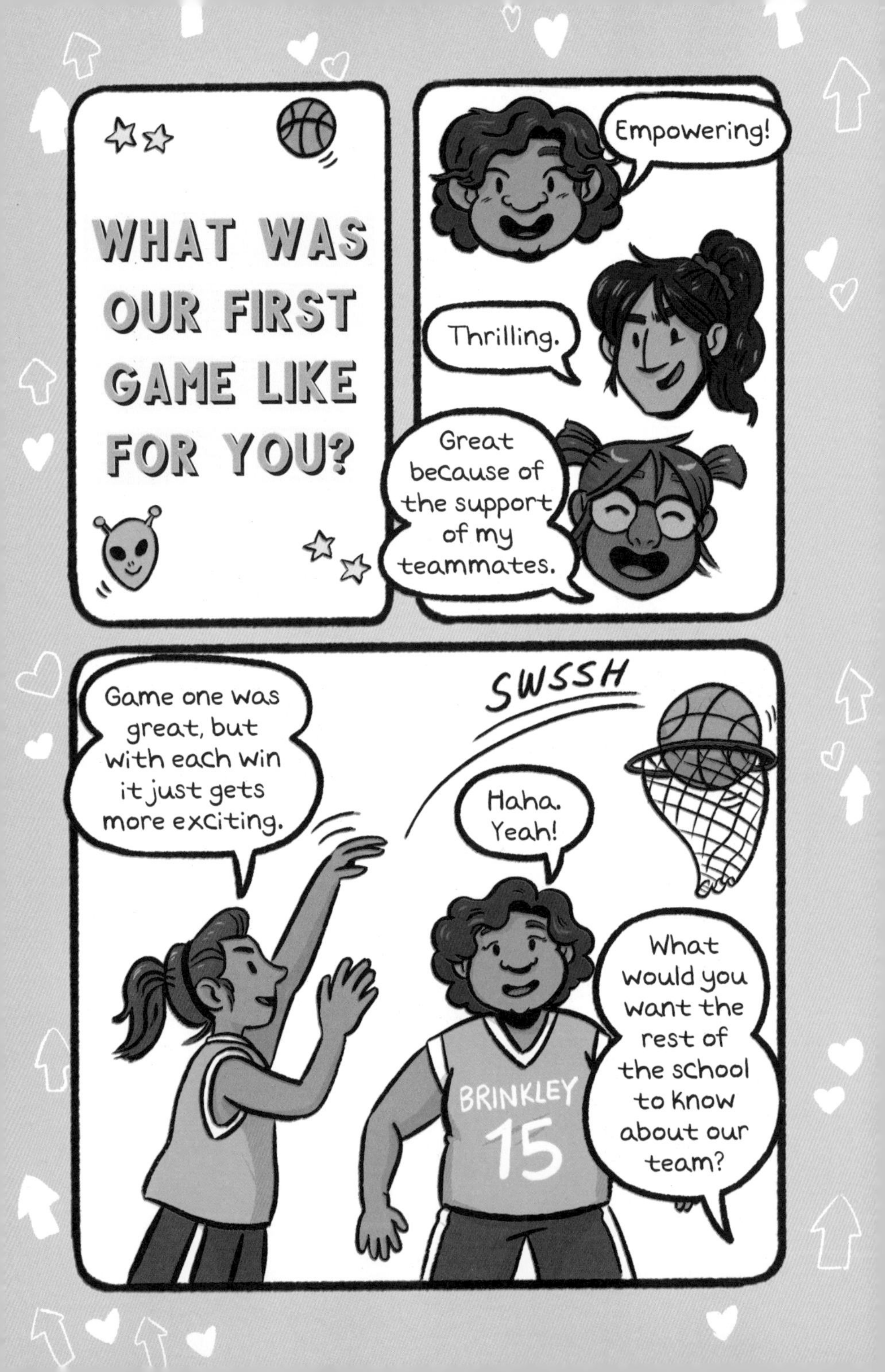
WHAT WAS OUR FIRST GAME LIKE FOR YOU?
Empowering!
Thrilling.
Great because of the support of my teammates.
Game one was great, but with each win it just gets more exciting.
SWSSH
Haha. Yeah!
BRINKLEY 15
What would you want the rest of the school to know about our team?

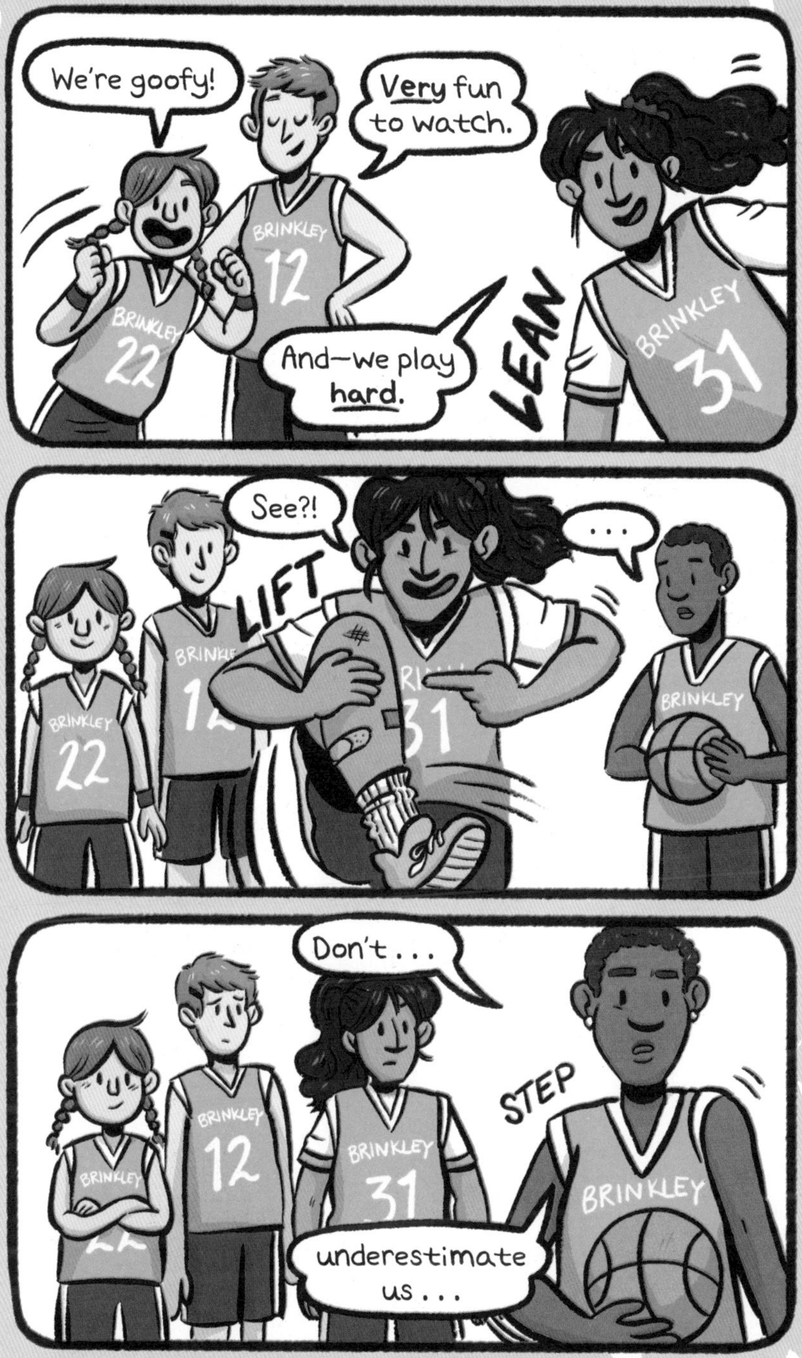
We're goofy!
Very fun to watch.
And—we play hard.
LEAN
See?!
LIFT
...
Don't . . .
STEP
underestimate us . . .

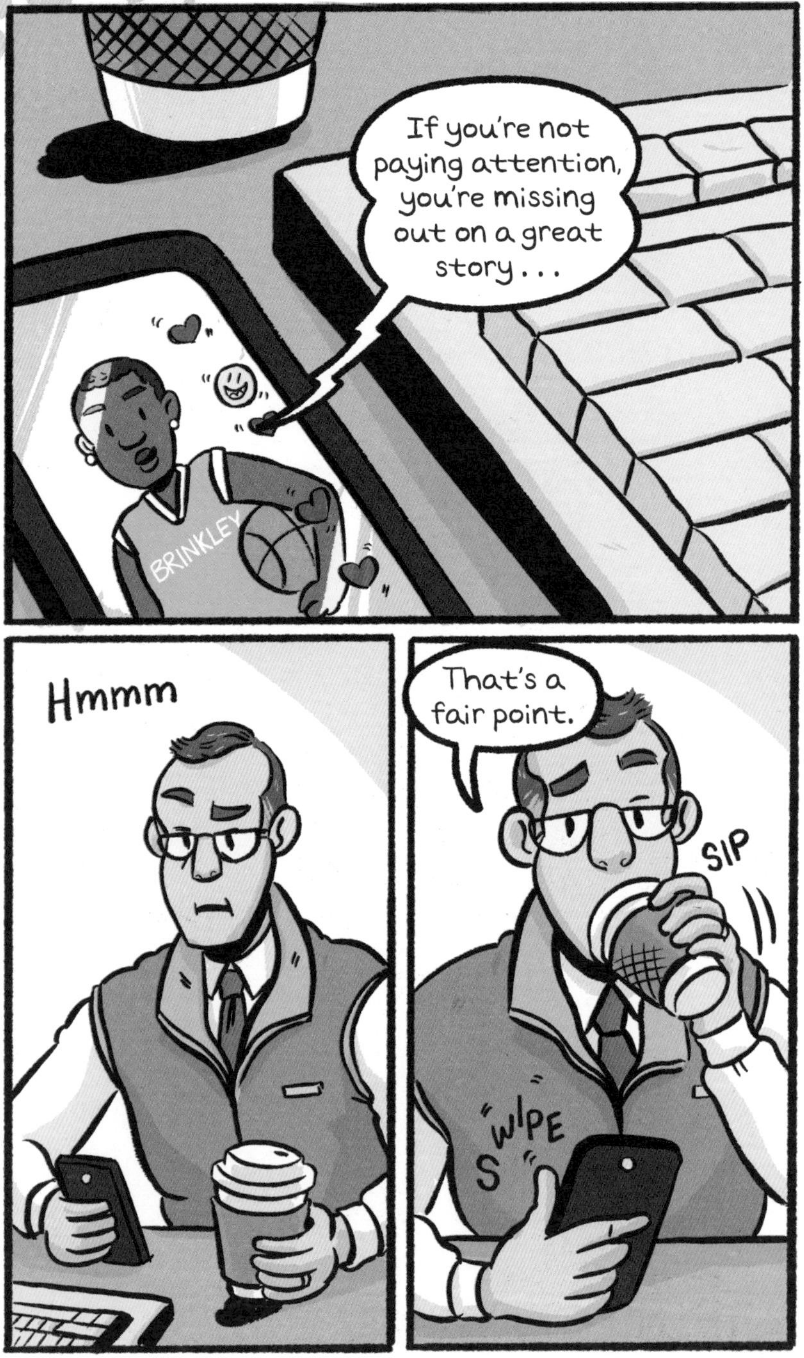
If you're not paying attention, you're missing out on a great story . . .
BRINKLEY
Hmmm
That's a fair point.
SIP
SWIPE

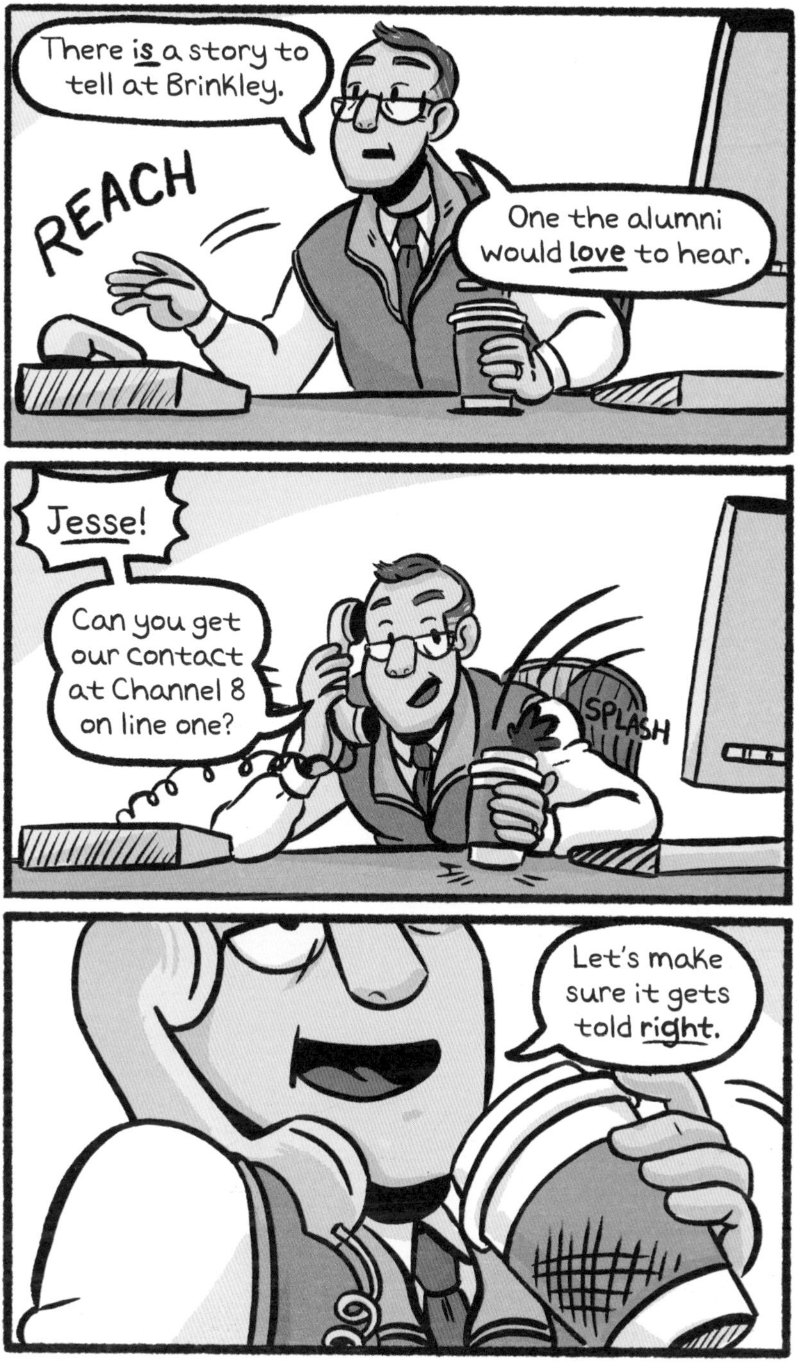
There is a story to tell at Brinkley.
REACH
One the alumni would love to hear.
Jesse!
Can you get our contact at Channel 8 on line one?
SPLASH
Let's make sure it gets told right.

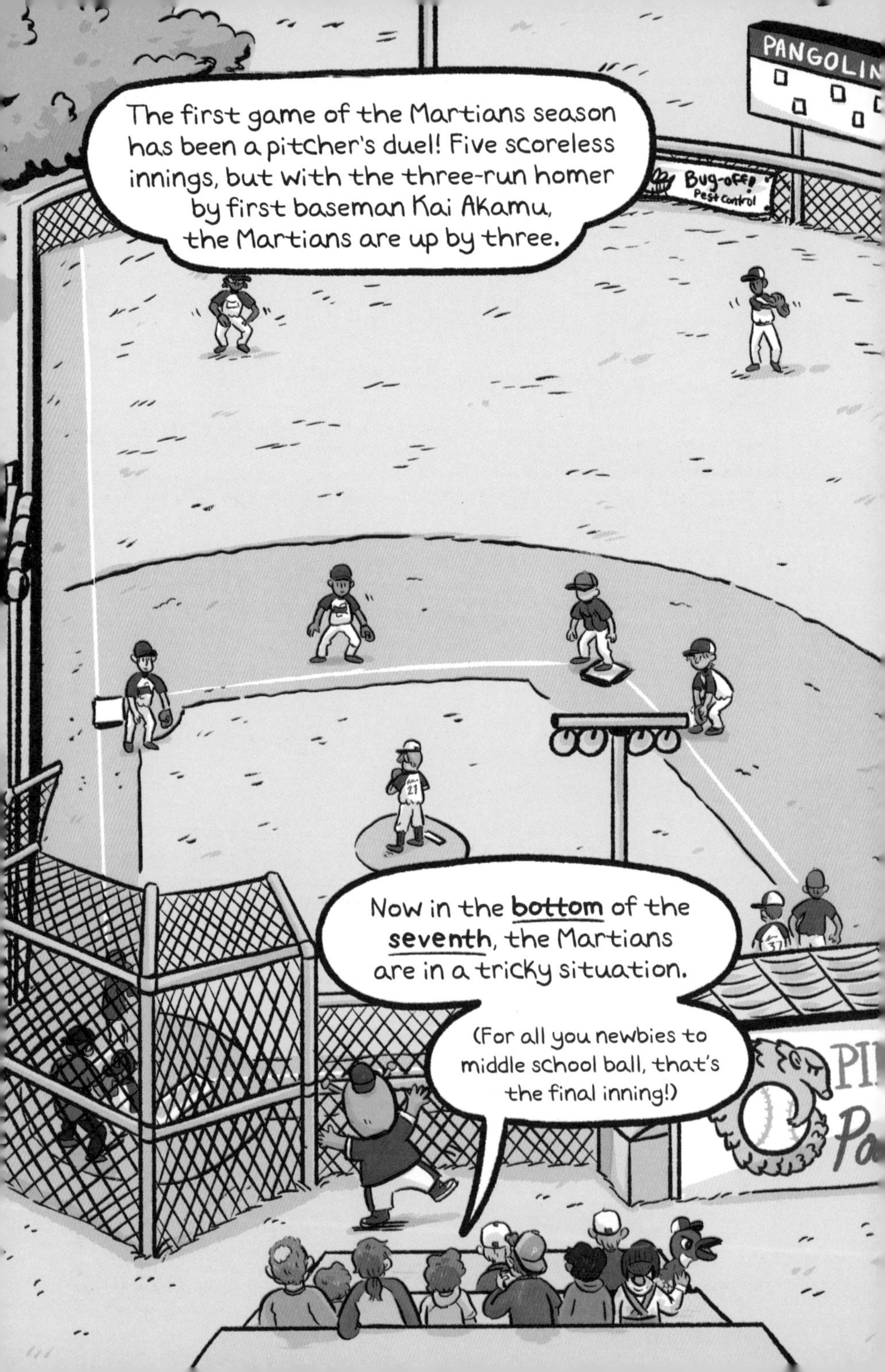

PANGOLIN
Bug-off! Pest Control
The first game of the Martians season has been a pitcher's duel! Five scoreless innings, but with the three-run homer by first baseman Kai Akamu, the Martians are up by three.
21
Now in the bottom of the seventh, the Martians are in a tricky situation.
(For all you newbies to middle school ball, that's the final inning!)

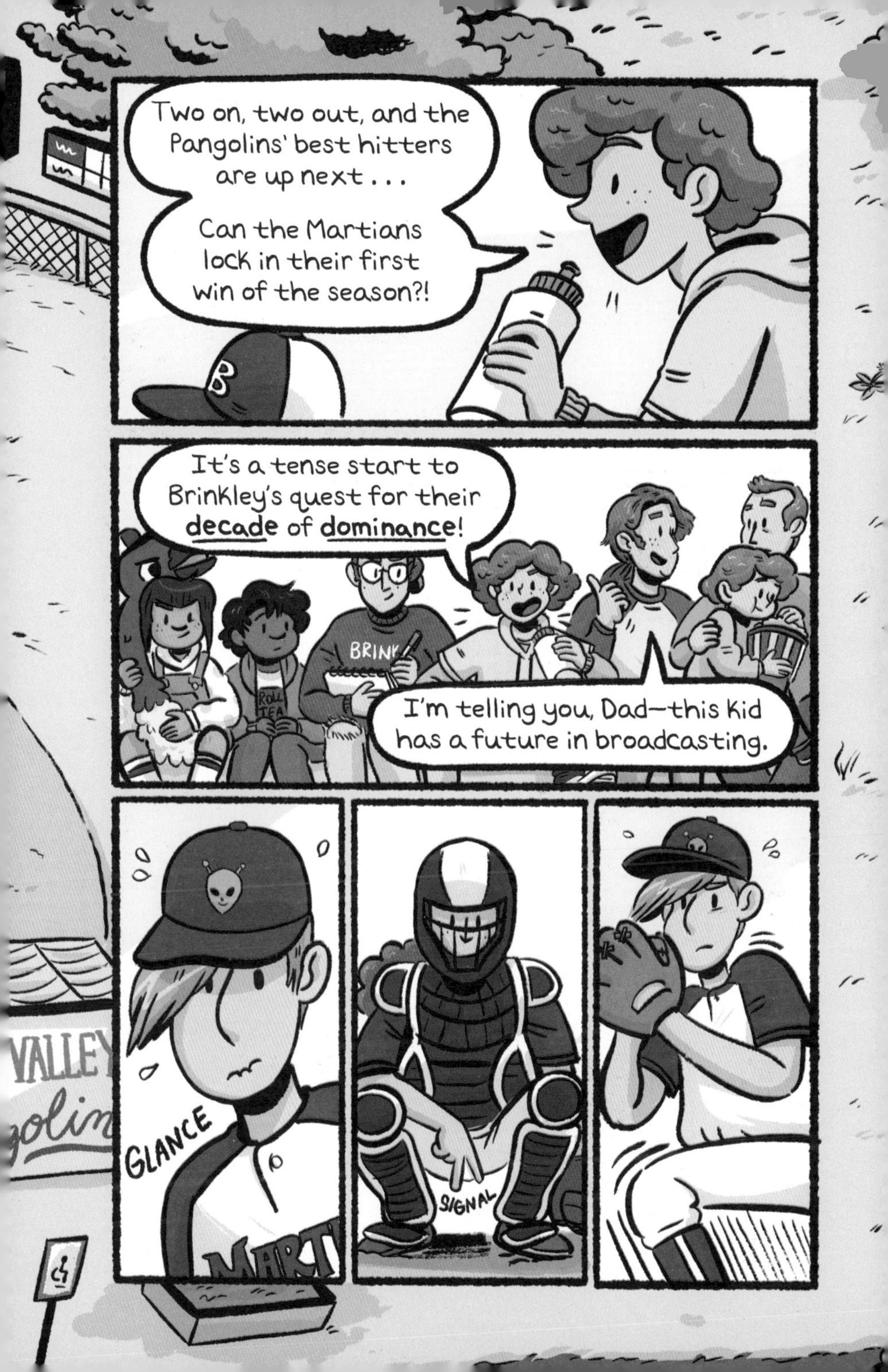
Two on, two out, and the Pangolins' best hitters are up next . . .
Can the Martians lock in their first win of the season?!
It's a tense start to Brinkley's quest for their **decade** of **dominance**!
BRINK
ROLL TEA
I'm telling you, Dad—this kid has a future in broadcasting.
VALLEY
golin
GLANCE
MART
SIGNAL

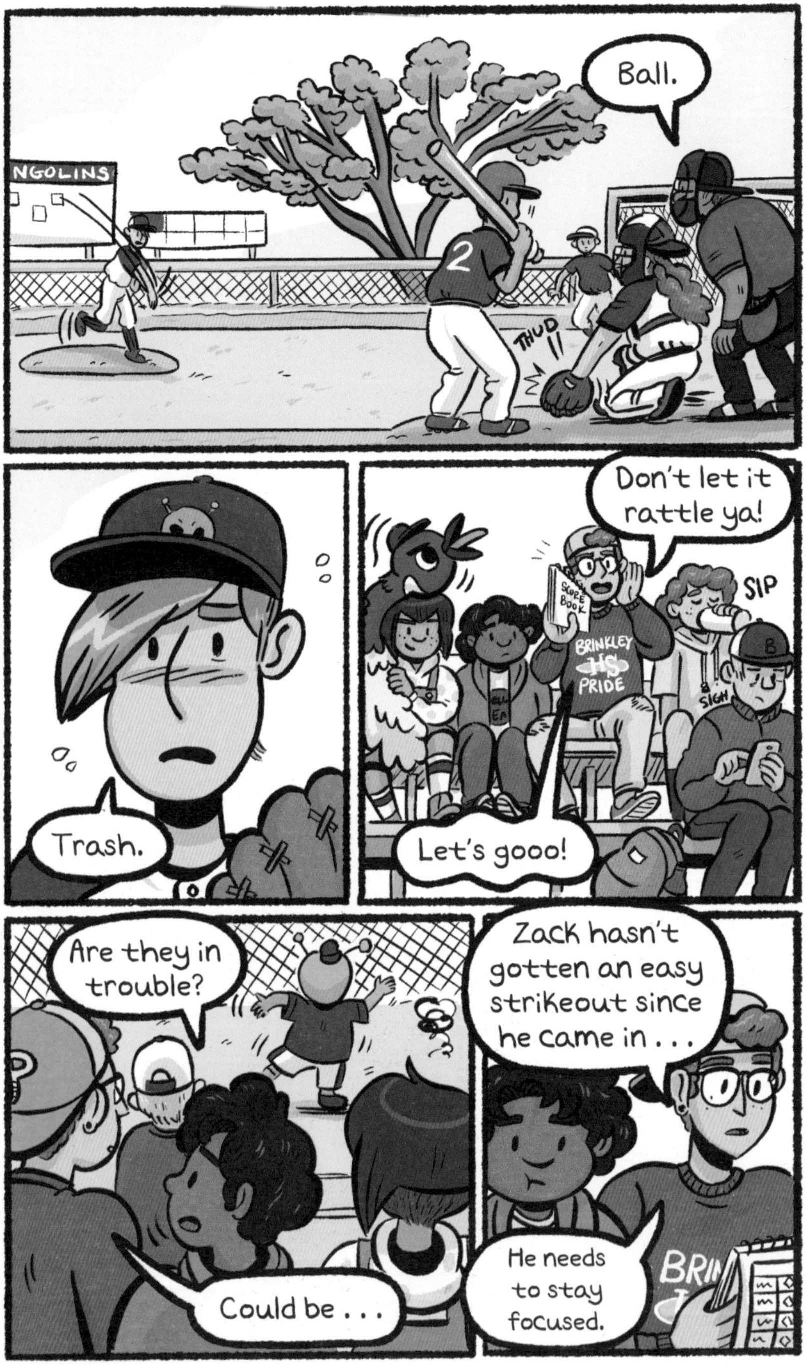
NGOLINS
Ball.
2
THUD
Trash.
Don't let it rattle ya!
SCORE BOOK
BRINKLEY HS PRIDE
SIP
B
SIGH
Let's gooo!
Are they in trouble?
Zack hasn't gotten an easy strikeout since he came in . . .
Could be . . .
He needs to stay focused.
BRIN

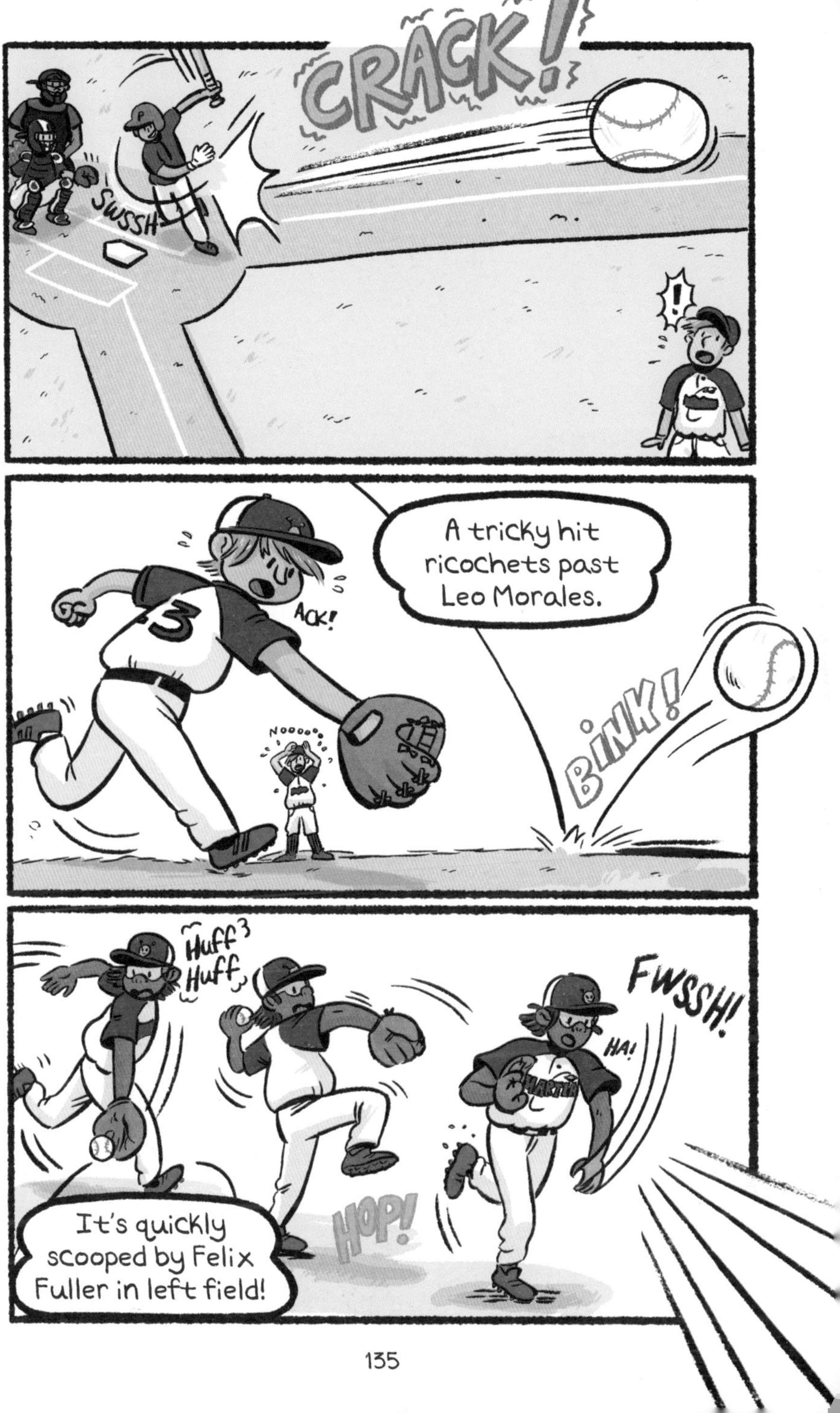
CRACK!
SWSSH
!
A tricky hit ricochets past Leo Morales.
ACK!
Nooooo
BINK!
Huff Huff
FWSSH!
HA!
HOP!
It's quickly scooped by Felix Fuller in left field!

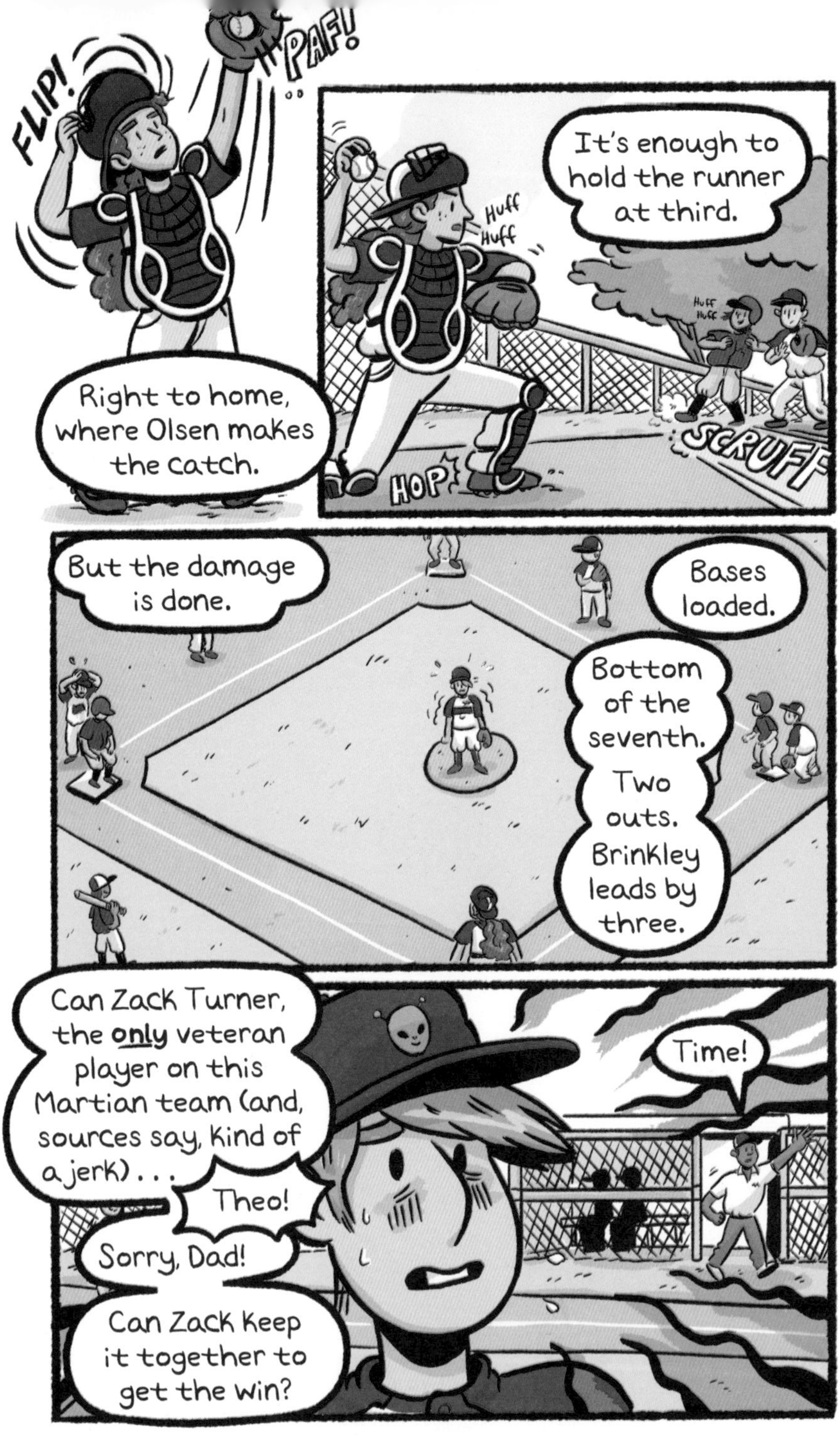
FLIP!
PAF!
Right to home, where Olsen makes the catch.
It's enough to hold the runner at third.
Huff Huff
Huff Huff
HOP
SCRUFF
But the damage is done.
Bases loaded.
Bottom of the seventh.
Two outs.
Brinkley leads by three.
Can Zack Turner, the **only** veteran player on this Martian team (and, sources say, kind of a jerk) . . .
Theo!
Sorry, Dad!
Can Zack keep it together to get the win?
Time!

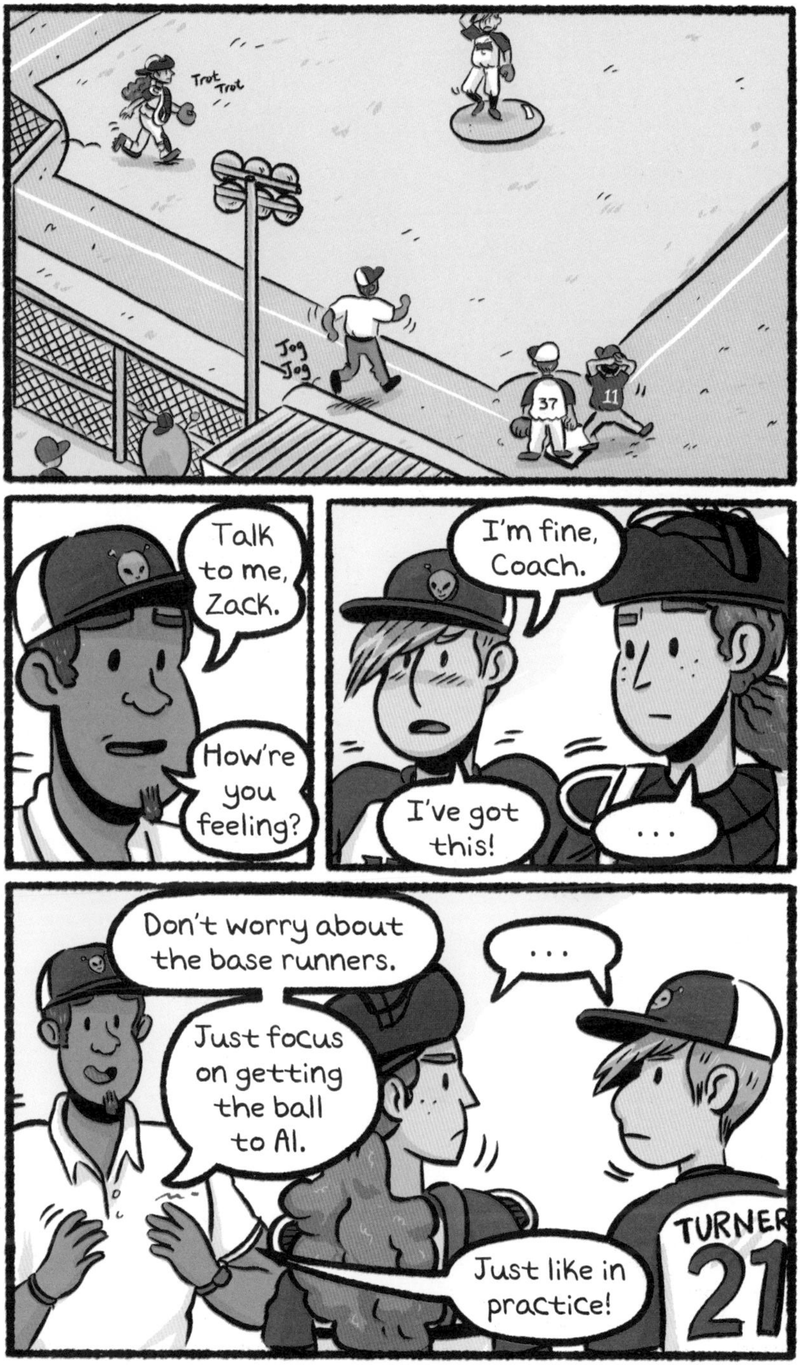
Trot Trot
Jog Jog
37
11
Talk to me, Zack.
How're you feeling?
I'm fine, Coach.
I've got this!
...
Don't worry about the base runners.
Just focus on getting the ball to Al.
...
Just like in practice!
TURNER 21

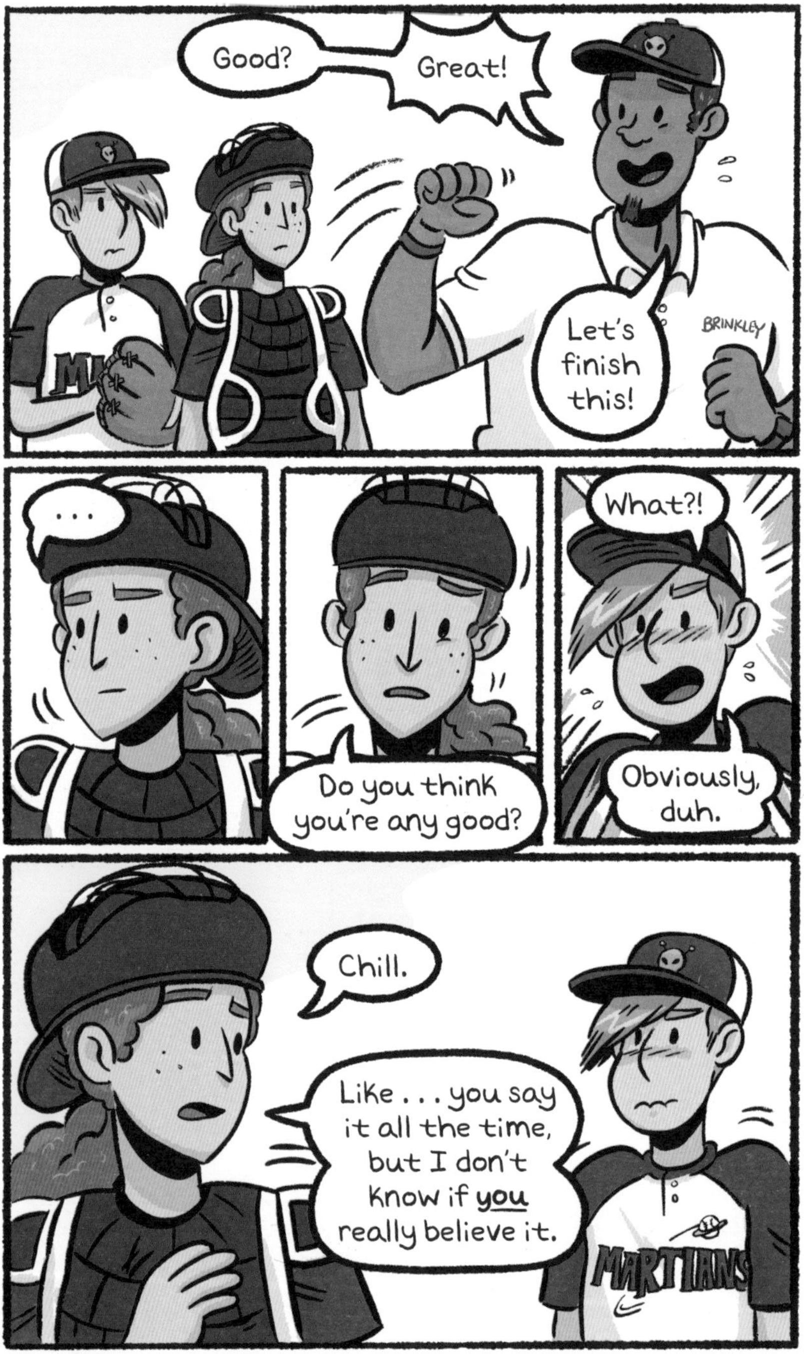
Good?
Great!
Let's finish this!
BRINKLEY
...
Do you think you're any good?
What?!
Obviously, duh.
Chill.
Like . . . you say it all the time, but I don't know if **you** really believe it.
MARTIANS

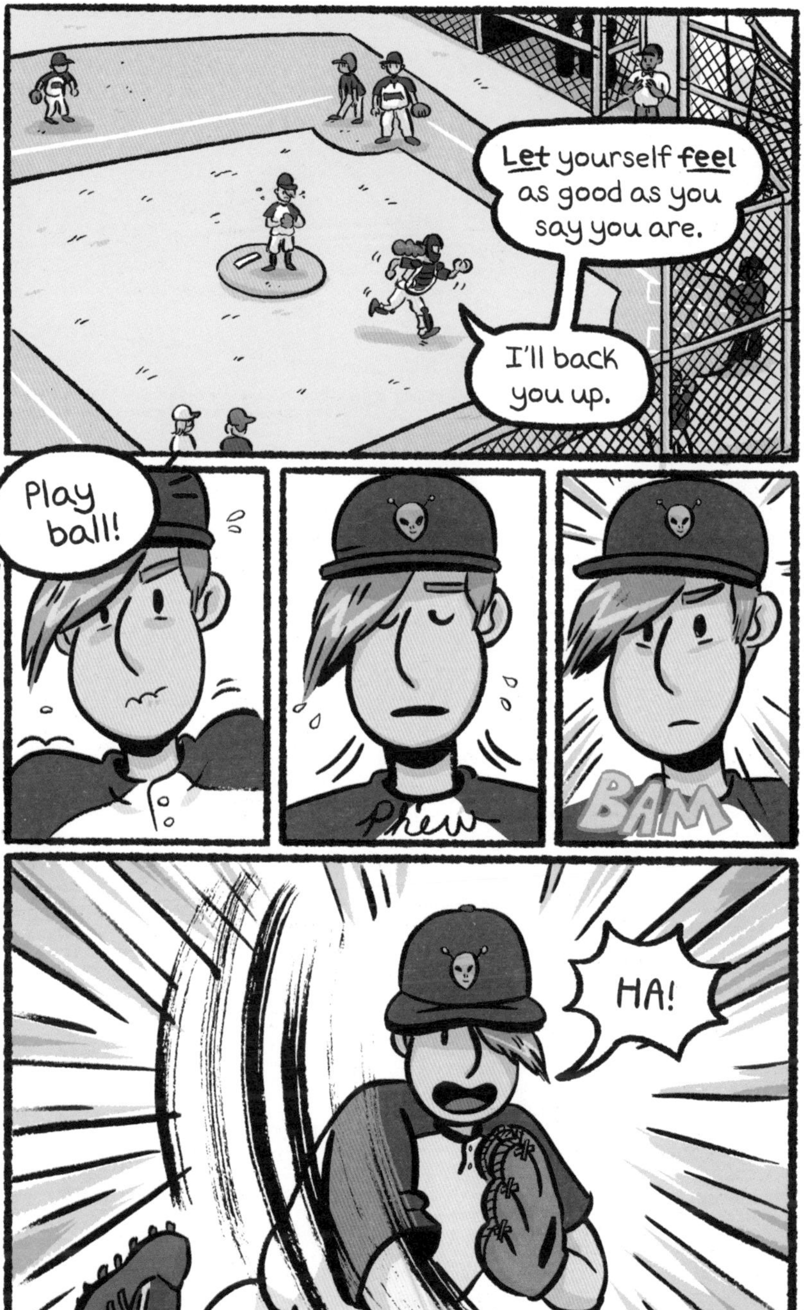
Let yourself feel as good as you say you are.
I'll back you up.
Play ball!
Phew
BAM
HA!

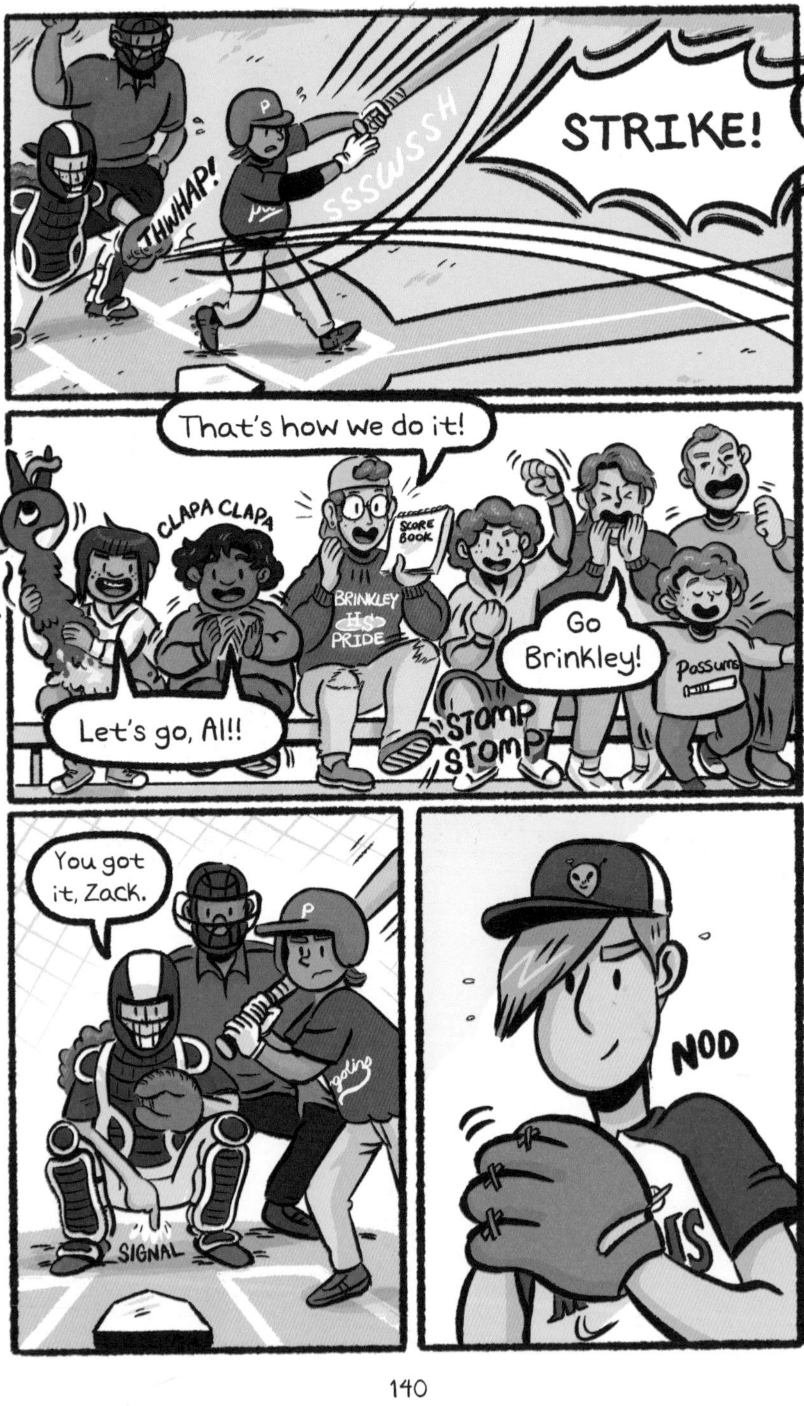
THWHAP!
SSSWSSH
STRIKE!
That's how we do it!
wiggle
wiggle
CLAPA CLAPA
SCORE BOOK
BRINKLEY HS PRIDE
Go Brinkley!
Possums
Let's go, Al!!
STOMP
STOMP
You got it, Zack.
SIGNAL
NOD

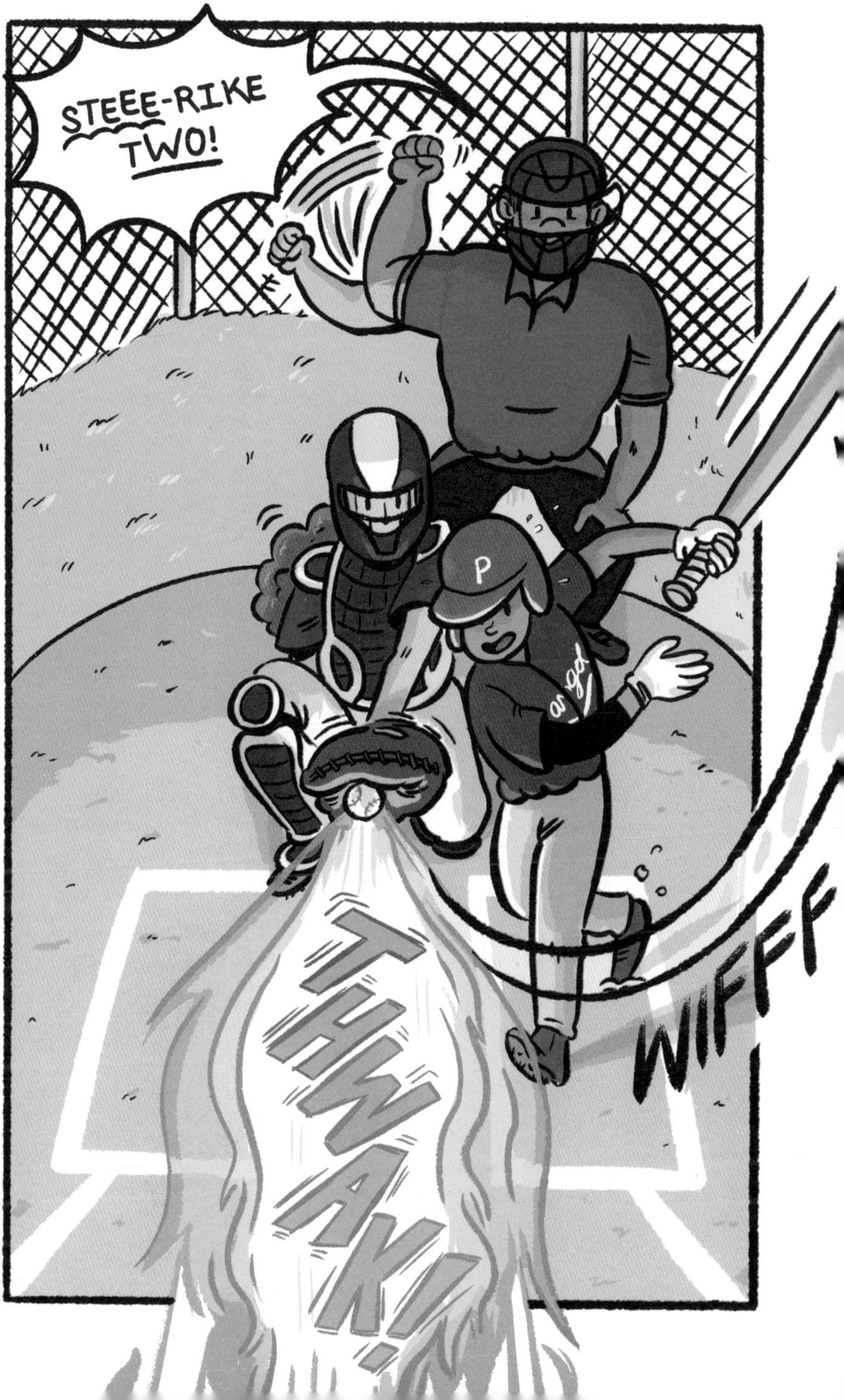
STEEE-RIKE TWO!
WIFFF
THWAK!!

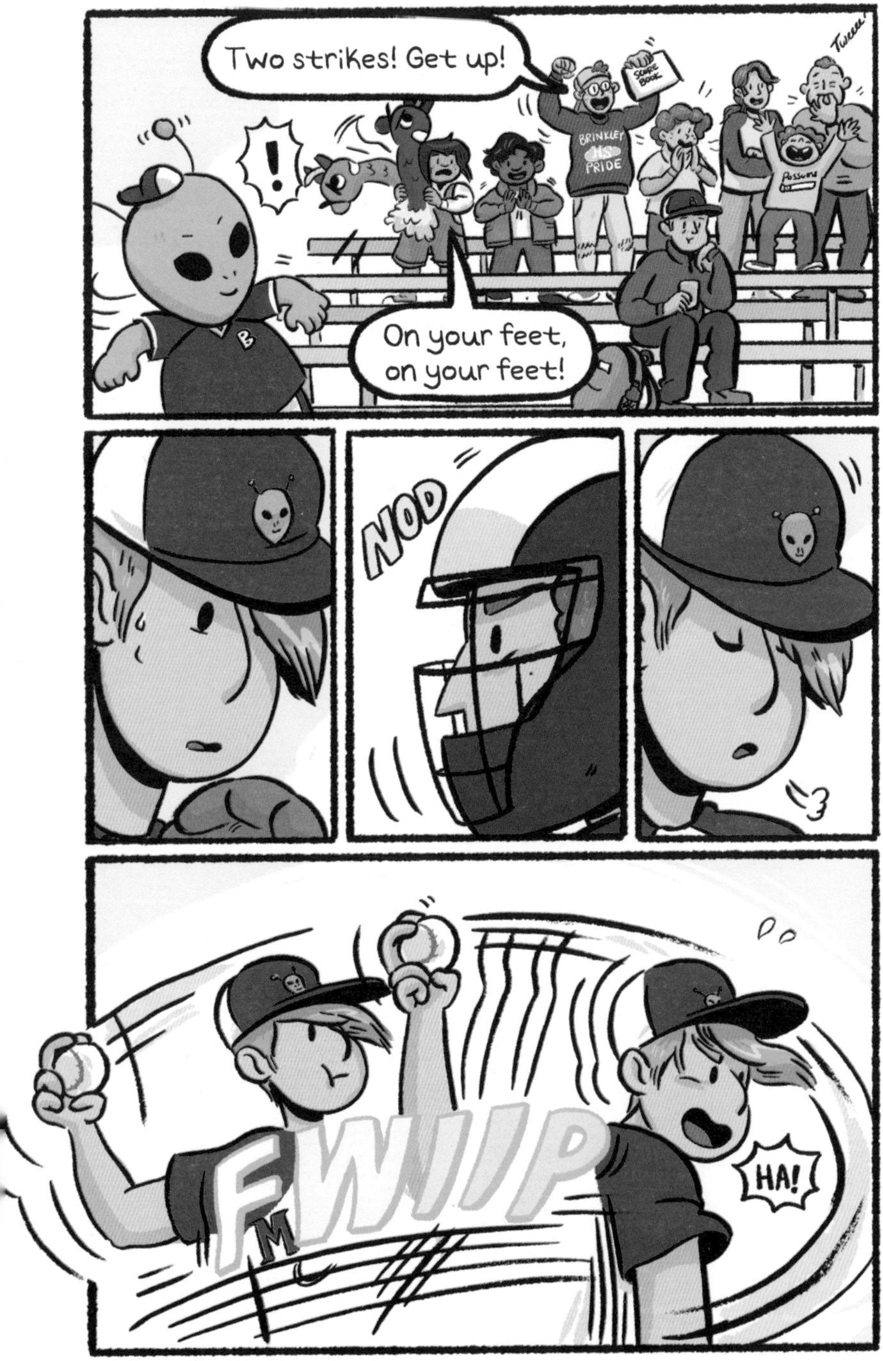
Two strikes! Get up!
!
SCORE BOOK
BRINKLEY HS PRIDE
On your feet, on your feet!
NOD
FWIIP
HA!

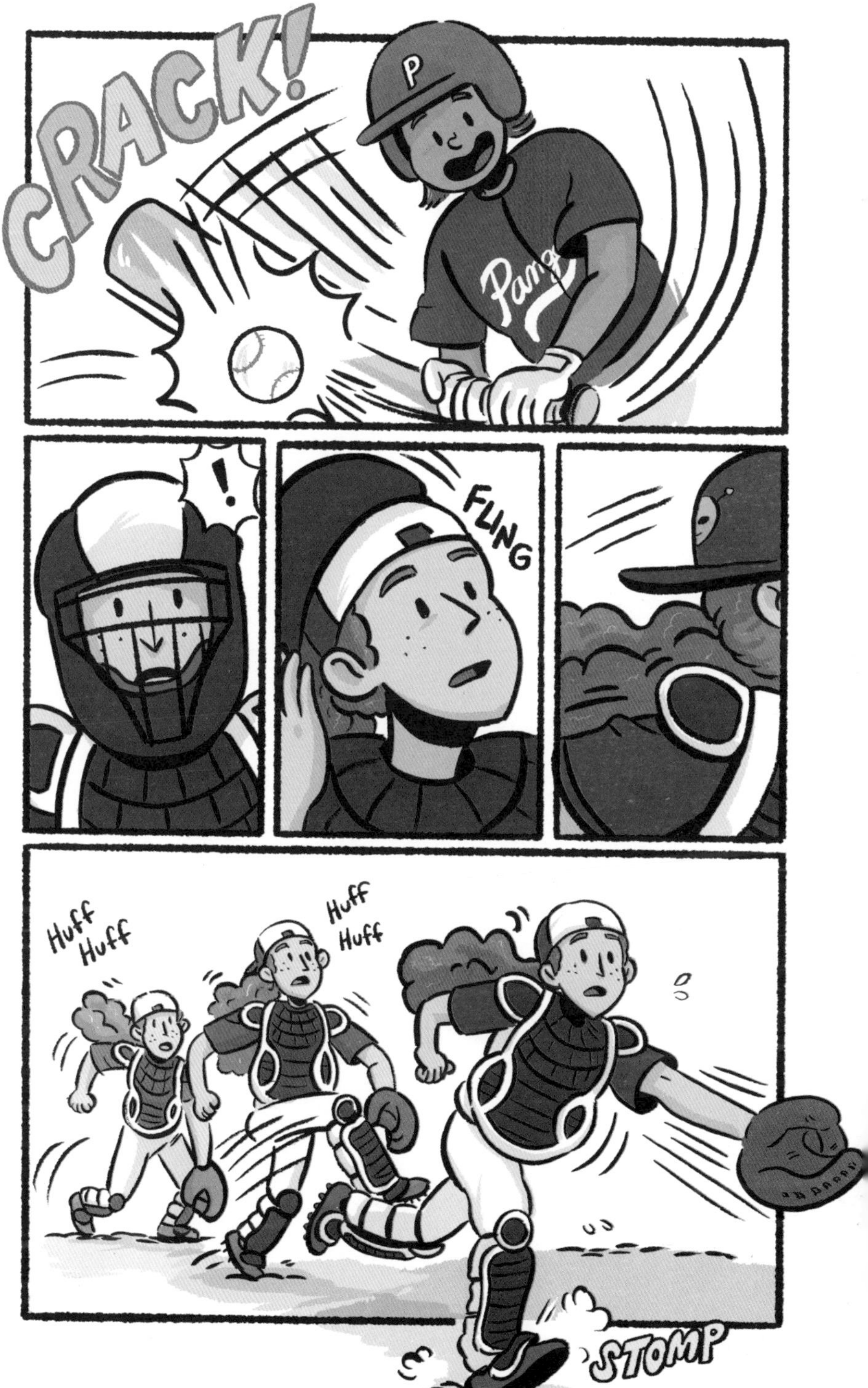
CRACK!
!
FLING
Huff
Huff
Huff
Huff
STOMP

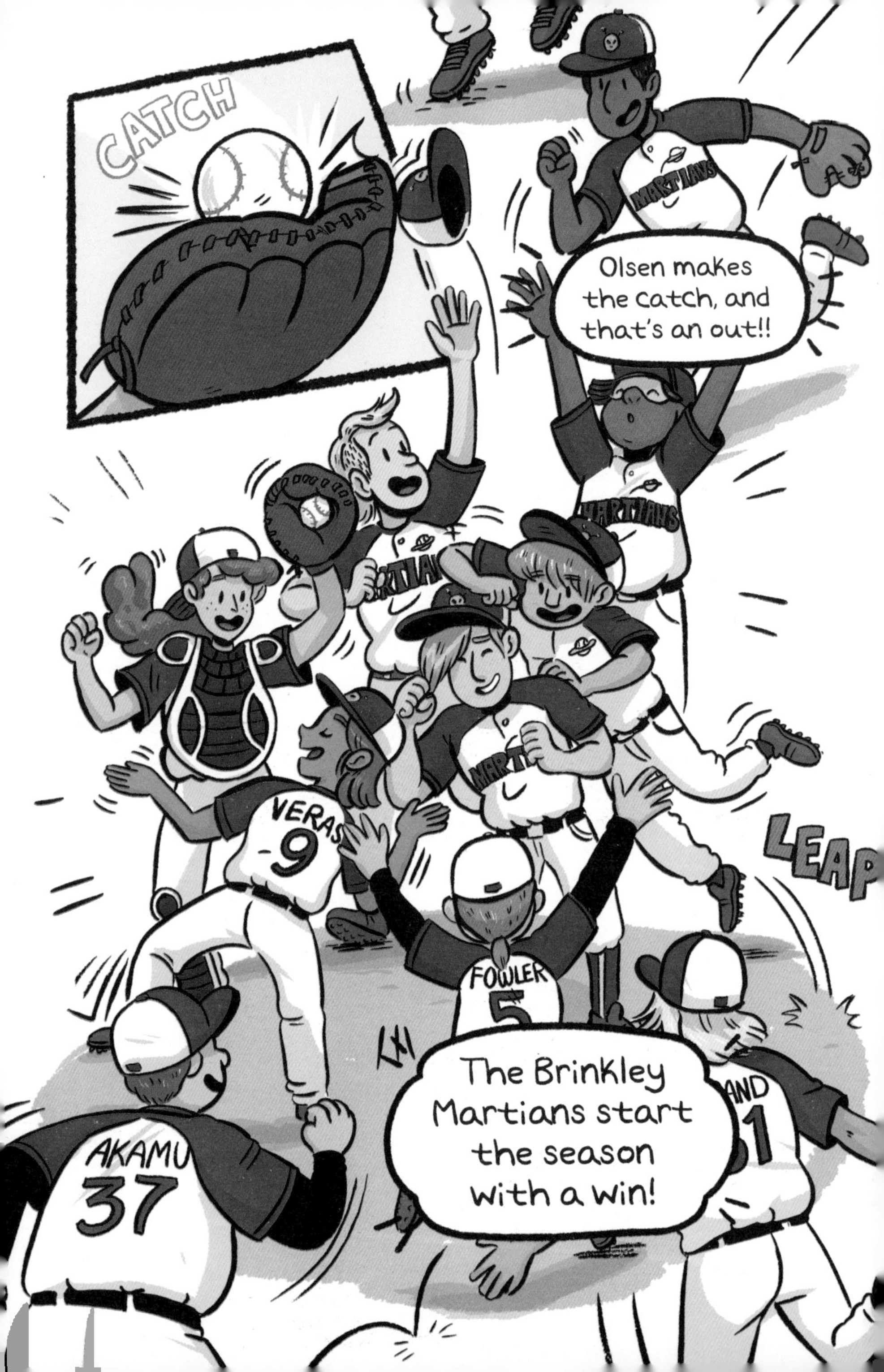
CATCH
Olsen makes the catch, and that's an out!!
MARTIANS
VERAS 9
LEAP
FOWLER 5
AKAMU 37
The Brinkley Martians start the season with a win!

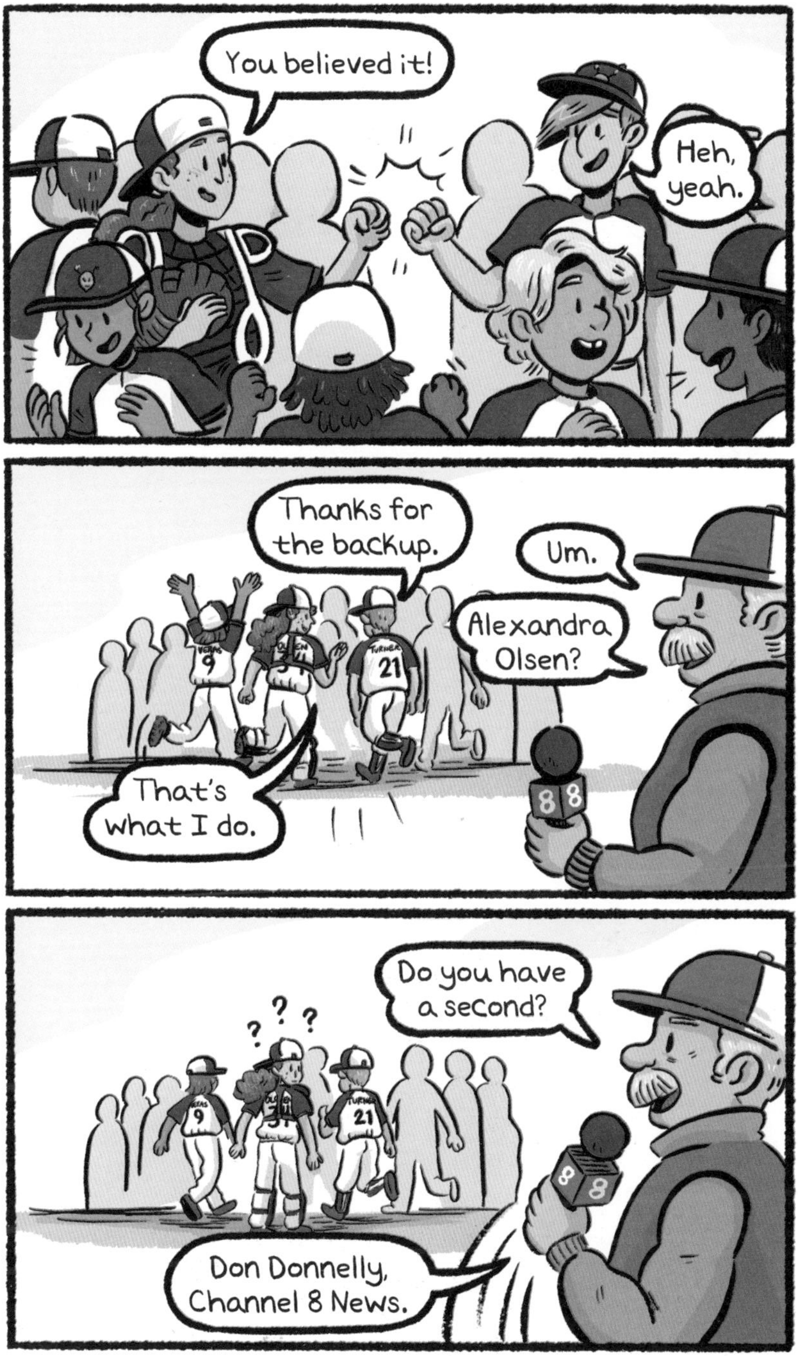
You believed it!
Heh, yeah.
Thanks for the backup.
Um.
Alexandra Olsen?
That's what I do.
Do you have a second?
Don Donnelly, Channel 8 News.

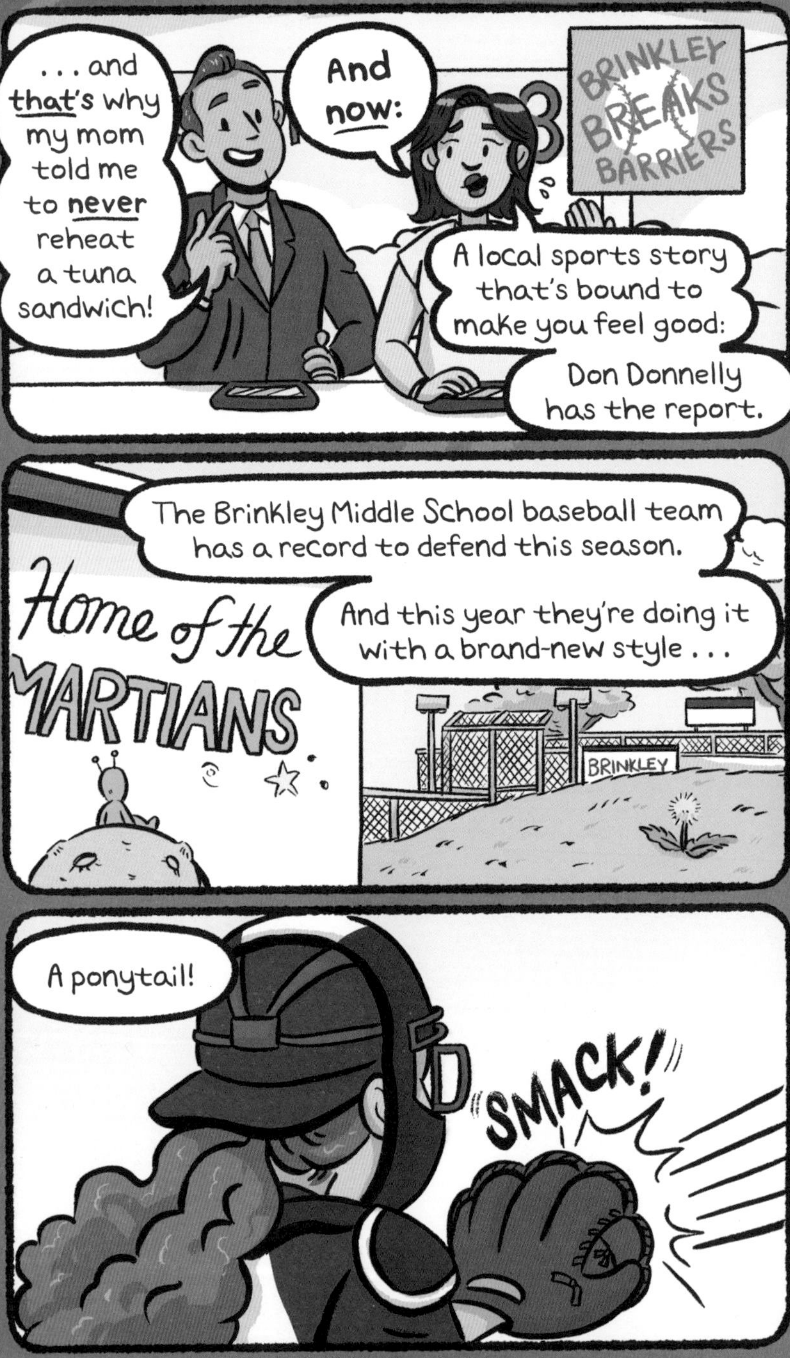

. . . and that's why my mom told me to never reheat a tuna sandwich!
And now:
BRINKLEY BREAKS BARRIERS
A local sports story that's bound to make you feel good:
Don Donnelly has the report.
The Brinkley Middle School baseball team has a record to defend this season.
Home of the MARTIANS
And this year they're doing it with a brand-new style . . .
BRINKLEY
A ponytail!
SMACK!

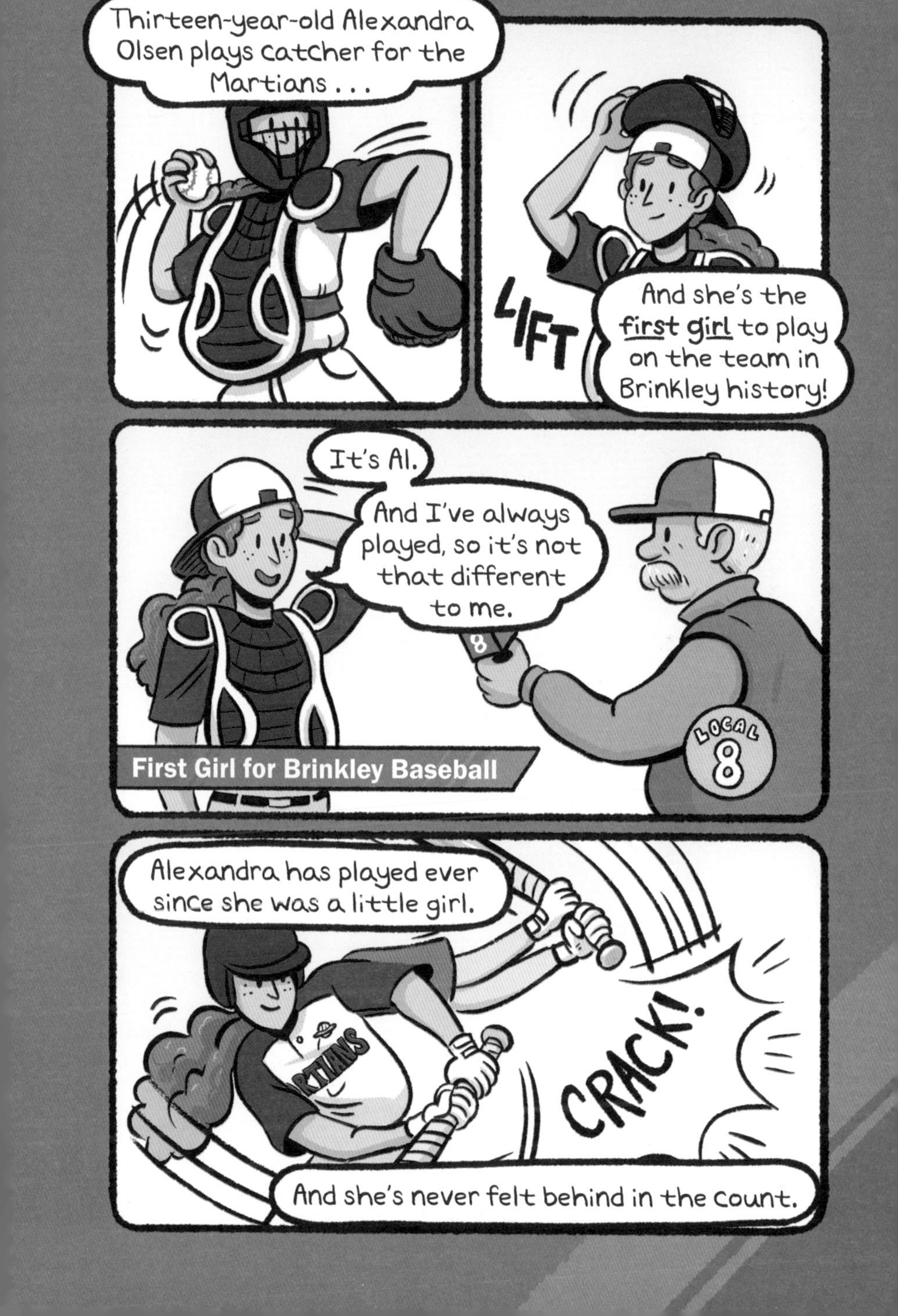

Thirteen-year-old Alexandra Olsen plays catcher for the Martians . . .
LIFT
And she's the first girl to play on the team in Brinkley history!
It's Al.
And I've always played, so it's not that different to me.
First Girl for Brinkley Baseball
LOCAL 8
Alexandra has played ever since she was a little girl.
CRACK!
And she's never felt behind in the count.

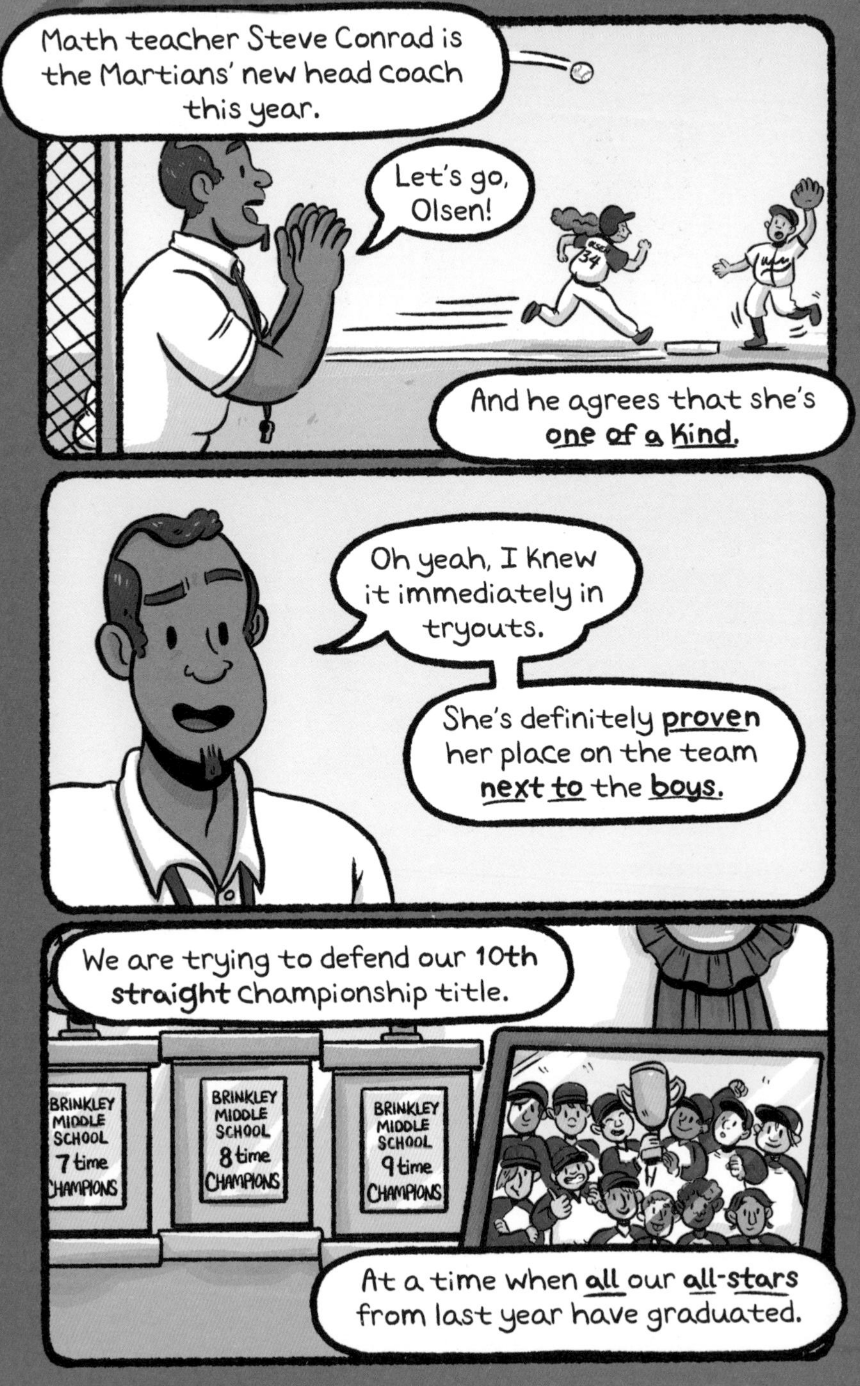
Math teacher Steve Conrad is the Martians' new head coach this year.
Let's go, Olsen!
And he agrees that she's one of a Kind.
Oh yeah, I Knew it immediately in tryouts.
She's definitely proven her place on the team next to the boys.
We are trying to defend our 10th straight championship title.
BRINKLEY MIDDLE SCHOOL 7 time CHAMPIONS
BRINKLEY MIDDLE SCHOOL 8 time CHAMPIONS
BRINKLEY MIDDLE SCHOOL 9 time CHAMPIONS
At a time when all our all-stars from last year have graduated.

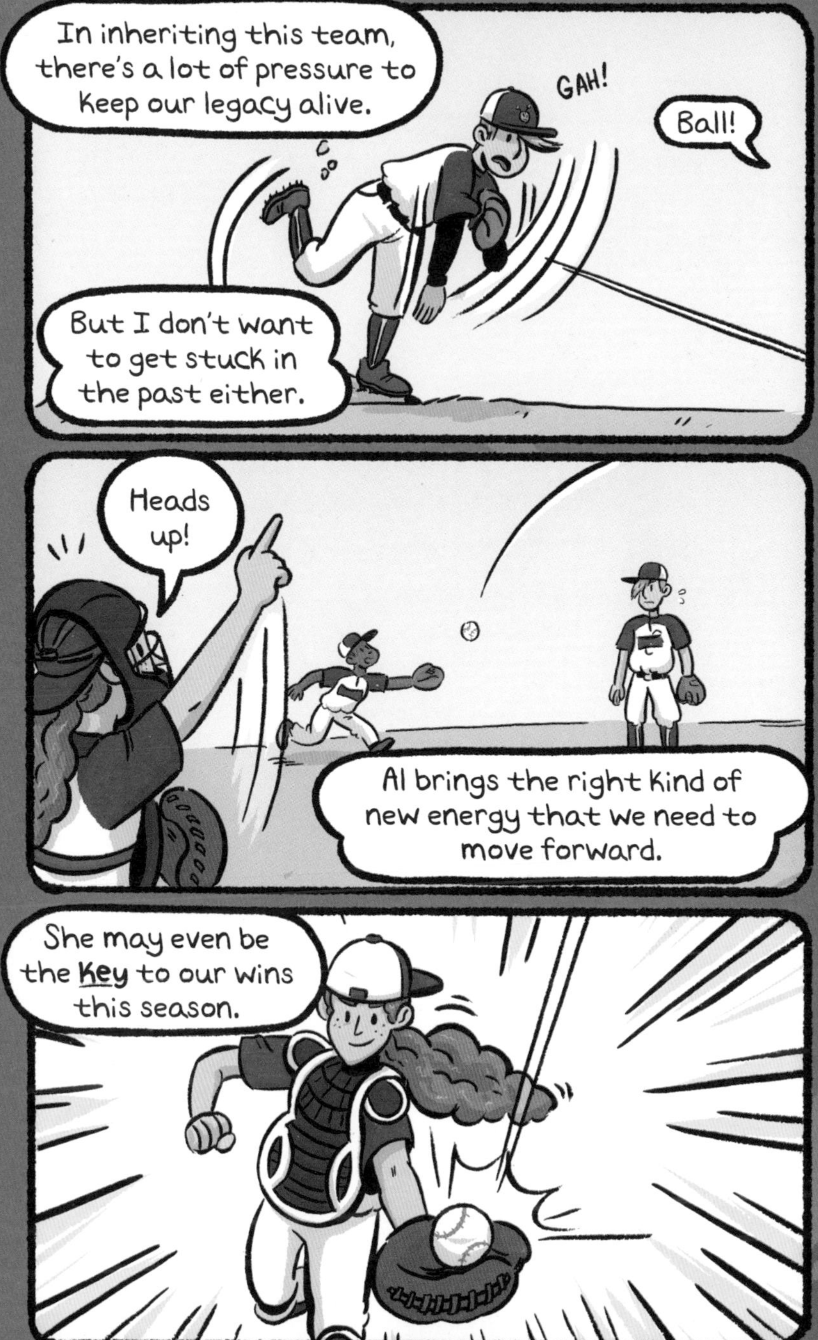
In inheriting this team, there's a lot of pressure to keep our legacy alive.
GAH!
Ball!
But I don't want to get stuck in the past either.
Heads up!
Al brings the right kind of new energy that we need to move forward.
She may even be the key to our wins this season.

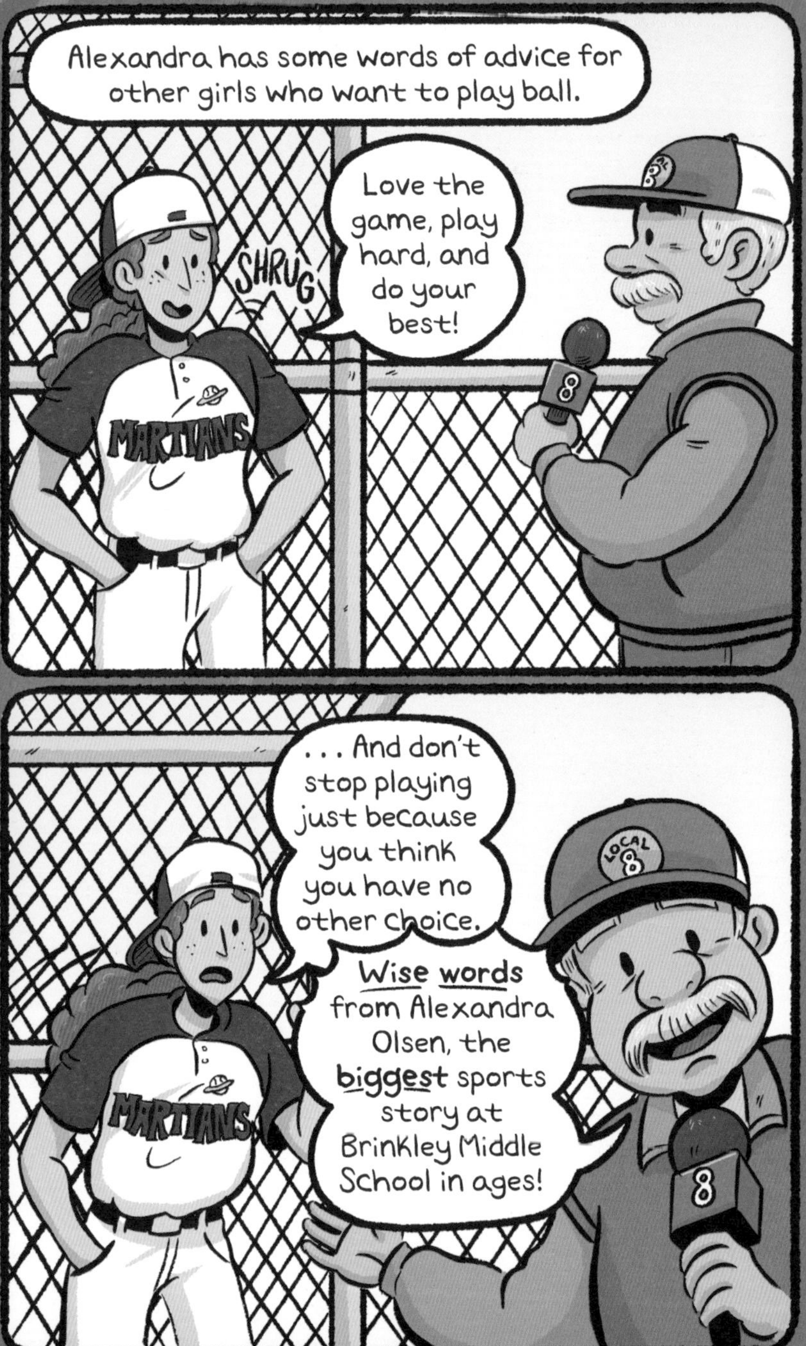
Alexandra has some words of advice for other girls who want to play ball.
Love the game, play hard, and do your best!
SHRUG
MARTIANS
. . . And don't stop playing just because you think you have no other choice.
LOCAL 8
Wise words from Alexandra Olsen, the biggest sports story at Brinkley Middle School in ages!

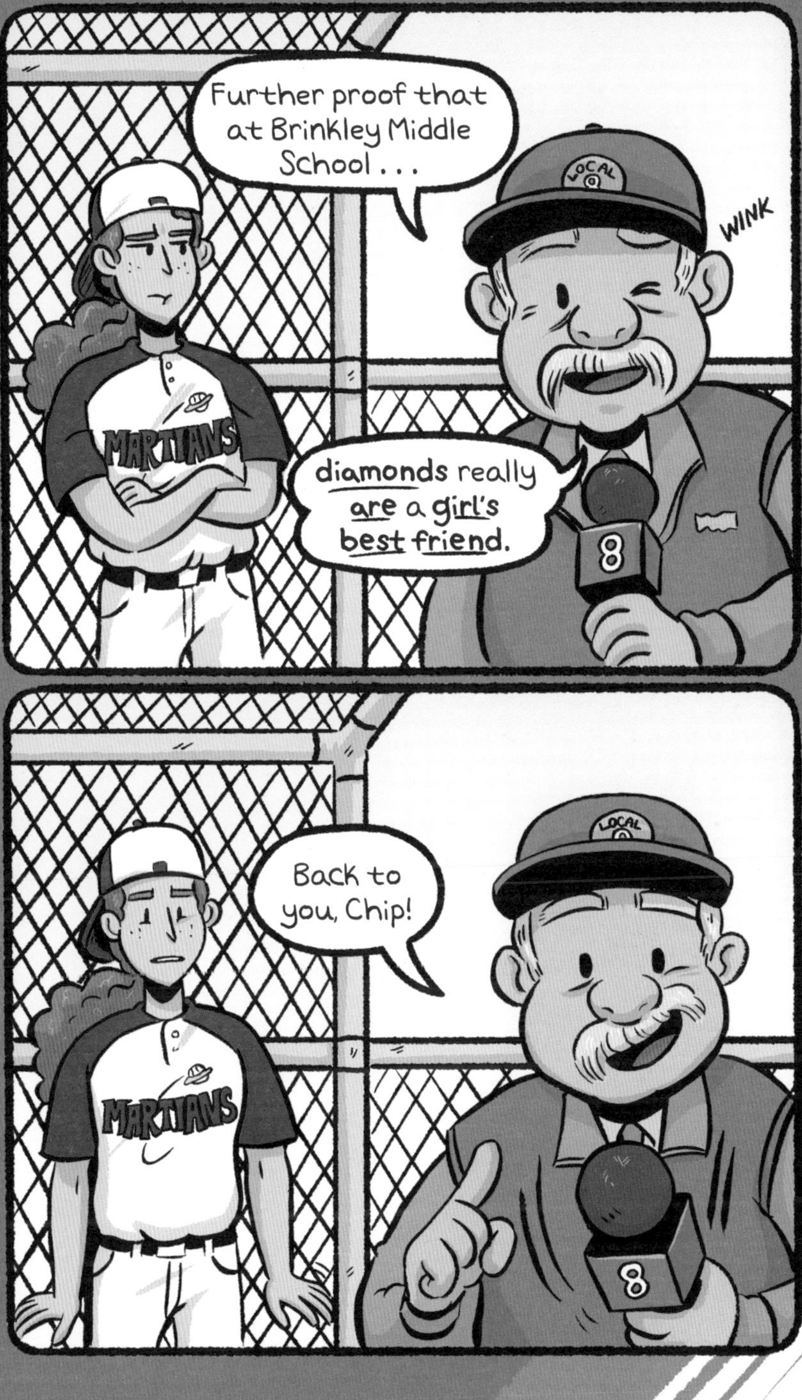
Further proof that at Brinkley Middle School . . .
WINK
LOCAL 8
MARTIANS
diamonds really are a girl's best friend.
8
LOCAL 8
Back to you, Chip!
MARTIANS
8

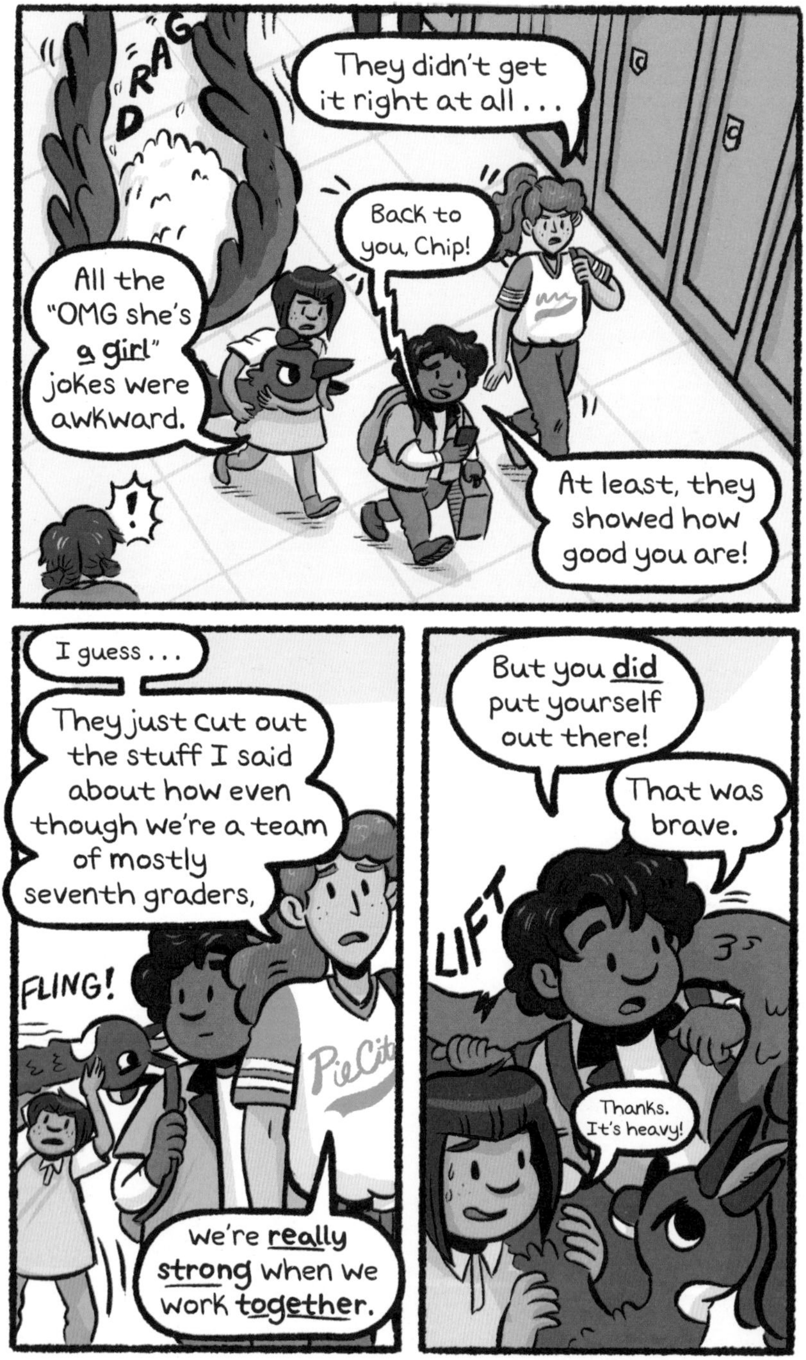
DRAG
They didn't get it right at all . . .
Back to you, Chip!
All the "OMG she's a girl" jokes were awkward.
!
At least, they showed how good you are!
I guess . . .
They just cut out the stuff I said about how even though we're a team of mostly seventh graders,
FLING!
Pie City
We're really strong when we work together.
But you did put yourself out there!
That was brave.
LIFT
Thanks. It's heavy!

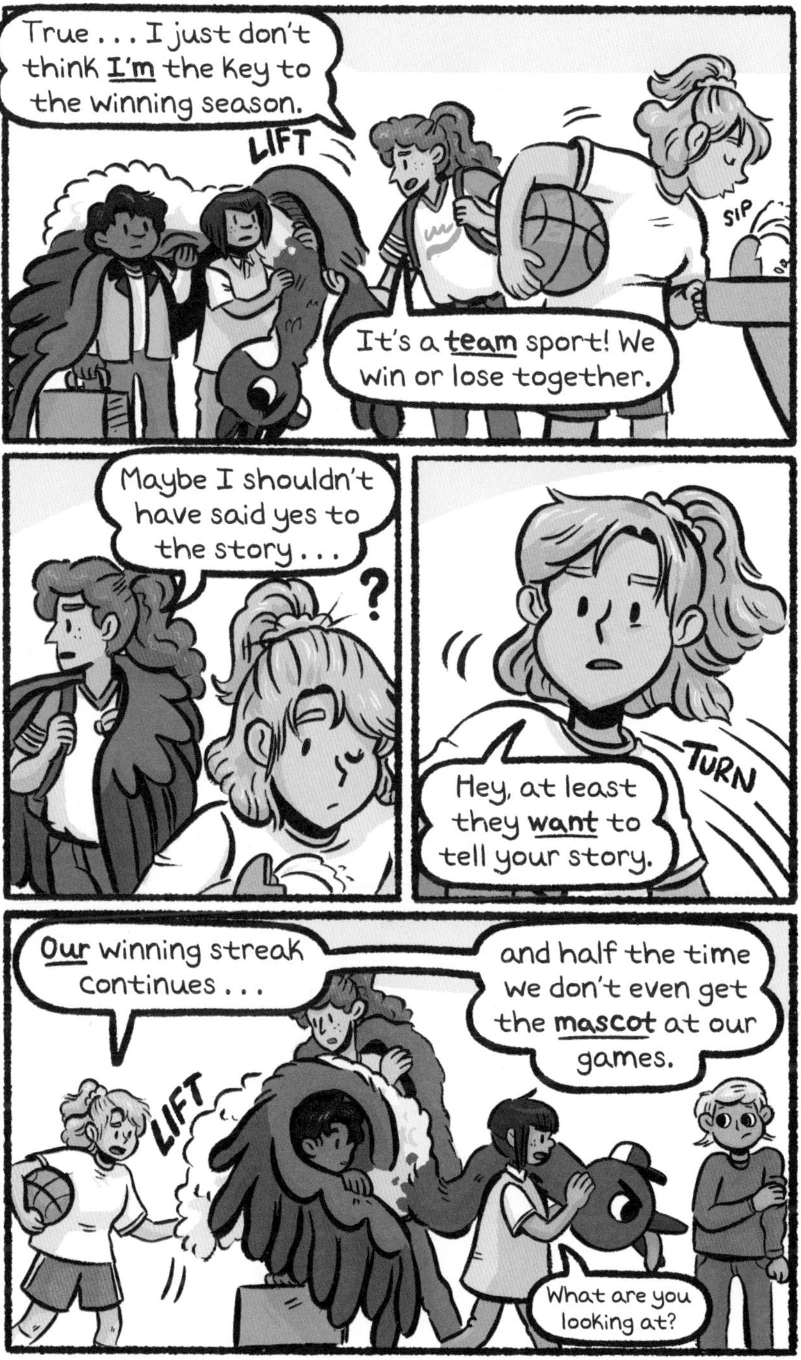
True . . . I just don't think I'm the key to the winning season.
LIFT
It's a team sport! We win or lose together.
SIP
Maybe I shouldn't have said yes to the story . . .
?
TURN
Hey, at least they want to tell your story.
Our winning streak continues . . .
and half the time we don't even get the mascot at our games.
LIFT
What are you looking at?

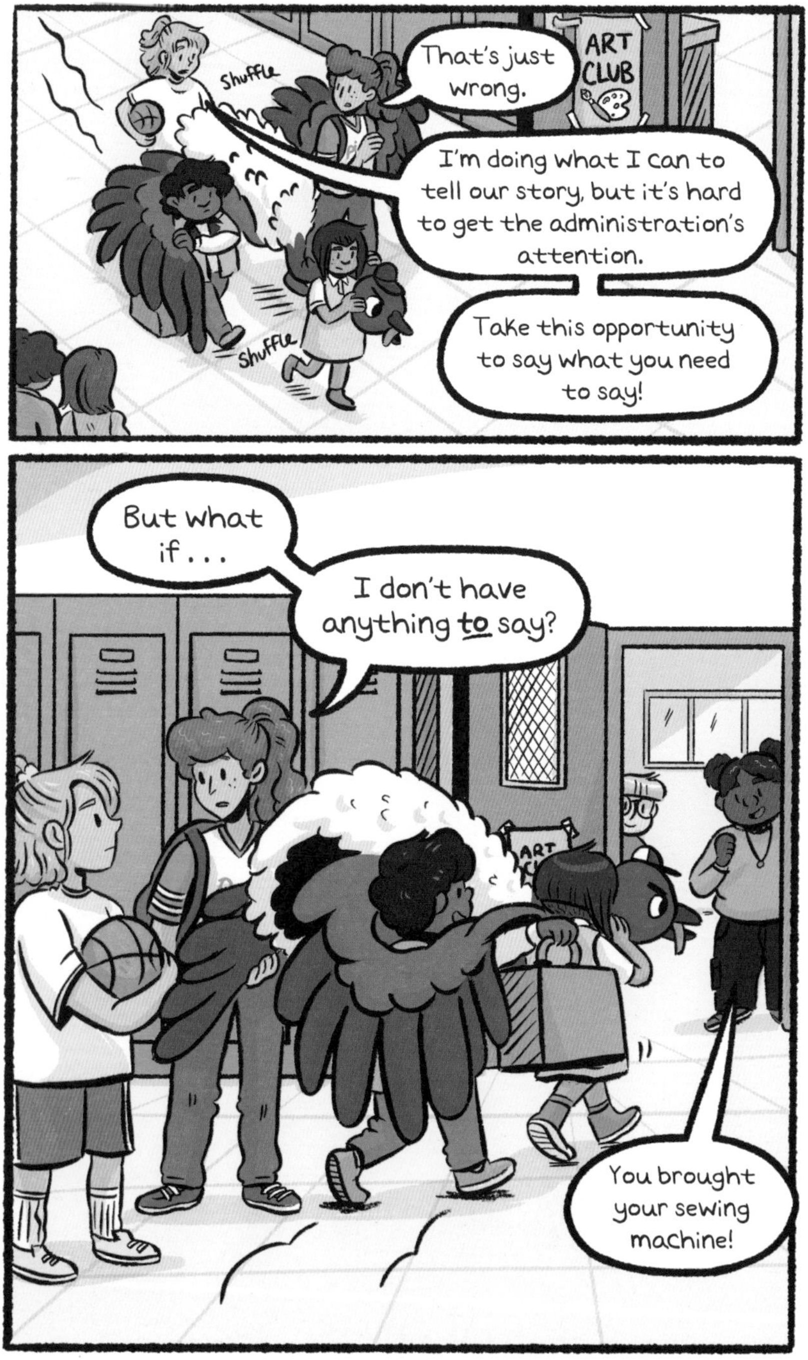
Shuffle
That's just wrong.
I'm doing what I can to tell our story, but it's hard to get the administration's attention.
Take this opportunity to say what you need to say!
Shuffle
ART CLUB
But what if . . .
I don't have anything **to** say?
You brought your sewing machine!

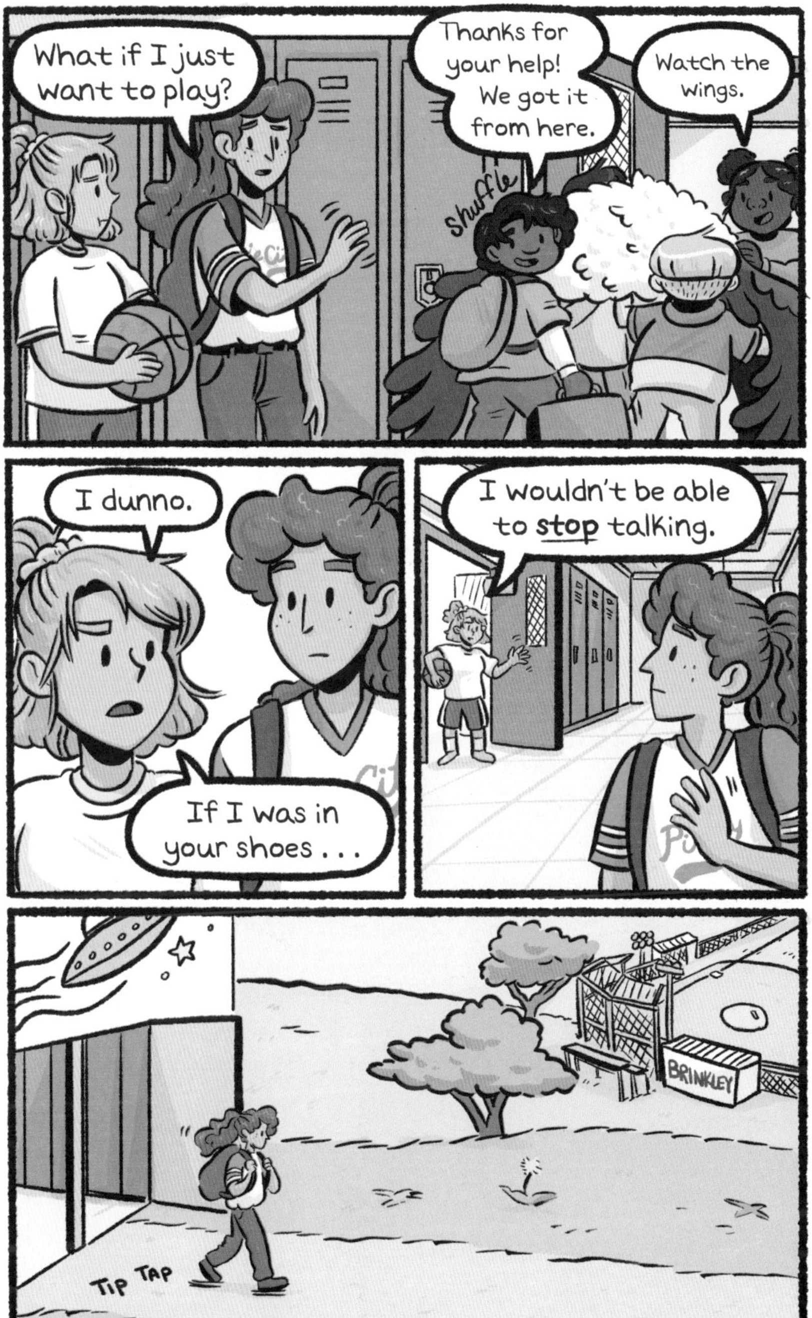
What if I just want to play?
Thanks for your help! We got it from here.
shuffle
Watch the wings.
I dunno.
If I was in your shoes . . .
I wouldn't be able to **stop** talking.
BRINKLEY
TIP TAP

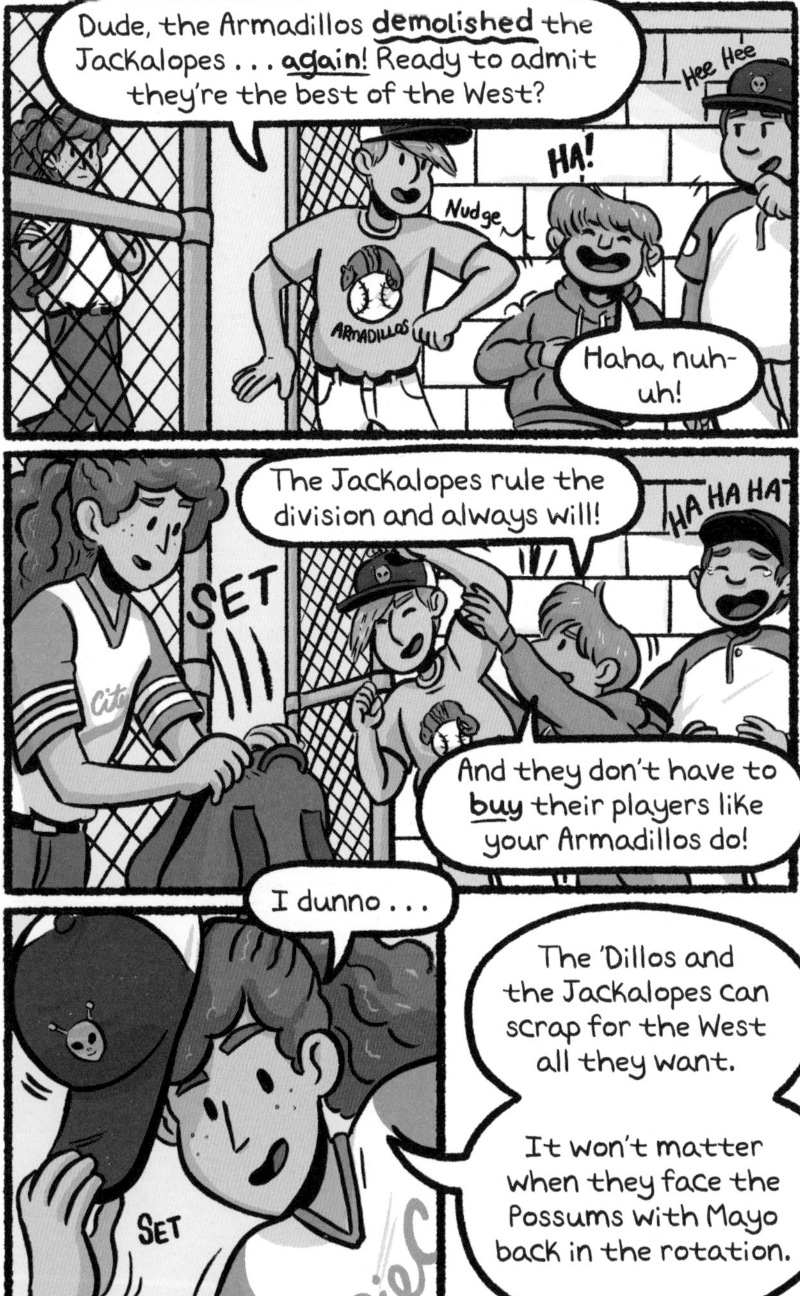
Dude, the Armadillos demolished the Jackalopes . . . again! Ready to admit they're the best of the West?
Hee Hee
HA!
Nudge
ARMADILLOS
Haha, nuh-uh!
The Jackalopes rule the division and always will!
HA HA HA
SET
And they don't have to buy their players like your Armadillos do!
I dunno . . .
The 'Dillos and the Jackalopes can scrap for the West all they want.
It won't matter when they face the Possums with Mayo back in the rotation.
SET

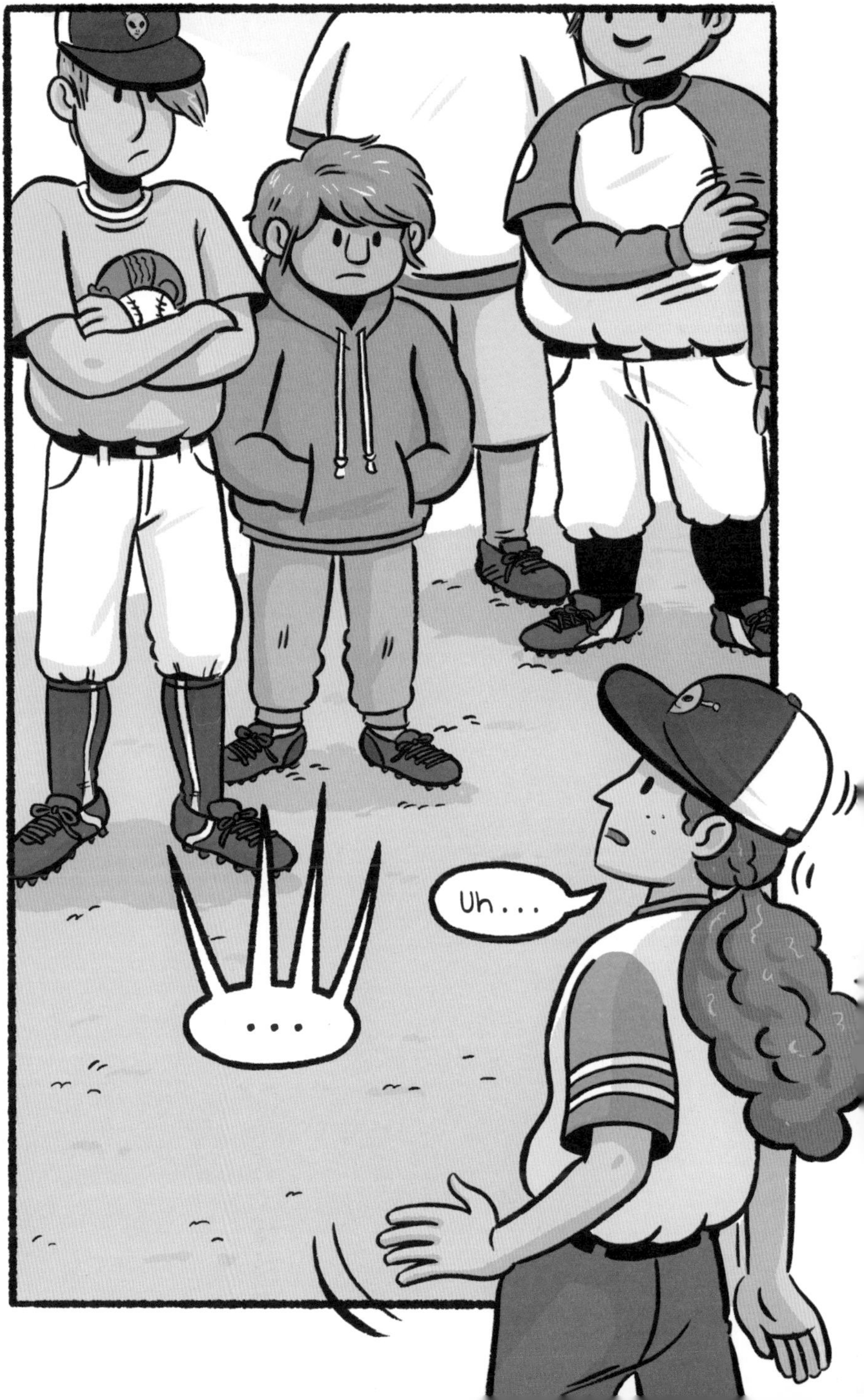
Uh...
...

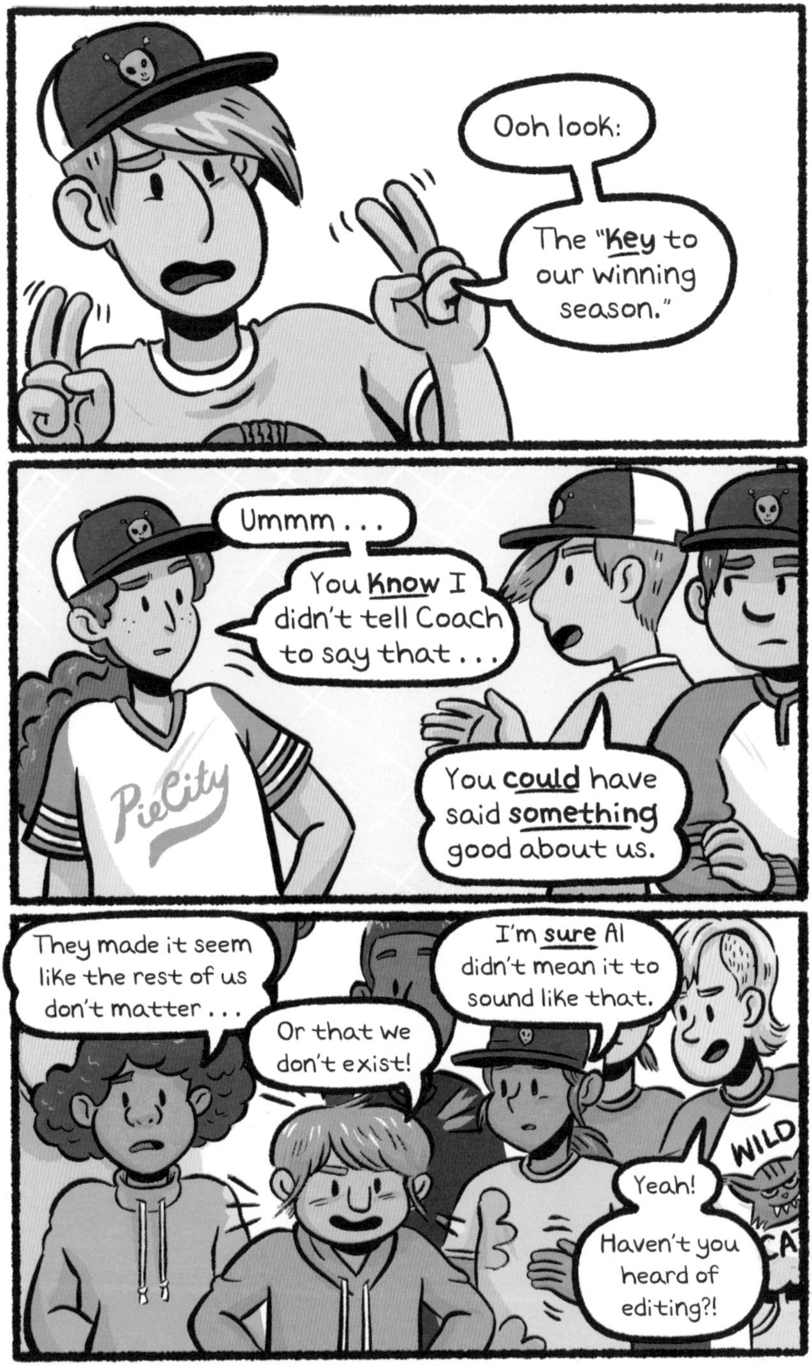
Ooh look:
The "Key to our winning season."
Ummm . . .
You Know I didn't tell Coach to say that . . .
You could have said something good about us.
They made it seem like the rest of us don't matter . . .
Or that we don't exist!
I'm sure Al didn't mean it to sound like that.
Yeah!
Haven't you heard of editing?!
WILD

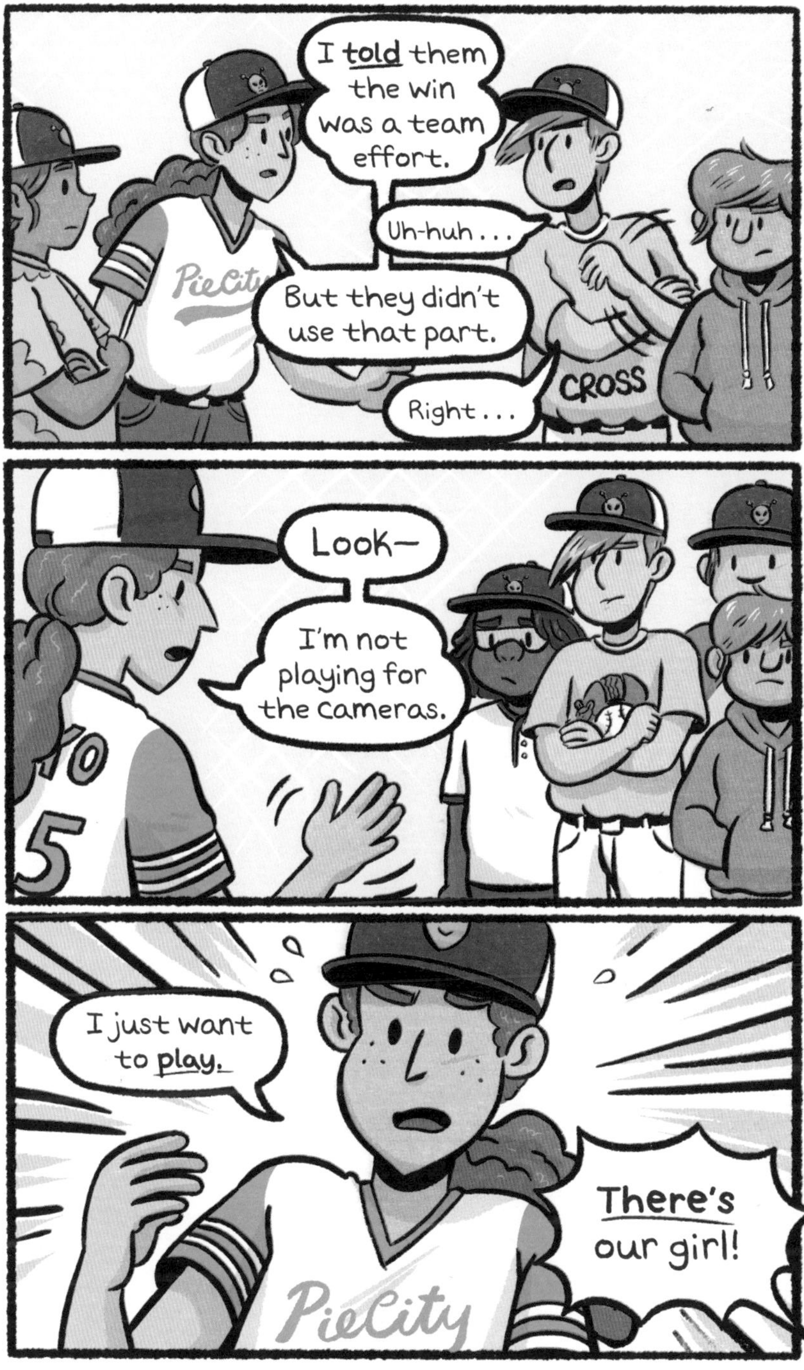
I told them the win was a team effort.
Uh-huh . . .
But they didn't use that part.
Right . . .
CROSS
Look—
I'm not playing for the cameras.
I just want to play.
There's our girl!
Pie City

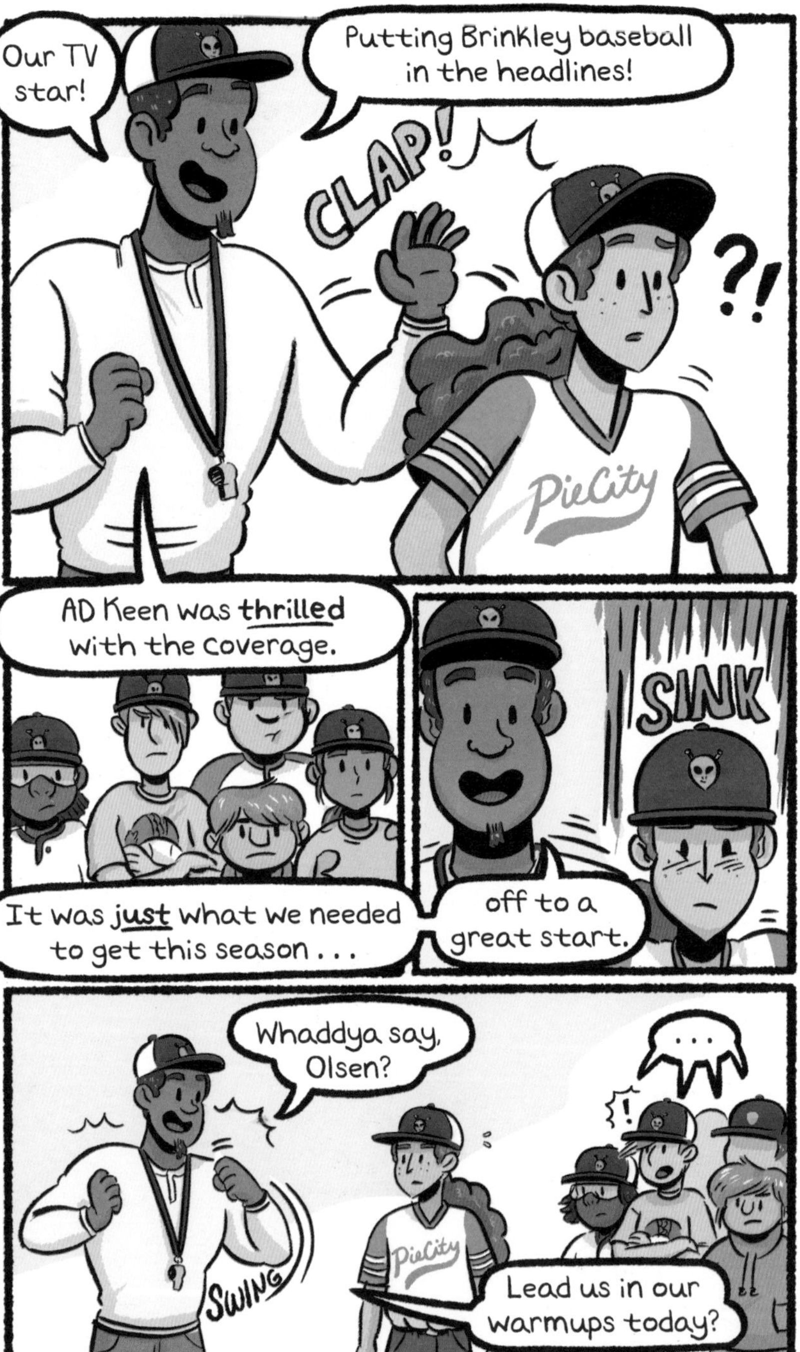
Our TV star!
Putting Brinkley baseball in the headlines!
CLAP!
?!
PieCity
AD Keen was thrilled with the coverage.
SINK
It was just what we needed to get this season . . .
off to a great start.
Whaddya say, Olsen?
. . .
!
PieCity
SWING
Lead us in our warmups today?

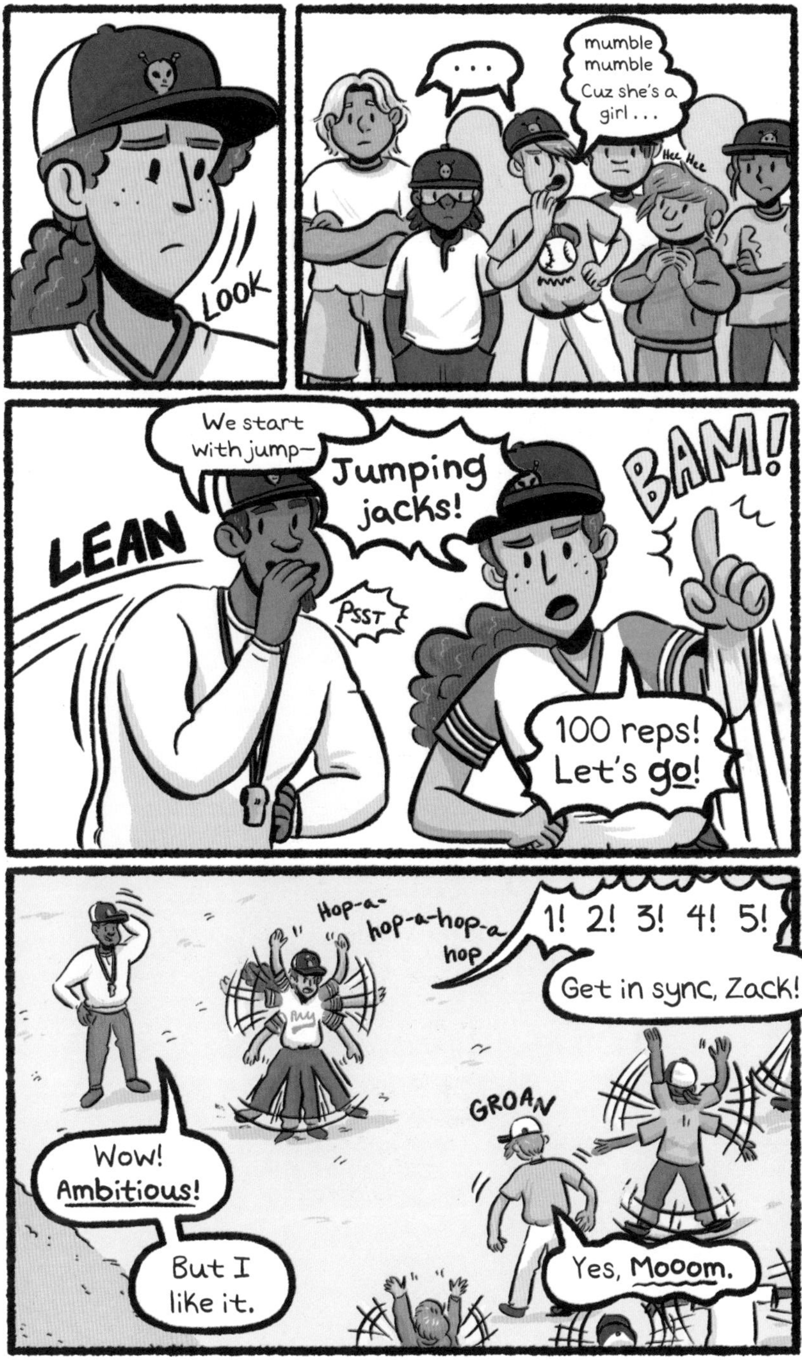
LOOK
. . .
mumble mumble
Cuz she's a girl . . .
Hee Hee
We start with jump—
Jumping jacks!
LEAN
PSST
BAM!
100 reps! Let's go!
Hop-a-hop-a-hop-a hop
1! 2! 3! 4! 5!
Get in sync, Zack!
GROAN
Wow! Ambitious!
But I like it.
Yes, Mooom.

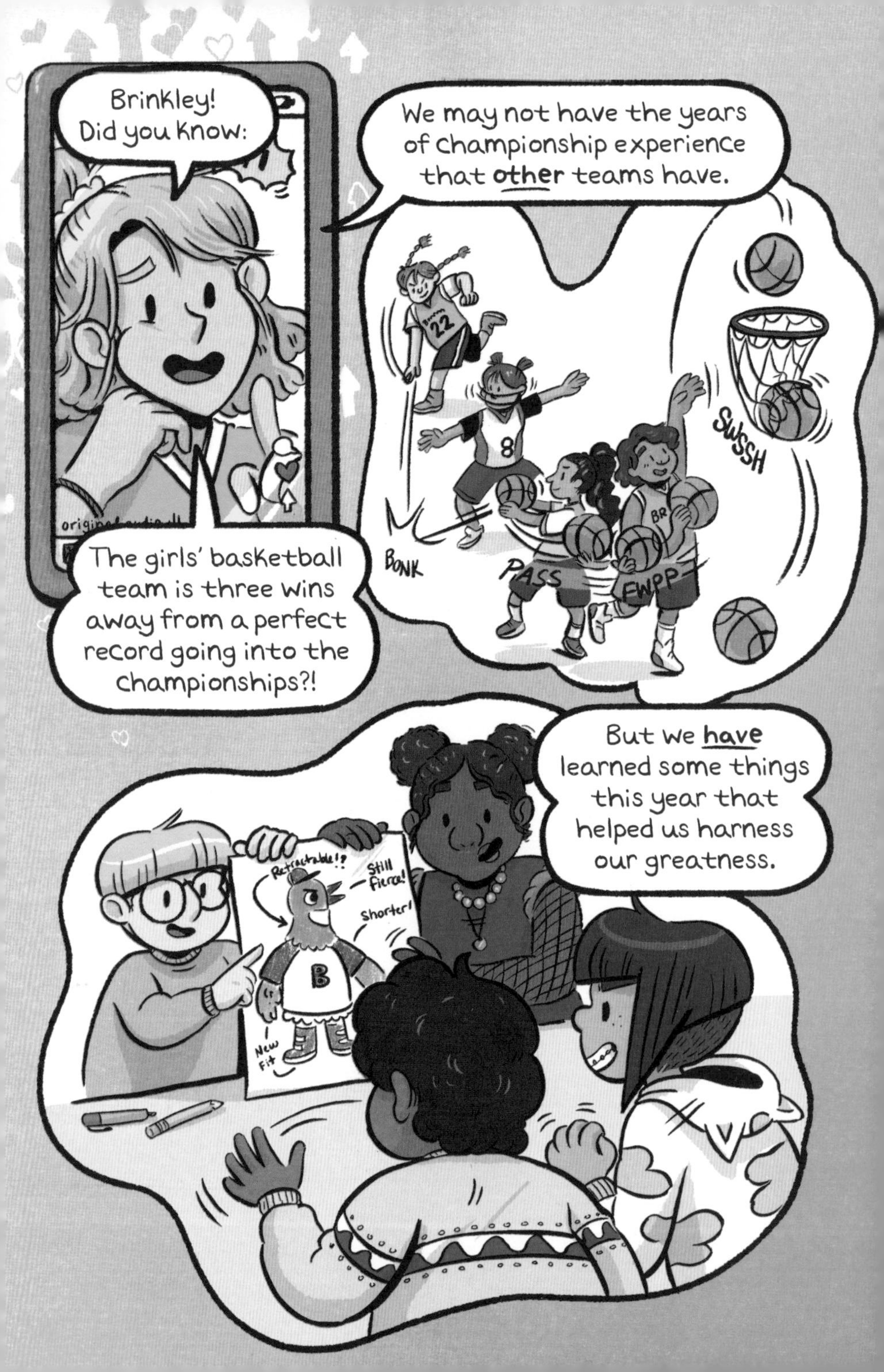
Brinkley! Did you know:
The girls' basketball team is three wins away from a perfect record going into the championships?!
We may not have the years of championship experience that **other** teams have.
BONK
PASS
FWPP
SWSSH
But we **have** learned some things this year that helped us harness our greatness.
Retractable!?
Still fierce!
Shorter!
New Fit

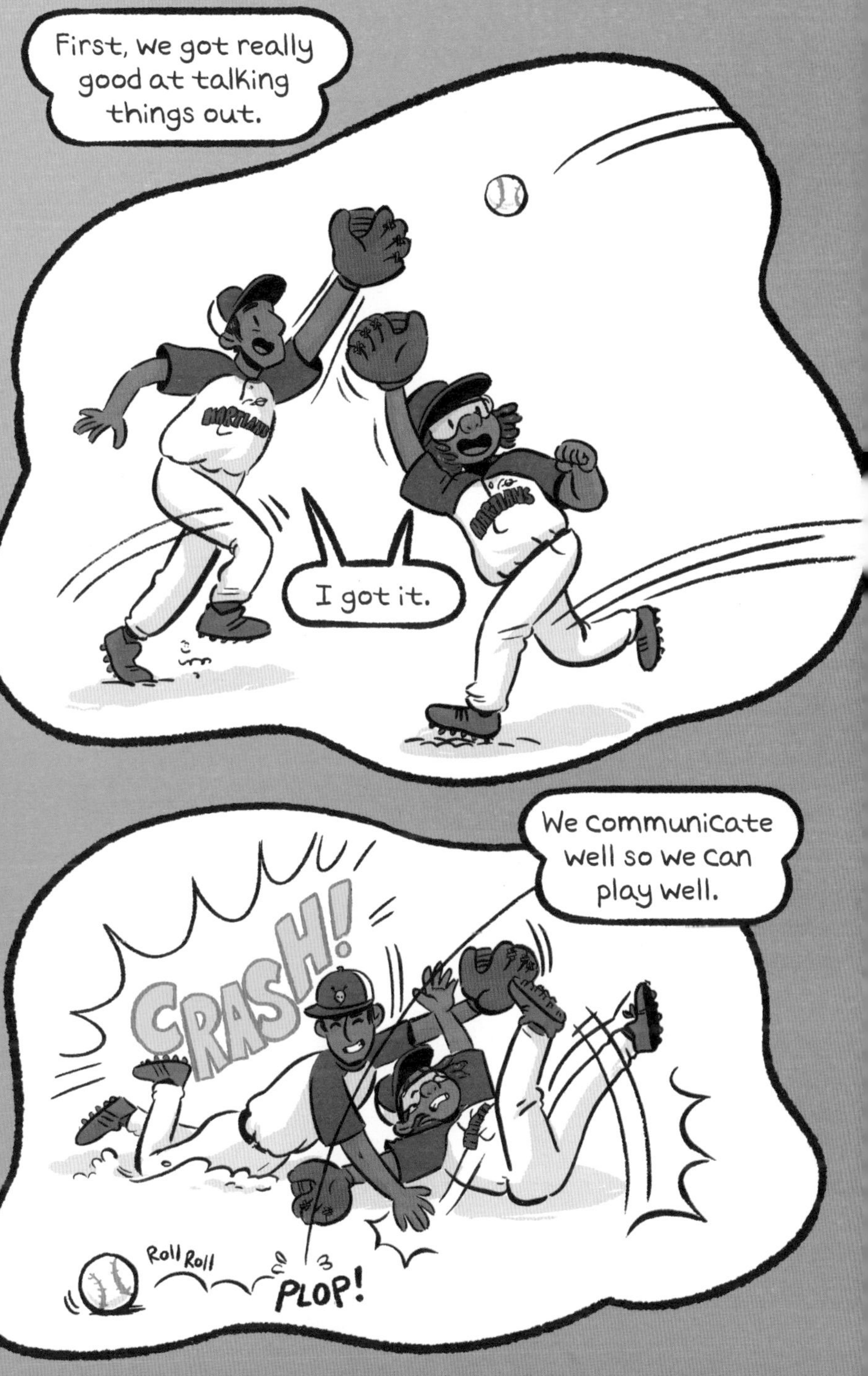
First, we got really good at talking things out.
I got it.
We communicate well so we can play well.
CRASH!
Roll Roll
PLOP!

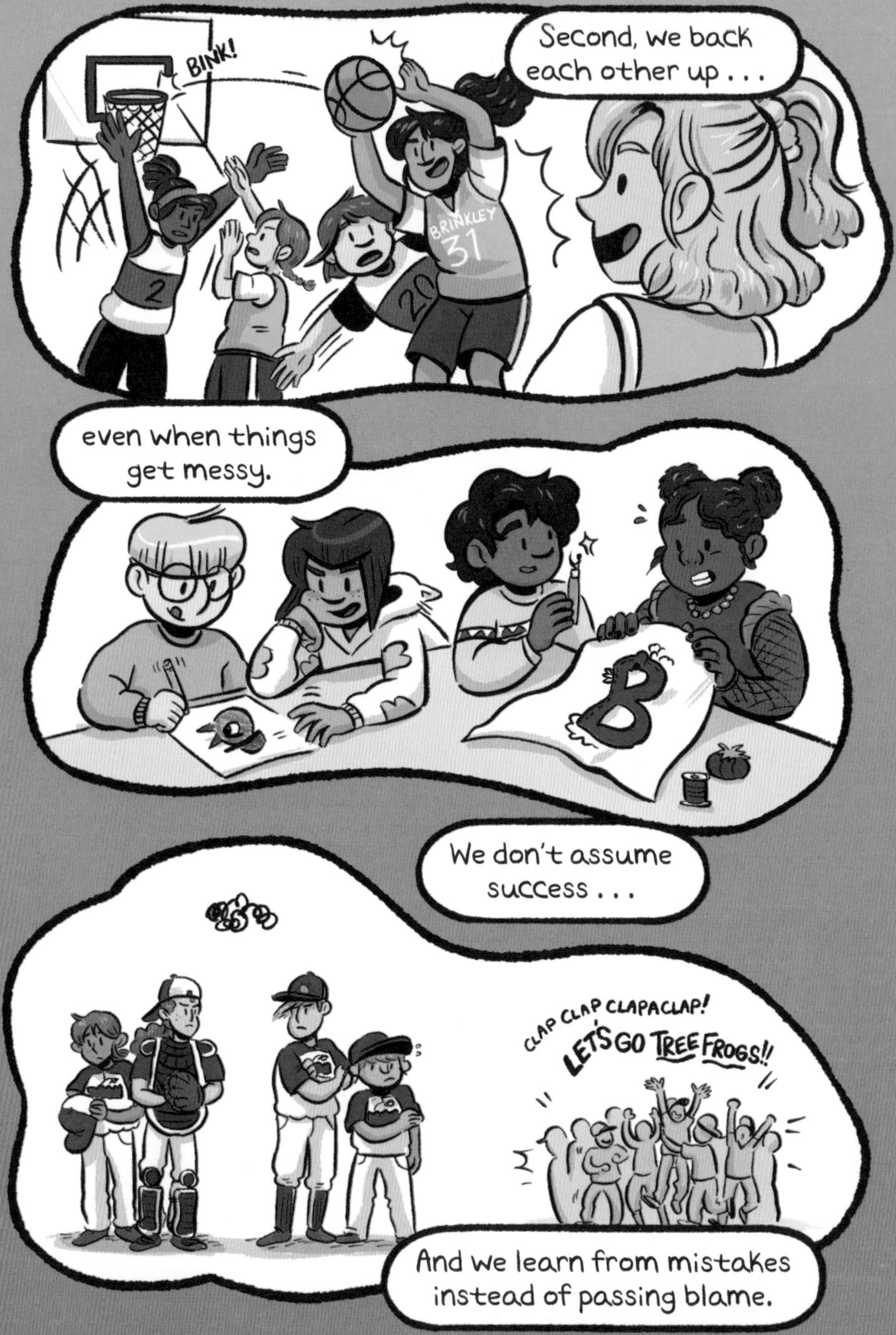
BINK!
Second, we back each other up . . .
BRINKLEY 31
even when things get messy.
We don't assume success . . .
CLAP CLAP CLAPACLAP!
LET'S GO TREE FROGS!!
And we learn from mistakes instead of passing blame.

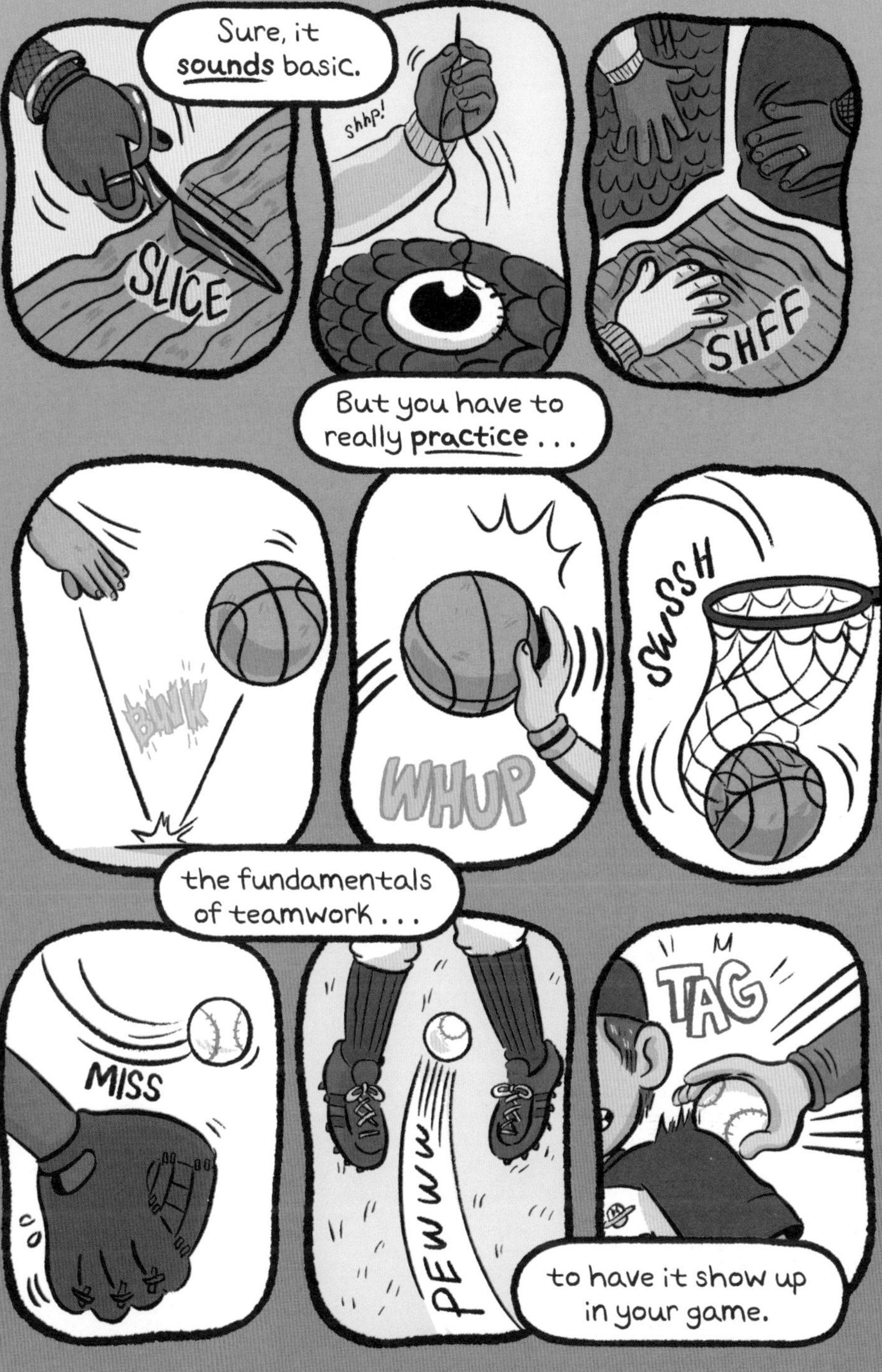
Sure, it sounds basic.
SLICE
shhp!
SHFF
But you have to really practice . . .
BINK
WHUP
SWSSH
the fundamentals of teamwork . . .
MISS
PEWWW
TAG
to have it show up in your game.

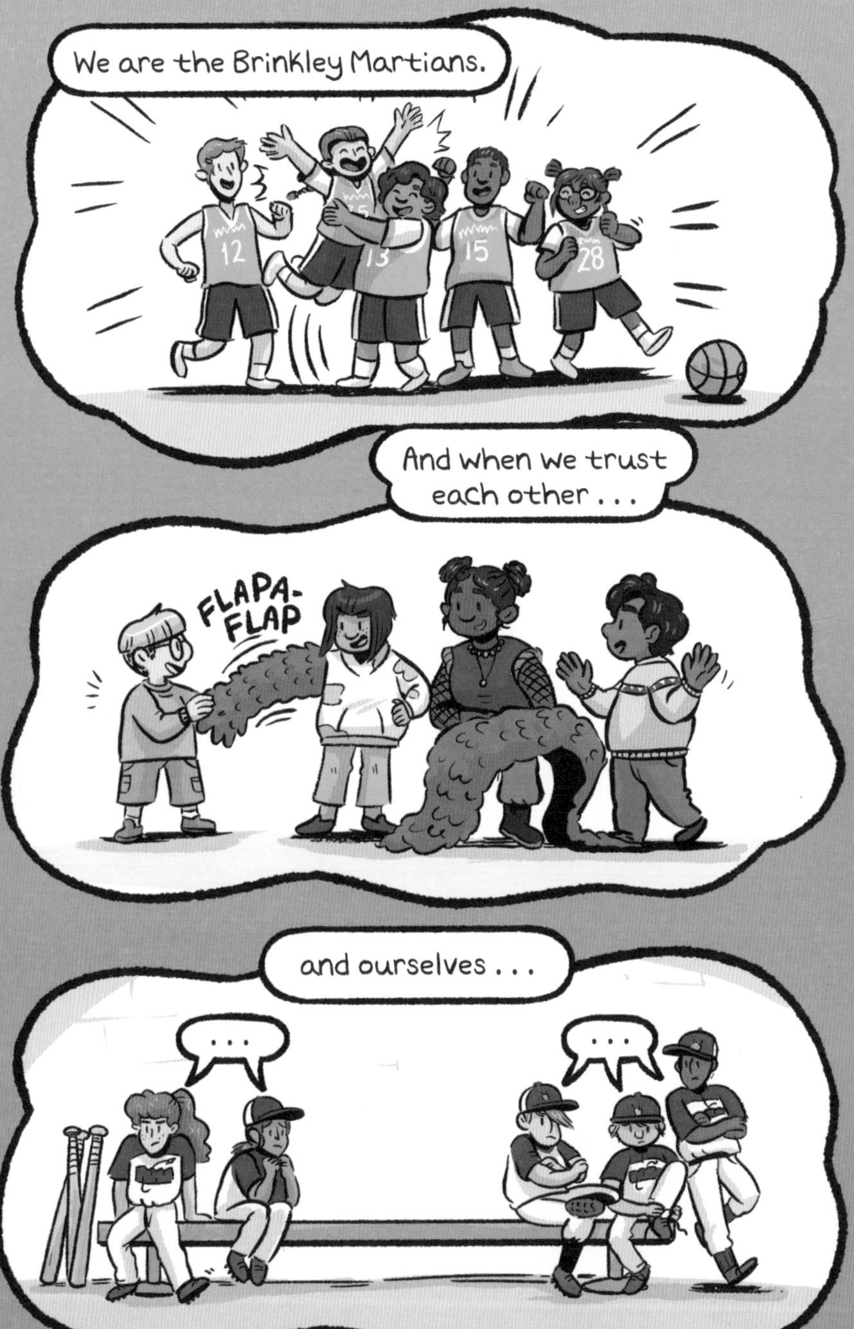
We are the Brinkley Martians.
12
13
15
28
And when we trust each other . . .
FLAPA-FLAP
and ourselves . . .
. . .
. . .

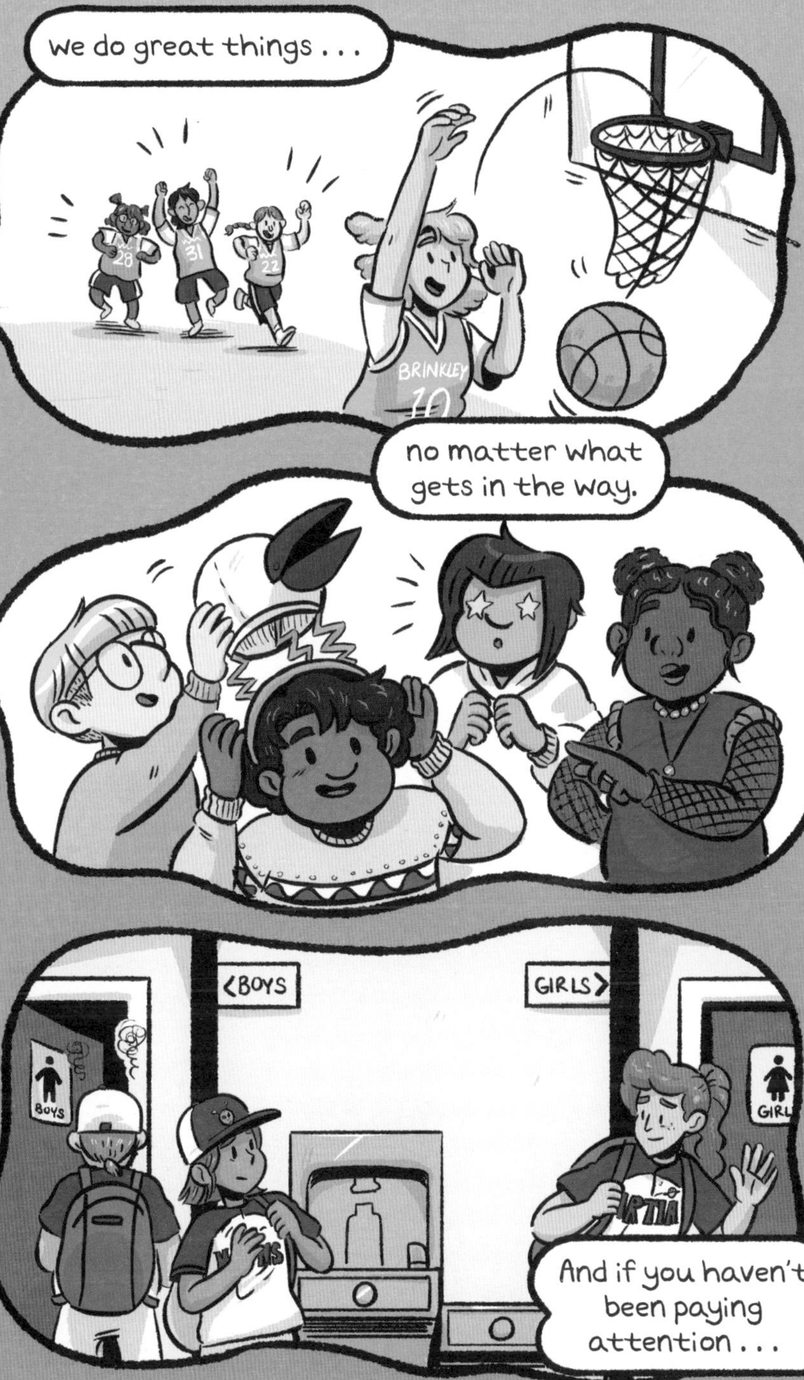
we do great things . . .
BRINKLEY
no matter what gets in the way.
<BOYS
GIRLS>
BOYS
And if you haven't been paying attention . . .

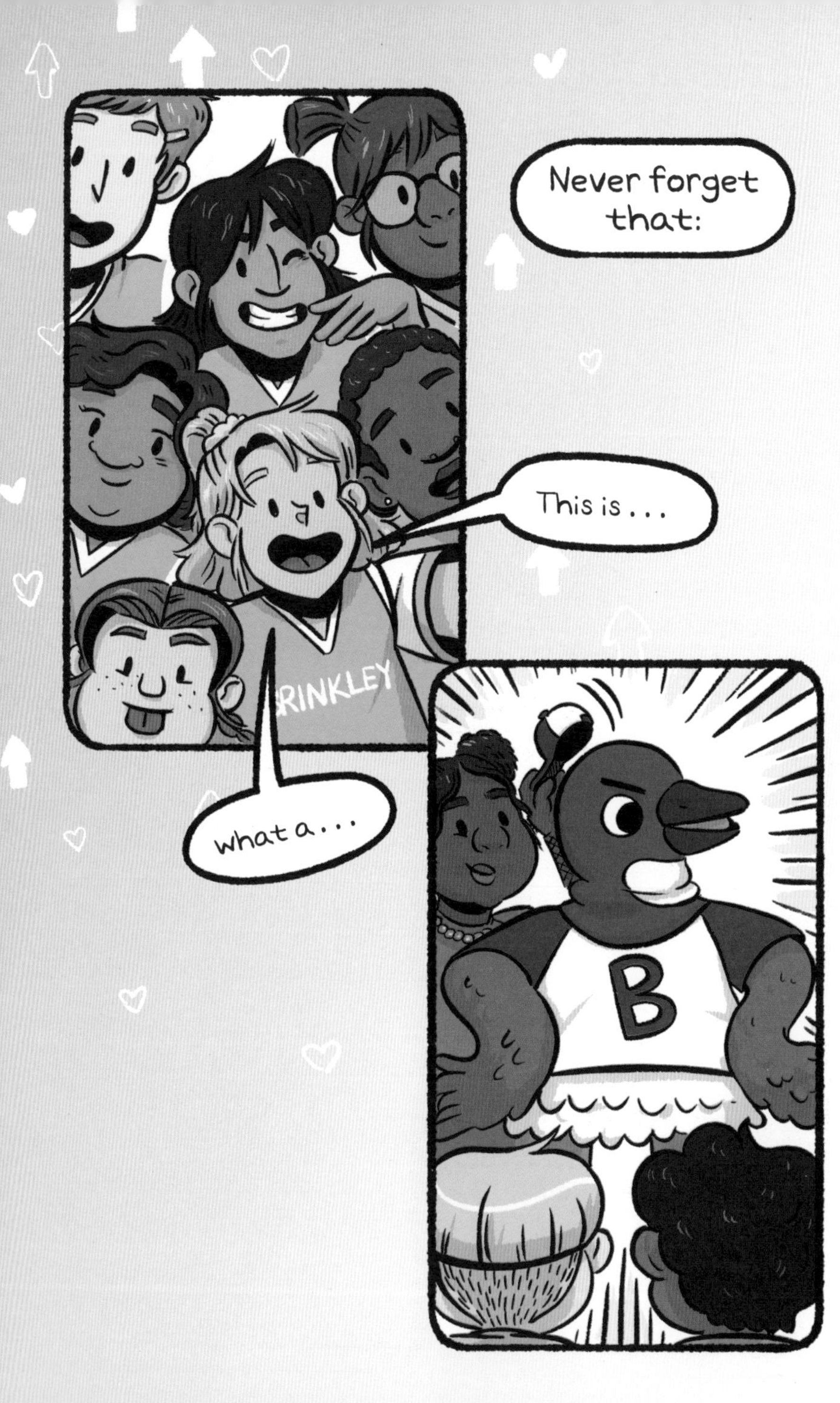
Never forget that:
This is . . .
BRINKLEY
what a . . .
B

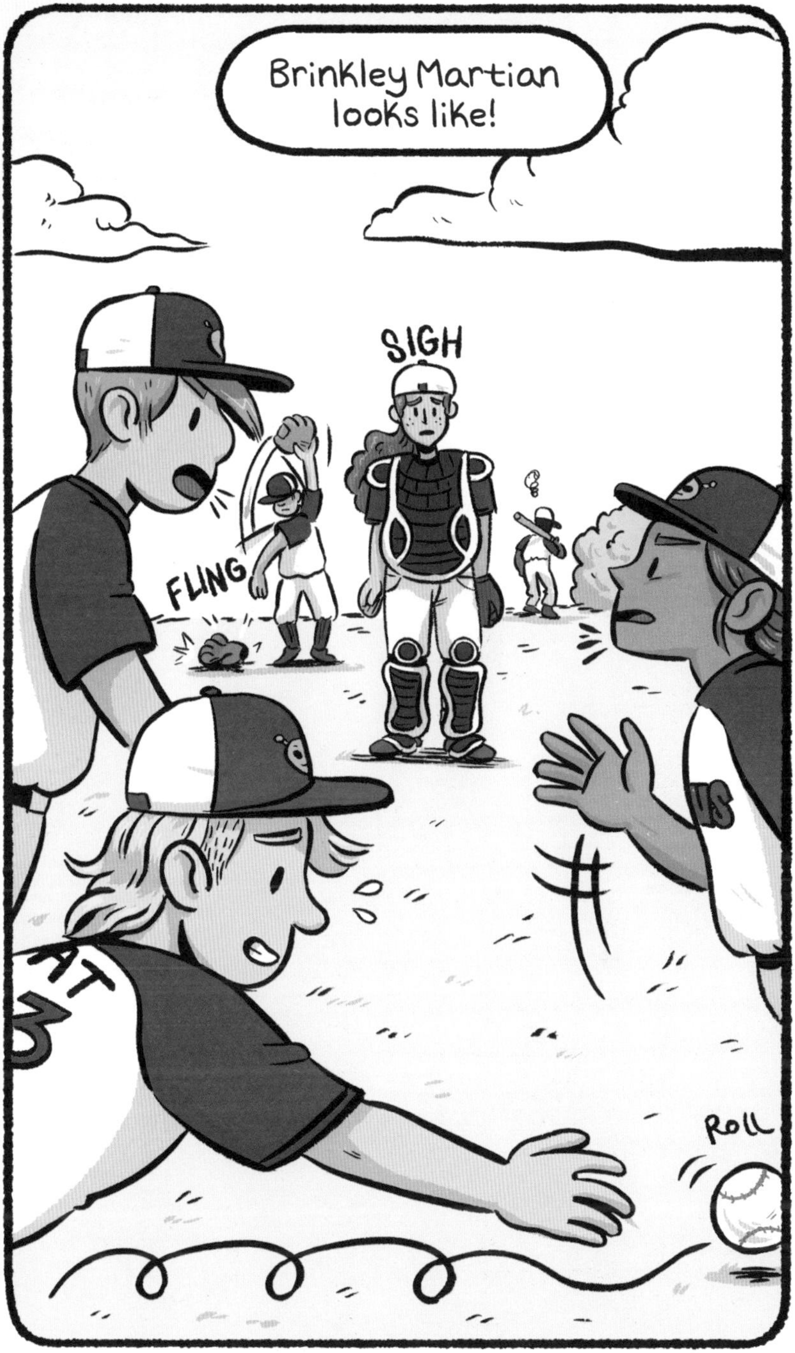
Brinkley Martian looks like!
SIGH
FLING
ROLL

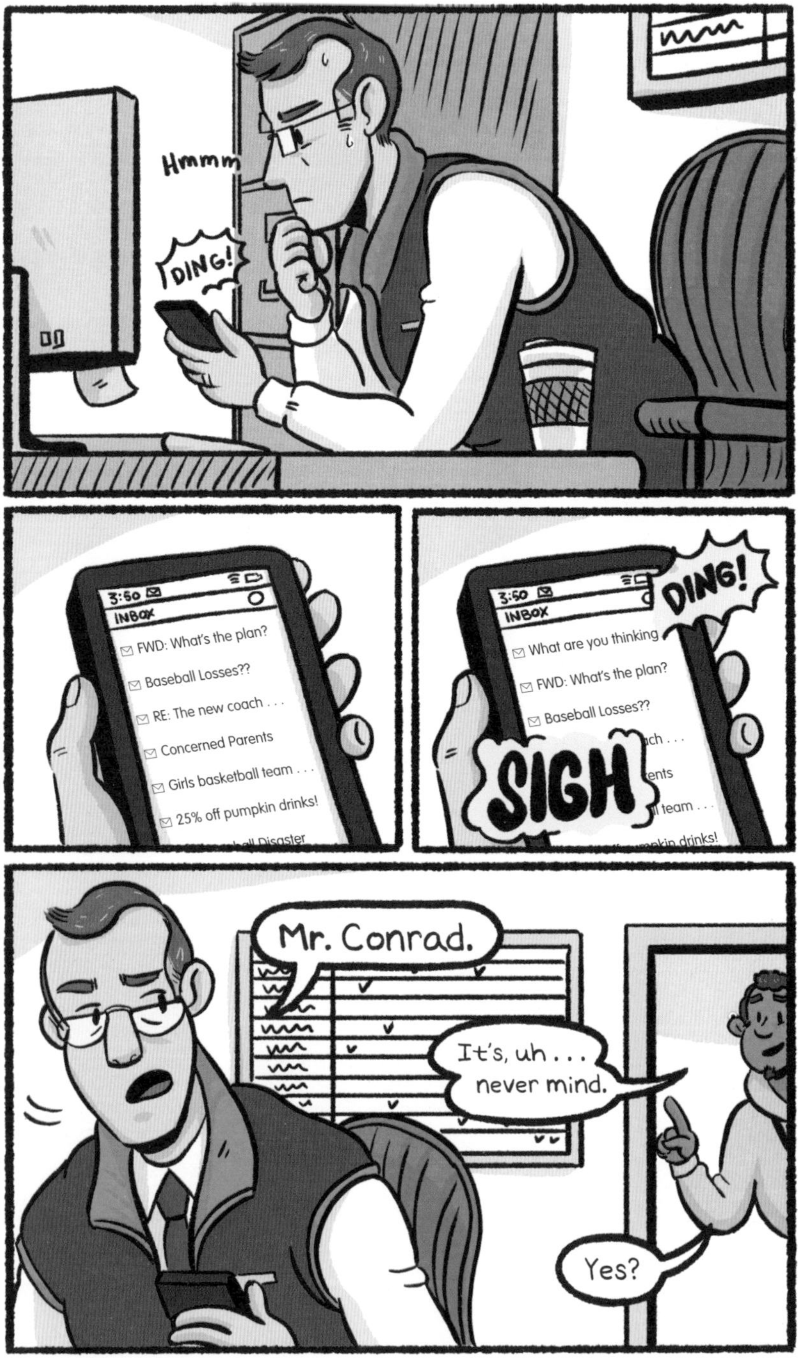
Hmmm
DING!
3:50
INBOX
FWD: What's the plan?
Baseball Losses??
RE: The new coach . . .
Concerned Parents
Girls basketball team . . .
25% off pumpkin drinks!
DING!
3:50
INBOX
What are you thinking
FWD: What's the plan?
Baseball Losses??
SIGH
Mr. Conrad.
It's, uh . . . never mind.
Yes?

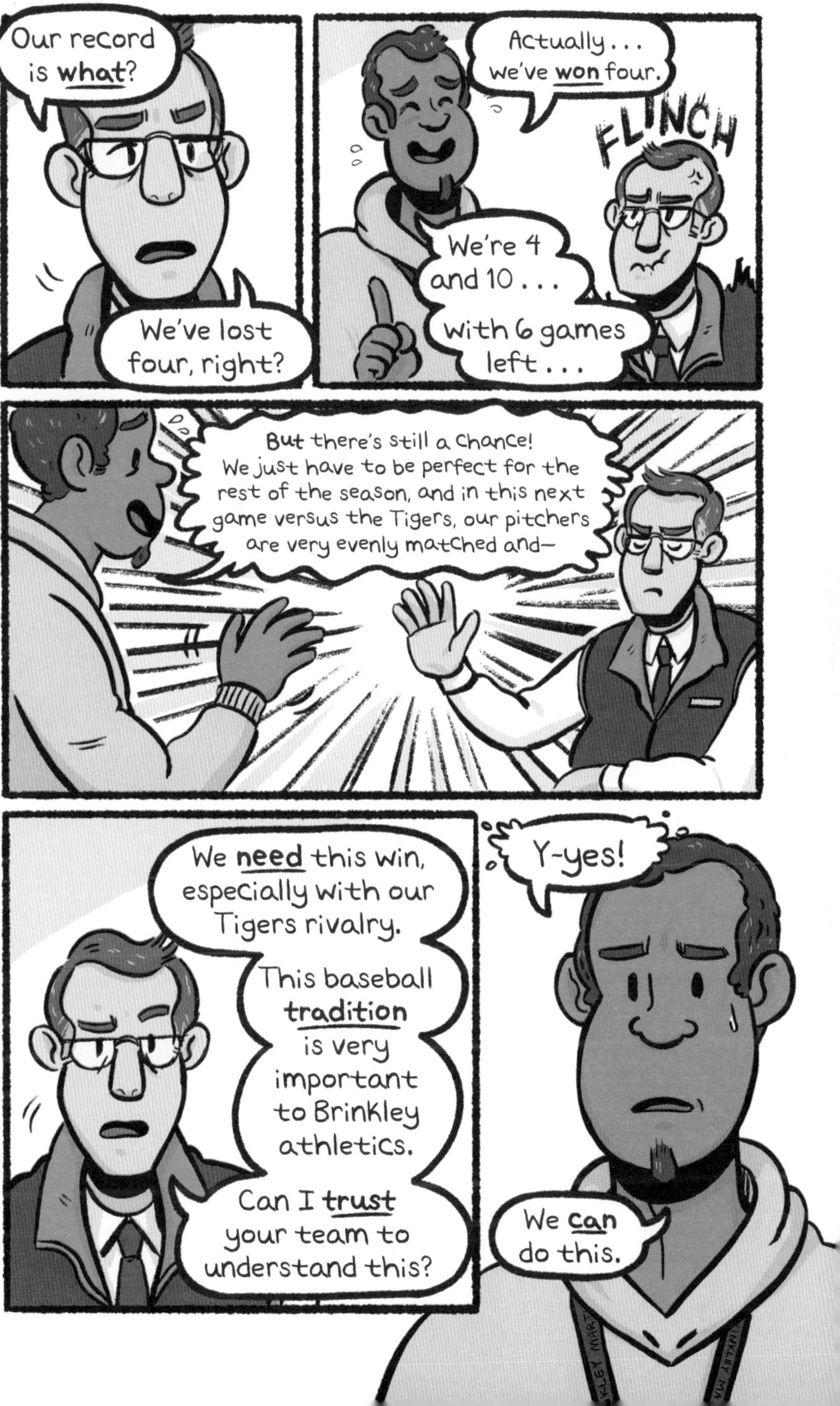
Our record is what?
We've lost four, right?
Actually . . . we've won four.
FLINCH
We're 4 and 10 . . .
With 6 games left . . .
But there's still a chance! We just have to be perfect for the rest of the season, and in this next game versus the Tigers, our pitchers are very evenly matched and—
We need this win, especially with our Tigers rivalry.
This baseball tradition is very important to Brinkley athletics.
Can I trust your team to understand this?
Y-yes!
We can do this.

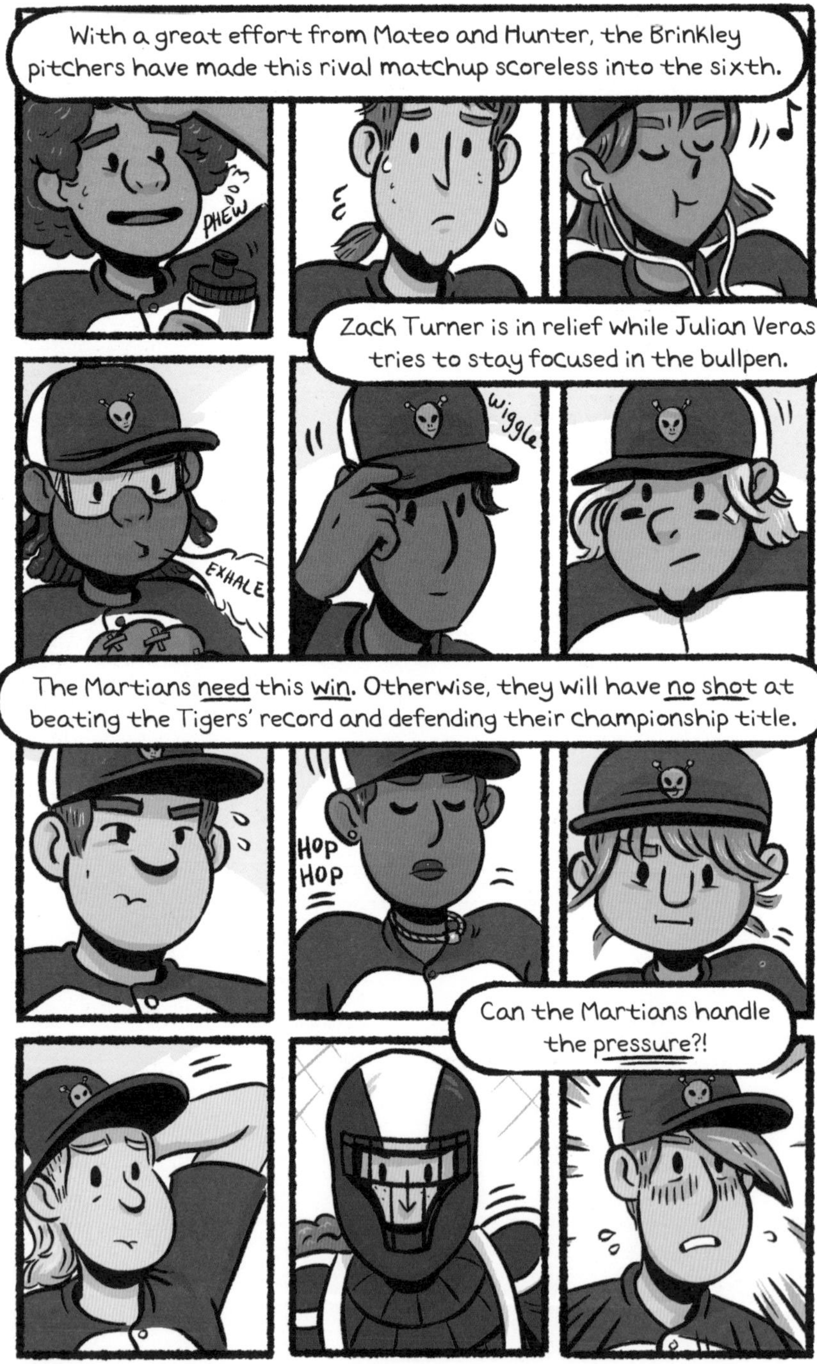

With a great effort from Mateo and Hunter, the Brinkley pitchers have made this rival matchup scoreless into the sixth.
PHEW
Zack Turner is in relief while Julian Veras tries to stay focused in the bullpen.
wiggle
EXHALE
The Martians need this win. Otherwise, they will have no shot at beating the Tigers' record and defending their championship title.
HOP HOP
Can the Martians handle the pressure?!

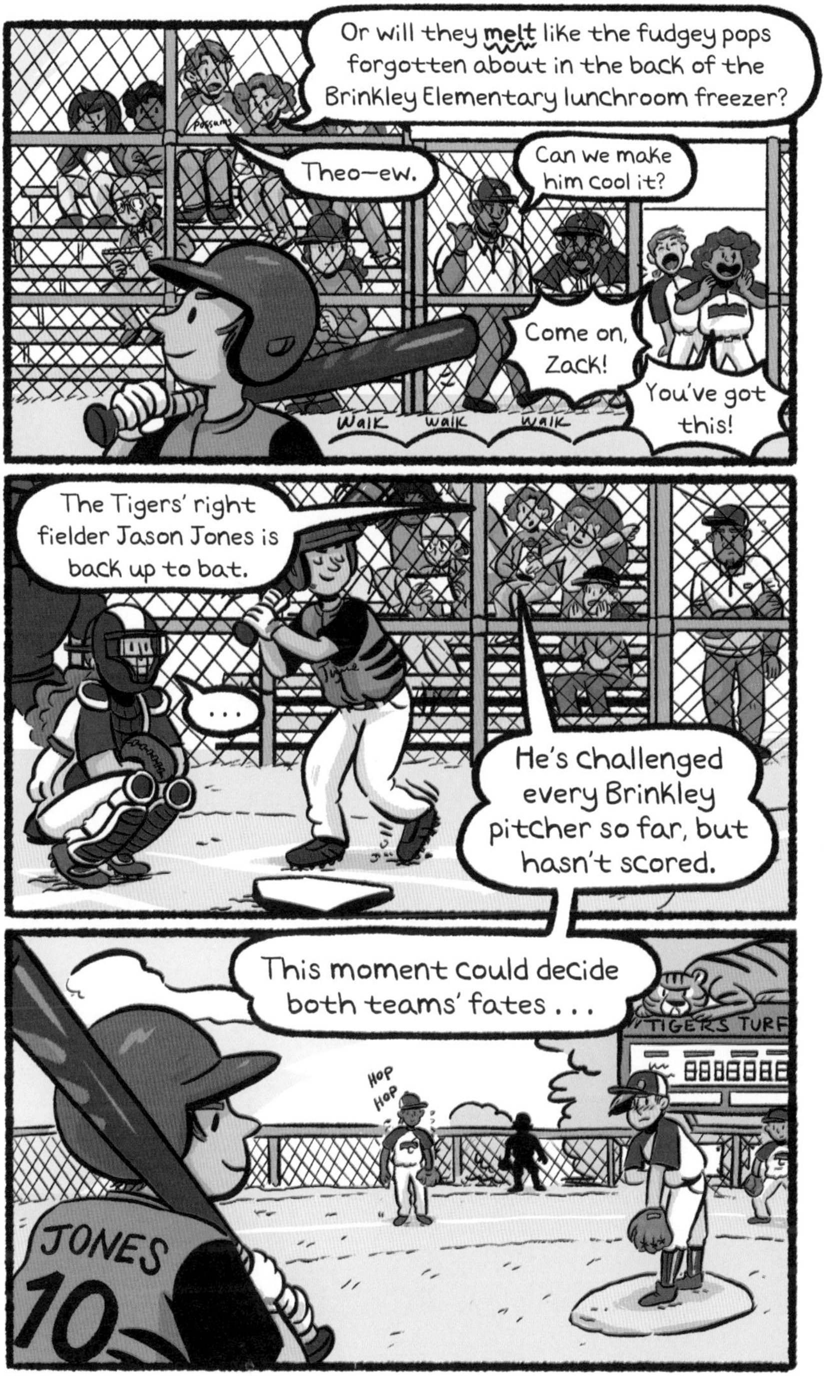
Or will they melt like the fudgey pops forgotten about in the back of the Brinkley Elementary lunchroom freezer?
Theo—ew.
Can we make him cool it?
Come on, Zack!
You've got this!
WALK WALK WALK
The Tigers' right fielder Jason Jones is back up to bat.
...
He's challenged every Brinkley pitcher so far, but hasn't scored.
This moment could decide both teams' fates . . .
TIGERS TURF
HOP HOP
JONES
10

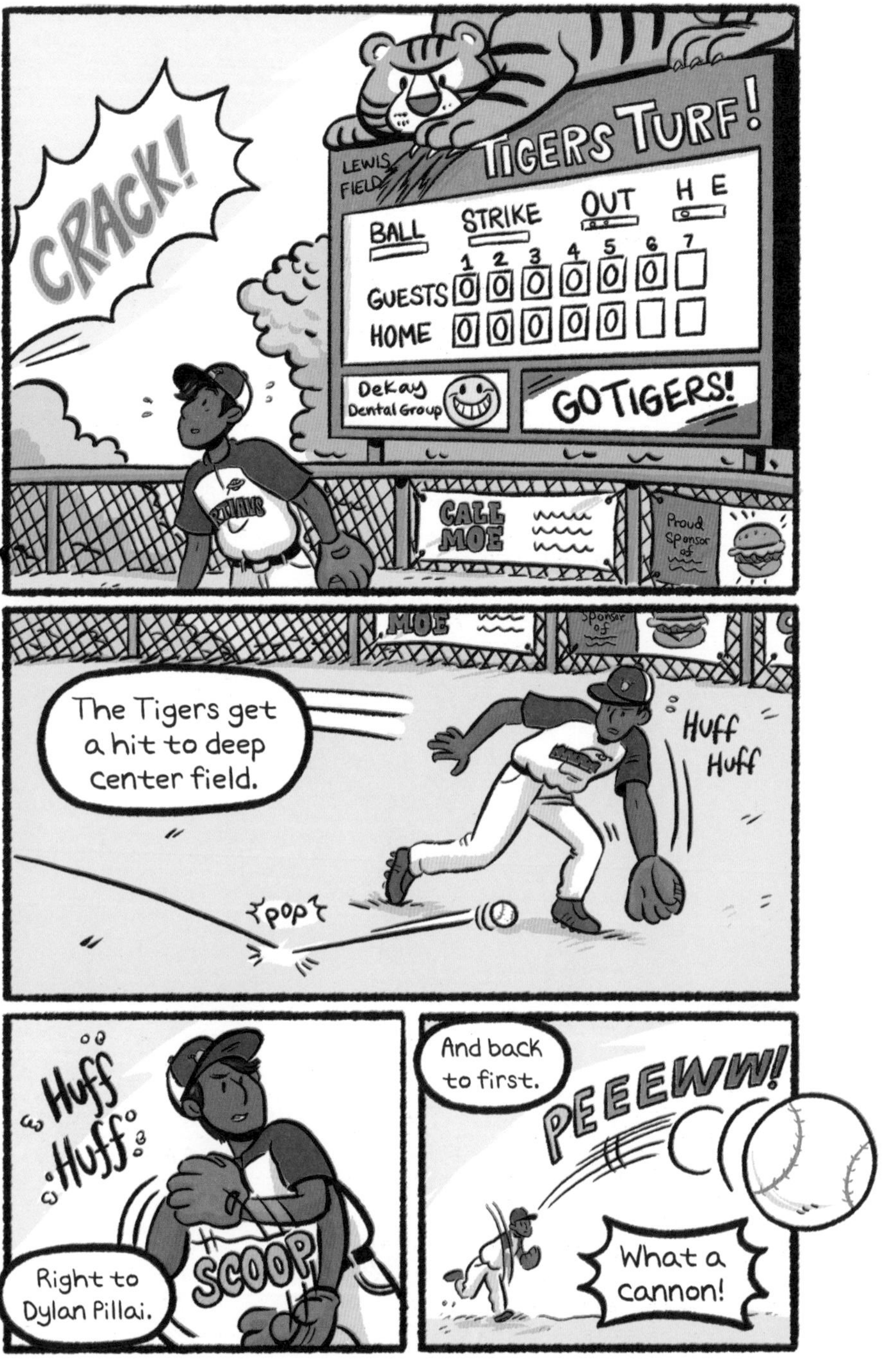
CRACK!
TIGERS TURF!
LEWIS FIELD
BALL
STRIKE
OUT
H E
1 2 3 4 5 6 7
GUESTS 0 0 0 0 0 0
HOME 0 0 0 0 0
Dekay Dental Group
GO TIGERS!
CALL MOE
Proud Sponsor of
The Tigers get a hit to deep center field.
Huff Huff
pop
Huff Huff
Right to Dylan Pillai.
SCOOP
And back to first.
PEEEWW!
What a cannon!

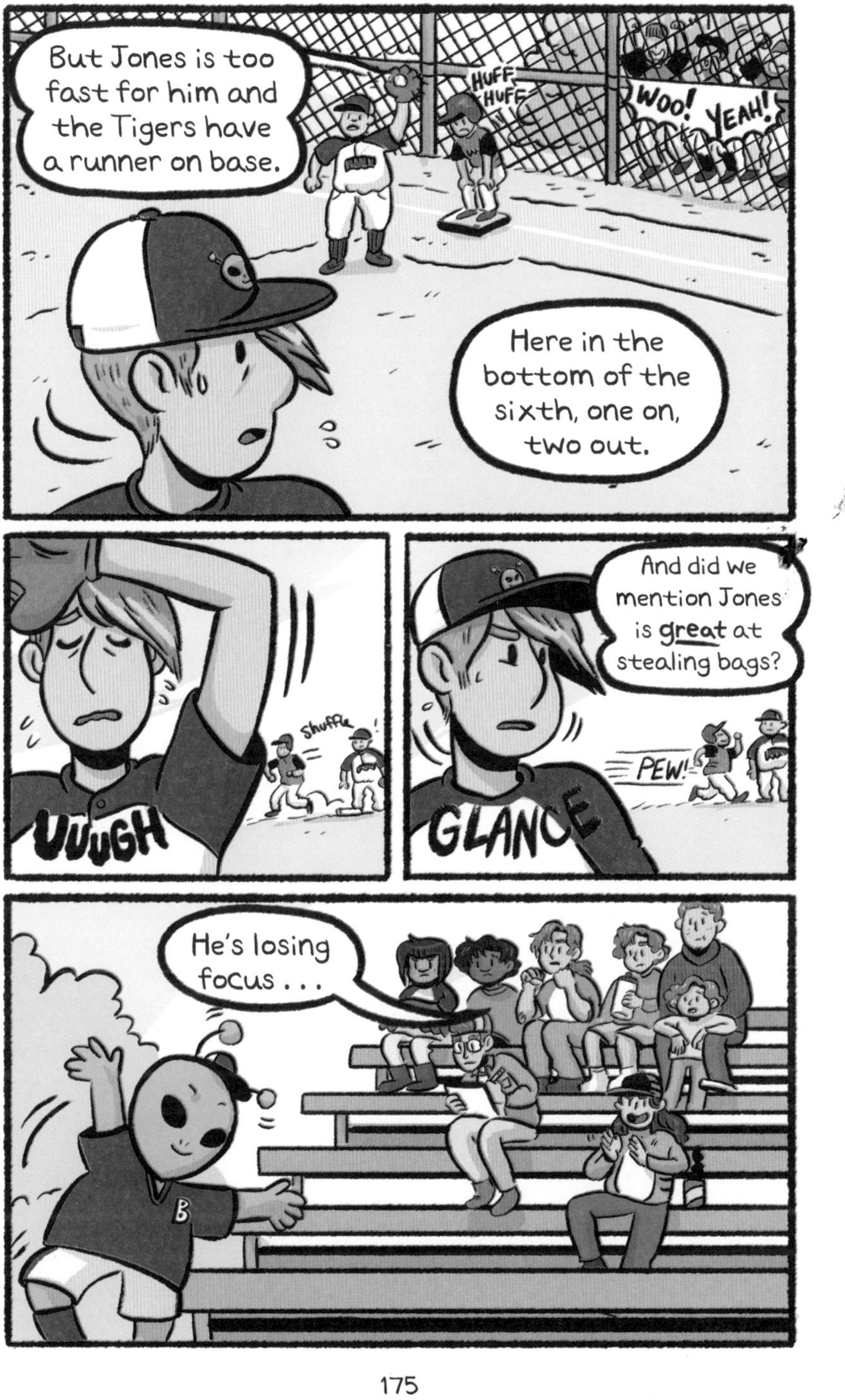
But Jones is too fast for him and the Tigers have a runner on base.
HUFF HUFF
WOO!
YEAH!
Here in the bottom of the sixth, one on, two out.
UUUGH
Shuffle
And did we mention Jones is great at stealing bags?
PEW!
GLANCE
He's losing focus . . .

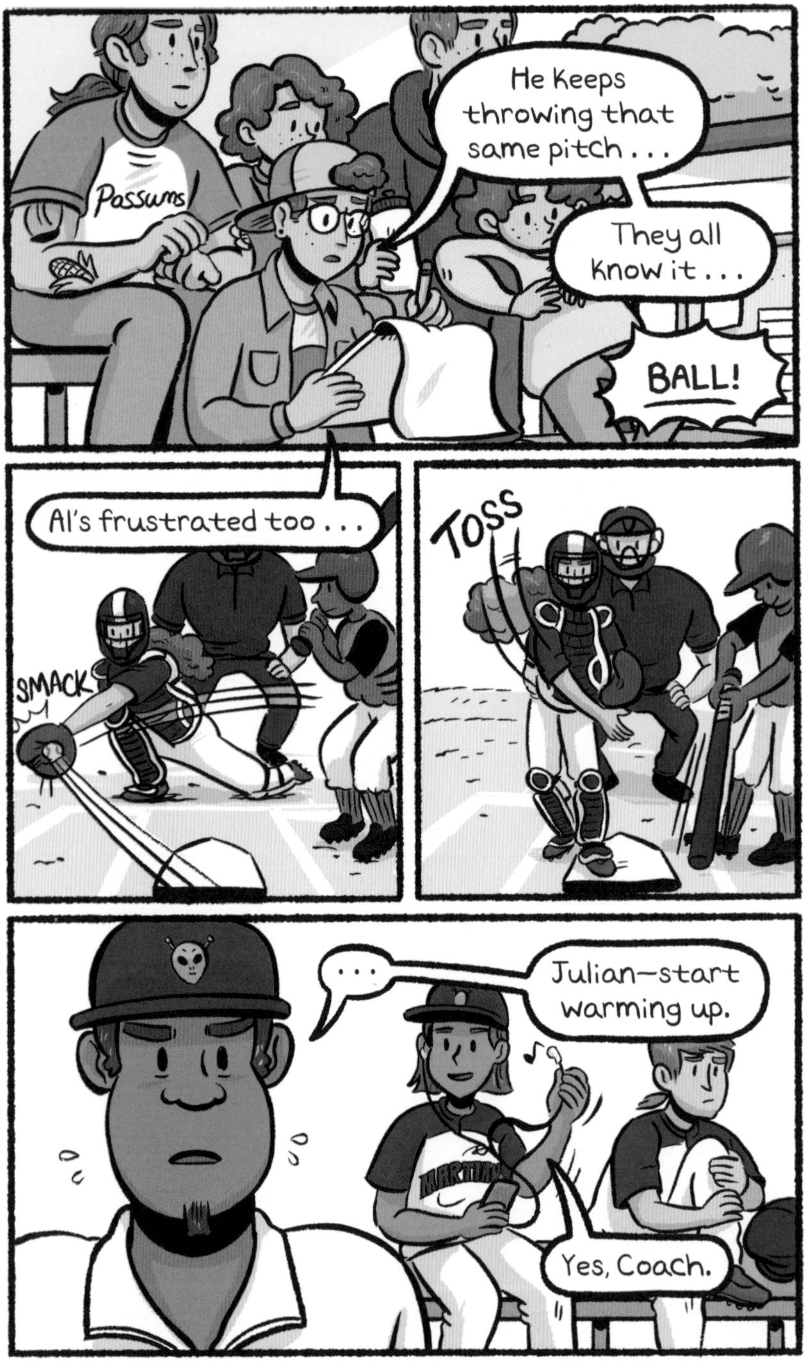
Passums
He keeps throwing that same pitch . . .
They all know it . . .
BALL!
Al's frustrated too . . .
SMACK
TOSS
. . .
Julian—start warming up.
MARTIAN
Yes, Coach.

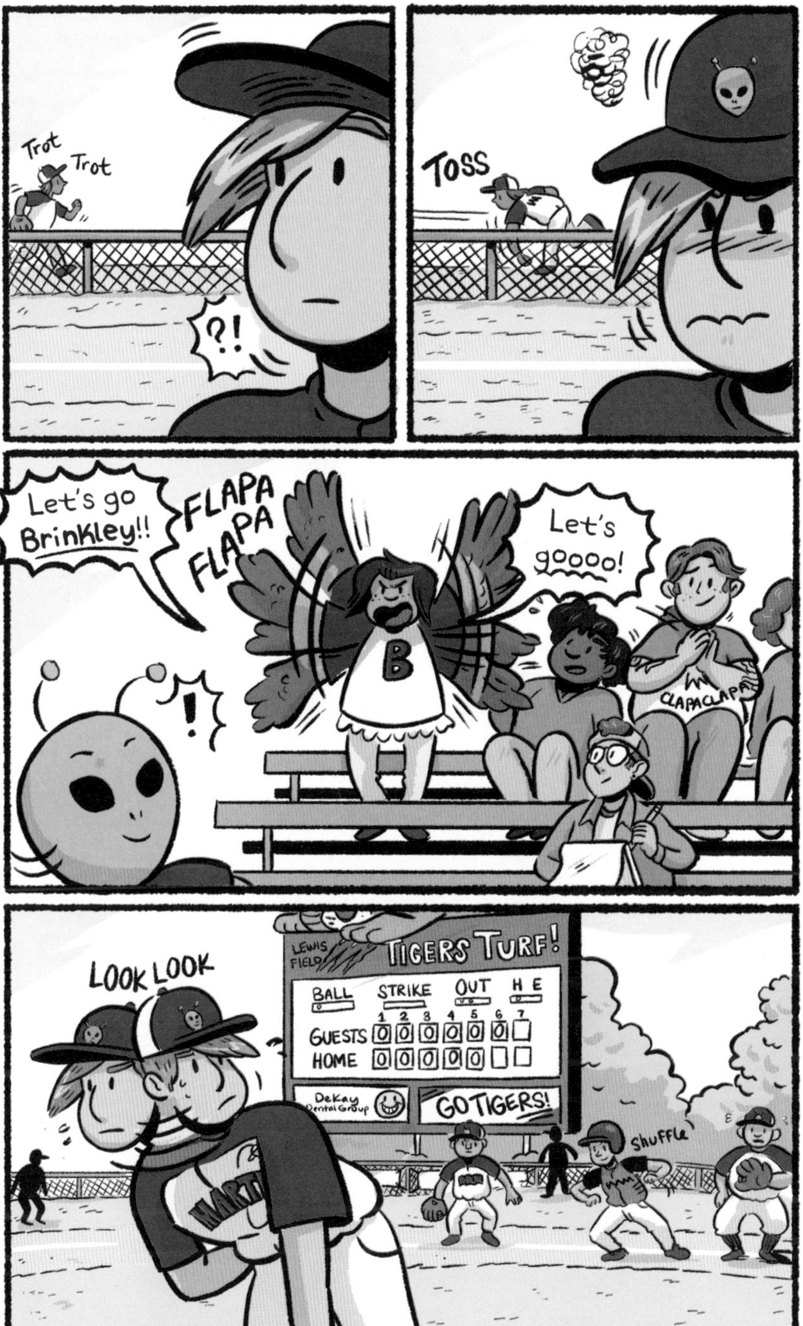
Trot
Trot
?!
TOSS
Let's go Brinkley!!
FLAPA FLAPA
Let's goooo!
CLAPACLAPA
!
LOOK LOOK
LEWIS FIELD
TIGERS TURF!
BALL
STRIKE
OUT
H E
1 2 3 4 5 6 7
GUESTS 0 0 0 0 0 0
HOME 0 0 0 0 0
DeKay Dental Group
GO TIGERS!
Shuffle

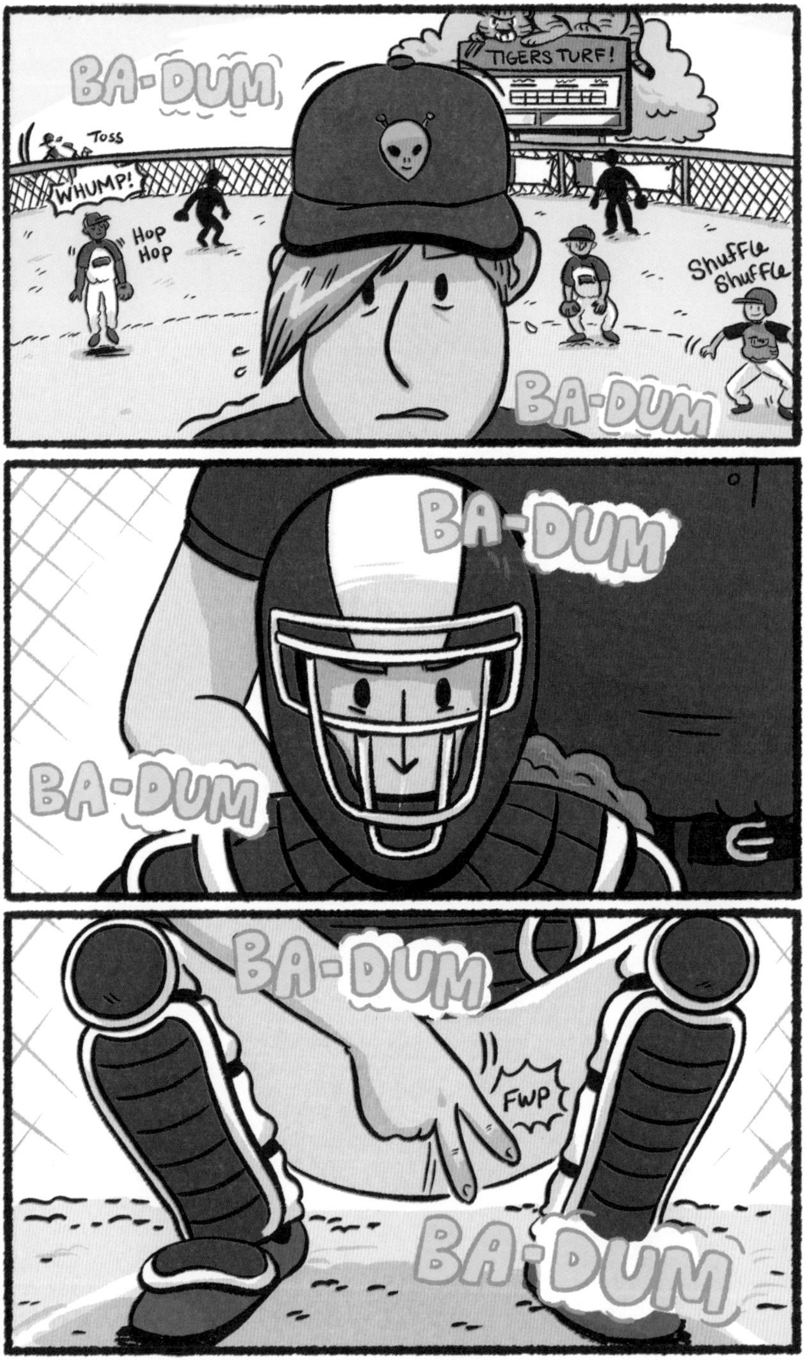
BA-DUM
TIGERS TURF!
TOSS
WHUMP!
Hop Hop
Shuffle Shuffle
BA-DUM
BA-DUM
BA-DUM
BA-DUM
FWP
BA-DUM

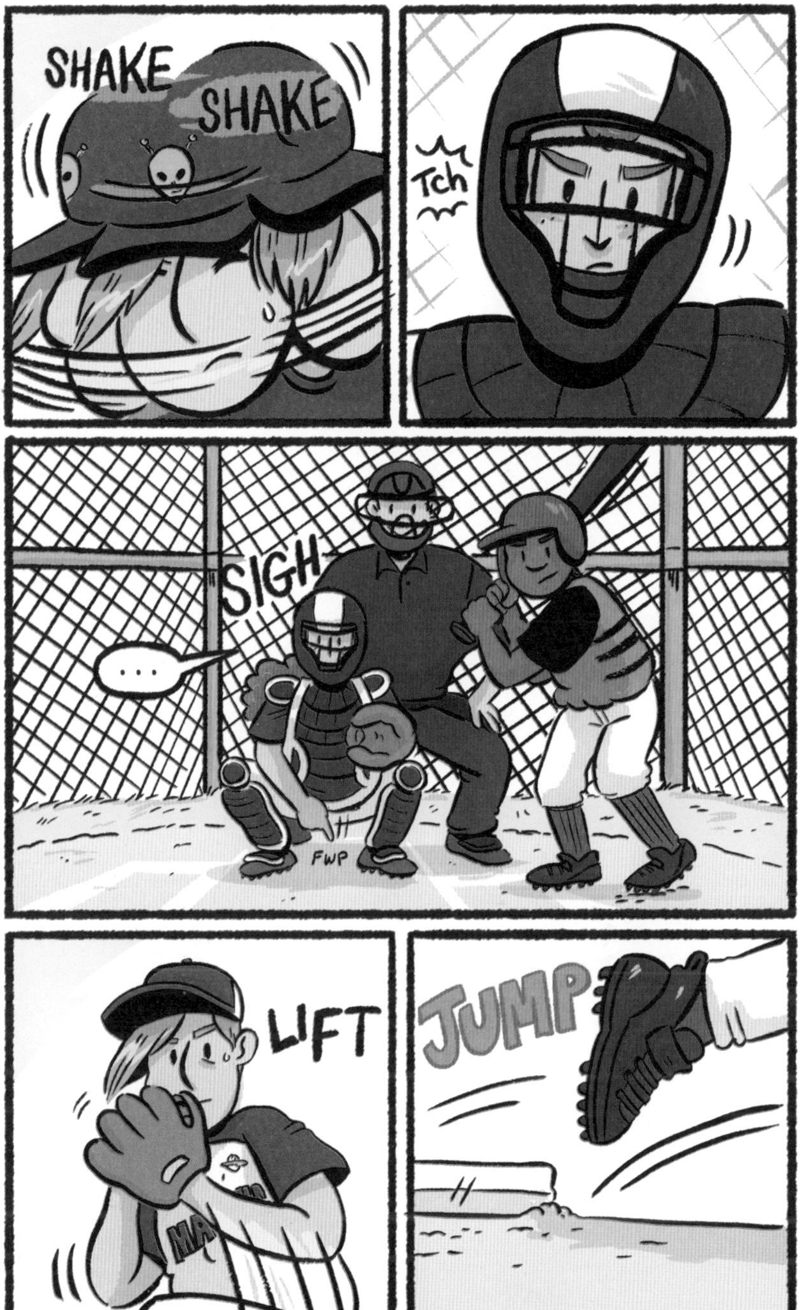
SHAKE
SHAKE
Tch
SIGH
...
FWP
LIFT
JUMP

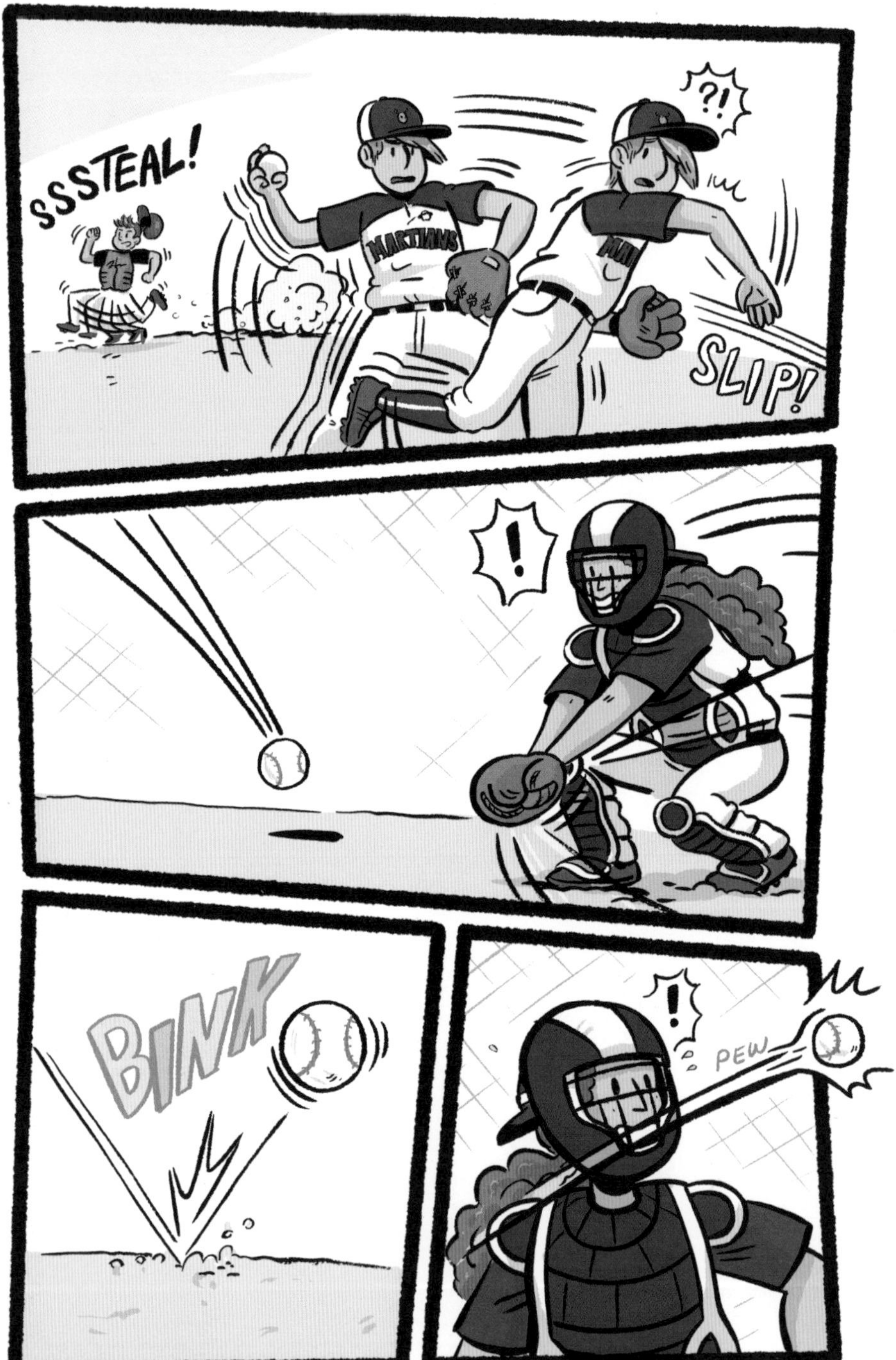
SSSTEAL!
MARTINS
?!
SLIP!
!
BINK
!
PEW

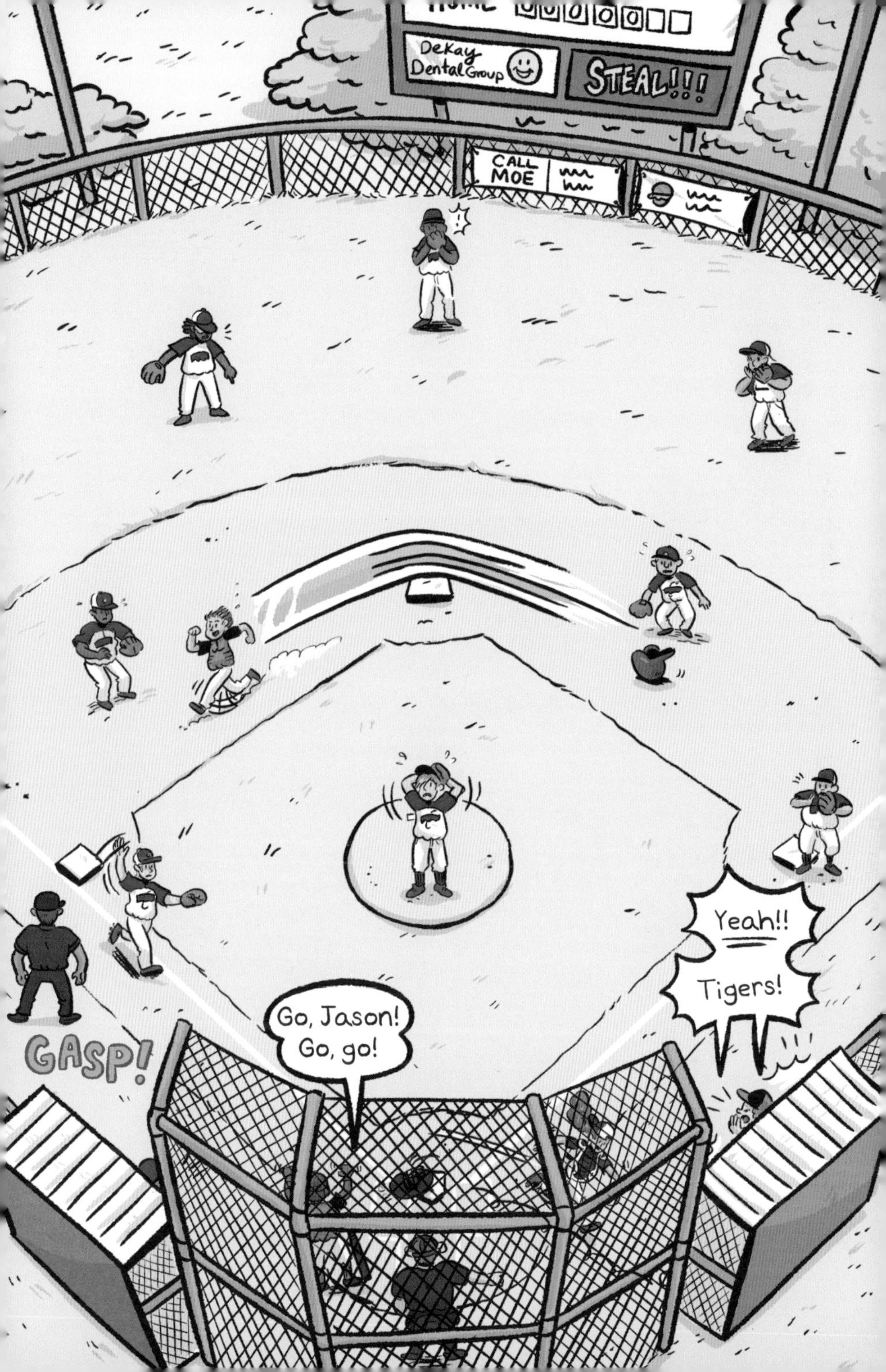
Dekay Dental Group
STEAL!!!
CALL MOE
GASP!
Go, Jason! Go, go!
Yeah!! Tigers!

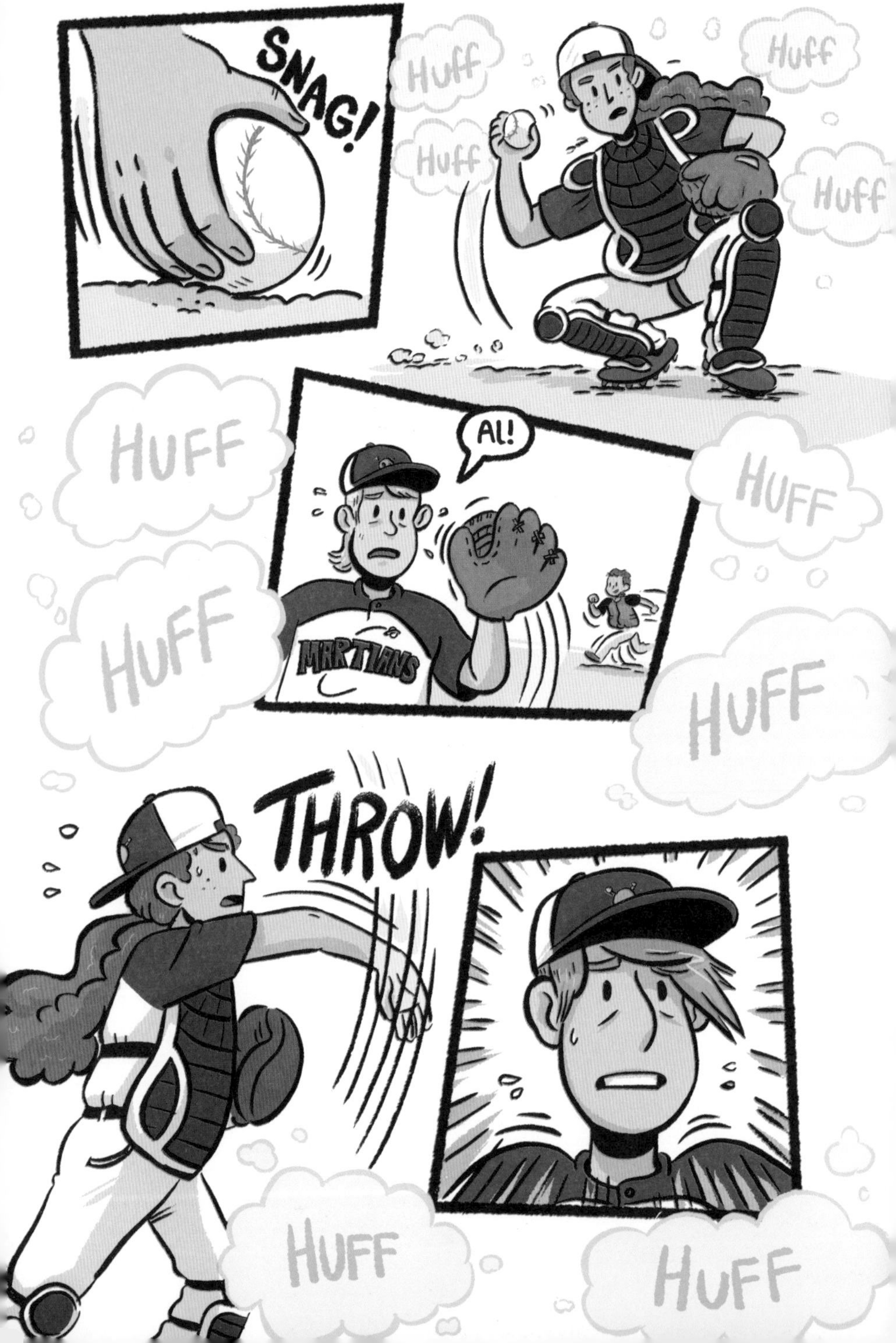

SNAG!
HUFF
HUFF
HUFF
HUFF
HUFF
AL!
MARTIANS
HUFF
HUFF
HUFF
THROW!
HUFF
HUFF

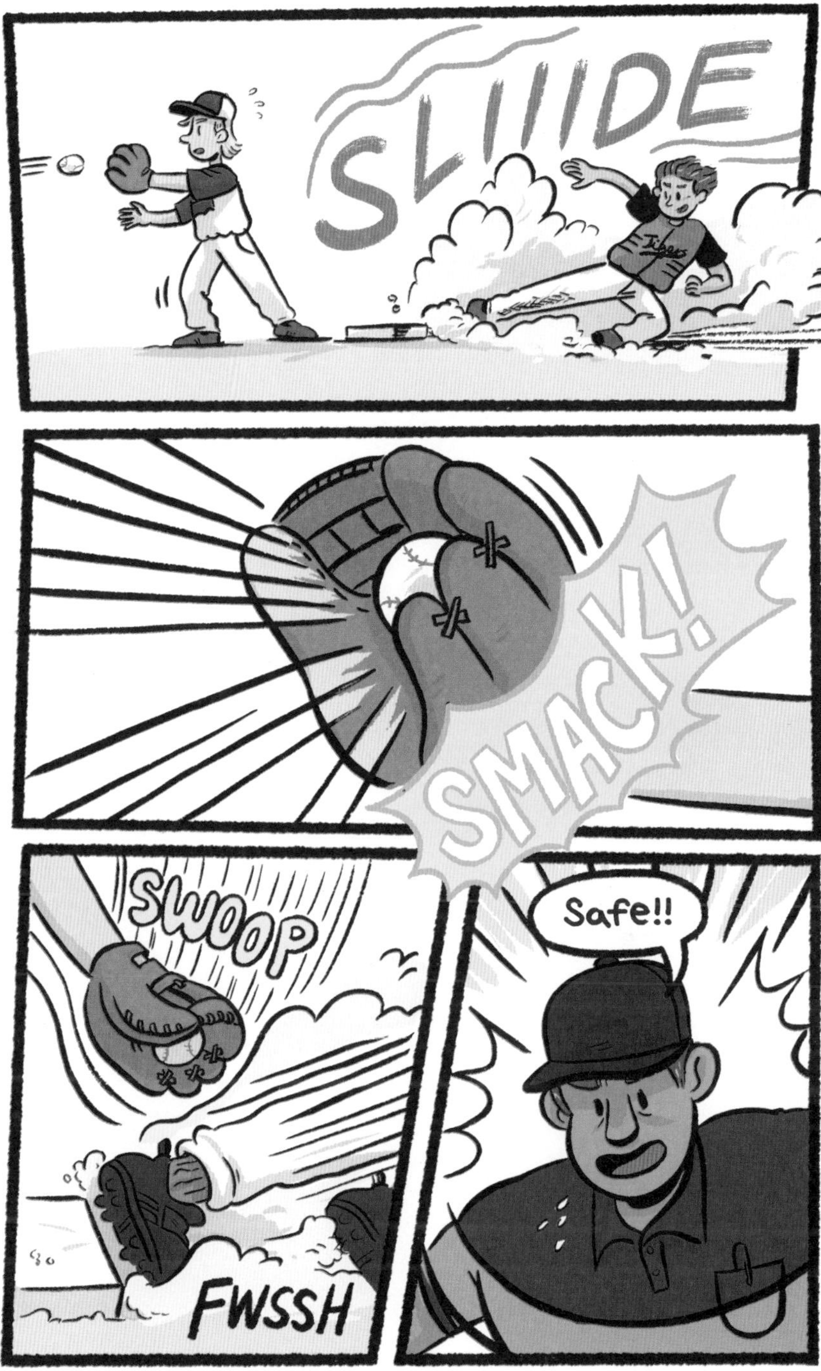
SLIIIDE
SMACK!!
SWOOP
FWSSH
Safe!!

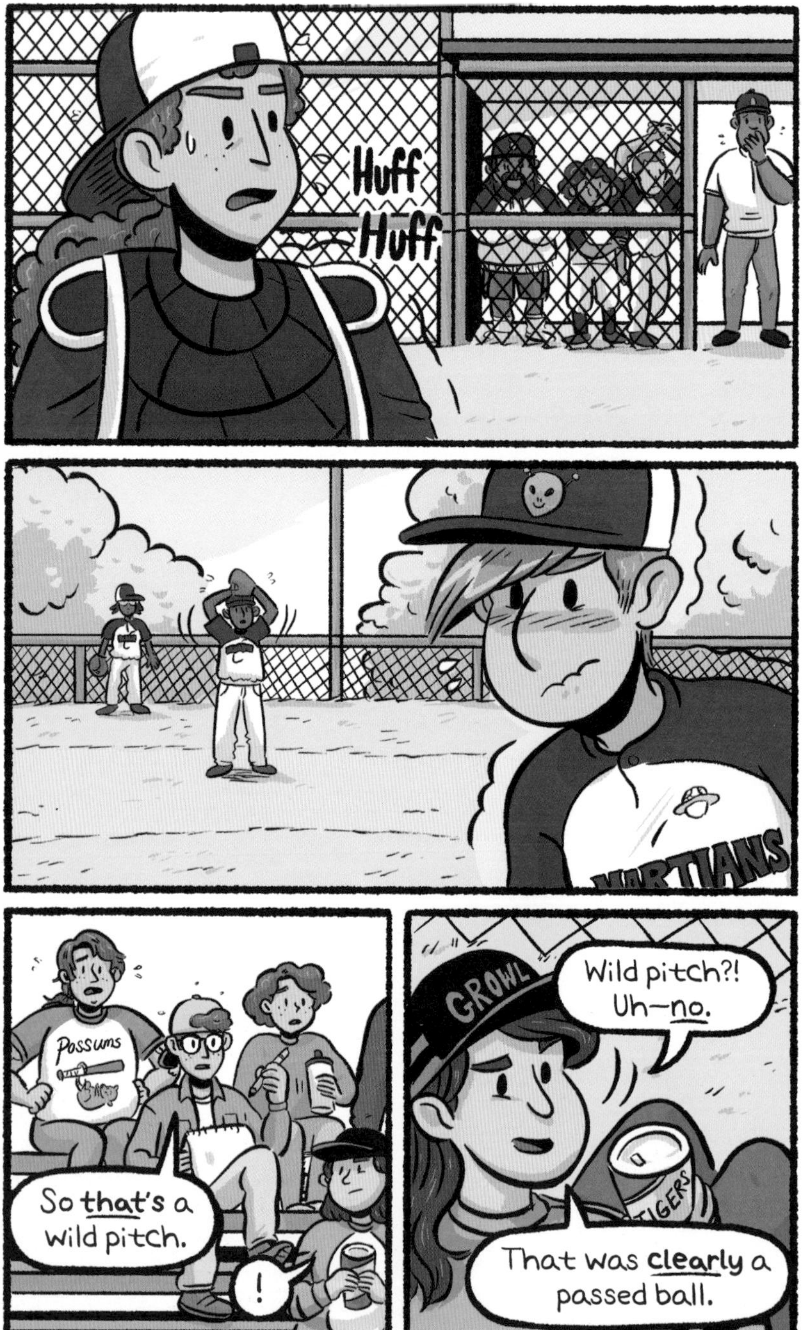
Huff
Huff
MARTIANS
Possums
GROWL
Wild pitch?! Uh—no.
TIGERS
So that's a wild pitch.
!
That was clearly a passed ball.

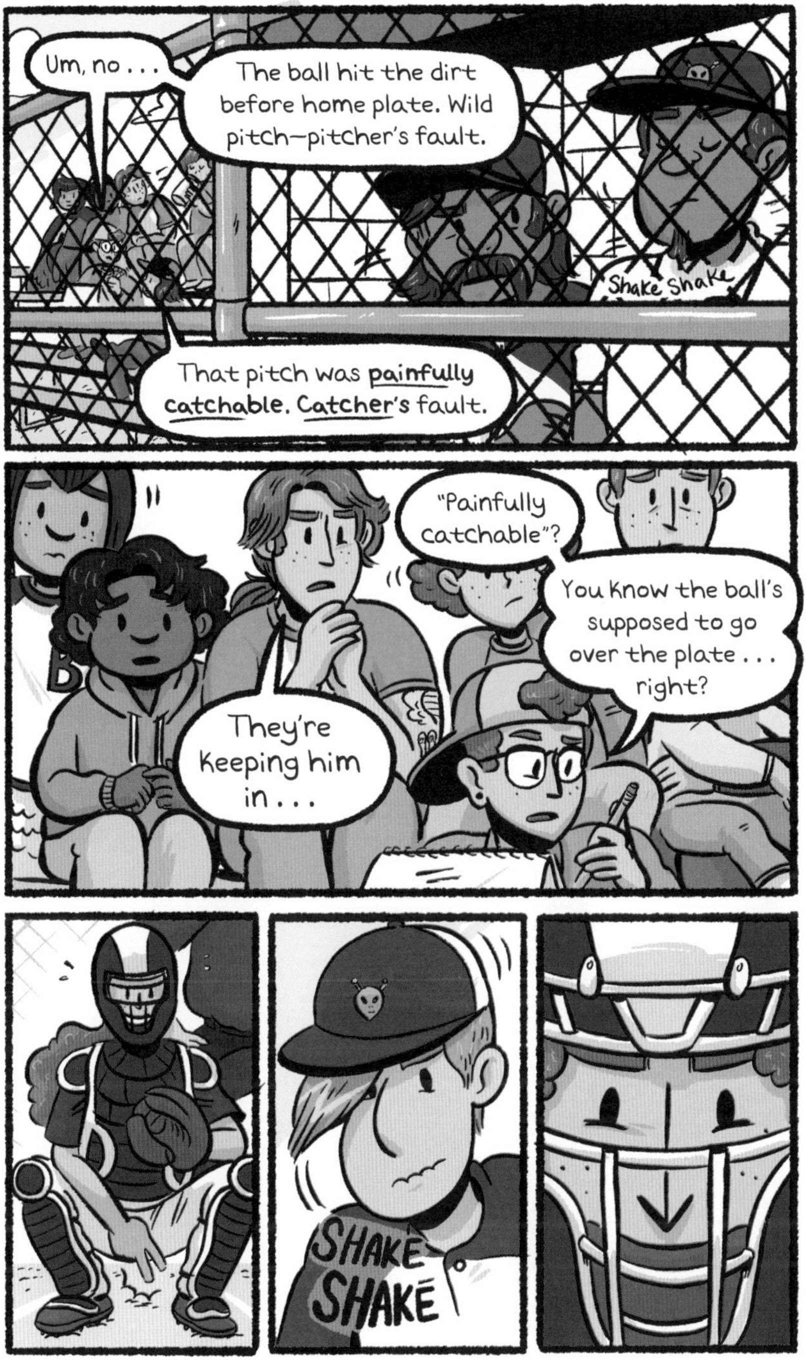
Um, no . . .
The ball hit the dirt before home plate. Wild pitch—pitcher's fault.
Shake Shake
That pitch was **painfully catchable**. **Catcher**'s fault.
"Painfully catchable"?
You know the ball's supposed to go over the plate . . . right?
They're keeping him in . . .
SHAKE SHAKE

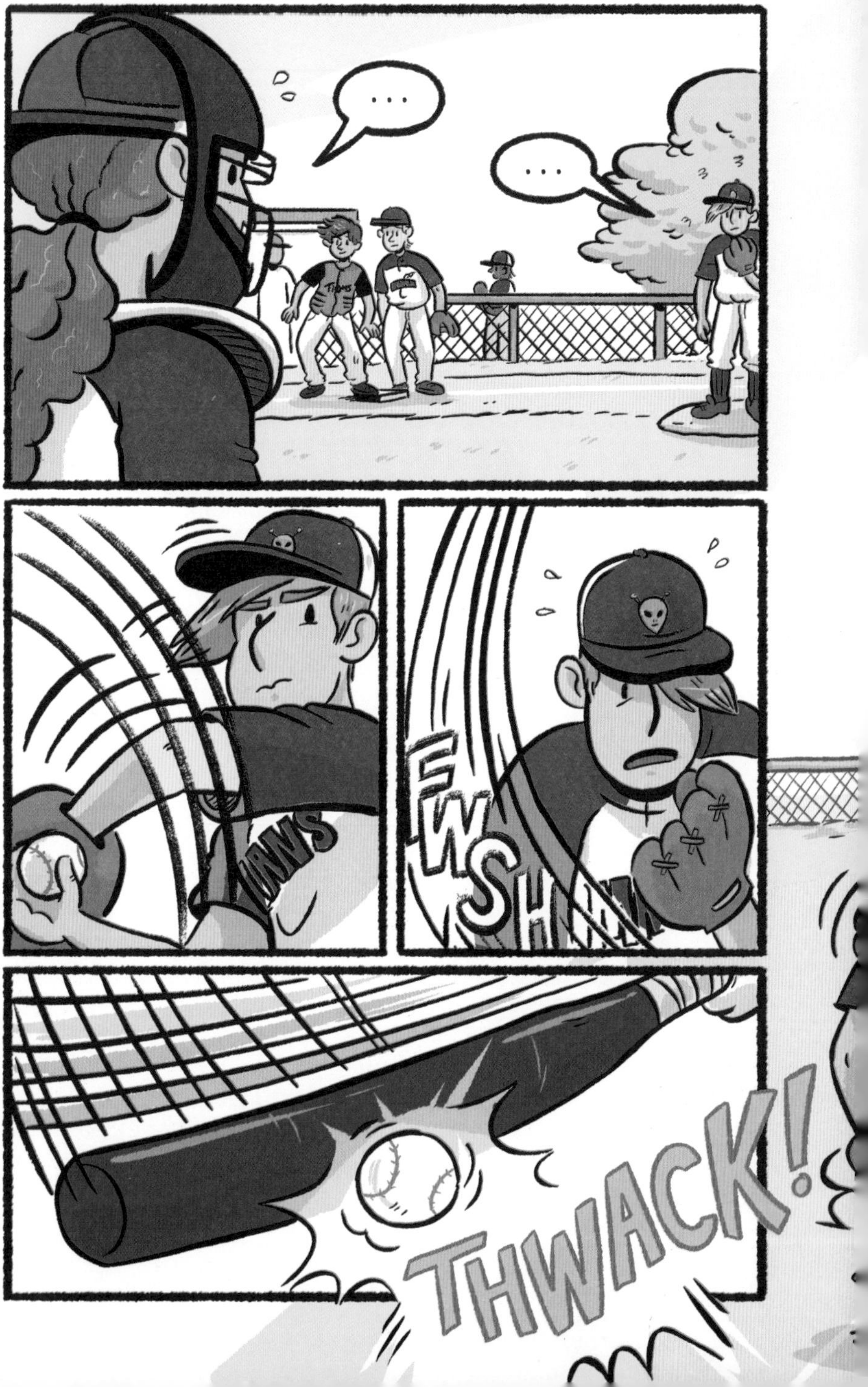
...
...
FWSH
THWACK!

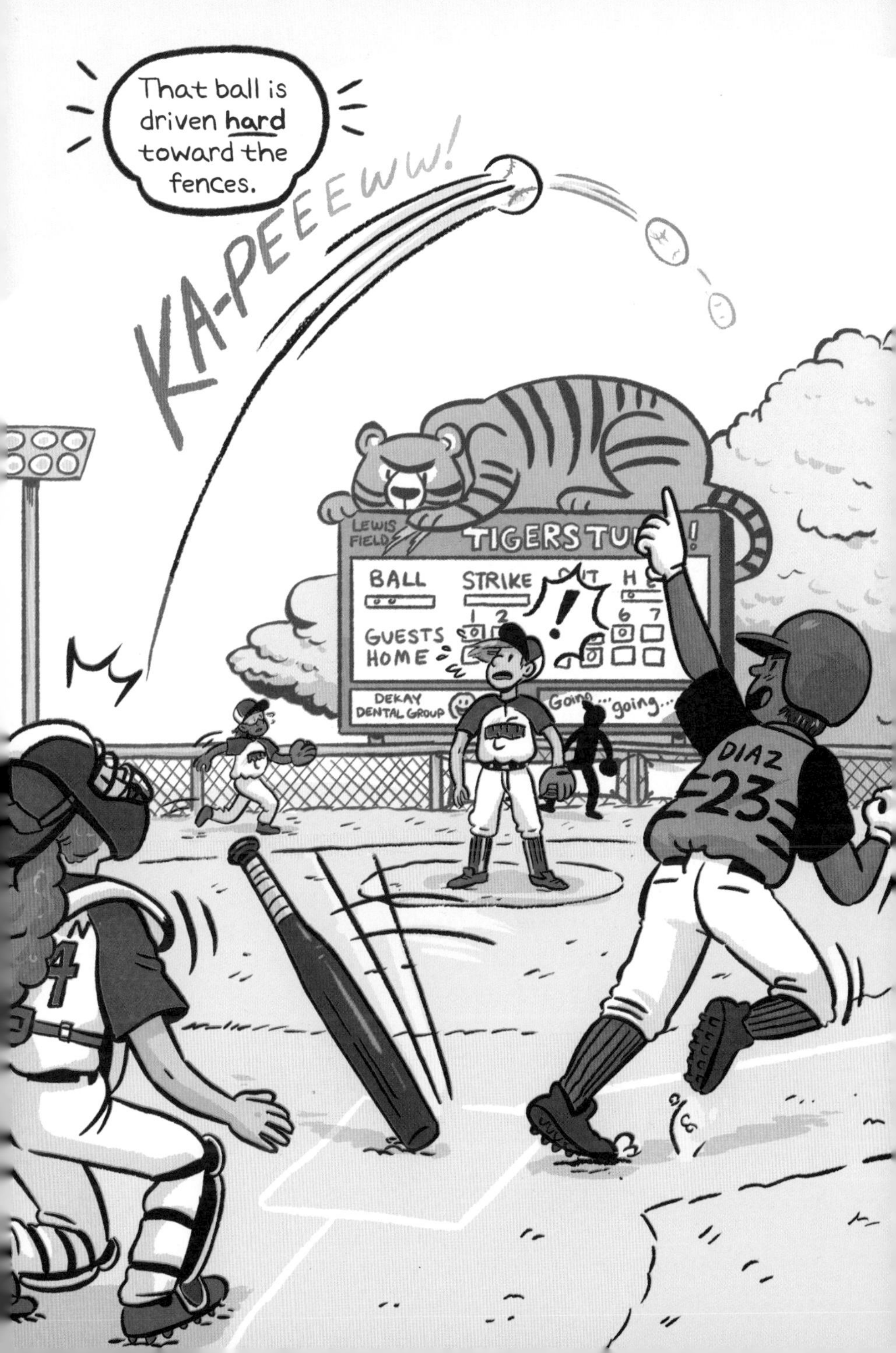
That ball is driven **hard** toward the fences.
KA-PEEEWW!
LEWIS FIELD
TIGERS TU
BALL
STRIKE
H
GUESTS
HOME
DEKAY DENTAL GROUP
Going... going...
!
DIAZ
23

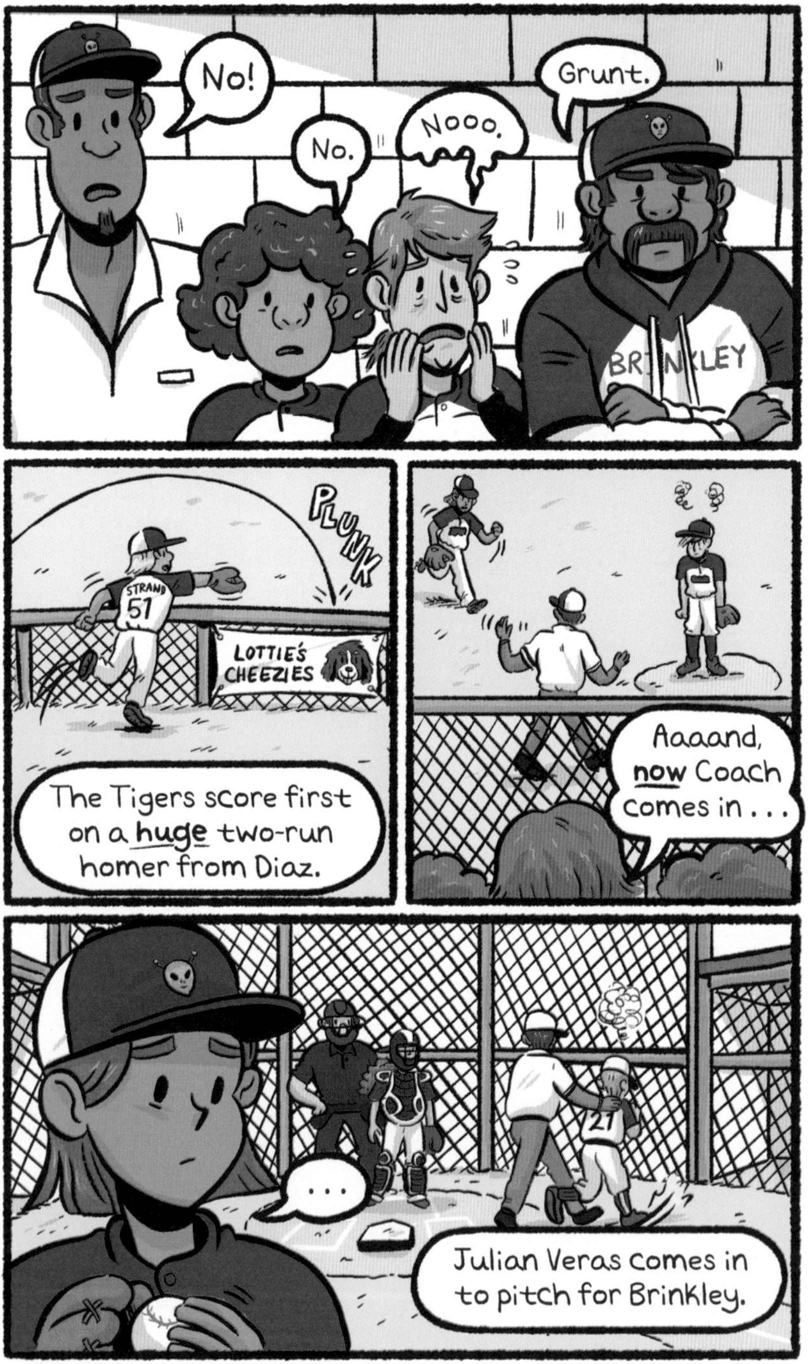
No!
No.
Nooo.
Grunt.
BRINKLEY
PLUNK
STRAND
51
LOTTIE'S CHEEZIES
The Tigers score first on a huge two-run homer from Diaz.
Aaaand, now Coach comes in . . .
. . .
21
Julian Veras comes in to pitch for Brinkley.

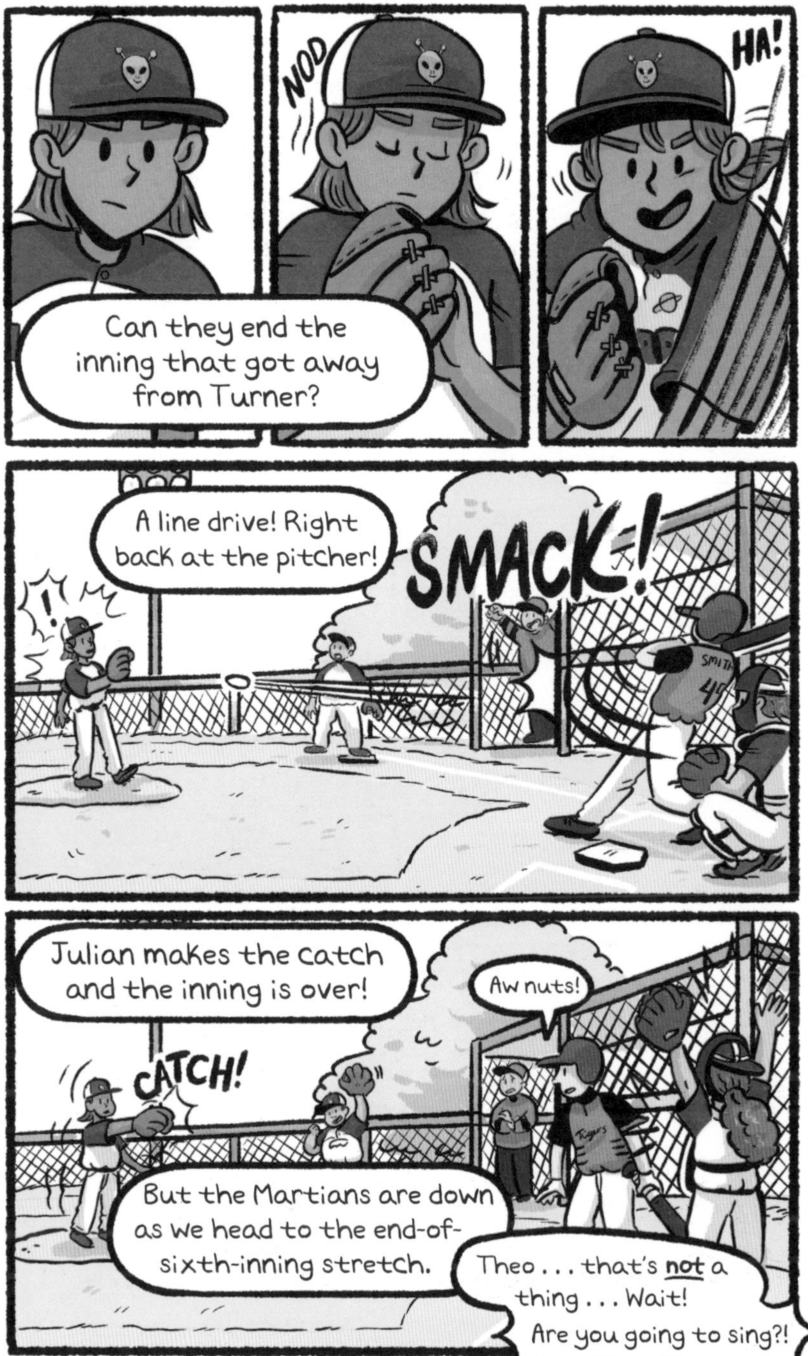
NOD
HA!
Can they end the inning that got away from Turner?
A line drive! Right back at the pitcher!
SMACK!
!
SMITH
44
Julian makes the catch and the inning is over!
Aw nuts!
CATCH!
But the Martians are down as we head to the end-of-sixth-inning stretch.
Theo . . . that's **not** a thing . . . Wait! Are you going to sing?!

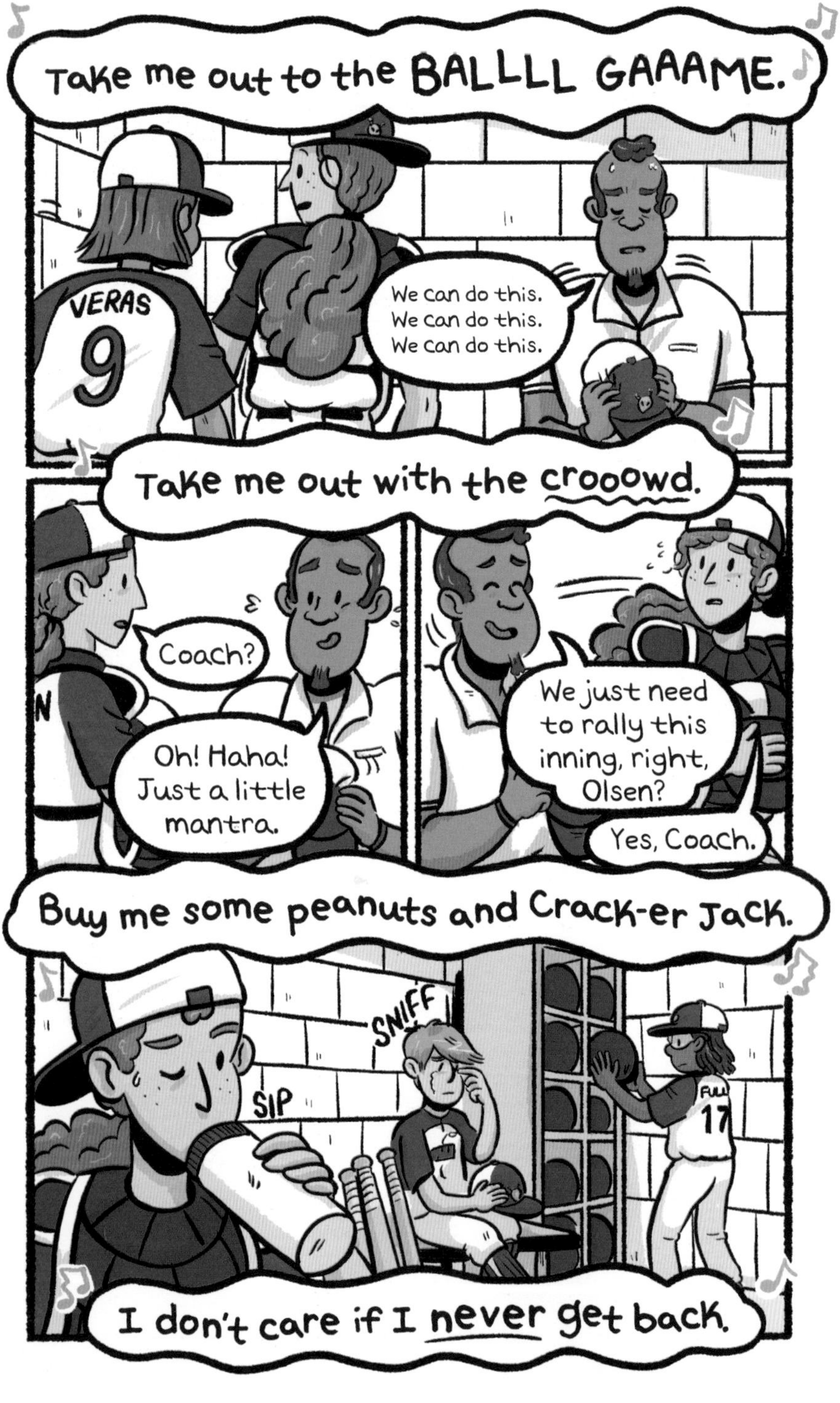
Take me out to the BALLLL GAAAME.
VERAS
9
We can do this. We can do this. We can do this.
Take me out with the crooowd.
Coach?
Oh! Haha! Just a little mantra.
We just need to rally this inning, right, Olsen?
Yes, Coach.
Buy me some peanuts and Crack-er Jack.
SNIFF
SIP
FULL
17
I don't care if I never get back.

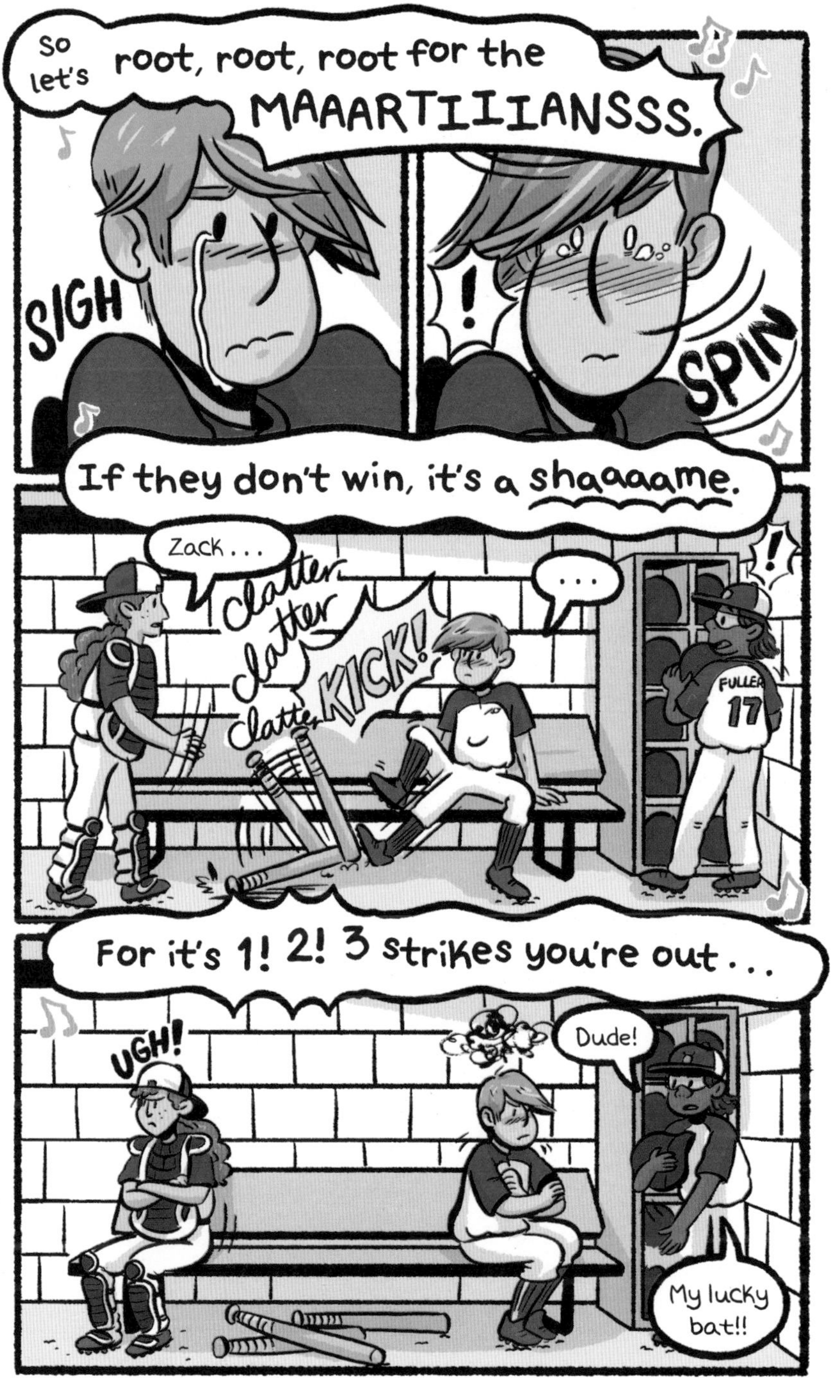
So let's root, root, root for the MAAARTIIIANSSS.
SIGH
!
SPIN
If they don't win, it's a shaaaame.
Zack . . .
Clatter clatter clatter
KICK!
. . .
!
FULLER
17
For it's 1! 2! 3 strikes you're out . . .
UGH!
Dude!
My lucky bat!!

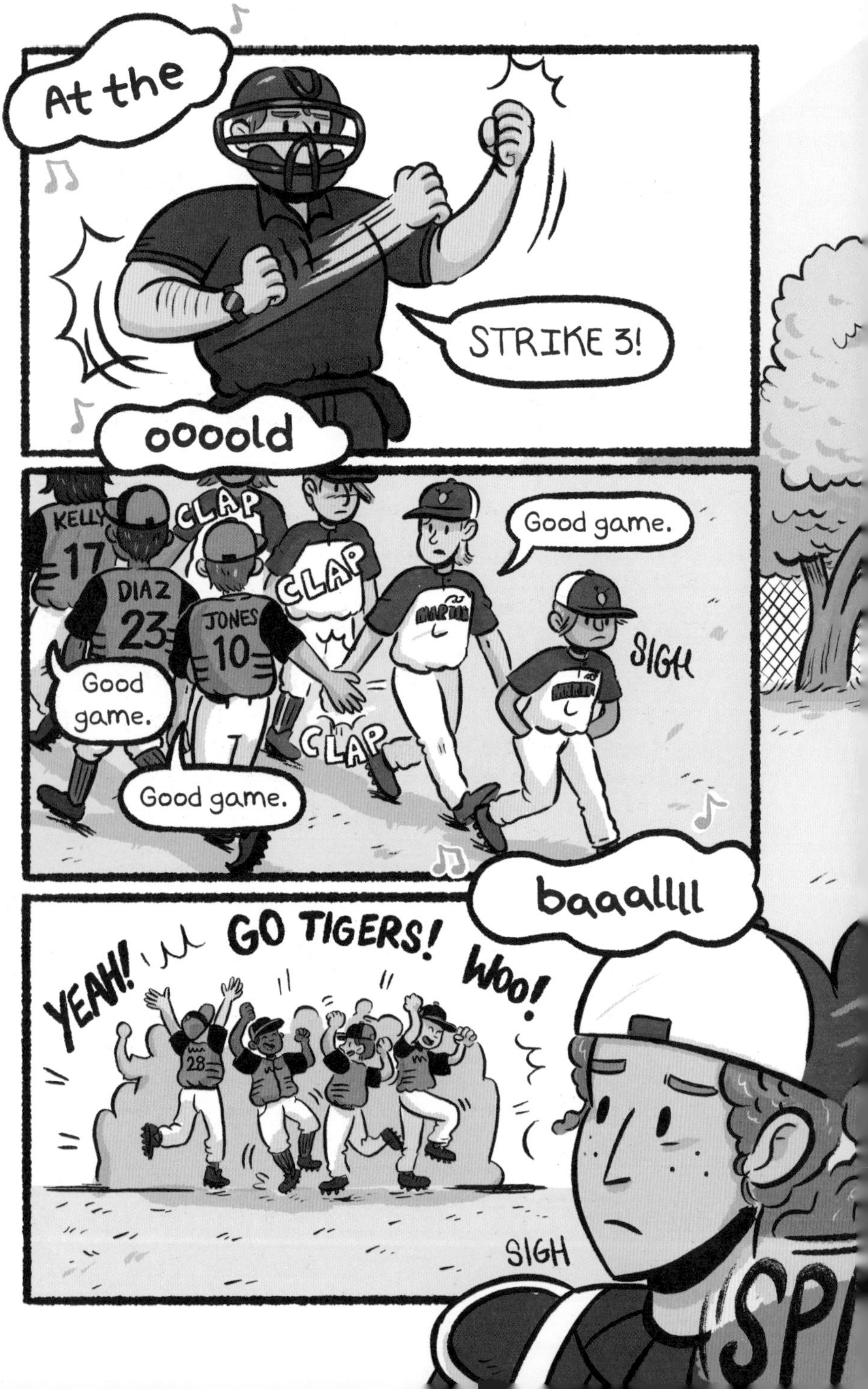
At the
STRIKE 3!
oooold
KELLY
17
DIAZ
23
JONES
10
CLAP
CLAP
Good game.
SIGH
Good game.
CLAP
Good game.
baaallll
GO TIGERS!
YEAH!
WOO!
28
SIGH
SPI

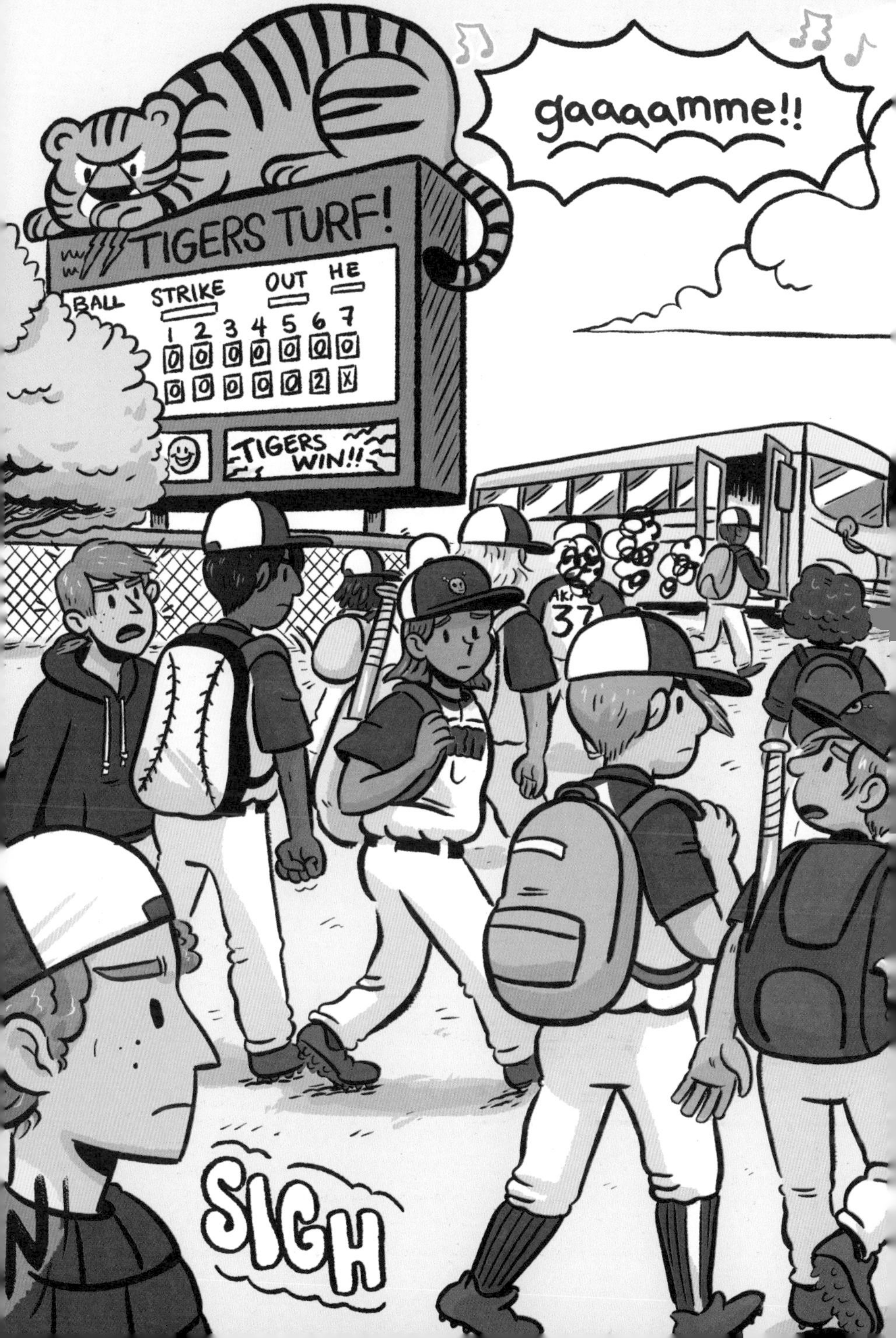
gaaaamme!!
TIGERS TURF!
BALL STRIKE OUT HE
1 2 3 4 5 6 7
0 0 0 0 0 0 0
0 0 0 0 0 2 X
TIGERS WIN!!
AKI 37
SIGH

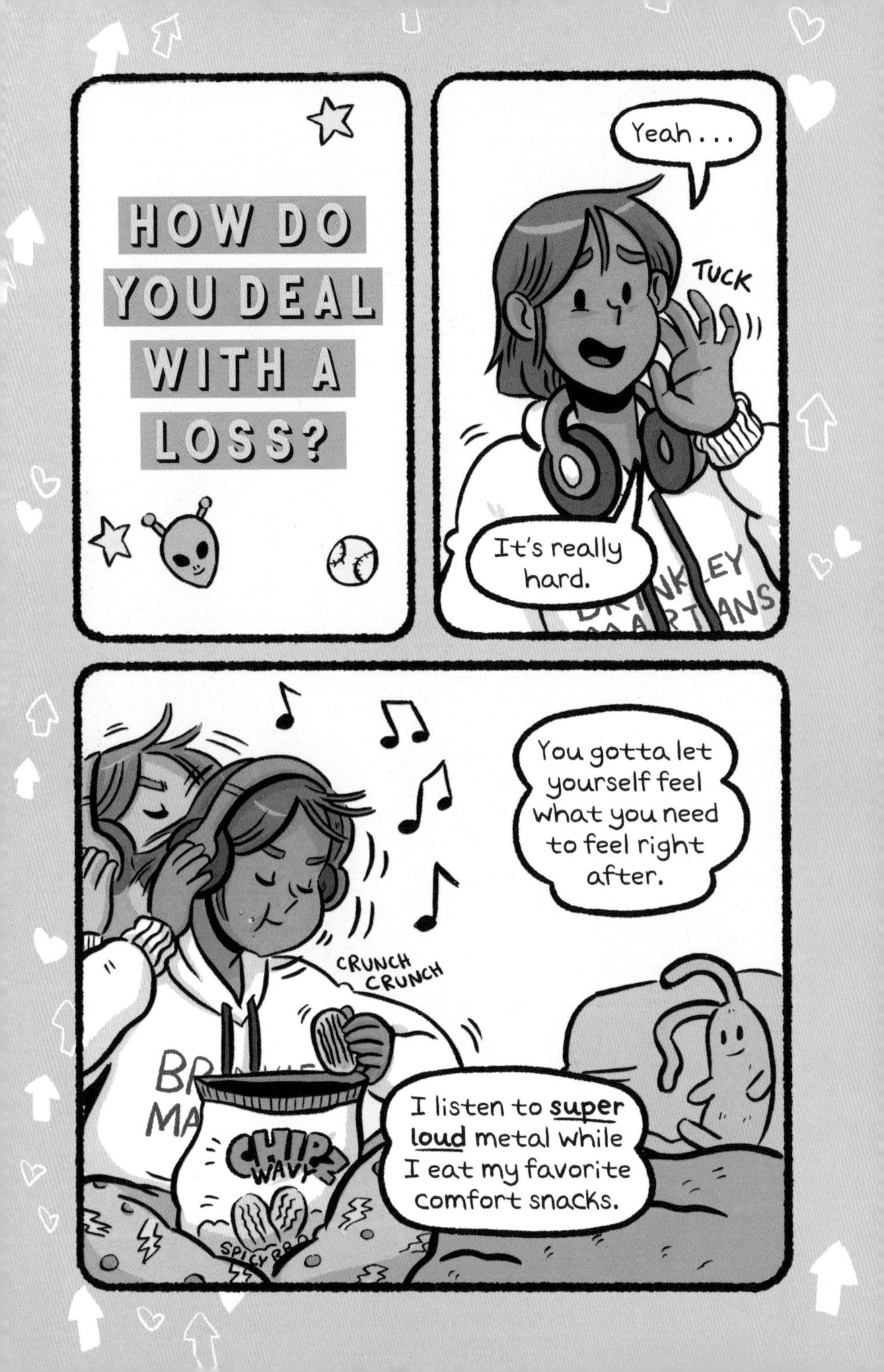
HOW DO YOU DEAL WITH A LOSS?
Yeah . . .
TUCK
It's really hard.
BRINKLEY MARTIANS
You gotta let yourself feel what you need to feel right after.
CRUNCH CRUNCH
I listen to **super loud** metal while I eat my favorite comfort snacks.
CHIPZ WAVY
SPICY BBQ

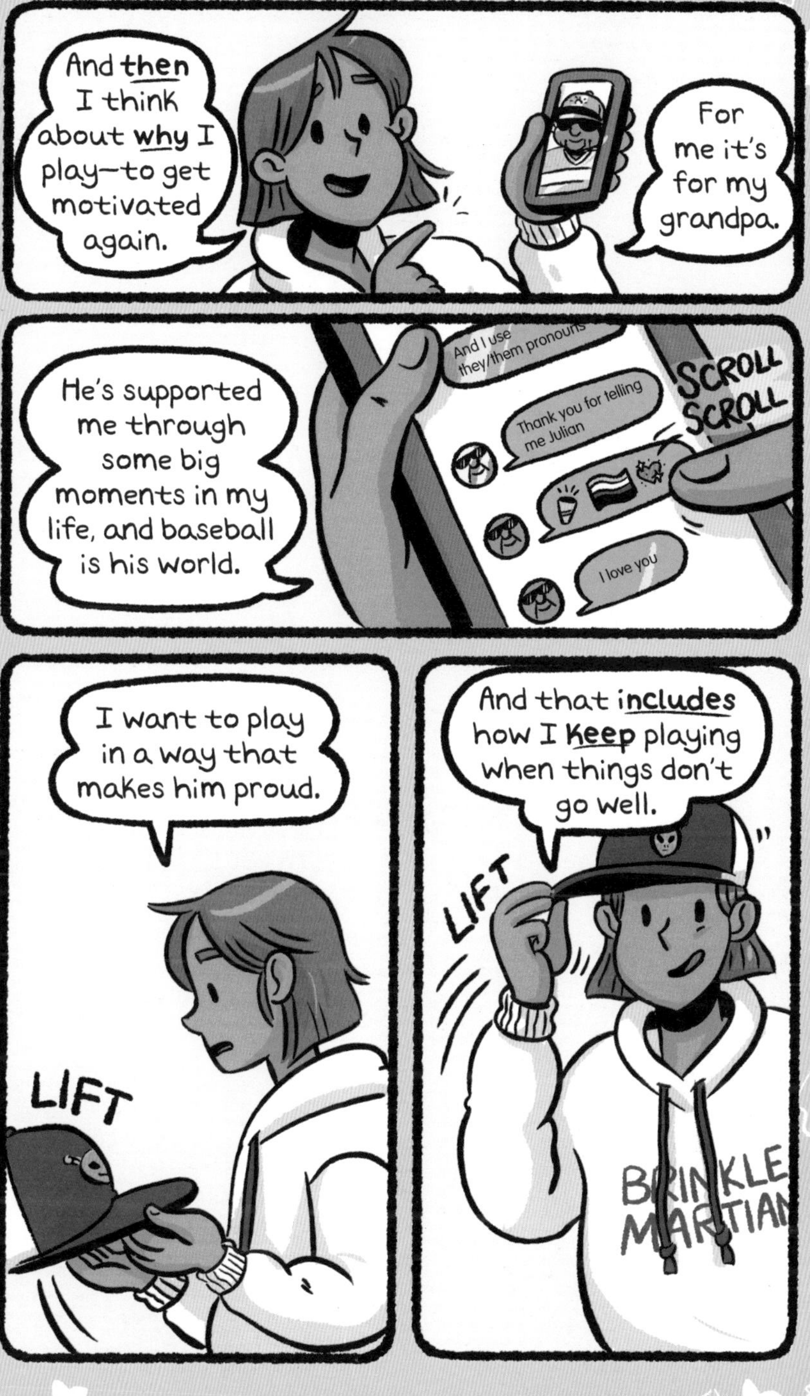
And then I think about why I play—to get motivated again.
For me it's for my grandpa.
He's supported me through some big moments in my life, and baseball is his world.
And I use they/them pronouns
Thank you for telling me Julian
I love you
SCROLL SCROLL
I want to play in a way that makes him proud.
LIFT
And that includes how I keep playing when things don't go well.
LIFT
BRINKLE MARTIAN

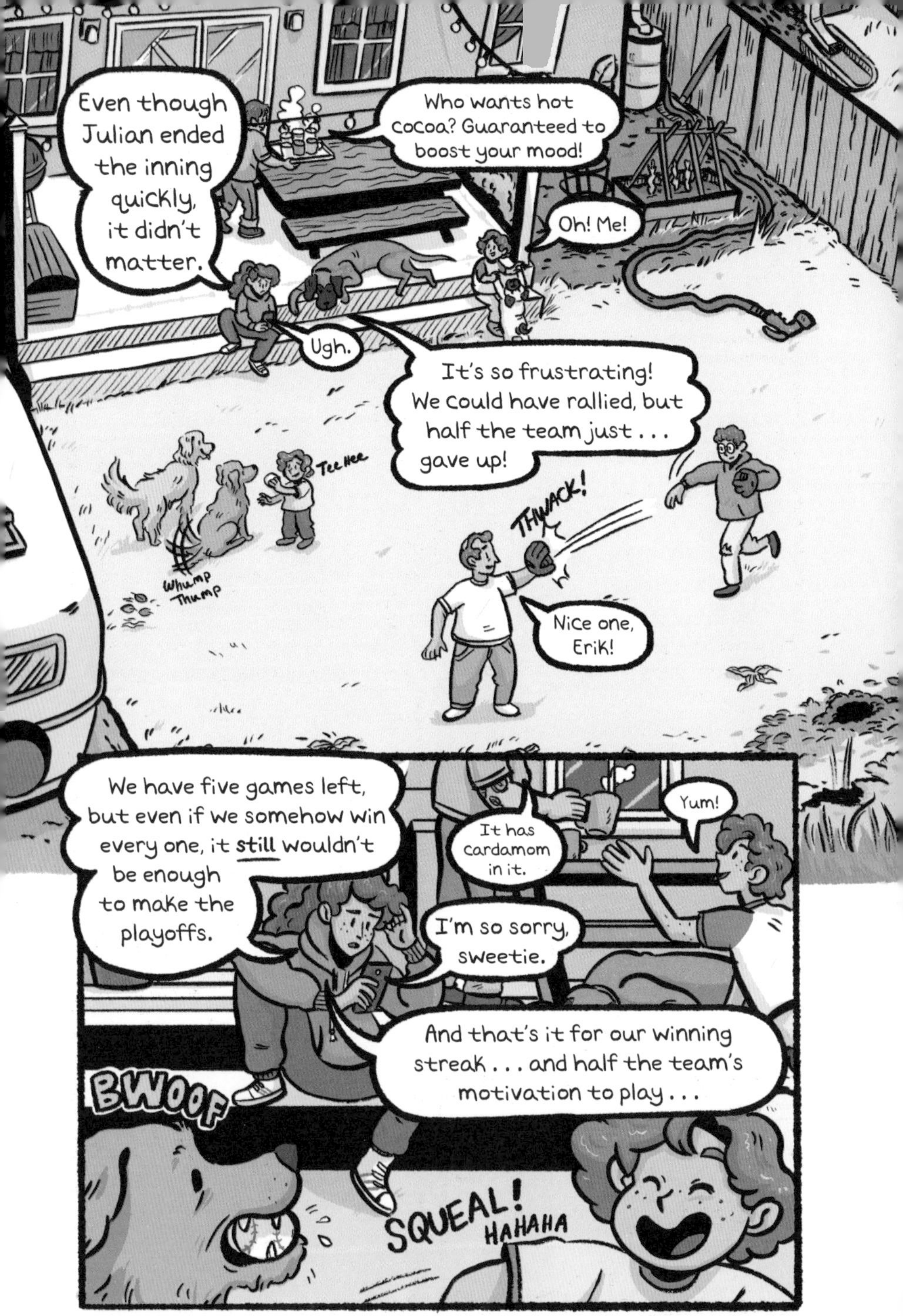
Even though Julian ended the inning quickly, it didn't matter.
Who wants hot cocoa? Guaranteed to boost your mood!
Oh! Me!
Ugh.
It's so frustrating! We could have rallied, but half the team just . . . gave up!
Tee Hee
THWACK!
Whump Thump
Nice one, Erik!
We have five games left, but even if we somehow win every one, it still wouldn't be enough to make the playoffs.
It has cardamom in it.
Yum!
I'm so sorry, sweetie.
And that's it for our winning streak . . . and half the team's motivation to play . . .
BWOOF
SQUEAL!
HAHAHA

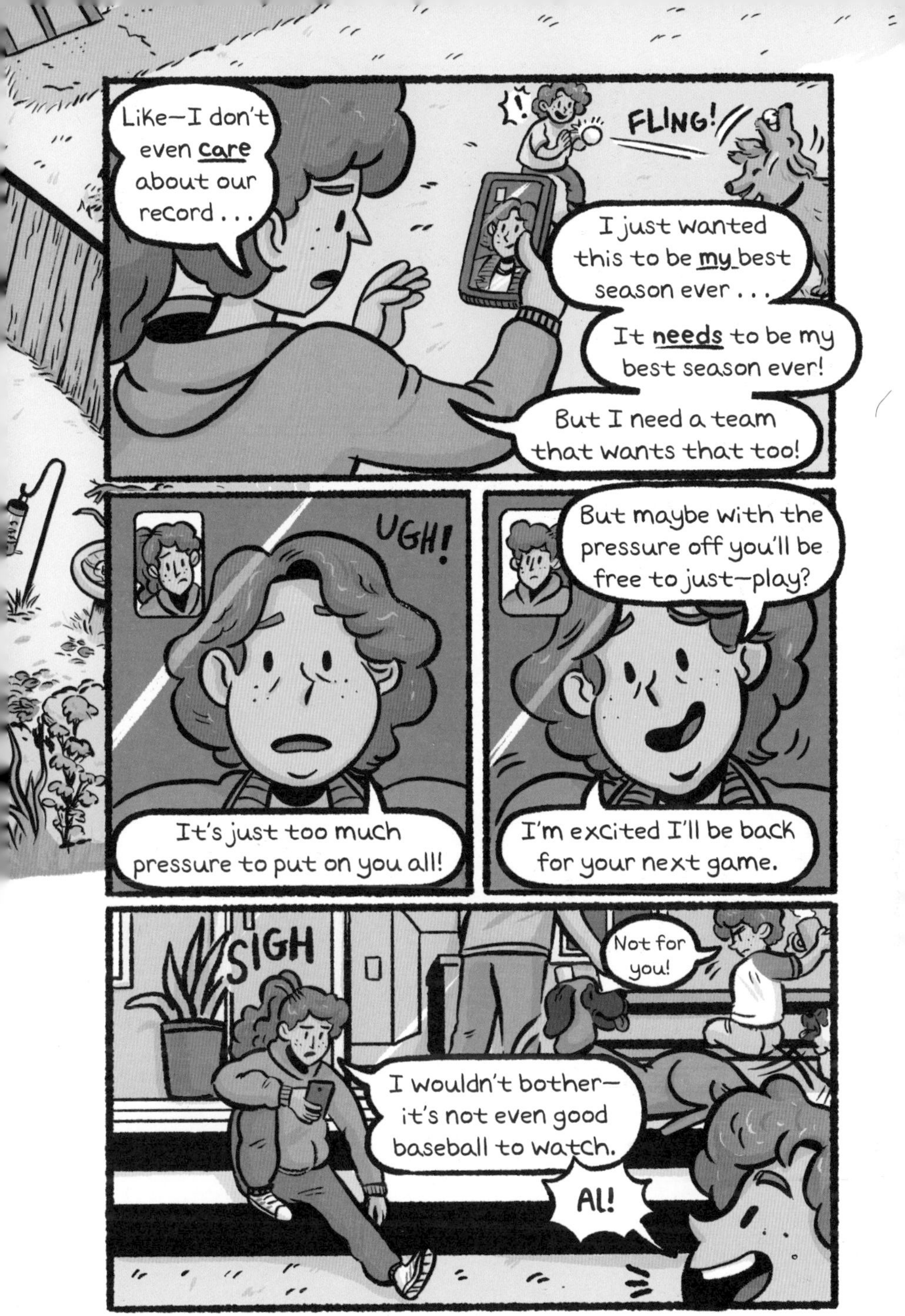
Like—I don't even care about our record . . .
FLING!
I just wanted this to be my best season ever . . .
It needs to be my best season ever!
But I need a team that wants that too!
UGH!
It's just too much pressure to put on you all!
But maybe with the pressure off you'll be free to just—play?
I'm excited I'll be back for your next game.
SIGH
Not for you!
I wouldn't bother—it's not even good baseball to watch.
AL!

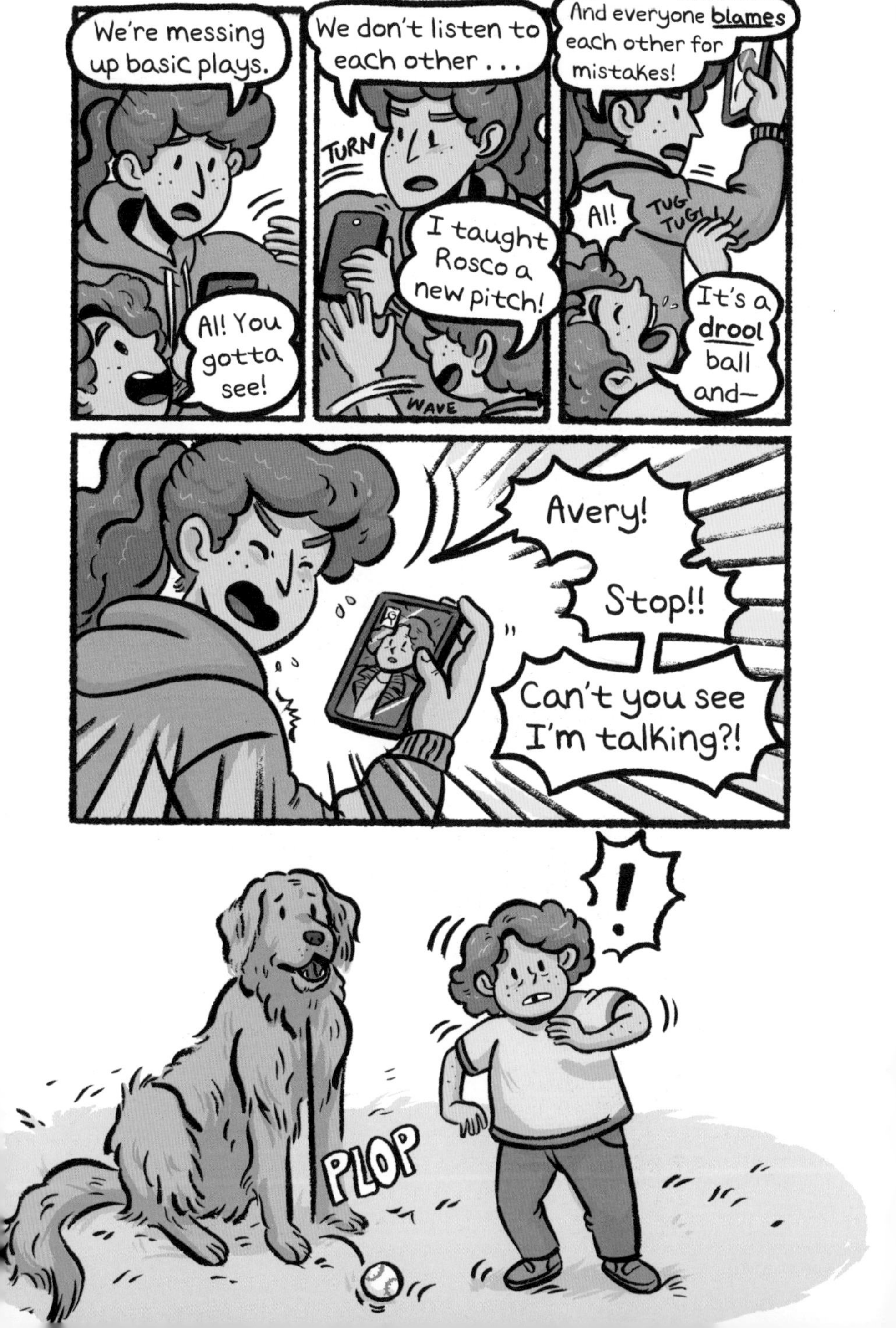

We're messing up basic plays.
Al! You gotta see!
We don't listen to each other . . .
TURN
I taught Rosco a new pitch!
WAVE
And everyone blames each other for mistakes!
Al!
TUG TUG
It's a drool ball and—
Avery!
Stop!!
Can't you see I'm talking?!
!
PLOP

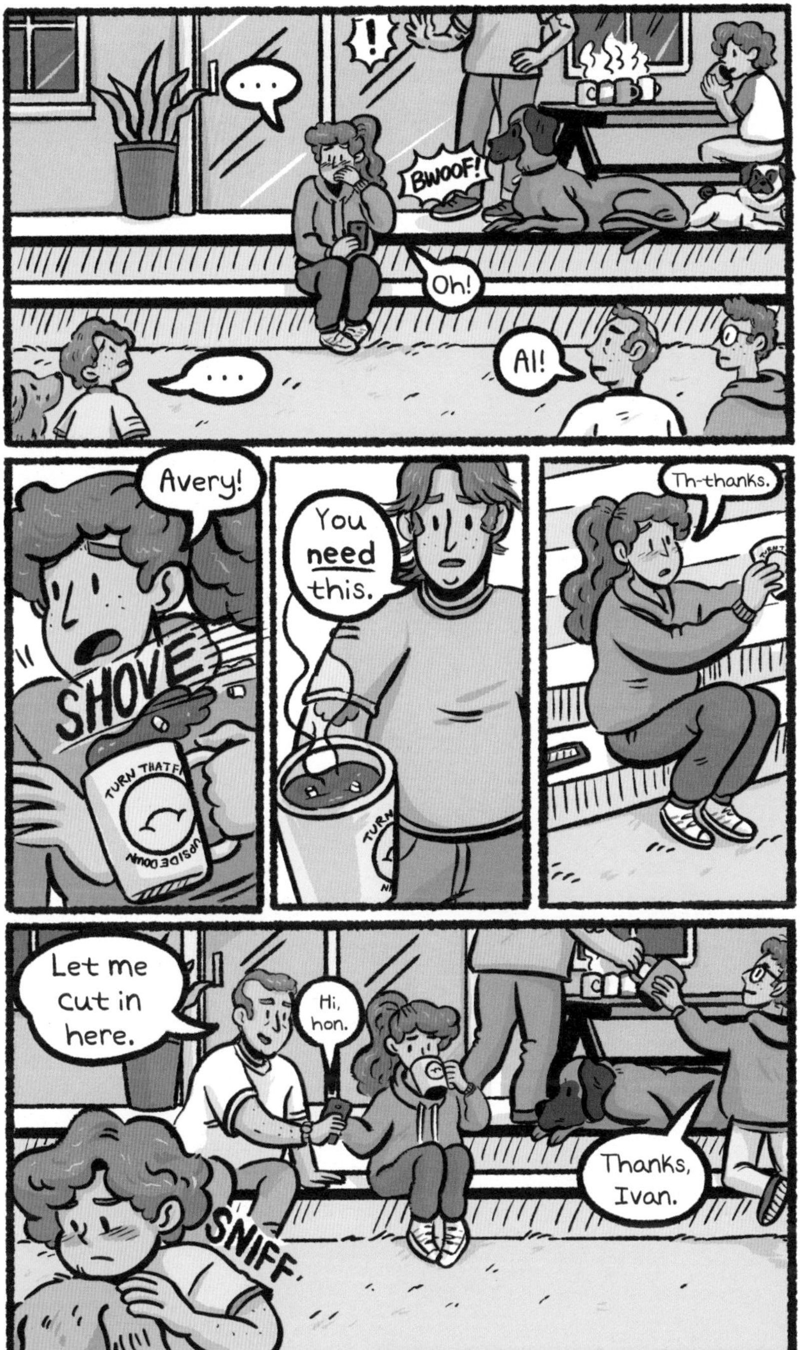

...
!
BWOOF!
Oh!
...
Al!
Avery!
SHOVE
TURN THAT F
UPSIDE DOWN
You need this.
Th-thanks.
Let me cut in here.
Hi, hon.
Thanks, Ivan.
SNIFF

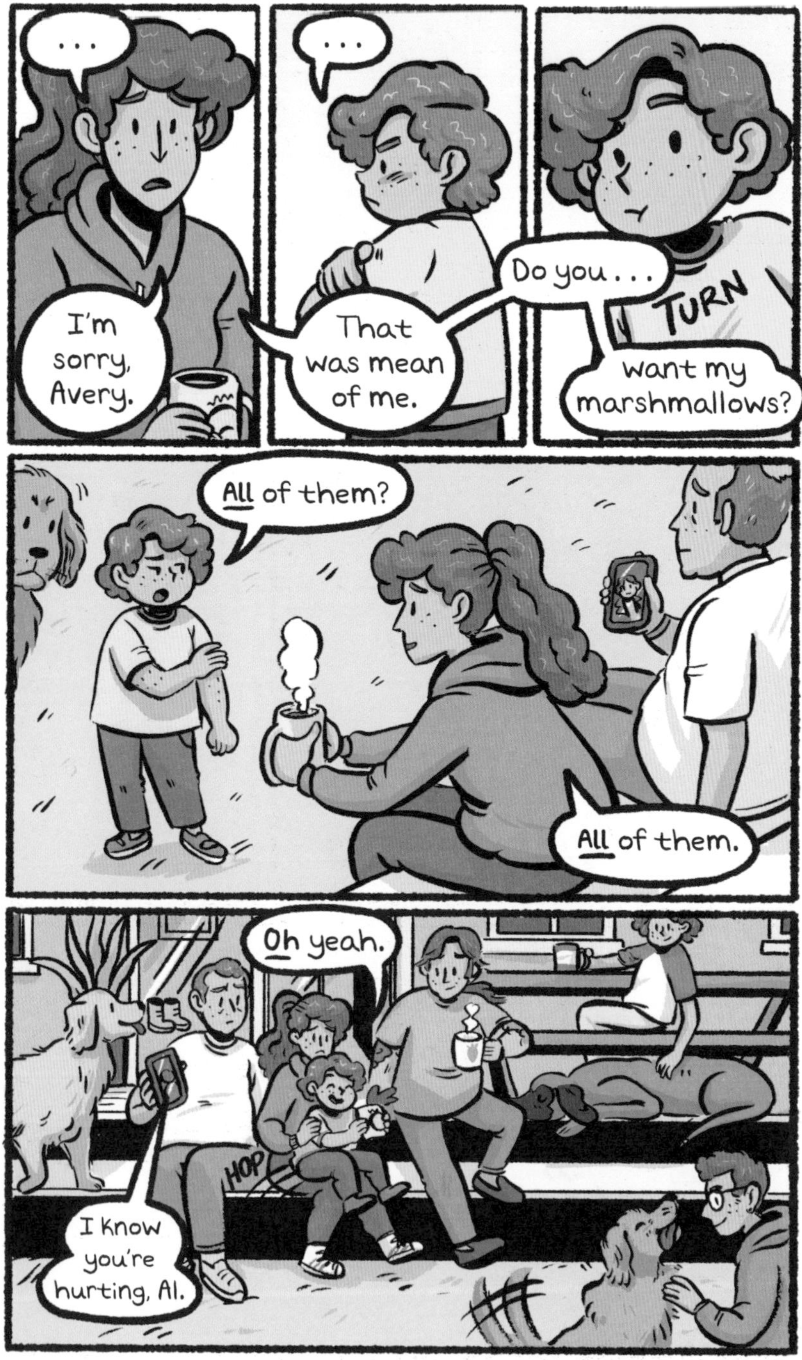
. . .
I'm sorry, Avery.
. . .
That was mean of me.
Do you . . .
TURN
want my marshmallows?
All of them?
All of them.
Oh yeah.
HOP
I know you're hurting, Al.

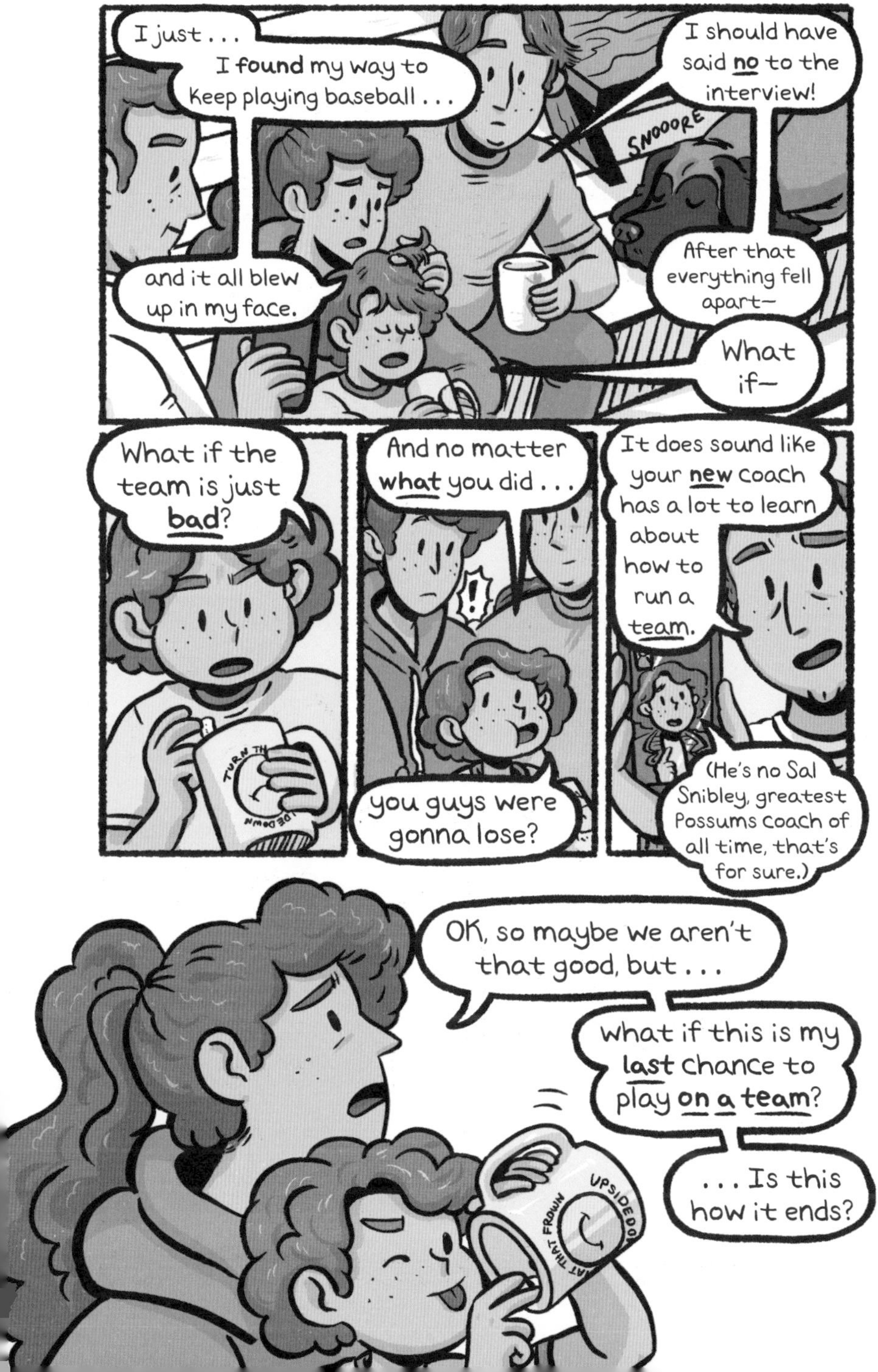

I just . . .
I found my way to keep playing baseball . . .
I should have said no to the interview!
SNOOORE
and it all blew up in my face.
After that everything fell apart—
What if—
What if the team is just bad?
And no matter what you did . . .
you guys were gonna lose?
It does sound like your new coach has a lot to learn about how to run a team.
(He's no Sal Snibley, greatest Possums coach of all time, that's for sure.)
OK, so maybe we aren't that good, but . . .
What if this is my last chance to play on a team?
. . . Is this how it ends?

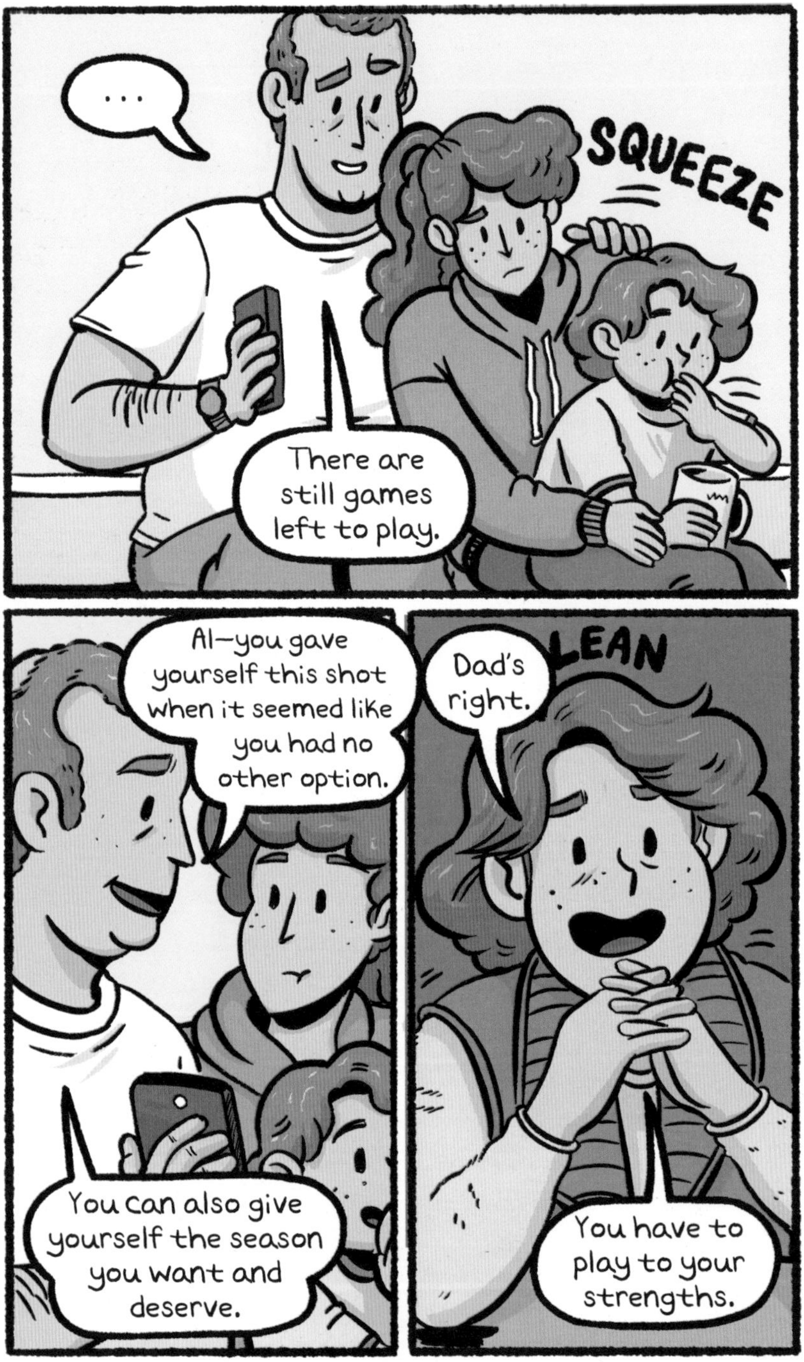
...
SQUEEZE
There are still games left to play.
Al—you gave yourself this shot when it seemed like you had no other option.
You can also give yourself the season you want and deserve.
LEAN
Dad's right.
You have to play to your strengths.

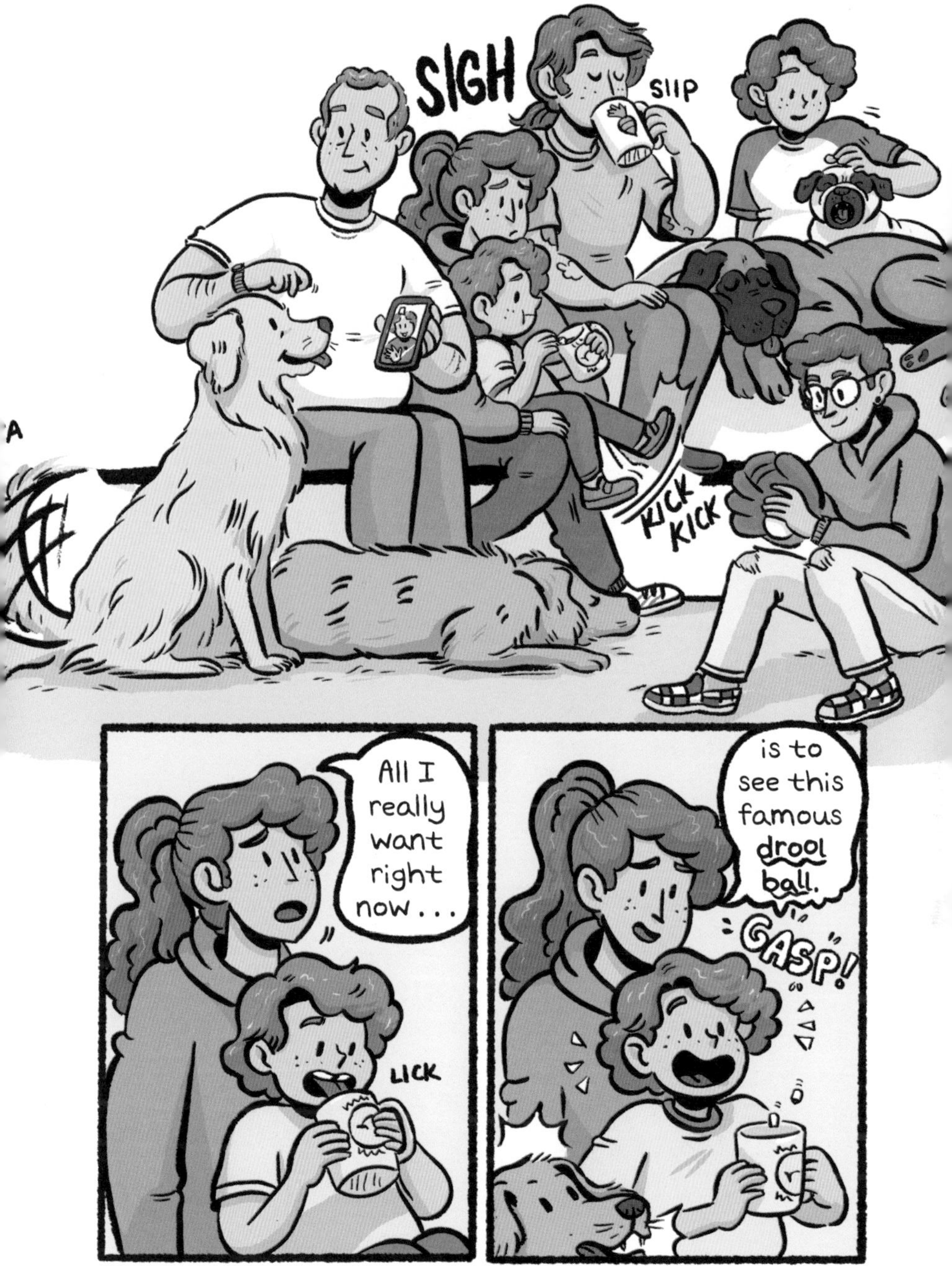

SIGH
SIIP
KICK KICK
All I really want right now . . .
LICK
is to see this famous drool ball.
GASP!

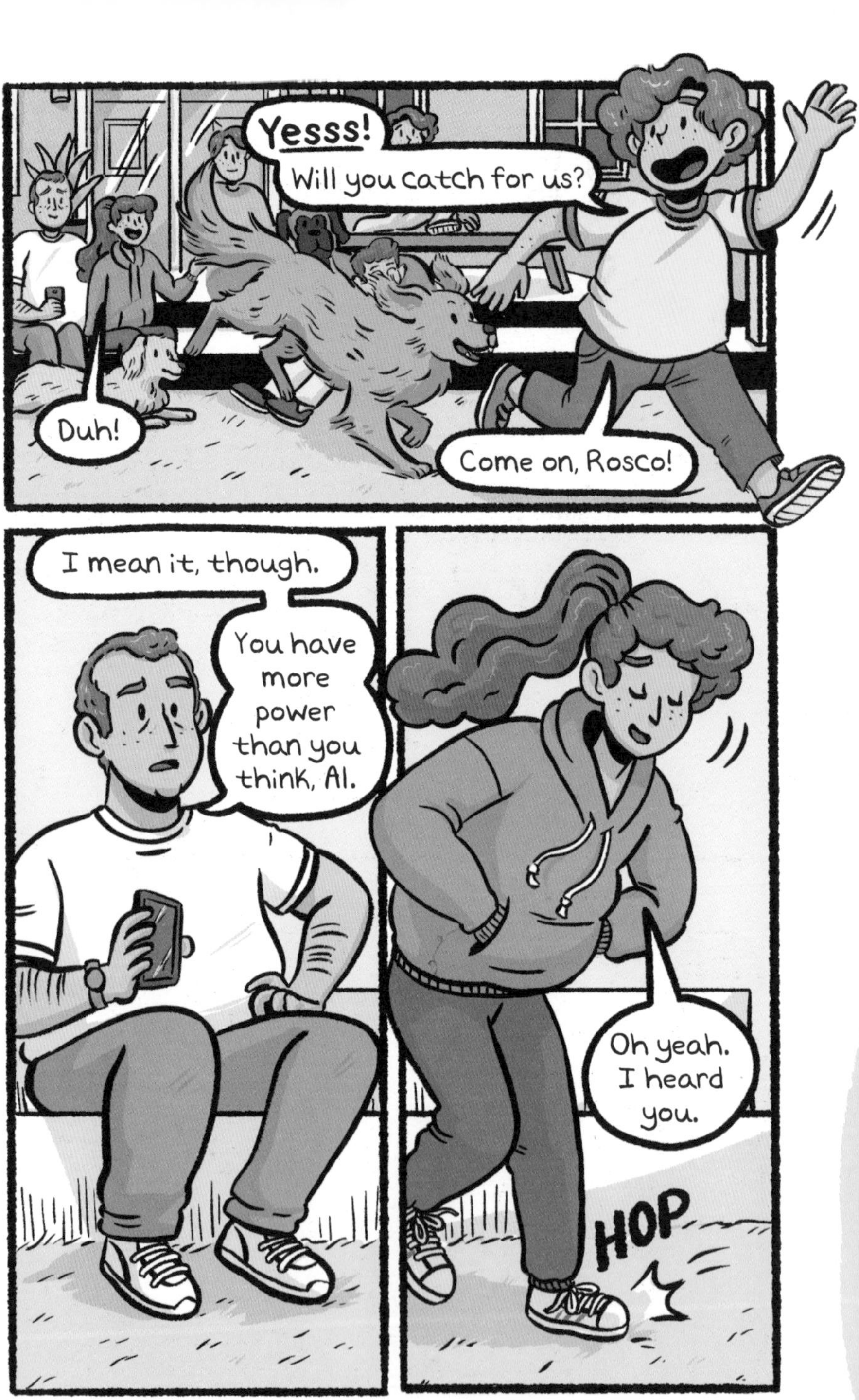
Yesss!
Will you catch for us?
Duh!
Come on, Rosco!
I mean it, though.
You have more power than you think, Al.
Oh yeah. I heard you.
HOP

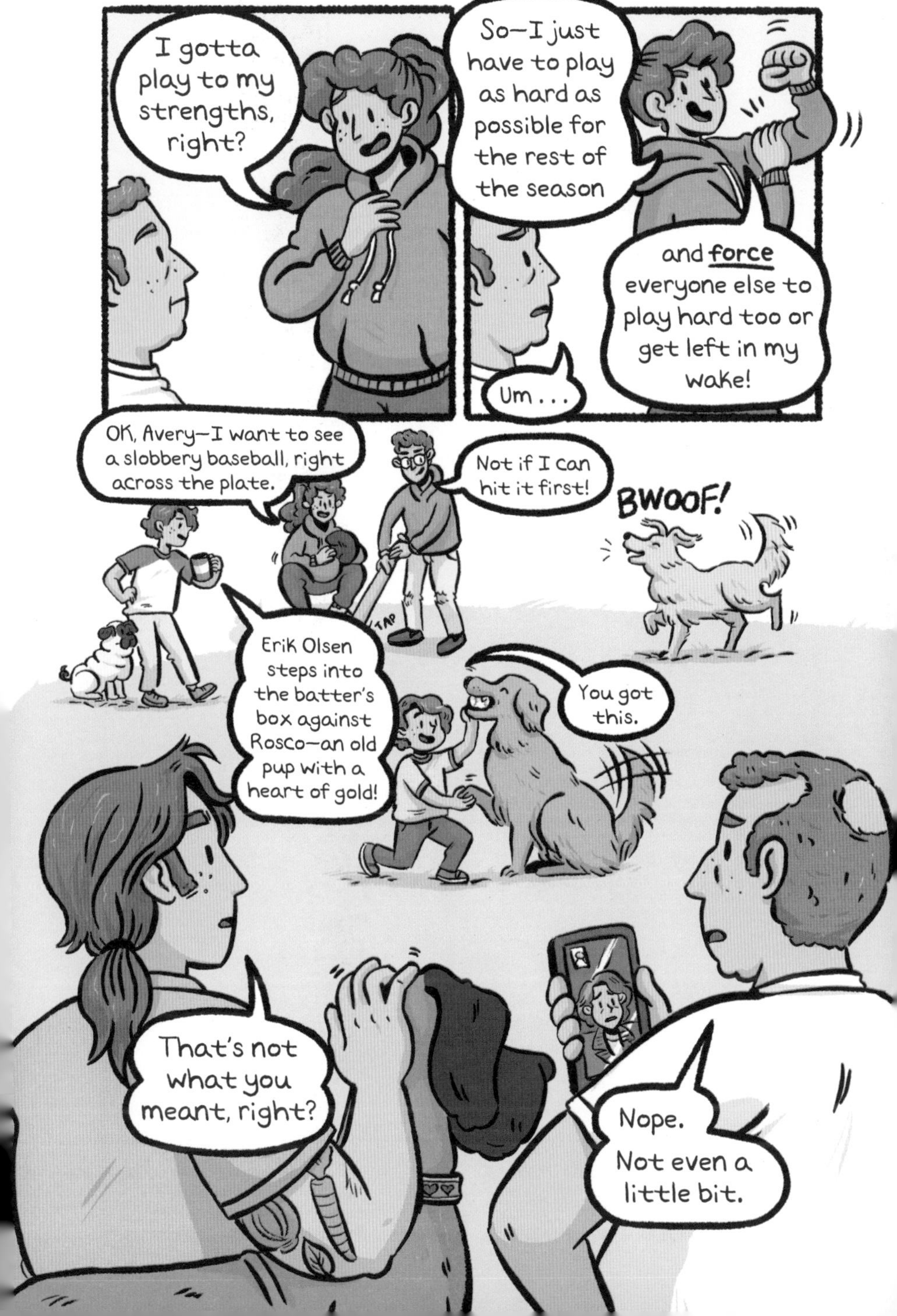
I gotta play to my strengths, right?
So—I just have to play as hard as possible for the rest of the season
and **force** everyone else to play hard too or get left in my wake!
Um . . .
OK, Avery—I want to see a slobbery baseball, right across the plate.
Not if I can hit it first!
BWOOF!
TAP
Erik Olsen steps into the batter's box against Rosco—an old pup with a heart of gold!
You got this.
That's not what you meant, right?
Nope.
Not even a little bit.

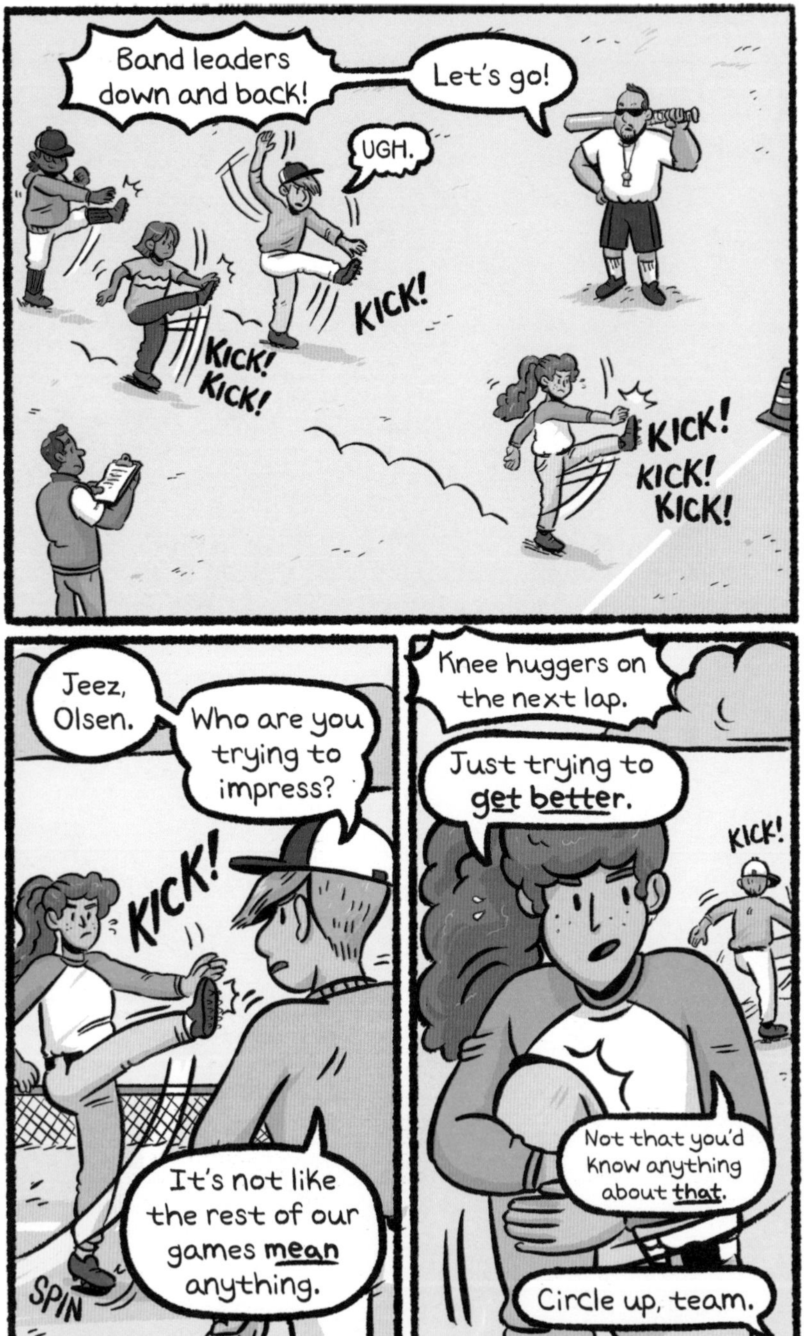
Band leaders down and back!
Let's go!
UGH.
KICK!
KICK!
KICK!
KICK!
KICK!
KICK!
Jeez, Olsen.
Who are you trying to impress?
KICK!
It's not like the rest of our games **mean** anything.
SPIN
Knee huggers on the next lap.
Just trying to **get better**.
KICK!
Not that you'd know anything about **that**.
Circle up, team.

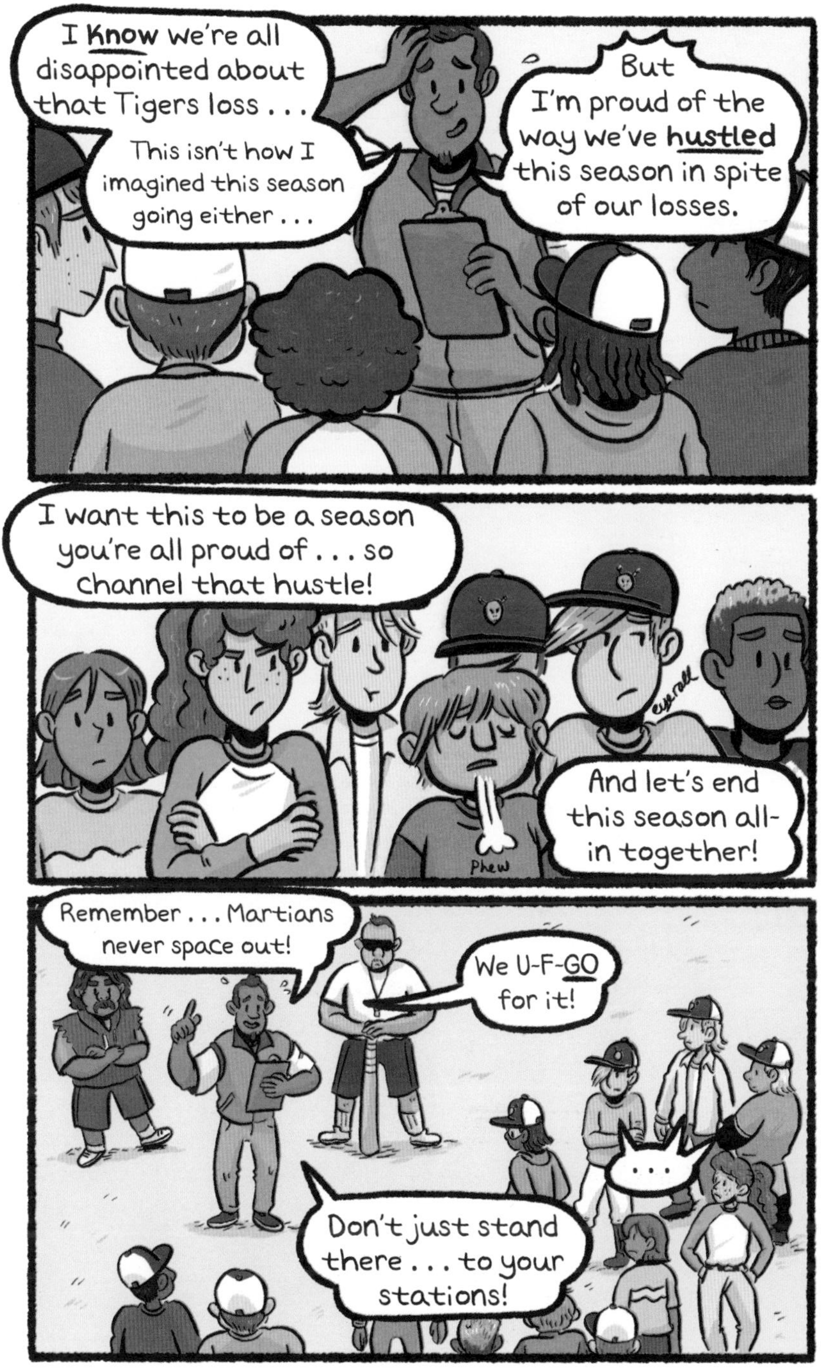
I Know we're all disappointed about that Tigers loss . . .
This isn't how I imagined this season going either . . .
But I'm proud of the way we've hustled this season in spite of our losses.
I want this to be a season you're all proud of . . . so channel that hustle!
eyeroll
Phew
And let's end this season all-in together!
Remember . . . Martians never space out!
We U-F-GO for it!
. . .
Don't just stand there . . . to your stations!

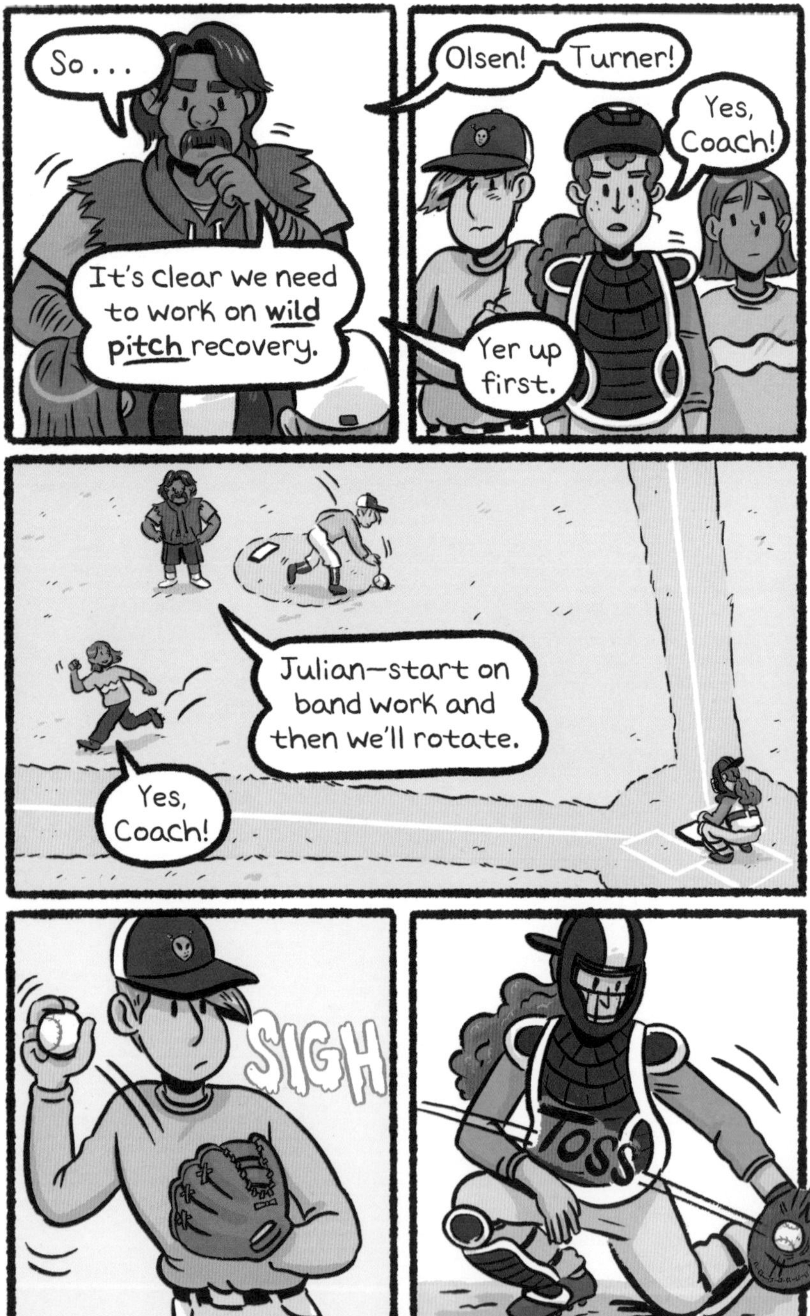
So . . .
It's clear we need to work on wild pitch recovery.
Olsen!
Turner!
Yes, Coach!
Yer up first.
Julian—start on band work and then we'll rotate.
Yes, Coach!
SIGH
TOSS

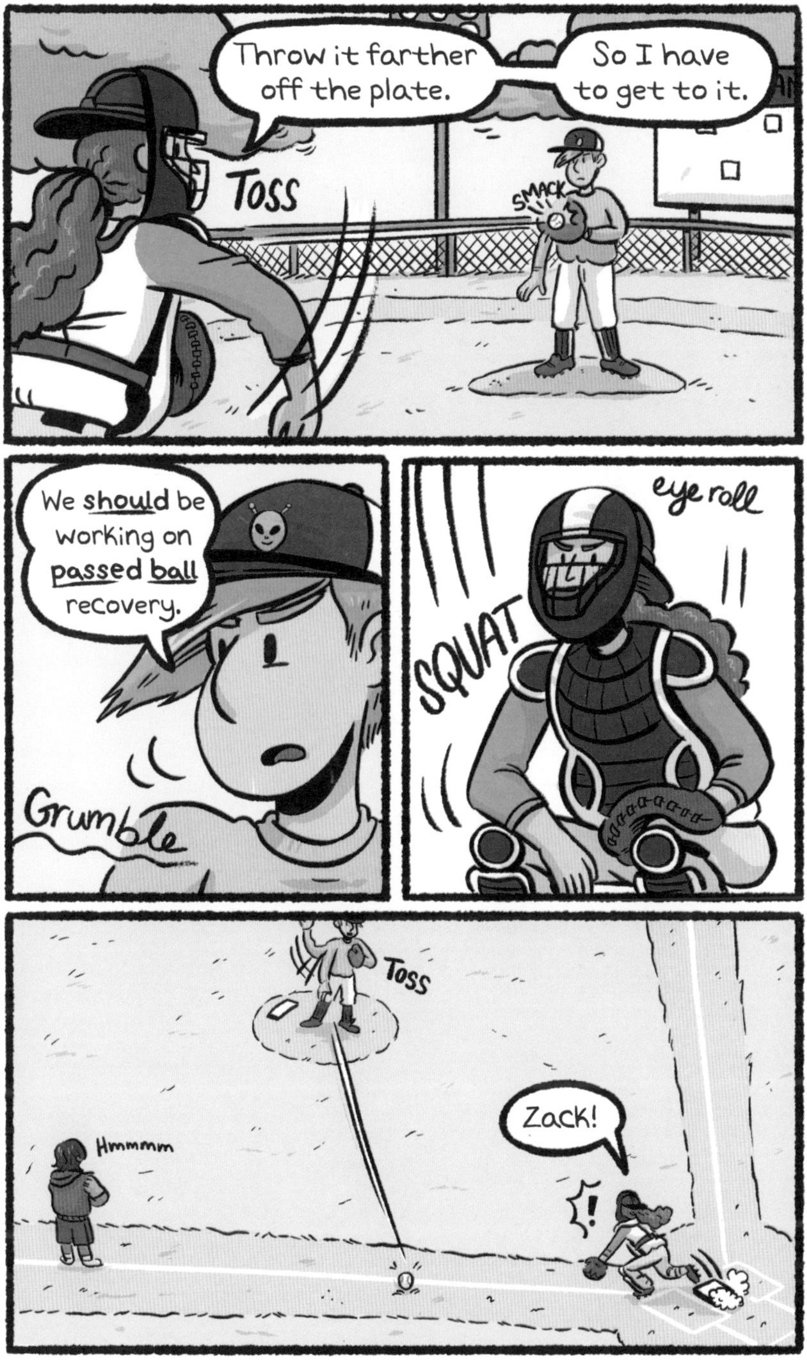
Throw it farther off the plate.
So I have to get to it.
TOSS
SMACK
We should be working on passed ball recovery.
Grumble
eye roll
SQUAT
TOSS
Zack!
!
Hmmmm

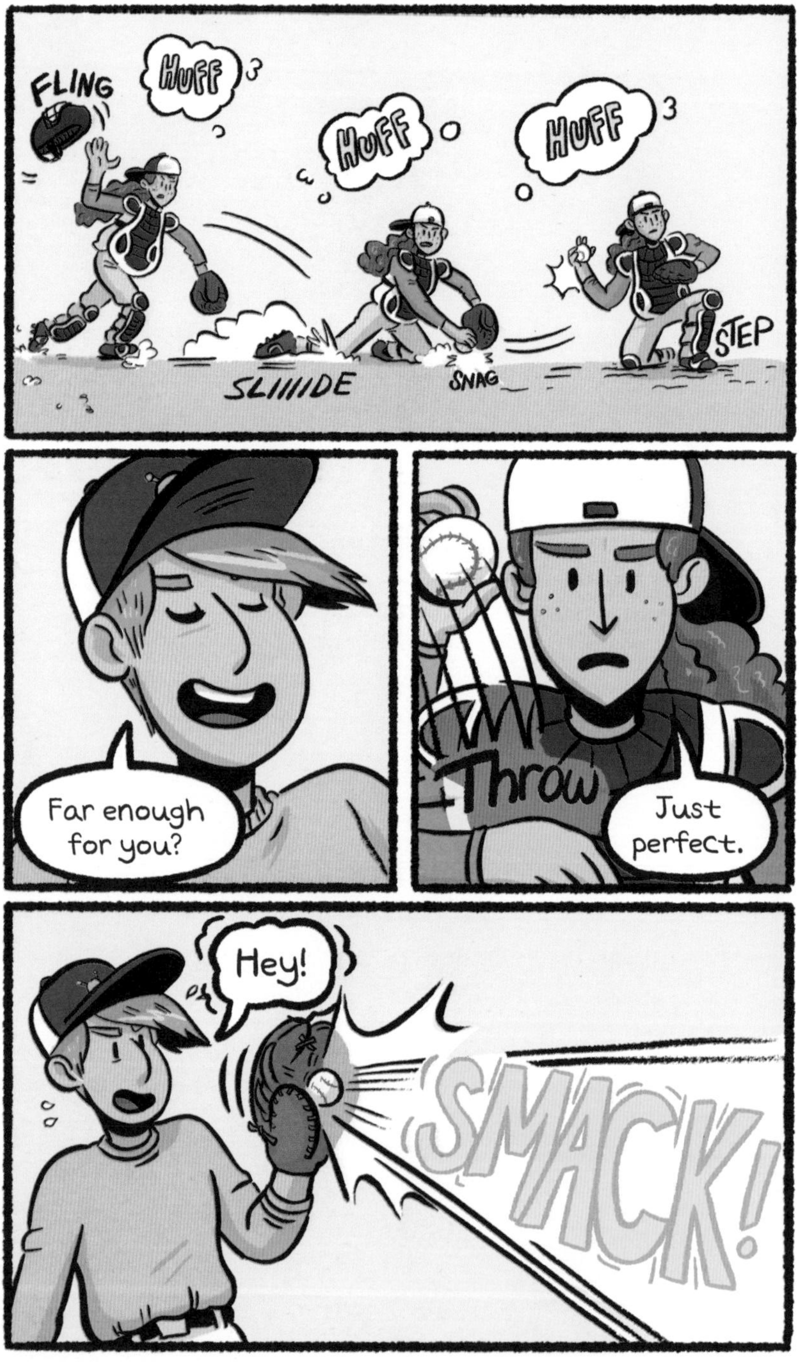
FLING
HUFF
HUFF
HUFF
SLIIIIDE
SNAG
STEP
Far enough for you?
Throw
Just perfect.
Hey!
SMACK!

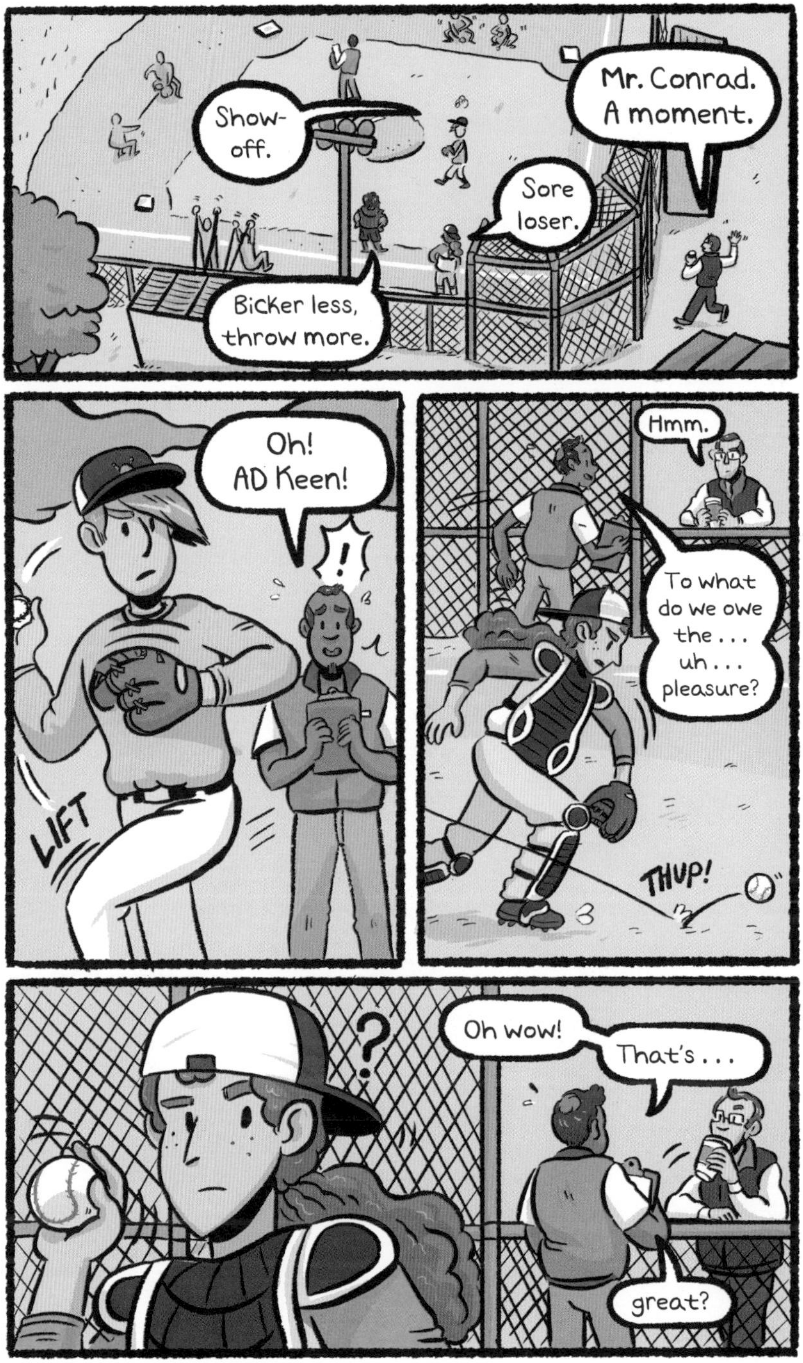
Show-off.
Mr. Conrad. A moment.
Sore loser.
Bicker less, throw more.
Oh! AD Keen!
!
LIFT
Hmm.
To what do we owe the . . . uh . . . pleasure?
THUP!
?
Oh wow!
That's . . .
great?

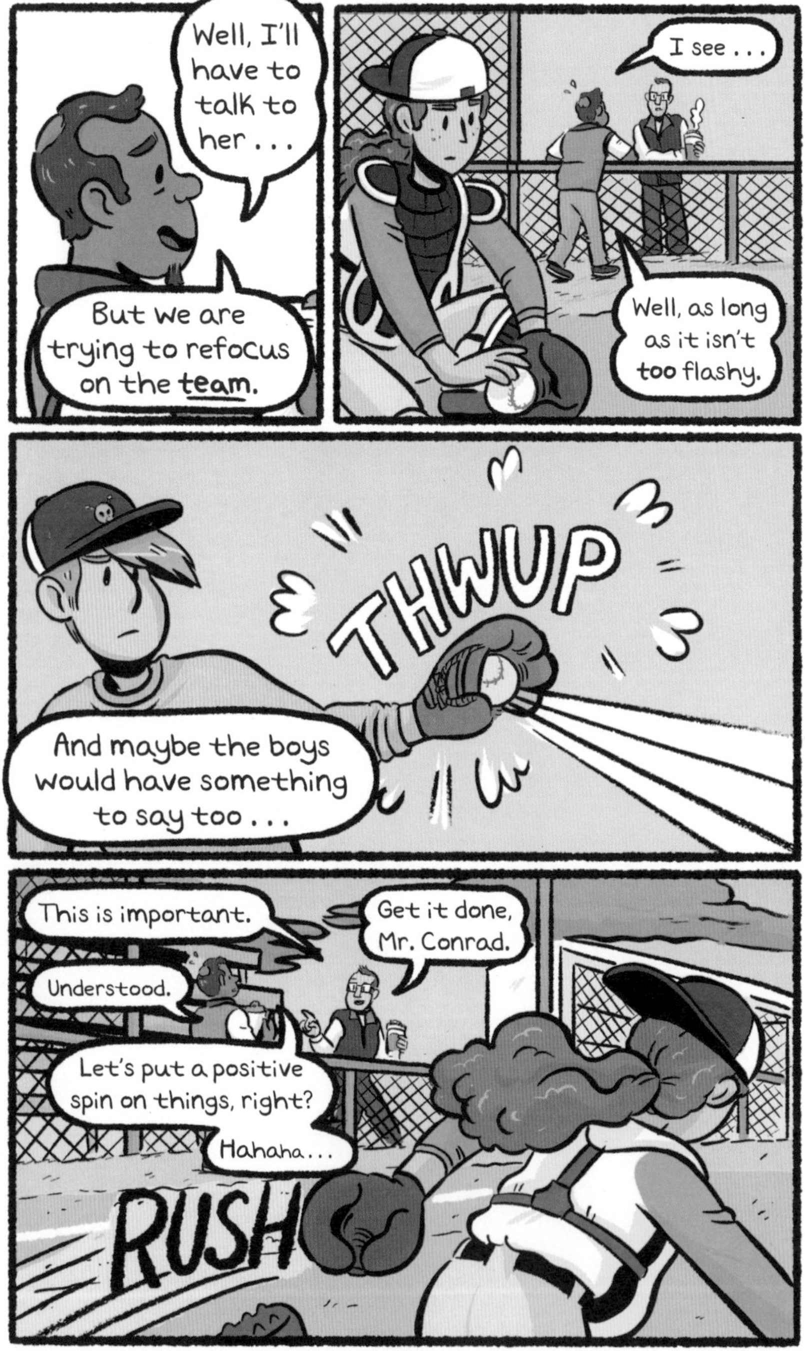
Well, I'll have to talk to her . . .
But we are trying to refocus on the team.
I see . . .
Well, as long as it isn't too flashy.
THWUP
And maybe the boys would have something to say too . . .
This is important.
Get it done, Mr. Conrad.
Understood.
Let's put a positive spin on things, right?
Hahaha . . .
RUSH

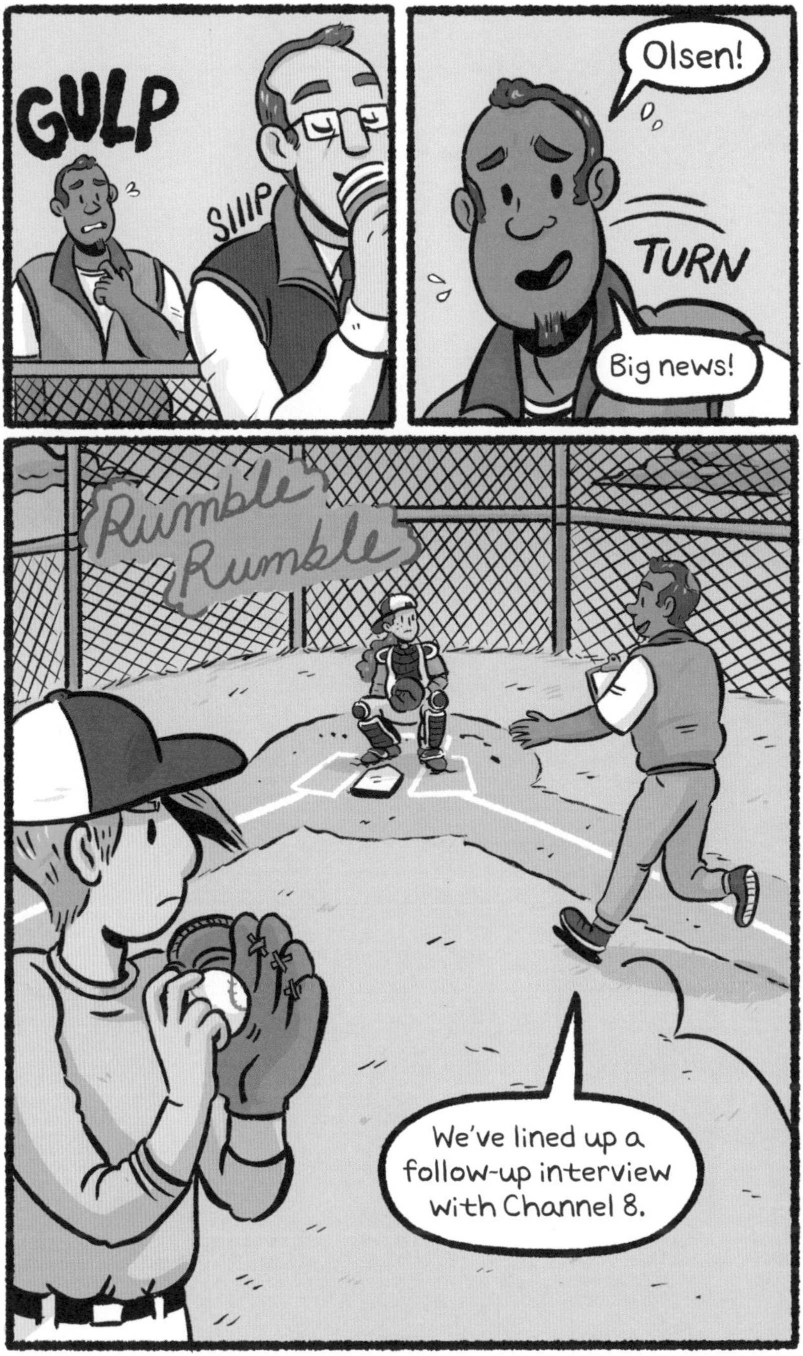
GULP
SIIIP
Olsen!
TURN
Big news!
Rumble
Rumble
We've lined up a
follow-up interview
with Channel 8.

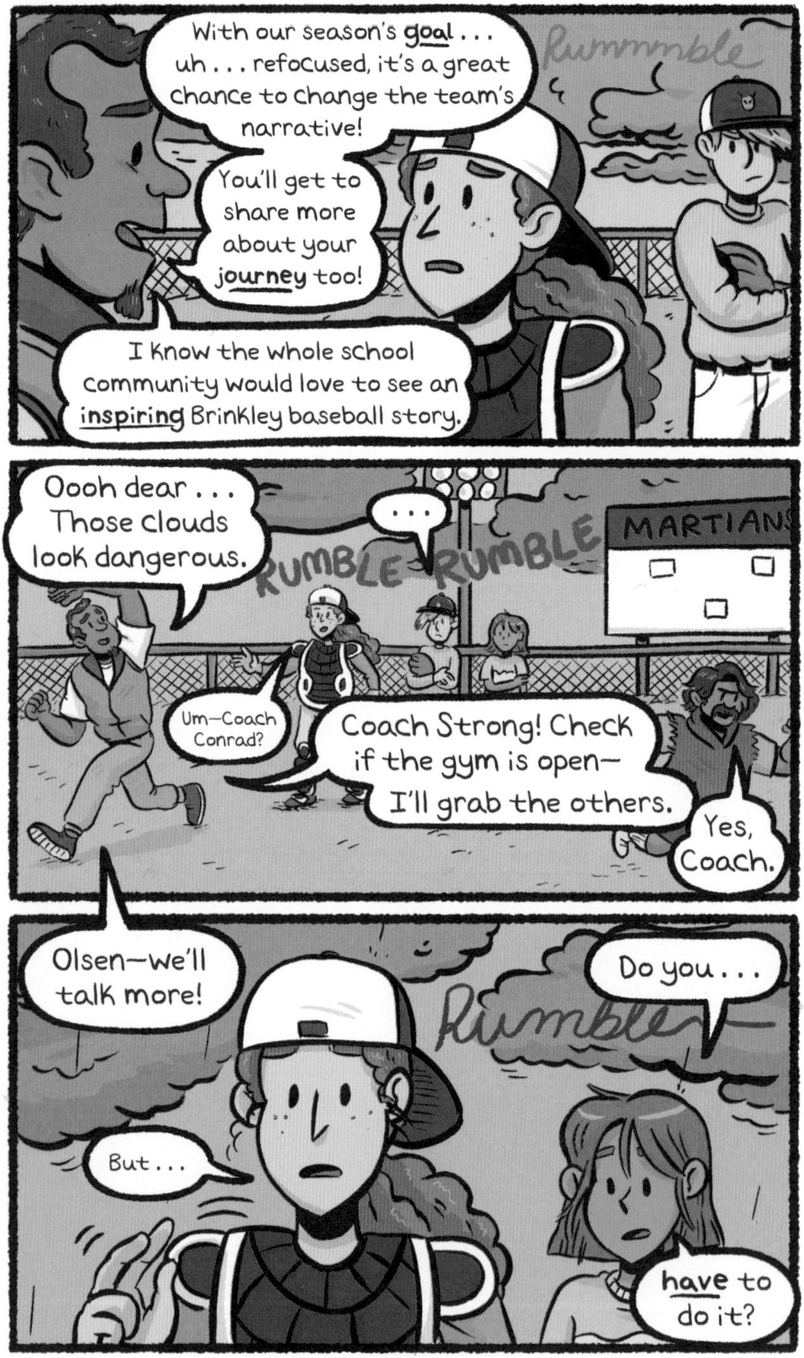
With our season's goal . . . uh . . . refocused, it's a great chance to change the team's narrative!
Rummmble
You'll get to share more about your journey too!
I know the whole school community would love to see an inspiring Brinkley baseball story.
Oooh dear . . . Those clouds look dangerous.
. . .
RUMBLE RUMBLE
MARTIANS
Um—Coach Conrad?
Coach Strong! Check if the gym is open— I'll grab the others.
Yes, Coach.
Olsen—we'll talk more!
Rumble
Do you . . .
But . . .
have to do it?

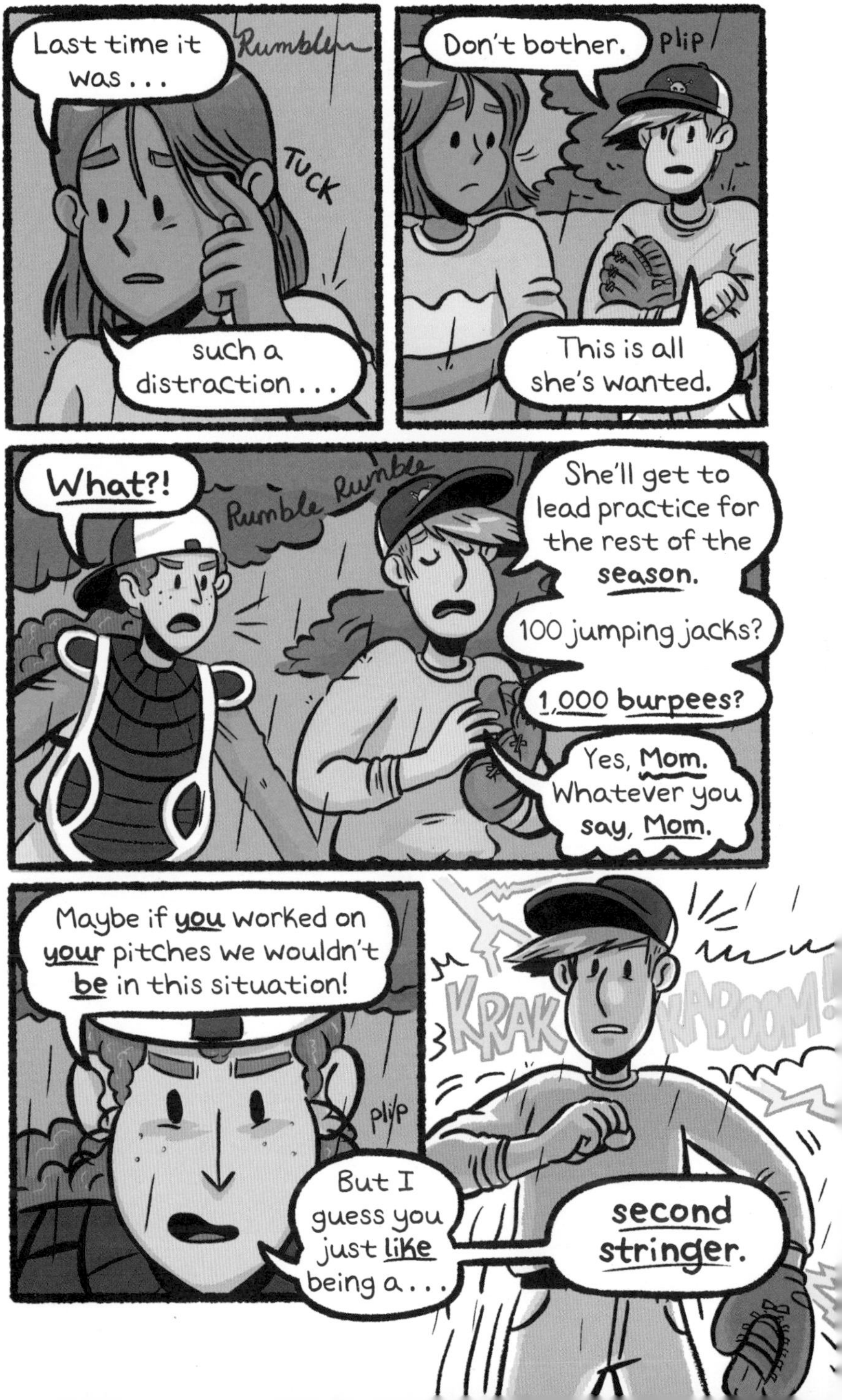
Last time it was . . .
Rumble
TUCK
such a distraction . . .
Don't bother.
plip
This is all she's wanted.
What?!
Rumble Rumble
She'll get to lead practice for the rest of the season.
100 jumping jacks?
1,000 burpees?
Yes, Mom. Whatever you say, Mom.
Maybe if you worked on your pitches we wouldn't be in this situation!
plip
But I guess you just like being a . . .
KRAK
KABOOM!
second stringer.

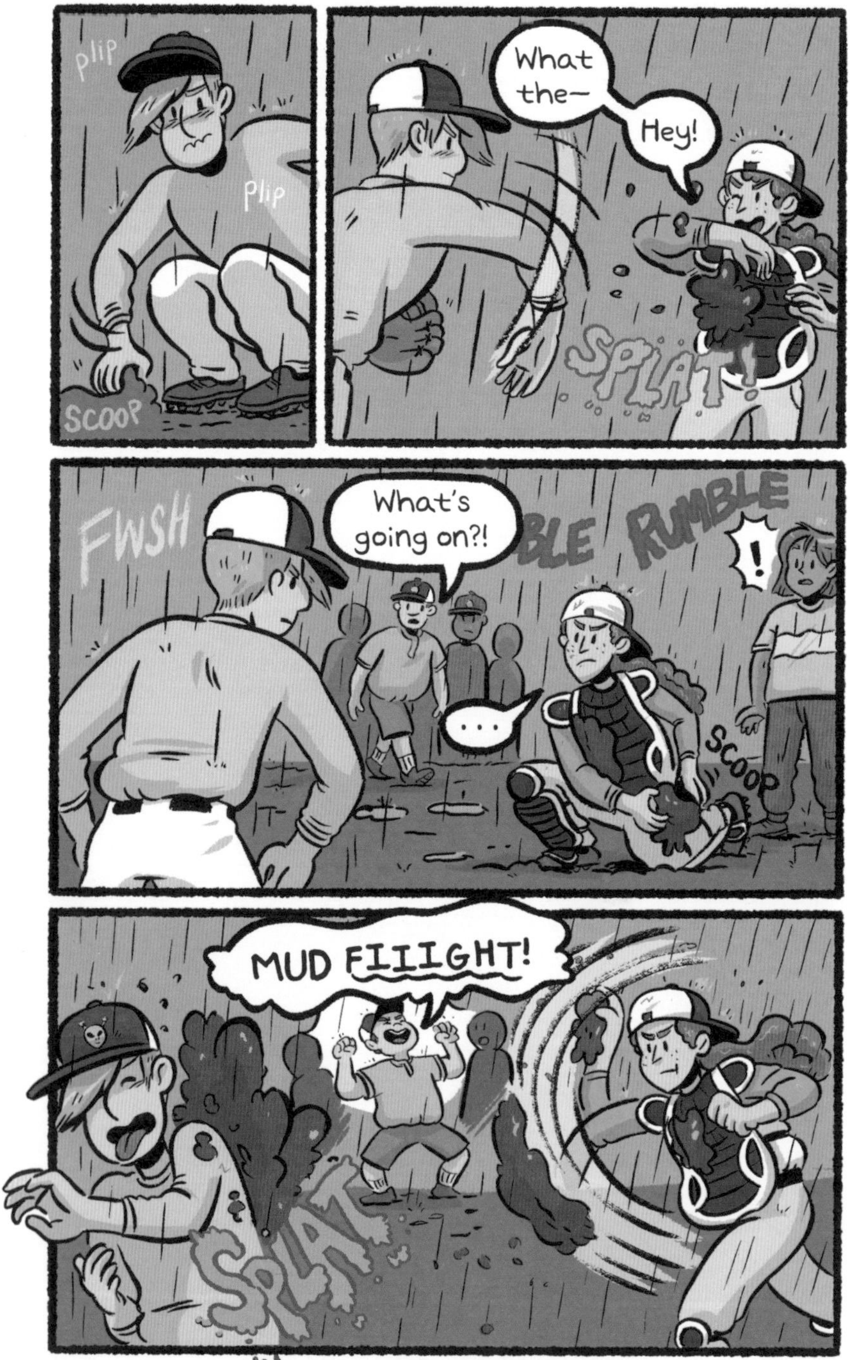
plip
plip
SCOOP
What the—
Hey!
SPLAT
FWSH
What's going on?!
BLE RUMBLE
!
...
SCOOP
MUD FIIIGHT!
SPLAT

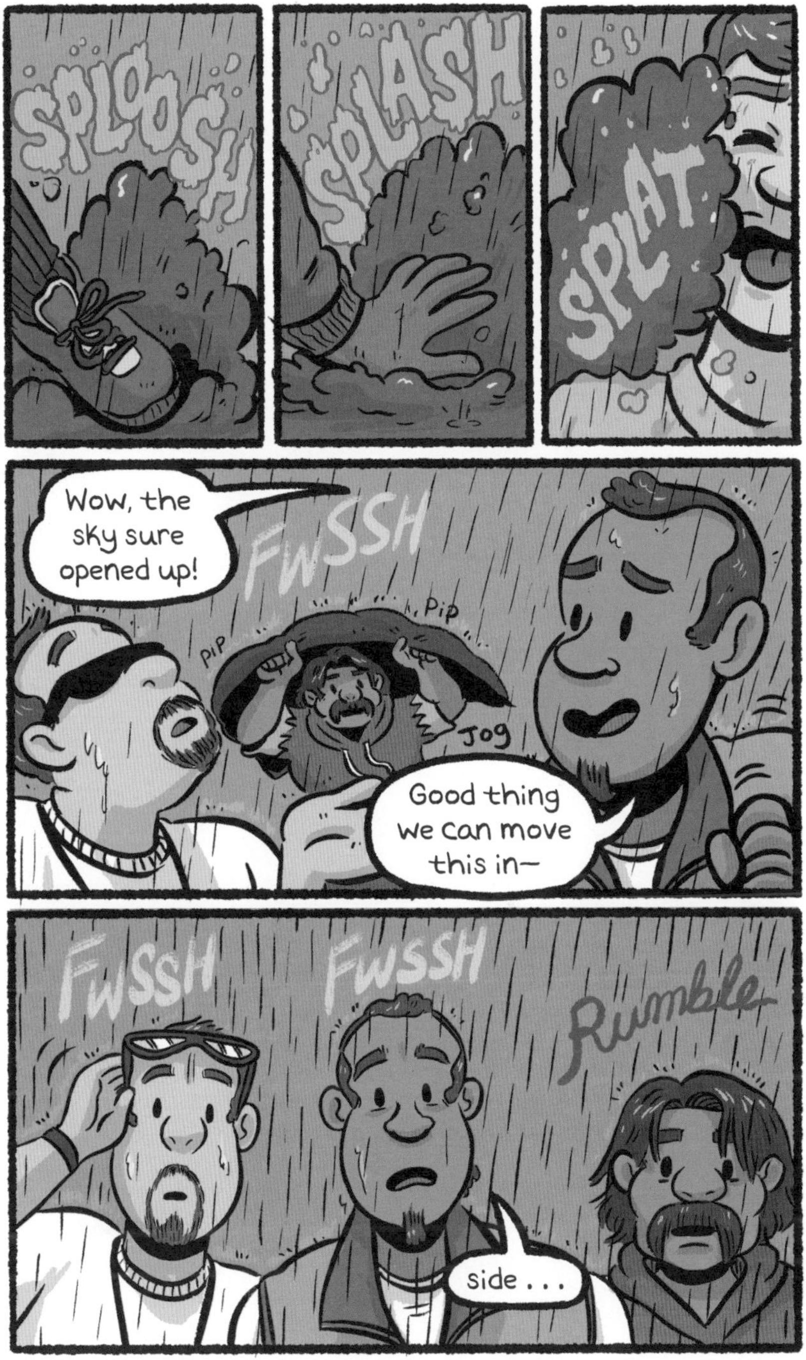
SPLOOSH
SPLASH
SPLAT
Wow, the sky sure opened up!
FWSSH
PIP
PIP
JOG
Good thing we can move this in—
FWSSH
FWSSH
Rumble
side . . .

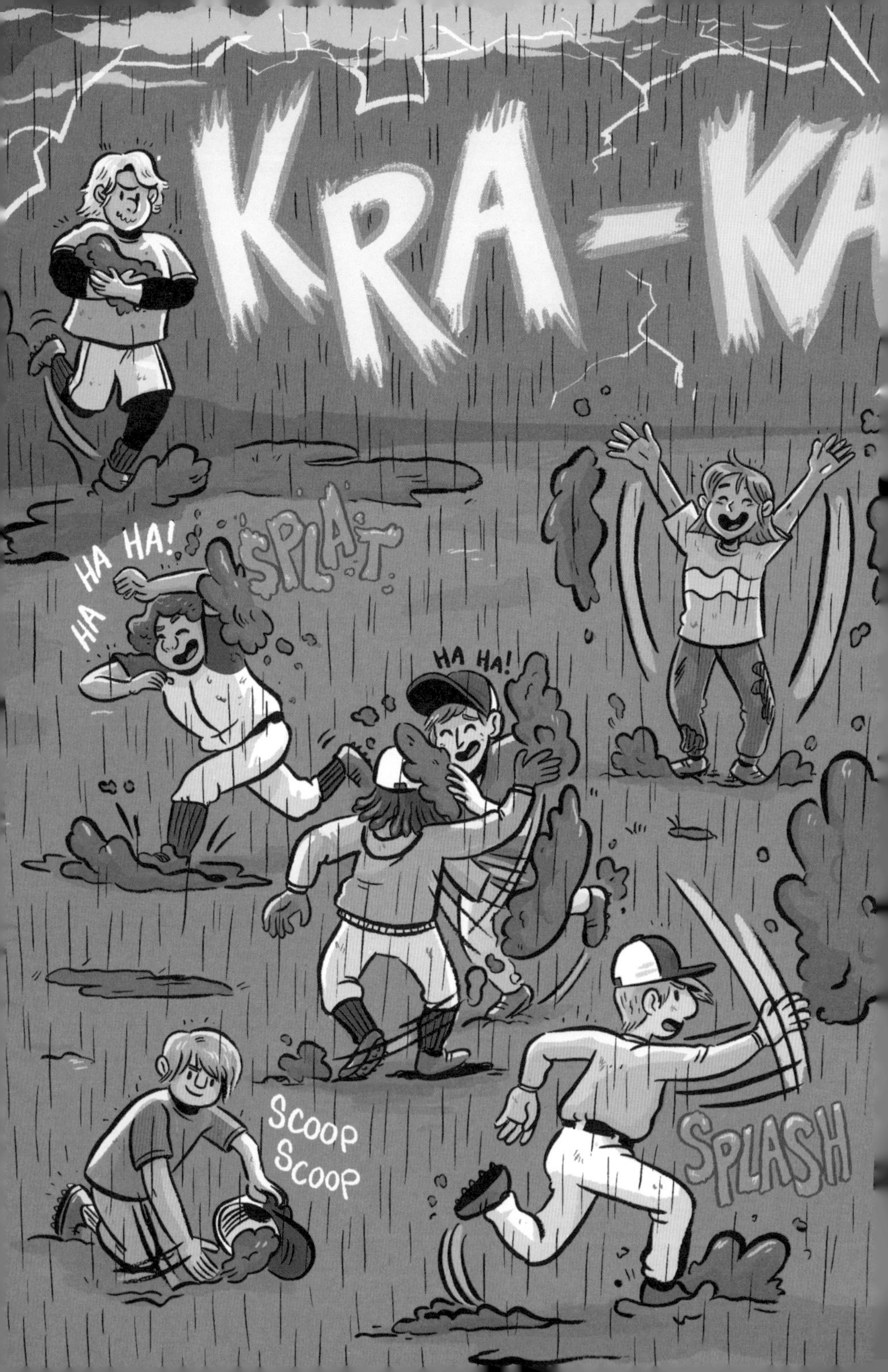
KRA-KA
HA HA! HA HA
SPLAT
HA HA!
Scoop Scoop
SPLASH

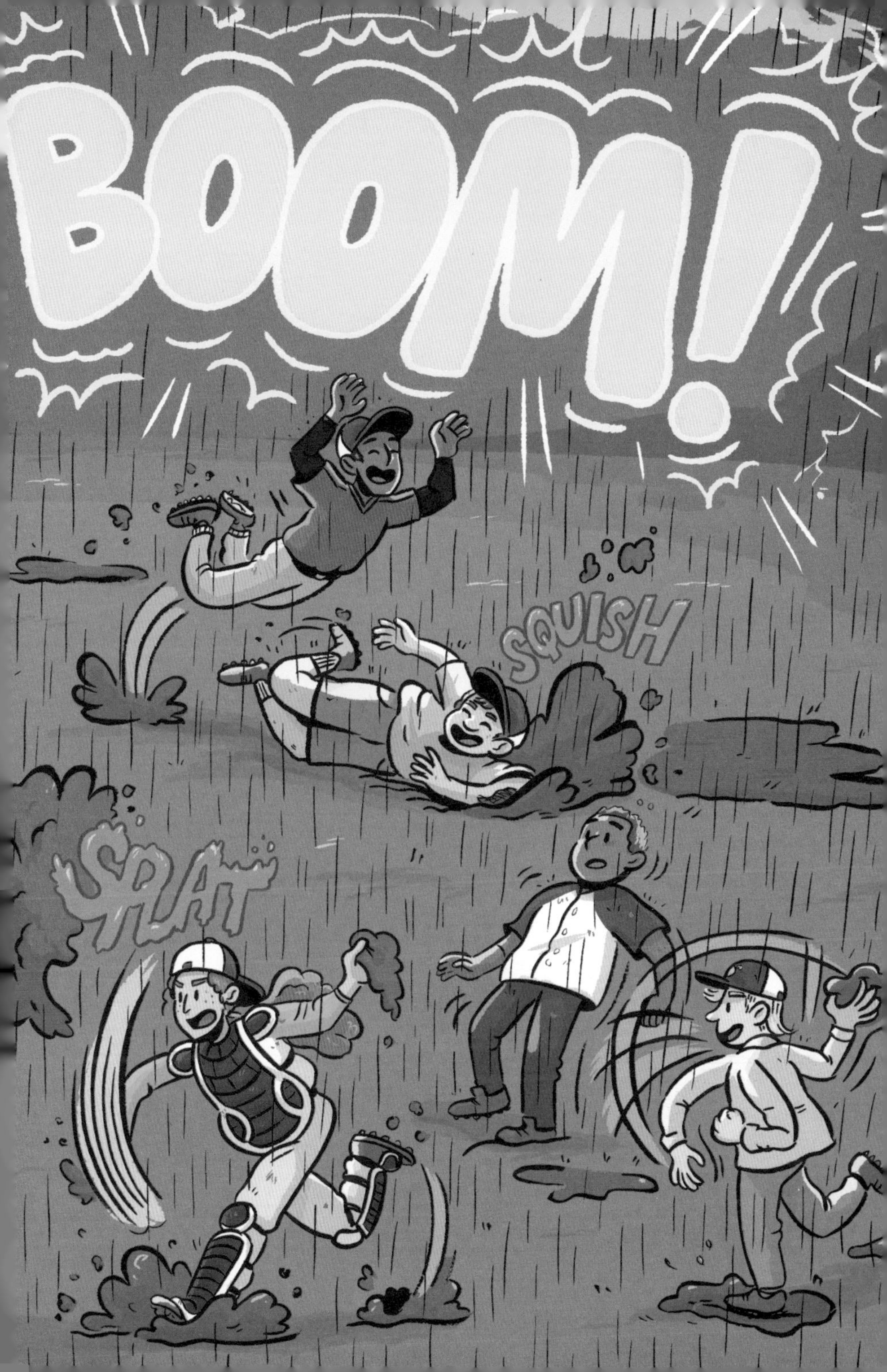
BOOM!
SQUISH
SPLAT

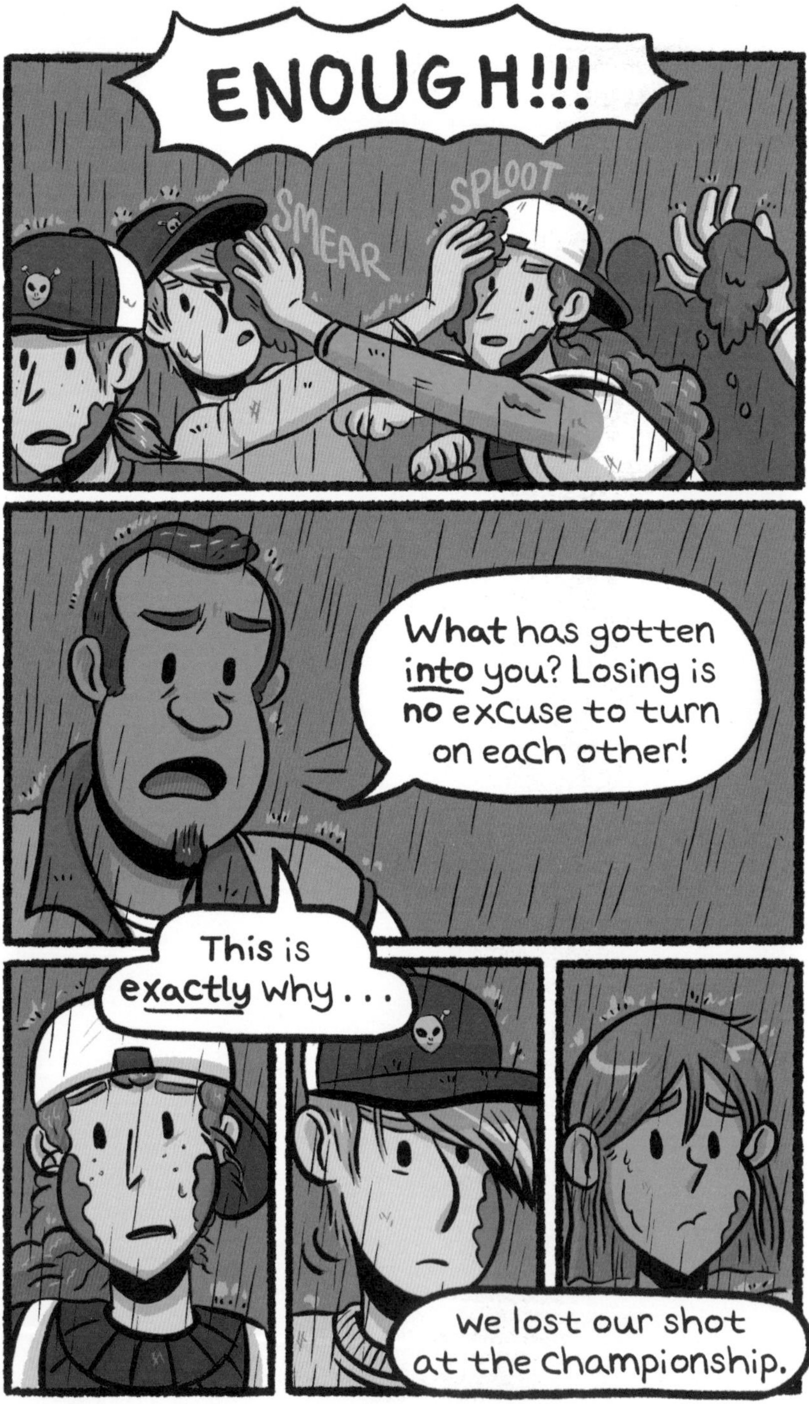
ENOUGH!!!
SMEAR
SPLOOT
What has gotten into you? Losing is no excuse to turn on each other!
This is exactly why . . .
we lost our shot at the championship.

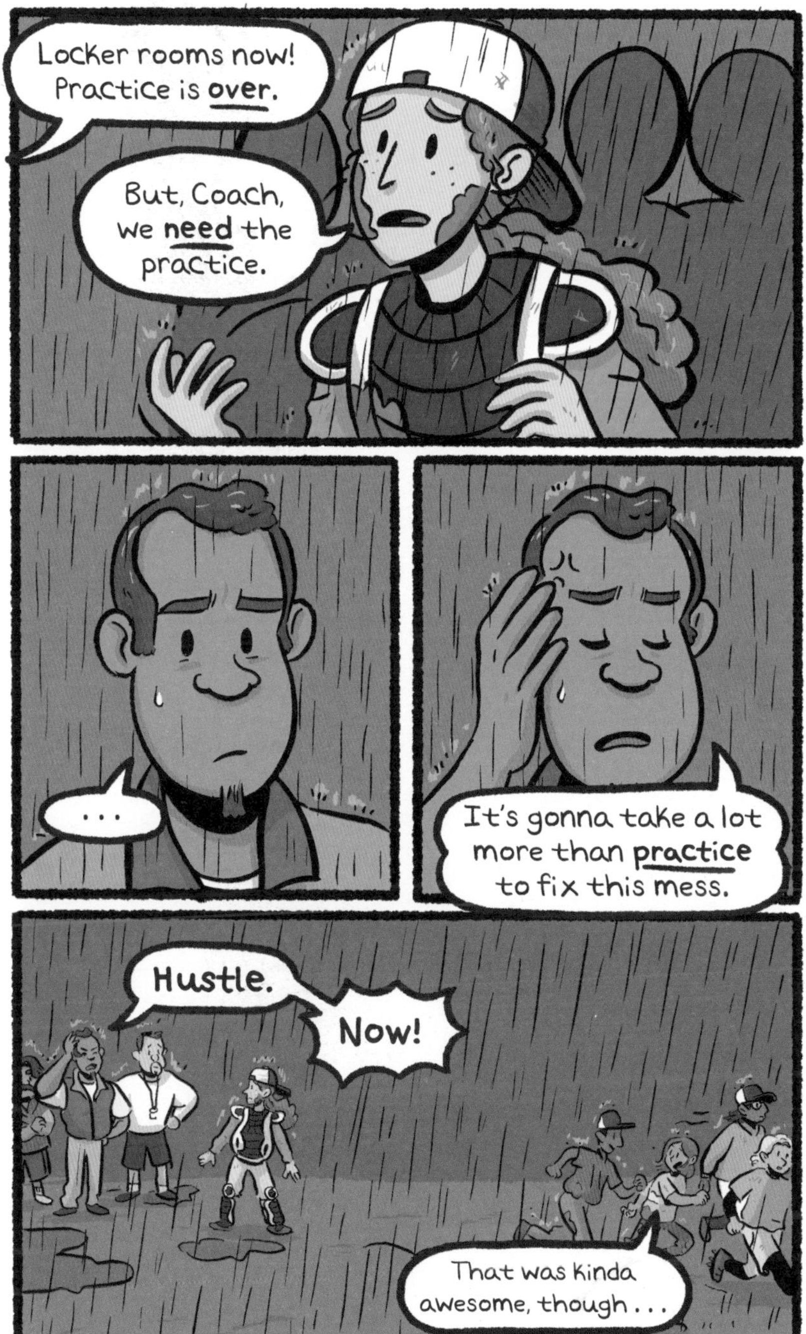
Locker rooms now! Practice is over.
But, Coach, we need the practice.
. . .
It's gonna take a lot more than practice to fix this mess.
Hustle.
Now!
That was kinda awesome, though . . .

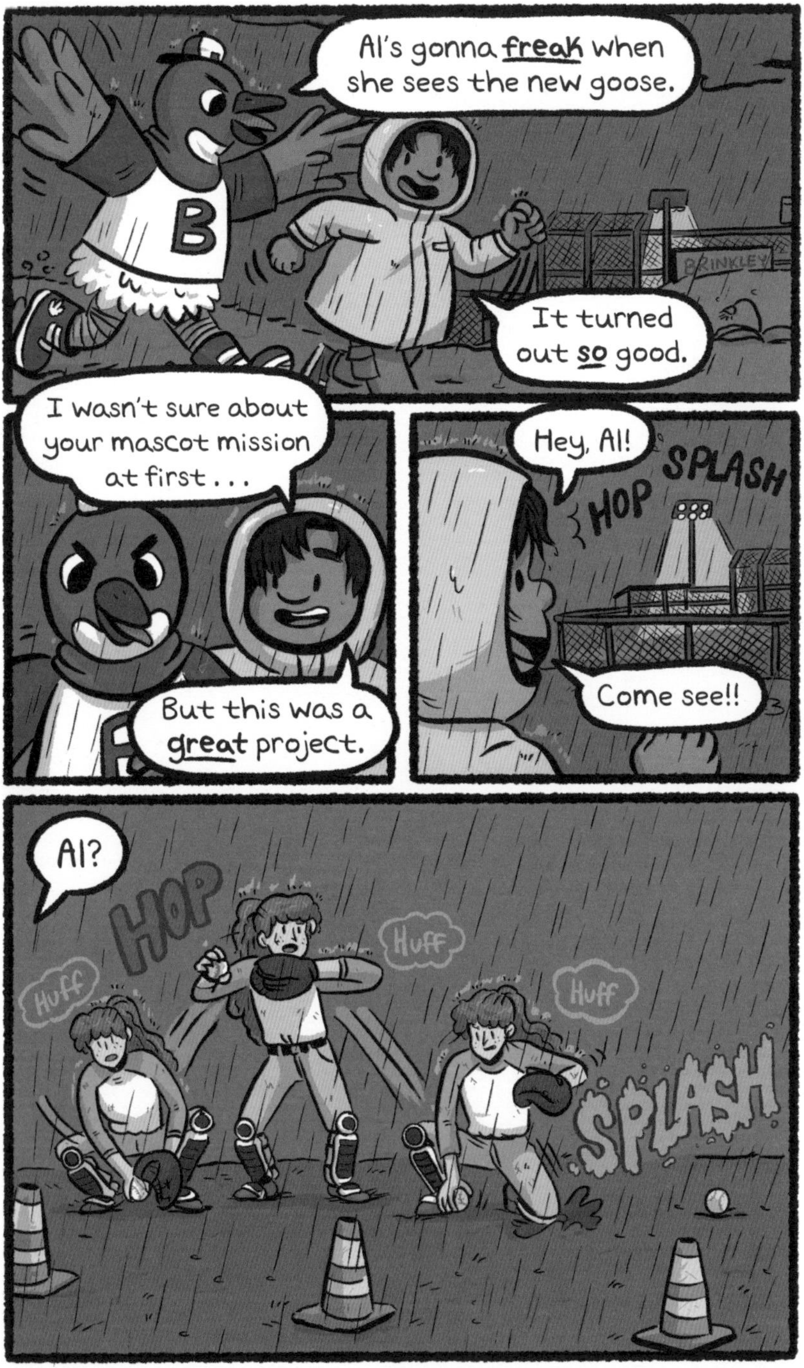
Al's gonna freak when she sees the new goose.
It turned out so good.
BRINKLEY
I wasn't sure about your mascot mission at first . . .
But this was a great project.
Hey, Al!
HOP
SPLASH
Come see!!
Al?
HOP
Huff
Huff
Huff
SPLASH

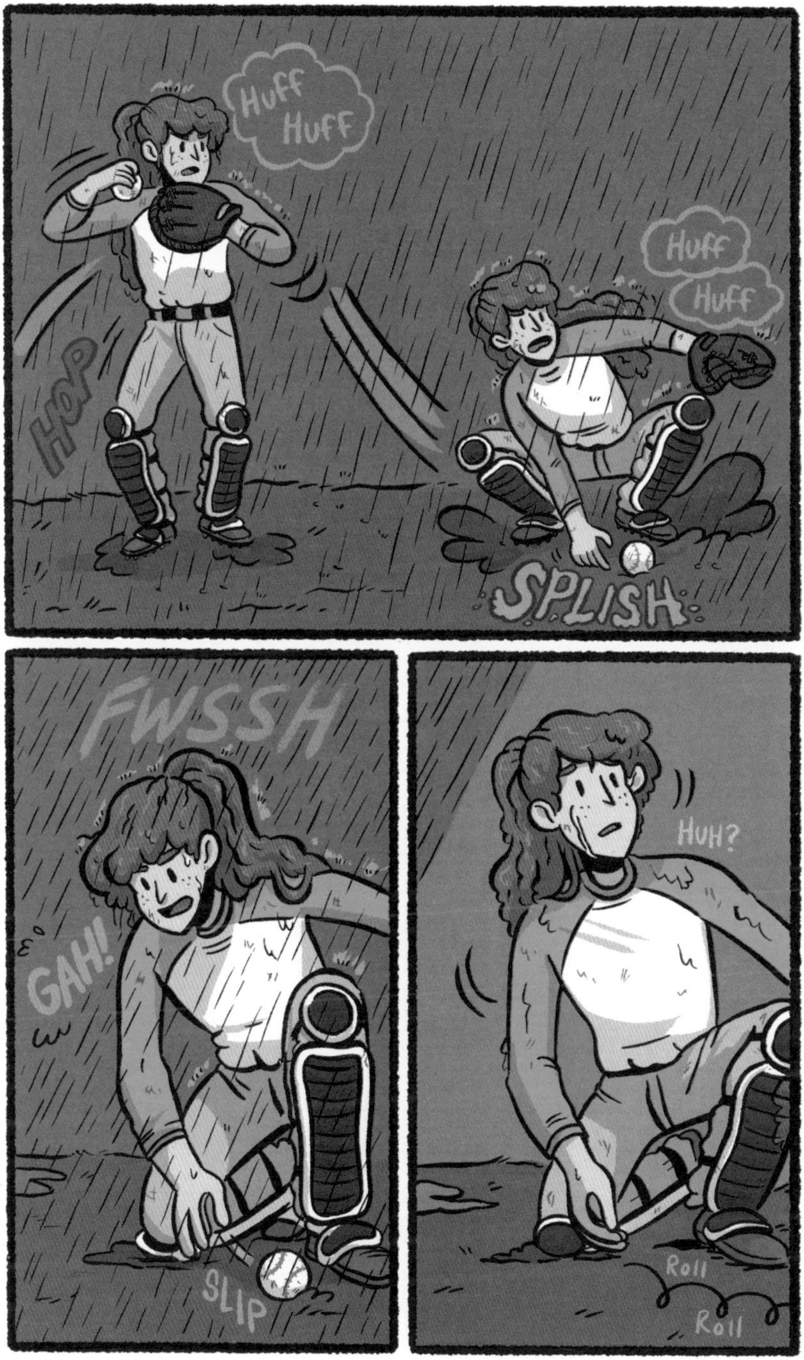
HUFF HUFF
HOP
HUFF
HUFF
SPLISH
FWSSH
GAH!
SLIP
HUH?
Roll
Roll

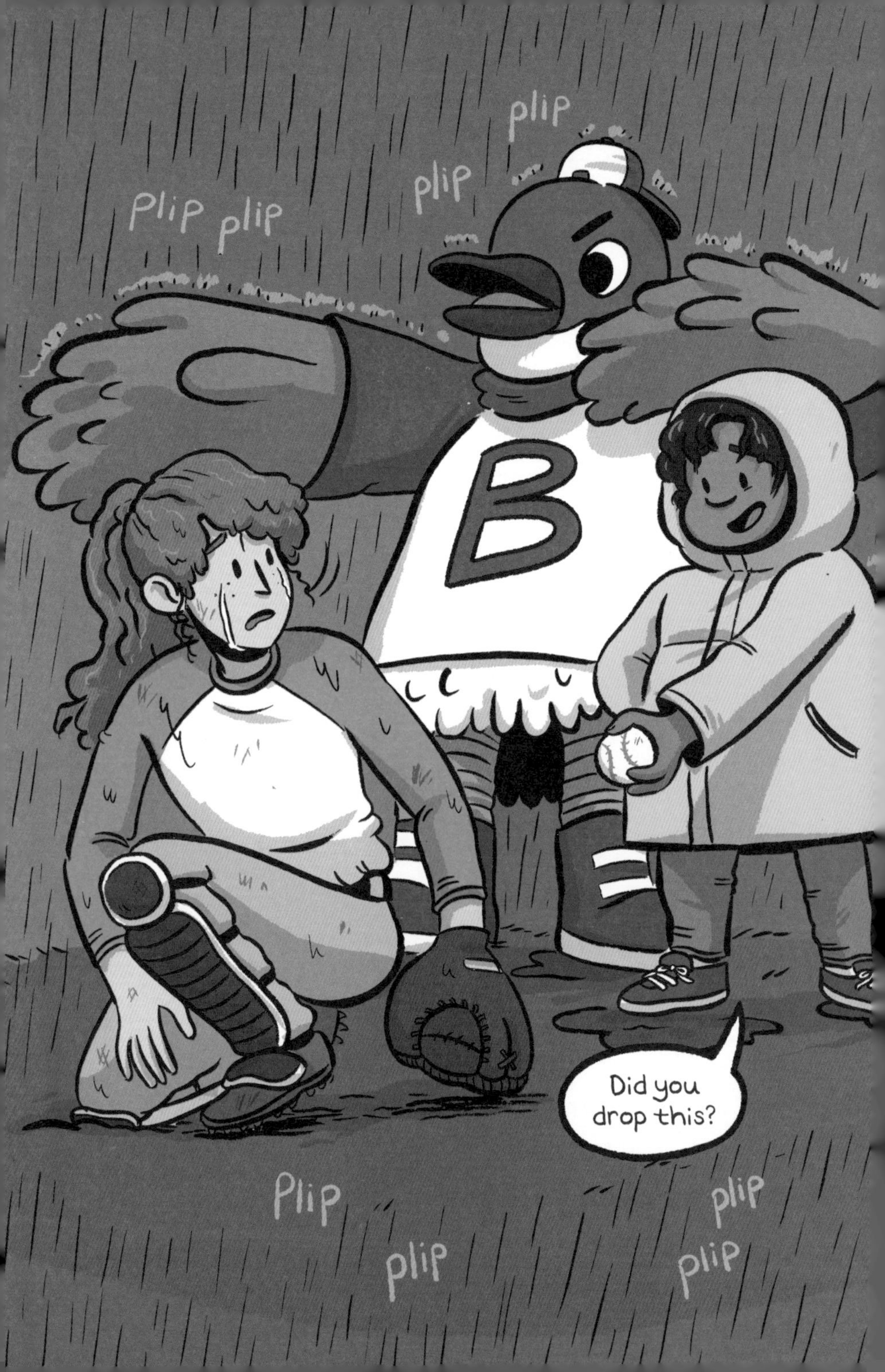
plip
plip
plip plip
Did you drop this?
plip
plip
plip
plip

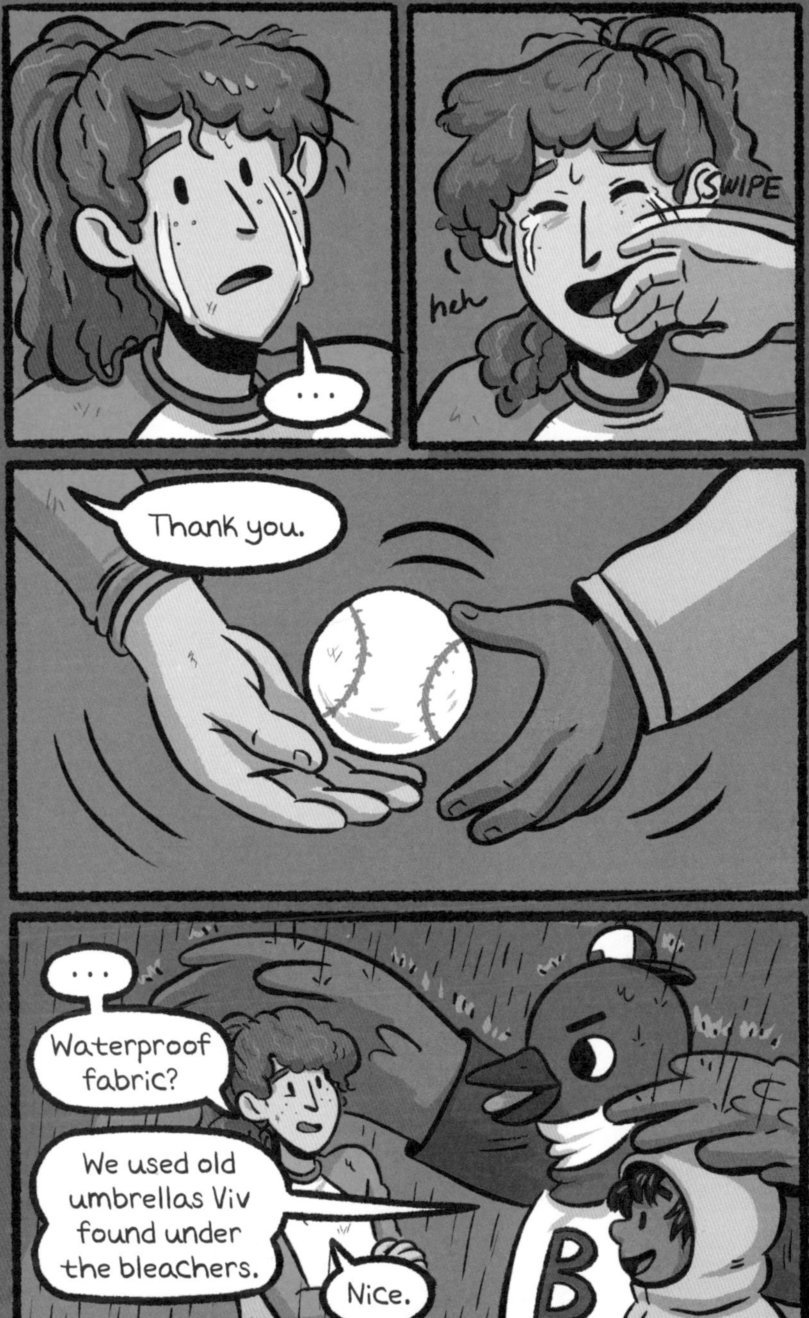
...
heh
SWIPE
Thank you.
...
Waterproof fabric?
We used old umbrellas Viv found under the bleachers.
Nice.

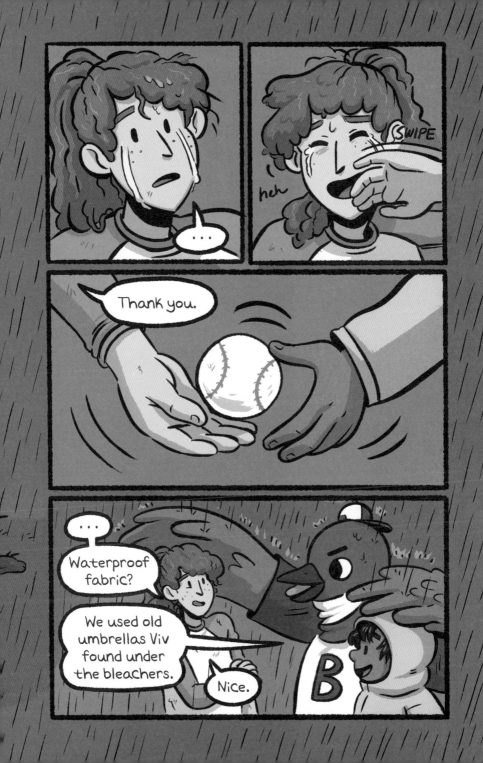

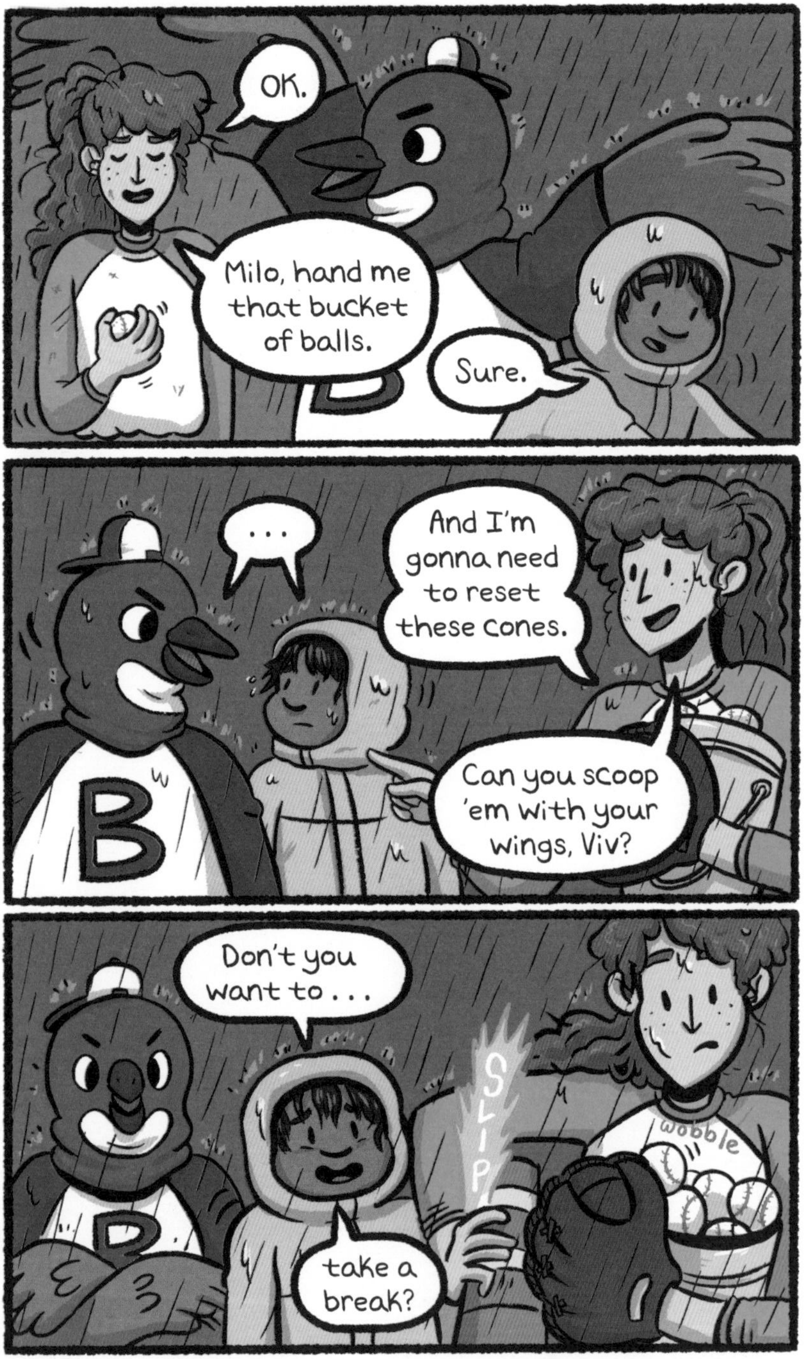
OK.
Milo, hand me that bucket of balls.
Sure.
. . .
And I'm gonna need to reset these cones.
Can you scoop 'em with your wings, Viv?
Don't you want to . . .
take a break?
SLIP
wobble

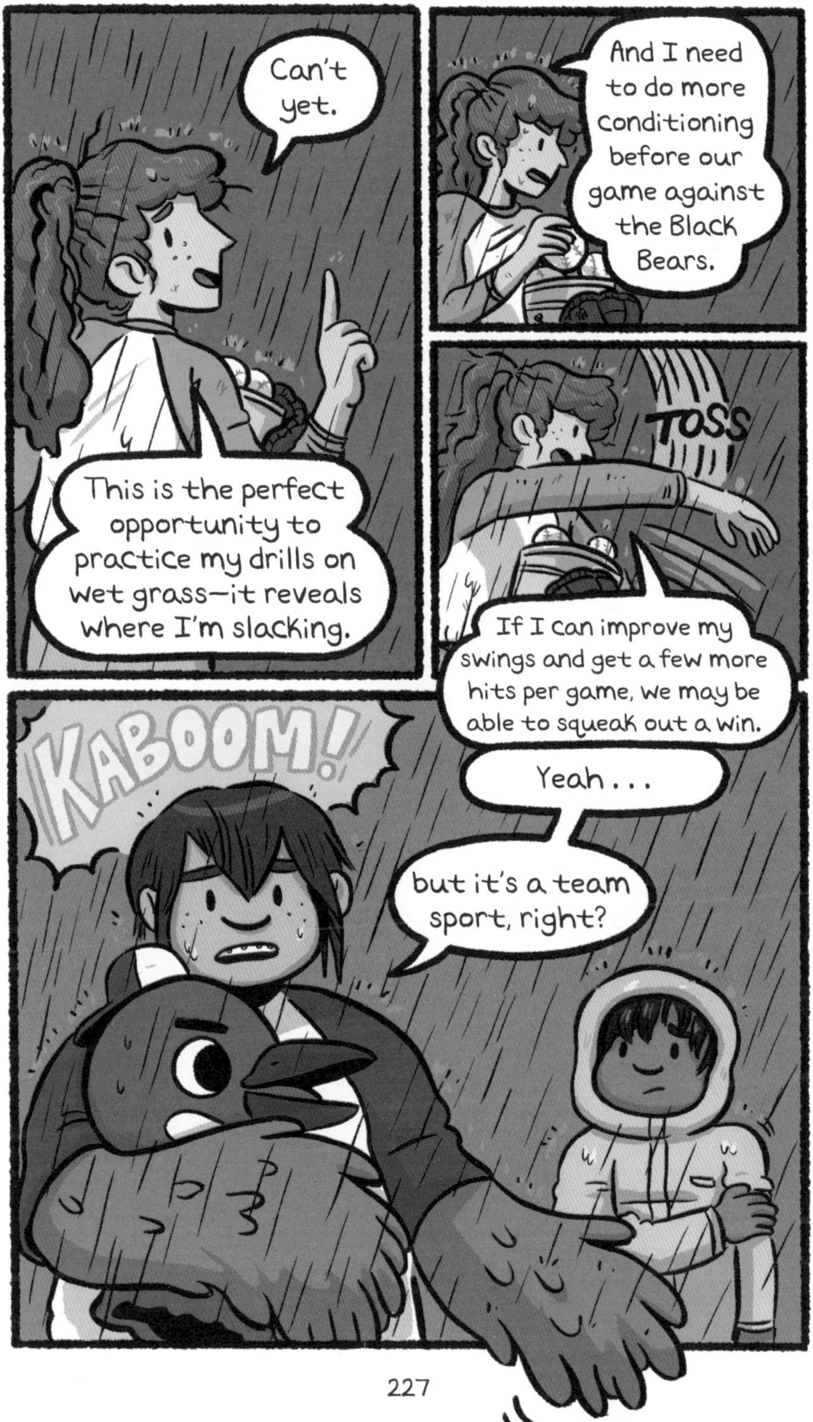
Can't yet.
This is the perfect opportunity to practice my drills on wet grass—it reveals where I'm slacking.
And I need to do more conditioning before our game against the Black Bears.
TOSS
If I can improve my swings and get a few more hits per game, we may be able to squeak out a win.
KABOOM!
Yeah . . .
but it's a team sport, right?

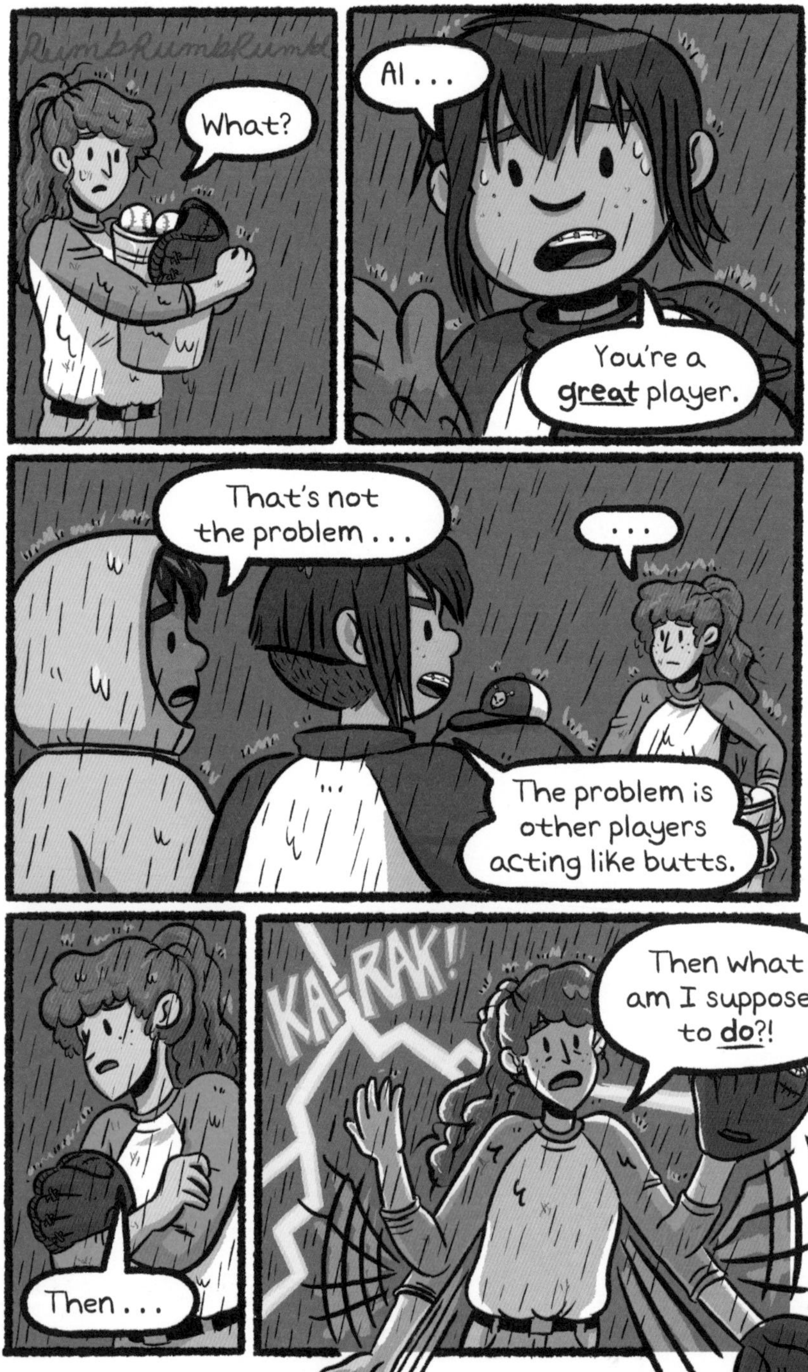
RumbRumbRumb
What?
Al . . .
You're a great player.
That's not the problem . . .
. . .
The problem is other players acting like butts.
Then . . .
KA-RAK!
Then what am I supposed to do?!

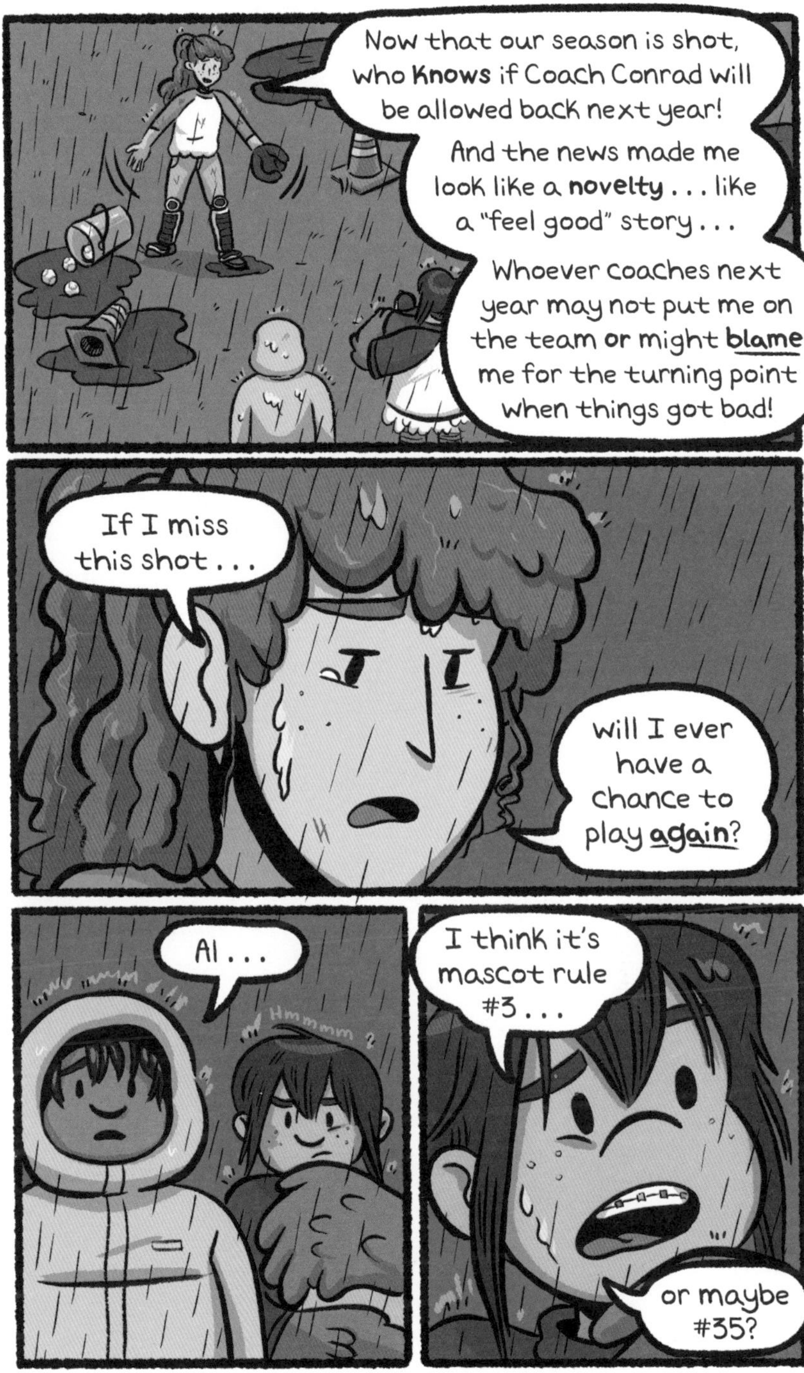
Now that our season is shot, who Knows if Coach Conrad will be allowed back next year!
And the news made me look like a novelty . . . like a "feel good" story . . .
Whoever coaches next year may not put me on the team or might blame me for the turning point when things got bad!
If I miss this shot . . .
Will I ever have a chance to play again?
Al . . .
Hmmmm
I think it's mascot rule #3 . . .
or maybe #35?

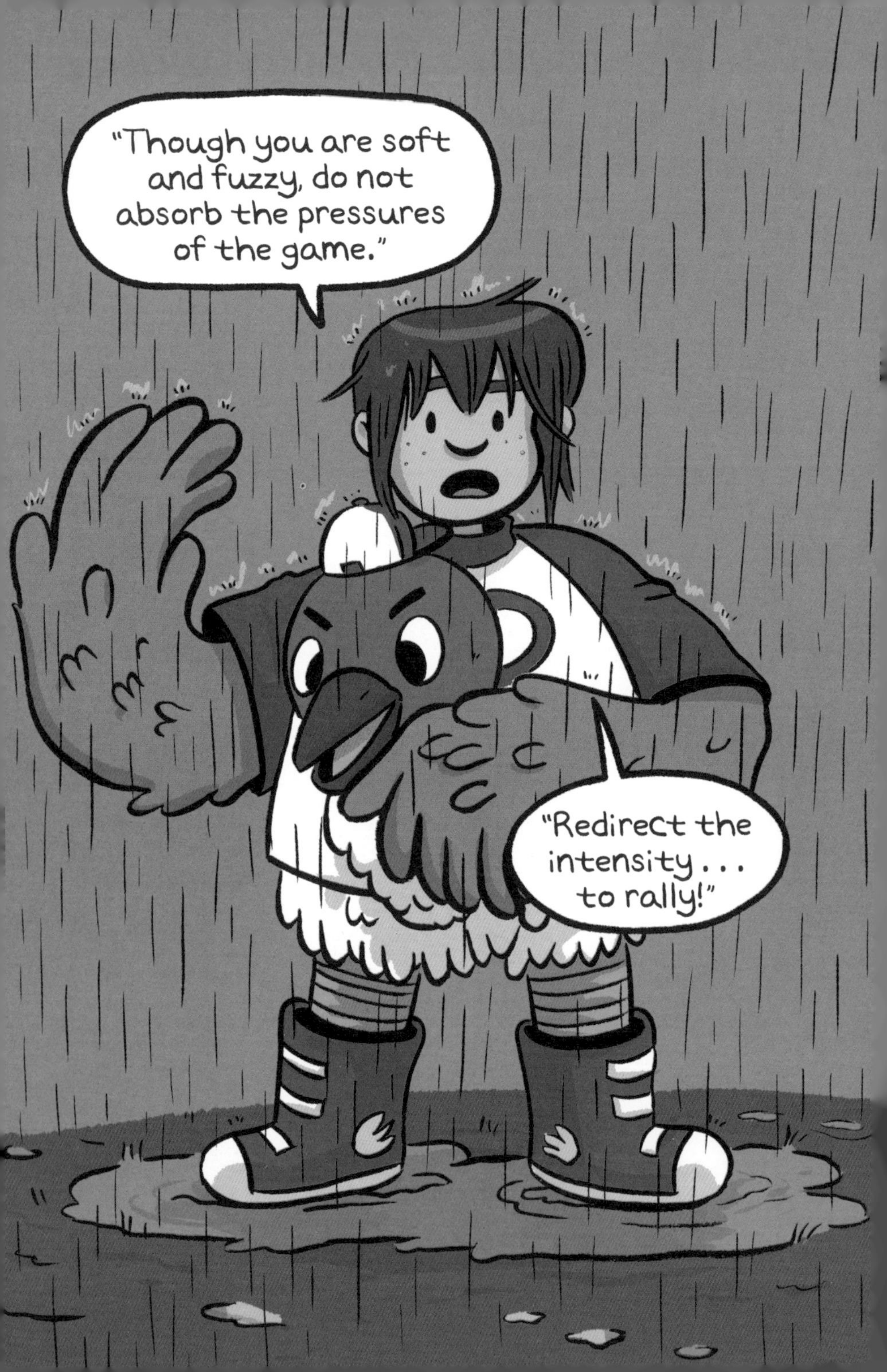
"Though you are soft and fuzzy, do not absorb the pressures of the game."
"Redirect the intensity . . . to rally!"

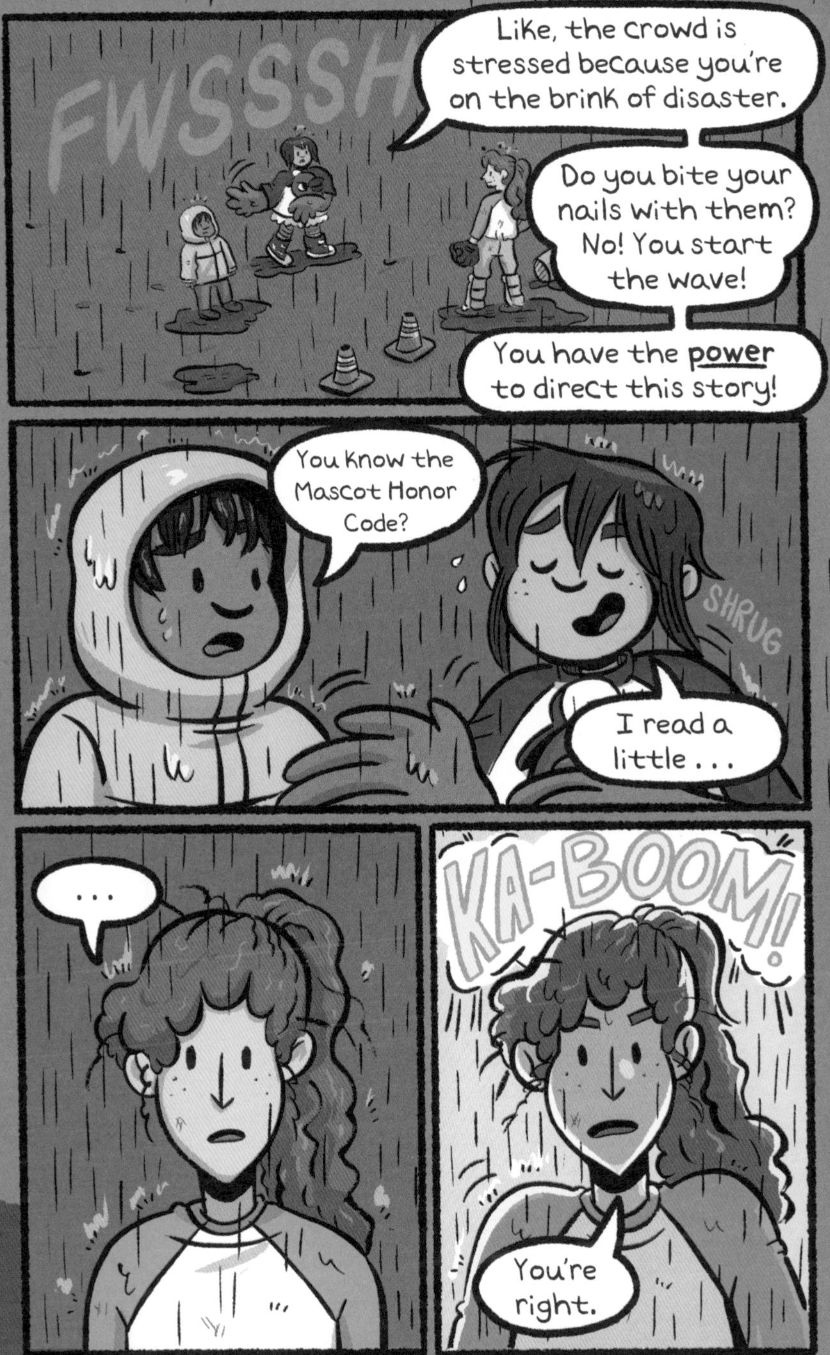
FWSSSH
Like, the crowd is stressed because you're on the brink of disaster.
Do you bite your nails with them? No! You start the wave!
You have the **power** to direct this story!
You know the Mascot Honor Code?
SHRUG
I read a little . . .
. . .
KA-BOOM!
You're right.

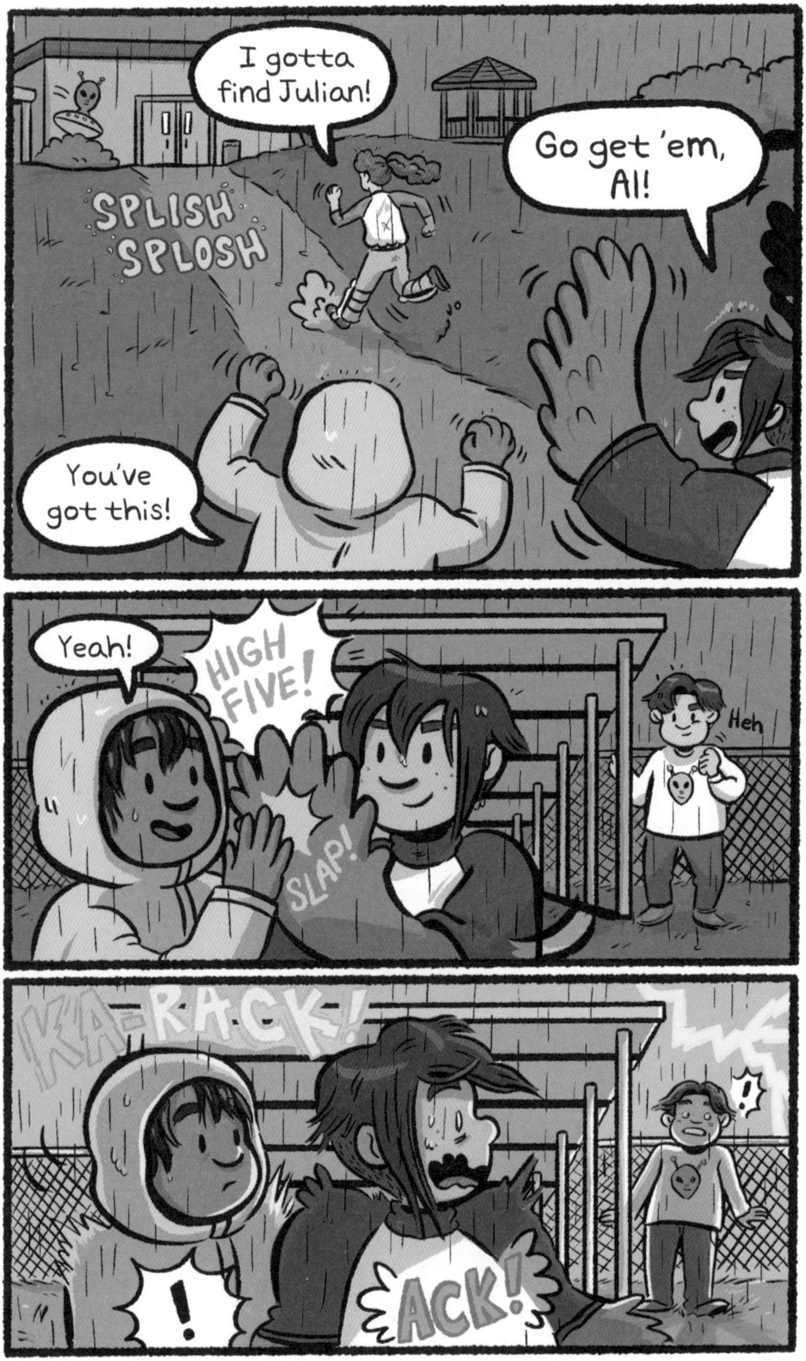
I gotta find Julian!
SPLISH SPLOSH
Go get 'em, Al!
You've got this!
Yeah!
HIGH FIVE!
SLAP!
Heh
KA-RACK!
!
!
ACK!

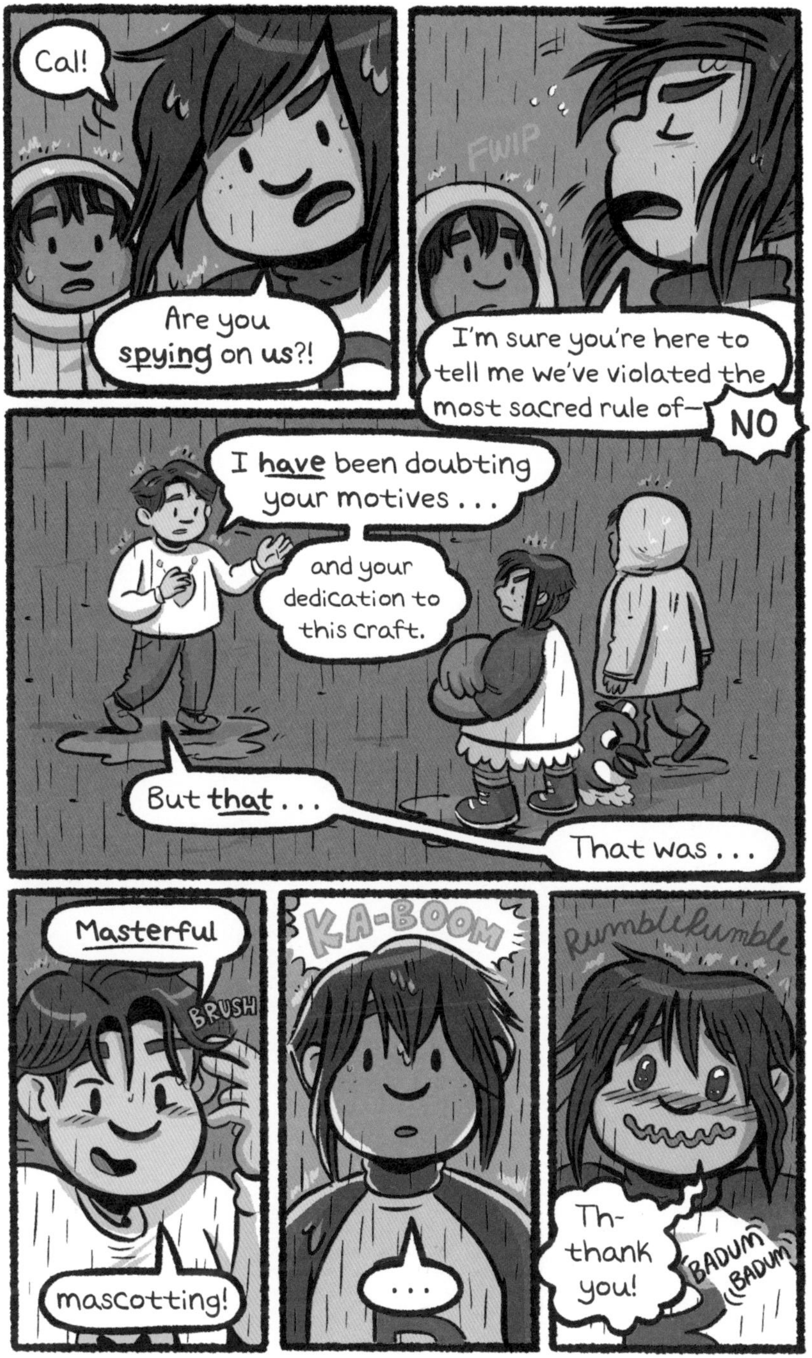
Cal!
Are you spying on us?!
FWIP
I'm sure you're here to tell me we've violated the most sacred rule of—
NO
I have been doubting your motives . . .
and your dedication to this craft.
But that . . .
That was . . .
Masterful
BRUSH
mascotting!
KA-BOOM
. . .
Rumblekumble
Th- thank you!
BADUM BADUM

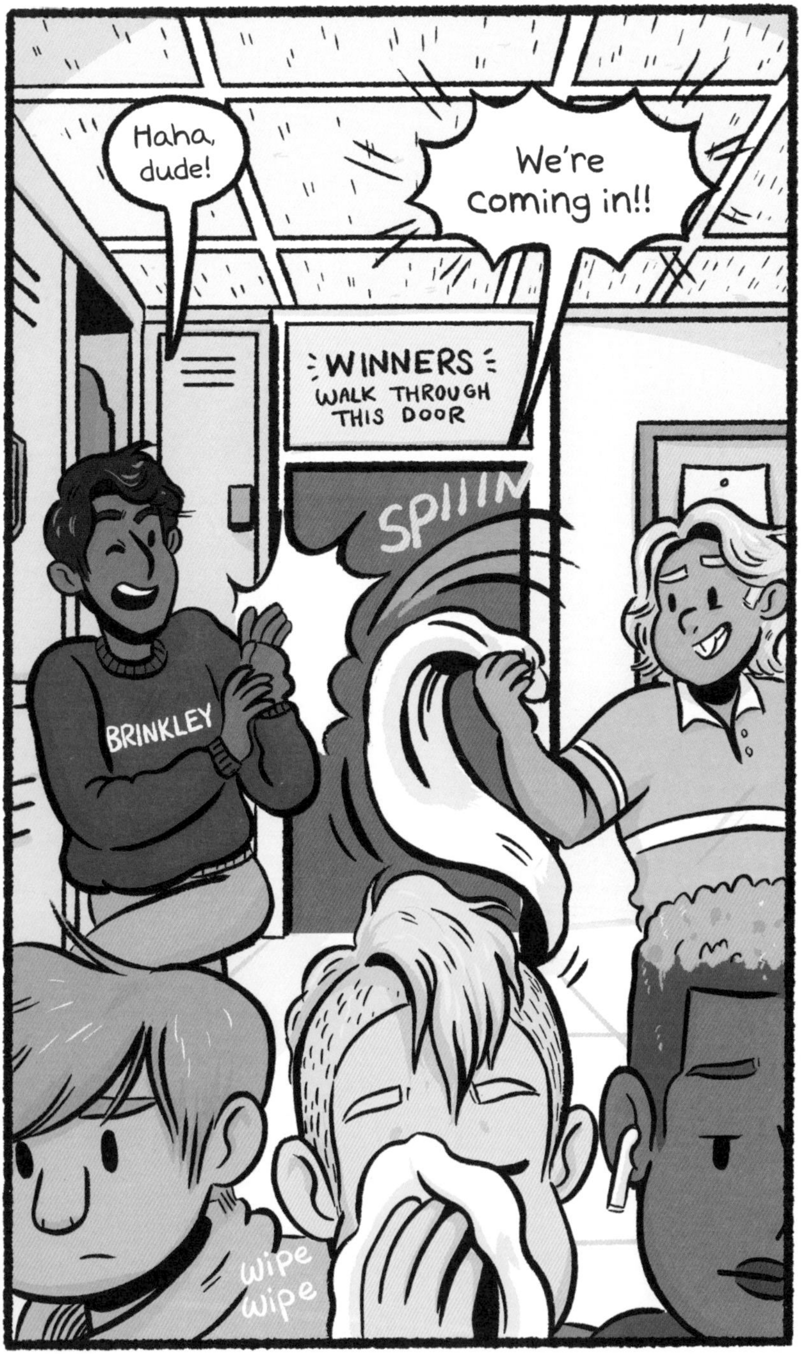
Haha, dude!
We're coming in!!
WINNERS WALK THROUGH THIS DOOR
SPIIIN
BRINKLEY
wipe wipe

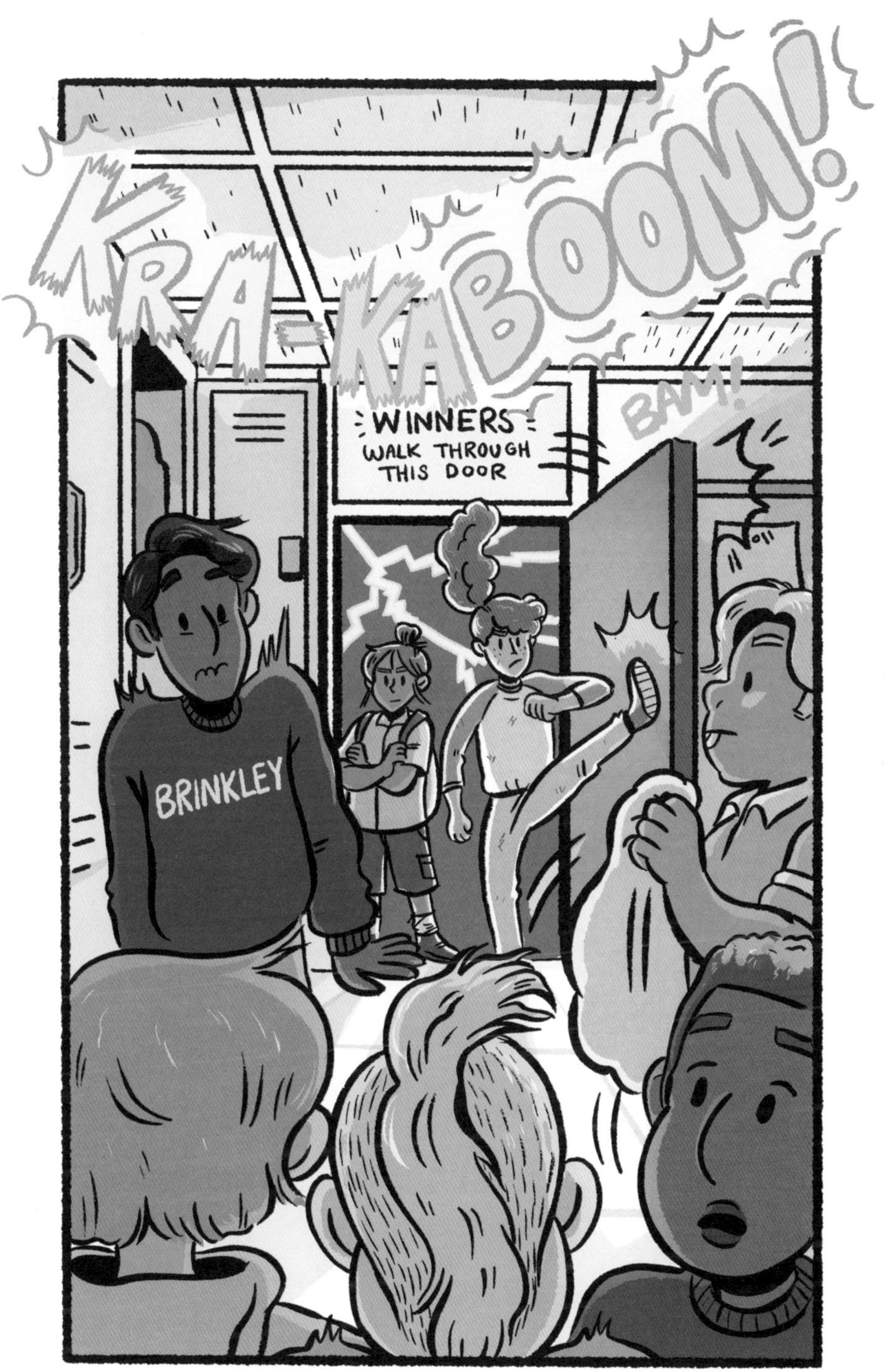
KRA-KABOOM!
BAM!
WINNERS WALK THROUGH THIS DOOR
BRINKLEY

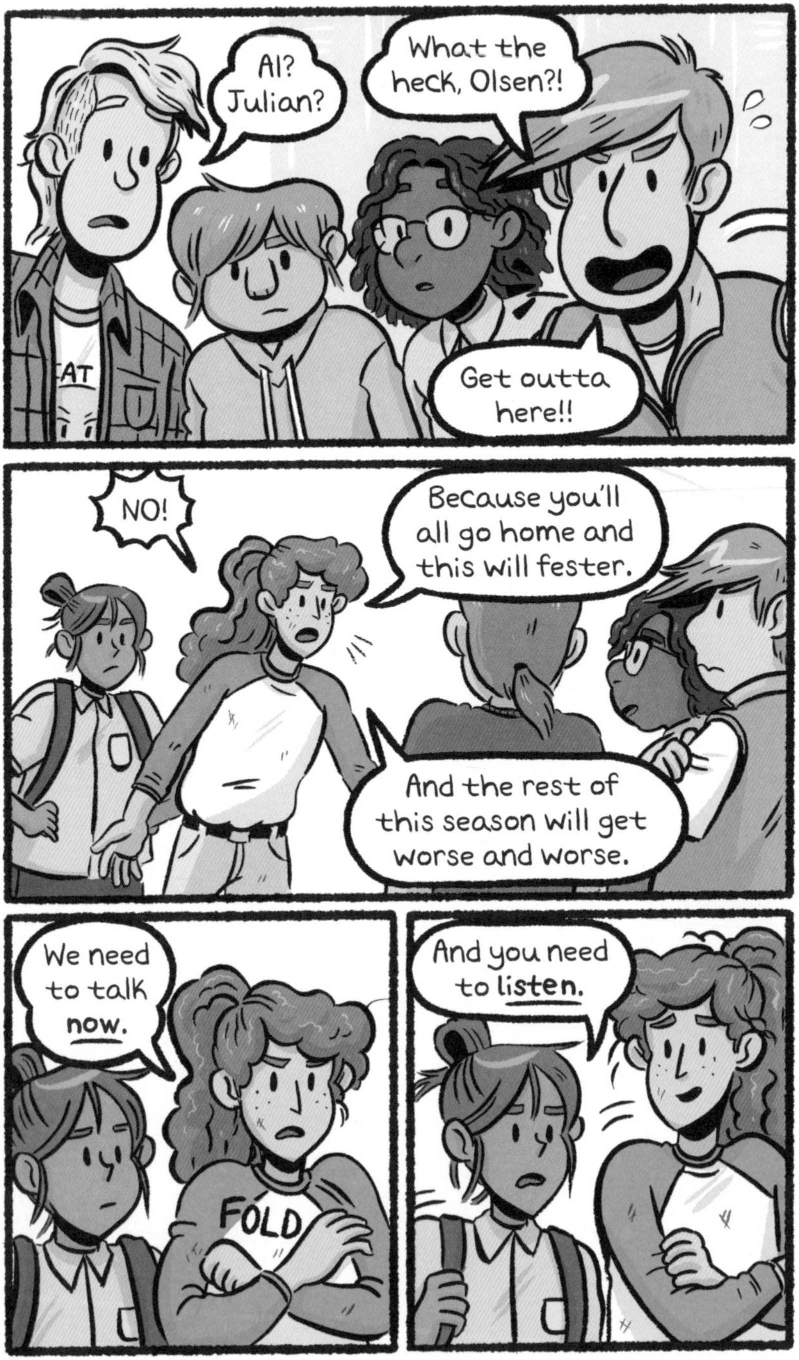
Al?
Julian?
What the heck, Olsen?!
Get outta here!!
NO!
Because you'll all go home and this will fester.
And the rest of this season will get worse and worse.
We need to talk now.
FOLD
And you need to listen.

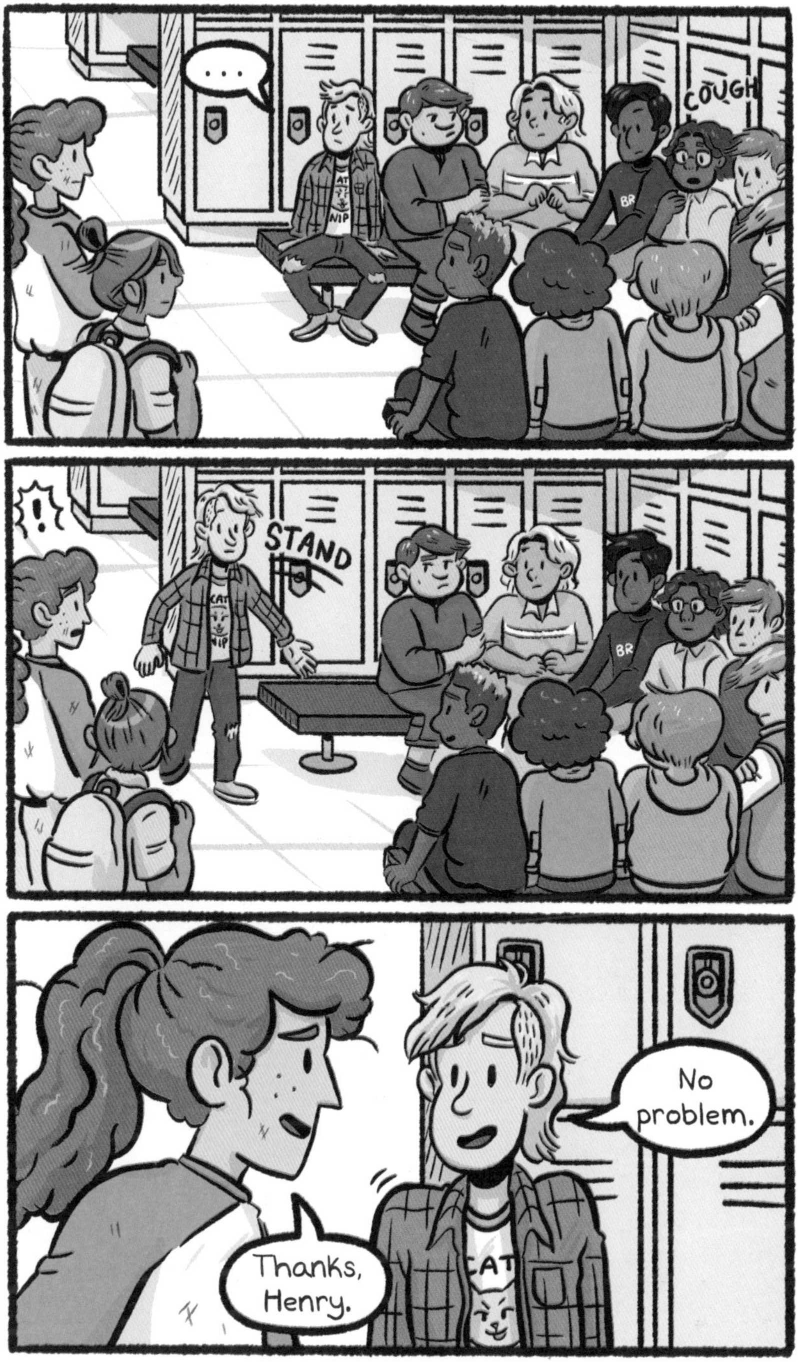
...
COUGH
!
STAND
Thanks, Henry.
No problem.

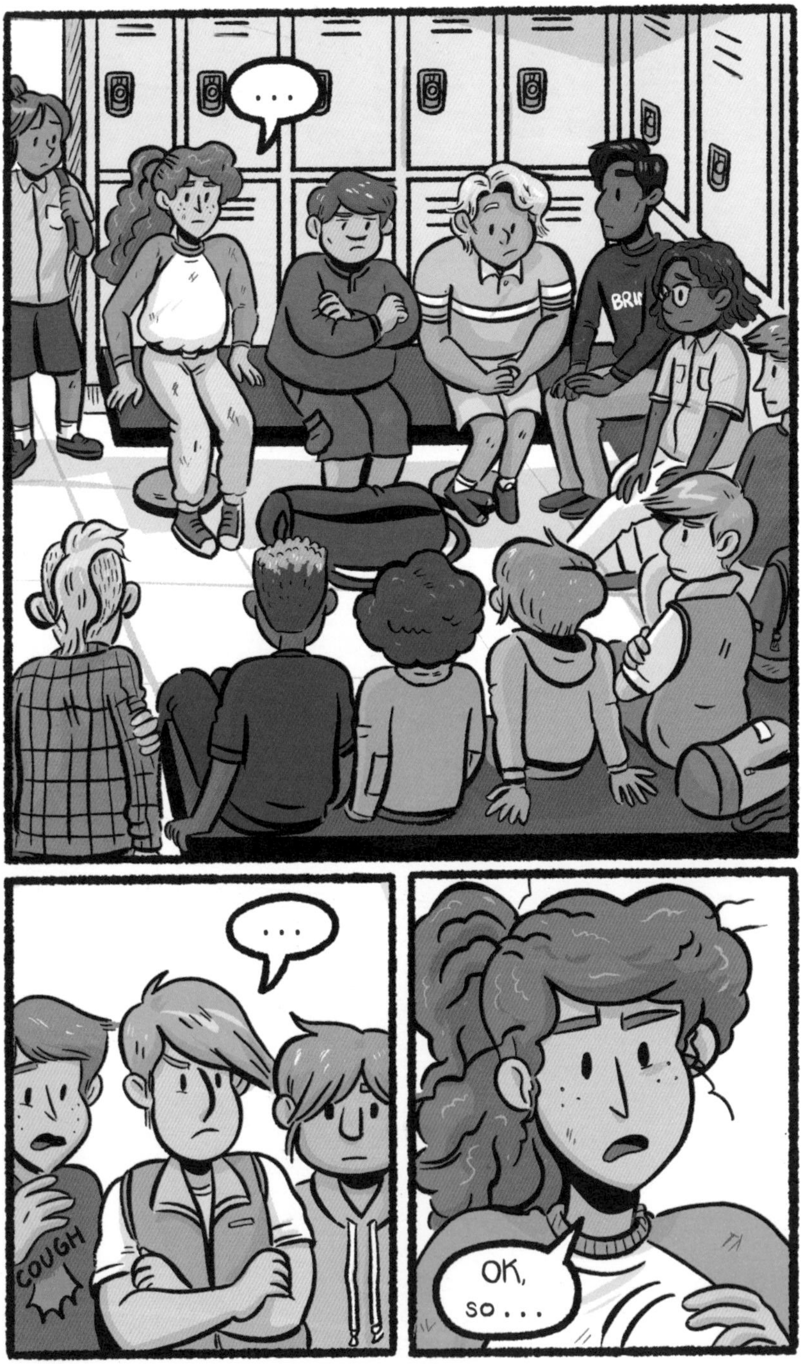
...
BRU
...
COUGH
OK, so...

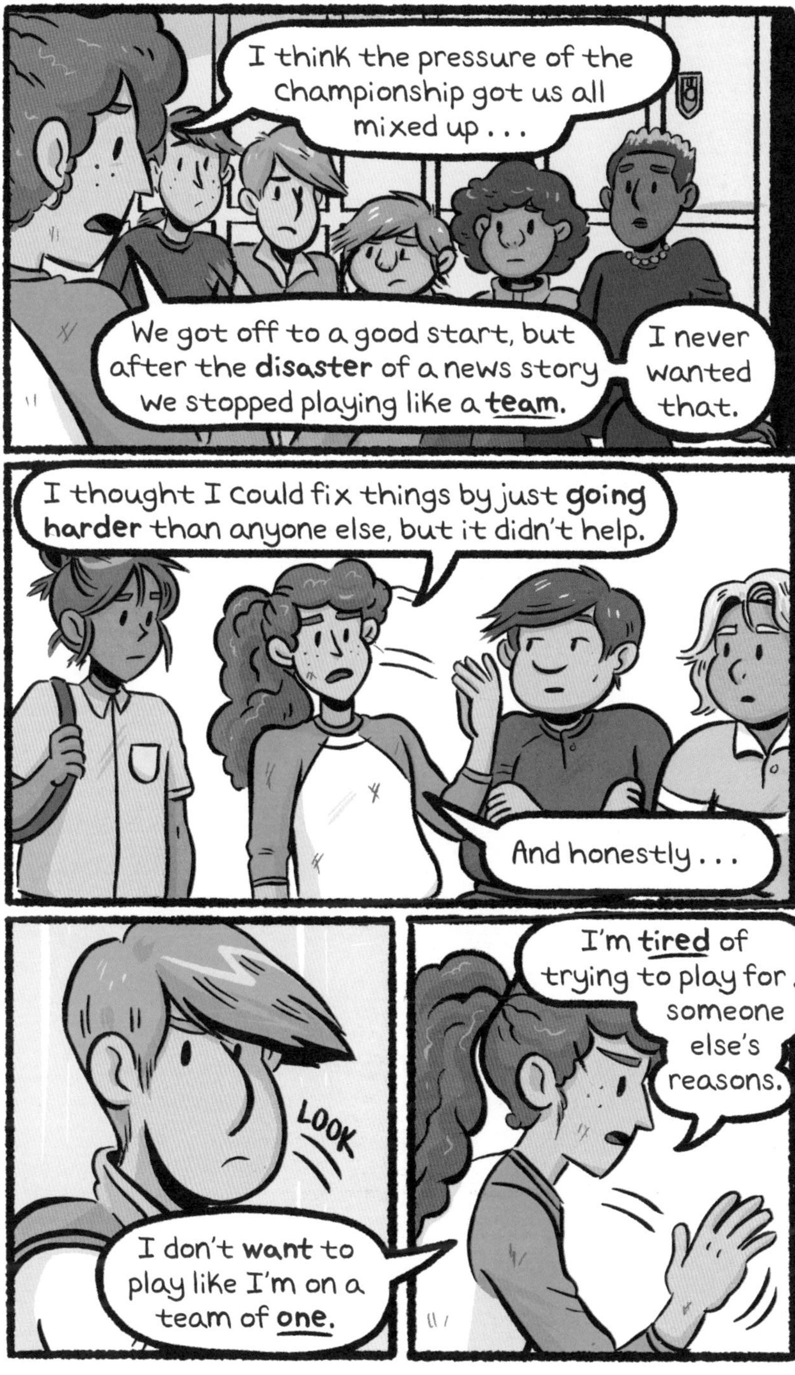
I think the pressure of the championship got us all mixed up . . .
We got off to a good start, but after the **disaster** of a news story we stopped playing like a **team**.
I never wanted that.
I thought I could fix things by just **going harder** than anyone else, but it didn't help.
And honestly . . .
LOOK
I don't **want** to play like I'm on a team of **one**.
I'm **tired** of trying to play for someone else's reasons.

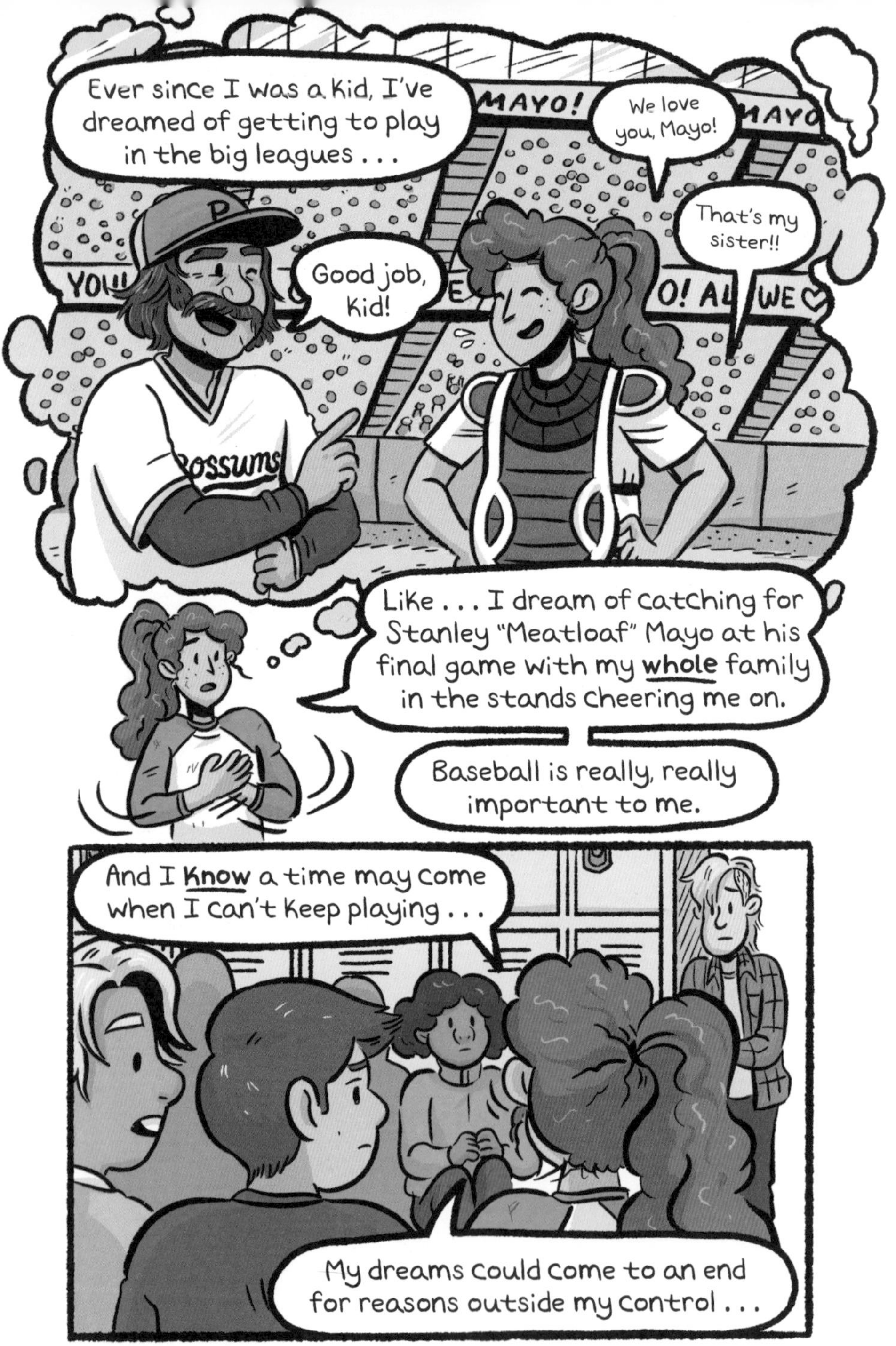
Ever since I was a kid, I've dreamed of getting to play in the big leagues . . .
MAYO!
We love you, Mayo!
MAYO
That's my sister!!
YOU
O! AL
WE
Good job, kid!
Possums
Like . . . I dream of catching for Stanley "Meatloaf" Mayo at his final game with my whole family in the stands cheering me on.
Baseball is really, really important to me.
And I know a time may come when I can't keep playing . . .
My dreams could come to an end for reasons outside my control . . .

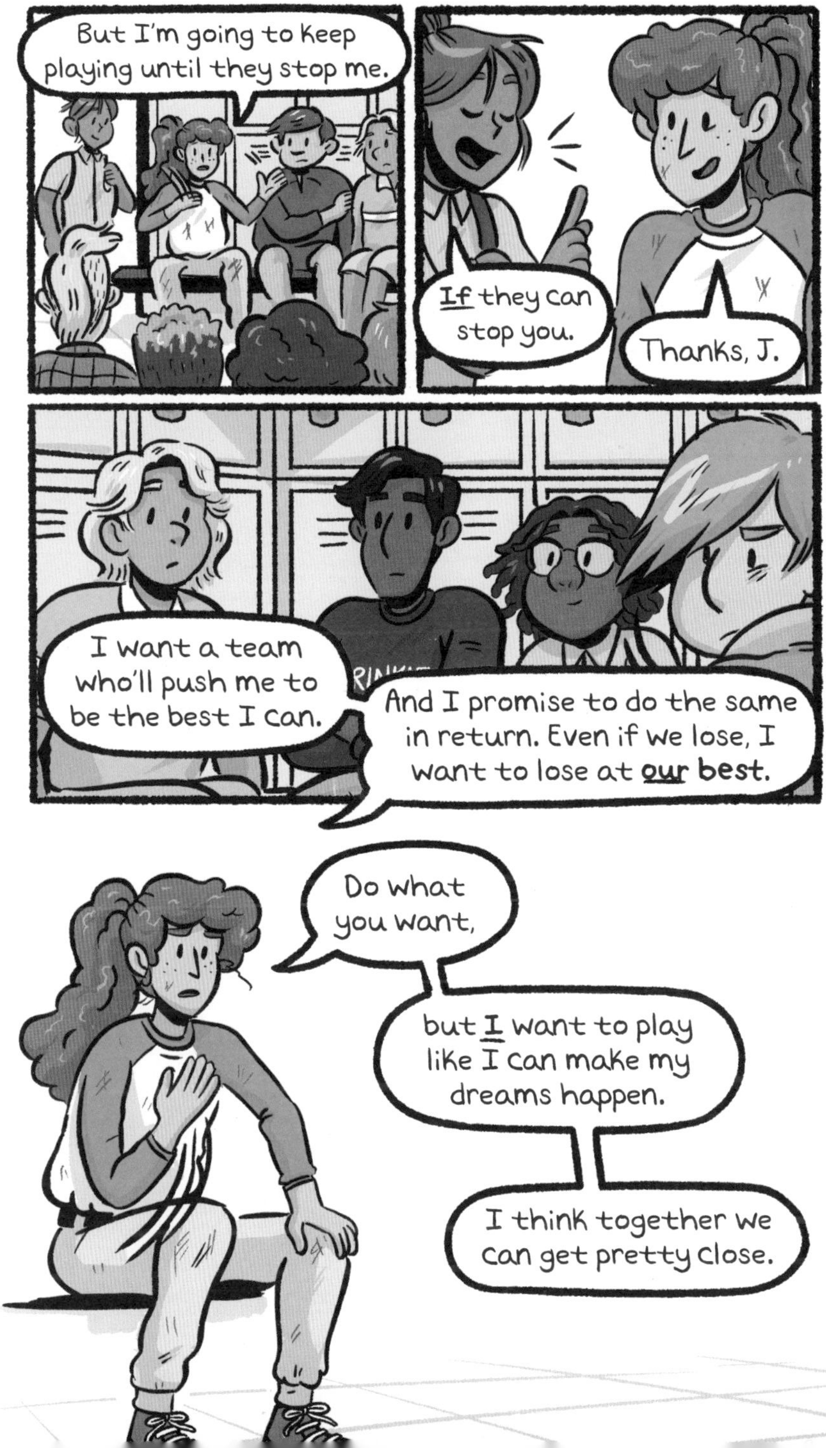
But I'm going to keep playing until they stop me.
If they can stop you.
Thanks, J.
I want a team who'll push me to be the best I can.
And I promise to do the same in return. Even if we lose, I want to lose at our best.
Do what you want,
but I want to play like I can make my dreams happen.
I think together we can get pretty close.

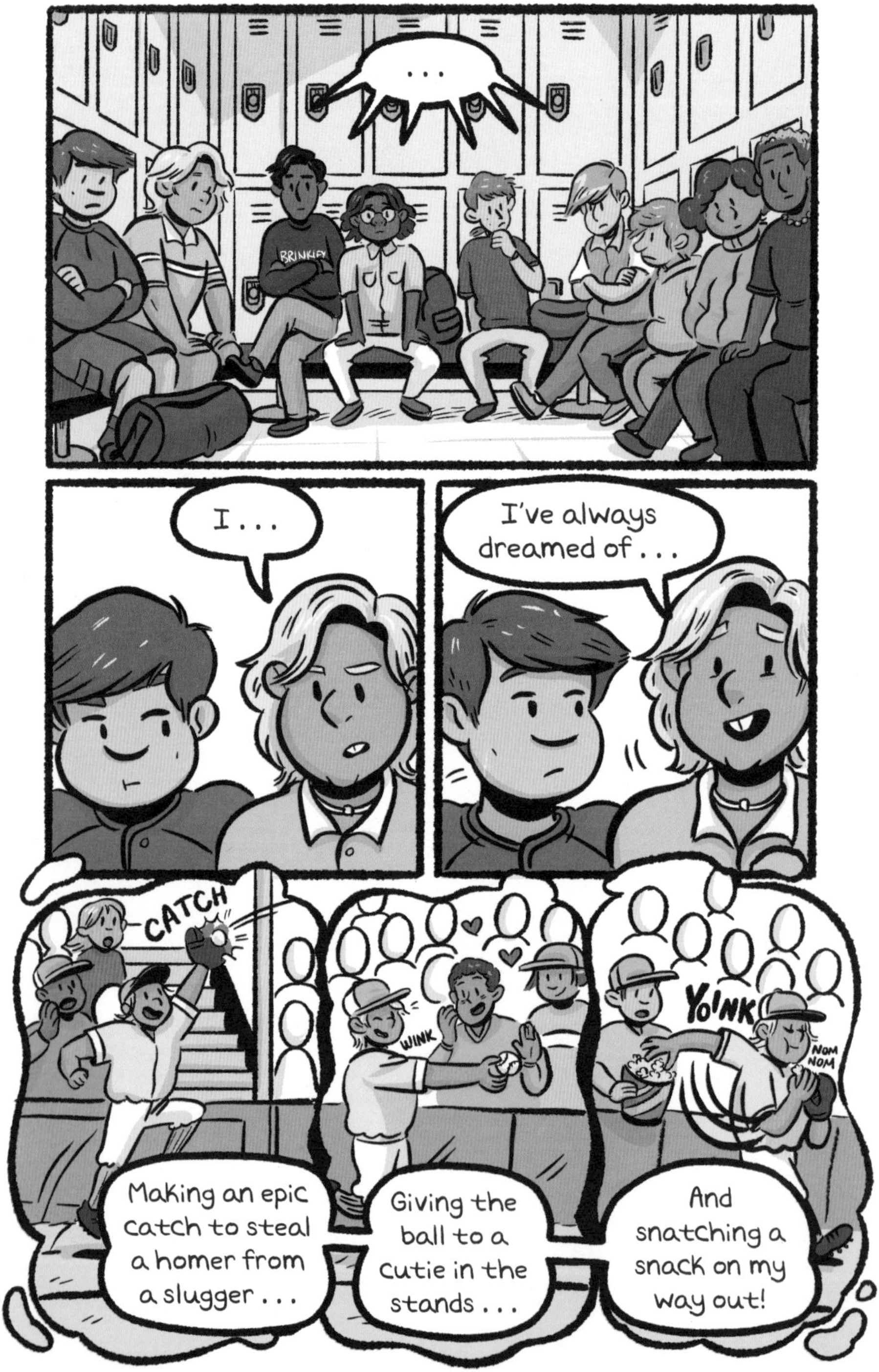
. . .
BRINKLEY
I . . .
I've always dreamed of . . .
CATCH
Making an epic catch to steal a homer from a slugger . . .
WINK
Giving the ball to a cutie in the stands . . .
YOINK
NOM NOM
And snatching a snack on my way out!

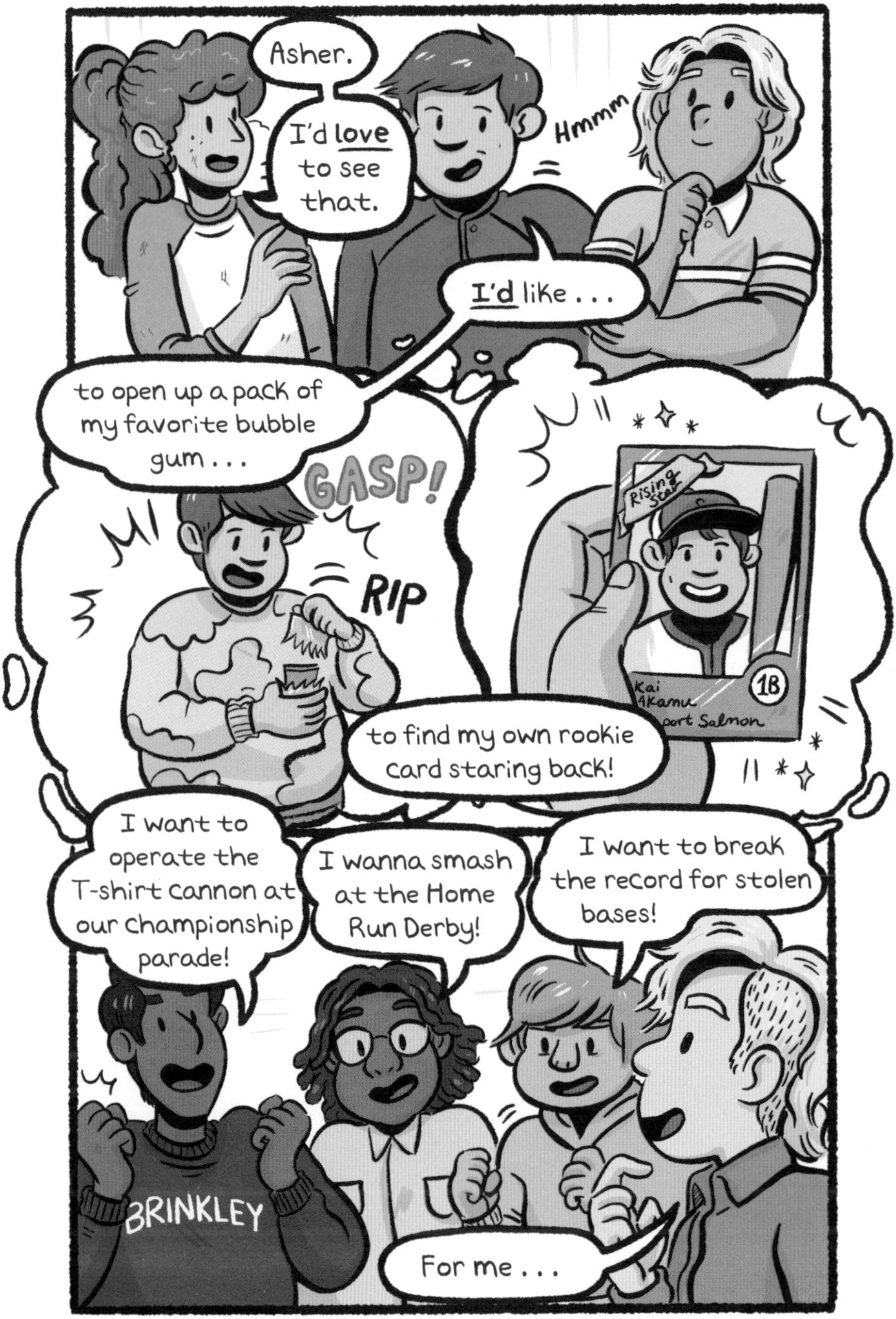
Asher.
I'd love to see that.
Hmmm
I'd like . . .
to open up a pack of my favorite bubble gum . . .
GASP!
RIP
Rising Star
Kai Akamu
1B
to find my own rookie card staring back!
I want to operate the T-shirt cannon at our championship parade!
I wanna smash at the Home Run Derby!
I want to break the record for stolen bases!
BRINKLEY
For me . . .

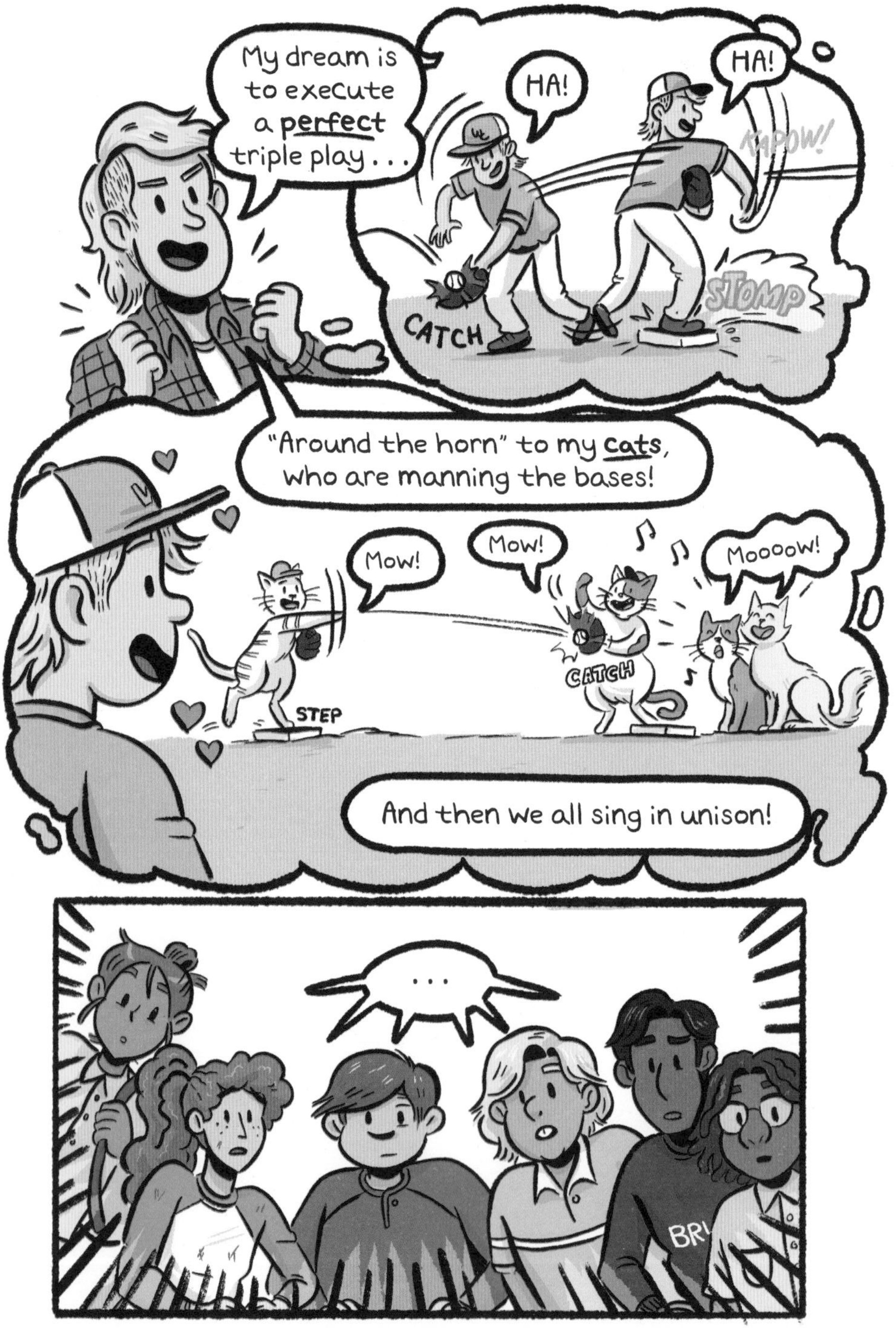
My dream is to execute a perfect triple play . . .
HA!
HA!
KAPOW!
CATCH
STOMP
"Around the horn" to my cats, who are manning the bases!
Mow!
Mow!
Mooooow!
CATCH
STEP
And then we all sing in unison!
. . .
BR

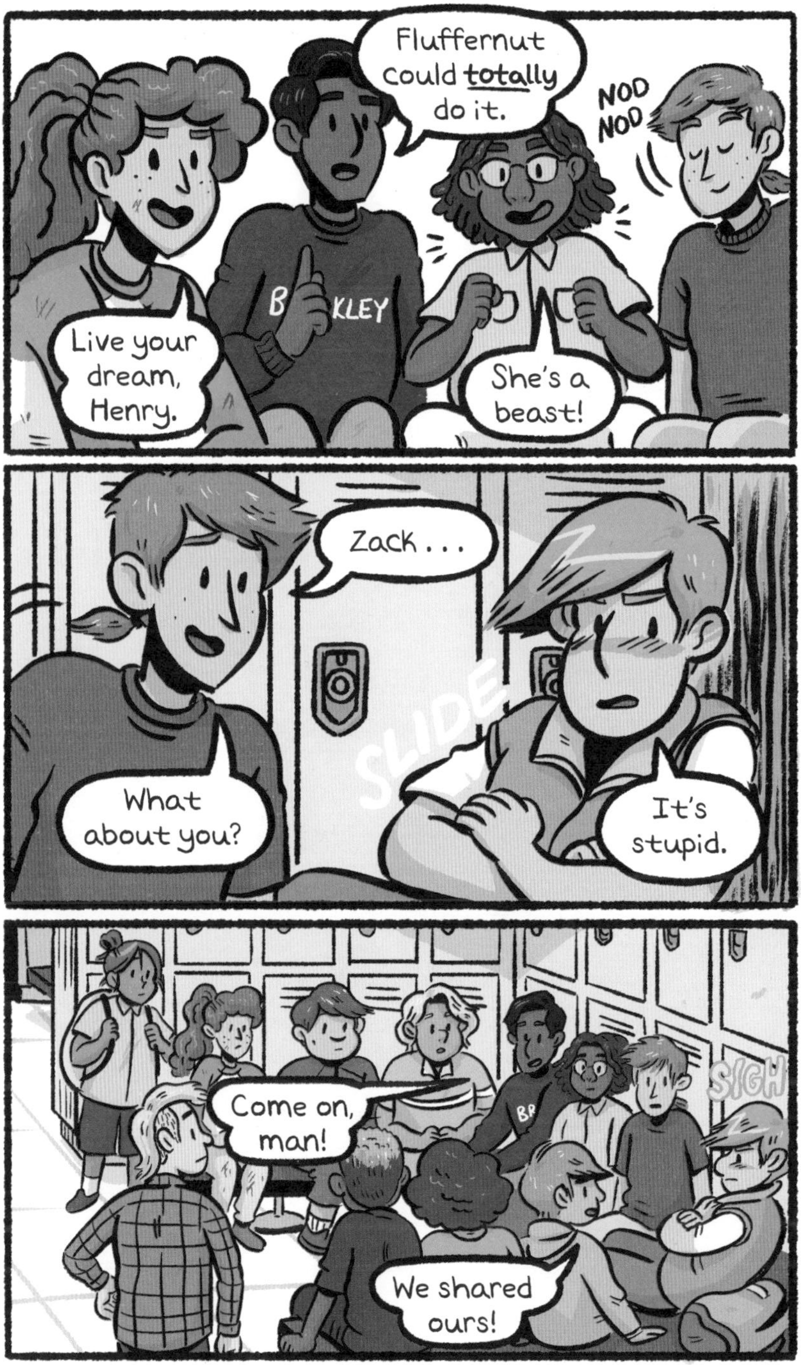
Fluffernut could totally do it.
NOD NOD
Live your dream, Henry.
She's a beast!
Zack . . .
What about you?
SLIDE
It's stupid.
SIGH
Come on, man!
We shared ours!

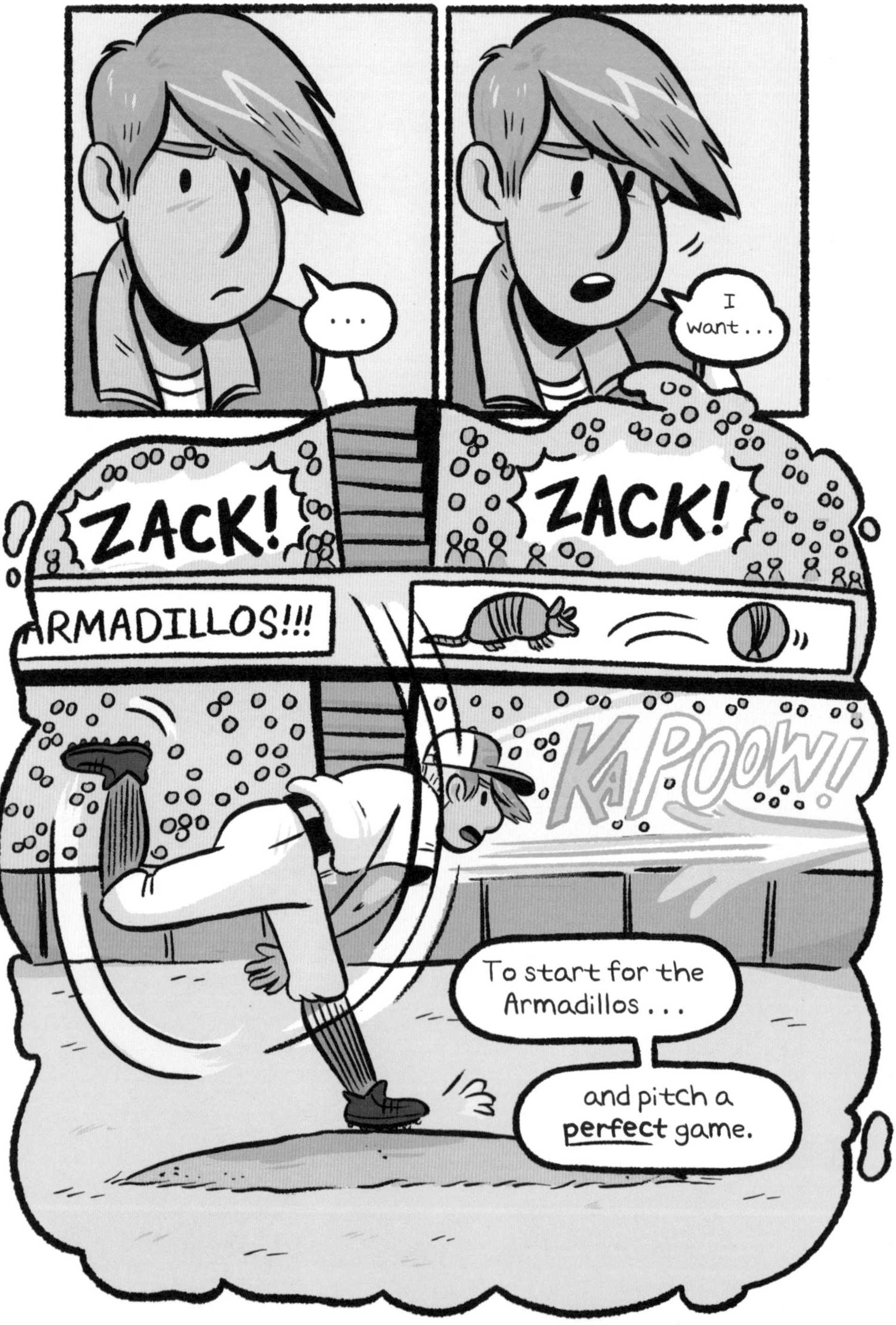
...
I want . . .
ZACK!
ZACK!
ARMADILLOS!!!
KAPOOW!
To start for the Armadillos . . .
and pitch a perfect game.

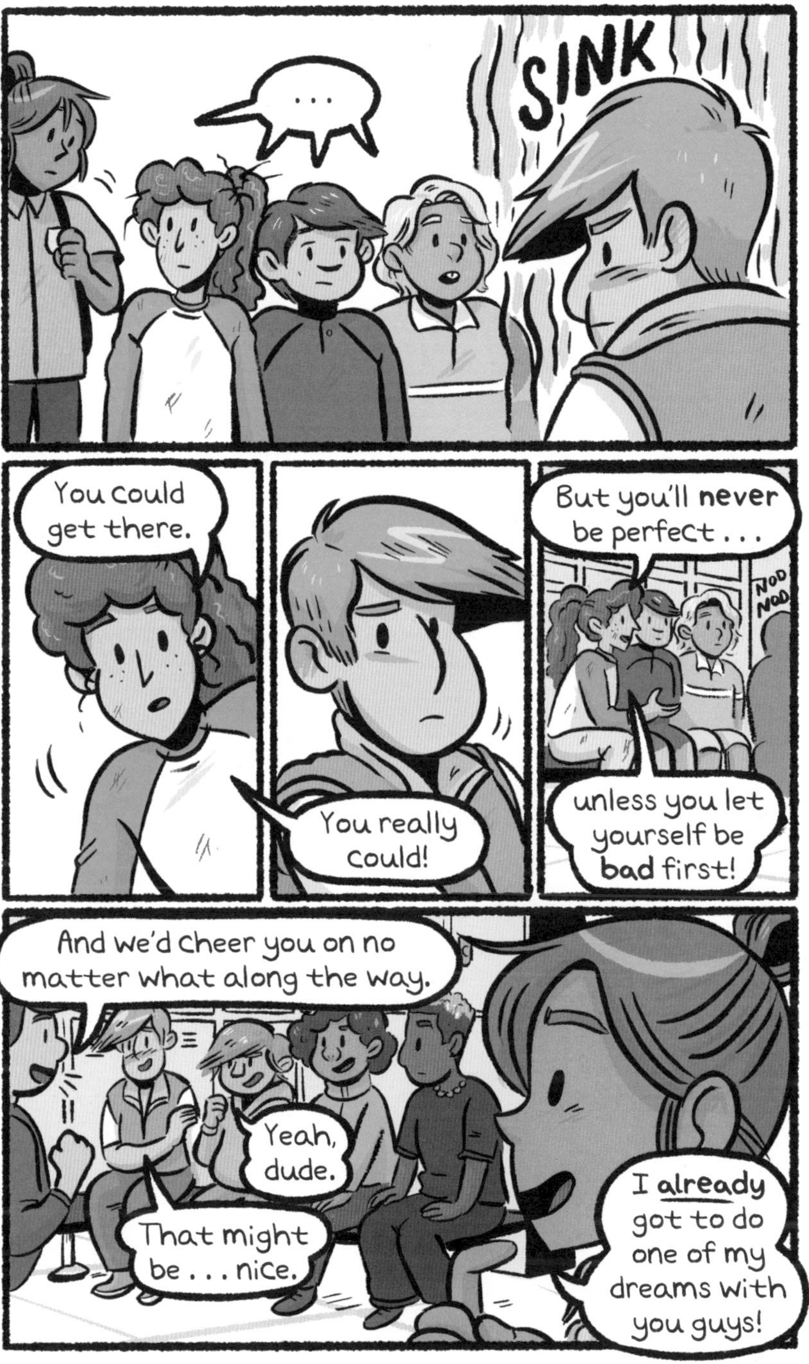
. . .
SINK
You could get there.
You really could!
But you'll **never** be perfect . . .
NOD NOD
unless you let yourself be **bad** first!
And we'd cheer you on no matter what along the way.
Yeah, dude.
That might be . . . nice.
I already got to do one of my dreams with you guys!

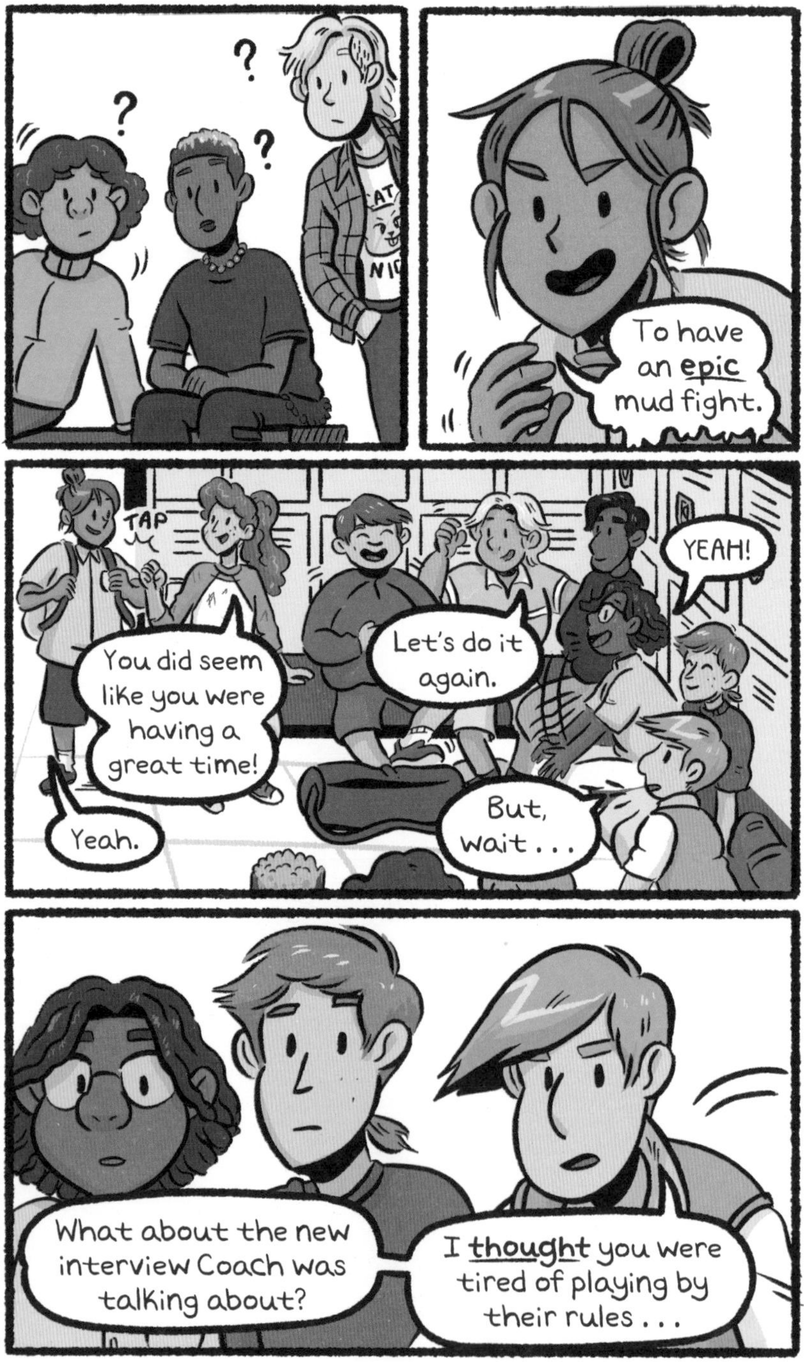
?
?
?
To have an epic mud fight.
TAP
YEAH!
You did seem like you were having a great time!
Let's do it again.
Yeah.
But, wait . . .
What about the new interview Coach was talking about?
I thought you were tired of playing by their rules . . .

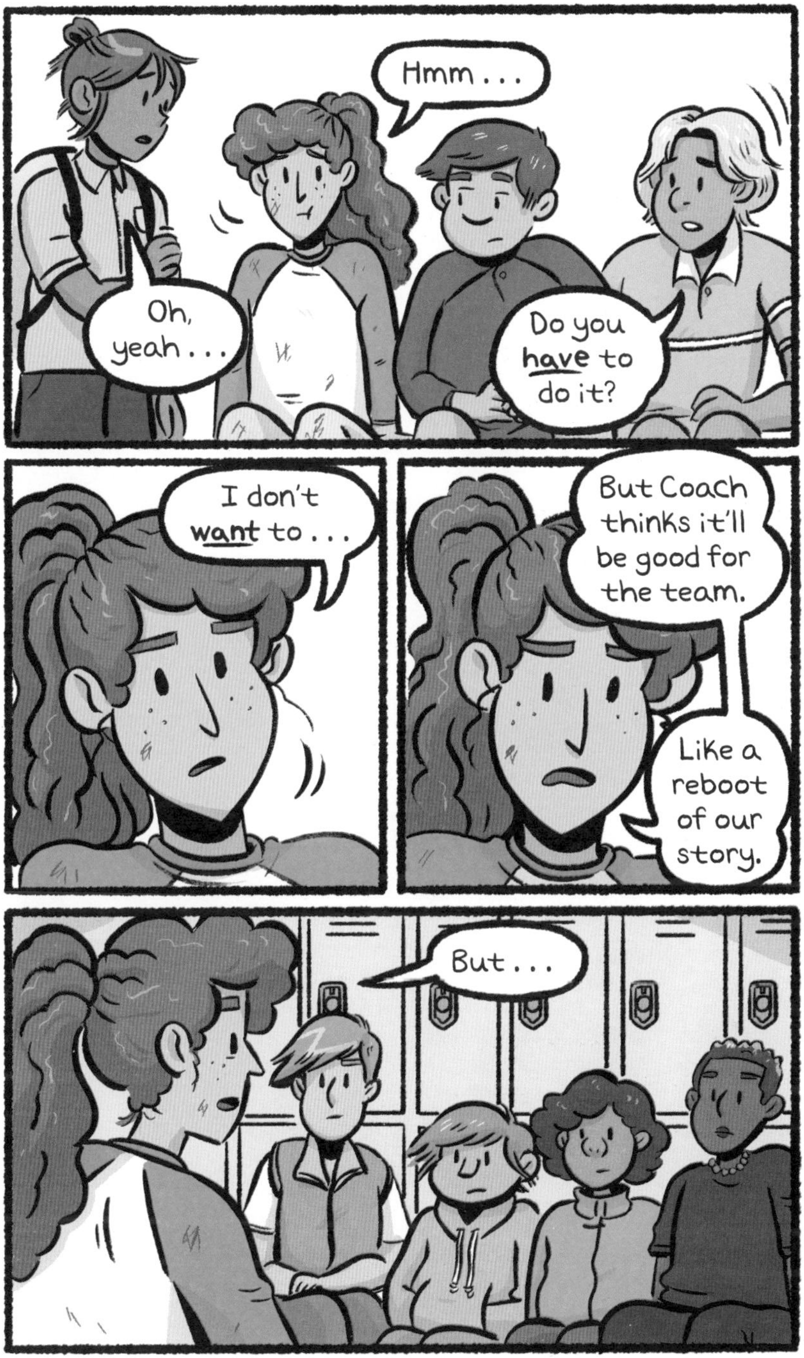
Hmm . . .
Oh, yeah . . .
Do you have to do it?
I don't want to . . .
But Coach thinks it'll be good for the team.
Like a reboot of our story.
But . . .

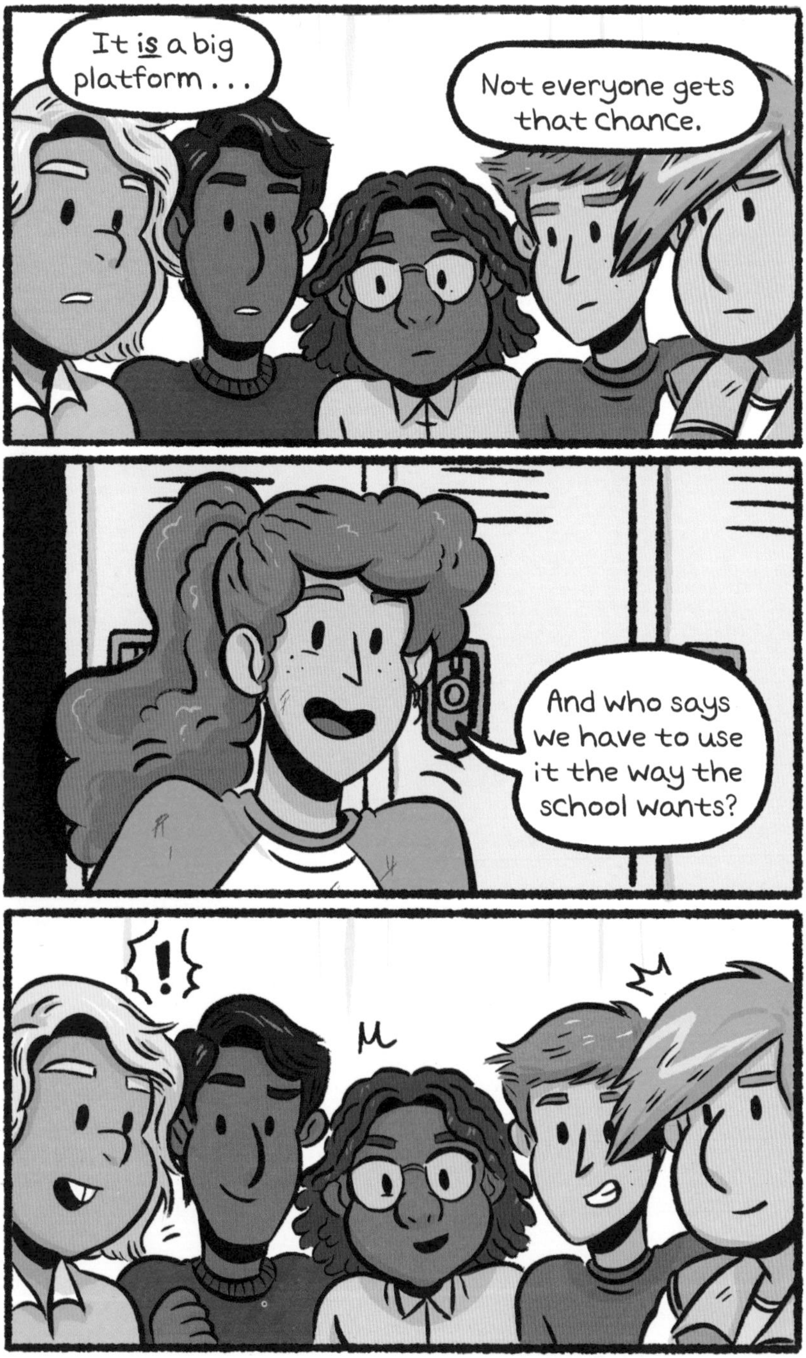
It is a big platform . . .
Not everyone gets that chance.
And who says we have to use it the way the school wants?
!

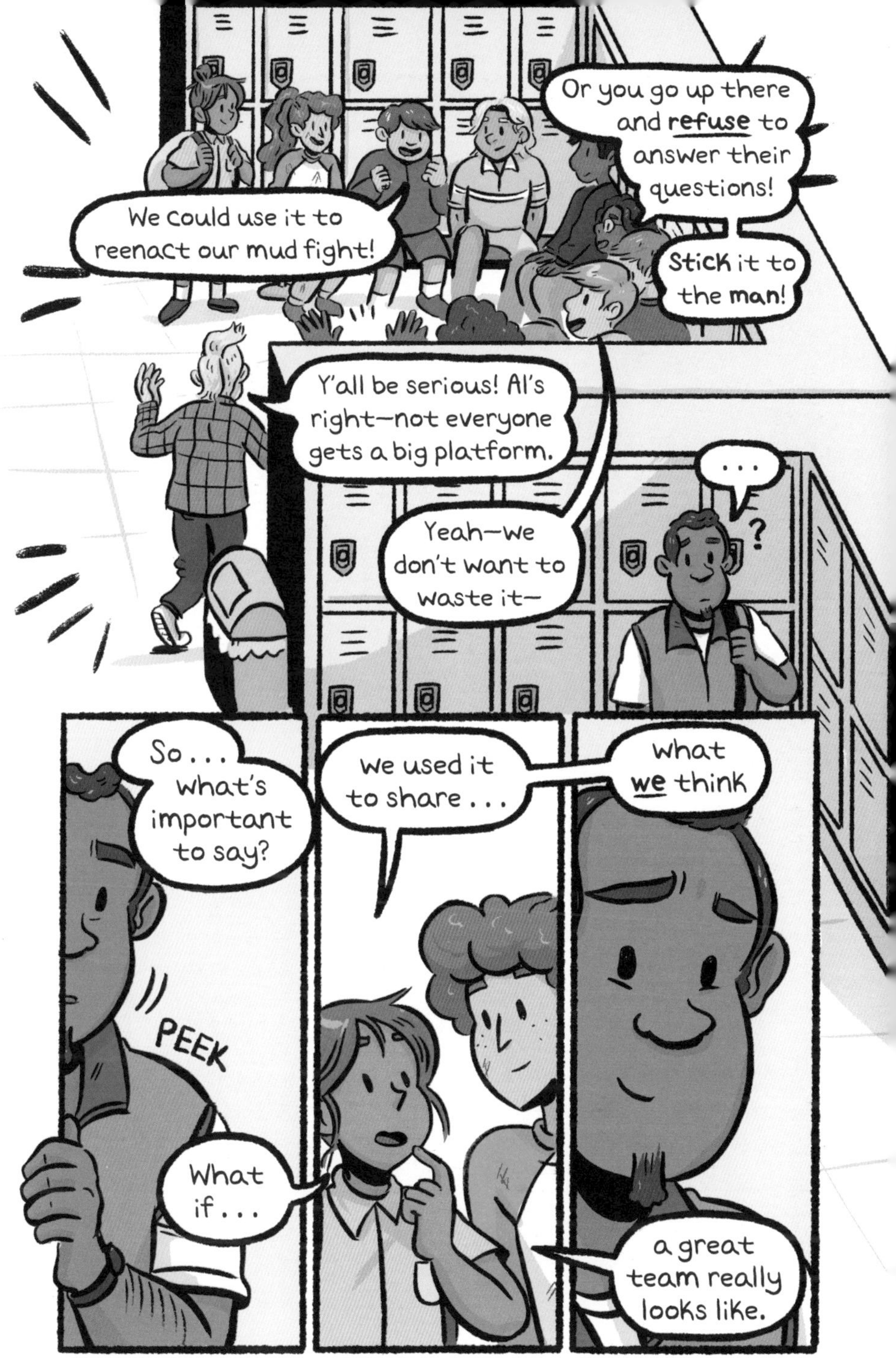
We could use it to reenact our mud fight!
Or you go up there and refuse to answer their questions!
Stick it to the man!
Y'all be serious! Al's right—not everyone gets a big platform.
Yeah—we don't want to waste it—
. . .
?
So . . . what's important to say?
PEEK
What if . . .
We used it to share . . .
what we think
a great team really looks like.

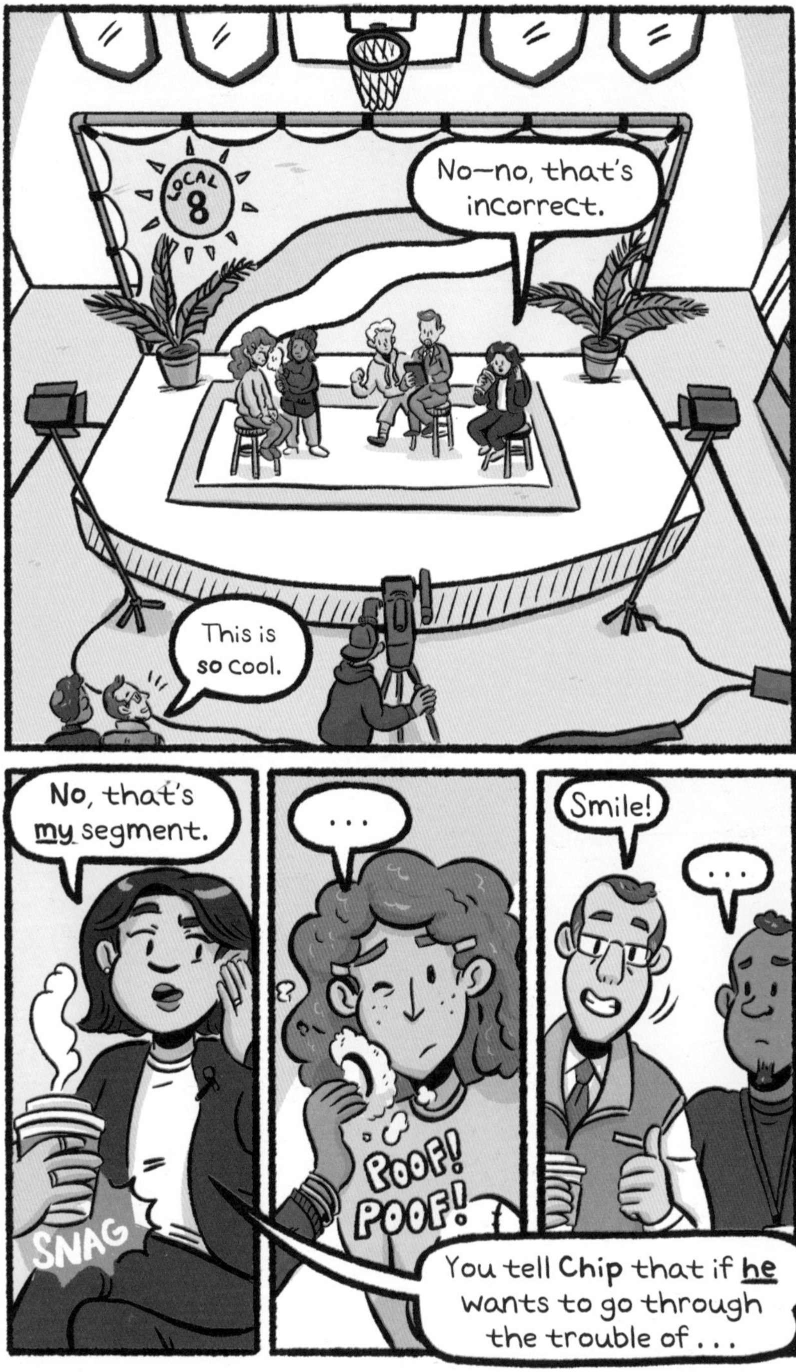
LOCAL 8
No—no, that's incorrect.
This is so cool.
No, that's my segment.
...
Smile!
...
POOF! POOF!
SNAG
You tell Chip that if he wants to go through the trouble of . . .

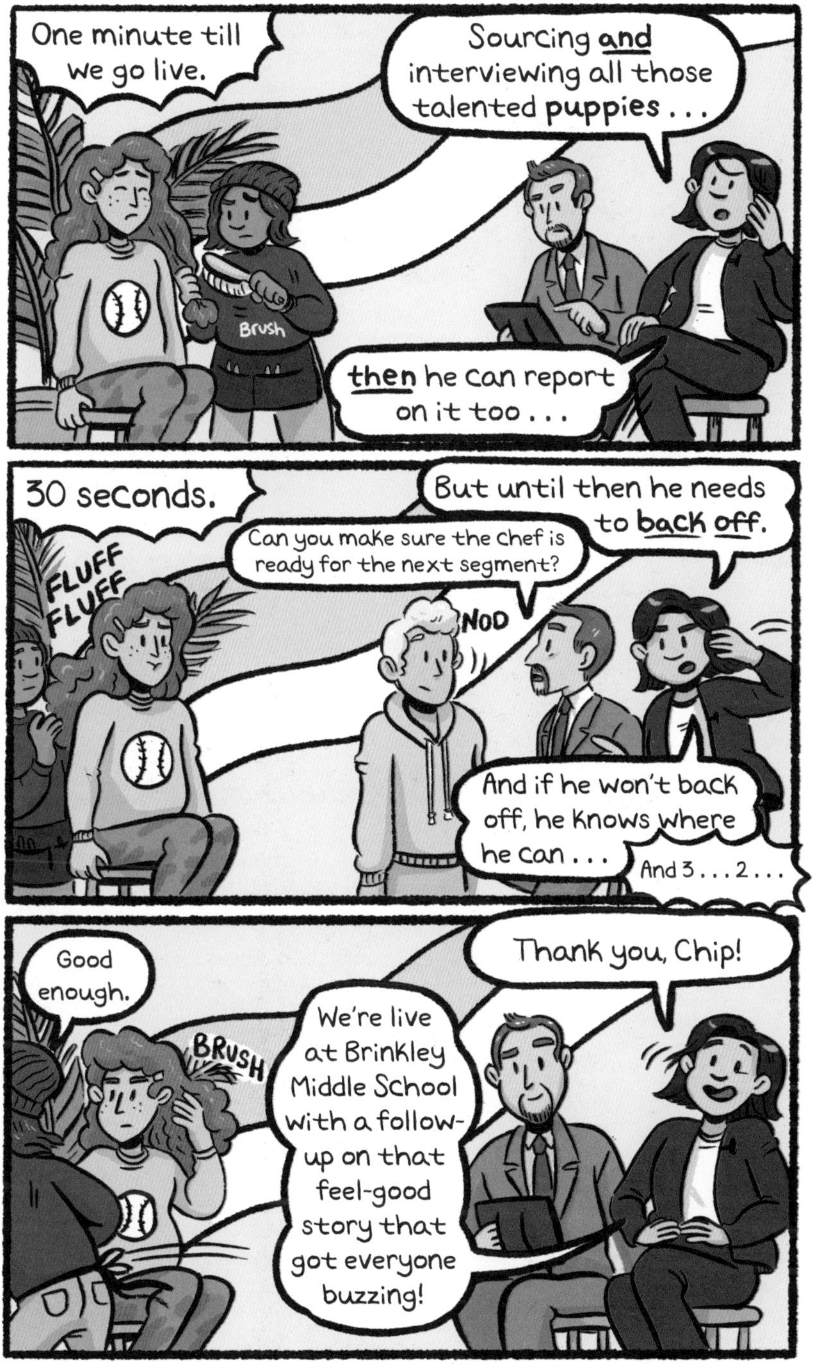
One minute till we go live.
Sourcing and interviewing all those talented puppies . . .
Brush
then he can report on it too . . .
30 seconds.
But until then he needs to back off.
Can you make sure the chef is ready for the next segment?
FLUFF FLUFF
NOD
And if he won't back off, he knows where he can . . .
And 3 . . . 2 . . .
Good enough.
Thank you, Chip!
BRUSH
We're live at Brinkley Middle School with a follow-up on that feel-good story that got everyone buzzing!

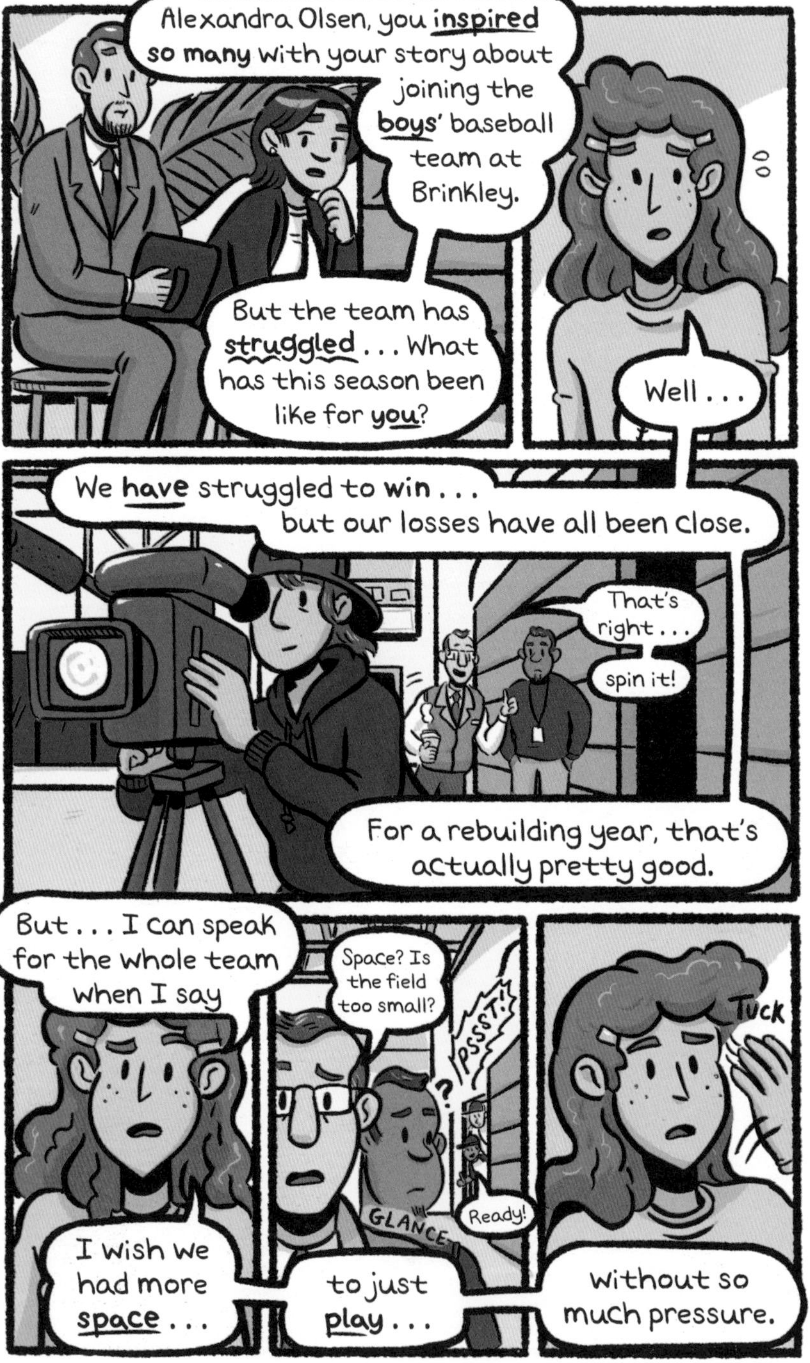
Alexandra Olsen, you inspired so many with your story about joining the boys' baseball team at Brinkley.
But the team has struggled . . . What has this season been like for you?
Well . . .
We have struggled to win . . .
but our losses have all been close.
That's right . . .
spin it!
For a rebuilding year, that's actually pretty good.
But . . . I can speak for the whole team when I say
I wish we had more space . . .
Space? Is the field too small?
PSSST!
?
GLANCE
Ready!
to just play . . .
TUCK
without so much pressure.

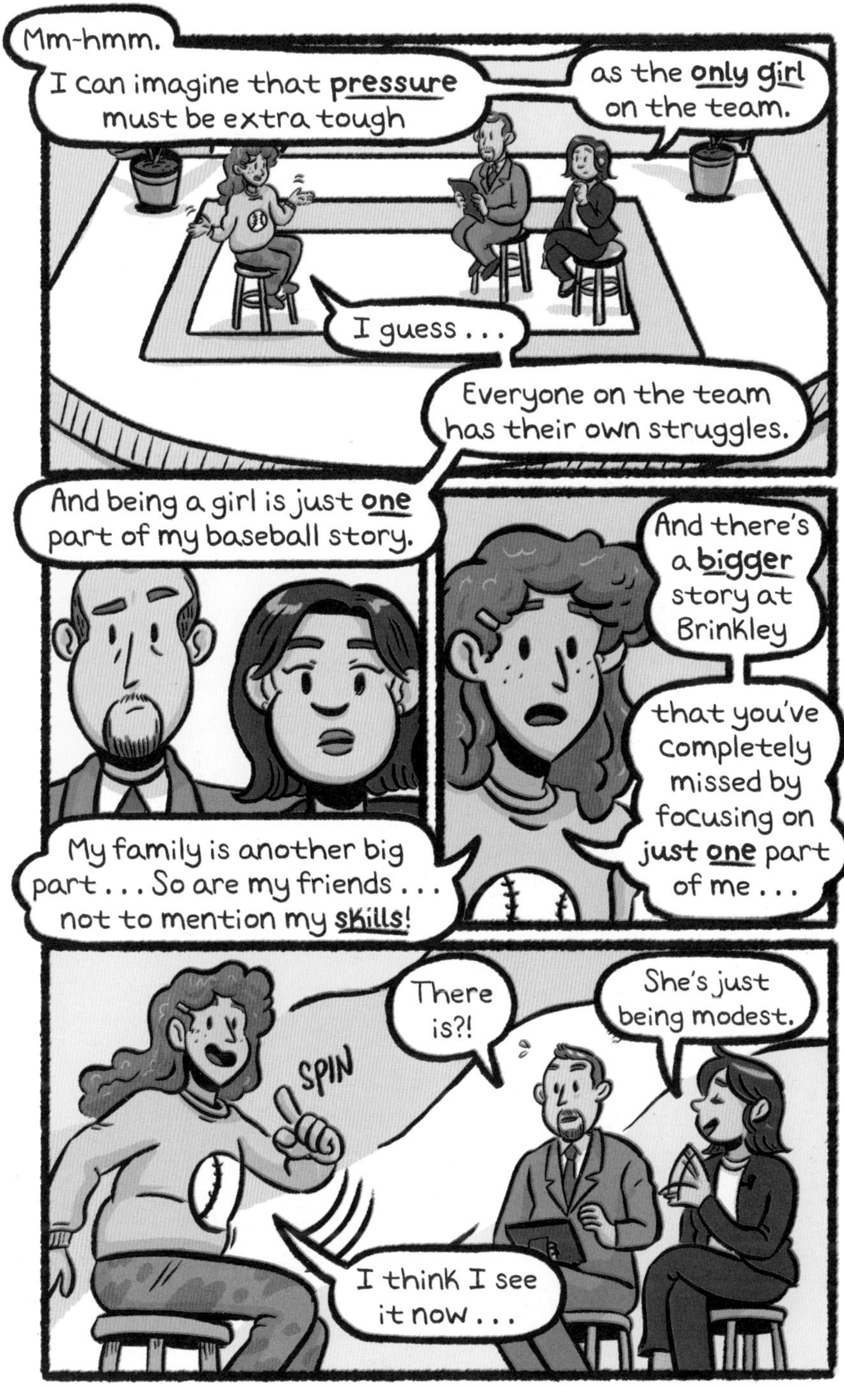
Mm-hmm.
I can imagine that pressure must be extra tough
as the only girl on the team.
I guess . . .
Everyone on the team has their own struggles.
And being a girl is just one part of my baseball story.
My family is another big part . . . So are my friends . . . not to mention my skills!
And there's a bigger story at Brinkley
that you've completely missed by focusing on just one part of me . . .
There is?!
She's just being modest.
SPIN
I think I see it now . . .

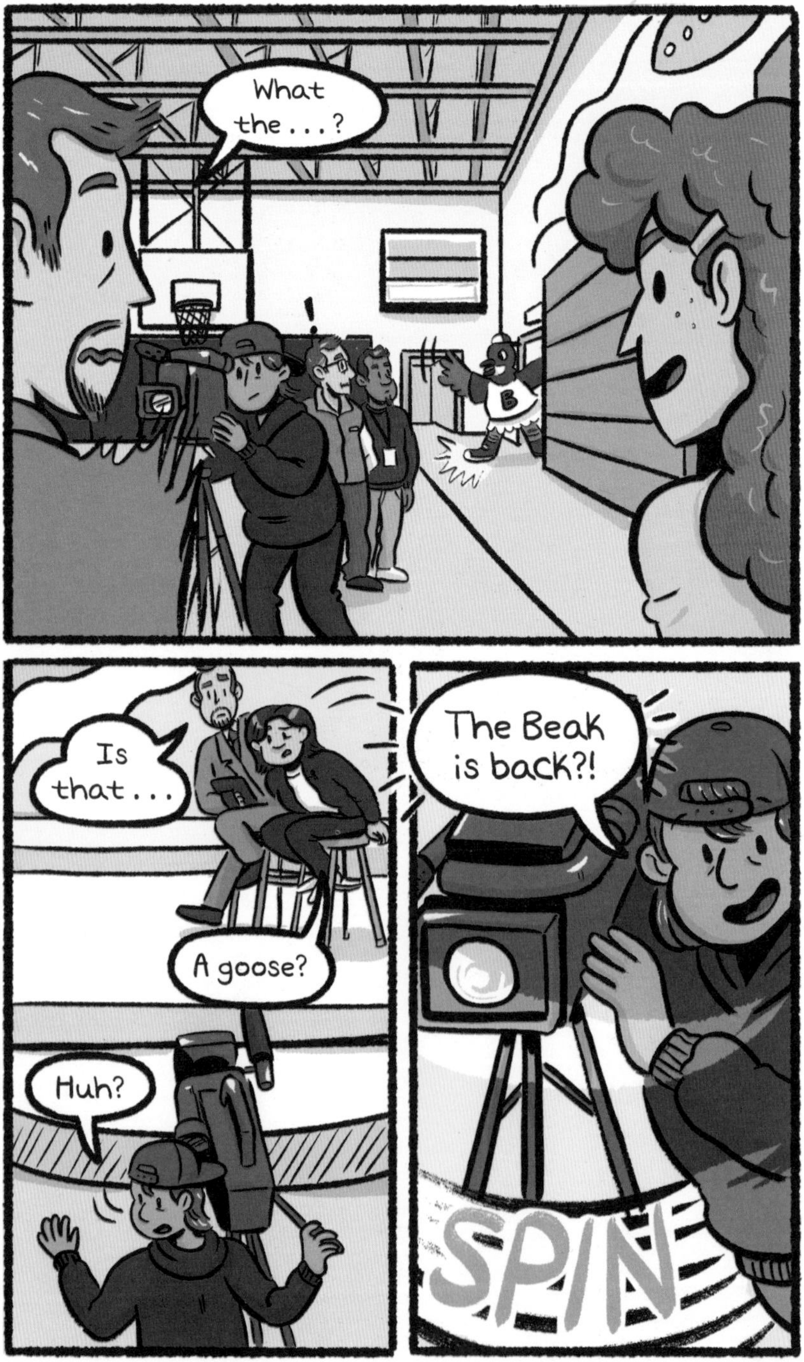
What the . . . ?
!
Is that . . .
A goose?
Huh?
The Beak is back?!
SPIN

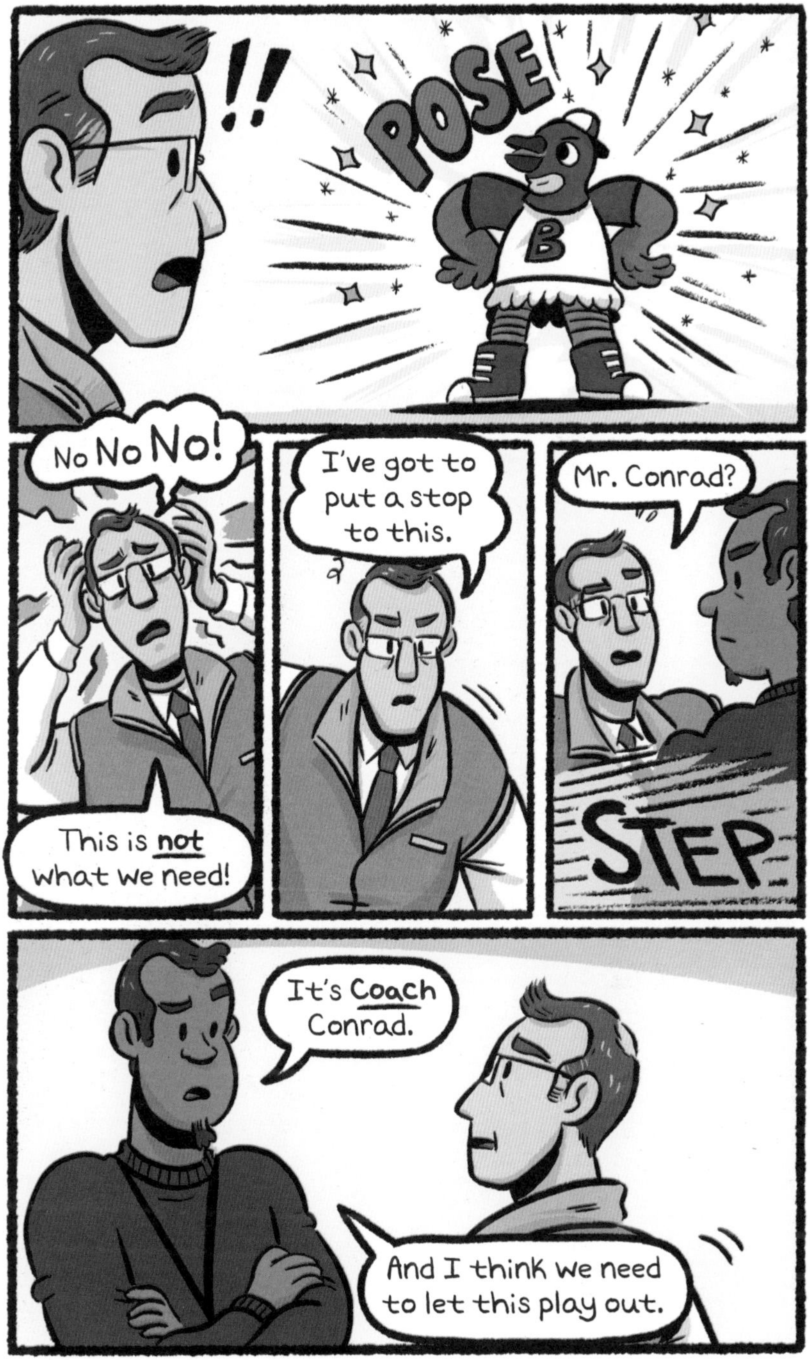
!!
POSE
B
No No No!
This is not what we need!
I've got to put a stop to this.
Mr. Conrad?
STEP
It's Coach Conrad.
And I think we need to let this play out.

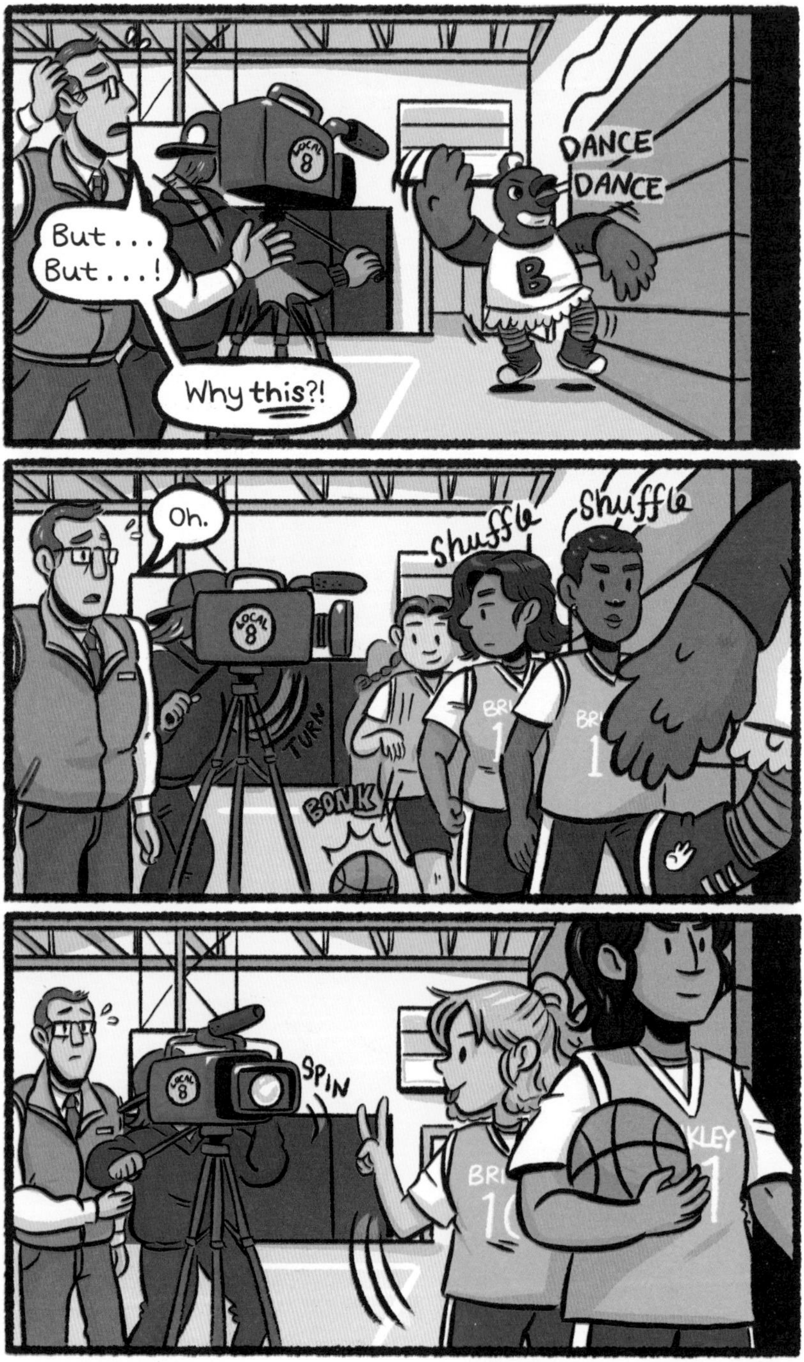
DANCE
DANCE
But... But...!
Why this?!
Oh.
Shuffle
Shuffle
TURN
BONK
SPIN

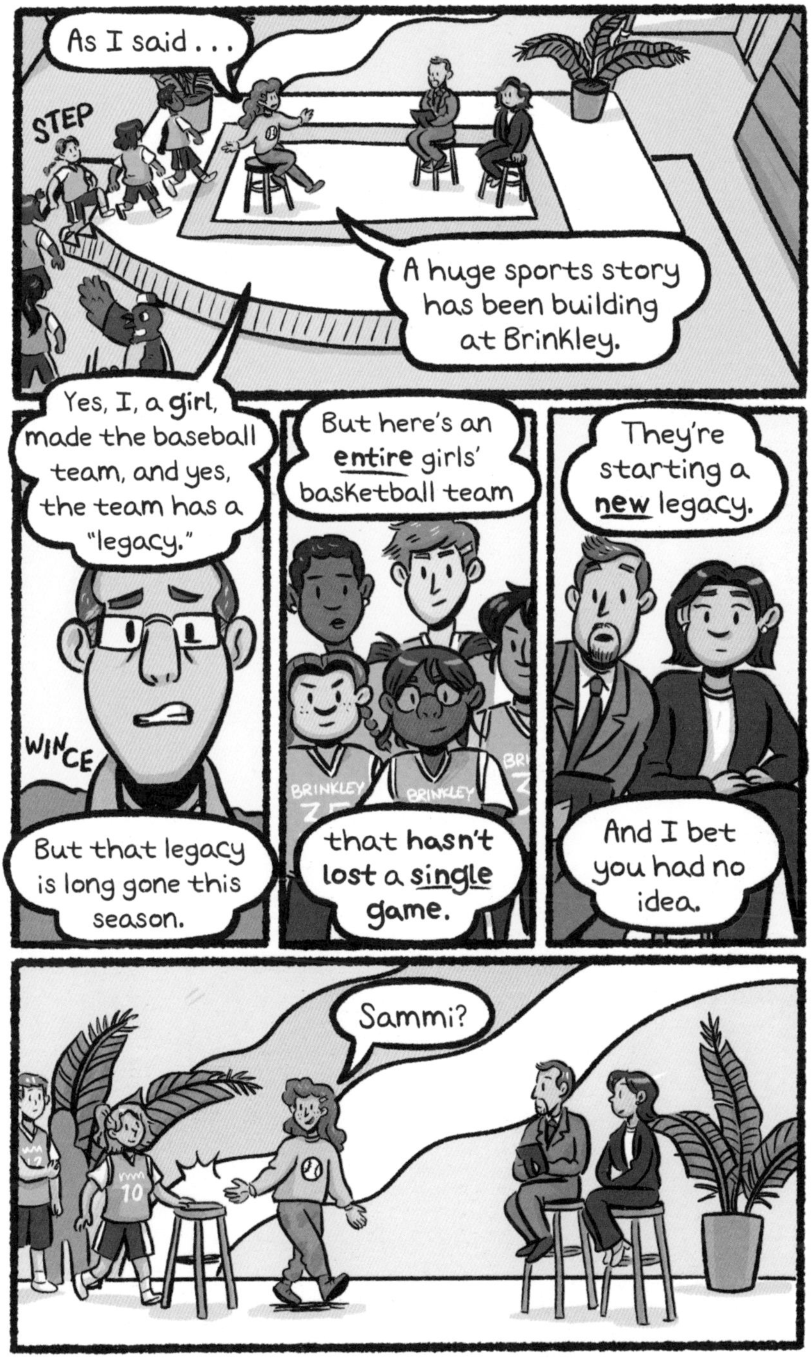
As I said . . .
STEP
A huge sports story has been building at Brinkley.
Yes, I, a girl, made the baseball team, and yes, the team has a "legacy."
WINCE
But that legacy is long gone this season.
But here's an entire girls' basketball team
BRINKLEY
BRINKLEY
that hasn't lost a single game.
They're starting a new legacy.
And I bet you had no idea.
Sammi?
10

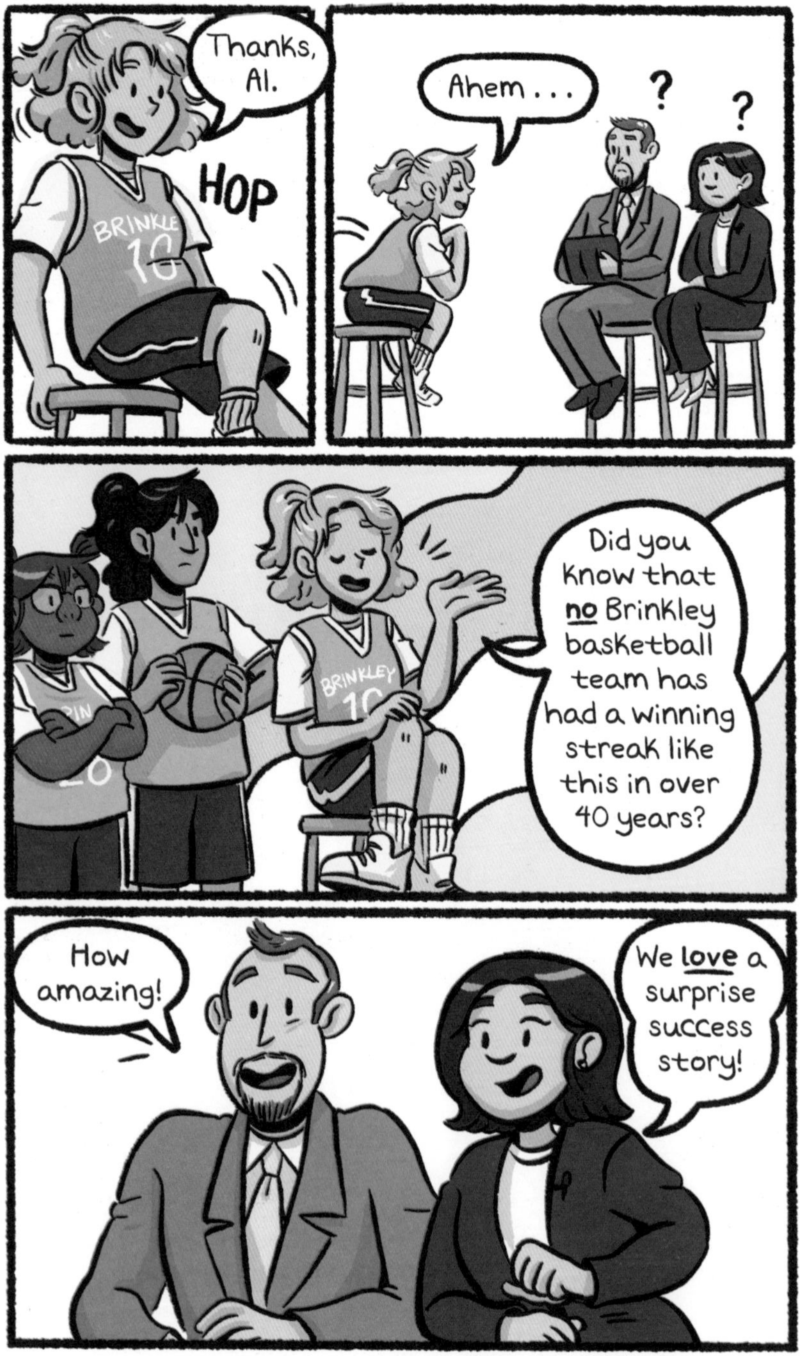
Thanks, Al.
HOP
Ahem . . .
?
?
BRINKLEY
10
Did you know that no Brinkley basketball team has had a winning streak like this in over 40 years?
How amazing!
We love a surprise success story!

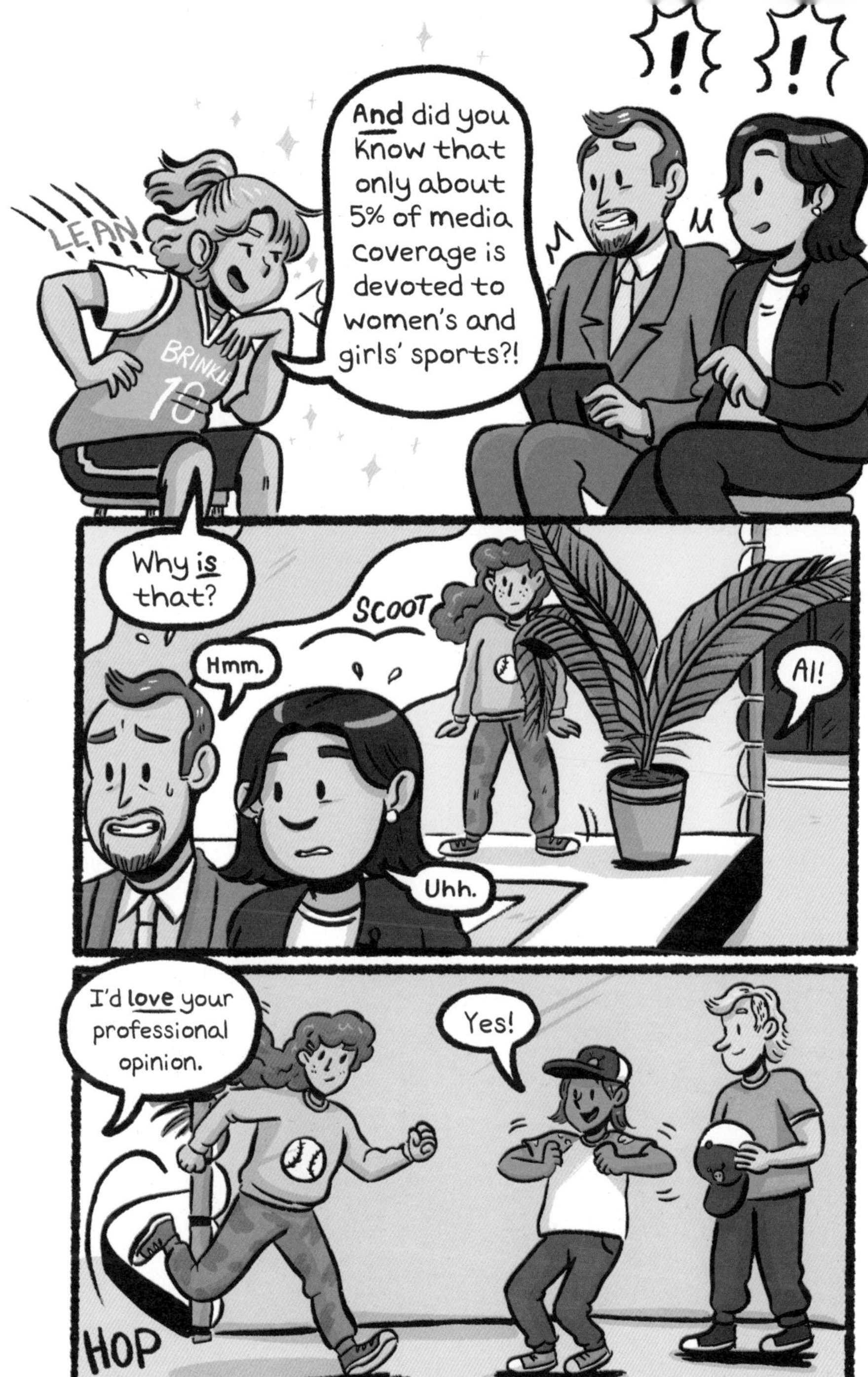
!
!
LEAN
And did you know that only about 5% of media coverage is devoted to women's and girls' sports?!
Why is that?
SCOOT
Hmm.
Al!
Uhh.
I'd love your professional opinion.
Yes!
HOP

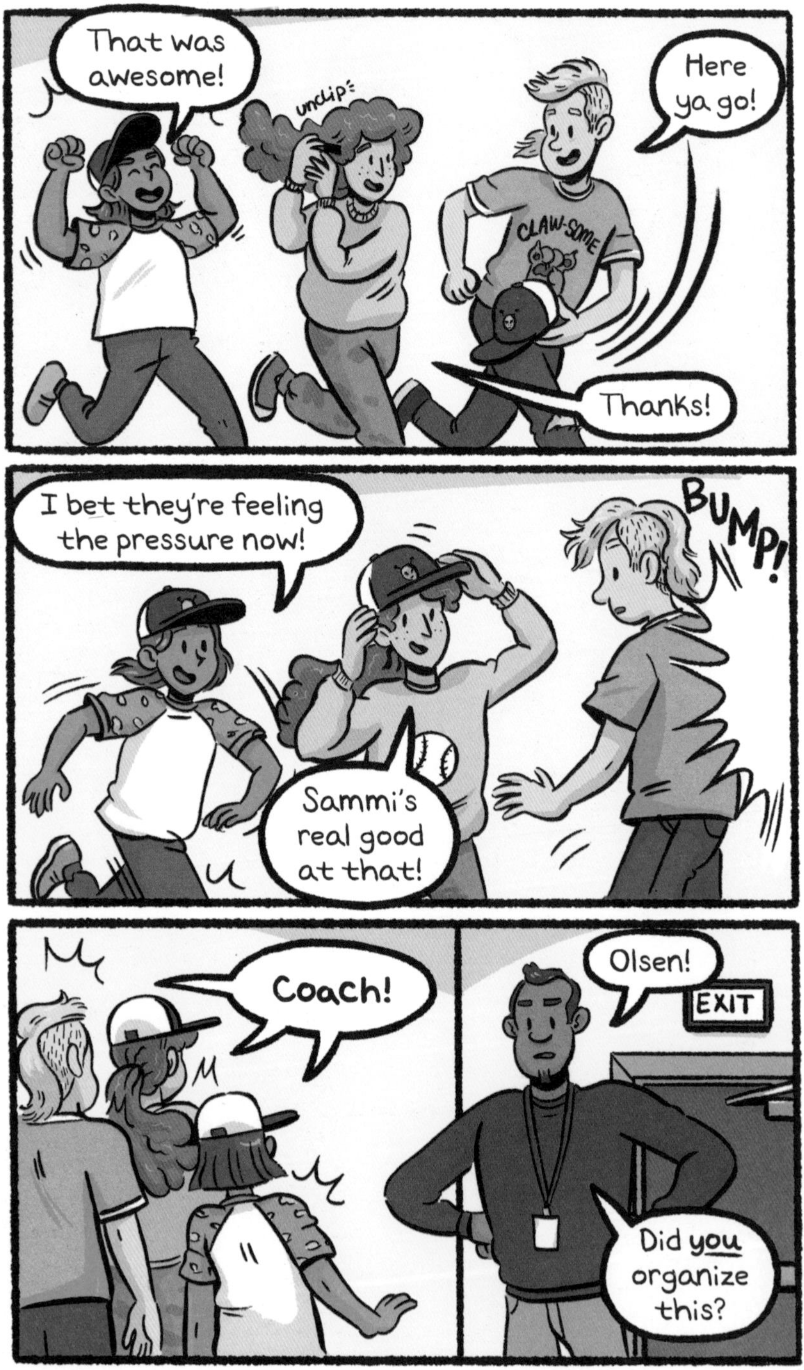
That was awesome!
unclip
Here ya go!
CLAW-SOME
Thanks!
I bet they're feeling the pressure now!
BUMP!
Sammi's real good at that!
Coach!
Olsen!
EXIT
Did you organize this?

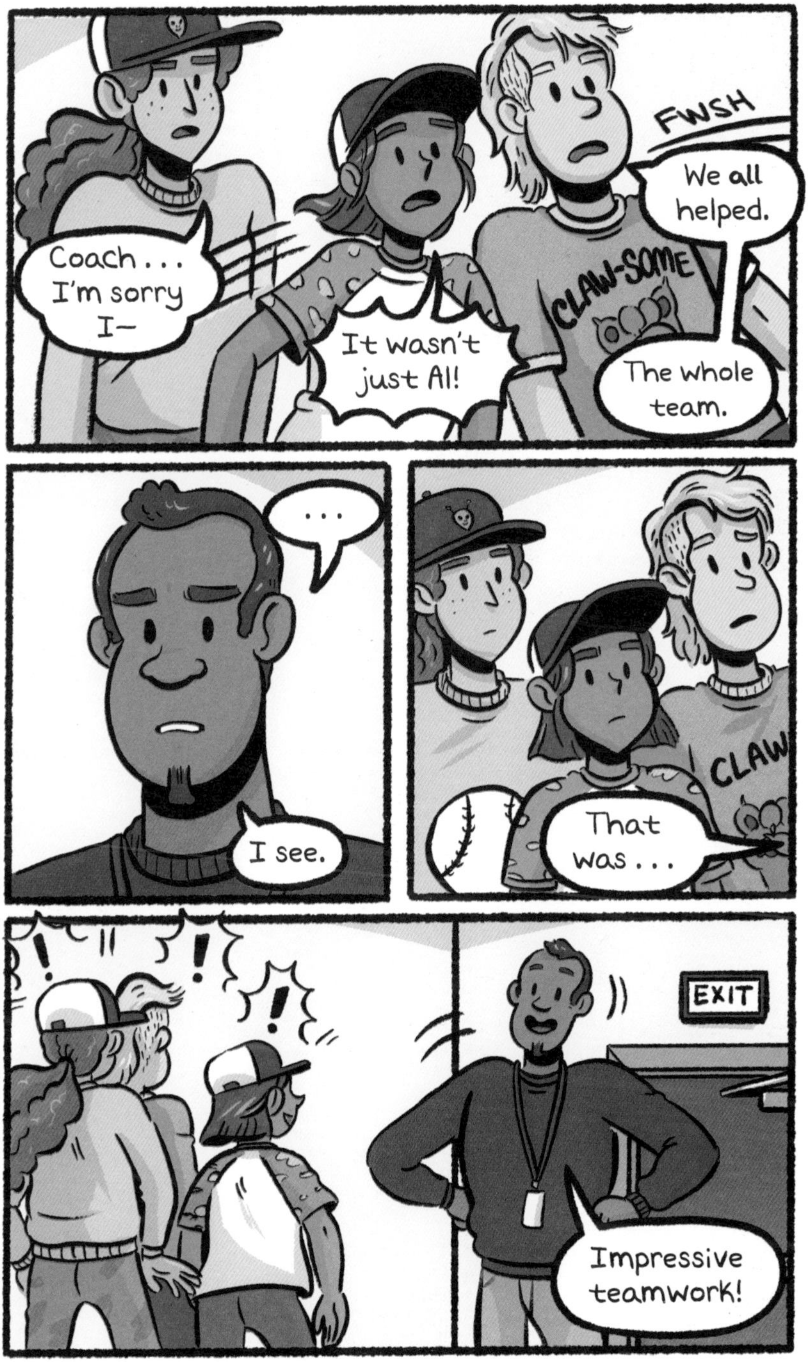
FWSH
Coach . . . I'm sorry I–
It wasn't just Al!
We all helped.
CLAW-SOME
The whole team.
. . .
I see.
CLAW
That was . . .
EXIT
Impressive teamwork!

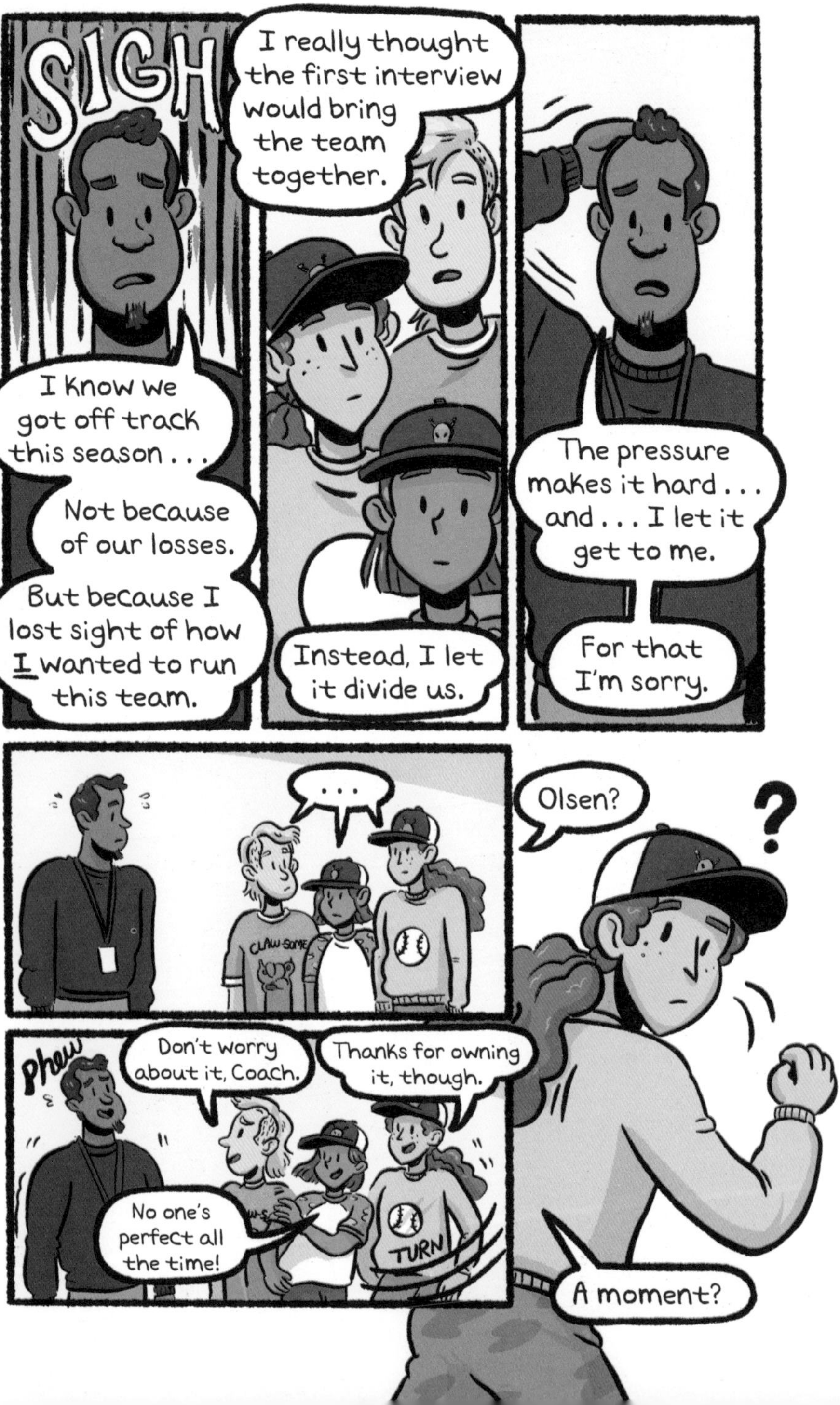
SIGH
I really thought the first interview would bring the team together.
I know we got off track this season . . .
Not because of our losses.
But because I lost sight of how I wanted to run this team.
Instead, I let it divide us.
The pressure makes it hard . . . and . . . I let it get to me.
For that I'm sorry.
. . .
Olsen?
?
Phew
Don't worry about it, Coach.
Thanks for owning it, though.
No one's perfect all the time!
CLAW-SOME
TURN
A moment?

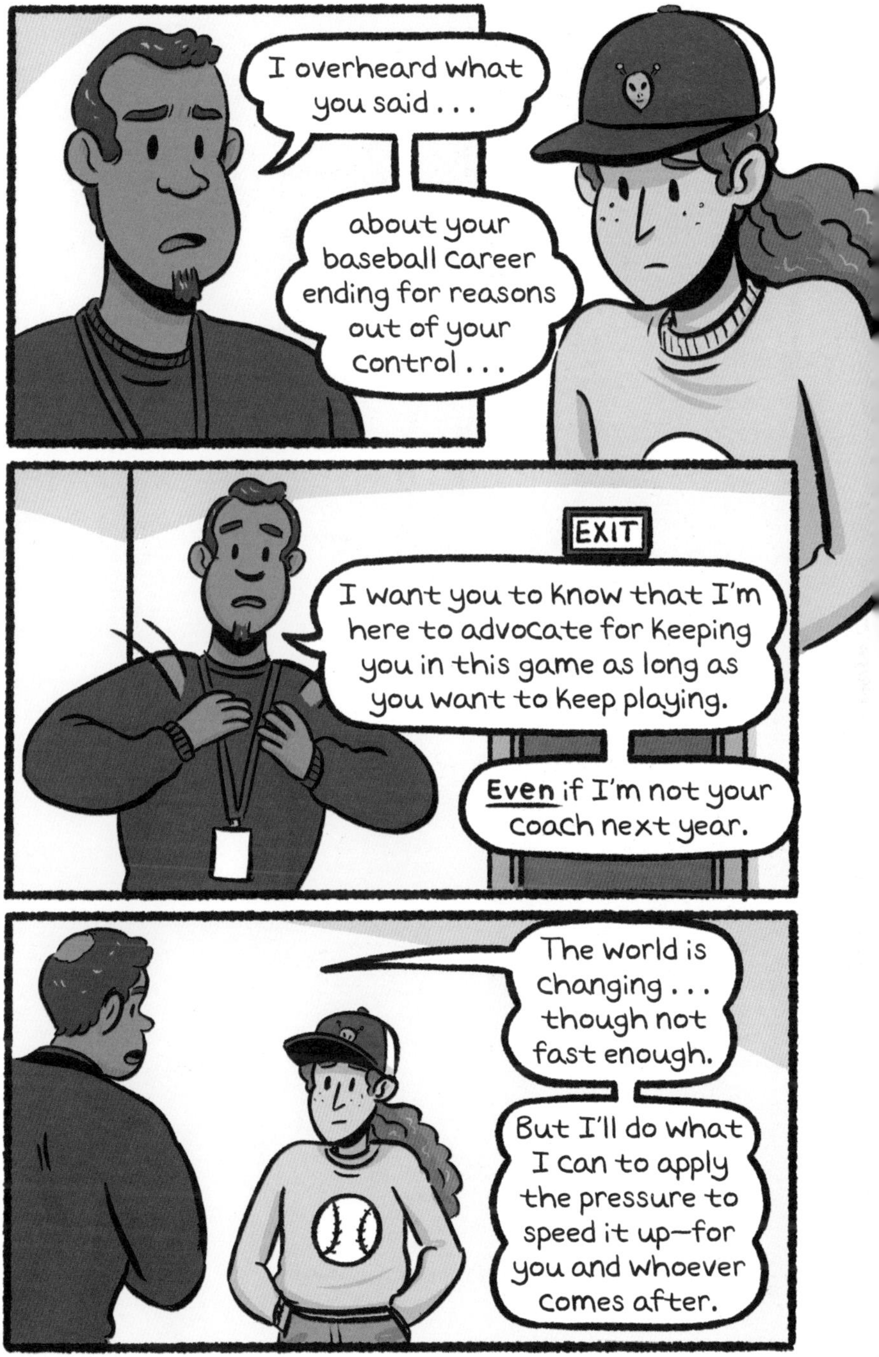
I overheard what you said . . .
about your baseball career ending for reasons out of your control . . .
EXIT
I want you to know that I'm here to advocate for keeping you in this game as long as you want to keep playing.
Even if I'm not your coach next year.
The world is changing . . . though not fast enough.
But I'll do what I can to apply the pressure to speed it up—for you and whoever comes after.

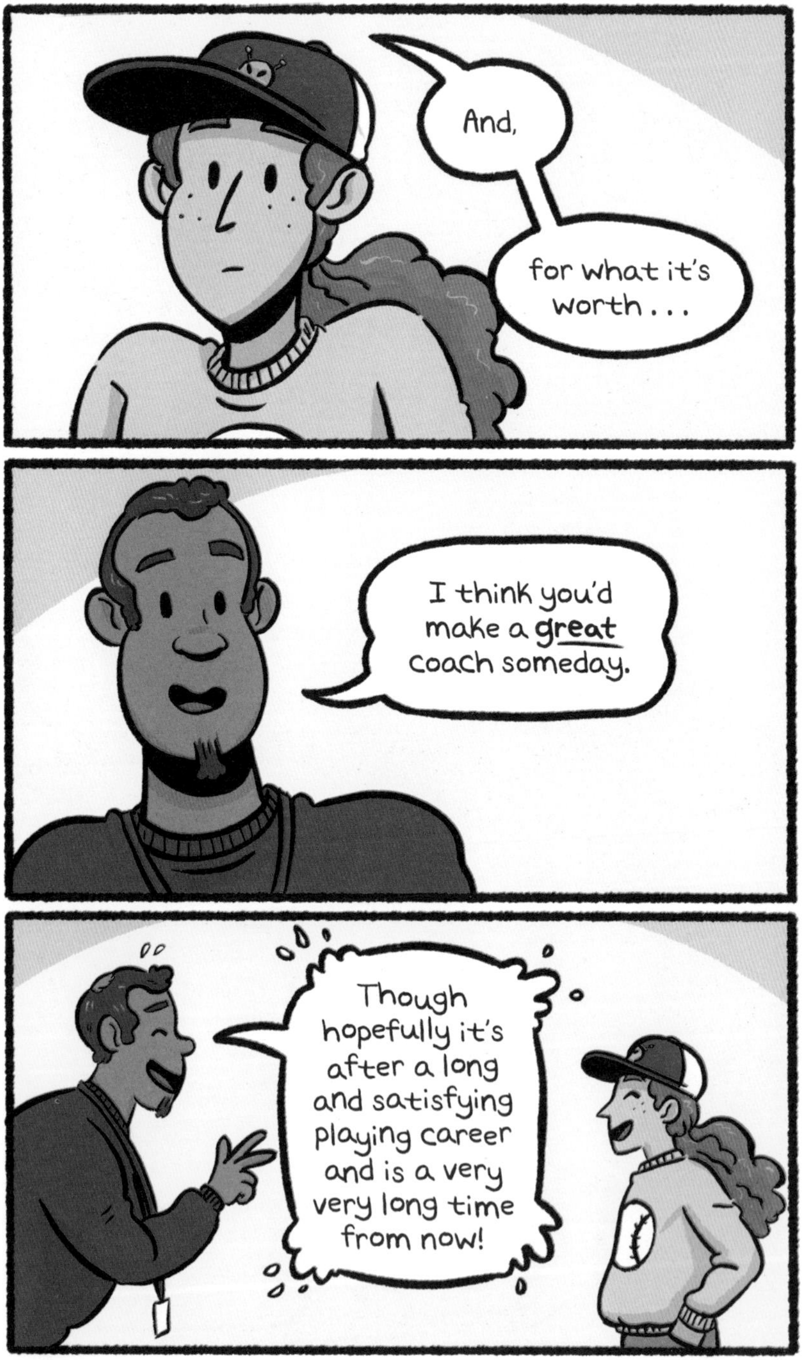
And,
for what it's worth . . .
I think you'd make a great coach someday.
Though hopefully it's after a long and satisfying playing career and is a very very long time from now!

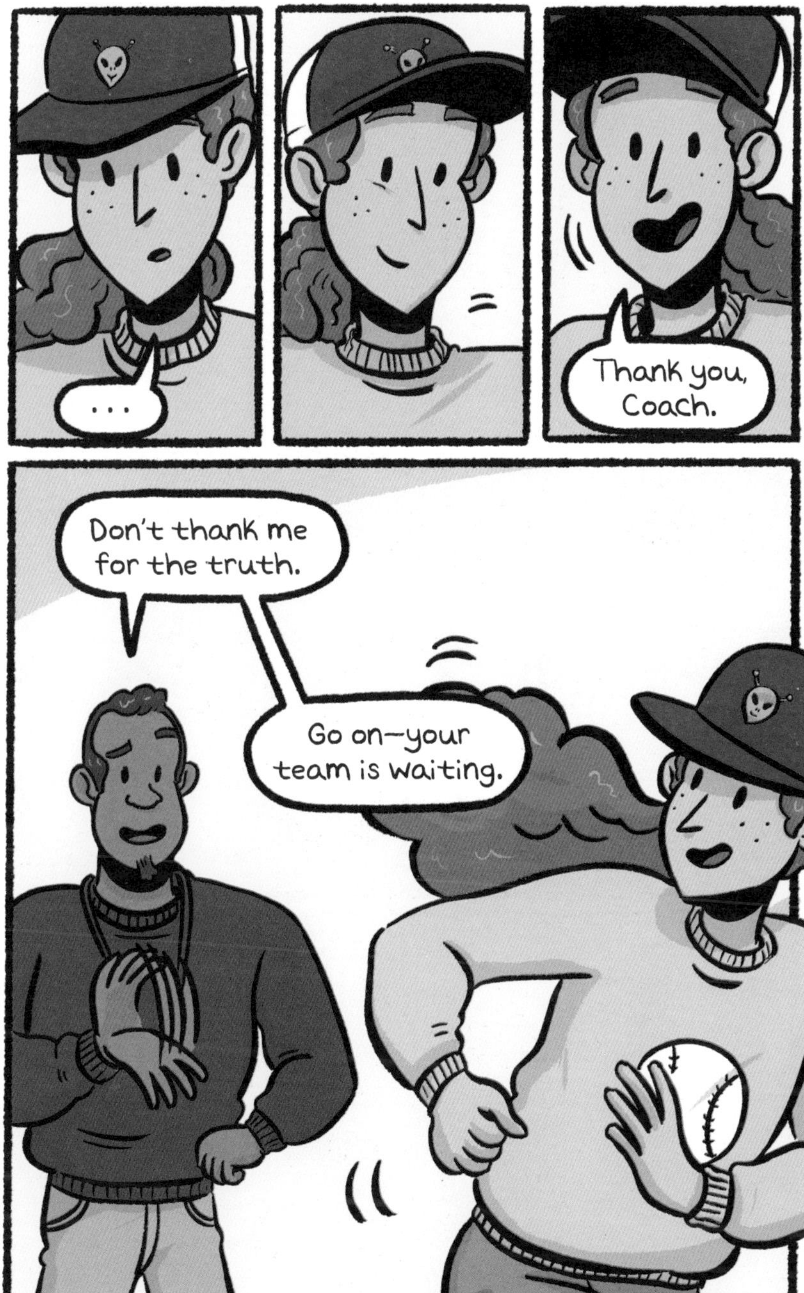
...
Thank you, Coach.
Don't thank me for the truth.
Go on—your team is waiting.

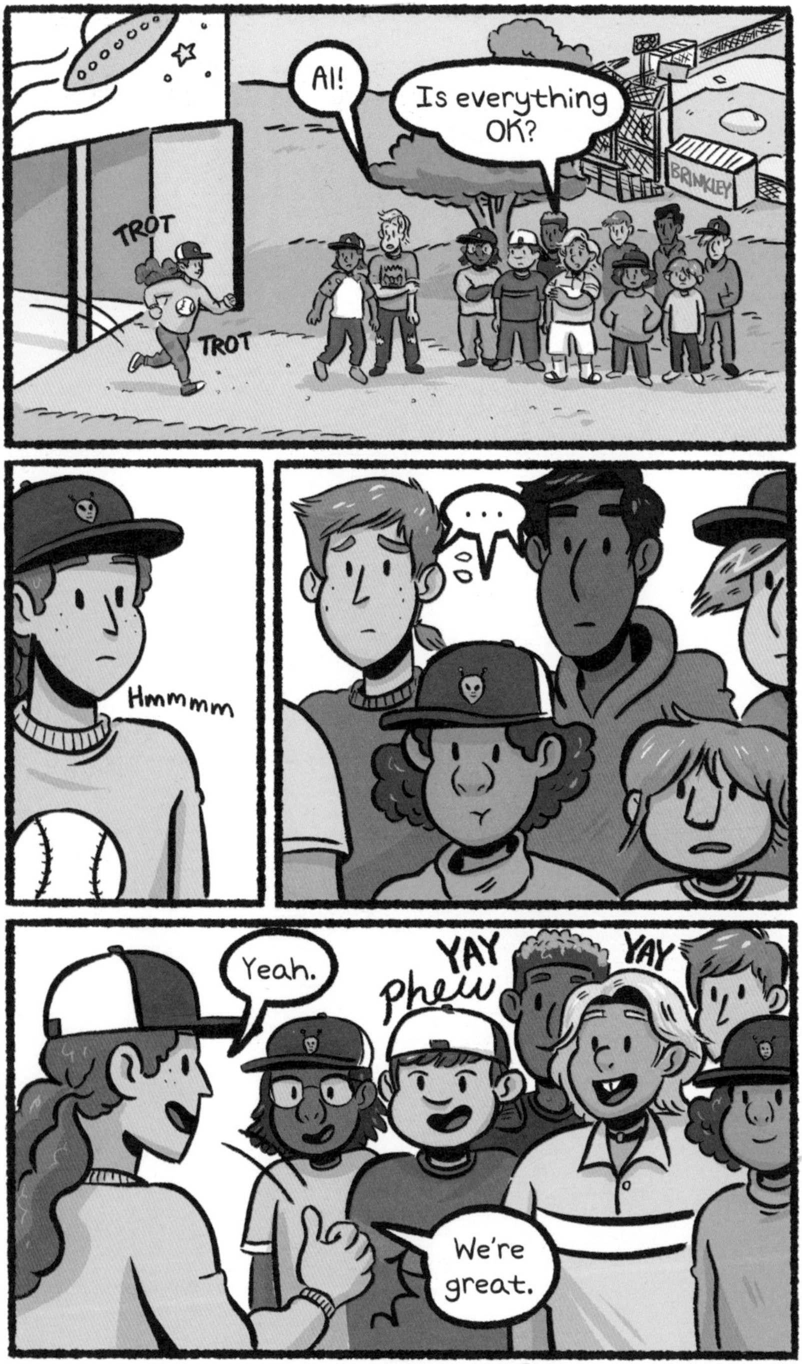

TROT
TROT
Al!
Is everything OK?
BRINKLEY
...
Hmmmm
Yeah.
Phew
YAY
YAY
We're great.

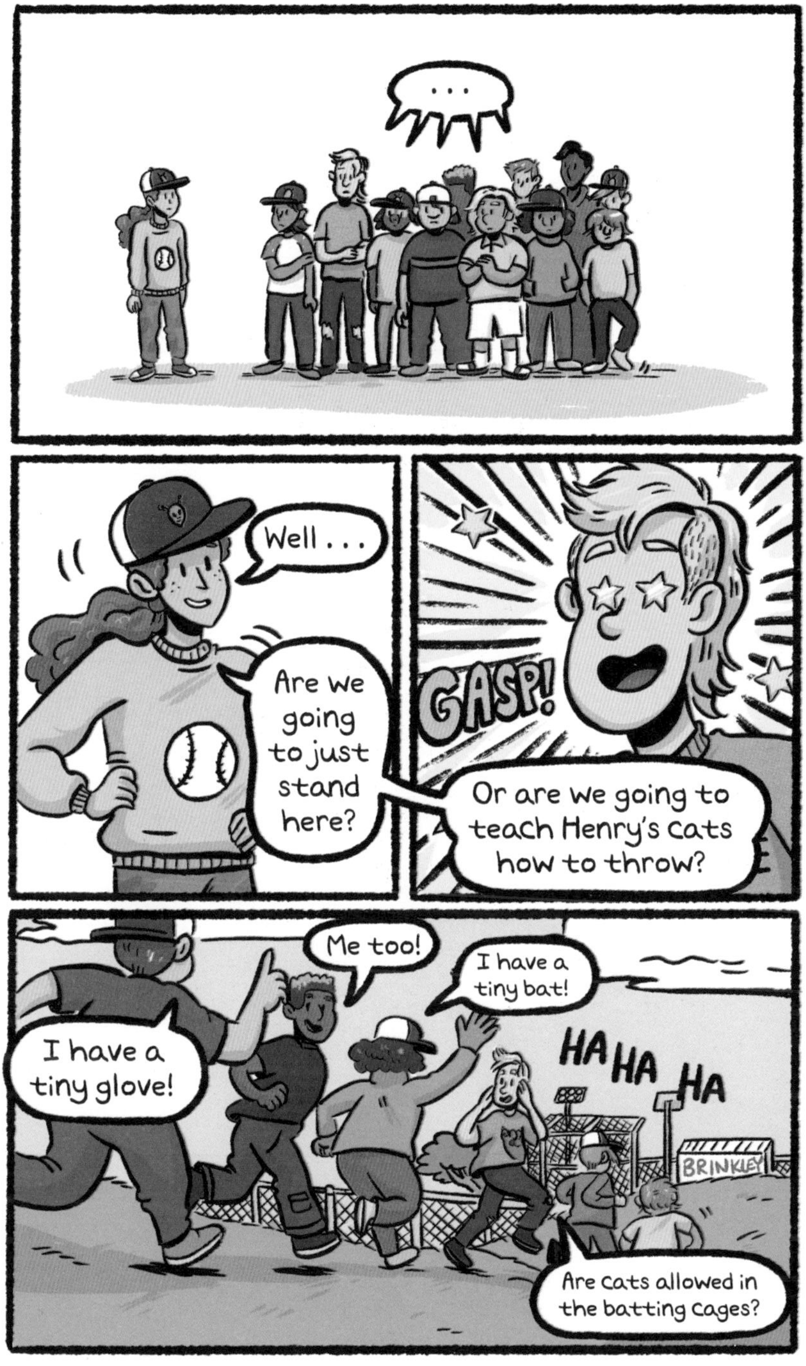
. . .
Well . . .
Are we going to just stand here?
GASP!
Or are we going to teach Henry's cats how to throw?
I have a tiny glove!
Me too!
I have a tiny bat!
HA HA HA
BRINKLEY
Are cats allowed in the batting cages?

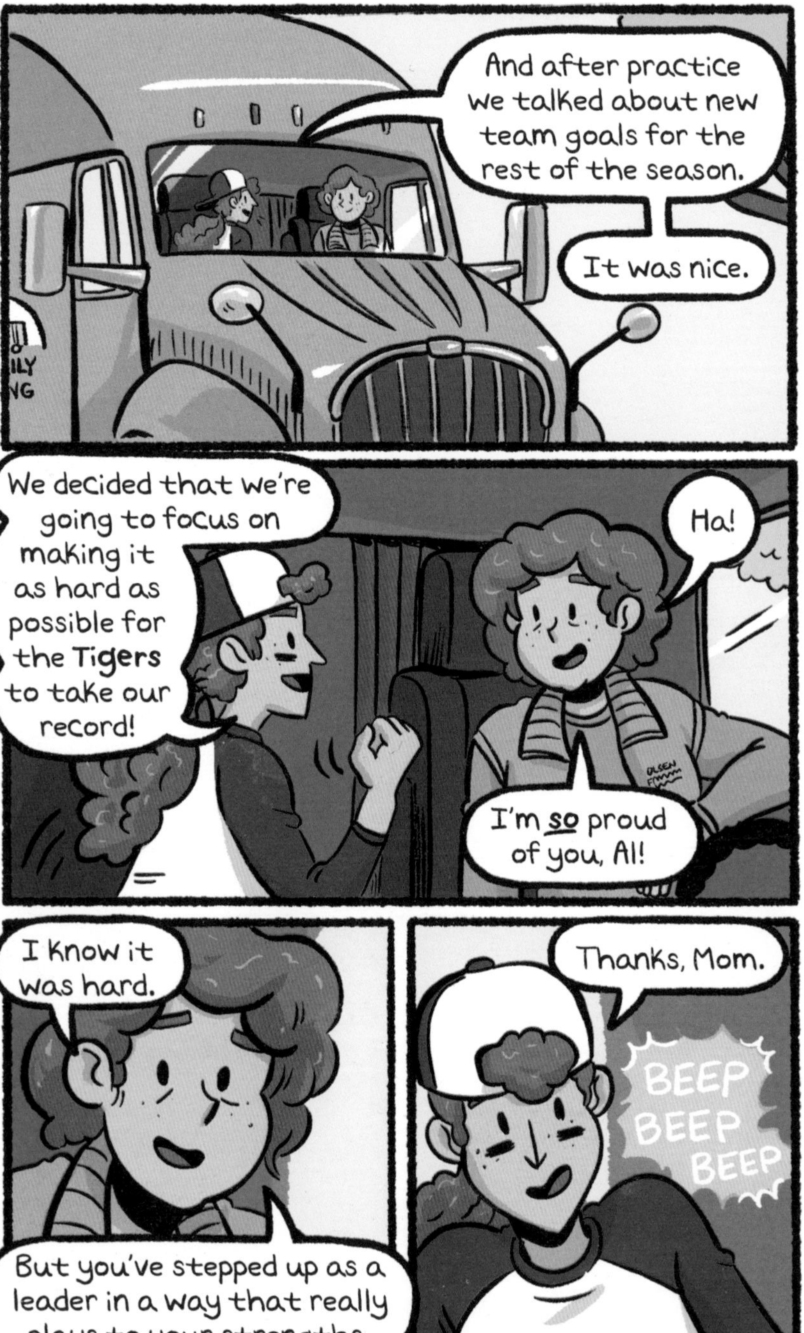
And after practice we talked about new team goals for the rest of the season.
It was nice.
We decided that we're going to focus on making it as hard as possible for the Tigers to take our record!
Ha!
I'm so proud of you, Al!
I know it was hard.
But you've stepped up as a leader in a way that really plays to your strengths.
Thanks, Mom.
BEEP BEEP BEEP

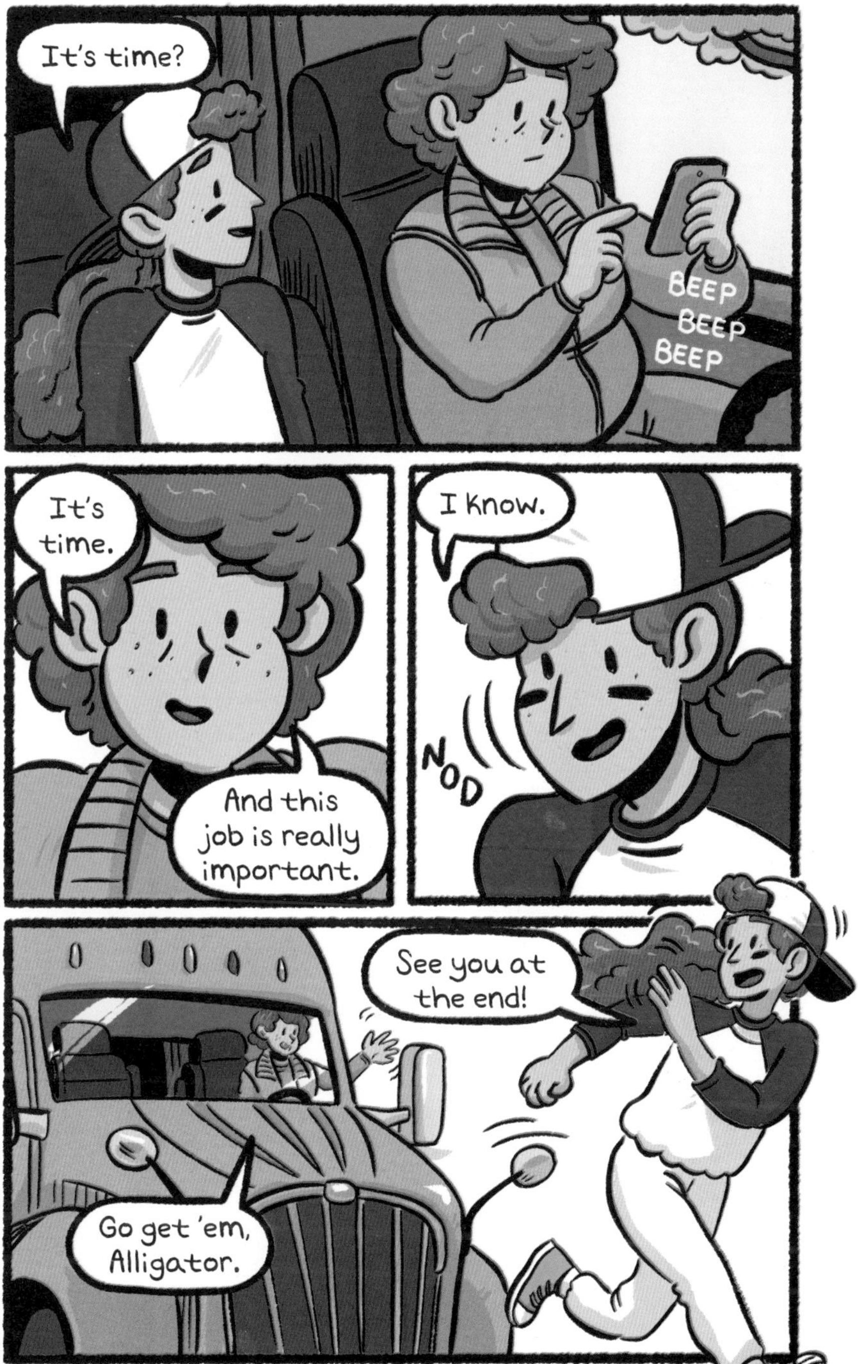

It's time?
BEEP
BEEP
BEEP
It's time.
And this job is really important.
I know.
NOD
See you at the end!
Go get 'em, Alligator.

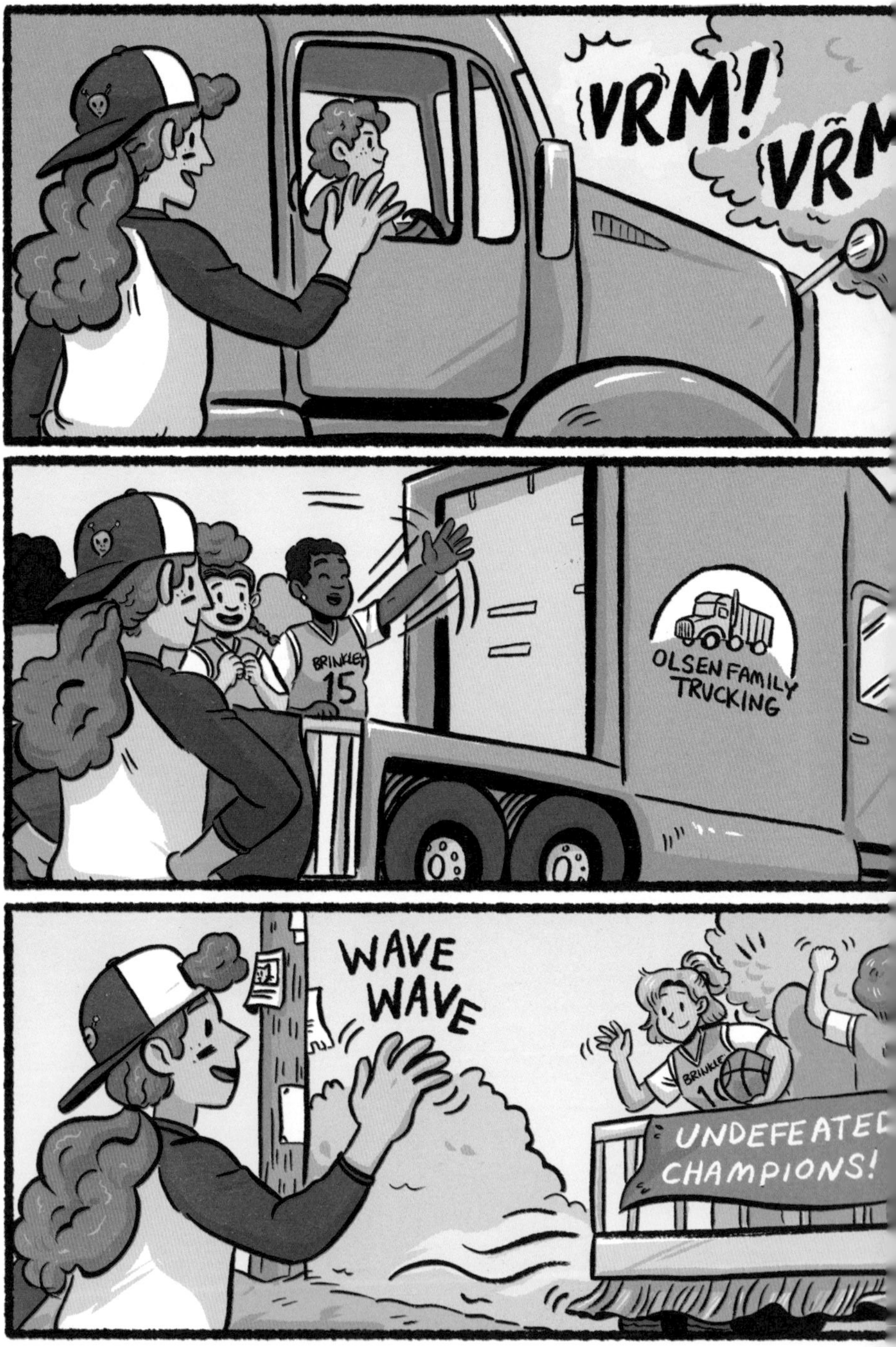
VRM!
VRM
BRINKLEY
15
OLSEN FAMILY
TRUCKING
WAVE
WAVE
BRINKLEY
UNDEFEATED
CHAMPIONS!

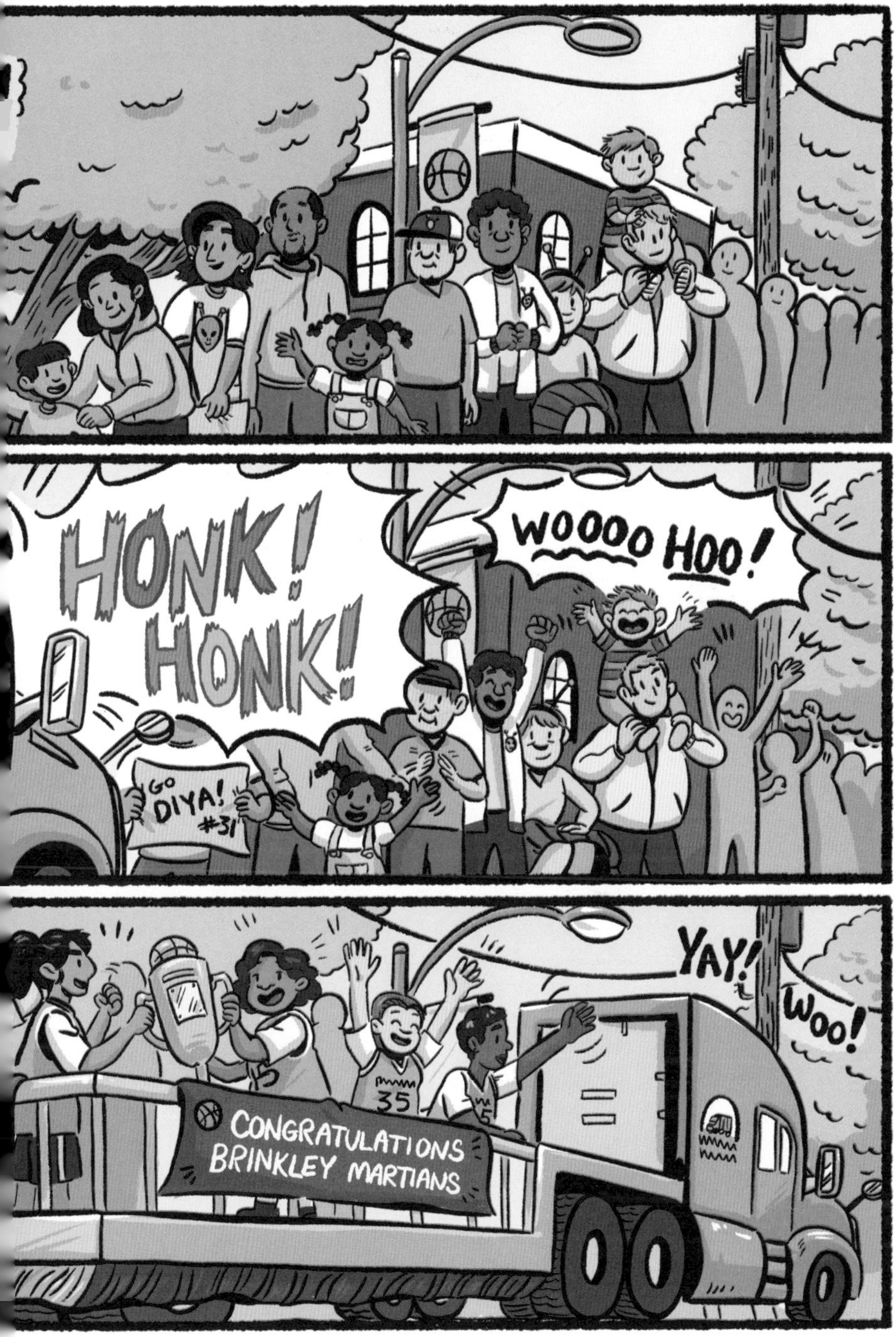
HONK! HONK!
WOOOO HOO!
GO DIYA! #31
YAY!
WOO!
CONGRATULATIONS BRINKLEY MARTIANS
35

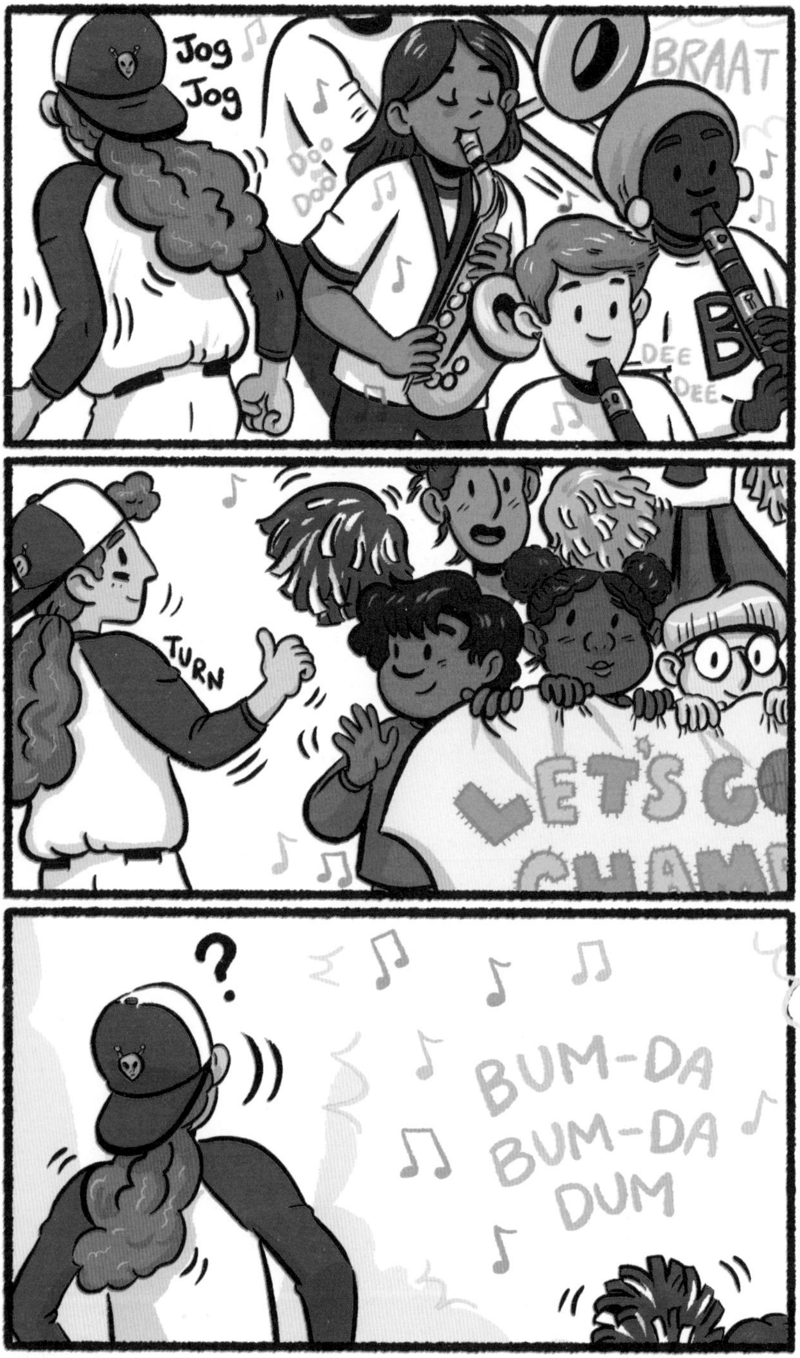
Jog
Jog
Doo
Doo
BRAAT
DEE
DEE
TURN
LET'S GO
CHAMP
?
BUM-DA
BUM-DA
DUM

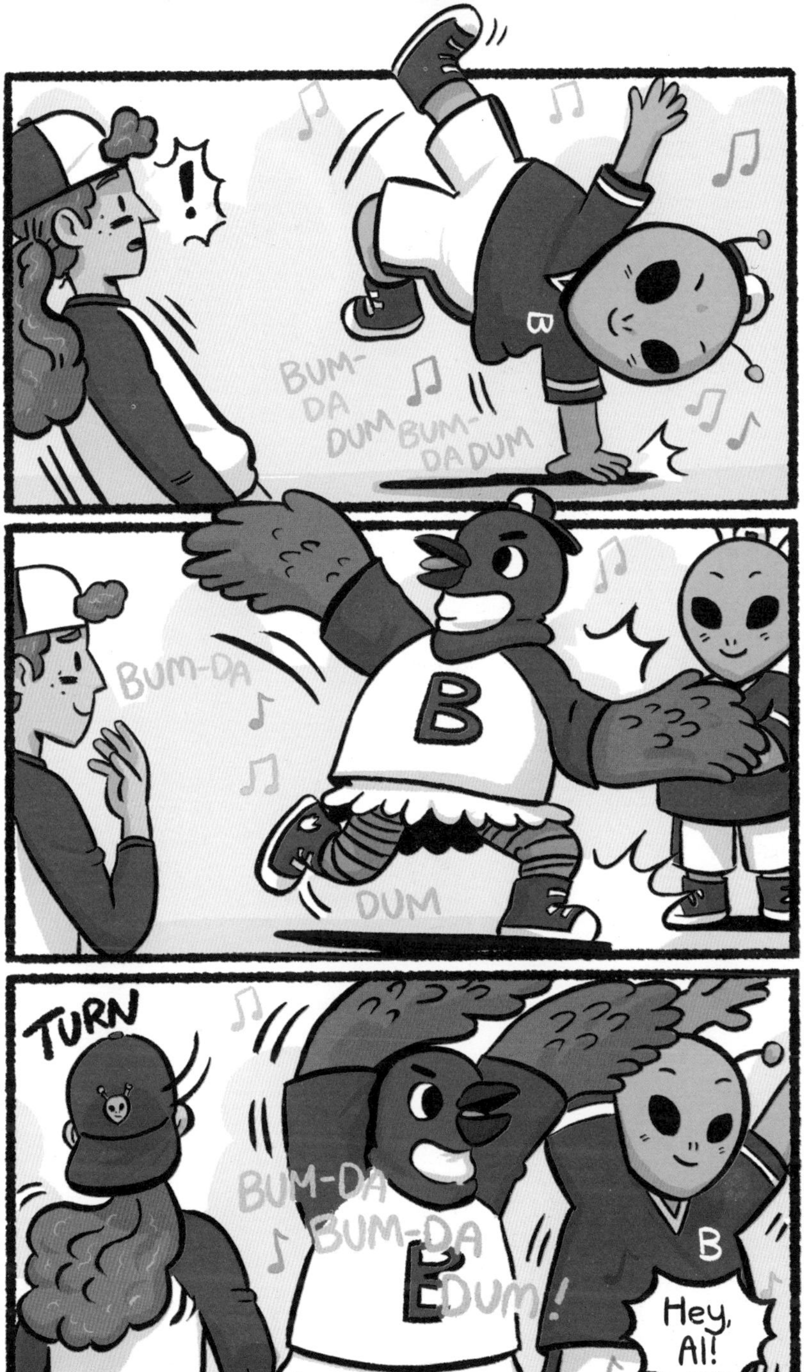
!
BUM-
DA
DUM
BUM-
DA DUM
BUM-DA
DUM
TURN
BUM-DA
BUM-DA
DUM!
Hey, Al!

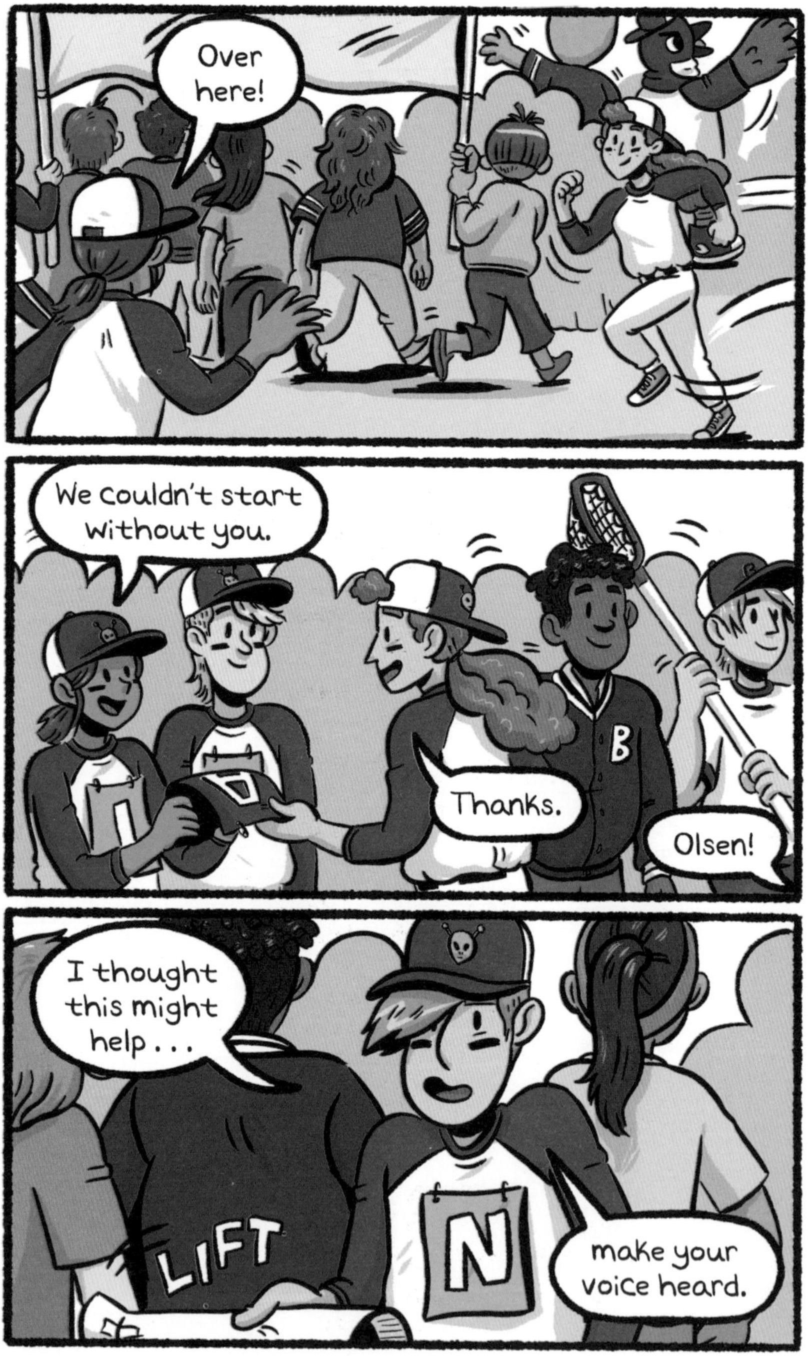
Over here!
We couldn't start without you.
Thanks.
Olsen!
I thought this might help . . .
LIFT
N
make your voice heard.

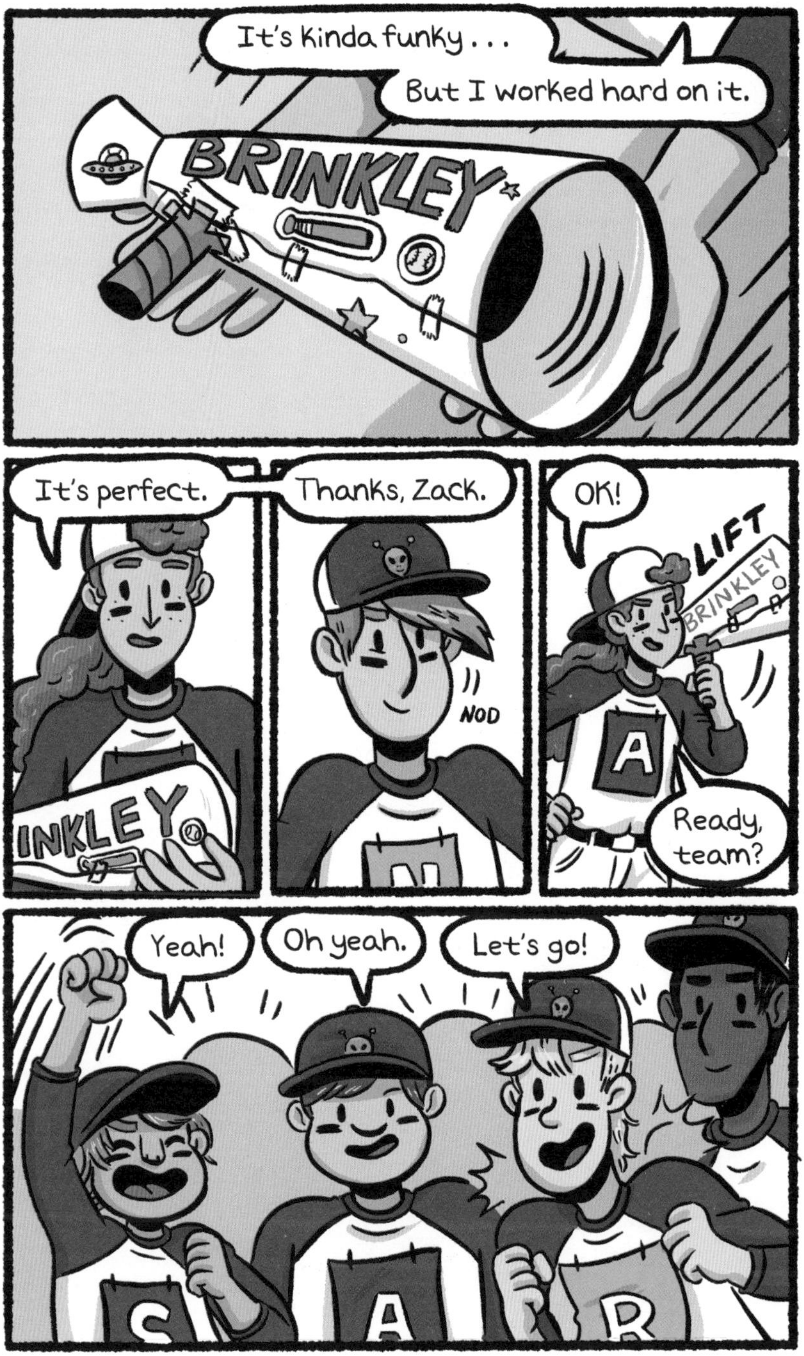
It's kinda funky . . .
But I worked hard on it.
BRINKLEY
It's perfect.
Thanks, Zack.
NOD
OK!
LIFT
BRINKLEY
Ready, team?
Yeah!
Oh yeah.
Let's go!

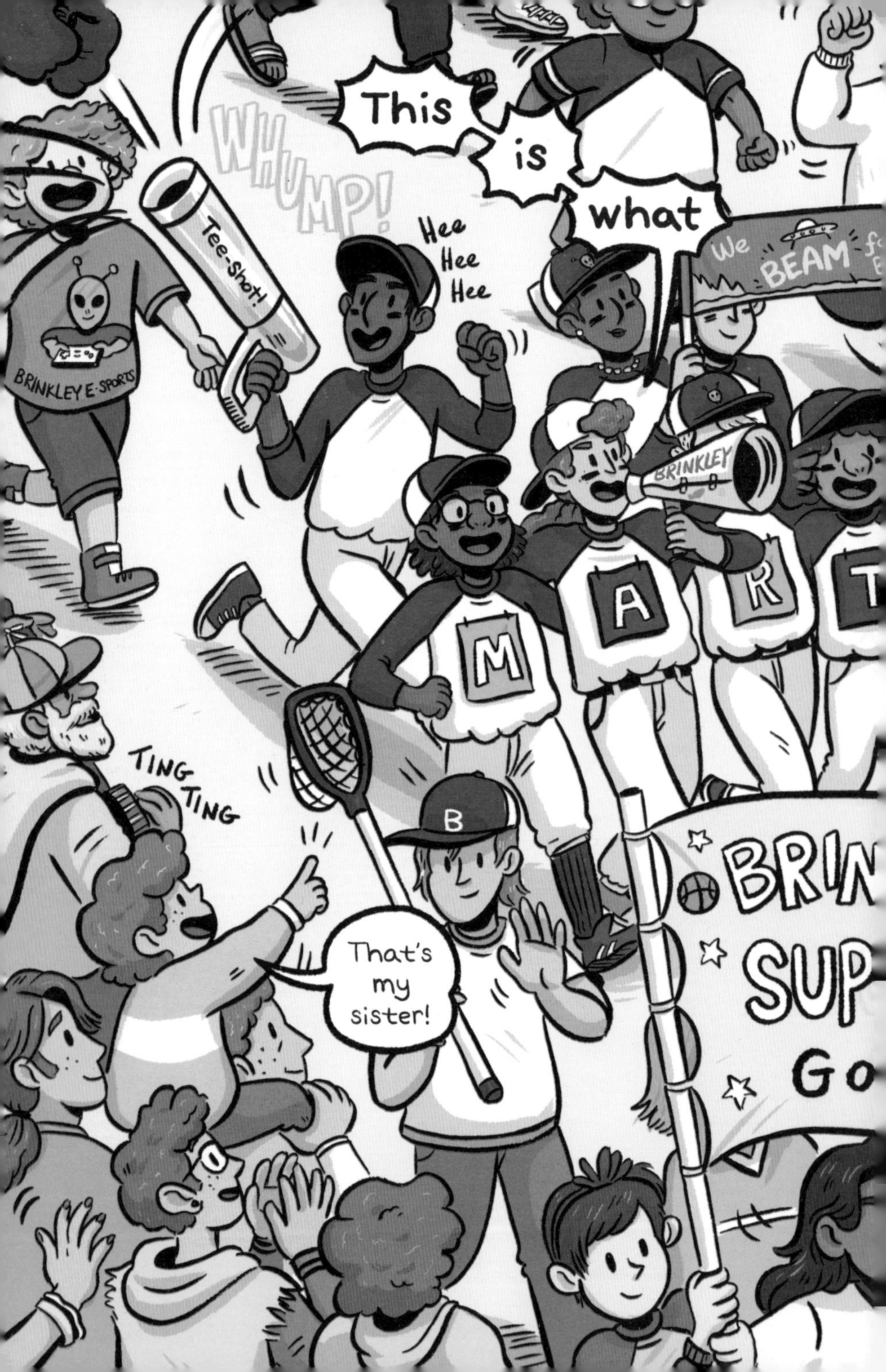

WHUMP!
Tee-Shot!
BRINKLEY E-SPORTS
This
is
what
Hee
Hee
Hee
We BEAM
BRINKLEY
M
A
R
T
B
TING
TING
That's my sister!
BRIN
SUP
Go

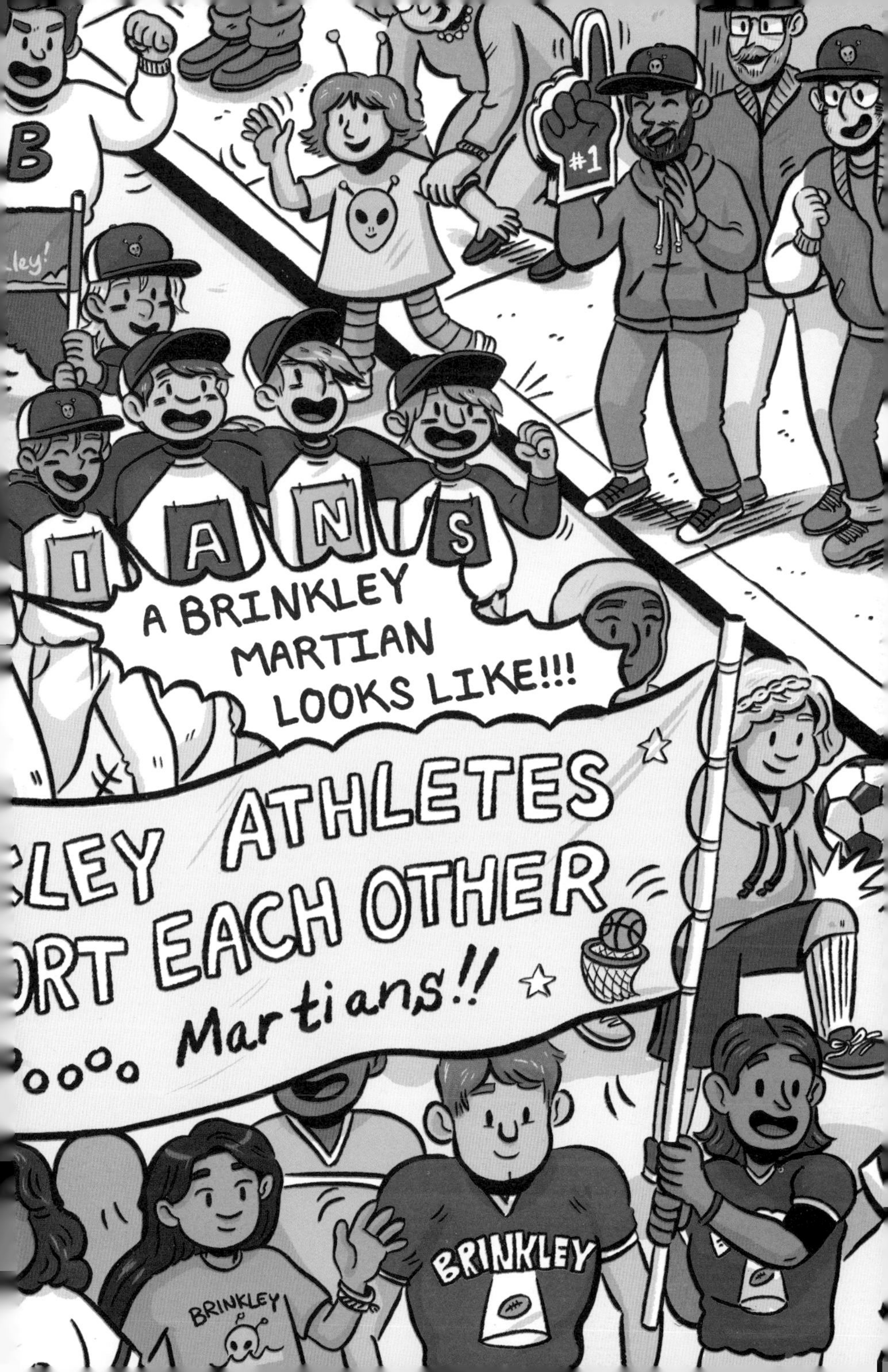

B
I A N S
A BRINKLEY MARTIAN LOOKS LIKE!!!
#1
LEY ATHLETES
ORT EACH OTHER
Martians!!
BRINKLEY
BRINKLEY

WE ARE THE CHAMPIONS!

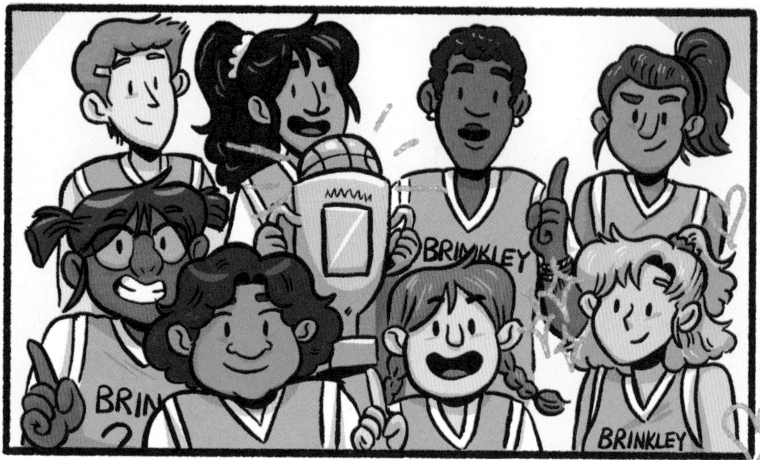
BRINKLEY
BRIN
BRINKLEY

The Brinkley Girls' Basketball team finished off an undefeated season with the first state championship trophy at Brinkley in over four decades!

Top (left to right): Rae Barker, Diya Wright, Grace Baker, Sunny Stevens
Bottom (left to right): Lily Chey, Ruby Reyes, Olivia Valk, Sammi Kimberly-Jones

BRINKLEY PLAYS FOR KEEPS

Zack Turner gets tips from Coach Strong on controlling his changeup.

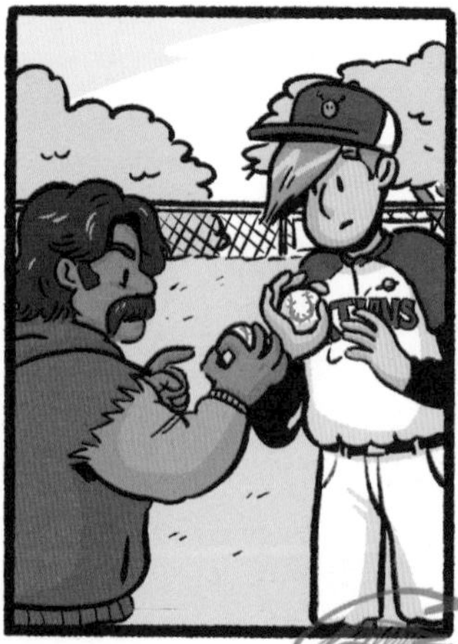

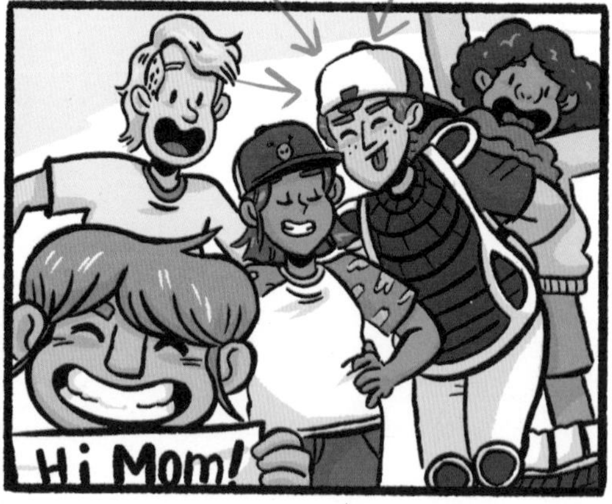
Hi Mom!

Henry LeChat (top left), Julian Veras, Alexandra Olsen, Mateo Adams, and Leo Morales (front) have fun as a team at baseball practice.

DOUBLE (MASCOT) TROUBLE!

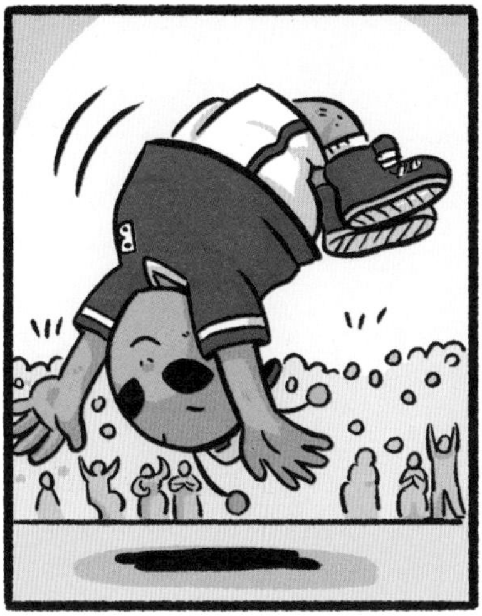

The Brinkley Martian (Calvin Yee) flips for Brinkley basketball.

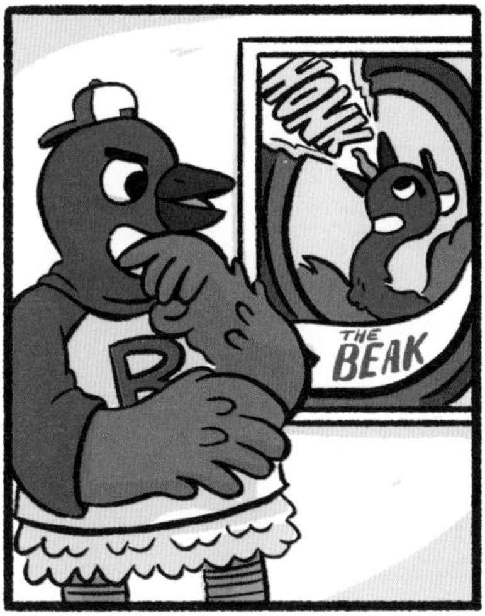
HONK
THE BEAK

The Brinkley Beak makes a comeback thanks to Viv Sullivan and Mr. Throm's Art Club.

??
?

CLUBS ARE "SEW" FUN!

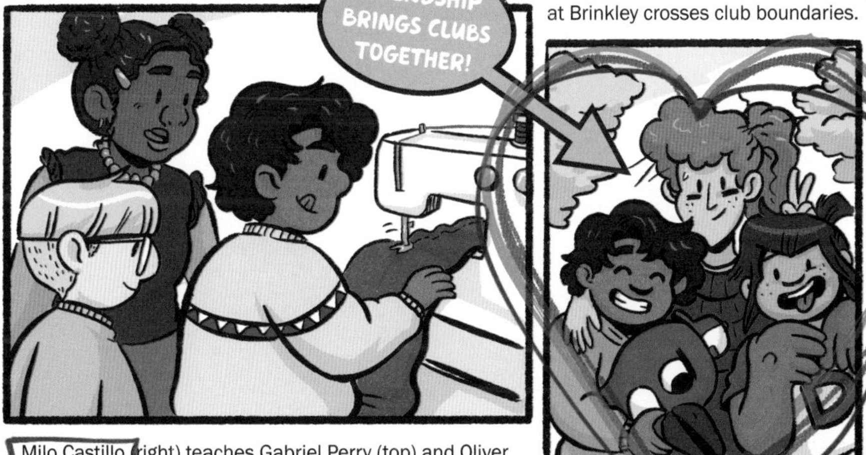
FRIENDSHIP BRINGS CLUBS TOGETHER!

Milo, Al, and Viv show us that friendship at Brinkley crosses club boundaries.

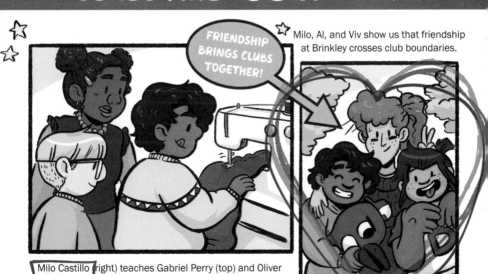

Milo Castillo (right) teaches Gabriel Perry (top) and Oliver Weisz (left) how to use a sewing machine during Art Club.

AUTHOR'S NOTE

I was not an athletic kid growing up, but I played a lot of different sports. From elementary school through high school, I tried soccer, basketball, track and field, and cross-country. As it turned out, I didn't connect with the "athletics" part of playing sports (see my photographic evidence), but I did get a lot out of being part of a team. For me, playing sports wasn't about competing—it was about the joy of memorizing all the Gavroche parts in *Les Misérables* with my friends while waiting for our turn to make a layup during basketball practice (sorry, Coach Turner). While I didn't come away from those teams with a love of the game per se, I did gain a sense of camaraderie and a sense of how to act in collaboration as part of a whole—and I got to try and push myself outside of my comfort zones.

There are so many reasons to challenge yourself to try out something new. Maybe, like Al, you have a deep passion that you want to pursue. Maybe, like Julian, you want to explore a skill that helps you connect more with a family member. Maybe, like Cal, you want to give your all to mastering a craft, or, like Viv, you want to reinvent it entirely. Or maybe, like Milo, you have hesitations around putting yourself out there, but once you find a way to incorporate it with something you love, you find that you're able to thrive. Whatever your reasons, they are all valid and all worth exploring.

During a time in which the stories of young athletes are being used to instill fear and to further division in our country, it is imperative to remember that the young folks at the center of these stories are whole individuals. It is so

easy for the entirety of a person to become simplified down in service of another person's narrative. Through Al's story, I wanted to explore what it feels like to be seen as just one part of yourself when you want to be seen for all your complexities—all that you bring to the table. In Al's case, the people framing her story think they are sharing it in an exciting, encouraging way. (She's the first girl on the team! She's breaking new ground!) And while that may be true, for Al, focusing on the story of being the first—and

only that story—reduces her years of passion and hard work to an element of herself outside her control and celebrates her breaking through a barrier that is arbitrary to begin with. In creating this book, I came across a number of organizations that are working hard to maintain your right to try out and take ownership of your story and the way that you want to show up on the field:

Baseball for All provides resources, programs, and playing opportunities for girls and women who, like Al, love baseball and want to pursue a path in the sport that they love: baseballforall.com

The Women's Sports Foundation provides resources, research, and advocacy for girl, woman, trans, and nonbinary athletes taking part in sports at large: womenssportsfoundation.org

GLSEN's Changing the Game initiative provides an inclusive framework for all K—12 students participating in physical education or competitive sports regardless of their sexual orientation or gender identity: glsen.org/changing-the-game

Growing up, I was given ample opportunities to discover new parts of myself through organized sports. I want to say emphatically to everyone reading this book: You deserve to have that same chance.

—Sarah

BRINKL

ACKNOWLEDGMENTS

A huge thank-you to the teams at Knopf and PRH who've worked to bring the stories of Al and her friends into the world with so much enthusiasm. Marisa—This series continues to evolve for the better under your editorial guidance. Thank you for trusting me to pull things together, even when I bring you ideas involving long-forgotten goose mascots! Jade—I'm delighted to have you on Team Brinkley. Thanks to your care, attention to detail, and killer design skills, *Tryouts* looks out of this world! Madison—Thank you for giving me the chance to put myself out there to represent the world of Brinkley and to try out new skills of my own!

Thank you to my wonderful colorist, Liana Sposto. I'm so happy to be collaborating with you on this series! Your tireless work brought a whole new dimension to Al and her story. You are the master of rendering a pitching flourish and your watchful eye kept me on top of the task of baseball-uniform consistency. (I'm *so* sorry for all the sleeves.)

Thank you to my endlessly fantastic agent, Molly O'Neill, without whom I would not be here finishing my second book! Thank you for always being ready with pep talks, publishing advice, or a delightful kitty conversation. Thank you to Colby Sharp and Sherry Owens for taking the time to talk with me about all things tryouts and coaching!

This book wouldn't be what it is without my Oakland Coliseum season ticket crew. Thank you to Owen and Joey for helping me appreciate the game of baseball on a deeper level. To Section 220: The Sandbar. Get that pitch count up!

Thank you to Stomper and Slugger for being very exceptional mascots. Cal's mascot code may be something of my own invention, but you consistently set the bar high for fuzzy excellence.

Adam: Your love and support help me do my best work. Thank you for always cheering me on, even when I'm ranting to you about minor-league baseball mascots.